S0-BFA-024

In & Out

In & Out

YEAR ONE
IN THE
Jumping for Gold Series

Barbara Moss

Caballito Books
WELLINGTON, FLORIDA

First printing 2005

ISBN 0-9765198-3-6
LCCN 2005920237

ATTENTION CORPORATIONS, UNIVERSITIES, COLLEGES, AND PROFESSIONAL ORGANIZATIONS: Quantity discounts are available on bulk purchases of this book for educational, gift purposes, or as premiums for increasing magazine subscriptions or renewals. Special books or book excerpts can also be created to fit specific needs. For information, please contact Caballito Books, 2513 Vista Del Prado, Wellington, FL 33414.

Chapter One

The town was Wellington, Florida. The street, a main drag—Forest Hill Boulevard. The place—Starbucks. Center of the universe, wasn't it?

He wheeled a vintage 1965 Mustang convertible into the parking lot and an empty space—black one, mint, ragtop down. Shut the engine off, and vaulted out without even bothering to open the door. Didn't lock her either. Just turned and headed for the door with long athletic strides.

Wellington was horse country, the winter show circuit resided here—top horseflesh, top prize money, top customers, top trainers. And this guy looked like he belonged in the thick of it...like he rode for sure. Mid to later twenties. Tall—just over six feet. Lean and hard—but then sitting on six to eight horses a day and hitting the gym pretty good afterwards would do that. Battered jeans, the seat and inner thighs almost white from saddle wear—hard muscles rippling visibly beneath the well-worn fabric. White tee shirt. Chestnut, sun-streaked hair pulled severely back and braided, the thick end swinging between broad shoulder blades in time with his stride—it would be one hell of a mane, let loose.

He approached the counter, frowned impatiently at the line in front of him. His was an arresting face even without the attitude, though not really handsome. Slashing brows over intense deep blue eyes, high cheekbones, straight nose, sensual mouth. Hadn't bothered to shave. Severe overall impression. But something hedonistic about him too.

The guy on the other side of the counter—one of the baristas—seemed bored, although he was taking orders at a pretty good clip and even bantering with the customers he knew. Like the Mustang's owner, he too was tall, maybe even taller. Blond chin-length shaggy hair, attractive—as in "drop dead" with sculpted Slavic features and soft bedroom eyes with long blond lashes—and he damn well knew it. Little growth of beard on his chin— kind of a man thing, but then he was barely in his early twenties so that probably meant something to him.

1

Mustang waited in line, not liking it, shifting from one foot to the other. Finally got his turn at the counter. If the barista's face looked bored, then his looked even more so—irritated too. "Latte," he muttered. His voice was deep, and a bit discordant. Unsettling.

Couldn't have cared less. "Size?"

"Venti."

Someone came up behind the rider and slapped him hard on the shoulder. He looked around sharply.

"Jericho," the newcomer said happily. He was older, looked affluent—big gold Rolex and the whole designer sportswear thing. Somewhat overweight, but not really fat. More out of shape and sagging in the middle. For sure this was no professional rider. Owner maybe. "So here you are. Cin and I have been looking for you—we've been calling you…don't you ever listen to messages? When did you get back in town?"

Kid behind the counter made a bit of a disbelieving face. *Jericho?*

"Richard." Reached over and took his hand—didn't really look that excited about it, although in fact, Richard Maitland was one of his better customers and patrons. Considering horses carried price tags that ran into seven figures, patrons could easily become important figures in a rider's life. "Me? About a week ago. Been having some trouble with the phones." Total lie, that. Sounded like one too. Covered it up with something more interesting. "Horses ship in today, yours included. Drop by the barn tomorrow afternoon. I'll ride Monterrey around three." He hadn't missed the look that kid had given him. Didn't like it much either. Slapped a Gold AMEX card down on the counter, with his finger still in the middle of it. Pushed it over to the clerk. "Got a problem?" he drawled amiably enough, while still effectively making it into a not too veiled threat.

"Not that I can think of." Obviously not intimidated in the least. He pulled the card over and ran it through the credit card processor, made a point of flipping it over and looking at the name.

Jericho Brandeis, it said alright. Christ, who had a first name like Jericho?

"So Jer, you still living over in the Polo Club?" his customer asked him.

"Yeah, same place."

"Are you going to rent your spare bedroom like you did last year? I know someone who might be interested."

Jericho shrugged like it wasn't particularly important to him.

Turned back around to sign the credit card receipt. Barista looked pretty interested now, was staring at him. Jericho took it personally, leaned in to him, one hand flat on the counter—actually looked like he might come over it, got right up in his face. "You know, if you have something to say, then say it," he invited in a deceptively silky undertone.

The man named Richard grabbed him by the elbow, laughing. "Whoa, whoa. He's a kid." Tried to cajole him out of it. "I see you haven't toned down that temper of yours one bit. Oh hey, that reminds me...Jude Crenshaw told me there's a rumor you were arrested a couple of nights ago." There was a nice dose of disapproval in his voice now too—like maybe he didn't like his trainer and top rider involved in a scandal. "Bar brawl, that's what Jude said. I told him, oh yeah, with Jericho, that's possible. Is it true, because you know we've talked about this."

Half-turned away from the Barista—Richard was right anyway, this putz *was* just a kid, albeit an annoying one. Let it go. Shrugged again, addressed the question about himself instead, although resentfully, but shit, he needed Monterrey in the barn and wasn't about to risk losing him. "Nothing's secret in this town, is it? But I'm telling you, it was bullshit. Drunk and disorderly. They had to drop the drunk part—I wasn't."

"What happens to the disorderly part?"

Wry grin, disgusted too. "Two thousand dollar fine." He leaned over and signed the receipt now.

Maitland's expression wasn't sympathetic, if anything he looked pleased about the fine—like maybe he thought it served him right. "Grab your drink and bring it outside. Cin's dying to see you. We have a table."

Brandeis nodded, though he didn't much look like he wanted to, and Maitland went outside—simply expecting him to follow as soon as he could. Jericho moved down to the other end of the bar and just stood there, trapped and annoyed by it, while the girl behind the espresso machine made his drink and the two or three in front of it.

Barista strolled over. Leaned up comfortably on the other side of the counter from him. Smiled, teasing but in a friendly way. Laid out a damn good imitation of Richard's New York accent. "I see you haven't toned down that temper of yours one bit."

Raised one slashing eyebrow. "Yeah, so?" Humor in his voice now too.

"Gonna go out and sit with those lamers?"

Eyes narrowed, but still his voice softly taunted. "Why, you want to sit with me? And those lamers pay me a lot of money."

Came out with what he actually wanted. "Not sit…just ask you a question. That guy said you have a room to rent. Do you? With show season, man its impossible to find anything—that doesn't cost a fuckin' fortune, that is. I know, I've looked."

The girl making the espresso drinks finally laid his Latte in front of him. Jericho wrapped his powerful hand around it. "Sounds like you're getting desperate."

Admitted it, but not the reason why. "I might be. Yeah, shit in a few days I will be."

Jericho looked him over slowly, thinking about it maybe. "How old are you?"

"Twenty…twenty-one in a couple of weeks." Gave him a brash look and a bit of a challenging comeback. Couldn't seem to help himself, even though he was trying to get something from him. "Yeah and how old are you?"

"Twenty-seven." Couldn't have cared less if this kid wanted to mentally bump shoulders with him—turned the questioning right back on the Barista instead. "Go to college—work here to pay for it?"

He shrugged, looked defensive about it. "Look, I pay for my own place, school…support myself."

"Do drugs?"

"Not really."

Looked at him skeptically.

"Come on," the Barista murmured. "Weed every once in a blue moon, that's it."

"Smoke?"

"Yeah. Is that a problem?"

Jericho smiled quietly. Shook his head in the negative. "Me too," he said. "Alright, maybe I'll let you have it if I'm feeling generous…and after the fabulous service I've had in here today…" Just let that slur lay out there.

"Cut me a break, was it that bad?"

"Five hundred." Last year, he'd rented the same room for $1250 a month. Wondered why he was throwing this kid a bone when five minutes ago he'd been ready to launch a fist at him. Didn't really know the answer, except that he liked scrappers and maybe this kid was that. Hell, he was too. And if he wasn't comfortable with the deal, he'd toss him out on his ass in the street inside a week. "Want to see it first?"

"If that's okay, or no, no…it doesn't really matter. Is there a bed or anything in it?"

Jericho picked up his drink, and although it was hot, took a long sip from it. "Christ, maybe you are desperate, at that. Fully furnished. Bed, television, stereo. House has a pool. I get the carport and the parking pad, you find a spot somewhere else." Barista seemed cool with that—excited actually. "My horses come in today, so I'll be busy. What time do you get out of here?"

"Three."

"Got wheels?"

"Sure."

Jericho pulled out his wallet, laid a business card on the counter.

"Call me on my cell phone. If I'm on a horse I don't answer. But I'll get back to you inside thirty." Laid a lazy stare on him. "Got a name?"

SALES

TRAINING

Brandeis Show Stables

Hunters/Jumpers

WELLINGTON, FLORIDA & EAST HAMPTON, NEW YORK

JERICHO BRANDEIS

561-596-5555

"Trevor Braeden. Brae for short."

"And you thought Jericho was lame?"

Smirked at him a little. "It is."

"We'll see about that." He picked up his Latte and simply walked away, looking for the Maitlands and resigned to spending the next hour or so with them.

———

They had a nice table on the corner of the small outdoor patio, shaded by a large green Starbucks sun umbrella. "You guys look great," he said as he approached, giving the obligatory flattering greeting. Laid his incredible blue eyes on Cin Maitland—man, she loved to flirt with him, and given the money she and Richard paid him monthly it was something he not only had to tolerate, but even had to participate in and encourage. Hated it, but so? "Cin, damn you darlin', you look good enough to…" Dropped it meaningfully there. The seat next to Cin Maitland had been conveniently left open, and Jericho laid his drink on the table and slouched over into it.

Cin laughed happily, while Richard protested good-naturedly, "Hey, hey..."

She reached over to him, and he leaned closer while she traced his stubbled jawline with beautifully manicured fingertips, and muttered a "Tsk, tsk," then lightly kissed both his cheeks—air kisses really.

Richard Maitland was probably 57, he was CEO of a major corporation in the Electronics Industry, and...had money, oh yeah. House in the Hamptons, spacious apartment in Manhattan, big home here in Wellington, and God only knew where else. He wasn't even really that interested in horses—that was the joke of it. But Cin was, and that explained that.

Cin. Appropriate name for the little bitch. She was probably 50, but if she'd said she was 40 or 41, no one would have contradicted her. Maybe could have even said younger. Cin lived the spa life—she took incredible care of herself—perfect skin, teeth and hair. Botox had removed any trace of crow's feet and a little nip or tuck here and there erased the rest. Same thing for her body—today she was wearing skintight breeches—the five hundred dollar kind—with a pair of equally expensive Manolo Blahnik slides on her feet, and a Ralph Lauren linen blouse fitted nice and tight to show off a slim waistline and her...really nice tits, Jericho thought. Not that he had the remotest interest in her except as a patron.

"Go to jail this week, Jericho?" Cin asked him, teasing, her voice just the littlest bit thrilled, her green eyes more so. Unlike Richard, she didn't seem to mind his wilder side one bit.

Shrugged, holding her gaze in his. "Couple of hours," he admitted. "It was fucking bullshit," he purred. Jericho cursed whenever he felt like it, but right now the profanity was solely for her benefit, and she smiled her "you're so bad" smile at him. Maitlands kept three horses with him...Cin's two hunters that Jericho trained and she rode in the adult amateur division, and the fabulously talented Monterrey—an eight year old Grand Prix Jumper, who'd try the moon and make it too if Jericho pointed him at it. Heart, guts, and talent—there wasn't much Jericho wouldn't do to keep him. And it wasn't like other trainers weren't sidling up to the Maitlands to vie for him if they ever decided to move him.

"Hmmm. Did they put the steel bracelets on you?" she kept at it, sipping lightly at her own iced coffee.

Had the good graces to look embarrassed, let his eyes fall away—even turned his head to the side, and shook it ruefully. "Stop."

"Oh, come on," she insisted. It was foreplay, pure and simple, he thought. He wondered if she fancied the image of him in handcuffs—and chained where? He didn't even want to follow that train of thought, but still it brought a perverse half-smile to his averted face.

"Might as well tell her, Jericho," Richard advised him. "You know how persistent she can be." Little bit of an order there too.

Relented. Swung his face slowly and deliberately back toward her, just far enough to send a deep blue sidelong glance her way. "For *a few minutes,* okay?"

Cin laughed at him again—liked putting him off balance…it was pretty rare. Charming too.

Richard wasn't quite done ribbing him on this topic either. "Anyway, Jericho, what were you doing to that poor kid behind the counter? I saw you talking to him after I came out here. You really need to…"

Looked up, innocent. "Who, Brae do you mean?"

Surprised, maybe not quite believing it. "You know him?"

He leaned back, and picked up his Latte, back in easy command— Richard wasn't the difficult one of this pair, not by a long shot. "Sure I do—met him here last year. He's a decent guy—working his way through college and all that. You didn't think I was really going after him, did you? No, hell no…he's between places. Might actually stay with me for a while."

"What time are the horses getting in?" Cin asked. Wasn't even remotely interested in talking about some clerk at Starbucks. She'd taken out her lipstick and was applying another glossy coat.

"Between eleven and twelve."

She looked him over again. "You're not riding today are you, Jericho? Richard has a golf game, but to be honest I'll be at home bored this afternoon."

Nice little signal that. He decided to miss it. "No, Cin, they've been on the road almost 24 hours, they'll be exhausted. I'll hand walk yours though, stretch them out a little bit."

"But I can come see them, can't I?"

She was a little more aggressive today than usual…he wondered what was up with that. "There's not much to see, but sure you can. I have to warn you though, we're still putting the place together." The stables he rented here in Wellington for the season were top shelf—paid for by his clients of course but that was only customary and this clientele wanted nice—really nice. Big tack room too—smell of leather, Oriental rug on the floor, prints on the wall, nice seating area for the customers. "You know I want it perfect for you, Cin." Then gave her the other piece of information he knew she was after. "The guys will be working till late to get it ready for tomorrow, and I'll be there until at least around five."

One of those Manolo slides had to be lying on the ground unoccupied right now, because he could feel silky, perfectly manicured toes sliding under the bottom of the leg of his jeans closest to her, slowly caressing the back of his calf. Had to admit, it felt pretty good, but passed a vulnerable and admonishing look at her—one he could see she loved.

"Well, maybe I'll stop by around four then," Cin said, wetting her lips but taking her foot away. "Bring a little something with me for you…and your guys."

"Marco still with you?" Richard asked, oblivious to the *double entendre* banter—or maybe he just didn't care—expected Jericho to police it for him. Or else.

"Yeah, he's here." Marco, his barn manager, head groom, whatever you wanted to call him. And he'd tell him to make himself painfully present—and in the way—this afternoon too.

What garbage he went through to ride Monterrey. But that was the game.

———————

The horses got there two and a half hours behind schedule. No big surprise that, and the shipping company had called ahead to say there'd been traffic delays last night around Washington DC…and don't worry, don't worry, all the horses were fine—Monterrey too. Still, most of the equipment was shipping in with them—meaning Jericho and his guys couldn't really start the barn set-up in any kind of efficient way until they arrived. Just bed the stalls down, fill water buckets, get the night feed ready early. Later, they'd be busting their asses because of this.

Twelve horses coming down, two specially equipped tractor-trailer rigs with air-ride suspension. When the first of the pair pulled down the long tree-lined driveway and into the yard, Jericho dropped what he was doing and went out to meet them. The driver was already climbing down—an experienced hauler, and one that he used regularly.

"They're all fine, Jer," the man said, fending off the question before it was even asked. "We stopped to water them about an hour and a half ago and everyone looks good. And yes, Monterrey is still alive and kicking."

"Damn well better be. Just open the frickin' door and let me see him."

Didn't even have to ask though. The shipper's men were already sliding the doublewide doors back from the inside and letting the ramp down. Jericho grabbed a hold on one side, and swung himself up and into the trailer. This rig had been specially done out to handle horses, and could be custom configured to provide the stall sizes the customers wanted for the trip—pretty much like picking between sending them first class or economy. This first truck was carrying all three of the Maitland horses, plus one more leggy four year old that Jericho owned personally. The rest of the show string was coming up behind them in trailer number two.

But it was Monterrey and Monterrey only that got his trainer's attention right now. Went over to him where he stood in the first large box stall, skirted under the door guard and went inside with him. The 17 hand, bay gelding turned at the sight of him and quietly nickered, then took a step toward him. Jericho smiled with satisfaction, the horse looked good.

"Hey, boy." He put a hand on his muscled neck and stroked along his sleek body, then felt down his legs to the knee—there were shipping wraps covering them below that. Stepped around and did the same with the hind legs. Monterrey responded, tried to follow him, reaching his neck out, nostrils wide and blowing softly. Nuzzled his jeans' front pocket. Jericho pushed him fondly away. "No beggar, there's nothing here for you." He went back to the front again. Ran his fingers down that perfect white blaze on his face, rubbed the baby soft muzzle for a few seconds longer. Then reached around and grabbed Monterrey's leather halter and lead, slipping the halter over the horse's head.

"Are you ready?" he asked the grooms.

"Ready."

They had the ramp down and the sides up on it. Jericho unclipped the door guard and led Monterrey out of the stall and toward it. No one handled this horse but him, no one—not when there was the slightest chance that he could be frightened and injure himself.

The big bay lifted his head and took in his new surroundings, snorting, dancing lightly on his feet. Saw the bright sunlight outside, so different from the trailer's dark interior. Jericho had a good grip on him, gave the halter a shake and murmured, "Settle down." Amazing how many horses kicked themselves or worse in those few moments of unloading, and he was staying on the alert till this jumper was safely away in his new barn.

Monterrey put one foot on the ramp, and immediately felt the change in the surface below him. Jerked to a halt, uncertain. Jericho just talked to him softly, didn't make a big deal of it. Let the horse get confidence from him. The gelding brushed his face against his arm, eyes wide but trusting, moved the second front hoof forward onto the ramp tentatively. And then he started to walk, coming obediently along with the man beside him.

Barking.

A dark shape flashed by at the foot of the ramp. Monterrey startled, started to go up on his hind legs, lost his balance and hit the side of the ramp, then panicked. Oh fuck, Jericho thought. For an instant, it looked like the bay might leap right over the side of the ramp, and damn it was too far to the ground. That just couldn't happen. He threw his body in front of him, blocking him—185 pounds of man versus 1100 pounds of horseflesh—telling him sternly, "Whoa now," at the same time. A hoof struck out, caught his thigh, sending pain shooting through it. The horse's shoulder hit his own with force, and that hurt like hell too, but he wasn't giving up control of his head, and he wasn't going to lose his cool either.

It was over in seconds—just a few volatile moments—and then the big bay was back in control again, and walking with huge prancing steps the rest of the way down.

"Whose fucking dog was that?" Jericho snarled to Marco as he led the snorting gelding into the large barn aisle way, and straight into his huge corner stall. Took his halter off, letting him loose in the enormous box, then closed the beautiful wooden door with its brass bars and fittings behind him. There was a flake of hay already waiting for Monterrey there, and he immediately fell to munching on it, looking up ever few seconds to nicker excitedly, then back to eating again.

"Get the leg wraps off him, and check him over," Jericho ordered one of his grooms. He didn't really think the horse had hurt himself, still it had been a close call, and man he didn't like that. When he found the owner of that dog, he was really going to give him an earful about it. Or better yet, kick his ass for him.

"You're hurt, Jer." That from Marco.

He looked down. Yeah, the side of his jeans was ripped where that steel shoe had connected and already tinged with a hint of red. "Alright, I'll take care of it."

Soft purring voice. "Nice job, cowboy."

Cin. He didn't even have to turn around to know it was her. Did turn though. "You're early, Cin. I didn't realize you were here yet."

"I was in the car. I just love watching you with him. He trusts you so much, you're the only one who can control him. I'm so glad I bought him for you, Jericho. You know, he's going to knock some people's socks off when you take him in the ring this…" She broke off. "My God, you're bleeding. Are you alright?" She came the rest of the way over to him—right up to him. Laid one hand at his waist on that side, then slid it lightly down the side of his leg and across the front of his muscled thigh where the injury was. "That looks bad."

Spoke brusquely. "No, it's fine." Blue eyes leveled on her as her fingers seemed to move around toward his inner thigh, and he breathed softly, "Christ, Cin…" She looked up at him, questioning but not really. Seemed tiny—only five foot four to his six foot one. But man was she in control right now.

"Come on," she suggested. "Lets put something on that."

He was glad for the opportunity to move away. "Yeah, there might be something in the tack room." Started toward it and she came with him. He wasn't limping, but the truth was it was throbbing a bit.

The room was still basically empty but for a sofa and coffee table he'd bought locally a day or so ago. But like the rest of this place he'd rented it was large and had beautiful fixtures.

"You should sit down," Cin told him. She laid a hand over his belt buckle. "And you should take these off."

Tolerant but chastising look. "Not with you in the room."

"Don't be ridiculous."

She went to undo his belt and maybe that was a sham, but still his hand wrapped powerfully around her wrist. He didn't say "stop" but he meant it. And she knew it. Her eyes lifted up to him while her free hand found the fly of his jeans, blatantly disobeying him. She lightly toyed with the zipper, teasing.

Then again, maybe it hadn't been a sham at all. Or maybe it still was.

Man, he didn't want to react to her, but tell his body that 'cause it sure wasn't listening. He was growing relentlessly beneath her suggestive touch, giving her something real to play with. Even through his jeans, his swelling erection was unmistakable. She found him, laying her palm like a ghost over his fly, almost exploring with her thumb but not quite, hinting how she might curl her fingers around him if she wanted to.

But he wanted command back, and just took it. His hand released her wrist and instead covered her fingers where they were hovering just over him. And he wasn't hinting anything. No, he was pressing—making her really feel him, and sweet Jesus that was bringing him up hard. "You want to tease me, Cin? Fine by me, I'll give you what you're asking for. But one of these grooms walks by, and I guarantee you everyone in Wellington will know about it before the day is through."

"Would that be a bad thing?"

"I don't know," he said harshly, cruelly even. "Did you sign a pre-nup with Richard?"

She looked a little exposed then. Wanted her hand back, but he wasn't having it. Not till he said so. "Yeah, I'd make a nice trophy," he quietly mocked her. "But come on, you'd rather have the lifestyle, the money and the ribbons. And see, I don't tame that easily." Released her, plenty of anger there.

But she hadn't given in. She stroked one finger down the length of him, very visible now and tantalizing. He was pissed with her, yes, but still very much aroused. As she was. "But I can keep trying, can't I?" Guilty smile, wicked. "I like it that you don't just kiss my ass, and I like the sexual tension between us. You're so fierce sometimes, and yes I absolutely love it that you're forbidden and dangerous." Lifted that lovely face of hers to him, eyes alive. "Maybe I'd even like to break you, Jericho. How does that grab you?"

Slid his palm under her jaw, laid a piercing stare on her. "Put a bit in my mouth?" he asked her. "Like that'll fucking happen." His fingers tightened, holding her face captive, staring dominantly down at her.

She let him have the moment, but still it didn't seem like she was through with him. Her hand trailed up over his bicep, then shoulder, then around the back of his neck, finding that thick chestnut braid and wrapping her hand around it. Then she suddenly tugged at the elastic band that held the end of it, pulling it loose. His hair was thick, silky and almost poker straight, and the braid immediately started unraveling. He lifted his face up, staring sharply down at her—shit, he'd give her one thing, she was a brazen little bitch—infuriating, but not even hateable, and that was an art form. He shook his head, freeing the rest of his mane, and it fell around his face, over his shoulders and down his back like a chestnut curtain. "Satisfied?" he purred.

"You know, I've known you for two years, and I've never seen your hair down, not even once, Jericho." She ran her fingers through it. "I'm jealous. Its even prettier than mine."

"Will you fuckin' behave?" he growled back at her. "Just how the hell am I supposed to give you a lesson tomorrow and watch that pretty ass of yours posting up and down in the saddle?"

Still tangling her hand through that mass of hair, the other finding the rough side of his face. "Mmmm. I love it when I hear you saying, 'more inner thigh, sit deeper.'"

"Yeah, I'll give you something to put between your legs, and you better sit deep on it cause its not going to be a tame ride, that's for God damn sure." Slapped her bottom and hard. "Now get out of here while I take care of this."

Cin slid her palm over his erection, it was beautifully full blown now. Practiced little fingers that promised and denied, brought heaven and hell simultaneously. "Take care of it how?"

Brought his hand to hers again and stopped it right there, deep blue eyes narrowed and reproachful, slowly shaking his head. "My *leg*, you little cock-teasing bitch." Smiled quietly at her, holding the moment a little longer. *"Out,"* he snarled finally, authority in his voice now.

"You're such a prude, Jericho." She backed up a step, moistened her lips, almost laughing—definitely enjoying herself. "See you tomorrow, darling. Ciao."

He watched till she left the room, then heard her voice from out in the aisle way. "See you tomorrow, Marco." He still couldn't quite believe her, worse yet, wasn't sure what she wanted—other than to tempt the living crap out of him, and probably never go further than that.

Wasn't even going to worry about it right now. Tomorrow would be whatever it was going to be—and the day after, too. He'd roll with it.

He pulled off his paddock boots and let them hit the floor with a satisfying clunk, then undid his belt and stripped his jeans off. Bruise on his thigh but localized, laceration at the point of impact, but not deep.

Marco entered the room. He'd been supposed to get in the way and make sure a scene like the one that had just gone on was impossible. Instead, he'd been policing the aisle, Jericho knew, giving him privacy, keeping everyone else away—the shit-eating grin on his barn manager's face told him that much.

Marco launched a pair of sweats at him. "Better cover that up, Jer," he snickered.

Didn't bother to look down. He had stretch briefs on under his jeans, but swollen like this, they wouldn't even cover him. Disgusted. "Just get me some antiseptic, will you?"

Chapter Two

Starbucks was working the drive-through window, and he had about 15 minutes left before his shift was over. He looked at the monitor and saw another car was pulling up. Good-looking chick in it—but then he basically spent the whole day flirting, so no news there. Liked that part of this job pretty well, to tell the truth. Why wouldn't he?

"Welcome to Starbucks," he purred to her, already laying it on pretty good. "What can I get for you today?" Somehow, even that stock phrase sounded infinitely sexy coming from him.

"Venti nonfat latte," she answered him, leaning in toward the microphone, obviously liking his voice. Smiling.

"Three-sixty. Come on down." He knew she was already wondering what kind of face would go with that voice, and hummed a little to himself as he punched in the order, and spun around to hassle his co-worker at the espresso bar in the meantime. Liked to play the fool—got away with it pretty easily, too. Then again, he was probably way too bright for this job, and was constantly looking for ways to amuse himself.

While he waited for her to appear, and for his drink order to be ready, Brae fingered the business card in his pocket. As soon as he got out of here, he'd give this Jericho Brandeis a call. Guy had been a bit of a pain in the ass as a customer, but he seemed cool enough to talk to. Brae wondered if he'd be a shithead of a roommate—he knew he could be fairly sloppy himself—one of the things that had gotten him in trouble where he was staying now…with his current and soon to be ex-girlfriend. Slovenly, she'd called him. Bigger problem though was that he was something of an alley cat and liked to play around. He knew she was about to toss him out. Not that he'd really miss her; he wanted to leave, too. Still, living out of the back seat of his Saturn wasn't something he was too thrilled about.

The chick's car pulled up. It was a cream-colored Audi TT sports car—cute and flashy. Better looking, though, was the driver. She was probably early thirties, short-short jaggedy ash blonde hair, streaked lighter—sassy. Designer sunglasses, gorgeous mouth. Looked trim and petite sitting there. She was wearing shorts, and seemed to have fairly nice legs. Right now she was staring at him—he was used to that, knew the effect he had on women of all ages. Gave her a grin. "How are you today?"

"I wasn't doing all that great, but you know what?" she said, flashing a set of perfect white teeth at him.

"No, what?"

"I'm doing a lot better now."

Starbucks smiled. He liked when the women started the whole flirtation routine; less work for him that way. This window put him up quite a bit higher than the customers, and he could really tower over them—hell, he was tall anyway. He leaned forward, laid that lazy pale blue stare on her—he kind of always looked like he'd just been thoroughly laid, but ready to go again, maybe—he tossed out softly, "How's that?"

She reached over and grabbed a digital camera from the seat beside her. "Now hold that pose, handsome," she teased him softly. Click, click, click—took a three-burst shot. Set it back down again. "Sorry, I had to do that. I'm a photographer, and that picture was just too good to miss." Her eyes traveled up from where his hand rested on the window's ledge, along his arm and shoulder, and back to his eyes again. "Ever think of making some money with that face of yours?" she asked him. Sounded on the level too—mixed with the flirting, of course.

"Every day," Starbucks purred.

She tossed him a scolding look. "Alright, you're not serious, but if you ever are…" Reached into her wallet. She handed him a five-dollar bill, and a business card. Smiled, winked, and then simply drove away. Didn't even wait for change.

He thumbed it thoughtfully, then looked down at the name before slipping it into his pocket with Jericho's card. Darien Revson-Marx.

Hyphenated last name like that could only mean one thing. Married. Best kind, really.

———————

Twenty minutes later Brae had shared his last bullshit line of the day with his co-workers, clocked out, and was heading for the parking lot and his beat-to-shit, eight year old Saturn. White underneath the grime. The insides were worse than the exterior—sand on the mats, old receipts stuffed into the side pockets, a leather jacket crumpled in a ball in the back seat. Well, the car got the attention it deserved.

He slid behind the wheel, turned the key in the ignition and pulled out, finding his cell phone from under a pile of CD's on the passenger seat. Had already memorized Jericho's phone number just by looking at it a few times, and dialed it as he wheeled out onto Forest Hill Boulevard, heading west toward the center of Wellington.

Rang a couple of times, then a sharp, "Yeah?" Sounded out of sorts—like he was busy. Harried.

"It's Brae...you know, from Starbucks." He'd felt compelled to add that, just in case this Jericho had a bad memory for names.

"Yeah well I'm at the barn, I'll be here a while...maybe pretty late." Sounded like he turned his head away from the phone then, and was yelling at someone else. "Did I fuckin' say to put that there? No, over here...no damn it, *listen* to me...*here*." Came back to their conversation with a brusque, "Sorry. Shipper showed up late and we're trying to hand walk all the horses, plus get everything ready so we can get down to serious work tomorrow. Tack room, feed room. Setting up jumps in the sand arena and out in the field...and...hell you don't care about that." Caught himself up short. Even though he'd been rambling, he wanted to keep this abbreviated. Went straight for the point. "So okay, you've thought about this and, what?"

Starbucks answered him the same way. "I want to do it...if you're still cool with it."

"When?"

"You tell me. I'll move in today."

A pause—it almost sounded like he was hesitating, but then Brae heard a noise that he recognized easily enough. Flare of a lighter. Jericho was firing up a cigarette. Then he exhaled, confirming the Barista's guess. "I guess I don't have a problem with that, but you'll have to get over here if you want a key. And at the house, my shit's all over the place."

"That's cool." Little bit of a laugh. "You some kind of slob?"

Dry humor. "Sometimes. Live with it, don't ride my ass about it, okay?"

"Doesn't bother me." Brae turned into the development where he'd been living with his girlfriend. She'd still be at work thank God, and he could move out without a huge scene—oh, sure, there'd still be a scene, but hopefully over the phone instead of face to face. Cowardly maybe, but a hell of a lot easier. "So I'm just gonna pick up my junk, and then I'll come over. Where are you?"

"Indian Mound Road. Know it?" It was an unpaved road, but the residents liked it that way—kept the traffic down. Some of the nicest stables in the area had been built there. Definitely prime property and not too far from the showgrounds either.

"Yeah, sure."

Gave him the farm's gate code, and directions to his place. Then a *non sequitor.* "Are you still at Starbucks?" Jericho asked him. There was maybe a tinge of longing in his harsh voice.

Brae laughed. "No, why? Are you hoping I'll bring you coffee? It'd be cold in an hour anyway."

A sigh. "Yeah, shit you're right. Listen, I'm hanging up on you. I'm up to my ass here. Call if you have a problem."

Brae looked at his phone, amused. Jericho had meant it literally, apparently. There'd been a quiet click.

He'd already disconnected.

It was probably more like an hour and a half later and turning dark when Brae and his disreputable Saturn pulled down the tree-lined entrance to this year's winter home of Brandeis Show Stables.

Real nice place.

Brick pillars and wrought iron gates out front. Long tree-lined entrance. The barn wasn't huge, but man it was fancy—stucco with an expensive slate blue tile roof. Inlaid brick aisles, all brass fittings, and dark oak stall fronts. Circular drive out front with a fountain behind it. Perfectly manicured grounds, lots of flowers to add color. Beautiful grass paddocks with immaculate dark wood fencing on the left side as you approached it, large sand jumping arena and then a grass one beside it on the right. Each arena was fitted with a set of Olympic-quality jumps that were still in the process of being erected.

Brae could see Jericho in the thick of it, busting his butt as hard as any of his crew. Sweat pants, shirt off, dirty, and carrying two heavy jumping rails laid across his shoulder—and irritably barking out orders at the same time. This soon-to-be roommate of his was a piece of work, he thought.

The Barista parked in the circular drive and got out. He'd actually taken the time to drive back to Starbucks to get a Venti Latte to go. What the hell, it wasn't like he'd had to pay for it. Grabbed it and strolled over casually, watching everyone else hard at it—and glad it wasn't him.

Jericho finished laying the rails in the cups of a jump, and then turned. Saw Brae approaching. Saw the coffee in his hand. Easy and grateful smile, but one that only lasted for an instant. Caught what his guys were doing out of the corner of his eye and snapped coldly at them. "Fuck me, just fuck me…how long have you been doing this? It should be an in and out, then two strides to that Oxer, damn you. And Christ, can't you see that's not a straight line?" Pause. Brutally sarcastic. "Well, fucking fix it, Marco."

Two of the grooms, both Colombian and long-time Brandeis employees, looked at each other. One muttered, *"Cantamañanas."*

Vengeful. "Yeah, I don't give a damn if you think I'm an asshole or not. You don't ride these lines, I do."

Starbucks came over and held the coffee out to him, happily mocking him at the same time, "Why am I giving you caffeine, man?"

Jericho took it from him, tossed a long swallow back. "Thanks," he said. Starbucks fished out a pack of Marlboro Reds from his shirt pocket. Took one and held the pack out to Jericho who shrugged and took one. "Yeah, alright, for a minute," he said. "I'll be here 'til midnight, anyway." Leaned in to the light Brae offered him. Inhaled deeply. Let the smoke just trail back out from his throat. "Key's inside. I'll get it for you. Can you go to Home Depot or someplace tomorrow and get another made? I have a spare, but no earthly idea where it is and I don't feel like hunting for it."

"No sweat." Nothing was for this guy. Life just rolled.

Jericho lifted his head sharply like a sentinel. Deep blue eyes narrowed. "What's this?" he muttered. "Like I need this now."

The farm's front gates were quietly swinging open again. Two cars came through, the first a navy blue Bentley with NY plates that read "Maitland"—Richard's car—and the second, a cream-colored Audi TT sportster.

Starbucks remembered both cars from work today. Knew the first one was that "I see you haven't toned down that temper of yours one bit" guy. The second was that chick photographer, Darien Revson-Marx. Small world.

Jericho sighed in exasperation. The Maitlands…and some of their friends. Unlike Brae, he didn't recognize the second car and had no idea who was in it. But damn, couldn't they wait until tomorrow? Even so, he grabbed his tee shirt from where it was lying on the ground nearby, wiped his face and chest with it quickly, then pulled it on and started walking toward the front circle where both cars were in the process of parking. The Barista tagged along in his wake, interested, amused. Curious to see how Jericho was going to handle this one.

Both Maitlands were out of the car now. They were dressed expensively, as always, but looking now like they might be on the way to dinner. Darien Revson-Marx got out of the other car. She was similarly attired. It was kind of an odd moment. Richard Maitland looked surprised to see Brae here, though he obviously remembered him—like he probably hadn't believed Jericho earlier when he said he knew the kid. Darien looked equally surprised, but pleased to see him. "Hi," she said with a laugh, and Starbucks gave her a boyish wave.

A look over his shoulder at Brae. Annoyed, but trying to deal with it. "I won't shake your hand, Richard," Jericho said in a surprisingly cordial voice considering his mood and the situation. He indicated his wet, grime-covered body wryly. The waistband and top two to three inches of his sweatpants were soaked through. A few chestnut strands of hair had worked their way loose and were clinging damply to his unshaven jawline. "God, I'm a mess. Just trying to get everything done outside before we lose the light and have to work in the dark."

He could see that both women were staring at him—Cin probably liked the fact that they'd caught him at a disadvantage like this, looking like a field hand. As for the younger one who'd been driving the Audi...hard to guess what she was thinking. Damn, he recognized her face but couldn't put a name to it. And something was nagging him in the back of his mind. Didn't like it. Uneasy feeling, that.

"Hi, I'm Darien Revson-Marx," she spoke up. "I see you ride at the shows all the time, but I don't think we've met. I'm a big fan of yours."

"Oh, I'm sorry," Cin interrupted before Darien got too much of her trainer's attention. "I should have introduced you. I just assumed you knew each other. Well, you've seen Darien at the shows too, haven't you Jericho?"

Yeah, he remembered her. "All the time. You train with Chip Langdon, right?" Chip and Jericho regularly rode against each other, and there was no love lost there. "I saw you win that class a month ago at the Hampton Classic. Great horse you were on—I love those bloodlines," he continued. That made her smile. Jericho looked around at Starbucks. "And this is

Trevor Braeden, my roommate…well, roommate as of tonight. He's moving in. Brae, these are Richard and Cin Maitland, good customers of mine." Shrugged. To the Maitlands, "Do you want to see your horses?"

Cin gave him a pretty little smile. "Can we, just for a moment?" Like he was gonna say no to that. *Right.* "I really want Darien to see Monterrey. I was telling her about him."

"Of course, Cin." He indicated the pathway leading up to the barn, but then took the lead himself while the others followed—Brae included. In fact, he fell into step with Darien. Tossed a look at her which she seemed to like.

"Are you a horse person?" she asked him.

Shook his head in the negative. Stayed quiet, though—nice and mysterious.

Jericho stepped into the aisleway and flipped on the lights. "Your horses are in the first three stalls," he told them, stepping up to the end and largest box where Monterrey was. He slanted a look around at Darien, still not completely comfortable with why she was here and what this was about, but playing along with it. He laid his hand on the horse's halter where it hung on a hook to the side of the large sliding wood and brass door. "Should I get him out for you?"

"Please," Richard answered him.

"How's your leg, Jericho?" Cin asked wickedly, then went on to explain to her husband and their guest. "Can you believe Monterrey kicked him this afternoon? It looked like a bad cut…bleeding and everything."

"Really?" Again from Richard, and more disapproving than concerned—like maybe he was asking if he'd been inattentive or something, maybe even hinting he'd caused the problem.

Jericho frowned. How like Cin to bring up that sexually charged scene from earlier. Little bitch, she was deliberately taunting him with it, and putting him in an awkward position as well. "No, it was nothing," he said, dismissively. "Some dog was loose on the property—startled him. Kicked out and caught me, but I'm fine. Must belong to one of the neighbors. Tomorrow, I'll find out who, and make sure it doesn't happen again." Why was he defending himself? But they'd made him feel like he had to.

He brought the horse out into the aisle and held him. Monterrey took a few sideways steps, eyes wide on the people around him. Jericho murmured low to him and he quickly settled.

Darien watched and wished for her camera. The horse had a gorgeous head and was lightly butting it up against the sweaty, rough-looking, but *so male* creature holding him. Sweatpants too large for his buff waistline and falling lower on narrow hips and just above that tight rider's ass—tattoo of some kind visible when he reached up and his tee rode up with the movement—located center back, below the waist. Nice, well cut arms on him. Sharp eyes that only softened when they fell on the animal. "You're good with him" she commented. "I like a trainer who doesn't just hand the horse off to a groom when he's done riding. Some of them are such prima donnas." She walked around Monterrey slowly, reaching out to pat his glossy hide.

Jericho took offense at that. *Yeah, you ride eight horses in a day…and wash them and groom them, too. See how that works.* But he kept his mouth shut, just turned that sharp blue stare away.

Darien caught that. Nice attitude on him, she thought—whatever his problem was. Continued right on talking. "Cin, Richard…he's just magnificent. And he's…what did you say? Eight? Have you been showing him, because I don't think I've seen him before. Are you taking him out Grand Prix?"

"This will be his first season Grand Prix," Cin was explaining. "Jericho found him for us in Europe on a buying trip for someone else…" She went on to detail the whole story, while her trainer just stood there and held the animal—wasting time when he needed to be working, he thought moodily to himself. Scratch the midnight thing. Now it would probably be even later.

Starbucks had, meanwhile, just taken a position leaning against the wall. Already knew his new roommate well enough to tell he was pissed. As for himself, he was just enjoying the view. The older of the two women, Jericho's client, wasn't bad at all—hot actually—but even better was Darien in a pair of tight black slacks and sexy white halter-top. Wondered how those pictures she'd taken of him had turned out, but didn't ask her.

"Brae," Jericho said, interrupting his thoughts. "If you don't want to hang, man, go in the tack room…second door down on the left. You'll see my jeans in there—keys are in them. Bring them back here and I'll pull off the house key for you."

Shrugged. Wasn't in a hurry, but shuffled off to get them, anyway.

"You can put him away now, Jericho," Richard Maitland said, pleasantly enough but tinged with a tone of authority. Used to being in charge, respected.

Then, as the Maitlands turned to show Darien their other two horses, he walked down to meet Brae who was coming out of the tack room, jingling the keys lightly in his palm. Jericho took the set, and pulled off a key in the middle. Slapped it into the Barista's hand, gave him directions. "Don't lock me out tonight," he warned.

"Right."

Overheard Darien ask Cin in a hushed but still audible voice. "Jericho's not gay is he?" Not really such an odd question—for whatever reason, many top riders were, including her own trainer, Chip.

Looked around at her pointedly and purred, "No, he's not."

Darien looked startled, turned her head toward him, her jaggedy blonde hair swinging with the movement. Opened that luscious mouth just a bit, momentarily mortified. Then she just smiled good-naturedly. "I'm sorry, I didn't mean for you to hear that." *Obviously—duh.* "It's just that…the two of you are both so handsome, and you live together, and well, so many of the male riders are."

Startled, Starbucks straightened up taller. Hell, she'd been thinking he was gay too! What the fuck?

Jericho looked at Brae, nodded his head toward the door—a rather clear signal that said "get lost", and the younger man accommodated him. Jericho moved back over to join his customers and Darien. "Most, but not this one." Wrapped one powerful hand around the stall's brass bars next to where she was standing and rested his weight against it, just staring down at her. Would have made a more overtly sexual comment if the Maitlands hadn't been there, but settled for, "Its not like I don't get hit on all the time though, especially here." Maybe he'd meant by other men in the equestrian scene…or maybe not. Could just as easily have meant by the rich, beautiful and very female horse owners who stayed in Wellington during the winter show season. Women like Cin.

"I'll bet you do," Darien chuckled. She didn't even look uncomfortable any more about what she'd said.

Jericho shrugged. "One 'no' is usually enough. Doesn't bother me most of the time." Lifted his eyes for a second and found Cin's—little meaning for her there. Dropped them to Darien again. Murmured to her, "And hell, I have nothing to prove."

Held that eye contact with her for just a second, then he turned and walked back over to Monterrey's stall. Jericho checked his water buckets—they were down just a little. He picked up a chart clipped to the front of the horse's stall and made a notation, then opened the lever that refilled the buckets, topping them off.

Darien was trailing behind him, curious—maybe a bit fascinated. "You watch them that closely, Jericho? How much they're drinking? Every time you fill the buckets?"

Expressive look in those deep blue eyes. Exposed—maybe caught in the act of doing something close to his heart. Spoke quietly but with underplayed passion. "For the first few days after a long trip, yes. Hell, they could get shipping fever...I've seen founder..."

Darien laid a hand on his forearm—he not only looked dirty, she could feel the sand on him. Caressed his arm just lightly—pretty familiar for having just met him, but sincere, too. "I'm not criticizing you. I'm actually...very impressed."

He stepped away from her, and back toward the exit. Half turned and sought out Richard—Christ, at least he was a man and an ally in that respect. "If you'll excuse me, I have to get back out and help my guys get this done. I want those jumps up perfectly and they won't be if I'm not watching them—don't get me wrong, it's a damn good crew and they've all been with me for years, but if you don't ride a line how can you really see it? And then we still have basically everything inside yet to do."

Maitland gave him what he wanted—release—and even a little approval now too. "Go on, Jericho, and thank you. We'll see you tomorrow."

"Oh, what time?" Cin asked him, coming over close to him for the first time that evening—then again she always behaved better when her husband was standing there watching her.

"Afternoon, alright?" It was hotter in the afternoons, and even ignoring that, most of the customers liked to ride in the morning so they had the rest of their day free. Of course, Jericho knew that so he was asking for leeway. "I want to hand walk again in the morning, then if they all look happy, do a light workout in the afternoon. I'll do one or two of my own first to get a feel for the footing, then you can ride if you want to and I'll do Monterrey at three."

"I'll be tired by two or three in the afternoon," she pouted, unmoved by his explanation, and not trying to make things easier for him. "You ride them tomorrow, Jericho. I'll just come and watch."

So instead of eight horses tomorrow, ten?

Yeah, alright. Wouldn't be the first time. Still, he coaxed her. "How are you going to beat Darien here if you don't practice?" Cin looked unconvinced, although she'd tipped her head and smiled at that. Darien had a wiseass little grin on her face now. Both women were focusing on him and he took advantage of it. "Come on, I'll make you a deal, Cin. I'll ride one, you ride the other, then I'll do Monterrey after that and you can sit there in the gazebo with a wine cooler and give me shit. Now you know you'd like that."

It was true, she would. "Alright, cowboy, you win."

Brusque nod from him, half-smile and nothing more. Turned and was gone. By the time the Maitlands and Darien had strolled outside again, he was already back in the field and stripping off his shirt, tossing it negligently over one of the finished jumps. His voice, like a deep discordant bark, carried over to them. "Marco I don't know why you put water in this Liverpool already, cause I can tell you right now it has to fuckin' move."

Protests coming back at him, Spanish curse words.

Darien stood for a second there at the entrance to the barn, just watching entranced as Jericho found his cigarettes where he'd left them on the ground, and fired one up. Was sneering back at his head man at the same time, "Yeah, too damn bad. I don't give a fuck if we're here 'til two A.M., okay? It's gonna be fuckin' right tomorrow when a horse sets foot in this ring."

"Is he always like that?" she asked the Maitlands, openly curious. She knew for sure that would never be Chip down there—he'd have kicked back with a beer at one of the local watering holes an hour ago…and never gotten his hands dirty or broken a sweat either.

"Like what? You mean a perfectionist?" Richard asked, trying to clarify her question. He chuckled to himself. "Or a son of a bitch?"

"Either…both."

"Oh, honestly, Darien…it's not that interesting," Cin said taking her arm. "You don't find him attractive, do you, darling? I mean, what's Bob going to say?" Bob, as in Bob Marx, Darien's husband, and a wealthy investment banker.

"Oh, stop it, Cin, you think he's cute, too." Scolding.

"Well I certainly don't," Richard Maitland laughed, opening Darien's car door for her. "And yes, he's always like that. Both—perfectionist and difficult. Gifted rider, dedicated…but on the downside, he's got one heck of a lousy temper...though to be fair, he never shows it to the horses or the customers. Right, Cin?"

Mrs. Maitland rolled her eyes. "Enough about Jericho. Are we going to the Player's Club for dinner?"

Darien looked over at the sand arena one last time, where the unwieldy Liverpool water jump was in the process of being moved. Yeah, he'd gotten his way on that one. "Have you told him yet?" she asked.

"Told him what?"

"That you might sell Monterrey?"

"No," Richard answered her quietly but with conviction. "And I'd prefer he doesn't find out, either. Nothing's happened yet, no reason to get him upset."

She disagreed. Plenty had happened. And she'd watched him with that horse—if this all came together he was going to be...going to be what? Furious? Hurt? Impossible to deal with? Or maybe all of the above.

———

Darien followed the Maitlands out the same way she'd followed them in. It wasn't very far to the Player's Club—nice upscale place, complete with piano bar and outdoor patio seating. A favorite of the horsey set—there was always someone she knew there. As she drove she felt really happy...and a little sad. But mostly happy. Monterrey really excited her.

And Bob said he'd buy him if she wanted him...which she probably did. A cool mil or more, but who cared what the price was? Lucky for her, Richard Maitland was seeing dollar signs—the chance to double his money. But what she saw was what it might be like riding him. If she bought him, she'd be moving him over to Chip's place, naturally. But hey, this wouldn't be the first time Jericho lost a ride he really wanted, she reasoned to herself. He was a big boy, he'd handle it.

She pulled her Audi into a spot in the Player's Club parking lot. Richard and Cin had driven up to the valet, but Darien didn't see a reason to. As she stepped out, she noticed something on the floor and reached over to pick it up.

It was her own business card, and someone had written on the back of it, "I'm serious." Darien smiled, and then gave in and laughed. The Barista. Only question was, what was he serious about?

Chapter Three

It wasn't actually two in the morning when Jericho pulled the Mustang into the carport. It was only 1:15, and he'd been working solidly since noon. Filthy and exhausted, that about summed it up. His leg was bothering him some, which wasn't good—tomorrow would start early, and he had all his horses to ride. He'd do some of the hand walking first—like Monterrey.

Walked up the sidewalk to his place with long slashing strides, but slower than normal—it was a nice house but not pretentious, located in the section of the Polo Club called Las Casistas—duplex houses really, though they didn't feel like that, basically just bungalows with one shared wall. Stucco exterior, nice tile roof. His was a three bedroom, he used one as an office. Big, oversized, caged pool out back overlooking the golf course. Comfortable.

The door was unlocked, and he pushed it open. Stepped into the small foyer...the living room lay in front of him. And there was Starbucks lying on the sofa—or more accurately, sprawled. The big screen plasma TV was on, but he wasn't watching it. He'd fallen asleep bunched up in the comforter from his bed, but for whatever reason had dragged it out here. The clothes he'd been wearing and his shoes and socks lying in two or three piles the middle of the floor. Empty bottle of beer on the floor close by where his hand dangled. If the place hadn't looked a wreak this morning, it sure as shit did now. Jericho could already see he was going to have to have the maids in more often. Truth was though, the messy room didn't bother him much.

As for Brae, he'd wake up tomorrow good and cramped if he stayed on the couch all night like this, but too bad. Leave him be.

He was stripping his own clothes off as he walked, dropping them on the Mexican tile floor just like his roommate had, and Christ they were disgusting. He was, too. Stunk of sweat, his whole body gritty. Man, he couldn't stand himself—no way he could go to bed like this, but at least the barn looked spotless. Instead he went into his bathroom and turned the shower on. In minutes he was standing under it, letting the water run over him. Disgusting mud-tinged water pooled at his feet, but it felt good, and he turned his face up to the spray and yanked his hair free. Worked a lather up and scrubbed down, taking particular care with the injury on his thigh, getting the dirt out of it. It probably took him twenty minutes, but at the end he felt human again—tired but good. He'd shave in the morning.

He rubbed a thick bath towel over his head and body briskly, then wrapped it around his waist. Padded barefoot back out into the main living area, through it and into the kitchen. Hadn't eaten but didn't care much about food right now. What he wanted first was a beer, and there was plenty of that unless Starbucks had gone through enough of it for a small army—and if he had, he was gonna be a dead man. Opened the fridge—found tons left on the shelf. Jericho grabbed one, twisted the cap off and lobbed it into the sink rather than walking around to where the trash was, tossed the bottle back and swallowed a good third of it.

Pizza box on the dining room table. He lifted the lid—only one piece sitting there and cold. Took a bite of it. Man it was gross but who gave a shit? He kept on eating till he'd finished it. Lit a cigarette, grabbed another beer to take with him, and started heading back to his own bedroom—the biggest and master. Starbucks was stirring as he walked past him, but Jericho ignored him. Just as he was disappearing into his own space, he heard a decided female and somewhat groggy voice saying, "Hey, who's she?"

Oh fuck man, he thought with disgust, stopping in his tracks at the entrance to his bedroom. Whoever this chick was, she'd seen his hair most likely and not much else—unbraided and wet it hung well down below his shoulder blades. Still…

Already tonight, he'd had Darien damn near calling him gay. Now Starbucks' bitch thought he actually *was* a woman. I mean, really—it was too much. Spun around and came back into the room, and now his attitude and walk were purely predatory. Laid his beer on an end table, and stubbed his cigarette out in an ashtray, then went over to the couch and stripped the covers back just far enough to find the pretty little thing. Her face, anyway.

She was closer to his age than Brae's, attractive but smudged a bit and her chin-length dark hair wild from his roommate's attentions and being wrapped up in the comforter. Jericho leaned over her, pressed one knee down into the soft fabric, separating her from what he assumed was Starbuck's body, half mounting her, weight carried on the hand he laid down directly between her face and Brae's. "Let me tell you this much," he murmured dangerously to her. "I'm totally fucking male."

The Barista jerked awake. "What…huh?"

"This your girlfriend?" Jericho demanded.

"No, not really."

"Good." Pushed, making more room for himself—squeezing Brae, who was closest to the back of the sofa, up and out of the way, and down to the other end of it. Leaned his face in closer, those deep blue eyes intense and demanding now, and totally leveled on hers. "Christ, I've been cock-teased too much today," he growled. No panic from this femme and no objections. He laid his mouth over hers, parting her lips, immediately deepening the kiss and laying claim. Delicate little arms went around his neck, accepting him.

He kept it up, kept kissing her, moving further onto the sofa over her. Heard his roommate chuckling, and knew this chick didn't mean anything special to him—more like he was enjoying watching this. Brae had even found Jericho's beer and taken it for himself, getting comfortable at his end of the large piece of furniture.

He lifted his head from her mouth, and looked back around at him, confirming an important point. "She's eighteen, isn't she?" Damn sure looked it, but you never knew until you asked.

Barista smirked. "Oh yeah. Knock yourself out."

Stripped the comforter back, and the towel off his waist. No surprise, he was up and damn hard already. Nice little body moving sweetly under him. He spread her knees with his own and slid in between them. "You're cool with this, right?"

He was asking Brae, not her.

"Totally, but watch it, huh? And don't kick me."

Didn't matter what Brae answered him anyway because Jericho was already positioning himself at that slick opening—then stroked himself up into her good and deep. She cried out softly, arching her back to take him, and he grabbed her ass and pulled her sharply to himself. Fully impaled now. He growled fiercely at the feel of her tight around him. Started moving over her immediately, staying up about six inches above her—weight easily carried on his right arm and knee. Not pressing his body to hers except where they were joined together, but there his position was really creating friction—especially along the upper side of his swollen erection and over that ultra sensitive nub of flesh directly above the entrance to her sheath. His knees pressed against hers, keeping her nice and open for him. She moaned and thrashed beneath him, panting, "Yes, yes, yes…oh God, yes," while he snarled like some wild animal, varying the rhythm…faster, then slow and tantalizing, and that made her really buck up, seeking more of him.

Really good show, Starbucks decided—beat the hell out of that lame porn they had on cable. He moved away to a chair that gave him a better view, lit a cigarette and swallowed what was left of Jericho's open beer—then pulled the cap off the second bottle and started in on it too. It didn't bother him at all that his roommate was fucking this chick's brains out…except it was a bit irritating that she hadn't sobbed and writhed quite like that when he was doing her. But, so what? He'd just have to practice more—maybe every night, right? Sounded like a pretty Goddamn good plan to him.

Had an idea suddenly. Brae looked around for his open suitcase—it was on the floor not far away. He groped around through it till he found what he was looking for. Smirked.

Jericho had now hunched up his powerful back and shoulders, nearly enveloping his companion's small form. His free hand was still possessively cupping her ass and lifting her in time with his rhythm, as he brought some real power to the way he was thrusting into her. Her words were incoherent now, except that she was nearly begging, or maybe really begging…for more…for him not to stop…for him to make her come. His lips plundered her neck, his long wet mass of hair hanging down, covering both of their faces and spilling over onto the sofa beneath her. She rolled onto it, trapping him there, and he didn't object one bit.

Oh yeah, world-class fucking going on…Brae had to give Jericho that much. He lifted the digital camera he'd fished out of his suitcase, turned it on, focused it…then remembered the pictures Darien had taken of him earlier, and reset the mode to three-burst. Looked through the viewfinder. Aimed again.

The chick beneath Jericho threw her head back and cried out sharply, and man he could feel her contracting hard around his throbbing cock…so mother fucking hard, and oh sweet Jesus it just pulled him right over the edge with her. He arched his back; the muscles were rippling, tight and as explosive as a drawn compound bow. Then reared up and threw his head back…*Click, click, click*…that long chestnut mane whipping over his head and flying wild behind him for an instant…eyes closed, lips drawn back in a guttural roar as his orgasm hit him with voracious force. The sound the camera was making *did* register with him, and he knew that Brae was over there taking a bunch of pictures while he fucked, but at the moment he was so consumed with release he couldn't really comprehend that, much less do anything about it. He pushed deeper, holding himself there while he emptied into her. *Click, click, click.*

Starbucks rose, put his camera away, and then strolled nude into the kitchen. By the time he returned, Jericho had almost returned to the land of the living—the femme, too, for that matter, but who cared? "Left hand," Brae ordered, and his new roommate lifted it on cue. Slapped a freshly opened beer bottle into it.

"Thanks…" Nodded his head to the very replete looking woman below him. "…for her, too…I needed it."

"De nada," the Barista murmured. He sat down on the floor next to Jericho and watched as he took a long pull on his beer, then leaned over the woman and fell to kissing her again, toying with her mouth, deepening it. Then getting more serious about it—like he wanted her again and damn soon. Managed to growl against her lips, "And no more fucking pictures, hear me? Erase the ones you already took."

"Oh, hell," he lied, laughing. "I was just busting you. I already did."

"Welcome to Starbucks."

Brae had been late for work the next morning, but nobody gave him much shit about it. They'd even clocked him in so that he'd be paid for the full shift. And now he was back at his customary place at the drive-through window—hair rumpled, unshaven, though that wasn't a big deal since he didn't have that much beard. Rakishly charming as always, drawing the customers in.

Sexy female voice. "Hi, Brae."

Of course that could be one of a number of his favorite customers. He looked up at the monitor, saw the Audi TT sitting there. Darien. "Venti non-fat Latte for you today?" he asked happily—making it sound like remembering her drink made her special, although the truth was, he had a pretty unerring memory for things like that. Upped the tips.

31

"Exactly," she laughed, flattered.

She was sitting in front of him a few minutes later. Handed him her money, and the business card he'd written on the day before. "What's that mean?" she asked him.

He feigned surprise. "Well, you said I should let you know when I get serious."

"Want to talk?" she asked him pointedly.

"Sure, I'll take a break. Can you stay for a few?"

"Okay. Should I wait for you out front?"

"Grab a table, I'll be right there." Truth was, he looked anything but serious. More like just seriously flirting…well, he never really did anything seriously, but the subject of women was the one where he got closest to it.

And of course, he really shouldn't be getting a break this early either, but knew the store manager would let him get away with it. He sauntered out a few minutes later, and came over to sit with Darien. She was sipping her Latte, and had her camera beside her. Lifted her eyebrows expressively—silently telling him this better not be just bullshit, but still smiling at him.

He flopped into a chair, reached for her camera and turned it in his hand, looking at it. "So what do you do weddings or something?" he teased her.

"No."

Held it up like he was going to take her picture with it.

Patient. "Brae…it always works better when you take the lens cover off."

Set the camera back down. "Yeah, I like taking pictures too," he baited her, a wicked sort of gleam coming into his pale blue eyes. More like naughty. Picked the camera up again and leaned over close to her, still pretending to be focusing on her, and still not removing the cover.

"Oh, do you?" Despite herself, she liked his ridiculous banter, and wasn't even annoyed that he probably wasn't serious about working with her one bit—well, not serious about having a portfolio of shots taken, anyway.

"I'm pretty good at it, I think," he went on. "I mean…could I show you some of my work?" He seemed sincere…and not sincere at the same time. Frustratingly impossible to read.

She raised her chin skeptically. "Are these going to be pictures you took of yourself looking like one of the three stooges?" Sipped her Latte again, but just couldn't quite hide the grin that was toying with her lips.

He reached over and grabbed her wrist, looked intent...almost. "No, honestly. I really think these are good shots, okay?" Cast his eyes down modestly, or even defensively. "You probably won't. Oh hell, forget it. So what did you want to say to me...I mean, you were the one who started this conversation in the first place, right?"

"Alright, show me your pictures," she relented, and he went loping off to his car without needing further encouragement.

Came loping back, same charming but foolish grin on his face. Get ready for anything—he knew that's what she was thinking as he dropped back into his chair again. There was a small digital camera in his hand now. He hesitated. Pulled out a cigarette and lit it.

"Well?" Darien encouraged him.

Finally set the camera down in front of her. "There's only a few shots on the disk."

Darien picked up the small unit, turning it over in her hand and looking at the controls. Not too difficult to figure out. She turned it on and set it in "Review" mode, so she could go through the images one by one. The first was a rather goofy shot of someone's Golden Retriever. Her brow knit, not getting it.

"No, no...not that," Starbucks said hurriedly. "That's just my ex-girlfriend's dog. Uhm, she took it. Keep going. Past that."

A few more of the dog, none of them remotely remarkable. The expression on her face was slowly turning to annoyed. Next shot at a cockeyed angle, and seemed to be a picture of a man's foot.

"Oh, hey," the Barista laughed, "That one was an accident. Yeah, keep going."

"I'm going to shoot you if you're wasting my time," Darien threatened, but scrolled forward to the next picture anyway.

She caught her breath, her eyes widened, and her gorgeous mouth grew slack. The image was unmistakably Jericho Brandeis...and it was heartstopping. Magnificent male animal, caught—not just in the sex act—but in the full throes of orgasm...absolutely no question about that. Hair flying wild around him—the movement stopped so perfectly that it was obvious he'd just reared up like this and thrown his head back. The expression on his face somewhere between ferocious and transcendent. The woman beneath him, just a means to an end. This was a picture about male carnal pleasure. Definitely not love or anything close to it.

What's more, the picture had been taken at an angle, which while explicit, wouldn't even be considered X-rated.

"Why did you show me this?" Darien asked him finally.

"You don't like it?"

"It's…" Boy, she hated even answering that question, not when she was this unsure of what he was doing and what it meant. Or how it was going to come back to bite her. "It's…really, really good." Yeah, he'd simply caught a moment and it was a great one, but still the picture could have looked amateurish, the lighting wrong, poorly framed…it could have looked like those dog shots. Well not really, but the point was the same, and this wasn't any of that. It was genuine art.

Starbucks smiled happily, basking in her praise and her obvious shock at what he'd produced. "There's more, keep going."

"All pictures like this one?"

"Well nothing actually shows," he pointed out, reaching over like he was going to scroll the camera forward himself.

But Darien wouldn't let him. She pulled it away and closer to herself, then moved on to the next picture, couldn't seem to help it. And then the one after that. And the next. Six frames in all. She could tell they were two sets of three-bursts images. One pagan shot after another, any one of them good enough to sell. But whether accident or talent, she didn't have a clue. And most likely Starbucks over there was just baiting her—wanting to see her face when he showed these pictures to her. Although…that didn't quite seem like him.

Finally, she set the camera down. Picked up her Latte and drank from it thoughtfully. "Jericho know you took these pictures?"

A shrug. "Took them, yes. But he thinks I erased them." Then he grinned.

A light breeze ruffled her short jaggedy blonde hair as she sat there. Inexplicably, she found herself smiling back at him. Was about to tell him to take some more pictures—not this subject, but something different. Something to show that this was more than rank beginner's luck. But before she could get the words out, another of the Starbucks crew came out the front door, and muttered irritably, "Brae, are you ever coming back to work?"

"Yeah, right now." He reached over and nabbed the little camera as he came to his feet. Said with some satisfaction in his voice, "Well now at least you know one thing for sure, don't you?"

"What's that?"

He was already heading for the door, but walking backwards so that he could still talk to her face-to-face. "Jericho and I—yeah, we room together. But we're not queer for each other, alright?"

For a minute she just couldn't even comprehend it, she was that stunned. "I'll kill you," she said, disbelieving, but feeling a chuckle coming on in spite of herself. ·

Was that what this whole thing had been about? Couldn't ask him though—he'd already disappeared back inside the store.

Jericho's day was proceeding in an orderly way, and he kept a pretty ruthless schedule for the most part, only relaxing when the customer's needs required him to slow the pace. Cin was on her horse now, and he was giving her a lesson. She looked perfect as usual, but had arrived late—also as usual. She hadn't even been there to see him work her first big hunter, Cabaret, but this one—a very expensive and very experienced competitor named Firedance—she really loved. Huge deep red chestnut, three white socks, perfect star on his face…and jumped like an angel. Since she did the adult amateur hunter classes, the jumps weren't all that high, but the horse had to take them flawlessly, and Firedance did that if ridden properly. He even did it when not ridden properly—or at least he tried.

Most trainers sat at the side of the ring when they were teaching—or in the gazebo, if they had one, and there was a large gazebo here, outfitted with expensive outdoor furniture in hunter green with tan trim—Brandeis Show Stables colors. Jericho, however, very rarely sat there. Instead he paced in front of it, or if things weren't going the way he wanted, he'd go all the way out to the middle of the jumping arena and walk around close to his student while he worked with them, maintaining an almost constant dialogue—or monologue, depending.

He was in the middle of the arena now, dressed as usual—worn jeans stuffed into tall black field boots and a white polo shirt with his stable's logo embroidered on it. Riding gloves tucked under his belt. Hair pulled severely back and braided again. Dark, narrow, rimless sunglasses. Riding crop in one hand that he played with and slapped negligently against the side of his boot as he talked. "Come on, Cin," he called to her as she worked over a line of three-foot rails with a final oxer. "You're bringing him in way too deep to the fences, and then he has to lurch to clear them. Yeah, they're clean but the picture's awkward. That's just points you're throwing away."

Looked up and saw Darien Revson-Marx had driven up and was walking over to take a seat in the gazebo. Skintight navy breeches and a white riding shirt, Dansko clogs and little Chanel logo socks, expensive Hermes belt—yeah, the outfit looked good on her. She and Cin waved to each other.

"Alright, do it again," he quietly ordered but with powerful authority, demanding his student's attention back again.

"Jericho, I'm tired," Cin pouted. "It's enough for today."

Looked up at her, laid a stare on her that was potent even behind those dark sunglasses, purred to her, "*Again.*" She looked annoyed but picked up her reins, and satisfied, he returned to his dialogue. "Do a 20-meter circle at the end there before you take the line. I want to see him balanced with more weight on the hind end. Cin...sit *deeper and push*...alright, alright, better." Pause. "No *keep* him that way. Do the circle again."

He lit a cigarette as he watched. Caught Darien staring at him almost transfixed. But when he looked over at her she quickly dropped her eyes— she looked embarrassed, and guilty. But when she thought he wasn't watching her, her eyes came right back to him—looking at him more so than at Cin and her horse. What was that about?

Drew on his cigarette, and then called out. "Stay on the circle 'til you get this. Cin, he's got to have weight on the hind end so he can lift his front legs from the shoulder to take the jump—he's got to bascule...to round over the fence, understand me?"

"Yes, master," Cin called back sarcastically, but teasing him at the same time, and doing better at what he wanted.

"*Right there,*" Jericho said emphatically. "Right there, do you feel that? That's where I want him. Keep that. Finish out the circle and take the line. And not too deep to the fences, okay? Come on, Cin...find your spot. Look up at it, not down at the horse." She came up to the first fence, and sailed over it. Real pretty. Then the second. Same. And finally the oxer—a bigger and wider obstacle. She rode into it, the horse gathered himself..."*Release,*" Jericho yelled to her.

Smooth, beautiful jump, nice and round, front feet tucked up tight and together. Perfect landing.

"*Good*. Pat him. You're through." He drew on the cigarette again, then tossed it. Swung around…Darien was staring at him again, and he muttered unhappily to himself as she pretended she hadn't been and turned to where Cin was pulling up instead.

"Great ride," she said, and Cin beamed.

From Jericho. "Walk him for five minutes, Cin, then Marco will take him, okay?"

"You're such a task master, Jericho," his client scolded, but not seriously. She'd loved that last line and knew she wouldn't have gotten it if he hadn't been after her as hard as he had.

"Yeah, well someone needs to push your ass," he said, lifting a sardonic smirk to her, satisfied himself. He was already walking around now, readjusting the jumps, raising them up to between three feet and three feet six. Not all of them either—just a few lines. Getting ready for his next ride.

Marco appeared at the entrance to the barn, leading a huge prancing bay, tacked up with Jericho's personal saddle and ready to go. Monterrey. Jericho watched them approaching for a few seconds, but then started walking toward them. As he did, he saw out of the corner of his eye the Maitland's big Bentley coming down the tree-lined drive. Richard, and here just in time to watch his big time jumper work. Good.

Marco and Jericho met at the edge of the sand arena, and Jericho took the horse's reins. Ran his hand down the animal's neck once, murmured to him. Checked the girth, the way the bit sat in his mouth, looked at the jumping boots that supported and protected the tendons between hoof and knee, and the little bell boots on just his front legs to cover the vulnerable coronet band at the start of the hoof. Satisfied with Marco's meticulous tacking job, he lowered the stirrup on his side, while his head groom pulled down the one on the far side and then leaned his weight into it so the saddle wouldn't shift while Jericho quickly mounted him.

The horse sidled to one side, and pranced anxiously with his head up and blowing as Jericho guided him into the ring. Huge walk on the horse, with the back feet well overstepping the tracks of the front and relaxing, which pleased his trainer. Jericho looked over and saw Richard and another man in his mid to late forties approaching the gazebo now. Darien had been watching him again he realized irritably—and not just at the horse, but more directly looking at him and probing—but now she turned and waved, rising as the second man came over to her, hugged her lightly and kissed her cheek. Husbandly look about him, so this would be Bob

Marx, Jericho guessed. Cin was off her horse by now and sitting there, too—Marco had taken it. So this was the Maitlands showing off for the Marxes. Alright, no problem there.

Jericho began warming the horse up slowly, lowering his neck and rounding out his topline at the walk first, and then at the posting trot, to stretch out his back muscles. The people in the large gazebo were helping themselves to refreshments from the cooler behind the small bar he'd set up, which was what it was there for, anyway, so that was more than fine with him. too. He picked up an easy canter, eventually working his way over to the gazebo to say hello.

Pulled to a stop in front of it. "Welcome," he said to all of them generally—first time he'd greeted Darien, though she'd been there for probably 20 minutes or more. Then looked more directly at the man he assumed was Bob Marx. Laid his left hand over both reins at the horse's wither and extended his right. "Jericho Brandeis," he introduced himself.

The man stepped forward and took it in a firm shake, then released him. "Bob Marx," he said, confirming Jericho's guess. "Darien's husband," he added. "Seen you ride often. Pleasure to meet you."

Simple head nod in return, but this guy looked pretty much to the point, and like he wouldn't want to be gushed over. Jericho took up the reins again, about to get back to what he'd been doing.

Richard's voice stopped him. "Why so low with the jumps? He'll barely even notice them, and you always say the higher they are, the better he likes them."

Something flashed through Jericho's eyes but he didn't vocalize it. Oh yeah, he thought, what he was doing wasn't showy enough for the Maitlands' taste—they wanted their friends to see Monterrey sailing over the big ones. "He only got off the trailer 24 hours ago," he reminded Richard with uncharacteristic patience. "He doesn't look tired, I know, but he's still tight and he's not used to this humidity. This first workout, I want to be easy. But if you insist, I'll have Marco raise a line toward the end of my ride so you can really see him. Just not anything over four feet, and nothing too wide. And I'd rather only ride it once…alright with you?"

"Sure, that's fine." Easy grin, but bothersome—maybe because it was more tractable than he usually tended to be.

Again, Jericho just nodded, but then added, "I'll have Marco come over and you tell him which line you want to see. Or hell, I can do two so you'll get a turn and a lead change, but then that's it." Didn't wait for, or want concurrence…or especially further negotiating. Instead, he pivoted the horse smoothly around and took off at an easy canter back toward the end of the arena closest to the barn. Raised his voice, and barked out, "Marco!" His man came out at a trot, moving quickly over to him and they conferred for a few minutes, then Jericho rode off going back to the workout while Marco stepped over to the gazebo.

For the next 15 minutes, he did only flatwork. Well, that would bore them, but fuck them—the horse needed it and they could socialize in the meantime. Took a five-minute walk break. Finally, he started facing Monterrey with the lower fences, keeping him at an easy lope, not pushing him.

Effortless.

Man, he wasn't even trying, but Jesus he could fly. Had to hold him back really—a delicate balance of subtle rein pressure and push from behind with seat and legs to keep him packaged—otherwise he'd stride in so big and plough the rails down, just because he wasn't paying attention to them. Jericho rode him with art, keeping him happy and relaxed—perfect two-point up to the fence, clean release without throwing away the contact. Total partnership between man and animal. Monterrey, trying hard to please.

Marco, he could see, had worked the line with the in-and-out to the oxer, and then of course, now he was raising the hardest line along the back side of the arena with a triple, to the Liverpool, to the Wall—how predictable was that? But alright, from what he'd changed so far, Jericho could see that Maitland had stuck to their agreement…though just barely. The in-and-out and oxer both were around four feet…the oxer maybe a tad higher, but not more than three feet wide, so okay. The triple was a bounce to a one stride, and the bounce had been set at three foot six—good. The one stride at four feet—okay. The Liverpool—a jump with water under it—was also set at four feet or a tad higher, and Marco was over at the wall, working on it now.

So fine, he'd give them a show, but it was gonna be a short show and they'd have to live with that. He picked up a nice easy loping canter and rode to the far end of the ring. But when he turned the corner to come back around and face the first of the two lines, that simple canter really changed. Jericho sat in, and spurred Monterrey, giving him more head, and the bay leapt forward suddenly like he'd been shot out of a cannon— the kind of breathtaking flat out gallop usually reserved for a timed, jump-off round. He could hear Cin's cry of delight as Monterrey hit the in-and-out almost full bore and cleared it like a stag—single bounce and huge leap out, right on his mark. Two strides to the oxer, feet scrambling a bit, head up, snorting and excited and still really moving like his tail was on fire. Jericho came up in the irons, lifting him into the take off, easy release, and he sailed over it clean.

Jericho signaled for a flying change of lead and then made an incredibly tight turn to the second jumping line to show just how handy this animal was, and heard his little audience really cheering, but kept his attention full on the upcoming triple now. Monterrey was loving the run, and had no problem with any of the triple's three elements—or with maintaining his blistering pace. Bounce, then one stride, over and out.

The Liverpool in front of them now…the horse looked at the water and the sun's reflection on it and might have hesitated or run out but for the man on his back who squeezed once with his legs, drove with his seat and then raised him up to it. Trusted his rider implicitly…tucked his legs and gave it his heart.

Bearing down on the wall now, only three strides to reach it, but *fuck, fuck, fuck,* Jericho realized…it was easily five feet tall, a monster obstacle, and he'd hadn't even been expecting it. About a second to react…and not enough space to turn the horse aside, cause man this big bay was moving like he had banshees right on his ass. Jericho found the spot with his eyes, cut the stride just a hair to hit it, faced the horse with it and asked, coming up himself in perfect balance…huge release to give him his neck… Monterrey had lifted from the shoulders in a beautiful bascule, then thrust powerfully from his hind legs in the take off. A massive jump, easily Olympic quality, and never, never, never even the hint of a stop from him. His rider said fly…and he flew.

Big landing, with Jericho staying well up off his back in two-point for the first two strides, and then coming right back to a perfectly controlled canter—the animal excited but happy, he even tossed in a little buck at the end of it to prove the point.

Jericho patted his neck, told him he was the most wonderful horse on earth, and Monterrey shook his head, full of himself, digging the praise and so very proud. His rider was equally thrilled with his performance, but man he wanted to punch Richard Maitland in the jaw—and Marco too, the prick, how dare he? How dangerous was it to raise that jump to that height without warning him they were doing it? Even if Maitland didn't understand that, Marco damn well did.

And did the Maitlands give a fuck that they'd just risked injury to their best horse?

"Fucking fantastic, Jericho!" he heard a man's voice call out to him. Looked around sharply at the gazebo. Saw Chip Langdon standing there, clapping along with the rest of them. When had he arrived?

Chip Langdon. And dressed to ride.

Felt like he'd just been punched in the stomach as realization hit him hard. *Oh Jesus, and fuck me,* Jericho thought, both enraged and sick at heart. Now he thought he understood why Darien had been watching him so strangely—she'd known that he was about to be blind sided...or less politely, screwed. Marxes weren't just here watching the Maitlands' fancy horse go around...not by a long shot.

No, he'd just shown them Monterrey to buy.

If he was right, the next thing that would happen would be that Chip would get on the horse.

"Jericho, can you bring him back over here," Richard Maitland called out to him.

Oh yeah, here it came...or maybe they still wouldn't tell him. Wouldn't have the decency or the guts.

He rode the Monterrey over at an easy, even trot. Pulled to a halt in front of the gazebo—but it was the only thing he planned to give them. Christ, he was gonna make Richard ask him to dismount—ask him to let Chip get on.

Completely awkward moment, that.

And man, he just held it there for a few agonizing seconds. No one saying a word. All five of them, Chip included, looking guilty as hell. Yeah, Jericho was enraged, but he was a professional above all. And yes, he dearly wanted to tell them all how fucked he thought they were. Didn't though...not that his silence was helping defuse the situation. His expression was harsh, despite the fact that dark glasses hid the brutal scorn in those deep blue eyes. *Assholes,* leaving it to him to salvage this...'cause it was obvious none of them had the fucking balls to deal with him. Kicked both feet out of the stirrups, vaulted off, then pulled the reins over the horse's head, and simply handed them to Chip.

"Jericho..."

Quelled him with a look—and he could stick that "I'm so innocent" crap up his ass too, cause Jericho sure as shit wasn't buying it. Chip had known in advance what was going to go down here—should have had the courtesy to warn him, but, no, he'd wanted the damn horse too much, that was clear enough.

He silently held his whip up, the condemnation in that simple gesture unambiguous, and Langdon wordlessly took it from his hand.

Turned and walked away—but not all the way away. Just down to the end of the arena, putting as much distance between himself and the gazebo crew as possible. Stood watching, arms folded over his chest while Chip adjusted the stirrups, and then mounted Monterrey and took him back out into the arena to ride and evaluate.

Yeah, he told himself, they were both professional trainers, but the truth was his style and Chip's were on opposite ends of the spectrum. Jericho spent a lot of time on groundwork and basics. He believed in a light consistent contact with the horse's mouth. Chip's schooling sessions were shorter—more time over fences, and he tended to saw the reins to keep control. Monterrey looked confused, and he wasn't liking it much.

Jericho swung his face vengefully back toward the barn, and bellowed, "Marco!" The head groom reappeared, but he was walking slow and looked reluctant. From the gazebo, they could see the two of them talk for a moment—whatever Jericho was saying it was slashing and harsh. And then Marco took off at a good clip back into the barn, to return sheepishly just minutes later with some kind of leather binder in his hand. Jericho coldly yanked it from him and started back to where the Maitlands and Marxes were sitting. But his eyes had never once left Chip and the horse.

Langdon had finished a brief flatwork session, and was now about to face the horse to a line. Appeared to be starting with one of the lower ones, not the two Marco had raised minutes earlier. At least he wasn't totally stupid, Jericho thought.

He stepped into the gazebo, basically ignoring his clients. Everyone there was silent, or at least they were now that he was near. Still watching Monterrey, he extended the leather binder to Darien. He was perfectly controlled, but underneath that, violence smoldered—frightening.

"What's this?" she managed to ask him in a hushed voice.

"Vet records, registration papers, show record," he said voice tight. "If you have questions, ask." Didn't even turn his face to her as she took the binder from him and opened it.

The first line Chip attempted was anything but beautiful—Monterrey was fighting the bit and he knocked the rail down on fence number one, coming in way too deep to it. Then he scrambled and took the second fence from too far out, tipping that rail out of the cups as well.

Jericho was standing there, just beside and slightly in front of Darien's chair. She could see his right hand ball into a powerful and dangerous-looking fist, and heard him snarl under his breath—no words, just a deep venomous growl. Man, he was pissed, and the truth was, she didn't blame him. All that wild, feral energy she'd seen captured in Brae's pictures had now turned to forcibly repressed temper...and as uncomfortable as it made her, it excited her, too. She longed to touch him, quiet him maybe. To be honest—and she always tried to be honest with herself—she hadn't been able to take her eyes off him all afternoon...kept seeing those six frames one after another in her mind. Was seeing them still.

"What are you doing tonight, Jericho?" Cin quietly dared to ask him.

His face turned to her. Silence, then in a virulent purr, "The same thing I was doing last night, Cin."

He meant working late...but Darien could only remember those six frames—relentlessly appearing in an erotic slideshow in her mind's eye. Imagined him with that same woman, working out his anger in another round of primal sex. Demanding an outlet—and just plain taking it.

"Why don't you join all of us for dinner?" Cin continued on bravely— or maybe she didn't totally understand how furious he was with them...or how betrayed he felt. "Around eight o'clock? We'll be at Nicole's."

No response.

Chip's second line was no improvement on the first one. Although the first fence was clean, it was also pretty wild, and then Monterrey simply ploughed through the second element of the line, sending the entire verti- cal, including the side standards, tumbling to the ground.

"*Oh, fuck me,*" Darien heard Jericho murmur viciously to himself, though she was probably the only one who was close enough to hear. That fist tightened yet again, and man it looked like it could be punitive. He stepped out of the gazebo with purpose, walking into the middle of the arena with long heated strides.

"Oh God," she whispered.

"No, don't worry," Richard told her with authority. He both looked and sounded smug—and even somewhat perversely amused. Pleased with himself. "He'll never do anything rash if the horse's safety is involved."

Possibly right, but pretty low, Darien thought.

Chip had pulled up and was waiting for him. "Alright, help me," he said plainly, but keeping his voice quiet as Jericho approached.

He'd stopped first to right the vertical they'd just tipped over—did it very deliberately, taking his sweet old time. Finally he lifted his eyes to Chip. "Tell me why I should."

Langdon had his number though, and played the only card he knew damn well would work with him. "Because you care about this horse. Because he's worked too long already today, and you want to see him go back to the barn—not stay out here tight and fighting it while I try to figure him out."

Those dark sunglasses only partially hid the wounded look in his eyes…and the very eloquent unveiled threat. "You lousy prick."

"Yeah, I am. Now help me with him."

Jericho laid a hand on Monterrey's neck, and got a rather desperate and insecure head butt back from him. "Chip," he warned in a deep savage growl, "You better fuckin' hide from me, cause if I see you after this, anywhere outside the showgrounds…man, I'll be in your face full force…and that's a promise, I swear to Christ it is." Both of them knew it wasn't an idle threat, either. He could see he'd really worried the other professional, and maybe that satisfied him for a bit.

Stepped away, paced a minute, then threw a punishing glare his way. "For Christ's sake, it's a big fucking horse," he lashed at him. "You have him way out behind himself, his back's hollow coming into the jump, and then you fuckin' jerk the reins instead of lifting him. And your release…" His voice was so utterly derisive. "Oh hell, you totally throw him away. You want a lesson from me Chip, then put him on a circle around me."

Jesus. Don't be such a cunt, Jericho." Yeah, he'd asked for help, but to make it obvious in front of his customers? How embarrassing was that?

Sneered at him. Didn't give a shit, frankly wanted to rub his face in it. "Do it."

"You bitch."

Slanted a vicious and thoroughly unpleasant smile at him. Waited…waited to be obeyed.

And finally, Chip acquiesced. It was humiliating for sure, but not worse than having the horse all over the place and knocking down everything in sight…and he couldn't even blame it on Monterrey, not after those incredible two lines with Jericho aboard.

"Canter," Jericho told him. Yeah, Chip could ride—it wasn't like he couldn't. But he didn't work hard enough at it…oh, but he was gonna fuckin' work right now.

Chip signaled for the canter and Monterrey picked it up without a hitch.

Words soft, taunting—but in another sense he was actually cutting Chip one hell of a break. After all, he just needed to raise his voice a little and the Marxes and Maitlands would hear every word he said. "*Come on,* damn you. You're a professional trainer. Is that canter good enough? He's not coming on from behind, and he's not round…are you gonna fuckin' fix that…or are you waiting for me to tell you?"

Really furious look back from Langdon, but he sat in anyway and tried to make it happen.

"Better," Jericho said. "Now do it in two-point like you were riding to a fence."

"What the hell's going on out there?" Bob Marx spoke up, not believing what he was seeing.

"Looks like Jericho's schooling him," Cin giggled. "Oh gee, that's rich."

It went on for 10 minutes…flatwork, then finally fences, but by the end of it he had Chip and Monterrey moving like a team, the horse flying over the obstacles the way he'd been born to do. And Chip, though he'd been shown up and dressed down rather handily…looked thrilled. He pulled up after his last fence, and said, "Oh man, this animal…" Looked around himself, confused. Jericho was no longer standing there with him.

He'd left the sand arena, walking past the gazebo but not stopping. Kept right on going to the circular driveway and to where his Mustang was sitting—top down and keys in the ignition. As a professional, he'd done what he had to do, fulfilled his obligation as Maitland's trainer. And he'd helped Chip alright…in the process losing Monterrey and all those classes he'd hoped to win this year. No one needed to tell him that Marxes would sign the deal after what they'd just seen.

Yanked the driver's side door open, jerked his tall body in behind the wheel, started the engine…and without a backwards glance, drove out of there—needing time to himself.

Chapter Four

Nicole's was a relatively new and trendy restaurant, located on South Shore Road, close to the intersection of South Shore and Forest Hill. It was about five minutes away from Starbucks, three minutes away from the entrance to the Polo Club, and maybe 10 minutes away from Jericho's stable—so very centrally located. Nice big bar area in the front with entertainment many nights, then a larger seating area behind that, comprising two rooms. During the horse show season, it was always packed.

The Maitland / Marx table was in the second room. Joining the two couples were Chip Langdon and his long time partner, John DeWinter. John wasn't a horse person himself—he painted, and actually made a living at it—but he sure knew the lingo and understood that at dinners like these, equines were the only topic…well, other than gossip.

There was an empty chair at the table too—there for Jericho, though no one really expected to see him. In fact, even the conversation had skirted around his name for the most part. It was the one down note in the otherwise celebratory atmosphere. Marxes had signed on the dotted line to buy Monterrey, and as long as he passed the vet check—which he would—he was theirs. The little group had already gone through two bottles of champagne toasting their transaction.

From where she was sitting, Darien had a pretty good view of the bar, and right now she was staring. A woman had just walked in…chin length, spiky, coffee-dark hair, very pretty features—huge eyes, slim straight nose, and a perfect mouth—slender boyish body but with a noticeable cleavage. And tiny—probably shorter than Darien herself. She wore tight black leather slacks, strappy high heel sandals, and a flashy chartreuse halter top—nothing expensive, but it definitely looked good on her.

She wasn't 100 percent positive, but Darien thought this might be the woman she'd seen in those pictures with Jericho, and that drew her attention like a magnet.

"Who in the world are you looking at, dear," Cin asked her, craning her neck around to check things out for herself.

"Uhm…I don't know her name, but she looks familiar." Darien fished a little bit. "Do you know her, Cin?"

Cin looked scornful. "Of course not. Well look what she has on…I mean, that outfit has to come from Old Navy, don't you think? It's certainly not Lauren or Gucci, is it? I'll bet she's a groom."

Chip laughed wickedly, and laid his hand on Cin's wrist. "I just love you," he giggled. "Listen to you, you are *so bad*."

Still, despite Cin's disparaging remarks, both Bob Marx and Richard Maitland were taking a pretty good look too. The subject of their discussion had taken a stool at the bar and ordered what appeared to be a Cosmopolitan. She was laughing and flirting with the bartender, who she seemed to know.

Was it her or not, Darien wondered. Jericho's lover, or just some pretty barn groom as Cin was suggesting? She'd probably never find out.

Bob Marx's eyes had returned to the empty chair at the table. "I'm not feeling good about the situation with your trainer," he said to Richard.

But Maitland brushed it off. "He'll get over it once Monterrey is out of the barn," he predicted, unconcerned. "He's getting a nice commission on the sale, that check should salve his feelings and put an end to it."

Chip made a face that seemed to say he disagreed, but he was too politically correct to contradict a guy like Richard Maitland. Marx noticed it though. "Alright Chip, out with it," he demanded good-naturedly. "What are you thinking?"

A shrug.

"Oh, come on," Marx coaxed again.

Little smile. "I'm so thrilled I got this horse, and I don't want anything to change that," he said, starting it out that way to be sure everyone understood that first. When Darien smiled warmly at him and said, "Nothing will," he felt safe enough to continue. "But understand, Jericho found this horse, trained him from nothing, and now he's ready for the big time…" Richard started to interject, but Chip waved him off. "Well, let me finish…I mean, its not a criticism, just the facts. See, Jericho…there's a guy with Olympic dreams…World Equestrian Games…you name it. And he has the talent, so it's not just bullshit. But he's never had the horse or…" Hesitated, then just said it. "…or the patron. I'm sure he thought Monterrey…"

47

Just left the thought dangling, didn't need to finish it, but did toss in, "And man, he didn't see it coming, did he?"

No one answered him.

More conversation, and some discussion of future plans for Monterrey …what shows they might take him to and which one would be his first.

Chip looked up, and surprise registered on his features. "Well, I'll be damned," he murmured. "Now there's guts."

The rest of the table turned to see what he was talking about, and there stood Jericho, having just come through Nicole's front door. Tonight he was dressed somewhat more formally than normal—somewhat. Black, long-sleeve tee shirt, pleated khaki slacks, sandals on his feet. Raised his head and searched the room. He'd come late enough that he wouldn't have to have dinner with them, but at least he'd showed—if for no other reason to hide how hard this was hitting him.

Saw them, and started over to the table. Didn't seem to notice the chick at the bar, and she wasn't looking at him either. Scratch that theory then, Darien thought.

Richard stood up as he drew near them, shook his hand and then clapped him on the shoulder. "Glad you could make it."

Didn't reject the friendly show, but didn't welcome it much. either. Shrugged. "I finished up at the barn around eight, showered, changed and came straight here."

Chip seemed shocked. "Eight o'clock, Jericho?"

Tossed him a rather unpleasant glare. "Well, I had three rides left." And he'd lost an hour to the whole deal with Monterrey, and another that he'd simply spent alone.

But Langdon was still protesting. "Well, couldn't a groom…"

Sharp quelling stare, sarcastic. "Yeah, a groom could." *And that's how you'd have handled it*, he thought derisively. Purred dangerously. "That's not what my customers pay me for though, is it?" Dropped his eyes away, wanted the subject dropped as well.

Actually his presence put an immediate damper on the conversation, not that he was saying or doing anything negative. He knew it, felt self-conscious, and mainly just stayed silent. Eyes wandering while they talked, wishing he could be somewhere else, but couldn't—and it wasn't like he really had anywhere else to go.

Looked idly up at the bar. Those deep blue eyes slowly narrowing with interest. Then more than just interest. Followed by the ghost of a smile.

Christ, that chick from last night, and here she was, he was sure of it. He rose quietly, with a predator's grace—his quarry sighted and ready to move in for the kill. "Excuse me," he murmured—odd, almost savage tone to his voice. "I'll be right back."

His tone of voice was so compelling, both Cin and Darien turned to watch where he was going.

He walked up to her, and she saw him coming…knew pretty well that he was heading over her way. But didn't seem to recognize him, looked puzzled. He stopped about a foot from her, a playful, mocking glint in his eyes. Reached back and grabbed the band that held his braid in place, and simply pulled it loose, shaking his head and tossing it back to let his hair fall free. "Recognize me now?" he murmured to her in a low, tantalizing growl.

Pale blue eyes widening. Soft sexy little laugh from her. She reached up and ran her fingers through that chestnut mane, untangling it. He permitted it for a long moment, then leaned against the bar facing her—in close enough to put an arm around her if he'd wanted to. Didn't yet. Looked over his shoulder and called quietly to the bartender, "Heineken," and seconds later, an open bottle appeared beside him. He wrapped one hand around it. Still no words between them. Her fingers ran lightly down his chest and then dropped away.

After a minute he spoke. "I'm Jericho."

"Is that for real?" Gentle lilting accent.

Realized he hadn't even heard her speak before, other than the words "yes, yes, yes," and her deeply erotic cries of passion. "Yes, it's for real. You're Irish?"

"No, but close. Scottish." Dark hair, blue eyes, pale skin…yeah, it fit.

Lifted the bottle to his lips and drank from it. Laid it down and leaned in closer. Although she was sitting on a barstool, he still easily towered over her. Ran his index finger down her jawline, turning her face slightly to him, the thick fall of his hair shutting the two of them in…and everyone else out. "Tell me your name," he demanded in a low rumble.

"You know, maybe it's better this way," she whispered back to him, her lids closing halfway and tipping her mouth toward his.

Yeah, his customers were probably watching him, but he accepted the invitation anyway, laying his mouth over hers for a few sweet moments.

Back at the Maitland's table the entire group was pretty much gawking. "Damn," Chip muttered. Then in a very exaggerated way added, "It's not like he doesn't hate me right now, but even so…why does he have to be straight?"

His partner, John, gave him an annoyed look. It was obviously a sham, but not entirely. He lightly punched Chip's shoulder. "Alley cat," he growled at him.

Darien was trying not to look as interested as she actually was. "You know, I think that's his girlfriend," she said, although…duh…anyone at the table could have guessed the same thing. She knew it sounded stupid and amended what she'd said. "*I mean*…I think I've seen them together or something." *Yeah in those pictures.* "That's why she looked so familiar to me before."

Cin was even more annoyed, but she certainly wasn't going to let on. "Richard," she said sweetly. "Why don't you invite Jericho's friend to join us too? He should have brought her over here in the first place—no reason for him to be stag." Actually, what she really wanted was to learn more about who this was…dig her claws in a little, get rid of the little bitch.

But Bob Marx was already on his feet. "Why don't I do it?" he suggested. Actually, he had his own motives, and didn't expect anyone here to object or try to stop him either.

And Richard simply acquiesced. "If you want to," he said.

Jericho knew he was basically fucked here—but not literally, which was what he really wanted, but figuratively for sure. He couldn't walk out on the back table—though to be honest while it had been important for him to make an appearance, once here, everyone—including himself—wanted him gone. Still he couldn't leave. Not this soon. On the other hand, this woman wouldn't wait for him. She might go home with him now, yes, but by the time he was free, she'd be long gone. And man, he didn't want that. "Come on," he begged her. "Cut me some slack. Spend the night with me."

"I didn't give you enough slack last night?"

"Not nearly."

She laughed. "So you're busy right now. With those people? Business?"

"*Yes,*" he murmured vengefully. "But I'll cut it short if you'll wait."

She licked her lips—already a bit swollen from the pressure of his mouth on hers—and teased him—tortured him. "I won't."

Murmured unhappily. "I know."

"You'll run into me again, though."

"Will I?" He tossed his hair back over his shoulder, and moved a few inches away from her. That deep blue stare growing colder. *Lousy, lousy fucking day, from beginning to end.* Picked up his beer again, and knocked another long drink from it back. "My mistake." he told her, more harshly now, faintly mocking—himself most probably. "You're right…I should have left it where it was." Uncurled from where he was leaning against the bar, slapped some money down to pay for his drink, looked like he was leaving.

That little rolling lilt stopped him.

"So spoiled, aren't you? I don't know what *you* want…but I want to see you again. I don't know when exactly, but soon. Tonight even…but I'm not going to sit here and wait for you, Jericho."

Frustrated. "Then tell me how to reach you."

Fingers stroked through that long hair again, tangled in it for an instant, pulling him closer. "I'll reach you. Tell me your last name."

Eyes on her. Powerful. "Brandeis."

"*You're* Jericho Brandeis?"

Whispered, but powerful. "*Yes.*"

Soft chuckle from her. "God, can you ride."

Sensual murmur. "I could say the same to you."

That pretty face tilted to the side and gently called him a liar. 'Oh, come on. You didn't care who I was last night, and honestly that's fine."

Contradicted her, or at least partially. "Yeah, maybe that was true. *At first.*"

She stroked the side of his face. "Good line, Jericho Brandeis." Slid down off the barstool. "And maybe you'll hear from me."

Murmured in dissatisfaction.

Pretty little laugh from her again, clear and charming. "Don't be a sore loser. I'm leaving. Kiss me goodbye."

His deep blue eyes were on her, reproachful—she was playing him, and doing a damn good job of it, and they both knew it. For a moment it seemed like he wouldn't oblige her, but then he seemed to change his mind. Laid his hand at her waist, stared down at her, and then moved in very close again…close enough that her hip brushed against the inside of his thigh, snarled almost inaudibly. Still hadn't kissed her. Both her hands came up to rest lightly over his abdomen, then curled around the fabric of his tee. She leaned up on her toes and touched her mouth to his, just lightly teasing him. But she'd let her hip move against his inner thigh in a very tempting and suggestive near massage. She heard him breathe, and then his mouth descended over hers forcefully, parting her lips and his tongue finding hers. Long seconds like that...and damn, he wanted more.

He pulled his face back from hers, that powerful stare running all over her. Stepped back a pace even. "Damn you," he swore, but then quietly smiled, accepting it.

She threaded her fingers deeply through his hair one last time, lifting it and laying it behind his shoulder again. Kissed his cheek. "Goodnight," she said, then turned sweetly and walked away...knowing, just knowing that he was watching her with that beautifully intent look until she was well out of sight.

Warm male voice coming up from behind him. "Score or not?" It was Bob Marx asking.

Jericho turned just his head and gave him a long sardonic look, but then admitted frankly, "Crashed and burned."

Marx tossed his head back and laughed out loud. He was still chuckling a moment later when he asked him, "Is she your girlfriend? A lot of speculation going on back at the table."

"I don't doubt that...and no. I just met her yesterday." Equivocated for a moment. "Hell, I didn't even really meet her, just..." *fucked her.* Gave a different version of the story to Marx though. "We were in the same place at the same time."

"Screw around a lot?" Darien's husband asked him point blank.

Yeah, and? "Not really." Shrugged, mocking now. "Sometimes, I guess."

"How old are you?" Bob Marx pressed him.

"Twenty-seven." *What's it to you?* Wasn't liking this third degree one bit, and man did it show—shoulders squared, more aggressive pose. The expression on his face harsh and shuttered closed.

"Well here's the thing," the older man told him—making a point he wanted to be sure was very, very clear. "Darien's a lot closer to your age than mine. She's thirty and I'm forty-five...but understand this...she's strictly off limits."

"Yeah, well I don't do that," Jericho purred back to him dangerously. "I draw a line, and my customers are on the other side of it."

Persistent and disbelieving. A little accusing, too. "Well she's not your customer. Is she?"

He dropped his eyes away and to the side, but they'd flared with anger. This guy was about three seconds away from getting a pretty cold "Fuck you," thrown in his direction. Jericho just stood there for a second—a long heartbeat. His face swung slowly back to him, and he emphasized every word. "Not now. But the world turns and things change. Anyway, I don't go there." He was close to saying a lot more, but just swallowed it. Still, his voice was loaded with scorn as he gave Marx the answer he was really looking for. "And yes...*I heard you,* alright?" Drew his breath in furiously, shook his head once in disgust, turned his eyes away again and then simply walked away from him...because the next thing he was going to do was launch a fist at this guy. Straight-armed the door and went outside.

His Mustang was parked close by, and he went over to it, raking his hair severely back, and banding it into a ponytail at the nape of his neck as he walked. The car's convertible top was down as always, and he fished inside and found his cigarettes, taking one and lighting it. Stood there smoking, and very close to just getting in and driving away. Right now, he didn't have a particularly good hold over his temper—just a little bit more of this, and he'd do something he'd regret tomorrow. He'd never decked a customer before, but there was a first time for everything, and this guy was damn near begging for it.

Felt a presence behind himself, turned and saw that Bob Marx had followed him. Jesus Christ, he thought vengefully, either the man had a set of brass ones, or he was just plain dense.

Marx was staring at him pretty hard. "Upset about the horse?" he pressured him again. He looked totally cool and collected, like he knew exactly what he was doing and didn't care.

Jericho laid his hand on the door handle. Didn't answer him. Jerked it open.

Marx even had the balls to chuckle softly. "Don't drive away till you find out what I want."

Brutal. Pure menace. "I don't give a fuck what you want." But instead of getting into the car, he closed the door again—closed it hard—and rounded on him, pinning him with a stare. "And don't you dare lecture me on professionalism. Am I upset? What do you think? But how I feel means shit, alright? You just tell me what you expect. You want me to ride the horse till you're ready to move him...fine. You want Chip to come over and ride him...fine...tell me what time he'll be there, and I'll have him tacked up and ready." Controlled, but not by much. "I don't have to like it...I know how to behave. Now get off my fuckin' ass." Tossed his cigarette out into the parking lot, muttering under his breath, *"Asshole."*

Marx was just standing there, taking it in. A slow smile spread across his face, maybe even a touch of approval. "You know what?" he said. "If you were an investment banker, I'd hire you on the spot. I keep watching you bunch that fist at me, but you haven't thrown it. Passion combined with control. How badly do you want to let me have it right now?"

Didn't understand this turn in the conversation one bit. Eyes narrowed intently. Looked down, and it was true, his right hand was clenched into what would be a pretty damaging weapon. He released it. "I'm not going to throw it," he breathed harshly, lifted his face coldly. "And here's all you need to know, Marx…I haven't shown your wife anything but respect, and I haven't done anything to damage this sale. That's not going to change. Who else I screw and what else I feel is my business not yours." Opened the Mustang's door again, and purred, "And for your information, I got my MBA at Columbia…and I haven't got the faintest interest in being an investment banker."

Got in, put the key in the ignition, and fired it up. Pulled it away without making eye contact again and without wanting, or even leaving room for a response.

The Marxes actually lived in midtown Manhattan—their main home, anyway. Then they had a nice place in the Hamptons where Darien spent a lot of time during the summer, and then a good-sized place in the Polo Club in Wellington.

After dinner, Darien had changed to a long flowing cotton dress that was just plain comfortable, and was curled up on the couch in the large living room watching television half-heartedly, and with more enthusiasm, looking through the Omnibus which listed all the hunter/jumper shows this season, making notes in a small spiral notebook—ideas about where to take Monterrey this show season. She hummed happily to herself as she looked through the book.

Her husband had opened a bottle of nice wine, poured each of them a glass, and came in to sit with her.

"Happy?" he asked, setting one glass of wine next to her and then taking a seat in the wingchair close by.

She looked up at him and smiled, picked up the glass and sipped from it. "Very. He's so beautiful. Thank you, sweetheart. And Chip is…well, he's beside himself. Ecstatic." She laughed, remembering all his excited banter over dinner. A more wicked smile touched her lips. "In a month, Cin Maitland will be green with envy, don't you think?"

"Totally." He had a Blackberry handheld with him, and was checking some stock prices at the same time, but seemed more interested in watching his wife pour over the Omnibus. Couldn't get enough of watching her, really, and he was glad now that he'd had that conversation with Jericho…whether the younger man liked it or not. Yeah, he'd been good and insulted—really pissed about it—and most likely it hadn't been necessary, but he felt better for it, just the same. And afterwards, he'd had gone back inside and made excuses for both of them…said that Jericho was planning to stay, but that he'd encouraged him to go find his lady friend instead. Everyone accepted that story, though Cin hadn't looked pleased—not at all.

"So are you going to tell me?" Darien asked, slanting a teasing look up at him.

Played innocent. "Tell you what?"

"What you said to Jericho that made him so angry?"

Boy, she didn't miss a trick, this little wife of his. "Angry?" he asked, still trying to get one past her.

Patient but knowing look from her. "Hmmm?" she asked again. Then laughed. "Come on, Bob."

"Alright, alright," he said, ruffling that jaggedy short hair of hers. "I told him I better never catch him looking at you the way he was looking at that woman at the bar."

"No you didn't!"

"Sure I did." He pulled her from where she was sitting and over onto his lap. Since he'd told her that much, he embellished it a little. "I said I'd kill him if he tried."

She laughed happily, putting her arms around his neck and snuggling in close. "You caveman," she teased him, then scolded, "I'll never be able to look him in the eye again." Maybe she was protesting, but she was flattered and happy.

"Good," he said, folding his arms around her and kissing her.

Their telephone rang…

Jericho was as tight inside as he'd felt in a long time. Didn't want to go home and face Starbucks and his antics—what he really wanted was to go somewhere and get in a fight. Didn't do that, either. Instead he drove around aimlessly for a long time and then finally headed to the barn.

It was about 10 o'clock, maybe closer to 10:30. The grooms had done night check on the horses about an hour earlier—given them hay, checked their water, made sure everyone was alright. Still, he drove up, parked, went into the aisle and turned on the lights.

Heard a noise he didn't like…it sounded like a horse thrashing or rolling. Monterrey? Instantly alert, he moved quickly to his stall and looked inside.

Oh fuck, he thought, grabbing the horse's halter and yanking his stall door open wide. The big bay was in trouble alright…he'd laid down facing the back corner, but too close, and now couldn't find enough room to get back up again. Like a turtle stuck on its back. *Cast.* Frightened and trapped, he was kicking and thrashing…was covered in sweat, eyes wild. Jericho spoke to him, tried to quiet him…to get close…but those hoofs were striking out viciously. Christ, he could injure or even break a leg this way, or just as bad, work himself up so much that he'd colic.

The horse was still for a second, and then began twisting and kicking again frantically.

"Whoa, boy," he murmured to him. It wasn't going to be effective though, he could see that. Monterrey had panicked and he needed help right now.

If any of the grooms had still been around, it would have been a hell of a lot easier. And when had they done night check, he wondered, because the horse looked like he'd been trapped for a while. He was gonna fuckin' kill them if they hadn't been there yet, or come early.

Jericho knew that if he could get the halter over the horse's head, he might be able to pull Monterrey far enough away from the wall that he'd be able to get up again on his own. Either that or roll him over so he'd be facing away from the corner instead of toward it. But that was 1,100 pounds of thrashing horse he was going to have to move by himself. He'd need to be in close and for more than just a second or two—and the way those legs were flailing now, he'd risk serious personal injury in the process.

Didn't care about that. Had to.

He opened the halter's snap, and approached from behind the horse's head—as far from those desperately kicking legs as possible, talking to

Monterrey constantly in a low calming voice. Ducked in low, lurched forward, making a grab for the big bay's head, though it was half-buried now in shavings. He began working to get the halter on, the horse swinging his head, striking out with those powerful front feet—didn't even seem to recognize his trainer, he was that worked up.

Jericho was panting, half buried in shavings himself now too. Could taste blood from where Monterrey's cheek had connected with his own. But he managed to slip the halter on finally, and forced it down the last few inches over Monterrey's ears. Snapped it closed. Didn't even take time to regroup...just wrapped his hands around the leather halter and the horse's neck and hauled backwards on him. Because Monterrey had been thrashing, the majority of the shavings around his body had been pushed aside—it would have been easier if there'd been a thick layer beneath him. There wasn't.

Leaned back and pulled. Moved him a few inches. Hauled again, and he wasn't going to stop until he'd moved this horse.

Agonizing minutes slipping by, and he'd moved him about a foot now. Rolled clear and encouraged him to try again on his own. Wildly flying legs...and then he'd found purchase and heaved his huge body to his front legs, and then followed by the hind. He was up and leaping forward. Jericho had to dive out of the way before he was trampled in the scramble of huge powerful limbs. Dragged himself up against the stall door, pulling it most of the way closed before the big bay bolted out of there. He took a few seconds to assess the condition of his own body—a few knocks here and there, but nothing of consequence—before turning back around to check the animal's condition. Monterrey was standing there, trembling and head hung low. Exhausted, sides heaving. Jericho murmured to him again, bent down and ran his hands over the bay's powerful but, oh, so vulnerable legs.

Felt along each joint and tendon carefully. He seemed to have escaped any real injury, but no way Jericho would leave that to so cursory an evaluation. He found the cell phone attached to his belt and pressed the pre-programmed code for *Palm Beach Equine Clinic*—his regular vet.

He'd need to call the owners too...was that the Maitlands or the Marxes...or both? Probably both.

Well, he'd wanted a bar fight tonight...and he'd gotten his wish.

Bob Marx," he answered the phone's insistent ring. Pleasant but business-like tone.

Single word answer. "Jericho."

Marx set Darien on her feet and stood himself. That tone of Jericho's had communicated. "What is it?" he demanded, raising a hand to stop his wife's questions 'til he knew more.

Christ, he had to tell them this and they weren't going to be happy. He'd already been through this with the Maitlands. Could see car lights approaching and was pretty sure the vet was here now, thank God. "I came to the barn a few minutes ago." Paused, really unsure how they would take the news. "I found Monterrey cast in his stall. I think he's alright, but I'm having the vet come over, anyway, he's pulling in now. I'll call you after he examines him, but don't worry. He'll be…"

To his surprise the question coming back from Marx was, "What's the matter? Are you injured?"

"No. I'm alright. Winded, that's all. Don't get excited…I'm not leaving him." Sounded angry, offended, like he thought Marx was after him again—accusing him of not putting the horse first, and he had been and still was.

"We're coming out," Bob Marx said.

"Fine, I'll be here."

Interesting contrast. Maitlands had told him not to call back unless the horse was critical.

By the time the Marxes arrived fifteen minutes later, Monterrey had been given a light sedative, and something for muscle pain. The vet was just putting him back in his stall. "He's fine," he told them. "Frightened and tired, but nothing serious. By morning, he won't even remember it happened. But I'll check him again first thing just to make sure." He made a point of adding in a serious tone of voice, "You have Jericho to thank for that, by the way. For coming out here and checking on him in the first place…and for risking his own neck to get him out. A cast horse is basically stuck on his back, legs up and flailing. Your trainer wasn't worried about himself—he was worried about Monterrey."

"Where *is* Jericho?" Darien asked, her face ashen.

"I'm here." He stepped back into the aisle way from outside, having taken a moment to brush the shavings out of his clothing and hair. Looked at the vet, quick professional look exchanged between the two of them—both knowing exactly how lucky they'd been tonight. "What time should I look in on him?"

Quiet tone from him. "In a couple of hours, then I'll come back at nine."

"Good. Marco will stay with him a little while. He's coming now." He'd gone over to Monterrey's stall again, and was looking in at him. The horse lifted his head and snorted gently, reached his nose out to him "Damn animal," he murmured to him, lightly stroking his muzzle through the bars. Lifted his chin and saw yet another set of car lights making their way down the long drive. "There's Marco," Jericho added, anger creeping into his voice now. Pushed away from the stall, and walked off to go out and meet him. Thought to himself, whoever had worked night check tonight was fired, no questions asked.

Marx just watched him leave, but turned to his wife when he was out of earshot. "Man, I like him," he observed quietly, eyes still following him. Smiled then. "Ready to go?" She nodded. And he put his arm around her, guiding her back to their car.

Chapter Five

Jericho called Marco one more time while he was driving home and checked on Monterrey, gave him the schedule for the next day. The horse was resting quietly, no heat in his legs. Still looked like he'd be fine, thank God.

And you know, he couldn't get over the Maitlands…had they even realized how close they'd come to losing their million dollar sale to the Marxes? Probably not, probably never would. Hadn't thanked him either, the pricks. And the hell with them, he decided. He'd call them in the morning—even so, he wouldn't hassle them on it. Cin still kept two horses with him, and she always paid her bills.

Starbucks was still out somewhere when Jericho got home from the Emergency Room, and he was glad of it…although he had to wonder who Brae was with.

Just went to bed. Alone. Yeah, and he told himself, he didn't care at all.

———————

Two days passed, falling into an easy rhythm. Monterrey had the time off, only getting hand walked, and for once Jericho just let Marco handle it. He still had seven rides, even without the big bay, and a handful of lessons to clients on top of it. Came home tired and generally depressed, but dealing with the sale of Monterrey, he told himself…he was coming to grips with the fact that he'd lost the best horse he'd had in years, maybe ever.

And who did he think he was kidding? Truth was, he was really down over it.

Early morning on the third day—just before 7:30 A.M. Jericho wheeled his Mustang into the drive-through line at Starbucks. He hadn't actually seen Brae for several days now, though there was evidence that the Barista came home at least once in a while. But for sure he was banging some chick hot and heavy, and most likely the same one, because he was gone every evening and sleeping somewhere else at night, coming home only to change and go out again.

"Welcome to Starbucks," that cheery voice came through the speaker.

"Yeah, fuck you and make me a Latte," Jericho purred evenly back to him.

"Oh, hey, dude!" Happy tone of voice, like he was really glad to see him. "So what's going on? Oh, shit, I've been…"

"Brae, for Christ's sakes," Jericho interrupted him, sarcastically. "I'm not gonna sit here and talk to a sign. I'll drive down."

"Cool." A goofy laugh. "Fuck you, too, man, okay?"

Don't I wish?

Nice deep rumble from the twin overhead cams, as the Mustang pulled to a stop at the second window. Starbucks stuck his body out from the waist up, leaning his elbows on the service shelf. Looked pleased with himself. Nothing new there, really. Waved away Jericho's money. "Nah, forget it. I got you covered. So what's new?" Pulled out a cigarette and lit it, but then handed it to his roommate. "Here you take it, I'm not allowed to, but give me a few hits on it, okay?"

Had to laugh. Took the fag and then a long inhale from it, then passed it back to him. "You moving out or something?" Jericho asked.

Starbucks took a long drag. Grinned—proud of himself, locker-room sort of thing, and showing off. "No, no, oh hell no," he said. "Nothing like that. Just been…you know, getting pretty lucky lately." Handed the cigarette back again.

Took it. Smoked some, held it out. Wasn't very happy about Brae's good fortune, but smirked back at him. "Good for you," he murmured. "So, where's my frickin' Latte?"

"Hey, what's up your ass?" Took their shared smoke back to his own lips again. "Don't you want to hear about her?"

"Haven't I already seen her?" More dangerous tone of voice.

"Nah, this is someone different." Leaned forward, almost fell out the window, had to really catch himself on the service shelf and the side of the Mustang to stop from sliding straight out onto the ground. Dropped the cigarette in the process too. "Ah, shit."

Jericho covered his face with his hand like he didn't even want to see this, and just shook his head. But, yeah, he was laughing. "Damn you, just give me my Latte. Tell me about it tonight at home, or you getting laid again?"

"Probably not. How about you?"

The car behind Jericho beeped.

Jericho gave the guy driving it the finger, ignored him. He answered Brae instead, taking his sweet time about it. "No. But man, I want to see that chick again though…the one you brought over. Haven't got a clue how to reach her. Do you?"

"Not really. Me bringing her home…? That was just a thing that happened."

Another beep from behind.

Jericho swiveled around, snarled, "Hey, fuck you! Sit on it, alright?" He looked at Brae and shook his head.

Longer defiant beep this time.

Jericho swung his car door open and stepped halfway out, like he intended to do something about it. Only one guy in the car anyway…asshole. Easy target. Brae was leaning way out the window again, watching and loving it. "Rearrange his face for him, Jericho," he encouraged his roommate.

But apparently the guy in the car behind him took one look at the tall aggressive figure about to come get right up in his face, pulled out of line and drove away, peeling some rubber to prove whatever point he thought he was making. "Yeah, you better leave," Jericho called after him. He got evenly back in his car. "Give me my Latte," he demanded again. "And do me a favor…get me her name and address."

Brae smiled…then laughed. Loved the fact that his roommate was such a hardass. "Will do, she's in here all the time. I'll get it," he promised, finally handing him his Venti Latte. "Anyway, I can tell you this much. Her first name is Ailynn."

Ailynn. Liked it.

"Cin, I don't have time for that."

She'd just finished up riding her two horses, and wanted Jericho to go look at a saddle she'd seen at the showgrounds. They were standing together in the aisle way—Jericho waiting for his next horse. "Oh, come on," she coaxed him. "You're not riding Monterrey today, you can take an hour out. Jericho, I don't want to buy it till you look at it first." And besides, she loved walking around the showgrounds with him—letting everyone see them together, and him very attentive to what she wanted and on her. She reached out and touched him lightly, pouted prettily, "Please?"

He laid that powerful stare on her, silently admonishing her. Stared at where her hand gently stroked his arm...but that only made her slightly increase the pressure, not lessen it or take those flirting fingers away. Richard had gone home that morning, and she was openly teasing him now. "They can't bring it over here?" he asked her, knowing damn well that any saddler worth a hill of beans would want to come to the farm—want to fit it to the horse. Hell, at three or more thousand dollars a clip, they were happy to do it.

"No. He said he can't," Cin lied—not sounding convincing and not caring either.

He thought about it. It was true that Chip was coming over later to ride Monterrey—Jericho wanted to be there when he did, but he'd ride another horse at the same time too. Didn't have another lesson anytime soon either. He actually could go over, if they kept it to an hour. And to be honest, the break would be nice. With Cin though..."Alright, for an hour," he said firmly. "I have to be back here in an hour. You know what? On second thought, I'm driving my own car and you take yours. That's the only way I'll go."

Not exactly what she wanted, but close enough. She smiled at him.

Fifteen minutes later they were there...and yes, there was actually a saddle that she'd wanted to show him. He didn't like it all that much, naturally, but made a show of looking at it, then took her away. "No, hell no, Cin," he told her as they slowly started strolling back over to where they'd parked. "If you want another saddle fine, but stick with the Hermes. Get Firedance one with a wider tree if you want to."

"If you say so." She'd slipped her arm through his and that got plenty of looks—both of them pretty well known around there.

It was still very early in the Season and the showgrounds were fairly empty, but every day they grew busier—many people stabled there the entire season, and they could see them moving in. Today, Sunday, was the second day of a small pre-season Dressage show. Cin looked down her nose at the horses and riders. "Why does anyone ride Dressage?" she asked.

Jericho stopped and leaned both elbows up against the fence that bordered a warm-up ring. There were probably as many as fifteen horse and rider pairs inside now, getting ready for their classes. He watched quietly, but then finally responded. "Dressage is a hard sport, Cin. So much precision, lots of difficult movements." Shrugged. "Hell, it's not for me either, but I respect it, and a lot of what we do on the flat has its roots in Dressage. It's the same fundamentals. Take a look at that horse." And he pointed.

Nice horse/rider team…the animal coming on from behind into a perfect round frame.

Something caught his eye, and he looked over to the far side of the arena. Jesus, he thought, and couldn't help chuckling. That had to be one of the ugliest mares he'd ever seen. Huge thing with a head like a block of wood, or like a railroad tie. Big mare ears, almost donkey length…well not really, but close. Thick, square but probably powerful body. Long legs. And solid brown—no white markings or even black points. Right now a groom was holding her, and she was trying her darndest to bite him. Cin followed his eyes, to see what had caught his attention. "My God, what a mule," she laughed wickedly.

For once, he totally agreed with her. "You can say that again."

Nothing could have surprised him more than to see who stepped out to ride her. Ailynn…or at least that's what Brae said her first name was. That gorgeous little slip of a femme, and such a huge moose-like mare. Talk about terrible fit!

"Jesus Christ, that can't be her horse," he murmured, shocked.

Cin threw her head back and laughed in delight. "God, Jericho, what horrible taste you have," she mocked him, putting one hand on his shoulder and leaning up against him full length.

He watched fascinated—ignored Cin.

In action, the pair looked even worse, if that was possible. The moose pulling on the reins, laying her ears back flat, just generally manhandling her small-framed rider all around the ring. Nose stuck out, back hollow, tail swishing angrily. And worse than all of that, Jericho thought, was the fact that Ailynn actually had a trainer coaching her from the sidelines…if you wanted to call him that. Reed-thin guy, and man he looked lazy—couldn't even be bothered to make comments that might have helped.

"Cross the diagonal and make a flying change," the trainer called out to Ailynn, though he didn't even seem to be looking at her. He was drinking a cup of coffee and eating a muffin at the same time, and that obviously was occupying him more than his student.

She didn't have a bad seat, Jericho thought, though man, she didn't know how to use it. Looked damn cute in those snow-white show britches, that much was for sure. At least she had that going for her if nothing else.

Ailynn had taken the diagonal now, although she had to dodge several other riders who were there in the practice ring with her to get onto it. Jericho's eye's never left her, as she slid her outside leg back to ask for the change of lead.

"Oh fuck," he murmured even before anything happened, but he sure as shit saw it coming.

The moose gathered those thick hindquarters of hers, lurched wildly into the air—almost as if she just been faced with a four foot obstacle. Totally unprepared for the move, Ailynn's body pitched back, and then snapped forward. She was still on her horse, but unbalanced and no longer centered in her saddle. As the mare's front feet touched the ground again, she finished off the maneuver by flinging that powerful hind end up high in the air, in a bone-jarring buck. Her little rider came about twelve inches out of the saddle then went sailing through the air, to land hard on the ground. The moose took off running—straight to the practice ring's out gate and onto the dirt path that connected the rings to the stables.

"Loose horse!" someone called out.

"Stay by the fence," Jericho ordered Cin, and then he moved. The big ugly mare had rounded the corner and was heading in their direction, head up and flat-out galloping. She had a wicked gleam in her eye—she hadn't been frightened one bit, had strictly done it for spite.

He spread his arms wide, creating an obstacle, and the mare hesitated, feet going every which way, but didn't stop. Still bearing down in his direction, he was closing in on her as well. Shouldn't be doing this, stopping a runaway horse was risky business no matter who was doing it, but that didn't stop him. The moose tried to skirt by him, but his arm lashed out like a snake and clamped down on the reins flapping loosely around her neck. Planted his feet.

Impact—the mare hitting the end of the rein and feeling his full weight dragging her to a stop…and him feeling that huge animal slam into the end of the slack—stab of pain along the whole length of his arm, but that only made him more determined to control this witch of a horse, and he jerked her viciously, dropping her down to her knees before she scrambled back up to her feet again, wide eyed, surprised and frightened now. She stood there staring at him, snorting and blowing.

He came the rest of the way over to her, keeping the tension on the reins. Snapped them down hard so the bit rattled in her mouth, forcing her to take a step backwards. Did it again, backing her up yet another pace. Then another. "Learn some respect," he growled at her, coming around to the near side of her. Backing her up still another step.

"Nice one, Jericho!" one of the on-lookers called to him.

He gathered the reins and vaulted on. No way he could put his feet in the stirrups—they were Ailynn's length—probably ten inches shorter than his…he'd have looked like a jockey with his knees up around his chin. Instead he just wrapped his legs around that hefty barrel and squeezed, forcing her up and into the bridle. Could feel the moose's back bunch up treacherously—oh fuck yeah, she wanted to buck, and he'd already seen how good she was at it. Lots of practice, he was guessing.

He looked down to those on the side of the fence watching him—and he'd definitely drawn an audience with what he was doing. "Crop," he demanded, and someone handed him one. Took it in his left hand and reached back.

Whack!

He'd laid it into that ugly brown hide, and now she was lurching forward. Squeezed with his legs…not enough response for his liking. Sat in deep…whack! Laid into her again.

Forced her back into the practice ring, and man, everyone else was scattering. The mare was twisting beneath him, trying to unseat him…but she was in for a big surprise 'cause this human wasn't going anywhere, and every time she stopped moving forward that whip was there on her hind end to send her jumping straight ahead again. It didn't take him more than a minute to convince her that bucking wasn't going to cut it with him. And she'd better damn well respect the mastery of those legs on her side too, because if she didn't jump to obey his command, he reinforced it hard. Her next ploy was to try running out the front end instead—to start running away. Wasn't counting on the force of that seat on her back and the unconditional "no" of the reins that brought her scrabbling back almost to a halt. Then legs again. "I said forward," Jericho said with authority, talking to her now.

He was completely cool and unruffled on her back—made that damn clear too. Rules. He had them, and they were absolute. Better figure them out.

He could see that Ailynn was up on her feet and unhurt, and simply went to schooling the mare. Inside five minutes had a nice collected canter under him—oh, it was mutinous too. The bitch knew she'd lost this battle, and she was nice and tractable now, but she'd need some heavy duty convincing before she really gave in. Still it was a decent start, and he reached forward and patted her neck, though he wasn't nearly through with her. Kept it up for another fifteen minutes—canter, flying change, canter the other way. Nice, round and biddable. He finally let the moose come back to a walk on a loose rein. She didn't even try to take advantage of it.

Nice little applause from the sidelines. Looked up and smirked. Headed her over to where Ailynn and her trainer were standing. Pulled up in front of them.

"You rode my horse on the showgrounds," Ailynn said with that soft lilt, but sounded upset. "Now I'm disqualified."

Jericho jumped easily off. He lifted the reins over the mare's head and handed them to her. Beautifully sarcastic response. "I charge two hundred fifty for a schooling session on a rank bitch like this one."

She looked stunned, was about to protest, but he cut her off. "Are you hurt?"

"No." Defiant—not so different from the horse.

Rules. Better figure them out.

Superior smile from him. "Have a trailer?"

"Yes."

Wouldn't mind taking a crop to that fine little ass either.

"Bring her by my place at three o'clock today." Soft murmur. "And no…I'm not going to charge you. But…*be there.*" Pause. "Understand me?" Jericho had the upper hand here and he knew it and he wanted her to know it too for a change. While he was at it, he sent a withering glare at her trainer that basically said…so tell me, what do you get paid to do?

She tilted her head to the side, looked up at him, and finally smiled. "Alright, I guess I can do that."

Probably that was as close as he was going to get to a thank you, but he was fine with that. Let a meaningful moment pass…before he nodded to her, and then turned and walked away.

And yes, it had been a stupid move. But damn, he wanted to sleep with her again, and cared a lot more about that than about the risk to himself. Didn't know why exactly, just did. He couldn't really even think about the other night too much without getting aroused all over again. And when he wanted something, he fought for it.

And that made him think of Monterrey.

It was just before three o'clock now. And Brandeis Show Stables was about to turn into a three-ring circus—almost literally.

Marxes and Chip Langdon had pulled into the drive.

Marco came down to take the horse Jericho had just finished riding. "Wait about five minutes and bring Monterrey out," he told him. "And in a few minutes another customer will be trailering in. Big bitchy mare—watch out for her. When she gets here put my saddle on her, and bring her out to me. Bring me Razz at the same time. Have we got a Dressage saddle?"

"That old one," Marco said dubiously.

"Get Juan to clean it up, and tell him I said do a good job of it," Jericho warned. "Put it on Razz. And use the bridle with the drop noseband."

Marco looked surprised, but didn't argue. In fact, no one in the barn crew was arguing with Jericho these days—not after he'd summarily dismissed one of them for screwing up the night check. Oh, he knew they had some choice names for him behind his back, but could have cared less.

Strolled over to the edge of the sand arena to greet Monterrey's new owners and trainer—he'd passed the vet check, even despite being cast three nights earlier. It was official now, and they planned to move him Tuesday morning—two days from now. And he was still gonna deck Langdon for that one some day soon, he thought viciously. Oh yeah.

But at the moment, he was pure professionalism. Curt but cordial greeting to Darien and Bob Marx.

"How are you, Jericho?" the mister asked him. They hadn't seen him since that night at the barn.

"I'm fine." Cool smile.

Chip was trying to be friendly. "Hey Jer, I heard about your little stunt at the showgrounds today. Nice."

Shrug—he wasn't buying the "camaraderie among trainers" thing.

"What stunt?" Darien asked.

Turned that deep blue stare on her. Penetrating. "There was a loose horse. It came my way and I grabbed it. Nothing."

Further conversation was halted by the appearance of Monterrey at the entrance to the barn. His first real outing since being cast. He was totally full of himself, and giving Marco something to really hold onto. Snorting, prancing like he had tennis balls for feet. He lifted his head and nickered. Thought he was some kind of herd stallion, Jericho thought fondly.

"God, he's so beautiful," Darien said with awe. Her husband just smiled.

Chip however looked a bit taken back. That horse was going to be a real handful to ride. He looked uncertainly at Jericho. "Shouldn't he be lunged first? You know, to take some of the energy out of him?"

Jericho slapped his crop idly against the side of his boot. He brought just the right measure of surprise and the faintest scorn to his voice. "You want him lunged, Chip?" His head turned as a nice looking crew-cab, extended wheelbase, duelley pick-up truck, hauling a matching two-horse trailer wheeled through the gate. Murmured to himself with satisfaction. "Marco will lunge him for you if that's what you want."

Chip clearly didn't like his rival's tone. "Well, wouldn't you lunge him?" he asked defensively.

"Me? No." That much was true. The horse was getting closer to them, and man did he look big. Jerking and pulling at the reins as Marco led him. Whinnying again. Couldn't even really walk, was jigging along beside the groom excitedly. Jericho's attention was on the truck and trailer rig, however. "Excuse me for a minute. I need to meet this horse and I'll be back. Just tell Marco what you want him to do." Strode away, but stopped, looked over his shoulder and called back to his head man. "Marco, Chip here might want you to lunge Monterrey…"

"Lunge him?" Marco asked, sounding confused. Or amazed.

"That's right…he'll tell you if he does and how long. If so, I need someone else down here to take this mare and get her ready. Maybe Javier." Alright, yeah…he was fucking with Chip here, but hell he deserved it. Making him look like he was afraid to ride the horse. And the truth was, he *was* scared.

Marco sounded concerned. "Jericho, you said this mare can be dangerous."

"That's right."

"Then I better take her," Marco went on.

"No, Monterrey comes first." Sneered. "Forget about it, I'll take her myself." And it wasn't as if any of this dialogue between himself and Marco had been planned either…well, maybe Jericho had planned it, but Marco wasn't in on that.

"Oh hell," Chip finally spoke up. "Listen, don't worry about it. If you don't think he needs lunging, then I'll just ride him."

"Well…I only lunge when a horse can't be ridden or is in a rehab program, so don't go by me." Brutal trap. "It's whatever you want." He caught Marx staring at him, and wondered what the investment banker was thinking—he was pretty sharp, and might have even guessed what was going on here, but fine if he had. The point was the same.

Jericho left them then. Chip would do what he'd do—either way, he'd been put at a disadvantage, which was all Jericho had wanted anyway.

Ailynn was out of her truck now, and standing beside the trailer. She'd changed from her show clothes into a pair of nice buff britches and dark green polo shirt—unknowingly wearing Brandeis Show Stables colors.

"Oh look who it is," Darien said, surprised.

Her husband turned his head. Smiled to himself. "I'll be damned," he said.

Jericho nodded to her, then toward the trailer. Smirked. "Is she gonna unload okay, or do I need body armor?"

Crystal clear laugh. "Body armor."

"Thought so." He looked over to the ring and saw Marco holding Monterrey in place—or sort of in place—while Chip tentatively mounted him. Snorted to himself. Terrified to get on him. Some fuckin' trainer. Like he deserved a ride like that.

Attention back on Ailynn again. "Marco and I will unload her, then. Just stand clear." He spoke good-naturedly to her, liked talking to her and having her watching only him, though she seemed wary—more so than the other night at Nicole's. Something up there. "Here's what I'm going to do in the next hour," he went on patiently. "I'll school your mare, and I have a nice five year old I want you to sit on at the same time."

She came nearer to him, drawn over to him, but also staying close to the side of the trailer like she thought he might reach for her—protecting herself almost. "Why? Are you trying to sell me a horse?"

She hadn't been like this with him the other night…ah, but she knew his name now, he realized. She'd checked his reputation, he'd almost bet on that…and there were plenty of those around who'd give him a pretty scathing report…some portions maybe deserved. He shook his head quietly in the negative, answering her question for her. "No, I just want to show you some things. You can live with that, can't you? I mean, I'm not into dressage, but I can ride a little…I might have something useful to say. It's possible, right?" Didn't even sound sarcastic, though he easily could have—normally *would* have. Was more coaxing her now, as he might with a skittish horse.

Soft. "It's possible."

"Good."

Between Jericho and Marco, they offloaded the animal without incident, although she'd pinned her ears and looked like she would have loved to misbehave. Her eyes were on Jericho though—she remembered him, clearly, and didn't risk it, but was still watching for any opening…any slip-up on his part. Didn't happen. Marco rolled his eyes expressively when he finally got a look at her, but said nothing. Moments later, he was leading the irascible mare, tail swishing angrily, up to the barn.

"Put your boots on and then come and join me in the arena," Jericho invited Ailynn. "I want to watch this horse go while we wait. What's the mare's name, anyway?"

"Elysia."

He barked with laughter. Could hardly think of a more inappropriate name for her.

"Well, its not like she has no talent," Ailynn said defensively.

"No, it's not. But if she were mine, I'd call her Shrew," he chuckled. Pivoted on his heel and returned to the ring.

Chip had been on board for about five minutes now. He was doing okay on the flat, although he hadn't cantered yet. But still, Monterrey looked explosive, tugging at the reins and periodically shaking his head. Back muscles tight, like there was a buck waiting in there someplace. Chip had him on a relatively small circle—between fifteen and twenty meters—trying to keep him contained that way.

Entirely wrong approach in Jericho's opinion, and he frowned, but said nothing. He was pretty sorely tempted to walk out there, but forced himself to wait—not unless Chip asked for help, and did it plainly. Interesting to see what would happen next anyway.

Felt Ailynn there beside him, but didn't turn to her. "Pretty horse," she said to him, meaning Monterrey.

"Incredible jumper," he agreed. Murmured unhappily, "He was my ride…but unfortunately I just lost him. Found him in Europe, trained him up from green."

"Disagreement with the owners?" she asked cautiously.

Oh yeah, she'd gotten the scoop on him—and someone had told her he had a wicked temper—he was more and more convinced of that.

"No. Dollar signs," he corrected her. "Totally my fault," he added bitterly. "Next time the contract's gonna say no sale without my prior consent."

Sighed with frustration, watching as Chip finally picked up the canter, Monterrey pulling against him, and pretty far strung out behind.

Little hand touching his arm just below the elbow. "I'm sorry." He looked down at her and she returned his gaze, pretty eyes soft and sympathetic. "It seems wrong." She nodded toward Chip and the horse. "He doesn't ride like you at all."

Marco and Juan coming out of the barn now, Marco leading Elysia and Juan, the big chestnut, Razz. Elysia tacked up in Jericho's jumping saddle, and Razz like a Dressage horse.

"This chestnut colt is five, but I promise you he's polite and tries hard," Jericho explained as they watched the pair of them drawing nearer. He was glad for the opportunity to turn the discussion away from the loss of Monterrey and how he felt about that. "His breeding is Oldenburg. I've schooled him as a Hunter. He'll go nice and round and on the bit for you, pretty much in the frame of a third level Dressage horse, okay? Ride him that way. He'll do a shoulder-in or haunches-in on the long side…well, that's just bending. I don't train half pass per se, but put him on the diagonal and ask for haunches-in and you should get it just fine."

Her slim fingers were still in place on his arm, and she ran them down to his wrist and back again. A definite caress. "Why are you doing this for me?" she asked him intently—maybe feeling exposed too. "Come on…you can probably get laid any time you want."

Good question, and he couldn't answer it. Dodged it instead. "Because whoever's training you is an asshole," he said with conviction—little bit of the hard guy routine too, but just a touch. "I watched you ride at the showgrounds. Your shoulders, back and seat are pretty…really pretty. Yeah, I'd like to see you use them more, but okay that'll come. But Ailynn, your legs are…every time you use them you tighten up. Your knees lift a good inch and sometimes your toes point out—you're spurring and you don't even know it. Forget everything else…without effective legs, you can't ride. Shit, you'll never do real FEI level Dressage. I'm gonna show you that, alright? That's it and that's all."

She looked hurt. His critique stung. "Boy, you're blunt," she said, walking with him now toward the horses.

Deep blue eyes fell away from her, and he murmured powerfully, "Tell me this then…do you want to *ride*…or not?"

They stopped directly alongside the big chestnut. "You know," Ailynn said. "Sometimes you have a look to you that's so…open. Vulnerable even.

I don't know if it's an act or not. If it is, it's a good one. But I'm not going to fall for you, I'm just not. I've heard too much…"

"Leg," he said sharply. Didn't need to hear more of this "I don't want to go out with you, so forget it" speech.

She sighed and let it drop. Turned to face Razz, taking the reins at the wither, and raising her left leg back and up from the knee. He wrapped his hands around it, and simply lifted her up and into the saddle. "Yeah, I could tell," he said harshly, leaving her abruptly and going over to Elysia. Didn't look back. Checked the girth on the big jugheaded mare—tightened it a notch. She stomped and swung her head around sharply like she might bite him for that…and got a stinging backhand across the muzzle for the attempt. Tossed her head up in the air, but didn't budge beyond that…almost as if to say, "Oh yeah, it's *you*…I forgot."

Marco laughed.

Jericho put his foot into the stirrup and swung cleanly up.

"Posting trot first, then stretching at the canter," he said flatly, emotionlessly to Ailynn. "I'll give you some comments…do whatever you want with them." Put his legs on the mare…and oh yeah, the moose remembered his lesson from earlier in the day, no doubt on that score. Jumped forward as soon as she felt his calves on her sides almost in a bunny hop. "Good," he told her, patting her, then pushing her immediately into a lope.

In the gazebo, Bob and Darien Marx had been watching both their own horse, and everything else going on with real interest. And with some disappointment too, though neither one had said as much. Monterrey had warmed up in an okay way, but not spectacular, and he still seemed explosive, and was fighting Chip's riding style—fighting it a lot.

"That horse is really horrid," Darien said, nodding toward Elysia. "I wonder why Jericho is riding her. She's truly ugly. And look, she's so rank…did you see there? She just tried to buck, but he really sent her forward."

Oh, and she *had* tried, really lifting her back muscles and croup in preparation…but very matter of factly, he'd reminded her what the crop was for. Sharp rap on her rump. End of discussion. Back to the lope he'd originally asked for—she was smart this mare, she got the point.

Jericho spent ten minutes with her in flatwork. Liked her. It wasn't a pretty canter, and it probably never would be, though it would improve with time and work. Still there was incredible jump and power in that stride. He couldn't wait to face her to a few fences—see what she'd do with them. As he worked he rode in close to Ailynn every so often, gave her his observations, instruction—critiqued her hand position, and especially her legs. And she was listening to him now—processing everything he said and really trying to use it, and that he loved. Good student. Give him a month with her…

He banished the thought. After what she'd just said to him, why even bother with her?

Chip and Monterrey had taken a jumping line. Jericho growled in anger. Same lousy Goddamn ride as the first time he'd tried him. Seemed to have forgotten everything they'd talked about. And hell, Chip was still perched tentatively on the big bay's back—like he was waiting, just waiting for him to explode. Three jumps in the line, and Monterrey had taken two rails down…and missed his mark on all three jumps, even the one he'd been clean over. And with the Marxes watching. Good. Now he'd show them a trainer who really knew how to ride.

"Marco," Jericho barked out. "Set the Oxer at three foot six, by three feet wide." Then called to Chip, "I'm taking this line."

Or in other words, stay out of my way.

The first two elements were verticals, and set low…under three feet. When Marco was finished, Jericho faced the mare to the first one, and man those mule ears pitched forward in surprise. He was guessing she'd never been schooled over fences, but could feel the excitement in her— could tell she wanted to give it a try. Bore down on the jump. Her jughead swung up, eyes and nostrils wide. Scrambling with her legs to try and find the take off point he was aiming her for. Missed the spot, but Jericho came up in his irons, lifting her anyway. And the big moose lurched wildly into the air at his command. Crooked over the fence, and she'd way, way over-jumped the small obstacle.

Standing near the gazebo, Marco giggled like a schoolgirl. "She looks like a kangaroo," he snickered to Darien, and she laughed along with him. Perfect description. Horrid horse, she thought again. Really an embarrass-ing mount.

Jericho rode out of the line and onto a circle. "Marco, raise the Oxer," he called to his man on the side. "Give me five by five."

"Jer, that cow doesn't have a clue what she's doing," the head man protested. "Five by five is huge."

Jericho didn't want or need his advice. "Do it," he snapped.

Spinning the horse around and cantering off on her, letting her stretch her neck out, there was suddenly a lot more cooperation on the moose's part. Well fuck me, he thought. She'd liked that, really liked it. Pulled her to a halt at the end of the arena and waited for the jump to be raised.

While Marco adjusted the fence again, he watched Chip taking another line. Monterrey shaking his head, seeming to hate the way his new rider sawed the reins as they approached. Clean over the fences maybe, but the horse jumping in a truly miserable form, and that would never cut it in the big time competition of the Grand Prix ring.

He had to turn his eyes away. Damn, it just broke his heart.

Marco had finished, and Jericho pushed the mare forward again, back into the canter. He abbreviated the line, going only for the Oxer this time, circling in to face it. And damn, that big obstacle got the mare's attention—she was riveted on it. Those mule ears signaling that she'd seen it, judged it, and had the courage to face it. He sat in and squeezed her forward for a second, then rose into two-point…tried to measure her stride although her powerful legs were going everywhere all at once. Snorting and really leaning into the jump—Christ, she wanted it! Came up, lifting her into the take-off, and felt those hindquarters bunch and thrust beneath him. Huge bascule, rounding into the air. He released, letting her stretch while still maintaining quiet contact. And oh, *Jesus fucking Christ*, this mare had just given him one monster of a jump—an easy foot of clearance over the top rail, and the landing had been well past the five-foot spread he'd asked of her.

Three consecutive hard bucks from the mare after she'd finished, but they were sheer exuberance, a celebration on her part.

He pulled her up. Patted her. Then picked up a posting trot to cool her out. Inside he was on fire though. Probably no one but himself would truly understand what she'd just done. But mother fuck, he thought…he was definitely buying this horse.

He rode over next to Ailynn again. She looked happy on the big chestnut colt, and gave him a friendlier smile now. "You know I'm sorry," she said in that lilting voice of hers before he could even get a word out of his mouth. "That sounded awful before, and I didn't mean it that way."

"Sure you did," he contradicted her. "I heard you, and I'll respect it." Softened the quality of his tone some, but not really much. "I want to make you a business proposition. Have dinner with me." At her skeptical look he added roughly. "Ailynn...I will *not* make a pass at you again, alright? I want to talk."

Surprised and not totally buying it. "About what?"

"Eight o'clock. Player's Club patio. Strictly business."

She hesitated, but finally said, "Okay, I guess it's fine."

"And the mare stays here tonight."

Her lips parted in an unconsciously sexy look that affected him far more than he liked. "Jericho, why?"

Repeated himself pointedly. "Eight o'clock. Player's Club patio. Hear me out then."

"Alright, I'll wait."

Chapter Six

It was about 6:00 PM, and Jericho had just finished up his last ride for the day. He strolled into the barn and wandered down to the stall where they'd put Elysia up for the night. *Elysia.* Yeah, it was an okay show name, but as ugly as this creature was it would always draw laughs, and if he bought her he'd change it—and forget about what was on her papers, he didn't give a shit about that.

Stared in at her now. The guys had washed her and brushed her down, but he still frowned in dissatisfaction. She was in sorry need of a real grooming…ears, muzzle and fetlocks trimmed, and some elbow grease put into that sorry brown hide of hers. Feet oiled up, mane pulled—he couldn't believe someone had actually taken her to the showgrounds like this. Then again, Ailynn's lazy trainer probably hadn't cared, and of course, this rank moose of a mare undoubtedly turned grooming sessions into a nightmare. Still, it sure as shit didn't meet Jericho's muster.

"Marco," he called over to his head groom. "I want to work a few of the horses tomorrow." It should have been his day off, but as of right now, he planned to spend at least the morning at the barn. "Put this mare first on the schedule—eight o'clock. But I'll tell you this much right now…I won't sit on a horse that looks like this."

"I was wondering," Marco said, disapproval in his voice too. And he knew his employer all too well. Jericho was meticulous—to a fault, if you asked the crew that worked for him. "Well, as soon as you're done with her tomorrow…"

"Oh, no. Hell, no," Jericho said flatly. "You and I are gonna do her right now. Go get me the clippers and the twitch."

Marco didn't look happy about it—already six o'clock, and this was going to take a while—the mare would be a total bitch, he'd be willing to put money on that. Even so, he just sighed and shuffled off to get Jericho

77

what he'd asked for…it wasn't as if his boss was likely to change his mind about it—he'd bet money on that too.

While he waited, Jericho grabbed the mare's halter and slid the stall door open. "Watch out, she kicks," Marco called back over his shoulder to him.

Boy, Marco had that number right. As soon as he stepped into the stall, the moose laid her ears back flat, and swung her hindquarters around, threatening him. If he'd made the mistake of backing away from her, she'd have lashed out at him with those wicked back hoofs. Instead he quickly moved in close, leaning hard into her hip and shoving her—even if she tried to kick him now, she wouldn't have the leverage to hurt him much. "Get around and face me," he growled at her. Slapped her rump open palmed—it would sting a little, sure, but he'd really done it because the noise itself would be intimidating, and this mare needed that. Shoved hard again.

Startled, the moose pivoted back around, and Jericho quickly turned and slid the halter over her muzzle—up and over those mule-like ears. "You know, you're going to learn something here, you damned alpha mare, and the sooner the better," he said firmly, giving the halter a shake. "I'm in charge, and you're not."

Sidelong stare coming back from her, the whites of her eyes showing, almost as if she'd understood what he said. She'd heard the tone though, and that was more than sufficient. Walking along beside him obediently now as he led her out into the aisle, he put her on the crossties. But this horse was one who tested authority—she'd try him over and over again, he knew that well enough. Over and over again, until he'd finally earned a place in her heart—and she wouldn't give that up easily. But if she *did*…if she could learn to respect and trust him, she was also the kind who'd go through hell and back to do what he asked of her.

Marco had returned, and he was grinning. "Have fun getting her out?" he asked innocently.

Cocky shrug in return. "Why? Was it supposed to be difficult? You let me know if you can't handle her, alright?" Added more seriously, "If I get my way, this mule's gonna be here a while. But only you and me, Marco. Tell the other guys to stay away from her, understand?"

His head man nodded. Jericho didn't need to say any more than that.

He fished around through the assortment of clippers they kept in a heavy-duty plastic grooming box. Found a medium-sized cordless model, and brought it over next to the mare. "Lets see what she does." He turned the unit on—it was designed to operate almost soundlessly, but even so made a quiet hum. He didn't try to touch her with it. Just wanted to see if she'd freak out when she heard the noise.

No reaction at all.

Suspicious. If the clippers didn't bother her, then why wasn't she properly trimmed? Maybe, just maybe, her trainer actually *was* that lazy—but even so, he didn't figure Ailynn that way, she was always perfectly put together herself.

Jericho bent down and went to touch the clippers to the front leg closest to him...and oh boy, did things change then. The mare squealed angrily and half-reared in the crossties—striking out viciously with that foot. Deliberate—not startled or frightened. Just a simple case of her trying to bully him around. He jumped out of the way before she connected, and smiled to himself, unperturbed. Alright fine—so she'd learn a few lessons today then. Number one, he didn't intimidate easily, if at all. And number two, there was only one acceptable form of behavior on her part...that she stood like a lady when he was around.

"Alright, let me have the twitch," he said.

———

It was 8:15 or so when Jericho pulled his Mustang into the Player's Club parking lot. Alright, he was late and Ailynn was probably already pissed at him, but her mare had been clipped—legs, muzzle and ears. Her mane and forelock had been pulled, and then braided to train it to lie on the proper side. Had conditioner brushed through her tail, and they'd banged it, snipping a ragged inch and a half off the bottom. Hoofs oiled...and Marco was still vigorously currying her coat out. Alright, he thought, nothing was going to change the fact that her head resembled a railroad tie, or that her coat was about as plain a color as you could find...but she looked cared for, and she'd stood there and accepted it...in the end.

Two hours of hard work. And he hadn't even had the chance to shower and change before driving here. Still, he was satisfied. Progress. The mare's world was changing on her, and that was good.

He parked the car and took the sidewalk that led around to the back of the Player's Club where the patio was. Opened the little gate at the side and came through it, looking for her. And thank God, there she was at a nice table overlooking the adjoining polo field—with an expression on her face that reminded him of a little tigress with her claws unsheathed. But at least she hadn't walked out on him.

He pulled out the chair next to her, and swung into it, eyes on her, apologetic. Looked down, and there was dirt on his arms, as well as clipper oil and tiny little pieces of clipped horsehair clinging to his shirt. Damn, he was a wreak, but so be it. "Sorry I'm late," he started.

"You had precisely three more minutes," she told him—not exactly cold, but not warm and friendly either.

Nodded, accepted it…didn't even give an excuse for himself. "I'm glad you stayed," was all he said. Looked around and over toward the outside bar, and waited till the barmaid looked at him, then signaled. "Do you want anything?" he asked Ailynn.

"No, and I'm not hungry either. Why don't you just tell me what you want, Jericho?"

Oh yeah, she was really annoyed with him.

The barmaid came to the table and he ordered a bottle of Heineken, then finally turned to her, and told her simply, "I want to buy her."

Now that shocked Ailynn. "Elysia?" The mare had actually been for sale for some time now, but the way she looked, went under saddle, and her horrible barn manners had pretty much nixed any hope of getting rid of her. Ailynn had been asking thirty thousand, but knew she was going to have to drop the price…her trainer had even suggested halving it. She lifted her chin to him stubbornly. "Well, I'm asking thirty-five for her."

"Bullshit," he replied. The barmaid had returned and set his beer on the table in front of him. He wrapped his hand around it, then knocked back a long swallow. Looked at her. "That's a rank damn mare…had many takers?"

Shrugged. "A few people are interested."

Flat out lie and they both knew it. Jericho asked her a different question instead. "What are you going to buy if you sell her? Have your eye on anything?"

An unhappy expression settled on her features, and she answered him more honestly. "Alright, no…I don't have any takers. So I can't really look, can I? I mean, you saw her today. I don't even get the chance to work on my own riding…all those things you said about my position. Half the time I'm just trying to hang on."

"Listen, you don't have to tell me, I understand," he answered her gently. "You tense up and we both know why. You're way over-mounted, Ailynn, and that's not a criticism of you. Whoever sold her to you should be shot." He was suspecting good old lazy boy. "Hell, she's a very difficult horse, and she's gotten away with it for a long time. I can only name a handful of guys who could ride her—and even less who'd want to."

She leaned forward, almost angrily. "Then why do you want her? Do you think maybe I'll be so grateful…"

Incredulous and angry himself now too. "Jesus Christ, do I strike you as someone that desperate? Either that or you've got an awfully high opinion of yourself. Do you honestly think I'd pay thirty-five thousand just to…"

Curt and defensive. Maybe she realized, she'd just given him the upper hand rather decisively—if he hadn't had it already. "No, I'm sure you're not. Scratch that. Forget I said it."

He sat back, expression hard, lit a cigarette, blew the smoke out. Not looking at her. Then just murmured to himself, "Mother fuck." Reached over and took her hand, and she let him. "Ailynn, damn it…straight up on my part and no bullshit, alright? I think she can jump. It's a crapshoot, no question, but I think she can, and I think for me she will. God knows, she's the most ill-mannered beast I've come across in a long time. I mean, look at me…" He brushed ineffectively at the front of his shirt. "It took Marco and I—*together*—damn near two hours to clip her…"

Look of shock on her face. "You *clipped* her?" she blurted. "God, Jericho, no one's been able to do that…not unless I get the vet to come and tranquilize her. And people look at me like I don't know how to take care of her, do you have any idea what that's like? I'd love to clean her up some, but…"

"Hey, you don't need to convince me. I just worked with her, it's not like I don't know." He sat back again, releasing her elegant little fingers though he didn't want to—didn't want to at all. Dragged on his cigarette again. "Look, its simple. You want to sell her. No…frankly, you *need* to sell her before you get hurt. And I want to buy her. So this discussion is only about the terms of sale." He trying to make her decision as easy as possible for her—it wasn't complicated. "If you want thirty-five, I'll give you thirty-five. Done, end of story. Or I'll trade you for Razz if you like him, and I'll tell you this much, Ailynn…he's mine and I have him on the market now for one-forty. I'll get it too, it's not like I won't."

She seemed stunned again. "But, you can't do that."

"Sure I can. I can do any Goddamn thing I want." He settled that deep blue stare on her, drove his point home hard. "Look, if I make something of this mare…*if* I do…she'll be worth some money—real money. I don't want you thinking I cheated you later on, or telling people I did. I want the deal to be good for you. Hell, I'll go one better. If you think you might want Razz but you're not sure, then try him for a month…just keep him at my place, that's all I ask from you. If you're happy with him at the end of the month, then take him. If you're not, I'll give you the thirty-five. We'll write up a contract that says that and sign it."

There was a spark of something in her eyes—excitement, but like she didn't dare to hope. "That's not a fair deal, Jericho. It's not fair to you."

By whose definition of fair? His voice was firm. "I want her."

"What if it doesn't work out? What if she can't jump? What if she's just a bitch of a mare that no one can deal with?"

He slowly smiled then—touch of arrogance maybe shining through. "My risk, my loss. Ailynn, I'm a professional, I know what I'm getting into. I'm not some amateur that someone conned…"

They both knew he was talking about her.

He pushed it. *"Come on…*you know that bastard you ride with just out and out stole from you when he sold you that mare—and now he tells you she's worth nothing, and takes no responsibility for that at all."

She could hardly answer him. Whispered expressively, "How can you know that?"

"It's true, isn't it?" Yeah, he was guessing, but man, the story was all too common, and it really burned him. It reflected on every horse trainer in Wellington when guys like her trainer pulled a stunt like that—and they did it regularly…sometimes to the same customers over and over again.

Ailynn just nodded. "You think I'm a total idiot, don't you?"

He pitched his cigarette over the hedge behind her. "Yeah, you're damn right I do." Mocking half-smile. Then more earnest. "Ailynn, ride with me for a month—while you're trying Razz, let me teach you. I'm not a Dressage trainer and I don't pretend to be, but I swear to Christ by the end of it, I'll take you to a Dressage show and he'll win for you. Try it, what can you lose?" Dropped his eyes for an instant and then turned them full on her again—that totally naked expression lurking in them. "This is what you're worried about, right? No, I won't make a pass at you, I won't ask you to sleep with me, I won't…"

"Stop it. I already said I was sorry for that this afternoon."

Sat back and just muttered angrily to himself, then said heatedly to her, "You know, I'm not gonna apologize for the way we met. You could have told me no, but you didn't. And God damn it, I loved it and yeah, I want to be with you again. So sue me. Fuck, I don't know what you heard about me, but I'll guarantee you a good half of it's accurate. Hot-tempered, yeah that's true. Perfectionist, holier than thou, know-it-all, I'm sure I come off that way. Do I screw around—yes. Hound dog, treat women poorly—I don't know, maybe. My work is the only thing that means something to me. With everything else…maybe I don't take enough time to…" Searched for the words. "…put myself out there. But when I offer you something on this deal? My integrity and everything I live for is on the line, and you better fucking believe it's honest and it's fair."

She leaned toward him and he responded, coming toward her too. She dared to run her fingers down his cheek. "I do believe you. And alright, yes. Draw up your contract, and yes, I'd love to try Razz for a month like you said. I'd…really love that." She was so close to him, and her touch along his face…it just promised. He wanted to lay his mouth hard over hers in the worst way. Didn't, resisted it. But all that passion and the intent were there in his eyes. She could feel the need in him, her lips had parted softly, almost expecting him.

He took that as an invitation—to try at least. "Don't slap me for this," his murmured. His lips brushed hers, just lightly drawing her lower lip between his teeth, coaxing. He felt her breathe in a sigh of longing, and thought, *protest all you want lady, but you want me just as much as I want you.* He kissed her a little longer, not giving her what she was looking for— or him what he was looking for, either. But this damn sure wasn't the place for that. He pulled back a few inches, and man, his deep blue stare was on her powerfully. And her return look seemed to acquiesce, or even more. His thumb brushed over that tempting mouth, and stroked the line of her jaw. "Ailynn, come home with me. Just be with me. God, *let me…I…*"

"Well, Wellington is certainly a small world, isn't it?" Deep male voice, and not one Jericho would have been particularly glad to hear under normal circumstances—and right now, man he hated it. He glanced over his shoulder sharply, resenting the intrusion.

The frickin' Marxes, Cin, and another couple he hadn't met.

Ailynn leaning up and whispering beside his ear softly, *"Yes."*

His eyes fell back on hers for an instant, caressing her hotly with just that look. And sweet Jesus, he wanted *inside* her again, he wanted…

"These are our friends, Carole and David Markham. Carole rides with me over at Chip's," Darien was saying pleasantly. "Carole and Dave, you guys have heard of Jericho Brandeis, surely."

Ah, hell. No choice in the matter. He couldn't completely ignore them, though he dearly wanted to. Customers needed to come with an "off" switch, but they never did.

He rose and shook hands with the Markhams, probably looking as unenthusiastic as he felt.

Not to be overlooked, Cin had to get her two cents in…and anyway, she wanted to know who this woman was that Jericho seemed so fascinated with. "Well Jericho, aren't you going to introduce us to your friend?" she admonished him, stepping forward, putting herself front and center in the little group.

Introduce her? Sure, he'd slept with her, and desperately wanted to tonight again, but he still didn't know her last name. But maybe she realized that, because she also rose now and quickly answered Cin. "Hi, I'm Ailynn McCrae." That little lilt to her voice made the name into music.

"A beautiful name," Bob Marx said graciously. "Where are you from Ailynn?"

"Just outside of Edinburgh actually."

"Lovely city…been there once or twice."

"I saw you riding at the showgrounds today," Cin interrupted the flow of the conversation to throw in the not too subtle dig and get back to her own agenda. "Lucky thing you didn't get hurt."

"Get hurt?" Darien asked. "What happened?"

"Yes, lucky," Ailynn mumbled, but looked mortified.

Jericho wanted to shake his client, the bitch. Anything to shut her up. He reached over and stroked Ailynn's silky dark hair, then held out his hand to her and brought her in under his arm and close against his body. She laid her head just against his chest, and let her arms drape around his waist. "Yeah, well it's not going to happen again," he said meaningfully, but not explaining.

Cin went blithely right on, laying it on thick. "Darien, Ailynn's got this beautiful big mare…" She said the word "beautiful" with just the right inflection—enough to let everyone there know she didn't mean it. "…but she started bucking right there in the practice ring. Bucking hard, right

Ailynn? Well, Ailynn's tiny—just look at her—so of course she couldn't stay on her, and my goodness dear, I mean you were really airborne there." She laughed sweetly—but not.

From Jericho, and a warning. "Cin."

She ignored him. "Oh Jericho's just being modest. You had to be there to appreciate it, but I just *have* to tell you this story." And she plunged right into it. "So Ailynn's mare bucks her off and then starts running flat out for the barn I guess. And Jericho jumps right in her path and grabs the reins and brings her up short...and he's got...what, darling? One or two broken ribs? But he doesn't care, and I have to tell you, our Jericho is fearless. Completely fearless. He just jumps on her back, no stirrups or anything, and she's bucking...but you certainly made her behave, didn't you?" she gushed, putting a hand on his bicep, feeling how tight it was and knowing exactly how much she was annoying him, but not even caring one bit.

Damn her, he thought. Ailynn was blushing as Cin described the scene, and then when she mentioned the broken ribs, appeared to be shocked. The Marxes were looking uncomfortable too—after all, their new horse was the one who'd kicked him. "You have two broken ribs?" Ailynn asked, horrified and obviously feeling terrible about it. "But when did that happen?" He sure hadn't had anything wrong with him the night they'd met.

He just glossed it over. "No, I don't have broken ribs. A horse kneed me the other day but it was nothing." Ran his hand down the faint trace of bruising left on his jawline. "And Cin's way exaggerating," he told the rest of the little group. "It wasn't that dramatic."

"Oh, no. She's not exaggerating," Ailynn insisted, unwittingly assisting Cin in making herself look...like she couldn't ride...like she'd caused a problem. "My mare was just being horrible. But Jericho, I had no idea..."

Man, he wanted to slap Cin.

"Have you two eaten dinner yet?" his oh so bitchy client continued. "If not, you should join us. I'm just dying to get to know Ailynn better." She smiled at her, and reached over to brush her hair fondly—adopting her as a friend almost, though nothing could have been less true. "I mean, I've never seen Jericho with the same woman two nights in a row, but I have to say, I think he's fascinated with you, dear."

Oh great—never seen him with the same woman two nights in a row—that was really going to help him here.

The Player's Club back patio was filling up nicely—it was almost like a cocktail party, with people at tables, but also milling around with drinks and socializing between the tables.

"No, look at me," Jericho protested. "I just left the barn and I haven't even showered yet…I mean, it wouldn't have been the first time I've cleaned up in the wash stall," he said with wry amusement. "But I didn't have anything to change into and…" Expressive look at Ailynn. "…I was already so late."

From Bob Marx. "You're at that barn dawn to dusk, aren't you?"

Shrugged. "After eight's later than I normally stay there, but Marco and I were clipping…"

Hard hand clapping him on the shoulder, then a firm handshake. Jason Coulder—another jumper trainer and decent friend—standing there with a drink in his hand, milling around and talking. He'd overheard that last remark. Smiled, but was also quietly mocking. "*Clipping*, Jericho? Jesus Christ, you have more grooms per horse than anyone I know, and you were still clipping yourself at eight o'clock at night? Get a life man."

Looked annoyed. "No, I don't normally clip," he said defensively—and yeah he knew the part about the grooms was accurate—most trainers had one groom to five horses, and he had one to three, but then he liked things immaculate—*all* day, not just at the end of it. "But this mare can be dangerous…"

"Oh, it was Ailynn's horse!" Cin interjected.

The woman beside him looked embarrassed again, and put her hand in front of her face, then said ruefully, "Oh God, she's just so awful. Jericho, I'm so sorry you had to stay till eight like that and Marco too…" Tipped her face delicately up to him now, her hand brushing down his side. "…and I was so mean to you for being late, and…"

"Come on," he murmured to her, the meaning just for her, although everyone else there could hear him. "You know damn well I do what I want to do…" His eyes lingering over hers.

Small smile, which really satisfied him. He liked the way she was subtly clinging to him too…the constant light physical contact. No, she hadn't changed her mind, and wasn't even vacillating. She'd leave with him from here and he'd take her home. Into his master bedroom this time. Lay her down and come over her.

Coulder was meanwhile introducing himself to everyone there—except Cin, whom he already knew…well, everyone who was anyone knew

Cin Maitland. She was occupied anyway, watching the dynamics between Jericho and Ailynn—and really, really, really not liking them. They were sleeping together, no doubt about that. And Jericho…looked like he'd claimed this woman for himself, and he was damned possessive about it…about her. The little bitch, with her ugly, frightful horse, and who was she anyway? No one.

"Well, Jericho," she spoke up again. "Why don't you go home and change, and Ailynn can stay here with us? By the time you get back, we'll just be getting around to ordering anyway. Jason, you stay too," she added.

Hell no, he didn't want that, though the truth was he needed to shower anyway, cause he sure as shit couldn't be with her like this.

"Sounds good to me," Coulder answered. "And while you're gone, I can try and steal all your customers," he joked.

"Marxes and Markhams have their horses with Chip Langdon, so steal away," Jericho corrected him, smiling tolerantly. And right now he was thinking he wouldn't mind losing Cin that much—so steal away on that score too.

"It's alright," Ailynn said, and her voice was softly making him a promise, but damn, she wasn't helping him here—in fact she'd pretty well backed him into a corner.

But he wasn't going to let it happen. He stroked that silky dark hair of hers, and said firmly, "No, we have other plans."

"Well, we understand that," Bob Marx answered for the group of them, though Cin glowered.

Okay, Jericho thought, Marx was a man and he knew what was going down, and he'd just thrown a bone his way—though why, he didn't know. Couldn't figure this guy out. "But Jericho, before you leave, take a walk with me," Marx added. His wife looked at him strangely—she obviously wasn't in on what he wanted to say.

Alright, so now he'd find out. Jericho nodded, then said to Ailynn, "I'll be right back, and then we'll go."

Smiled at him again. Sexy little tilt to her head—playful. Soft voice. "Okay."

He grabbed his Heineken from off the table and stepped over next to Marx, and then led the way to a more private area of the patio. Turned around and faced him, lifted one slashing eyebrow questioningly.

Straight to the point from the investment banker. "Can Chip Langdon ride my horse?" he demanded.

Didn't get much blunter than that. Still Jericho called him on it. "You saw him riding him today. So what's your question? Can he ride him…yes."

Annoyed look coming back at him—as if to say "you know what I meant." But reworded his question anyway. "Can he ride him well enough to win?"

"Hard to say." But, you know…this irritated him. Purred back to him, "He's been on the horse twice…give him a fucking break." No, what he'd just said wasn't in his own best interest, but it was the truth, and he wasn't going to undercut another professional trainer that way.

Marx looked more than surprised. "What are you saying?"

Just let him have it. "What am I saying? This." He took a long swallow of his beer, taking those few extra seconds, because he could feel his temper rising relentlessly. *Fucking owners.* "Chip Langdon owed me a phone call when he knew I was being blind sighted on the sale of Monterrey…but then I might have gone to the Maitlands and talked them out of it, so he screwed me instead. But just because that bastard has no professional courtesy, doesn't mean I'll do the same to him. Talk this over with Chip…not me. I'm biased as hell anyway."

Long moment of silence from Marx. "You can't mean you don't want the horse back."

Harsh. "No, I don't mean that, you're right."

Marx's eyes narrowed. He was definitely analyzing this conversation, and hard. He tossed out quietly, "You don't like me much, do you Jericho?"

Turned his face away coldly. Murmured, "Like I'd actually answer that."

Aggressive. Perceptive. "And of course that *is* an answer, isn't it?"

Lifted that deep blue stare to him. No response.

A soft laugh. "Fine, you don't need to tell me." Paused thoughtfully. He clearly wasn't done with what he wanted to say, but appeared to be thinking about how he was going to handle it. Resumed. "You know, Chip told me the other night that you have the talent to make an Olympic run…interestingly enough, he didn't say he did. Just you."

Shrugged. "Maybe he was being modest." Though the truth was, Jericho couldn't see Chip making the team—even with Monterrey. Even if he worked harder at it, and he wouldn't—Chip was comfortable where he was. "Did you ask him about it?"

"No." But Marx countered him. "Was he right about you?"

Jericho finished his beer, reached over and set the bottle down by his feet. "Maybe. Why would you care?"

Marx ignored the question. "He said you've never had the right mount or the right patron. Patron, because I assume an Olympic run costs plenty. Is Monterrey an Olympic quality horse?"

Despite himself, this conversation reached in and grabbed him by the heart. It touched on everything he wanted or cared about—promised and withheld. And man, that hurt, and he'd been used and lied to way too many times before. By people like the Maitlands. "You know what?" he growled. "Don't toy with me, Marx, and don't test my integrity—don't dare. I already told you, talk to Chip first about Monterrey. Is he Olympic quality? I have an opinion, but it's an opinion and nothing more." Seemed like he wouldn't answer that question, but then said harshly, "Handled properly? Oh yeah."

"So what *is* the cost?"

"Plenty. I mean…you know you just missed it, right? The Games in Athens? So are you asking me about annually, or for the whole three and a half years?" He still looked angry, very angry and even more distrusting …and then he said why. "You know, I hope you realize you're putting me in the position where I'll be forced to call Chip personally. And I say to myself, if you'd screw him, you'll screw me anytime you want. You're gonna dangle something in front of me that you're pretty damn sure I'd kill to get, and then make me…" Broke off. Marx didn't respond though, the bastard. Just let him stand there, just waited until he went on. "Alright, alright," Jericho murmured brutally to him. "You want to hear this, fine. These are my terms, and they're not negotiable. Do the right thing with Chip or I will. Then if you're serious, I'll draw up a contract. I have absolute control of the horse for the next three and a half years, including no sale without my written concurrence. I pick where he shows and when, including Europe. You pay for everything." Stepped in closer and looked down at him aggressively. "And I need two mounts."

Sarcastic, and pretty much stunned. "Well you don't want much, do you?"

Shrugged. "It's an easy five million out of your pocket. But if I'm doing it, I'm really doing it, not some half-assed try…and I'm sick and tired of being fucked."

Tired of being fucked? Marx tossed a smartass glare in Ailynn's direction, went to open his mouth with some off-color comment.

Moved in closer. "If you say it…" Jericho threatened him so very quietly. "If you say one word about her…then remember that fist I didn't launch at you the other night?"

Marx backed away from him, couldn't even believe it. "You're a fool," he said coldly. "Brash, arrogant, and just plain stupid too. Grow up. I offered you something tonight, but no…you had to throw it in my face and make a point. Well, point taken, Jericho." Unpleasant smile from him. "Goodnight."

He'd gone back and collected Ailynn, but something obviously had changed. Walked silently out to the parking lot with her. Stood beside her at the door to her car.

"What happened?" she asked him.

Lowered his head and sighed. "Marx just offered to sponsor my run for the next Olympic Games…three and a half year's worth."

She looked stunned and so excited for him. Reached over and hugged him. "My God, Jericho, that's wonderful! Oh my God!"

He took hold of her, and moved her back a step, stared down into her eyes. Pain—masked, but there if you wanted to find it. "It would be, if I'd accepted it."

"You didn't?"

"I had to know if he was serious…and he doesn't even understand this about himself, but no, he's not. Doesn't have a clue what he's talking about." How could he explain it to her so she'd appreciate why he'd said what he'd said, done what he done? "He wants to own me the way he owns that horse…Marx, he's the one who bought my jumper out from under me. Ailynn, I'd have to kiss his ass constantly to keep him as a patron for the next three years. And I can't work like that. I can't live like that…or with the constant threat that he'll take it all away from me any time he damn well pleases." Pulled her back against his body and just held her. "Hell," he murmured against her hair. "I'd do it in a heartbeat and kiss his ass too if he'd give me a contract to protect myself. Yeah I know, he puts in the money…but I put in everything else, including three years worth of sweat and dreams. But he won't…he's too controlling. So, game over. And I have to stand there and realize what he could mean to me…and then watch it all dissolve."

"I'm sorry. I'm so sorry." She laid her hand on his chest and stroked him. "Jericho, do you want to be alone now? I won't mind if you say yes."

He lifted her chin up, looked at her, murmured, "Hell, no."

Chapter Seven

Three weeks had passed, and it was pretty much official, Jericho and Ailynn were an item, and not just hot...on fire. Seen together almost every day, him staying at her place or her with him virtually every night. But that wasn't lessening his desire for her one iota—almost unheard of for Jericho...by now, his eyes would normally have been roving far and wide, searching for something new to amuse himself with. They weren't. Even in public, his hands finding a way to touch her, one arm thrown around her, lingering kisses...his stare possessive and fierce on her. And Ailynn, dainty, pretty, adoring.

Pretty much everyone in Wellington had that number down by now. And it made great gossip too. How long could it last? Lots of speculation on that score.

He'd seen the Marxes around...more often Darien, but also both of them...but from across the room in some restaurant or bar or shopping center. He hadn't tried to talk to them, or them to him. Monterrey had been picked up on Tuesday as scheduled, with no further word coming back about him. And though he tried not to think about it, the whole conversation with Bob Marx still haunted him, and would for a long time to come. Did he regret what he'd said to the investment banker? Maybe. Would he do it differently if he had another chance? Had to be honest with himself. No, probably not. End of that.

Fell back into his work again. The mare was first on his schedule every morning—first, because that early in the morning no one but his guys would see her go, and he wanted it like that. As for the rest of it...the sale was official, the contract signed, he'd changed her name to QL and done the paperwork on it.

"Why QL?" Marco asked him. "What's that stand for?"

Smirk in return. "Something a damn sight more appropriate than Elysia." Felt superstitious about it, but decided to tell him anyway. What the hell? Marco was Marco, he wouldn't talk. "QL...for Questionable Lady."

His head groom chuckled. "That's perfect," he said.

Schooling sessions with QL were always...interesting. Marco stayed down in the ring with him most days, raising and lowering jumps, picking up the rails and resetting them if she knocked them down. She was a wild thing to ride, always challenging him, moving like a horse on fire sometimes, always ready with a hard buck of protest, but growing more and more trusting and really loving the work, despite herself. Fiercely independent, she hated when he shortened her stride or picked a spot and made her hit it, but she was learning that this man demanded her attention, demanded precision...and he didn't put her in places she couldn't handle. In fact...*shock, shock*...he seemed to know what to do better than she did. If she followed the cues he gave her, then she could really be free to jump.

And she loved to jump.

Big, big and wide...solid and imposing, airy and ethereal...it didn't matter at all what the obstacle was. This alpha mare was as fearless as the human on her back. And she liked that about him...and he loved that about her.

He spent time with her outside the jump ring every day too. Worked side by side with Marco when he groomed her, especially during the weekly clipping sessions, and she was getting used to them...or more accurately, getting used to letting them happen without creating chaos in the process. All in all, QL was slowly becoming a jumping horse, and Jericho her partner. She'd never be a servant, but partnership with him? Maybe it didn't totally suck.

And then there were...oatmeal cookies. Forget apples, forget carrots ...sugar was nice but not something she'd really try very hard to earn. But this particular human occasionally handed out those incredible round flat things...and now those were something a mare could really sink her teeth into. Oh, he broke them up into pieces and doled them out sparingly...but if she really, really pleased him, out they'd come. Like when he clipped her legs and she left all four of them on the ground the whole time...oatmeal cookie, pat on the neck, and "Good."

"Good," even by itself seemed to be worth some effort. "Good," came with treats sometimes, it came with soft murmured words and stroking. And it came with really fun and exciting jumps. "Good" was good.

"No," was also becoming a sort of a friend to her. "No," set boundaries. She could do anything she wanted until she ran into a "No." And if she stopped what she was doing and respected the "No"…now this was interesting…it was usually followed by something she really liked…"Good."

Next on Jericho's daily schedule was Ailynn with Razz—official show name, Razz Ma Tazz. The big chestnut gelding seemed to like his new profession—Dressage horse. And he liked this little slip of a rider—he was liking her better and better as she grew more confident. To Marco and the boy's disgust, they now had a Dressage ring on the property, and Jericho had talked around to some of the Dressage trainers he respected—he wanted someone who'd come over to work with Ailynn. Yeah, he could still teach her for a while, but eventually she'd need a trainer who specialized in that sport, and he didn't want her moving out…where he wouldn't see that sweet little ass of hers riding every day. Lots of erotic thoughts going on when he taught in the Dressage ring, no doubt about that.

Marco came into the small office one day to find him making show entries. "Where are we going first?" he asked.

"The National." The National Horse Show Outdoor Championships, the last week of November. The NHS was huge, and even had national level television coverage from ESPN. It had classes for Hunters, Jumpers, Dressage and more. Yeah, it was a big show, but most of his string was good and ready for it.

"Who's going?" Marco asked, coming over to take a look.

Jericho pushed the entry forms over to him. Cin's two Hunters, Cabaret and Firedance, doing the Adult Amateur Working Hunter classes…another client's two geldings, Maximus and Rebel Yell, who Jericho rode in the Open Hunter Division…his own colt, Laredo, an Open Green Hunter and for sale…Ailynn on Razz, doing Third Level Dressage, tests one and two…and QL.

"QL?" Obviously that one stunned Marco. "But Jer, you've only been riding her a few weeks."

"You're right, and she's not ready for it," he agreed, not elaborating. But there were two $100,000 Grand Prix classes at the National. He only planned go for the first of these—more than that would be way too much. "But hell, Marco…there are qualifying rounds early in the week, and if nothing else, I'll put her in those for the experience. If she makes the finals, fine, but who cares if she doesn't? And frankly, I might not show the finals even if she does make it. Forget about the prize money—I just want to get her in the ring."

"But she's not qualified," Marco protested one more time, although he could see that Jericho was getting annoyed with him.

Shrug. Smug smile. "Yeah, I know…just let me handle that, alright?"

The show started Wednesday…QL's qualifier was Wednesday too. In fact, Wednesday promised to be one bitch of a day, with all seven rides Jericho's, and QL's the last of them. Thursday was lighter, but then Friday, assuming the horses qualified in the early rounds…straight from hell.

Wednesday

Class	Horse	Rider
Regular Working Hunter Round 1	Maximus	Jericho
Regular Working Hunter Round 1	Rebel	Jericho
Regular Working Hunter Round 2	Maximus	Jericho
Regular Working Hunter Round 2	Rebel	Jericho
First Year Green Working Hunter Round 1	Laredo	Jericho
1001 The Palm Beach Post National Welcome Qualifying Stake, CSI	QL	Jericho

Thursday

First Year Green Working Hunter Round 1	Laredo	Jericho
Regular Working Hunter Round 3	Maximus	Jericho
Regular Working Hunter Round 3	Rebel	Jericho

Friday

2721 Amateur Owner Hunter 36 & Older Round 1	Cabaret	Cin
Amateur Owner Hunter 36 & Older Round 1	Firedance	Cin
Third Level, Test 1	Razz	Ailynn
2003 NHS Hunter Championship Open Division Phase 2—Round 4	Maximus	Jericho

NHS Hunter Championship Open Division Phase 2—Round 4	Rebel	Jericho
NHS Hunter Championship Open Division Phase 2—Round 5 (Final)	Maximus	Jericho
NHS Hunter Championship Open Division Phase 2—Round 5 (Final)	Rebel	Jericho
Amateur Owner Hunter 36 & Older Under Saddle	Firedance	Cin
1003 The NHS Jumper Championship, CSI-W	OL	Jericho

A few days later, Jericho gave Marco the schedule with a curt, "Make sure you and the boys have this damn well memorized—the horses ready in the warm-up ring when I need them, the guys ready for tack switches between horses—and I mean fast, not fumbling around. And Marco, I need you to be on top of which ring I need to be in and when. I have to ride, I need you to handle everything else."

As if Marco didn't know that after all the years with him.

On Sunday before the show, Marco grabbed Ailynn and pulled her into the tack room. "The horses will go to the showgrounds Tuesday morning, and you'll practice over there Tuesday and Wednesday—probably in the afternoon sometime. I'll make sure you know when." She nodded, understanding. "But Ailynn," Marco went on. "I need to tell you something. At the show...Jericho..."

"Will be an utter beast," Cin spoke up. She was there too, sitting on the couch and putting her boots on before her lessons with Cabaret and Firedance. She laughed. "He always is. Barking out orders, snapping all the guys heads off. He's polite enough with his customers, but barely says more than two words other than coaching."

The subject of their discussion strolled in. "Marco, do we have the stall drapes ready? And I mean cleaned and pressed?"

"Yes, Jer." No, would have been a very bad answer.

Nodded. "Show me the stall chart." He wanted to be sure he approved of who they put where—especially QL.

His head man went to retrieve it.

"Jericho darling," Cin continued, getting up now, ready to ride. "Are you really going to show Ailynn's mare in the Grand Prix?"

"She's *my* mare now, Cin. And yes I am."

Teasing little smile, as she came over and tapped his shoulder lightly with her riding crop. "Well, you know what? I can't wait to see that one. Are you going to beat Monterrey?" Clearly, she didn't think so.

Shrug. Single word answer. "Try," he said.

———————

Tuesday at the showgrounds…man what a zoo.

Jericho had space in the permanent barns there—twelve stalls, small tack room, feed room, two tack stalls, and a space out front that was fixed up as a sitting area for customers. One of the guys had spent most of the last week over there in preparation…putting rubber mats in the aisle way, bedding the stalls down, setting up feed and water buckets in each stall. Monday, Marco and the whole crew went over and hung the stall drapes out front and on the sides, set up the customer area with some wicker furniture, small refrigerator, refreshment center, wood chips on the floor and some nice potted plants around. Absolutely first class.

Tuesday they brought in the horses and the tack—and that alone took two trips. Then the feed, hay and shavings. Grooming equipment. Saddle pads, polo wraps, splint boots, bell boots. All the horses had to be bathed…those with classes the next day got a show grooming, including special shampoo, whitener on any white markings…braiding of manes and tails would be done early the next morning.

Jericho picked up show packets for each of the horses. He checked the schedule again for the next few days, resolving conflicting ride times with the Horse Show Office. And then, when all of that was done, he had to teach both Cin and Ailynn and finally ride his own mounts—all of that in the practice rings, dodging other riders, sharing the fences. QL he did last, when the activity had died down some. Still his ugly mare drew comments and some on-lookers, including USET Showing Jumping Chef D'Equip, Chuck Frankel, standing back in the shadows away from the edge of the ring—but watching, curious. Jericho saw him, though he didn't acknowledge him. And the reverse didn't happen either.

Still Frankel had his eye on him, and that was a very good thing.

He mainly did flatwork with her. A couple of fences, but hell they were set up poorly here, and he wasn't going to make Marco redo their course for them.

"Just set up a few four footers for me to take her over," he asked him. Then set to jumping them. Nice session from her—she was more insecure here in unfamiliar territory, and was really leaning on him for encouragement and support, but actually trying hard. "Good girl." Patted her. Done.

He looked up and was surprised to see Ailynn and Brae sitting on the fence now—Brae with a Latte in one hand…Jesus, great roommate. The Barista also had a camera in the other, and had been taking pictures. Jericho rode over to them, reached for the Latte and took a long drink from it…no longer really hot, but still damn good. "Thanks."

Brae waggled the camera. "Want to see them?"

"Sure. Back at the barn, okay?" He ran his eyes over Ailynn. Long, meaningful, lingering look. Then just rode off—him, the mare, and the Latte. Ailynn and Brae started back together too. It was a bit of a hike from the practice ring to where their stalls were. As they walked along laughing and joking, Darien Marx came driving by in a golf cart, but she recognized the two of them and immediately pulled to a stop. "Hi. Want a ride?" she asked.

"Nah, we like the exercise," Starbucks told her before Ailynn got the opportunity to accept—which she probably would have. "But hey, look at these pictures before you go, see what you think." He set the camera on "Review" and advanced to the first of them, then stuck it over almost in her lap. Goofy grin from him.

She almost hated to take a look. Cautiously she lifted the camera and quickly glanced at the image cued up on the small screen. She couldn't believe it, but here he was completely surprising her again…really, really nice shot of Jericho on that ugly moose of a mare. Taken at the apex of clearing the fence. It appeared to be a four-foot vertical, but the mare was so far above it, she could have easy cleared five or more feet with that jump. And what was really interesting was that even though the horse was solid brown, Brae had managed to get beautiful detail, including her expression. Yes, this mare had a head you wanted to put a bag over…but still the look about her face was so bold and joyful, that she almost seemed beautiful. And then there was Jericho in nearly perfect balance and quiet release.

The pictures Darien took were quite often horse related, and of course she did jumpers all the time. But this was a picture she would have loved to have taken herself, it was that good. She handed the camera back to him. "We *really* have to talk. After the show, okay?"

He shook that disheveled blonde hair out of his eyes, laid a compelling stare on her. Easy smile. "Okay."

As Brae and Ailynn walked the rest of the way back to the stalls, a man neither of them knew came up to them. Said it looked like Brae had been taking pictures. Yeah, he had. Asked if he could see them. Sure, no problem. Offered fifty dollars for the disk.

Starbucks sold it to him.

Wednesday. Overcast day, lots of humidity, but not oppressively hot. From the standpoint of showing, a little breeze might have been nice, but otherwise it wasn't half bad—as long as the rain held off, and thus far it had.

Brae came over as soon as he finished up at Starbucks—he was kind of getting off on watching his roommate at work, although he knew absolutely nothing about the horses. He slipped in next to Ailynn at ringside. "How's it going?" he asked, giving her a hug and a little kiss—kind of bad boy look on his face as he did.

Ailynn just let him, though when she looked over at Jericho, it was more than obvious where her affections lay. "Just look at him," she said. "He's so…"

Starbucks rolled his eyes. "I should have never introduced you to him."

Sexy little laugh from her. "Well, he basically introduced himself, didn't he?"

The Barista looked even more annoyed, but agreed, "Yeah, he did."

The truth was, Jericho *was* a real figure at the showgrounds—in beige breeches and high black boots that Marco constantly rebuffed…a tee shirt during times between classes, formal shirt, tie and jacket in the ring. And of course, those ever present slim, rimless sunglasses. His long braid had been folded under twice and actually sewn neatly into place by Marco—exactly as he did with the horses' manes. Ailynn was still watching him—she couldn't take her eyes off him really. "You know…he's like a machine. There's always someone talking to him, asking him questions. Either that, or he's riding. And Brae, you should have seen him today…both Maximus and Rebel qualified through the first two rounds of the their classes, and Laredo looked so good that someone asked about buying him."

"Cool." Smirked. "I'll bet he's impossible though, right?"

Oh yeah, that was also true. As Cin predicted, he'd been a tyrant all day, harshly demanding as always—but even more so on the showgrounds than at home. On the other hand, everything in his stable ran like clock-work—no missed classes, no wrong numbers on the horses, no screwed up tack. Clockwork. An hour later it was finally time for QL's qualifying class.

And it was a big mother fucking class. Forty-two entries, and less than half would go on to the finals Friday. Jericho's ride was about mid-way through the pack. Chip and Monterrey were just three goes in front of him, meaning he'd be in the warm-up ring when they went through—but he still hoped to see most of it.

He'd changed into slim-fitting white breeches, white shirt and white tie, and would wear a formal black jacket and hunt cap in the ring—tradi-tional attire for this class. Ready, he came up to the ring to watch while they set up the fences. When they were done, the riders were allowed to walk the course, as always. He stepped out into the arena and began step-ping them off. Twelve elements in total, but fifteen individual jumps since one of the elements was a triple and one a double. Time allotted for the ride, only 71 seconds. He knew this course designer—she focused on test-ing both heart and precision. QL was short in the precision area, but she made up for it in guts. Still he was worried about the series from the double, fences 7A and 7B…flying change of lead…to a tight right hand turn, and into the vertical at fence 8. Otherwise, Jericho thought, his mare would handle it okay.

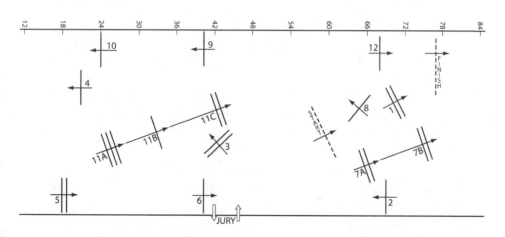

Perfect course for Monterrey.

Chip Langdon appeared beside him almost as if he'd conjured him up. They walked out the strides between the second and third elements together, not speaking. Both stopped in front of the huge oxer that was element number 3.

"I know what you did for me with Marx," Chip muttered. "He told me. I didn't deserve it either."

Jericho, lighting a cigarette. "No, you didn't."

The two of them, moving on now to element numbers 4, and 5 and 6. Nice airy vertical at 4, turn to another spread jump at five, and a set of planks at six.

"This is a hard combination for Monterrey, isn't it?" Chip went on conversationally—he wasn't really picking Jericho's brain, but wouldn't mind hearing his opinion on it.

"No, no," Jericho responded. "Just keep him sharp over this last one. It looks too easy to him, and he won't put the effort in if you don't make him. And look how shallow these cups are. These rails will fall at the slightest hit."

They finished walking out the course together—uneasy conversation, all about the jumps themselves with a bit specific to Monterrey. But Jericho knew what this was—Chip apologizing to him, and yes, he was basically accepting it.

He stood at the fence and watched the first two horses go around the course, then turned and walked to the warm-up ring where Marco was waiting with QL. He passed Ailynn with Brae again on his way over. Also saw the Marxes standing together and looking nervous, and the Maitlands—both Cin and Richard. But didn't say a word or acknowledge any of them. He'd gone totally inside himself now, mentally riding that course, thinking about his mare.

Put his left foot in the iron, and swung into the saddle, gathered the reins and started QL out at a walk. Then into the posting trot and the rest of his flatwork. Nice, round, obedient…well, tolerably so anyway…and at least her attention was on him, nowhere else.

The sky had darkened some, and he gave Marco his sunglasses. The air was heavier too, and for a few minutes it even sprinkled a bit, but lightly. Jericho ignored that, and QL did too.

Chip was already up on Monterrey. One eye on them. He and Monterrey were anything but a match made in heaven. The big bay hadn't learned to like his riding style any better in the last three weeks, and was tossing his head off and on—which also meant he was hollowing his back— something he'd never done before, but it almost looked habitual now. Jericho growled to himself, but forced himself to look away. QL was his problem at the moment, and he had to stay totally with her. Started taking her over a single fence or two, nice and easy, nice and calm.

It seemed like almost no time, and Chip was over near the In-gate, putting on his jacket and helmet. Jericho pulled up next to Marco, and took a minute to put on the rest of his own gear too. He could see that Chip was going in now, and there were only two rides between them—71 seconds per ride, plus maybe another 30 seconds each with the riders coming and going. Anyway, he was only minutes away from his turn in the ring.

While Marco wiped down his boots one last time and made sure his number was securely attached, Jericho stood up in his irons to see as much of Monterrey's go as possible. Okay over Fence 1…but fighting around the corner, not settled and prepared for the airy element at Fence 2. Rail down. Murmur of disappointment from the crowd, and Jericho cursed sharply. Better form over the big Oxer at Fence 3, followed by a perfect lead change, and then moving straight on to Fence number 4. They had a nice run over both 4 and 5, and then…fuck…he'd let Monterrey muscle him right into that plank jump. Rail down there too.

Shook his head bitterly, didn't watch the rest of the go. Caught Bob Marx looking over at him as he took QL back to the canter and over the single practice vertical again. Ignored him…but at least Marx had done the right thing and talked to Chip—Jericho gave him that much. More than he'd expected from him.

Jericho stroked QL's neck and murmured to her. She definitely knew something was up and was clearly excited about it. Big jump from her over the practice fence, but she'd gone in right where he wanted her. Nice landing, with Jericho staying up in two-point for three or four strides after the fence. He leaned forward and patted her. "Good."

"817 on Deck," the ring steward called out to him. Jericho had already gone through the bit check thing so he could head directly to the In-gate. He pulled QL back to a walk and took her at an easy pace toward it. Passed Chip handing Monterrey to a groom on his way over—Langdon didn't look happy, and neither did his owners. But Jericho couldn't think about that now, though he wondered how many faults the pair had ended up with. Eight at least.

The ride in front of him was finishing up and the steward opened the gate. Jericho picked up the canter and went into the ring.

He could see that the ring crew was resetting the fences—meaning the pair in front of him had knocked some down. There hadn't been many clear rides so far today, he thought to himself, and that was in his favor. If he could keep his big mare listening and relaxed, they had a decent chance of making the final round.

He put QL on a controlled but relaxed 20 meter circle at the canter, though her big mule ears were twitching like mad—processing this ring with it's big obstacles, the huge crowd on the sidelines making noise and talking...and wondering what in the world was going on. A few comments about his big ugly moose of a mare drifted out to him, but that just made him smile faintly.

See what you think 71 seconds from now, he thought unconcerned, and even amused by it.

"Next to go is number 817, QL, owned and ridden by Jericho Brandeis," the announcer's voice came over the loudspeaker. The big mare snorted and even let out a surprised whinny at the sound, lifted her head, but rounded again immediately at Jericho's light pressure on the reins and drive from his seat.

The bell that signaled that he could begin his go sounded. He rode to the ground jury, pulled his hunt cap off with his right hand in a smart salute, got their return acknowledgement, then shoved it hard back into place on his head.

Now or never QL.

Jericho circled back out to the right at the canter and around to face the starting line. There were timers there would mark the start of his run when he passed through them. A fine mist of rain was falling now, and the sky was dark and threatening again, but his mount was ignoring that and so was he. With luck, they'd be out of here before anything real started. He sat in and pushed QL into a strong working canter, passing through the start standards and timers. And then they were facing directly into the first obstacle, a big Oxer, four-foot-six by four feet wide. Nice solid looking jump. QL leaned toward it eagerly, pulling and fighting him a little but wanting it. Jericho sat in to bring her to her spot, came up in his irons...lifted. Big round jump, nice landing. She bucked enthusiastically as he turned her to the right and headed her to obstacle number 2, drawing an appreciative laugh from the crowd.

Took the vertical at 2 without a problem, though the jump was a bit wild and flat…but she was clear over it and that was all that counted. Still he knew he had her moving too fast into the huge Oxer that was fence number 3. Jericho set her back hard on her haunches, then pushed again, coming up and launching her at it. Big mule ears swinging to the fence, then back at him again, then back to the fence again…powerful take-off, tucked those hind legs up and to the side…soared like a bird. Touch down, flying change as they passed between the second and third elements of the triple they'd face later in the course, and aimed straight toward the airy jump number 4.

A big splat of rain hit Jericho's cheek, and oh fuck, he thought…not yet, not yet. At times he really hated this Florida weather…fine one minute, downpour the next. *Just give me fifty seconds more, damn it,* he prayed inwardly. But that big splat was ominous—it meant rain was imminent.

Over jump number 4, then around the bend and approaching the spread at 5. Another cold splat of rain. The sky was darkening up like a mean bitch too. Whatever was coming was rolling in hot and heavy now, bringing a stillness to the air that promised a major downpour and soon. QL knew it too, and she felt edgier beneath him. Her back was tense, and her legs churning as she picked up her speed coming out of the turn. She launched before her spot—well before—almost jumping out from beneath Jericho, and he threw himself forward to stay centered over her, releasing immediately to avoid hitting her in the teeth with the bit. They were clear over 5 but only because of her huge jumping ability. Most horses could never have made that high of a fence from that far out.

The planks next—the jump with those so shallow cups that Chip and Monterrey missed minutes before. Jericho focused her on it hard, made her look at it. One mule ear kicked directly back at him, the other pointed intently at the big five foot vertical. Good. At least she was back thinking about her work. More large drops of rain hitting him in the face…coming one right after another in rapid succession, and he knew damn well now that he wasn't going to get out of here dry. Faced her with it, lifted her into it. Take off! Another soaring effort.

As QL's front feet came back to the ground, the sky lit up above them. Huge lightning strike somewhere close, and then as her back feet landed…BOOM! Incredible earsplitting crack of thunder.

The mare letting out a scream of terror—not pretending like she usually did, this was the real thing. They were heading unswervingly into the double elements of 7A and 7B—the jumps that Jericho had known would be difficult for her under any circumstances, and her legs were scrabbling hard, desperate now. Slowing for a fraction of a second like she might stop, then speeding up like a crazed thing instead. Completely erratic…the mare was nearly frantic…and then the skies opened up. Teeming rain came down on them.

Snap! Snap, snap! Snap, snap, snap!

Umbrellas coming up all around the ring. A sea of unfurling monsters, all different patterns and colors. Moving. Shimmering in her field of vision. And hard on the heels of that thunderclap. QL hollowed her back, and threw her head up hard, screaming…smacking Jericho right in the face with the back of her skull, snapping his head to the side and back with the impact just as they approached the first fence of the double.

Standing at the fence line Chip Langdon sucked his breath in sharply…in dread. "Oh, Jesus Christ," he breathed.

The mare in panic, Jericho off-balance and momentarily disoriented, unable to see in the pouring rain. And bearing wildly down on 7A. Every competitive rider's nightmare.

QL couldn't stop, and didn't know what she was doing anyway. She plunged straight through 7A, barely even making an attempt to jump. The whole obstacle went down as she powered straight through it—rails flying, one side standard toppling over to the ground.

Collective gasp from the crowd. *"No…God, no,"* from Chip. His fingers gripped the fence, knuckles white from the pressure he applied.

And the mare was falling…Jericho could feel it happening. Her front end was going down…and if she tumbled and rolled…it spelled terrible injury for her, and for him too if she landed on him. He could have bailed, but that maneuver just wasn't inside him—he did the only thing he knew how to do instead…came up in his irons, tightened the rein contact and absolutely muscled her head up, lifting her by his own strength. The second fence, 7B right there in front of them, and if he didn't make this happen they'd hit that too—crash through it and really go down this time. "Come on," he growled to her. *"Come on!"*

Her feet thrashing beneath her, everywhere at once. One knee had touched the dirt, but she was up now. *Fence.* Jericho launched her…and *Jesus mother-fucking Christ*, the heart in this beast! Huge thrust from those powerful hindquarters, those front feet tucked so tight to her chest. Airborne!

That rail fell too, but they'd survived it, and she was back up and had her balance again. Flying change of lead, and following his direction into the tight turn, but flat out galloping and still plenty scared—still basically out of control.

"Pull up, Jericho," Chip was nearly snarling at the sideline. *"Retire…God damn you!"*

A hand reached over and grabbed hold of the fence just beside his. Soft voice, but lots of authority. "He'll never retire." Chip swung his head. Chuck Frankel, Show Jumping Chef D'Equip was standing there, a fierce look in his eyes.

Fence number 8 was a wall, and to take it QL would have to jump directly facing that sea of umbrellas at the edge of the arena. Rain coming down so heavily that Jericho could barely see the jumping rail at the base of it, and his mare was galloping like she had hellhounds hard on her ass. No choice…he just guessed. Rose and lifted her…and they were too far out. Way too far out. Threw his body weight forward, asking, asking… asking for what she shouldn't have been able to give him.

Huge bascule, mammoth jump.

Clear!

More thunder and lighting, but this big moose of a mare was figuring something out. She was still okay…she was safe because of the creature on her back, and she and he could actually *do* this. And she trusted. She trusted this man thing…she'd do anything he asked her to.

He knew when it happened, felt it…knew the feeling, and God it was gratifying. That moment right there in that Grand Prix ring was when she gave her soul to him.

The rest of the course…fences 9 and 10…the big triple combination at fence 11…and the final vertical, number 12…done in a teeming rain that made the surface beneath them slippery and sloppy, a downpour that turned sighting the obstacles into an exercise in ESP, that had soaked both of them and made the leather of her reins almost impossible to hold…still, the rest of their ride was a celebration of that new partnership for both man and beast. QL, cued in on him so tightly—fearless in the face of huge obstacles, umbrella monsters, and puddles on the ground that resembled miniature lakes. Didn't matter. She listened, she jumped. She flew at his command.

When the round was finished, Jericho pulled QL back to a trot, amid a roaring applause. Eight faults, but who cared? Not him, and no one on the sidelines either. And that big moose of a mare, stepping daintily…like she was the prettiest mare on earth—runway model. Swinging her mule-eared, block-of-wood, jughead proudly.

See what I did.

Pat on the neck as they left the arena. "Good girl."

Marco was right there, and Jericho vaulted off as soon as he was out of the ring. The two of them checking her over for injuries after plowing through that fence, but this equine tank looked perfectly fine. Marco had the oatmeal cookies in his pocket, and this time she got a whole one. Chomped happily on it, butted her thick head against Jericho's chest.

Marco ran a hand over his boss's cheek then.

"Bad?" Jericho asked.

Wink from his head man. "No worse than when you get in a bar fight, Jer."

A hand clapped Jericho on the shoulder, interrupting the two of them. Quiet compelling voice. "That might have been the ballsiest round I've ever seen."

Jericho's intense blue stare swung around to identify who was speaking to him. It was Chuck Frankel…just standing there, with his hand still resting on his shoulder. Frankel, whose opinion could potentially mean so much to him. "Chuck, she's green as hell, but yeah…she's got a heart the size of Texas," he replied with passion. "Just give me some time with her, then I promise you'll see what she can do."

Frankel just smiled, then clarified himself. "I meant you Jericho. Not the mare. Let's talk soon. Monday?"

Nodded. Deeply interested stare. "Give me a place and time."

"How about my house? Do you know where it is?" Again Jericho nodded. "Good," Frankel continued. "Five o'clock then."

They'd stopped the competition to let the heaviest part of the rain pass, which it did in less than ten minutes. Anyway, the press corps and fellow riders alike had crowded around Jericho…asking him about his go…about the mare…about what he'd done to stop her fall…about the fact that he'd elected to go on with the round, rather than pull up. Finally, he was able to break free of them, and head back to the barn.

With eight faults he'd be on the borderline of those who qualified—maybe he would, maybe he wouldn't. Didn't care. He wasn't planning on showing the finals with her anyway. The money be damned. What he wanted now was to take her home and go back to work with her. There'd be plenty of shows during the season he could bring her to—one nearly every weekend. And what she'd given him this afternoon was more than enough. Way more.

He didn't see Ailynn anywhere as he headed back to where his stalls were, which disappointed him a little, but with the rain as strong as it had been, he didn't really blame her. He'd undoubtedly find her waiting for him when he got back there. He walked with that long slashing stride of his, oblivious to everything until a golf cart pulled up alongside him. The Marxes and Chip. "Jump in, we'll drive you," Bob Marx invited him.

Jericho was good and soaked by this point. Even his high leather field boots were wet clean through, and his socks beneath them. But, what the hell? It had been a tough ride, and a tough day, and the truth was he was exhausted. "Thanks," he said, climbing aboard.

"Christ, you amaze me," Chip said once they were moving again. "And how's your face?"

Small smile in return. "Feels like someone sucker punched me."

"Yeah, it looks like it too," the other trainer said and laughed. "But I'll tell you this much, Jericho…I don't know how you picked that mare up and got her over that fence. Man she hit you so hard, I never thought you'd stay on her. And then to complete the course? No lie…I can't think of anyone else I'd expect that from. I mean, damn…" He seemed pretty much at a loss for words after that.

"Come on," Jericho muttered. "That's bullshit, Chip, but thanks anyway. You'd have done the same thing. I was just trying to save my ass."

Marx pulled up in front of the Brandeis Show Stables stalls. He looked at Jericho meaningfully…in a way that clearly told him, "We'll talk again." But he let him get out now without a word and without pressuring him.

Jericho ducked inside his aisle way. He was already stripping off his helmet, jacket…then his tie and shirt. Marco tossed him a towel, and when he'd dried off his chest and arms, a tee shirt. He quickly pulled it on, then tossed him the towel back.

"Put a bracer on her chest and legs, and give her a really good rub-down," he ordered.

Voices. Jericho looked down the aisle, and toward the end of it he finally saw Ailynn. But she was standing with a man he didn't recognize. Tall, harsh features, salt and pepper hair, wearing an expensive navy blue suit and tie…definite businessman look to him. Lawyer type. And they were arguing. And Christ, he wasn't standing for that. He strode down the aisle with purpose, stopping just short of the two of them, and said coldly, "This is my stable. I don't know who you are but you're trespassing. Get out now. I don't want to ask you twice."

The man turned to him. "You're Jericho I take it?" He had a nasty, whining type of voice.

Brutal. "That's right."

"Well, my name is Coleman McCrae." He even dared to take a step in Jericho's direction. "And whether you realize it or not, Ailynn's my wife," he ground out, good and angry himself. "From what I hear you've been trespassing on *my* property…on a nightly basis, if the gossip's right. So we're even, aren't we?"

Jericho muttered a savage curse, but otherwise he was speechless. He looked harshly at her, and she wasn't denying it. If anything, she looked horribly guilty. She opened her mouth, like she wanted to tell him something, but just couldn't.

A wall of rage rose up inside him. His fist curled, and he brought it up to waist height—more than just threatening. "Then take your property," he snarled softly. "Take your property and get out of my sight…both of you. Leave…while you still can—while I'll still let you."

McCrae grabbed Ailynn by the wrist, and walked away with her.

Chapter Eight

Sunday night after the show.

Brae had taken a slew of pictures at the horse show. He came home, downloaded them on his computer, and sat alone in his room looking through them. He—like everyone else—had been steering clear of his roommate. Ever since the scene with Ailynn…probably the biggest gossip of the NHS this year, once the word got out…Jericho had been deadly—fiery tempered one minute, stone silent the next. Just doing what he had to do with the horses and leaving immediately afterwards.

And only Brae knew this one…Friday night Jericho had gone to some dive bar in the neighboring town of Lake Worth, and managed to take out his aggression in an argument with one of the locals, coming home with badly bruised and swollen knuckles but no other marks on him—the other guy probably couldn't say the same thing. If he'd been detained or arrested for brawling, he didn't mention it.

Starbucks turned on the television, and sat back to take a second run through his pictures. They were pretty damn decent, if he did say so himself…and he *did* say so. Especially the shots of Jericho on QL. Even through that pouring rain, the ones of the mare crashing through jump 7A, Jericho picking her back up and then launching her over the second obstacle at 7B were…well, spectacular…if he did say so himself…and he did.

Grin. Well, he'd show them to Darien tomorrow, that should blow her mind as usual. He wasn't working, but he knew what time she normally came in, so he'd just go over, have a few smokes, bullshit with his co-workers, and flirt with all his regular chicks till she got there.

Tough life.

He heard the front door open. Slam shut again.

Refrigerator door opening next. Closing again.

So Jericho was home, and he'd gotten himself a beer. Brave it or not? Starbucks decided to go out and see what was up with him—maybe even cajole him into a better mood.

He came out into the hallway, and then around to the living room. "Hey, get me one too," he called out to Jericho.

And surprisingly enough, he did. Even brought it out to him. Brae took it, tapped the neck of the bottle against the one that Jericho was holding for himself, then screwed the cap off and tossed it on the dining room table.

"Christ you're a slob," his roommate muttered angrily, watching the path of the cap through the air and it's touchdown on the tabletop's glass surface.

Shrug. "No worse than you."

"True." Said begrudgingly though.

Brae took a swallow. "Win anything at the show today?" he asked, ignoring the rancor in the other man's tone.

"Yeah, one class—the Open Hunters. And some seconds and thirds." Cin had been third in the Adult Amateur class for one thing, beating out Darien Marx among others—a major victory for her. The Maitlands were ecstatic, and that was good, he supposed.

"But not that ugly horse, right?"

Looked disgusted at him. "You know what?" he snarled back, then knocked back a long pull from his own drink before continuing. "'That ugly horse, as you call her, is the best thing I have in the barn right now." Added bitterly. "Yeah, she's a bitch, but at least she's honest."

They both knew he was making a reference to Ailynn.

"Oh, come on," Brae said, possibly taking his life into his hands, but not really realizing it—or maybe just knowing he could get away with it. "Jericho…shit, bro…that whore banged both of us in the same night. Prolly her husband, too…so tell me, what did you expect from her? Everlasting love? Man, what you need is to go out and get laid, and I mean seriously. I can have girls over here in fifteen minutes if you want me to." Ignored the flare of violence in that deep blue stare coming back at him. Blithely changed the subject. "Hey, I've got some incredible pictures of you and Ugly knocking down that fence, want to see them?"

Now that caught Jericho's interest. Getting laid right about now was starting to as well.

"Yeah, okay," he answered harshly…maybe to both.

"They're on my computer," Starbucks answered, nodding with his head toward his room.

Well, that would be the pictures, not the chicks, but Jericho came along willingly enough, falling into step beside him. Brae went into his room and flopped down cross-legged on the king-sized bed, and Jericho sprawled across the other side of it, half-lying, half-sitting, with his weight on one elbow, one leg stretched out, the other knee drawn up...drinking more of his beer. Starbucks turned the screen so they could both see it, and then started through his pictures. Jericho sat up and paid more attention. "Christ, those are good," he said.

Brae tossed back that disheveled blond hair of his and looked pleased. And smug. "Press this button to scroll forward, and this one to scroll back," he said, reaching for the phone on the nightstand beside him. While Jericho went through the slideshow, Brae dialed.

"Oh, hey, Marcia," he said glibly into the telephone. "Yeah, what are you doing?" Pause while he listened. Jericho's eyes going over to him, not really believing this. "No, no," Starbucks continued. "I'm meeting someone later...yeah...no...well, I was actually calling about my roommate, Jericho...yeah sure, Brandeis. Well, it's his place and I rent from him...that's right." The Barista took a long swallow from his beer now too. "Yeah...well, it's actually almost a pity fuck kind of thing...ow, man!"

Jericho had kicked him—he looked offend and incredulous but was laughing in spite of himself. Hell, it was impossible to be angry with Brae. He was just such a fool, you couldn't help yourself.

"Well, come on," the Barista protested, talking to him now, ignoring the femme on the phone. "I mean, you haven't been laid in at least five days."

Superior growl. "What makes you think that?"

"Oh, wait a minute," Brae told whoever this Marcia chick was. "He's telling me something here. So when did this happen?" he asked Jericho, clearly not believing him.

Casual reply, "Well, I had to fight to get her, but Friday night."

Bark of laughter from his roommate. "Cool, man...so where'd you do her?"

"Mustang."

The Barista giggling stupidly. "Alright, check that..." he said back into the phone again. "So it's only been two nights, but still he's mean as a snake...yeah, yeah, he wants to do it." Listened. "No, I swear to God...yeah sure I've seen him fuck…oh yeah, world champion…well, Christ, I have to listen to the screaming from his bedroom every damn night…" Dodged another kick. Laughed. "So, Marcia…no, you come here, he's too much of an asshole to pick you up…absolutely…I promise you, all night long." He looked up at Jericho, smiled, gave him the thumbs up sign. "Yeah, okay…I'll make him do it. Thirty minutes? Thanks, Marcia."

"Make him do what?" Jericho demanded, drinking more beer, but he looked thoroughly amused now.

"Take your hair down."

"Oh, fuck me." He rolled his eyes, smirked. "That's the only reason I keep it long. Pain in the ass but the chicks dig it…don't ask me why."

"Yeah, well this chick will be here in thirty minutes, and she wants to…" He raised his voice a good octave and simpered, "…see that mane of yours first hand."

"Fuck me," Jericho repeated derisively.

"That *is* the point," Starbucks pointed out.

"True." Looked quickly back through the pictures one more time, then rose stripping his clothes off as he went, heading for the shower.

Brae arrived at Starbucks the next day, late morning. He was dressed as only he could get away with…black sports jacket but bare-chested beneath it, khaki pants that were riding low down on his hips and that were so long that he was walking on the backs of them, sandals on his feet. Big pair of dark sunglasses. Hair a mess as always, hadn't shaved. All the women sitting outside turned to watch him approach—some openly, some hiding it, but pretty much unanimous.

He went inside, got himself a Venti, then brought it back out and found a centrally located table to hold court from—laughing, telling stupid jokes and generally flirting with all the ladies.

Eventually Darien drove up. She'd gone through the drive-through, but waved as she pulled out and spotted him there. He waved back and beckoned, and no surprise, she quickly found a parking place. Got out with her coffee in hand, and started over to join him.

She wasn't riding today—it was Monday, and the day after a show—all the horses got time off. So instead of breeches, she was wearing a sexy little pair of shorts and halter-top. Nice legs. Sweet little bounce to her breasts too as she walked.

"Hi," she said, smiling and taking a seat beside him. "What are you up to?"

"Nothing. Relaxing," Starbucks said.

"Not working?"

"Nope." He grinned at her. Too soon for the pictures, but he'd get around to them.

"So how's your roommate?" Darien asked, sipping her coffee. "I felt so bad for him, he looked really upset."

"Jericho?" Brae scoffed. "Oh, hell no. He's way over it."

She looked skeptical. "I don't think you're right about that."

Innocent. "Oh sure...I mean, he's back screwing other chicks, so he can't be too torn up, right?"

Now that surprised her. "He is? Are you sure, Brae?"

He paused, seemed to be thinking about it. "I don't know...maybe I'm wrong." Got a confused look on his face. "But what does it mean when I hear a woman in his bedroom with him last night, and she's going..." He did his female voice imitation again. "...Oh God...oh God...*oh God!*"

Darien burst out laughing. "Last night?"

Nodded. Looked disgusted, then added, "Last night, *all* night. We're talking three in the morning here." Did it one more time for effect. "Oh God, Jericho...oh God...*oh God.*"

She reached over and slapped his shoulder. "Is that true?"

"Swear to God," the Barista smirked.

"Well, he's fine then," she pronounced.

"That's what I said." He sat back and looked at her through those dark sunglasses—nice pose.

She studied him. He was as hard to read as Jericho was, but in a totally different way. Always clowning around, it was impossible to tell when he was serious. But when he looked like he did right now, she could just envision him in a magazine ad...well, you'd certainly have to dress him up a little better, but that was nothing. "You know, I still want to take your picture," she told him. "...a bunch of different shots. You need a portfolio—you could make money with that face. I keep telling you that."

"I like *taking* the pictures better," he admitted, seemingly on the level. "Hey did you watch Jericho ride that skanky looking brown horse in the rain when the damn thing almost fell down? Oh yeah, sure you did, I saw you there." He produced his camera and set it on the table between them. Laid that soft blue bedroom eyes stare on her…and held it. "I got some great pictures of him. Go on, you know you want to look."

She really did want to see them. "There's nothing off-color on here, right?" she asked, just to be sure.

"Right."

Darien picked up the camera and looked through what he had on it. All the pictures were professional quality to be honest, but the ones of Jericho and QL at that double were "take your breath away" good. Looking at them, you could just see the imminent peril, and then Jericho muscling the mare up and finally her gallant take off over the second element. "Oh, come on," she said finally. "You just have to sell these. At the very least, all the local horse mags will want them…maybe even bid for them. And I can even make a contact for you over at API."

"Oh no," Brae said, unimpressed. "I just keep them a while and then delete them."

"Don't you dare!" She shook the camera at him. "Brae, think of it this way…if these pictures got some national publication, how good would that be for Jericho? Attention like that brings sponsors…money."

"Really?" He was grooving on having her coax him like this. Wondered how difficult it would be to get her to go to bed with him.

"Yes, really."

He shrugged. "Well, okay…do you want to keep the disk?"

Nodded. "Yeah, I do…is that okay?"

Smiled at her.

"And I want to do something else too," Darien went on, hoping that he was actually listening to her. "I'd like to have you take some shots with a few of my cameras. They're more sophisticated than the one you're using—lots more functions. Don't you want to see what you could do with them?"

Actually, he wanted to see what he could do with her, but didn't say that. Instead, he leaned forward and stared intently at her. "When do you want to take my picture?" he asked. Wondered if he could get her to come to Jericho's to take pictures of him. Wondered if she'd do a nude shot of him, or almost nude anyway. Lots of possibilities swimming around in that head of his. "I'm off during the day on Wednesday, and all day Friday."

Wondered if she'd squeal in bed the way that chick Marcia had. "Oh God...oh God...*oh God.*"

That had been pretty good.

———————

Five o'clock, Monday night, Chuck Frankel's place.

Those had been the instructions, and Jericho damn sure wasn't going to screw them up. It had been an unusually light day for him—he hadn't ridden—just got up late, dropped Marcia at her condo, checked the horses, then went to the gym. Came home, did a few laps in the pool, slept for a while, hung around doing nothing. A couple of minutes before four, he finally showered, shaved and put on something halfway decent—white short sleeve shirt with the "Polo" logo. Sandals on his feet. Hair tightly braided, as always. Clean but well worn jeans—but then again, all of his jeans were beat to shit from riding, and it wasn't like Chuck gave a hoot about that.

Frankel's house was in a new section of Wellington off Lake Worth Road, called the Equestrian Club. Jericho had been to a few social events at Chuck's place, so he knew where it was. Drove there in the Mustang, arriving just before five o'clock. As he pulled up to the stucco, hacienda-style house, he was surprised to see Darien Revson-Marx's Audit TT in the driveway, and another car beside it also with New York license plates.

No room for him in the driveway, so he just parked the Mustang out front. Swung his long legs out of the car.

The front door opened, and Darien appeared—she was leaving. She waved to Jericho, and when they met on the sidewalk, took hold of his hand and squeezed it, but not explaining what that was about. Still it was a friendly gesture, and her fingers seemed to linger in his. As if a sudden fancy struck her, she leaned up and kissed him on the cheek. "Talk to you soon," she said, dropping his hand and heading for her car without a backward look.

What was that about, he wondered, though the truth was he'd liked it. He had a lot of mixed feelings about her anyway—anger and resentment over her purchase of Monterrey and the way she and her husband had handled it. But mingled with attraction too—he still remembered the first time he'd met her—standing by her at Monterrey's stall, the way she'd caressed his arm.

Unimportant right now though. He rapped twice on Frankel's front door, opened it a few inches, and called out, "Chuck?"

The Show Jumping Chef D'Equip was standing right there. He grabbed the doorknob and opened it. Shorter than Jericho by probably four inches, but lean and hard like him—maybe fifty years old. Weathered face, neatly cut dark hair streaked with gray. "Come on in, Jericho. We're over here," he said.

We?

Frankel led the way over to a nice sized dining area. There was a round glass and chrome table there, with matching chairs. Bob Marx sitting in one of them, a drink—probably Scotch—on the table in front of him.

So this was the "we." Marx. Made absolutely no sense what he'd be doing with Chuck.

And that was definite cause for suspicion...nervousness too. Jericho laid a powerful look on Frankel, but got nothing back from him other than a matter-of-fact, "Sit here." He'd pulled out the chair where he wanted Jericho—the one opposite his own. The wall behind Frankel's chair was mirrored—meaning Jericho would be staring at his own reflection the whole time. Hated that.

The whole thing didn't feel good—too formal, too much like being interrogated.

Jericho slung his tall body around evenly and into the chair. Frankel had meanwhile gone into the kitchen. He came back and laid an open bottle of Amstel and an ashtray in front of him.

Worse, Jericho thought. Chuck didn't smoke, and if he thought his guest was going to want to or need to, what did that say about what this conversation was going to be like? He sat back, eyes flicking once to Marx, but then away again—instead narrowed and intently focused on the man sitting opposite him. And damn, he was going to let Chuck start this. Took a long drink from his beer and waited.

"Incredible ride Wednesday," Frankel said in opening. Seemed friendly enough, but with Chuck it was hard to tell.

"There were moments," Jericho answered, voice low and compelling—asking too...*what the fuck is this?* He didn't say, "thank you"—wasn't sure yet that Frankel was even complimenting him.

The Chef D'Equip nodding thoughtfully, picking his next words carefully, it seemed. "Incredible...but do you want to tell me...how many of those fences do you think you missed your spot on?" It wasn't just a rhe-

116

torical question either. He seemed to want an answer the way he was leaning back and staring. Waiting.

Nice slap in the face, that. *Oh fuck yeah.* Jericho paused, breathed in slowly. Not pleased—it was one thing if Chuck wanted to critique him, but the way he'd just started in with no preamble made it seem like more of an attack. "Counting the double?" 7A and B, the one she'd knocked down.

"Without that."

Soft purring resentment. "Maybe four."

"Try six."

Half the course, in other words. Oh sure, but forget that it had been driving rain with his mare terrified and him fighting to control her on top of it. "Alright, six then…I'm sure you're right. My goal was simply trying to get her through the thing."

Frankel seemed to be processing what he'd just said, though damn, Jericho thought, Chuck had been a big time competitor himself. He had an eye—he'd known what Jericho was facing better than almost anyone else would. Finally the older man looked over and commented casually, "Big jump on the mare. Looks awfully heavy in the hand to me though…and not disciplined. Not disciplined at all. Is that the way you're schooling them these days, Jericho?"

Chuck was really taking him down here, looking for things to criticize and making it personal. Why?

And Marx…watching him with interest—judging the way he was handling this. He could see that in the mirror too.

Jericho looked down, buying time and tempering his answer—'cause the words that jumped to his lips were anything but polite. *"Come on…is that what you think?"* he answered him sharply. "You think I short change the horses on their training? Does that sound like me? You *know* me, and you know that's not true. I can't even believe you said it. That mare? Christ, I've only had her three weeks…and she wasn't even a jumper when I found her, let alone been in a Grand Prix ring before."

"Hmmm." Frankel stroked his jaw. "Is that right?"

"Yes, it's right."

Oh, and he felt it coming. Chuck was leading him right into this.

"Well, if that's true, then explain something to me," Frankel said, staring at him dead on. "How does a mare that's never jumped before wind up in a national level, invitational class?" Hesitated meaningfully, obviously wasn't through with what he was saying yet...just wanted to let the full weight of his question sink in. Then added pointedly, "Because whoever let you finagle your way into that class should be fired for it...and I ought to damn sure see you formally disciplined. Berths in that class are earned, Jericho, not bought."

Jericho murmured under his breath—something that both looked and sounded like a quiet snarl. Tossed a cold, derisive stare at Marx. Thought he understood this now. Marx had lodged a complaint—that was pretty Goddamn obvious. Didn't look at him again, 'cause if he did...

He rose. Swallowed the rest of his beer, and laid the empty bottle on the table. He lit a cigarette too, then walked away from them. Stood facing the kitchen for a moment, then muttered vengefully, "How many years have you known me, Chuck?" Rounded on him. "You make it sound like I bribed someone in the show office, and that's complete and utter bullshit, and I hope you damn well know it is too."

"Do I?"

"God, I hope so. Yeah, you're right...QL wasn't invited to participate in the National. *I* sure as shit was...but my mount got sold out from under me less than a month before the show. And Chip fucking Langdon—who earned *nothing*—rides him instead."

"That's the horse show world," Frankel commented without much sympathy.

"Yeah, that's the horse show world," Jericho repeated coldly. He paced silently for a moment, then pivoted and went into the kitchen, retrieving another beer. Twisted the cap off and sent it spinning across the countertop—taking his anger out there—trying to keep it out of what he said as best he could. Came back and leaned against the doorjamb between the two rooms, body tight, looking dangerous. "Alright Chuck, I'll tell you exactly what I did, then you judge. Yeah, I made some phone calls. There were some empty berths from late cancellations...and they were just gonna stay empty cause it was too late to get someone else."

"That always happens."

"Yeah, that always happens, that's why I called and asked. Hell, I only rode the qualifying round, and I scratched the finals...so you tell me what the problem is. I didn't take a berth from someone else, and I didn't go for the prize money either." He took a long drink from his second beer now, then murmured passionately, "Just fuck me, Chuck...I can't believe you'd call me dishonest."

Calm, even tone of voice back from Frankel. "Maybe everyone can do that then, and forget about it being an invitational...how would that be? Is that fair to the riders who legitimately qualified?"

Came over and laid his beer down on the table, but didn't sit. Instead he turned, towering right over Frankel. "Fine, Chuck. You'll do what you want to do. File a complaint and request a disciplinary hearing. Coming from you it'll carry enough weight to get action. I'm just asking...while you're making recommendations remember...it's not like I drug my horses, cheat my customers, sell animals under false pretenses...and we both know plenty of that goes on. Yes, I got into a class where I wasn't invited. So what?'

"So what?" Frankel pushed it. "So what? Can you really afford to be sidelined?"

"Sidelined?" He drew his breath in. Man, that stunned him—scared him too. He swung back into the chair again, leaning forward. "You'd do that? You'd actually go that far? Damn it, you know that would break me—most of my customers don't even ride. I show their horses. Sideline me during season, and I'll lose a good half of them."

Wasn't getting an answer, just a hard stare.

Jericho sat back. Looked miserable. "Alright, I hear you. At least you warned me. I'll call my attorney in the morning." Sat silently for a moment, then looked Frankel in the eyes and tried one more time. "Chuck, push for a fine if you want to—make it punitive, I don't care, I'll find a way to pay it...just Christ, don't sideline me for season over something like that." Shook his head again and sighed, then added in a low, forceful tone, "It's not like I didn't work to be there. You of all people know how hard, how many hours I put in...hell, I've been long-listed for the last three years. I *made* that horse..." They both knew he meant Monterrey, he didn't have to say it. "But as soon as he's worth money, man I lose the fuckin' ride."

He didn't need to listen to more of this. What he needed was to get away—come to grips with it. Stubbed his cigarette in the ashtray, rose quietly, ready to go.

"Well, you know, you bring up an interesting point. Actually more than one," Frankel told him.

Jericho stood there, worried all over again. Knowing there was more. Asked nervously, "What? Have you got two barrels you want to level at me, Chuck?"

The Chef D'Equip issued a calm order. "Maybe. Have I said I'm done with you? Kill the attitude, Jericho. Sit down."

Oh fuck.

His deep blue stare swung to Marx one more time, then back to Frankel…then dropped away as he growled harshly, "First you criticize my training program. Then you question my honesty, and threaten me with charges. I don't know what's up your ass, Chuck. If you feel some burning need to dress me down personally…fine, maybe you've earned the right. But Jesus fucking Christ,…in front of an audience?"

Completely ignored the comment. Launched another stinging question his way instead. "You're the one who brought it up, so yes, I want to go there. Can you explain why a rider with your talent is long-listed for the Team—not short listed?"

Fired back at him, "No, can you?"

Perfect lead in. Frankel actually had the nerve to smile. "Well I don't know…maybe it has something to do with that fiery temper of yours." He also looked at Marx now, then back to Jericho. "See I could almost feel sorry for you, until I found out you turned your back on a perfectly good sponsor…*and* the horse you claim you're so unhappy you lost."

"Man, that's bullshit."

"Is it?" He rose himself now, standing directly in front of Jericho, since he didn't seem like he'd sit back down. "You didn't tell him you were going to throw a fist at him?"

Oh, low blow…Marx had told Frankel about that, but not about why?

"And you know what?" the Chef D'Equip continued, right up in his face now, and really hitting him where it hurt. "That's the reason why I can't push anyone to sponsor you, Jericho. Including the Maitlands. Sure, I could have talked to them last summer, but I decided not to….decided I couldn't, in all good conscience. And do you want me to tell you how much that frustrates me? Here I've got a Team quality rider…one I know cares—hell is passionate about it. One I know puts the effort in. But he doesn't have enough control to behave like an adult half the time."

Couldn't really answer him. Some of it fit maybe. Not the way he was making it sound, but it wasn't like he was dead wrong either.

Frankel tapped his fingers against the knuckles of Jericho's right hand. They weren't swollen anymore, but the bruising was easily visible. "Can't be more than a few days old," he said with scorn. "And here's the worst of it," Frankel continued. "I watched you ride that class last Wednesday…your mare hit you in the face and hard, she was falling beneath you. But you never panicked at all. Cool, levelheaded—you knew what to do, you were strong enough to do it, and you got the job done. Jericho, I don't know three other American riders who could have survived that situation without going off—let alone have the balls to finish out the ride. But I ask myself, why the *fuck* can't he act that way with the rest of his life?"

Hell, who was he kidding, Jericho thought? It wasn't that *some of it fit*—no, Chuck had him dead to rights. Gave in some, murmured to him expressively, "Alright."

"And here's my nightmare," Frankel went on, really driving his point home. "I'm on ESPN in Aachen trying to explain to the American public why one of my best riders is in jail instead of competing."

Jericho grabbed his beer and walked away from him. Drank from it, then just let it drop to his side. He took a deep breath and blew it out, laid his head back and closed his eyes for a few seconds...then looked back around sharply at him and said flat out, sounding tired—or beaten. "Alright. That's completely fucking fair, I'm not arguing."

"Thank you," Frankel said, shaking his head, disgusted though. "At least you're willing to admit it."

"Am I that stubborn, Chuck? You think I have that big a chip on my shoulder?"

No relenting. "Answer your own question."

Just swore.

Complete *non sequitur* coming back from the Chef D'Equip. "Do you work Monday's, Jericho?"

"No." Equivocated. "Yes. *Usually*...but not a full schedule. Eh. I'm not supposed to be there, but I always am."

"Well, you'll ride Monday...work it out."

Now that took him back, and confused him too. "Ride where?"

Warmer, but still superior glare leveled straight on him. "Ride for me, Jericho."

Exposed look in those deep blue eyes—not even daring to hope he had this right. After Chuck kicking the crap out of him for the last forty minutes, was he actually telling him he'd been added to his coaching schedule? "Where?" he asked.

"Your place, ten o'clock...the mare first, Monterrey second."

Monterrey. And that was the real reason why Marx was here, wasn't it? In fact...Jericho turned and looked at him now...Marx was the one who'd engineered this, not Chuck. Chuck hadn't intervened for him before and still wouldn't—he'd said that much, and nothing had changed it. Except Marx. It was Marx who'd rearranged the playing field—put his money down and used it to get what he wanted.

And man, Jericho had sure shot his mouth off to Marx before—more than once. Not all of it undeserved, but yeah, handled stupidly.

"Alright," he told Frankel.

"I don't want to wait till next week, so this week I'll come Wednesday. Pick up Monterrey tomorrow morning first thing, you'll have one day to re-school him. And I don't want to hear any excuses about Chip Langdon screwing up the horse," he warned.

Actually, Chuck was still kicking the crap out him, just in a different way. "Understood."

The Chef D'Equip came closer to him. "And Jericho," he warned him. "I'm still going to report you for that class last Wednesday...mainly because I don't want it biting me in the ass later on. I'm going to recommend a stiff fine, something really punitive—something harsh enough that the topic of sidelining you doesn't even come up. You won't fight it. You'll plead "no contest", and you'll pay." His head swerved to Bob Marx. "And don't you dare give him the money to cover it."

The investment banker laughed quietly. "No, I won't."

Frankel looked at Jericho again, wanting to hear him agree. Demanding it.

"Yes, Chuck, alright," he said...wondering exactly how large "really punitive" was, but almost not caring.

"And you're not short-listed, Jericho."

"I know."

"But I'll tell you one thing," Frankel promised him sharply, still not completely done taking him down. "If it gets back to me that you're brawling, or God forbid get arrested again...you're out and you're out for good. Make absolutely sure you hear me on this, because you will *not* get another chance. I'll put the time in, but damn it, you *are* going to get serious, and you *are* going to work."

Jericho answered him fervently. "Come on, maybe I screw some things up..."

"Maybe?" he interrupted him.

Man, he thought, there was no leeway here for him tonight. "Alright, alright...I do fuck some things up, and yeah I even go out and pick a fight sometimes—and yes Chuck, I totally heard your warning, you'll drop me if I do it again. Satisfied? But me putting the work in? That can't be something you're worried about."

Gave him that much. "You're right, its not. You're a perfectionist, and you're relentless too. Yes, you work. Listen to me, Jericho…you're a top technical rider, but guess what, I already have technicians…current team members who are better at it than you. But here's what you are, and why I'm willing to coach you…you might be the toughest son of a bitch I know. You've got the heart and the balls to ride out any situation, and Jesus Jericho, you're strong…*and* you ride cool." Frankel clapped him once hard on the shoulder, left his hand there, even gripped with it. "What does that mean to me? It means I can put you at anchor when the rest of the Team's gone to hell and know you won't fold under pressure. It means I can put a rank talent under you like that witch of a mare you're riding now. Get out of your own way—stop fucking around. Think about it." Paused. "Now get out of here—I'm done with you tonight."

Marx, still sitting calmly at the table, sipping his drink. Watching. Not even interjecting a word. Didn't have to—he was producing and directing this little drama. Jericho laid a meaningful look on him again. "I owe you," he said harshly, but harsh from the depth of his feelings not anything else. "Don't think I don't understand that."

Nod from the investment banker. Quiet smile.

Chapter Nine

The fact that Chuck Frankel was coming out Wednesday to coach Jericho was no secret—although he wasn't spreading the word, personally. Early Tuesday morning, Jericho and Marco drove the two-horse trailer over to Chip Langdon's place and picked up Monterrey. After that, his schedules had to be re-arranged, and of course it was obvious that Monterrey was back, so the Maitlands found out in a heartbeat. Cin spread the word to the rest of Wellington, and Marco and the boys told anyone she might have missed.

Wednesday morning, there was already a good-sized group gathered in the gazebo. Darien and Brae were there by nine—Darien having brought several cameras with her—different lens, advanced functions, which she was now explaining to him in detail. Cin and Richard came early too, maybe a little jealous that Monterrey was no longer theirs and that the Marxes were the center of attention instead of them.

At ten after nine, Bob Marx and Chuck Frankel pulled in the driveway together in Frankel's swanky Ford 350 pick-up truck.

"So what are you planning to do today?" the investment banker asked him.

"Mostly just evaluate where Jericho is with the horses," Frankel answered, shrugging. Small secretive smile...then he gave it up. "And see what it takes to completely wear him out." Truth was, Frankel's coaching sessions were notoriously brutal—always intense, and his comments biting and harsh. It wasn't even all that unusual to find his riders leaving a session close to tears.

Marx laughed. "Boot camp?" he suggested.

A brusque nod as the Chef D'Equip opened the driver's side door and got out. "Same principle."

The two of them strolled over to the sand arena together, and entered the gazebo. Jericho was in the process of riding Maximus in one of his normal schooling sessions. He'd only just started, and looked over in surprise as Frankel's suddenly appeared at the side of the ring.

Shit, he'd said ten, hadn't he?

Bellowed for Marco, then started trotting Maximus over to greet them—not just Chuck, but Bob Marx too. Had to treat Marx a lot better than he had been, that was for Goddamn sure. But Frankel was already stepping out into the arena, and headed him off. "Ride to me, Jericho," he said.

Did it. "You're early, aren't you, Chuck?" Jericho said as he pulled up next to him. "Anyway, it doesn't matter. I'll have Marco take this horse and bring QL down." His head groom had already appeared at the barn entrance, and was hotfooting his way down to the jumping field.

"No, you're right, I'm early. Don't change anything. I'm still planning to start at ten o'clock," Frankel said matter-of-factly. "But lets get Marco and maybe someone else from your crew out here. I'm going to want to rearrange the ring. Just go back to schooling this horse like you normally would…this is the gelding you won the Open Hunters with, isn't it?"

So Chuck was aware of that—man, he didn't miss much. "Yes."

"Owner's happy?"

"Oh yeah."

Smile. Nod. But that was just conversation. He quickly got down to what he was really standing out here for. Laid a hand on Jericho's saddle. "Drop your irons for me," he quietly ordered. Jericho took his feet out of the stirrups, wondering what this was about but not questioning it. Frankel removed the stirrup closest to him, both leather and iron. He wordlessly walked around and removed the other one as well. "You'll ride without stirrups from now on till I say differently…on all your horses. Understand me?"

"Sure." Didn't seem concerned about it even though it meant hours and hours of work like that.

Seemed pleased with the easygoing response. Slapped the horse's rump. "Go back to work." Then simply turned and headed over to the gazebo.

Jericho pivoted Maximus and cantered down to meet Marco.

"Is he getting on your case already, boss?" his head man asked with a little smirk.

"Maybe. Stirrups off on all my saddles for starters, especially for these next two rides," he said, relaying the order from the Chef D'Equip. "And go and see Chuck—he'll tell you how he wants to set things up."

Back in the gazebo, Cin was laughing. "No stirrups, Chuck? He's done that to me once or twice…one time for almost twenty minutes. Boy, that was misery."

Frankel looked smug. "It's going to take a damn sight more than twenty minutes to bother him, but lets see how he's doing two or three hours from now."

Cin giggled wickedly, but it was Brae—leisurely playing with all the settings on Darien's cameras—who casually spoke up. "Oh hell, that's not going to bother him." He lifted a camera with a telescopic lens and sighted through it.

"Who are you?" Frankel asked sharply, eyes running over the slovenly young man sprawled in one of the chairs with the best view of the jumping ring.

Darien interceded. "Oh Chuck, this is Brae…Trevor Braedon, actually. He's Jericho's roommate, and an excellent photographer. Wait till you see his work. Brae, this is Chuck Frankel…he's…"

"Oh yeah, I know who he is. Jericho told me." Sounded completely unimpressed. Watched his roommate riding, although he really knew nothing about the sport. Still it was obvious to even the most uneducated viewer that the work was effortless for him. Legs in perfect position, body balanced comfortably over them—coming easily into two point to lift and launch his horse over a jump. "Nope," Brae repeated happily but with authority. "That kind of stuff he can do all day." Sighted through the camera again. Took a few shots.

Ten minutes passed. No change in Jericho's classically correct position. Frankel turned to Brae, seemingly more interested now. "Do you ride yourself?" he asked. "Do you have any idea how much strength that takes?"

"Oh hell no, I don't ride…not horses anyway," the Barista said blithely, tossing in the subtle off-color remark. "But here's what I'm saying…my roommate over there is a strong fuckin' guy. A lot stronger than he looks, that's for sure."

Bob Marx jumped into the conversation, protesting, "I don't know, he looks pretty damn strong to me."

"Well, that's my point." An inane grin spread across his face. Darien should have known to stop him—she'd seen that look before, but it just never crossed her mind that he'd come out with something as wild as what he said next. "Well here, I'll give you an example any guy can relate to, okay?" Starbucks waited until he had their complete attention, then just

126

gleefully laid it on them. "Jericho…this is true…can do a chick one-handed. I mean straight-armed, like a one-arm push up…his other hand underneath her, holding her up off the mattress too. And he can keep it up for…oh hell, a long time. Now hey, I don't ride, but *that* I've tried…fell right on top of the femme I was with…couldn't even hold it for more than a second or two." Smiled foolishly again, not even remotely embarrassed. "Man, that's when I got some respect for the guy."

Stunned silence…then an outburst of laughter. Frankel trying to hide the fact that he was grinning too.

Jericho looked over, saw Brae holding court there and sure as shit didn't trust that. Wondered what the hell they were all laughing at…and felt pretty uncomfortable when most of them turned to look at him. Ignored it, went back to schooling Maximus.

"So you don't think I can tire him out?" Frankel asked again, definitely probing for information.

"Ha! No," Brae scoffed, trying a few more pictures—Jericho and Maximus taking a fence, beautiful form—you'd have to know he was riding without stirrups to even notice it. He handed the camera over to Darien so she could take a look. Tossed out another comment to the Chef D'Equip. "I mean, after all…riding…he's sitting down most of the time, isn't he? Oh yeah, he grips and all that, but that's nothing. Comes up before the fence and stays up over it, but even that's just a few seconds, right? Won't bother him. Do it all day. Now those chicks? There, I'm talking a good twenty minutes solid…and he only stops then because…well, not because he's tired." He raised his eyebrows expressively.

The entire group in the gazebo broke up one more time. Cin especially squealing in shocked but fascinated amusement and staring hard, first at Brae, then at him. Jericho cursed to himself…knew damn well Brae was talking about him, and there wasn't a thing he could do about it. Later on he was gonna find out what the little shit had said.

Frankel seemed to have decided Brae had a point—though truth was, he'd coached a lot of riders, and work without stirrups would do most of them in fast. Still Jericho had been at it a good fifteen minutes already, and his legs hadn't budged an inch. He looked as fresh and relaxed as he had at the beginning of his ride.

Frankel stepped back a few paces out into the sand arena. "Jericho, stay up in two-point till I tell you to stop," he called out to him, then watched while his rider came cleanly up—balanced, weight carried evenly between his lower legs and his knees. Strolled back again. "Lets try that then," he said, smirking quietly. "Thank you, Brae."

"Welcome." Goofy grin.

Meanwhile, Darien was showing the pictures Brae had taken to her husband. Marx looked surprised—like he hadn't expected much from this clown of a kid. He handed the camera on to Frankel, who stared at the images without speaking. But when he handed the camera back to Brae, he made a request. "Can you take pictures for me of these next two rides?"

No problem for the Barista. He liked doing it.

———————

Halfway through the coaching session with QL now. Chuck was keeping him up in two-point without stirrups—no breaks either, and no letting up. He was really, really getting on his case about measuring the mare's stride too. Hard to do without using his seat as a driving aid, but he had to admit that Chuck's comments—while bitingly sarcastic at times—were showing him things he hadn't realized about the way he rode this moose of a mare. Jericho totally threw himself into it, and to hell with the fact that his thighs ached like a son of a bitch, he could live with that.

Flatwork done, and now they were jumping—fences of varying sizes and with some subtle and some not so subtle changes in the length of stride required. Stretching QL out wasn't a problem, but reining her in…she voiced her objection to that, tossing her jughead and pulling—pulling hard.

"No. Again."

Brought her back around, and redid the line.

"Better. Again."

In fact, "again" seemed to be the Chef D'Equip's favorite word.

"Alright, yes. Like that. Exactly like that. Now do it again."

An hour and fifteen minutes before he finally said. "Good, she's done."

Jericho cantered over to the sidelines where Marco was already waiting with Monterrey. Vaulted off, switched horses with his head groom, and then casually—unassisted by a leg up or mounting block—vaulted cleanly onto the big bay.

Frankel had returned to the gazebo to retrieve a bottled water from the cooler for himself. Looked at Brae, shook his head, and commented, "Well, you were damn sure right. Fucking legs of iron…I take that as a challenge." Turned and went back out.

Jericho hadn't waited for him, was already warming Monterrey up at a posting trot. Frankel beckoned to him, and he turned, riding over to him. "Alright, tough guy," the older man mocked him. "Can you ride without stirrups in two-point for another hour?"

Intent, deep blue stare coming back at him, equally mocking half-smile. "If you want me to, Chuck."

They went back to work.

At the very end of the hour, Frankel mapped out a short course for Jericho and Monterrey. "What wins a jump-off round?" he asked him, then answered the question himself. "Precision and speed. So gallop this for me," he said. "And don't miss your mark like you usually do…*try* Jericho. Put some effort in." Walked away.

Totally unfair comment, but man did it spur him on.

Standing back in the gazebo, Frankel watched along with the others as horse and rider descended on the course with intent. He just shook his head, amazed at the strength that Jericho had left—not to mention the way he rode light and sensitive with Monterrey, but drill sergeant tough with QL—versatility. "Jesus, you made a damn good decision here, Bob," he said to Marx with passion. "I've never given this guy a chance—couldn't gamble with Team money, frankly—but I've always liked him. Good God, can he ride, and what a horse you bought." Then screamed scathingly to Jericho, *"Come on, damn you, show me something!"*

Incredibly tight turn, dead on spot, came up as boldly over the horse as if he were riding with the Valkyries—lifting Monterrey into the huge obstacle, taking off without even slowing that flat-out top speed. Perfect release.

Over and clear.

"Alright, you're done," he called out to him, no hint of approval. "Work on all that. See you Monday." Got the picture disks from Brae, shook hands again with the Marxes and Maitlands, then simply turned and walked back to his truck—drove away.

———

"I hate her," Cin pronounced over lunch at the cute little restaurant known as Backstreet's. "Doesn't she just think she's the cat's meow sitting there watching Monterrey? Richard, why didn't we ever sponsor Jericho?" she pouted. "Now Marxes are everything and we're nobody."

Richard smiled tolerantly, but didn't answer her. He set down the Wall Street Journal that he'd been reading, paying that much attention to her at least.

"And what's a million dollars to you?" his wife continued. "It's not like you care about it."

"A million dollars?" he asked incredulous. "Of course I do."

"Well, Bob Marx doesn't." Nice little competitive jab she threw at him. "But then I *know* he's very successful..."

Maitland frowned. It wasn't as if he didn't give his wife damn near everything she wanted. "Cin, you have two beautiful hunters," he argued reasonably. "And you beat Darien Marx in the ring just a few days ago."

"Yes, but wait until she brings her other horse over to Jericho...well, it's only a matter of time isn't it? She won't stay with Chip," she predicted gloomily. "And then he'll be fawning over her, and she'll get the best ride times, and..."

God he hated the whining. He'd do almost anything to stop it. "Well, what are you saying? You agreed you wanted to sell Monterrey—you said you weren't riding him, so why did we want him, remember?" Reached over and patted her hand. "Jericho's still going to pay attention to you, darling."

Bottom lip stuck out, tears unshed in those pretty eyes of hers. "But not like Darien." She leaned toward him. "Richard, can't we find a horse that will beat Monterrey? I mean, not this second, but can't we look a little bit?"

He picked up his Journal again. "We'll see," he answered vaguely, smiling at her. Started reading...subject closed for the moment at least.

But not closed for Cin...when she wanted something, she rarely gave in till she got it. At the moment, she didn't keep harping on it, but she'd planted the seed. While Richard read his paper, she sat back, sipping her ice tea...and thinking about those stories Brae had been telling about Jericho...imagining that one-arm technique. Brae...beautiful child, really...and a nice stepping-stone to what she really wanted. His roommate.

I hate her," Darien told her husband, sitting out beside their pool, relaxing for the afternoon.

Marx was leaving the next morning for New York, and liked laying low like this. But his pretty little wife didn't want to just sit—she had something to say.

"Who, Cin?" he asked, although he knew the answer very well.

"Well, sure. I mean, doesn't she sound like they still own Monterrey?" Darien said crossly. "And the way she looks at Jericho...and even Brae."

"Honey, that's Richard's problem," Marx said patiently. "Jericho can take care of himself, and though I suspect he's something of an alley cat, I can't see him involved with clients and married women on top of it. And as for your friend Brae...he's lucky he even remembers the names of the girls he's been with—and he won't remember Cin Maitland's name either, if she does something foolish with him." Marx actually chuckled.

Darien smiled fondly. "Yes, he's atrocious, isn't he?" She rather like the picture her husband was painting...of Cin chasing the Barista, then being dumped by him...and him forgetting her name. Now that was rich.

"But talented," Marx continued thoughtfully. "We might get him to take some more pictures of Monterrey...a little publicity in the horse publications wouldn't hurt one bit."

Darien smiled happily. She had her horse, she had her husband...and everything was starting to fit.

———

During season there were always parties. Every year, in the first week of December, Jason Coulder, the jumper trainer who'd teased Jericho about clipping that night on the Player's Club Patio, had a pool party at his house. He and his wife Kate had a modest sized home, but with a huge, heated, caged pool—perfect for entertaining. Without fail, Jason's party turned into a raucous affair—with people being thrown into the pool, people swimming in their underwear...swimming with *no* underwear...what have you. Lots of good stories coming out of the Coulder party every year.

Jericho came late as he almost always did to functions like this. He had Brae in tow—the Barista had officially managed to survive beyond his twenty-first birthday just a few days earlier. They found a spot to park the Mustang and strolled together up the sidewalk that led to the Coulder's front door, laughing at some locker-room joke Starbucks had come up with, and smoking. Jericho rapped at the door, but then just opened it and walked inside. Together they would have made a great magazine ad—both in jeans and casual shirts—Brae with his blonde, disheveled, good looks…Jericho with his harsher features and severely pulled back hair, a sharp contrast. Darien, who was in the living room looked up, saw them and waved…and wished for her camera.

Cin was close by too. She walked over and intercepted them before they could go over to Darien first.

"There you are, you bad boys," she said with a sexy laugh. She gave Jericho a kiss on the cheek, then turned to Brae. Gave him a wicked smile and told him, "You're so handsome, I just have to give you a kiss too."

He raised an eyebrow to her, but didn't seem to mind, leaning down to accept the kiss, but accidentally-on-purpose turning his face ever so slightly so that his lips brushed against hers for an instant. Murmured, "Mmmm," so low that only she could hear it. Sure she was probably old enough to be his mother—Jericho's too for that matter—but who cared? She was hot looking and seemed easy—and married—just the type he liked.

His roommate watched him in action with a touch of amused scorn on his face, but hell, Brae could do what he wanted to do, and no one controlled Cin—that was for Goddamn sure.

"I'm getting a beer," Jericho announced, looked at Brae and asked him, "Want one?"

"Yeah, thanks man."

Strolled off and left the two of them together. This would be interesting.

Darien caught up with him in the kitchen, after he'd retrieved two beers from the refrigerator. "Hi, so how are you?" she greeted him. Cute little halter dress on her, clinging in all the right places.

Humor in those deep blue eyes. "Do you mean, am I sore?" he laughed. "Hell, yes. Chuck's a madman."

She nodded appreciatively. "I think you really surprised him though—I don't think he had a clue you could ride three hours in two-point and with no stirrups like that. And you should feel good—he seemed really impressed overall."

Jericho snorted. "You weren't hearing the comments he was giving me. And I thought *I* was a perfectionist."

"Happy though?" she asked.

"Yeah, I am." Serious expression then. "I don't really know what to say to you and your husband, I…"

Again, that dainty hand caressed his arm, just like it had the first time they'd met…but maybe that was just a habitual gesture of hers. If so, it was sure erotic. "We're kind of a team now, right?" she said softly, looking up at him.

"For sure."

"And Chuck's behind you too."

He frowned for a moment.

"What?" she asked.

Jericho sighed. "I'm not so sure. You know he's filing a complaint against me, don't you? " Didn't wait for her answer, assumed she did. "I'm living in dread of that call." He'd paused there like he was finished, but then went on, telling her something he wouldn't have told many other people. "I asked around…I might be facing as much as a twenty-five thousand dollar fine."

Darien looked shocked.

"But oh well," he went on. "Would I have gotten this chance if I hadn't ridden in that class? Would your husband have sponsored me? I keep telling myself to look at it that way…telling myself I'd have paid almost anything to get on Chuck's schedule. And if that's what it takes, then that's what it takes." Sighed again, obviously hadn't really convinced himself, and then said as much. "I don't know. It's just that USA Equestrian makes any disciplinary action public. Everyone I deal with…all my customers… they'll all know about the complaint, and Chuck told me flat out not to fight it. I'll look guilty as hell…and maybe I am."

Her hand still lingering on his arm. Delicate question, but she asked it anyway. "Will you be able to pay it?"

Nodded, but didn't look happy. "Sets me back hard, but yeah. It's all the profit I'll get from selling Laredo—shot—and I won't be able to replace him with another sale horse. But yeah, I can pay." Dropped his eyes away, momentarily vulnerable. "But here's what I keep asking myself…put all that aside…alright fine, Chuck adds me to his coaching schedule, but does he really want me there, or is he only doing it because your husband pushed him into it? I get hit this hard, but maybe it's for nothing." Looked up sharply. "I mean, fuck, Darien. Maybe I'm just kidding myself. Maybe guys like Chip Langdon have the right idea, and…"

"Hey, bra…where's that beer?" Starbucks—arm slung around Cin— sauntered up to them.

Jericho handed it to him. "Sorry…talking."

133

Horrible time for the interruption. Darien knew what he was saying to her. In fact, she was touched he'd opened up that much. Self-doubt. Driving himself crazy wondering if he was good enough. She so wanted to tell him he was…but not with Cin and Starbucks standing there. Instead, she had to settle for, "Let's talk some more, okay?"

Looked at her, nodded.

Cin, making matters worse by interjecting the mocking comment, "Boy, Chuck Frankel sure gave you some shit today, huh Jericho?" She laughed merrily—had said it loud enough for others to overhear. "I mean, it's a little embarrassing, isn't it? No stirrups? Kind of a beginner's lesson, if you ask me."

Darien wanted to accidentally spill her drink on her. What a bitch! "Gee, I don't know," she piped up, slipping her arm through Jericho's. "You said work without stirrups was misery, and you don't consider your-self a beginner, do you Cin?"

"Well, I beat you, darling."

Little mini catfight taking place.

"It was a great session," Jericho responded, trying to calm things down before this got out of hand. "Honestly, I took a lot away from it." His eyes wandered the room, and out to the pool area. Things were already starting to get a bit wild—people getting pushed into the pool, a few well-known figures around Wellington…stripped down to almost nothing. His eyes narrowed suddenly, and he lifted his head, sharp intake of breath.

Cute little bottom covered only by a black thong—if you wanted to call that "covered." Man, he knew that sweet ass all too well. Skimpy little black bra on the top half.

"I was going to tell you she was here," Darien said quietly.

Ailynn.

She looked none too steady on her feet. Was carrying a drink and wavering along the edge of the pool. Jason Coulder, their host, walked up to her and put an arm around her, and she snuggled happily against him. They turned and seemed to be heading back toward the house.

"Fuck, I'm leaving," Jericho said vengefully. He laid his beer—un-touched—on the countertop, looking like he meant right then and there.

But he wasn't going to be quick enough. Coulder was steering Ailynn right into the kitchen where they were standing, and her eyes lit up with recognition. She broke free from him, and took a few uncertain steps in their direction, saying joyfully, "Jericho!"

He muttered a curse, turning his face away from her in warning—a warning she didn't notice or heed one bit. Came directly over to their little group. Muttered, "Hi, Brae," but barely looked at him. Straight up to Jericho, placing both hands—drink and all, spilling some—and then her head against his chest. Her body draped against his. Tipped her face up, and said in that lilting soft voice of hers, "I've missed you." Then giggled and added, "I'm drunk."

Duh. *Really?*

Damn, she was all but naked, and she looked good. Starbucks was staring openly. Smiled. Liked the view.

Jericho put his hands on her upper arms and moved her back a step. Poignant expression on his face. "No," was all he said.

Ailynn tossed her spiky dark hair—it had recently been wet, and looked a bit wild now. "Jericho doesn't like me any more," she announced. She pouted. Announced to everyone there in the room, "I guess he heard that Cole said he's going to ruin him. Cole's that way." Smiled. Took another swallow of her drink. She really looked looped.

"I'd like to see him try," Jericho murmured, more to himself than anyone else. "Like I was the one who did something to him." He turned to go, wasn't going to stand here and have this conversation with her in front of half of Wellington, especially considering the state she was in. And God, it wasn't like her nearly nude form didn't bring back deeply erotic memories. Hours of heathen passion, that tight little body beneath his own, welcoming him into her again and again.

Lying. Always a lie. A promise and a lie.

Her hand gripped his wrist, and she stumbled a step or two. "Jericho's mad," she observed.

"Ailynn, stop," Darien told her firmly. "Don't do something you'll regret later."

"Oh, I won't regret it," she insisted. Her drink slipped from her hand, falling to the floor, the glass shattering. "Oops." Barefoot and surrounded by glass shards.

Cin had jumped backwards in disgust. Backwards tighter into Brae's embrace, of course.

He didn't even realize that he was quietly snarling. Just reached over and picked her up, carrying her away from the glass like she was weightless. Her arms went willingly around his neck, her skimpy top riding up in the process to reveal round, full breasts.

Nice fuckin' scene…everyone watching them—turning around to stare. She was whispering in his ear, and at least that, no one else could hear. Oh, but he could. Telling him how she wanted him. Wanted to feel his weight on her…to feel him pressing into her.

He could hardly have been more dangerous than he was at that moment. Little bitch. Fucking little bitch. He set her down again clear of the mess, handing her off to Brae, who didn't seem to object at all to holding this almost naked chick up against himself—Cin scooting out of the way, horrified. Fished the Mustang's keys out of his pocket, and slapped them in Brae's hand. "Take her home," he said sharply. "I'll walk." It wouldn't be a short walk either.

"Jericho, I'll take you," Darien offered, bringing sparks of jealousy to Cin's eyes.

"No," he said coldly. Spun away, and was gone.

Brae whistled low. "Watch out," he pronounced. "Someone somewhere's going home tonight with a broken nose, and it won't be Jericho."

"Oh, no," Darien whispered, terrified that it was true.

───────

Maybe a half an hour had passed since the little scene in the Coulder's kitchen. Well, first there had been all the amazed gossiping about it, and then the floor had to be swept and vacuumed. The party had resumed and by now it didn't even look like anything unpleasant had occurred. Everyone enjoying themselves.

Brae was gone with Ailynn now too.

Darien sighed to herself. She was really worried about Brae's prediction. If Jericho went out and got into a fight over this…he'd lose everything. That just couldn't happen. It couldn't. Unable to stand it, she gathered her purse and went out to her Audi TT—she was going to try and find him, wanted to take him home where he couldn't get into trouble, even though he'd refused a ride from her before. Maybe he'd cooled down some, maybe he'd be more reasonable.

The top was down and the breeze ruffled her jaggedy hair as she followed the most logical route between Jason and Jericho's places. With that long stride of his, he'd have covered some ground in a half an hour—maybe even be home by now, but she was still going to try.

And he probably would have been home…but he'd stopped about halfway, and was leaning up against a lamppost just staring out into the street and smoking. Darien pulled up next to him. Got a very forbidding stare from him for her trouble.

She just looked at him at first, and finally he came over and sat up with one leg resting along the passenger side door, the other straight beneath him, foot on the curb. Neither of them had spoken yet. Shook his head, pitched his cigarette butt into the street. Seemed to think about it. Stood up again, opened the door and swung into the seat beside her.

"Where are we going?" she asked.

"Not home, not yet."

"Okay. Want to check the horses?" she asked.

It was a pretty good suggestion, actually. Distract him. "Alright." And after a minute or two, "How fucked up was that? Christ, I've never seen her drink like that."

Maybe she's very unhappy, Darien thought, but she didn't vocalize it. She reached over and touched him quietly instead…then put her hand back on the wheel. They drove the rest of the way to the stable without conversation.

Once inside the barn, Jericho switched the lights on, and slowly walked down the aisle, checking each horse, stopping to top off a water bucket or two. Darien just walked along at his side.

At the last stall, he opened the door and went inside. QL. She no longer swung her hindquarters around when he entered, but instead came over to nuzzle against his shirt, searching. "No, nothing for you," he said in a low voice, rubbing her forehead, and then those big mule ears.

Maybe he'd gone in to her because this had been Ailynn's horse…or maybe he just liked her fierce independent nature. She'd sure performed for him today. Oh, she was still dead green, but she learned so quickly. Rubbed her for a minute more, then turned and left the stall again, with QL following him right up to the door. One more pat, then closed the door behind himself.

He put an arm around Darien's shoulder and walked with her down to the first stall again—Monterrey was back inside it…the place of honor, top dog. The big bay nickered to him too.

"All the horses love you," Darien observed warmly. She wasn't object-ing in the slightest to the loose way he held her—liked it. "It's so obvious."

He half-turned, leaning his shoulder against the bars. Let his arm drop away, but then lifted his hand up and brushed her cheek with it. "I love them too," he told her. "They're honest. They put everything out there."

"You really liked her, didn't you, Jericho?" Maybe it was an ill-advised question, but she seemed to sense he needed this.

"Still do," he admitted, letting his eyes fall on hers. Long eloquent look. How easy…how easy it would have been to lower his mouth to hers in that moment. She wouldn't have pushed him away either, and he knew it. But Christ, he had to control himself…hadn't that been Frankel's whole message to him Monday night? He held back, just staring at her…wanting the contact, but denying himself.

And then Darien took the decision away from him. She stood up on her toes, and brushed her lips over his, then pulled back a hair, her eyes searching his expression to see if it had been okay…if he'd wanted it. Found permission there. Closed her eyes and tipped her mouth up and over his again, her lips more active now, playing with his, coaxing a response.

Jericho deepened the kiss. It was still essentially closed-mouth, and yet his lips were just parted in a very erotic tease. His hand slid behind her neck, his powerful body all but surrounding her, though still not pressed to her. A long, slow kiss. Then repeated. His mouth on her throat, by her ear, and then back on her lips again, lingering.

He pulled back from her, sighed deeply, eyes expressive and wanting. "Darien…"

"I know," she said, stroking his cheek. Leaning in and kissing him just lightly one more time. "That was wrong of me, I'm sorry."

His one hand slid out from behind her neck, along to the point of her shoulder and down her arm…pausing to brush across her breasts, even locating and touching a nipple, but then down to her soft abdomen, to her side and around to curve over her buttocks, and finally over her thigh…pushing up the hem of her dress and splaying his fingers lightly across the front of it…his thumb just barely touching her between her legs before falling away. A short but very thorough journey—not remotely lewd, more like awed, respectful. "I'm sorry too," he said, and made himself turn away. It was clear he wasn't apologizing for his actions, just voicing regret over what could never be.

Chapter Ten

Frankel returned on Monday, pulling in around ten to the appointed hour. He strode over to the sand arena, but made a small detour first to where Marco was standing off to one side. For a few minutes he just stood silently next to Jericho's head groom, both of them watching him school another of his sale horses—this one a young four-year-old colt named Landrover. He'd obviously followed the Chef D'Equip's instructions, and had no stirrups...was up in an effortless two point, only sitting in rarely and that only for schooling purposes.

"He's riding all the horses that way?" Chuck asked Marco in an off-hand manner, chewing on a blade of grass.

"Oh sure," Marco laughed. "Hasn't seen a stirrup since the last time you were here. The first couple of days, he'd give up on the two point after the fifth or sixth horse, but by the weekend he was riding the whole eight hours that way." Certain pride there, the way a pit crew chief would talk about his driver.

"Look tired by the end of the day?"

A nonchalant shrug. "Marches down the aisle barking out orders like always." Marco turned around to face Frankel. "You know, I've worked for a lot of jumper riders in the last ten years...including some of your team members." He seemed to have decided not to go any further along that train of thought, and just turned away again.

"And?" Frankel prodded.

Marco just spoke off into the wind, almost like he wasn't speaking to Chuck. "And none of them tops this guy...for ability...or guts."

Interesting opinion, and coming from someone who'd been behind the scenes for a long time. "Put his stirrups back on QL and Monterrey... none of the others."

The slightest smile from the head groom, and a nod of understanding. Without another word, he walked off toward the barn to get QL and bring her down. Frankel went over to the gazebo. Darien and Bob Marx had arrived to watch too, and as he was greeting them, the Maitlands appeared, carrying a very expensive looking picnic basket filled with brunch type goodies.

"Where's our photographer?" Frankel asked, looking annoyed.

"Working, I think, Chuck," Darien explained. She grinned. "He works the drive through at Starbucks actually."

"Well, that's ridiculous," he grumbled irritably. "I need him here. Those pictures he took for me last time were a great training aid, and I have to measure Jericho and the horse's progress weekly." Looked up at Marx. "I'll look to you to arrange that," he said, laying an assignment on the investment banker, who just smiled tolerantly.

"I'll take care of it," Darien promised.

Relented and chuckled a bit. "Kind of miss his commentary, actually."

"It's hard not to like Brae," Cin agreed, drawing the Chef D'Equip's attention to herself, and by association...Richard.

And it was actually Richard Maitland that Frankel addressed next. "Remind me, you and I need to find a time to get together...alright?"

Didn't have a clue what this was going to be about, but Richard nodded, and Cin spoke up, making sure she was included too. "We'd love to, Chuck. Let us know when."

Accepted that without turning a hair. Tossed out a time. "Eight o'clock tonight. Let's go in to Palm Beach...how about Café L'Europe?" Anyone who knew Chuck Frankel knew he hated high-class restaurants like the one he'd just named—something local and very casual suited his taste best. Only one reason he'd suggest a place like that...he wanted privacy, wanted to talk somewhere outside of Wellington. Both couples looked curious as hell.

"Sure Chuck, sounds great," Richard answered for both of them.

But Frankel was already striding out into the middle of the arena. Jericho was up on QL now. He'd been surprised to see the stirrups back on his saddle, but Marco had only smirked, and Jericho didn't ask about it. He rode over to meet Chuck.

"Alright, I'm convinced," Frankel said after he'd pulled up alongside him. "But keep the stirrups off for the rest of your rides. I don't want to hear any excuses. I expect you to be the strongest rider out there, understand me?"

Indicated that he did. Satisfied look in those deep blue eyes, but didn't make a point of it.

"What's on your schedule after this?"

"Whatever you say, it's my day off."

"Fine. Go to work then." He didn't explain why he'd asked, just leaving Jericho to guess. Started right in with, "This mare lacks back muscle. She hasn't been ridden round."

"I know. I'm just starting to get her to lift." Just from that comment, he already knew what this session was going to be like—Chuck riding his ass for something he hadn't had a chance to fix. Steeled himself for an hour of derisive, stinging commentary, but okay…this was what he needed to work on with her, and no one's eye was better than Chuck's. It would be a hard but invaluable ride.

"Fine," Frankel said again. "We'll work on that. Show me what you're doing."

"Mostly all flatwork," he said, giving him an idea of what he was about to see.

Scornful look from his new coach. "Well, I would fuckin' hope so, Jericho." Then added witheringly, shaking his head. *"Ride."*

Almost two and a half hours later, and just finishing up with Monterrey. Jesus, Chuck had been scathing today, in both rides. Jericho felt mentally raw as he rode the big bay back toward the barn, but oddly satisfied too—he knew there'd been some great moments with both horses, and once again he was taking a lot away from this that he could use. The rumors about Chuck's coaching style were sure true though…he was brutal, really took you down. But that only made Jericho try harder—and he *was* going to get Frankel to see the skill in what he did…earn some respect from him.

No mean trick, that—still he wanted it.

"Awfully tough on him, weren't you?" Marx commented as Frankel stepped back into the gazebo.

Didn't look concerned about it—in anything, he seemed pleased. "That's a grown man and a professional, and a damn fine rider…but he doesn't need to hear that from me—what's the value? Or if he does, he's the type who'll never hold up to international competition and I'm wasting my time with him. No, I want him hungry. On-fire hungry."

"You know why I'm asking." Nothing coming back from the Chef D'Equip. A sigh, and then Bob Marx conceded the point. "You know best, Chuck."

"Damn straight," he muttered as he said goodbye to the group, promising to see the Maitland's later, and then headed up to the barn himself. Walked in just as Jericho was pulling on a clean polo shirt. "I was just about to come out and find you," Jericho said.

Frankel nodded toward the door. "Let's go someplace else. I have to talk to you."

That made him nervous as hell every time he heard it. Statements like "I have to talk to you" always meant bad news. Didn't ask though, just yelled out to Marco, who would be somewhere close by, "Marco, I'm leaving."

Head stuck out from the tack room. "Sure boss."

Jericho fell into step with Frankel, heading out to Chuck's pick-up, and whatever bomb he was about to lay on him now.

Inconsequential conversation only while they drove, which worried him more. Chuck wasn't even going to give him a hint until they were sitting face to face. Which meant it could only be one of two things. Either it had to do with the disciplinary action he was facing…or Chuck was dropping him. Oh God, it had to be one of the two. He tried not to let it eat him up inside, but his stomach was tight. He rolled the window down and lit a cigarette, and Chuck didn't even complain about it. Bad sign. They took South Shore to Forest Hill, and hung a left, both silent now.

The place Frankel finally parked in front of was a local watering hole called Jalapeño Harry's. It was downstairs in a small mall located off Forest Hill Boulevard. Both men walked in and down the single flight of stairs. Big bar dead ahead with some pinball machines and a pool table beyond it—a few wooden tables and chairs for diners off to one side. Chuck stopped at the bar and got two beers, then led the way to one of the tables. He pulled out a chair and set one of the beers in front of himself, the other at the place beside it.

Jericho took that seat. "Alright, tell me," he said. He'd waited long enough.

Frankel leaned back and took a drink of his beer, staring at Jericho the whole time. Then he just laid it out there. "You're going to be suspended."

Just breathed in, turned his face to the side, away from him. Oh fuck man…the impact of that statement was sinking in hard. His business…he was going to lose his business. Suspended. Sidelined. "Why?" he finally managed to ask, still not believing it. "Why suspension instead of a fine?"

"Not instead of—both…suspension and fine."

"Jesus, a fine too?" Could it get any worse? "How much?"

"Twenty-five thousand."

Fuck, very steep—close to maximum. Forced out another question. "And how long?"

"Sixty days."

Yeah, his business was gone. "Well, fuck Chuck," he murmured viciously. "Why don't I just go out and get a construction job now, cause I sure as shit won't be a horse trainer much longer."

"Jericho…"

"Don't "Jericho" me…you know the economics of this business as well as I do," he lashed back at him. "I'm fucked and you know it. The debt I have to service is huge…house here and one in the Hamptons, my truck, my car, the two-horse and six-horse trailers…working capital to finance the sale horses. Hell, I lose money on the board like everyone does, make a little on the training…but its prize money and sales that I live on. *Come on*," he murmured in an ugly tone. "If I can't ride for sixty days I'll lose most of my customers…and I won't get them back when the suspension ends either. *And* I won't be showing and selling horses either. I'll be in default in a month."

"Calm down and listen to me."

Ignored that. "I haven't had a hearing yet—Christ, I haven't even had a chance to explain my side…and you're telling me they've already made up their minds how to handle it?" Wrapped his hand around the beer, but didn't drink from it. Added vindictively, "Chuck, I have you to thank for this…oh yeah, you just had to lodge a complaint. Well, I hope you're satisfied, you self-righteous son of a…" Just broke off, snarled under his breath.

Frankel lowered his eyes at Jericho's accusation, didn't accept the comment, but didn't exactly fight it either. "Don't shut down on me, there's more you need to hear. For starters I'm going to tell you this…you'll find out anyway. I'm the one who asked for the suspension."

Now that hurt. Anger swelling inside him. "After you said you wouldn't? After you promised me? I guess that's what your word's worth." Total scorn in his voice now. "You bastard…just fuck you. Why did you even come over to my place this morning?" Pushed the beer away, took out a ten dollar bill from his pocket and slapped it down on the table.

Sharp. "What's that for?"

"I don't want you to buy me a beer, Chuck. I'm not bankrupt yet." Pushed his chair back and rose harshly. "And I'm fighting this."

Even tone of voice coming back from the Chef D'Equip. "Don't you even want to know why?"

Cold derisive look. "I know why." Cutting. "Oh yeah, I know why… Bob Marx. He forced me on you, didn't he? And you made him contribute to the whole Team, not just sponsor me. Sure you did. Something substantial. Something you don't want to lose. But now it's not a problem, right? I'm out of the picture…and next I suppose you'll want my recommendation who to put Monterrey under Chuck, cause we both know who you don't want him under."

"I want him under you."

He grabbed the back of the chair he'd been sitting in and shoved it under the table forcefully, not buying it one bit. "If you wanted to get rid of me, Chuck, you could have talked to me about it…fuck, did you have to drive me out of the business to get what you wanted?" His eyes were accusing and hot. Kept right on goading the older man. "You've got a reputation for being one brutal motherfucker…man is that deserved."

Some of what he was saying was hitting the mark, he could see that. Chuck reacting, eyes narrowed, lips curled into a frown. "Done venting?" he snapped at him.

"Yeah, I'm done venting. I'm done talking too." Tossed out a cold threat at him. "I may be out of the business—congratulations, you accomplished that. But I promise you this…I'm going to expose the fucking way you operate on my way out. God damn it, I hate dishonesty."

Frankel came to his feet now too. "Watch yourself. Want to launch a fist at me too, Jericho?" He got nothing more than a sneer in return…and Jericho turning away from him. But Chuck's arm snaked out and wrapped around the younger man's forearm, stopping him.

His head swung back to him. Deep blue stare falling on him hard. "You like living dangerously, don't you?" Jericho purred.

"You're not leaving till you hear the rest of this. Then go if you want to. A second complaint's been filed against you, and it's much more serious in nature," Frankel told him, meeting that piercing stare head on. "I looked into it, and I consider it frivolous, but coming right on the heels of the first one, it was going to get some big time attention and publicity. That *would* be the end of you. Even if it's eventually dropped."

Nightmare. This whole conversation. "What are you talking about?" he demanded.

"Coleman McCrae."

What had Ailynn said at that party? "Cole's going to ruin you" or something close to that.

Furious. "What can he possibly accuse me of? Fucking around with his lying bitch of a wife? Yeah, I did that."

Frankel's grip on his arm tightening. "Look, I'm hitting you with a lot here. Breathe deep. Suck it up. Stay calm. Listen to me…I've been working on this almost solid for the last four days. And Marx? He knows everything I know. He's still behind you."

"McCrae," Jericho demanded again, not buying this sudden turn in Chuck's manner with him. "What could he possibly accuse me of? What?"

"Fraud in the purchase of QL."

"Jesus fuck me," Jericho cursed savagely. "Nothing could be further from the truth. *Nothing*."

"I've looked into it pretty thoroughly, and I happen to believe you. But he wants to make an issue of it…frankly, Jericho, he's a con man through and through in my book, and I think he's done this before. And that wife of his…she's part of the set-up. He's threatening civil action…against you, against USA Equestrian too. He's looking for a big settlement. That's why you're suspended."

Temper only barely contained. "USAE…throwing me to the wind?"

"No." Stern again. "Making it clear that you aren't given any leeway when you're in the wrong…and backing you one hundred percent where you're not."

Jerked his arm free. "What difference does it make, Chuck? I'm ruined either way."

Softened. "No, you won't be. I've put a lot of thought into this, so has Marx—he's been stanch behind you—you need to know that. Even came to several private meetings…flew to New York on his own dime. You'll weather this, Jericho. Sit down, let me talk to you." Wasn't getting much trust coming back at him, and no relenting.

Murmured powerfully, "You know what, Chuck…I can't even listen to you right now. What you're telling me is that even though I have a spotless record, I'm getting about as harsh a punishment as the rules allow…at *your* recommendation…on a minor offense…and why? Because someone's threatened to sue USAE—someone you call a con man straight out. But hell, we have to protect the damn USAE, don't we? So I lose everything, and life goes on, right?"

"That's one way of looking at it, you're not totally wrong," Frankel said bluntly. "But it's not the whole story either. You're damn right—I'm protecting the USAE and the Team too, I have to. And yeah, it's a tough penalty on a minor infraction, and I told you I wouldn't ask for suspension, and then I did it anyway. And now I'm asking you to suck it up, and that bites, doesn't it?"

Caustic. "Yeah, doesn't it?"

"Yeah, it does. Do it anyway."

"Do it anyway? Fuck you."

Didn't even faze him. "Cooperate. Plead guilty on the first complaint…"

Even angrier. "Last week you said plead 'no contest'."

Repeated it. "Plead guilty, accept the disciplinary action. If you do, your suspension will start as of December 1st—we're backdating it by a week, which helps you some. It will run through January 28th, and then you'll be fully reinstated. Think about it, there are no shows to speak of in December anyway, so you'll miss January…one month. I'm going to personally call every one of your customers and ask them to stand behind you…as a personal favor to me. I'll explain the circumstances, tell them you're cooperating even though you got a raw deal…that you're doing it for the Association and for the Team—to help us beat this lawsuit."

Snarled incredulously at him, "Man, I haven't even been consulted in this whole thing. You just make the decisions and lay them on me. And what you just said…about what you'll do for me if I don't fight you? That's damn near blackmail. Either I let you play God with my life, or you bankrupt me. That about right?"

Frankel shrugged, admitted it. "You're right, I'm sure it feels that way. But see if this makes it go down any easier. After you're reinstated, I'll short-list you."

"Don't stroke me, Chuck. I'm not stupid. I could be short-listed for the rest of my life, but who gives a crap? We both know you'd just be doing it to shut me up." Turned his head and sighted the door. Wanted out of there. "You know what, I'm leaving. I've heard you out, and now I want to think through all the incredible options you've given me. Choice A—bend over, Choice B—just get fucked standing up." Laid his eyes on him expressively. "Besides, what good is your word? You've already lied to me and you won't hesitate to do it again if it suits you."

"Fair comment," the Chef D'Equip said, once again conceding Jericho's point. "And the truth is I'm going to take some pretty good flack over this from the whole riding community—they'll think I screwed you. Maybe I did."

Jericho came back at him with real passion, "Why did I ever let you reel me in…with all your bullshit about coaching me? Christ, I'm so fucking stupid, I deserve this." Cynicism, scorn—directed brutally at himself. "Maybe I'll just move to the Mid-West somewhere…you know, open a little jumper stable. Teach kids and fat old ladies." He'd had enough, turned to leave.

"Jericho, you don't have a car," Frankel said quietly after him.

Looked back around over his shoulder and smiled without the slightest trace of humor. "Well there's a preview of things to come, isn't it?" Muttered a curse under his breath, then just kept walking—out of there.

Frankel sighed, and then went back to the table and sat down. He'd promised to call Marx when this conversation was over, and took out his cell phone now.

Marx was driving with Darien when the call came through—he'd filled her in on what was happening, and that Frankel was breaking it to Jericho now. She was looking pretty anxious, so he put the call on speakerphone so they could both hear. "Bob Marx here," he answered, but caller ID told him this was Chuck, so he just went ahead and asked, "How did it go?"

Pretty confident voice coming back at him. "I don't know, I think he handled it pretty well."

"Bullshit. Did he walk out on you?" Marx quizzed him, not believing it.

He chuckled guiltily. "Sure. But he listened all the way through to the end, that was something. Didn't even lift that fist of his to me…I was kind of proud of him."

"Is he going to agree?" Marx insisted, trying to get a real answer from him.

"Pretty much has to, doesn't he?"

"No. He's stubborn and proud. He could fight it."

"No he can't," Frankel said with authority. "He needs me to make those phone calls and he knows it. In the end, it all comes down to that. From his point of view, I'm the one who put him in this position…and I'm probably also the one person who can get him through it alive."

Just could not fucking believe it when Frankel appeared in his jump-ing arena early the next morning, Marx in tow. Jericho wasn't even sure how he felt about the investment banker now, cause he was sure participat-ing in this big time. Just couldn't figure him out…if he was actually a stand up guy or just some egotistical bastard—another fucking puppeteer.

He hadn't called Frankel back—hadn't given him an answer, and that was probably why they were here, he knew.

Max went in and took a seat in the gazebo. Frankel stepped out into the ring. Jericho was up on QL. "Rounder," the Chef D'Equip called out sharply. "Take her more over her back…didn't you hear me yesterday?"

Jesus, what was this? Did he actually think he was going to come out here and start coaching…or was he just busting his balls? Probably the latter.

Ignored him. Cantered off to the far end of the field.

"Rounder!" Chuck screamed after him.

Furious, Jericho sat in and pushed her deeper.

"Good. Fence," Frankel demanded.

There was an Oxer pretty much dead ahead of him. Obviously Chuck meant that one. Jericho sighted it, shortened her stride and lifted her into it.

"Alright, better than yesterday…but *deeper* on the approach. When I say deep I mean her head at her damn knees…now *do it!*"

Fifty electrically charged minutes later, Frankel called out, "She's done. Get Monterrey."

Jericho rode up to him, his eyes on fire, and he was spitting mad—hadn't ridden that way—rode with ferocity maybe, but cool. Now he looked hot. "What's this about?" he demanded. "You just show up at my place and start giving out orders?"

"You don't need the coaching?" Frankel mocked him. "Too good for it?"

Marco—ever tuned in to what was happening was already walking Monterrey down from the barn.

"You're here because you haven't heard from me," Jericho said, dis-missing the question about coaching. "So yes, Chuck…*yes*. I'll plead guilty to your fucking charge. Happy? What choice do I have? So now I'll just sit back and see if your promises mean shit." He sat there, looking down at him—not a hint of respect in him. "Now you've got what you came here for…so leave."

"Not till you ride Monterrey for me."

Scorn. "You're coming every day now? Why are we pretending?"

"Yeah that's right, every day ten o'clock, like it or not. And before I go today I need your customer list too. Names, horse's names, phone numbers. And I'm leaving you a list of shows I want you to enter."

Jericho was nodding as he was saying the first part of that. He'd already put together the list…thought the truth was even if Chuck did make the calls like he'd said he would—how much effort would he really put into it? He was completely at his mercy here—and fucked if he didn't do all that much. But when he mentioned the list of shows, those deep blue eyes flared with anger again. "You know I can't enter a show right now."

"Fill the entries out, give them to me."

Vengeful. "Damn you, just damn you."

Frankel just took the criticism, didn't even flinch under it. "You really don't trust me at all, do you Jericho?"

"Not at all."

Actually, he had more that he needed to tell him about…but decided now wasn't the time. "Fine. Do it anyway. Change horses, lets get to work."

Jericho was back in the barn a couple of hours later. Both Frankel and Marx were gone—they'd left immediately after Monterrey's ride, Marx not even speaking to him—and maybe he was reading too much into things right now, being oversensitive, but that bothered him too.

He found himself standing at the far end of the aisle…at QL's stall—it was becoming something of a habit—but just liked being there with the big, jugheaded mare. Something about her comforted him. He fed her some cookie pieces, and finally walked away. Time for Cin's lessons, and there she was coming into the barn now.

She waved to him. Perfectly dressed as always, and something of a smug little look on her face. Called out happily to him, "So you got suspended, huh cowboy?"

His eyes fell away from her. She knew already? Nice greeting too. Had to face it. "Yes, Cin. Who told you?"

"Chuck…over dinner last night." She came right up to him, still smiling superiorly. "Big fine too…ouch."

Chuck. Over dinner last night. And he'd never even mentioned it this morning. He was starting to deeply dislike the guy. "Did he tell you why? Cin, can I at least tell you why?"

"Oh, he explained it," she said, dismissing it, reaching out to lay a hand on his chest and then leaning up to kiss his cheek. "Big rah-rah speech about how you were doing it for the sake of the USAE. Oh Jericho, I told you not to get involved with that little bitch, Ailynn," she smirked. "Are you going to be broke, darling?"

She was loving this, he decided. Remembered her telling him once that she'd like to break him herself. "Pretty much so," he admitted. Then tried to change the subject. "Cabaret's ready, lets ride."

But Cin didn't seem to want to leave the topic alone. She moistened her lips with a wicked little grin. "But here was the amazing part, and I really couldn't believe this…last night, I mean. Can you imagine Chuck suggesting that we buy that horrifying QL horse?"

"What?" he demanded, body tightening, really looking mad. "QL is mine, how dare he? Christ, I haven't said she's for sale."

"Well, maybe he's just assuming you'll sell anything, Jericho." Innocent little look on her face. "You know, I've always liked your car, so if you're thinking…"

"I'm not." Harsh. Man, he was wishing that Frankel was still there, cause he'd love to tell him off. God damn him. "Put your boots on, it's time to ride," he said again.

"I don't know, Jericho," she mocked him. "I don't feel like riding today. That's what I came to tell you."

"Come on, Cin. Then stay and I'll ride them for you."

"No, cowboy…I really don't want to." Smiled at him. "Ta, darling." She gave him another little air kiss on the cheek, then spun around and sashayed out of the barn, stopping once to turn and wave goodbye.

The Maitlands were leaving him. He knew it beyond a doubt.

"I thought that was your car."

Jericho had been sitting by himself at the far end of the bar at Nicole's. It was about eight o'clock, and he'd just finished up—hadn't changed, didn't even want to go home. Felt more like getting drunk. He lifted his eyes, though he didn't need to—he recognized that voice. Marx.

"Yeah, it's my car at the moment," he murmured bitterly. "Cin offered to buy it when I get strapped enough."

Marx sat down next to him without asking if he'd mind the company—signaled the bartender, ordered a Scotch. Big patron—Jericho guessed he'd earned the right to join him.

"You'll be fine, Jericho. I know it doesn't feel that way right now."

"Do you know how it feels—getting manhandled around like this? Not to mention how it's going to feel, knowing everyone's talking...looking, speculating. By tomorrow, it'll be common knowledge." He looked depressed, sounded that way too. Added quietly, "I'm pretty sure the Maitlands are leaving me. I've had them three years now. Cin's come from...well, a nothing rider, to third at the National, and I've bought and sold two horses for them where they turned a huge profit, but no one cares about that, right?"

"Chuck thinks..."

"Chuck," Jericho interjected sharply, voice rife with dislike. "Your friend Chuck tried to sell QL to the Maitlands last night. Christ, he didn't even have the decency to ask me first...and I don't even have her on the market. I guess he just assumed I'll be that hard up." He snorted. "Hell, I could have told him the Maitlands would never buy her anyway—they'd never own an ugly animal, and of course they can't see the beauty in her and never will. I wouldn't want them owning her..." Turned and laid that deep blue stare on him. "...even if I do get that desperate, and the truth is maybe I will."

"Suppose I want to buy her?"

He snapped out a biting response. "What is it with you and Chuck? Just fuck me. No. Absolutely not." Silence for a long moment, with Marx studying him quietly. Reconsidered the tone he'd just used with him. "Look, I'm sorry, alright? I shouldn't have mouthed off to you that way. My temper's really short, and Chuck...he just keeps dicking me around."

"I'm not Chuck Frankel. What I am, is very serious," the investment banker repeated. "The first time you and I talked about this you told me you needed two mounts to make a legitimate run for a berth on the Team. I didn't understand that, so I asked Chuck why, and he explained it...horse pulls a tendon right before a big show, or something else happens...and you're left with nothing to ride."

"It happens all the time," he conceded, but added resentfully. "And in your case, maybe you'll need two trainers too...just in case."

Amused smile. "No Jericho, I'm backing you...and Monterrey...and if you'll let me, QL."

"Why?" He really meant it, didn't understand. "I haven't even been all that polite to you, but Chuck says you've been strong behind me—even in private sessions with USAE." Looked scornful all over again. "...though coming from him, I didn't know whether to believe it or not. So tell me why," he asked again. "It's a ton of money and I'm completely unproven in international competition. There are easily ten or more riders who'd be safer bets."

Shrugged. "I've liked you since the first time we talked—it was right here, in this bar, remember? And I'll never forget standing by your car with you—and you're clenching and unclenching that fist like I'm about three seconds away from feeling it crush my jaw."

Looked embarrassed. "Yeah, it's a bad habit. I wasn't going to hit you though."

"You told me that too. Look, I know you're pissed at Chuck, and frankly, I don't blame you, but he's sure changed his mind about you since the first time we talked. Believe this...he wants to see you make the team this summer. And maybe I want a picture to hang in my office...my horse taking a victory gallop, the rider I sponsor with a medal. Maybe I'm just that competitive, and..." He chuckled a little. "...and I sure as shit won't be winning it myself."

"So you'd back a suspended rider on the verge of bankruptcy? Come on, you've got to know Chuck will tell you anything if it gets you to contribute more."

"You won't go bankrupt if you sell QL to me," he reasoned, simply dropping the part of the discussion that related to Frankel—Jericho and the Chef D'Equip would have to work that out between themselves. "And think about this...I can afford to send her to Europe to compete this spring, can you? Could you, even before this?"

Looked at him. Picked his beer up and slugged some down. "No. Or I don't know...with Team support, and maybe if I sold my house."

"Would you actually do that? Sell your house just to compete?"

Nodded. "Oh yeah."

"You think she's that good?"

"For sure."

"As good as Monterrey?"

Nodded again, but then added, "She's not for everyone. In all serious-ness, she's a really, really difficult ride…I won't kid you. And he's not, he really tries. But talent…yards of it. Heart…ditto."

Marx thought about it. "Then sell me half of her. You retain control. I pay her expenses, you train her at no cost. That's a fair deal. How much?"

Couldn't believe this—he didn't trust it either. So little had gone right lately, he didn't dare. "You're serious, aren't you?" he quizzed him, wanting to be sure. Even launched another warning at him. "And you're not going to like the number I toss out."

Pretty firm. "Try me."

Pretty firm coming back too. "Ask Chuck first. Get a figure from him so you'll have something to check it against."

Marx smiled.

Jericho just shook his head. "So you already have? Man, I've got the two of you coming at me from both sides, and I'm just sitting here clueless. Alright, you want a number? Two hundred thousand."

He didn't seem fazed in the least. In fact, he looked happy about it—like maybe Chuck's number had been higher. "Done," he said. "I'll have a contract drawn up and wire you the money. How's that?" He held his hand out.

Hesitated. Then reached over and clasped it. Bargain with the devil maybe, but done and well struck.

Chapter Eleven

Nine o'clock the next morning, and Jericho's barn phone rang. "For you, boss," Marco said, holding it out.

Took it. "Yeah, hi. It's Jericho."

"Jason Coulder, Jericho." He paused for a moment, and then he went on. "I called to let you know the Maitlands were over here yesterday afternoon...looking for a place to move their horses."

Jericho sighed and shook his head. "Thanks for the warning. It doesn't surprise me though. Ah hell...just let them walk, they will anyway." He sounded really down...like he wouldn't fight to keep them, like he wasn't even going to try. Blew his breath out. Gave up the reason why, expressive tone of voice. "I'm suspended, Jason."

"Heard it," Coulder said back to him—quiet and sympathetic. "The news broke this morning. Hell, it's basically all anyone's talking about. And I'll tell you what, Jericho...it's a real blowjob. To you of all people? Hey, what you did was nothing—we've all done something just like that at some point in our careers—and no one gave a shit that you rode in that qualifier."

"Yeah, well someone did." Angrier now.

Really biting and critical response. "*Frankel*...what an asshole." Paused meaningfully for a few seconds. "Look, I told the Maitlands "no" alright? Told them I didn't have room—bawled them out too. Told them I was shocked they weren't supporting you...after all you've done for them?"

Jericho couldn't help but chuckle at that, sounding more like himself. "Christ I'd have loved to see that...especially Cin's face when you said that to her, she hates criticism. And thanks, Jace...but you didn't need to turn them away."

Harsh. "Oh hell yes I did, and if I had my way every trainer in Wellington would do the same thing." Went on with some passion, "You need to know this…the community's behind you, Jericho. Swear to God, we'll close around you. You have sale horses, don't you?"

Jesus, the conversation really surprised him. "Sure."

"I'll bring some customers by, take a look at them. Tell me about them."

Did that, then added, "God, I'd be incredibly grateful for the chance to show them to you. Tell your customers I'll be more than reasonable on the prices."

Strong. "No you won't. They have money, let the fuckers pay. And Jericho, I love sitting on the horses you make, its no favor on my part. The whole thing bites, man. Sixty fucking days in the middle of season…*and* twenty-five thousand? That's criminal. A couple of the riders are getting together this afternoon to talk about it…you don't need to be there, but I'll let you know what goes down, alright?"

Couldn't even begin to describe how this was making him feel. "Fuck…I have no words for you, Jason…"

Warm laugh. "You don't need to. Jericho, you'll come through to the other side of this. You won't go down…alright?"

"Alright."

"But I'm curious," Coulder went on, sounding it too. "Rumor is Frankel's got you hot and heavy on his coaching schedule. That true?"

Resentful. "Comes every fucking day now…even Mondays."

"What the fuck's that about?"

"I wish I knew," he told him. "It's not like I kiss his ass, far from it. I tell him to get off my property, but no…he just stands there barking out instructions like I haven't said a damn thing. I ride the frickin' horse, and he rides my ass at the same time. Maybe you can figure it out, cause I can't. Maybe he just likes jerking me off." Added viciously, "He's pretty good at it—loves it too."

"Stranger than fiction," Coulder muttered. "That bastard trains you like he wants you for the Team, and then he tries to break you? Watch out, Jericho…there's more behind that."

"Tell me about it."

They talked for a few more minutes, with Coulder assuring him one more time that he'd get through this, that the other trainers in Wellington were going to make sure he did. "If you really get strapped, you call me, Jericho. Hear me?"

"Loud and clear…and I owe you, I really owe you. Anything, anytime. My word on it, man."

"Already knew that, Jericho." Warm goodbye.

————————

Marx and Frankel having lunch together at Yano's Italian Deli—small place, basically all riders inside it, lots of take-out orders. Their table was near the door where everyone walked past it—both on the way coming in, and again on the way out.

Marx was on the phone with his office, talking some financial transaction he had underway. Frankel drinking a coffee.

Two young women—probably early twenties, and both in breeches. They strolled slowly by, heading for the door. One covered her mouth, and said pretty loudly, "Asshole," but made it sound like she was sneezing or coughing. Even so, the word was enunciated clearly, and the rest of the room snickered.

Frankel shook his head in anger, looked away stone-faced.

Marx got off the phone. "What was that about?" he asked, staring after the two girls.

"Jericho," Frankel smoldered. "Word's out about the suspension and I'm being painted as the bad guy. Nobody cares that he didn't belong in that damn class. No—they all think he got screwed. And I've been getting the cold shoulder from one end of Wellington to the other."

Marx just chuckled. "You asked for it, Chuck. Literally."

"Yeah, and I was right," he said defensively and pretty strongly too.

The investment banker shrugged, short on sympathy for him. "Jericho sucks it up…now you do too. Fair's fair."

Grumbled about it. Knew it was true.

————————

Delivery truck coming in to the Brandeis Show Stables. Grand Prix Shavings, it said on the side. Jericho bought pretty much everything from them…hay, feed, supplements, and shavings. Good product, fair prices… still it came to a hefty bill weekly with twelve horses in the barn.

Today the owner was driving. Jericho came over to him with a check.

Pocketed the thing, smiled. "Thanks," he said, giving Jericho a long look. "You've been a good customer for a long time," he added. Then said vaguely, "I don't normally extend credit, but sometimes I can be talked into it."

Knew exactly what he meant. "Appreciated."

Nod of approval. Got back in his truck again.

Later in the afternoon Darien came into the stables. She found Jericho just hanging up the telephone, and approached him. "Hi, how are you?" she asked.

He turned, his deep blue stare falling on her, reading her—knowing there was more to her question than just a casual greeting. She looked tentative, didn't have a clue what kind of mood he'd be in, that much was obvious. She probably knew most of Wellington was buzzing about him, and thought he'd be good and upset about it too. But that wasn't even remotely what was running through his mind. He'd been attracted to her from the first day he met her—but deliberately stayed away. Hell, she was married, and to Marx of all people. But that was before last week, right here in this aisle way...her kissing him, him kissing her. Maybe it was just rebound after Ailynn, but damn did she look good today in that tight pair of breeches—it stirred him in a way he hated to admit. Covered it though. "I'm fine...no, actually, I'm completely overwhelmed," he told her. "The phone's been ringing off the hook."

"Ouch."

"No, it hasn't been like that...that's what I thought too—figured I'd be besieged by gossip hounds looking for fodder. But honestly everyone who's called has been super to me—most offered some kind of help."

"Really?" She looked so happy for him, like she really cared. That gorgeous mouth slightly parted, curving up in a warm, personal smile. "That's wonderful. How satisfying it must be for you." She came the rest of the way over to him, laid her little hand on his arm again—like always—that incredibly innocent caress that reached right in and grabbed him, made his body react. "Bob told me he wired you the money for QL today, so the deal's done right? And she's half ours?" At his nod of agreement, she asked him. "Will you show her to me up close, Jericho?"

It actually surprised him. For some reason, he'd been thinking of the partnership in QL being with her husband, and wasn't even recognizing that Darien was part of it too. Stupid of him. "Sure, of course. She's down in the end stall…so now your horses are like bookends, first and last boxes." Smiled. He slowly strolled down that way with her. "I need you to listen to me now, okay?" he said, demanding her attention and getting it with a more serious tone of voice. "QL isn't like Monterrey," he warned her. "Don't go in the stall with her…ever. Promise me that, Darien. Always let Marco or I bring her out, okay? Even the other guys don't handle her. Just Marco and myself."

She looked taken back. "Wow, is she that vicious?"

Shrugged. "Vicious, I don't know. Potentially dangerous, yes. She's a very strong alpha mare…you understand what that means, right?" He'd stopped in front of her stall, and grabbed her halter. QL nickered, coming over to him, and he brushed his fingers over her nose.

"Well, its like top dog, I guess." She watched him as he played with the horse's upper lip, and those big mule ears twitched toward him. "She certainly looks docile enough though." Darien took one step forward. *Instant reaction.* QL's thick skull swinging sharply around, ears lying flat back on her head—teeth almost bared. Darien jumped back. "Oh my God," she breathed.

"That's right," Jericho laughed softly, "And don't forget it." He slid the door open and came inside. "Cut it out," he said sharply…and that block of wood face reached over to nuzzle him sheepishly. "Yeah, you're sorry," he grumbled to her. "Show some manners, witch." QL snorted softly, then lifted her front foot, pawing with it in the air just a little. "No. No begging." He slipped the halter on her, clipping it shut. Foot still waggling in the air. Rapped her shoulder. "Put it down." She did. Patted her neck, and told her "Good girl." Slipped something from his pocket into her mouth, and she chomped happily on it.

Darien watched fascinated. "I know I keep saying this, but you're just amazing with her—with all of them. Look how she listens to you."

He snapped the lead shank on her. "Yeah, well we've come to an agreement. The first time I walked in here, she swung those hindquarters of hers around and tried to nail me with them…and stand back, okay?" Darien did as he asked, and he led QL out into the aisle way. Didn't put her in the crossties though, just stood with her, so he had control over her head. "Stand in front of her…no, not there, over a little. Right there. Now she can see you for a minute. Let me see what she does. This isn't a bad horse, but she needs to be handled by a professional. And you always need to respect what she is."

QL looked calm with Jericho beside her. Still Darien remembered that big head swinging aggressively at her just moments earlier. Scary. "So alright, what is an alpha mare?" she asked him.

"I'll explain. Step a little closer to her." Jericho reached his arm out and settled it around Darien's shoulders. He moved her nearer...to the horse, and to himself too. Lingering perhaps longer than needed before letting it slip away again. "In the wild, stallions don't really lead the herd the way most people think they do," he explained. "They have one purpose...well maybe two...covering the mares, and making sure other stallions don't. Ever actually see horses mate?"

She looked a little embarrassed, shook her head in the negative.

He'd moved in behind her, could feel the proximity of her and even smell the faintest hint of perfume, but without any sort of real physical contact. "Christ, its beautiful. Savage almost, the way the stallions cover the mares." Quiet smirk from him. "Way too short for my taste, but..."

"You're bad," she murmured, not looking around, but hearing his tone. And he was letting her just sense him there...tall behind her...male, and in close. Coupled nicely with the image of a stallion rearing up over a mare.

Ignored her scolding, just continued. "The stallions live outside the herd mostly, they're loners. The strongest mare is the one who keeps the group together, finds green pastures and water, fights off wolves and other predators. She's the alpha mare, and she has to be fierce. By the way, it's why mares tend to have bigger ears—they're always listening for danger." Chuckled. "Now this mare has...really big ears." QL looked offended, almost as if she'd understood. Jericho laughed, reached past Darien to stroke her...his arm just brushing the woman in front of him as he did.

Soft intake of breath from her at the feather-light contact. Trying not to acknowledge the way it affected her. "I never knew that...about the alpha mare."

"Most people don't." He murmured in a low compelling way when he spoke...to both her and the horse. And both were reacting, focusing on him...Darien letting him nearly surround her now. "The alpha mare is aggressive, she's independent—refuses authority, but man is she strong. Damn hard to work with from a rider's standpoint, but if she gives you her heart, she'll lay down and die for you...she cares that much."

Standing this close to QL, Darien could see that she was huge. No, she wasn't beautiful, but she was awesome, that was for sure. "May I touch her, Jericho?"

"Yes. Actually, I'm getting to that. Trust me, you'll see." *Trust me.* Did she? Better question…should she?

The next words out of Darien's mouth completely surprised him. "I want to move my hunter, Roué, over here Jericho, will you have a stall for me?"

"Sure, but why? You're happy with Chip, aren't you?"

Soft smile—hard for him to see from this angle, but there just the same. "Well, actually he suggested it," she told him. "He got a new client in, so I think maybe he's short on room himself. And he said it's going to be hard for me, going back and forth between here and there every day, and that's true."

Jericho looked down, knew what this was. Chip—tossing some income his way. Nice of him. "God, he doesn't have to do that," he muttered. "Darien, between your husband and the community down here, I'm surviving…I'll still be in business at the end of this. I sure didn't think so when Chuck first told me. But then I never expected this level of support."

"You're respected, that's why. Anyway Jericho, I'd really like to move Roué here. I'd like to ride with you…if it's alright."

"Sure it is." He reached down. "Give me your hand now."

She tensed for an instant, little flare of excitement, lifted her hand a few inches and back toward him. He slid his behind it, taking the back of it in his palm and just holding it for a second, then brought it over and laid it on QL. Nervous dance from her hoofs, quickly quelled by his firm command, "Just stand."

He knew what Darien was feeling, and maybe it was a little bit of an ambush on his part—maybe more than a little. The mare's sleek coat beneath her fingertips, the animal's warm body, his own hand completely covering and enveloping hers, his thumb curled around hers. Light but commanding pressure from him, and Christ to him it was erotic. Just that little touch, and nothing else…and with her so close in front of him, his arms all but around her. He stroked her hand down the length of the horse's powerful neck. Did it again. Then let his own hand drop away, and she was patting QL by herself.

Jericho moved out from behind her, and back over to QL's near side—not what he wanted to do, but what he had to do before he did something stupid with his patron's wife. Slid a piece of cookie into the mare's mouth, murmured to her, "Good." Lifted his eyes back to Darien. Eloquent look there. Held it. Then quietly began pointing out some of the finer points about QL—just horse talk, but making it seem private, intimate. "Look at the slope of her shoulder. It's what gives her that freedom of movement..." He went on for probably the next five minutes, patiently telling her about the horse that she and her husband had invested in.

He could tell he'd completely entranced her—and her him for that matter. The rest of the world gone...nothing else in it but the two of them and this mare named QL.

From Darien: "I think she's really special to you, isn't she?"

Powerful response, and he wasn't talking about QL either. "I'm...completely drawn to her. Maybe I shouldn't be. Fuck, I know I can't be..."

Then Marco suddenly bursting the bubble with, "Jer, your horse has been ready for twenty minutes...you ever gonna ride?"

"Coming now, Marco."

End of it.

Two weeks later and almost Christmas. The Maitlands' two horses were gone now, but Roué was there instead, so down one in total. Maximus and Rebel maybe leaving too, though Christ, he was fighting hard to keep them, and Frankel had pitched in full force on that one too—had to give him that much.

It was still early, eight-thirty, and Jason Coulder was there with two customers, a couple named Bayland. Jericho planned to show them Landrover...and hopefully get them in and out of there before Chuck's daily visit from hell. "I think he could go either way...hunter or jumper," Jericho was explaining. "But I've been schooling him as a hunter, and that's what you're interested in, right?"

Confirmation back from Coulder. "Right."

Marco was leading the big flashy black colt up now—impeccably groomed, and beautiful. Jericho looked at the pair of them and his eyes narrowed. He muttered something under his breath—something that probably wasn't polite. "Marco, where the hell are the stirrups on that saddle?"

"Well Jer, Chuck told me not to put stirrups on unless you're riding Monterrey or QL." Innocent look from him, but Jericho knew he wasn't stupid. They were showing this horse for sale, not schooling him. What did Marco think he was proving?

"Go and get them," he ordered. "Yeah, I ride him that way, but that's not what Jason and his customers want. Christ's sakes, Marco." Disgusted with him.

Coulder was chuckling though. And he sounded amazed. "Chuck's making you ride without stirrups?"

Jericho rolled his eyes, then just shook his head. "You can't imagine, Jason. No stirrups and up in two-point…six out of eight rides a day."

Whistled low. "Oh man!"

"Yeah, right?" He reached for the reins. "Look, while Marco's getting the stirrups, should I warm him up for you? You can see what I'm doing with him that way too."

"Absolutely…we hoped you would, actually." He looked at the Baylands, and they nodded too.

"Fine." He grabbed the pommel of the saddle, and just vaulted on. Pivoted the horse cleanly around to face them. "I'll do some flatwork with him, then pop him over a few lines. Marco should be back by then, and you can sit on him if you want." Again Coulder agreed, and Jericho swung the young colt away from them, and rode off at the posting trot. Did that in both directions, and then moved him into a long and low canter to stretch him out. Flying change of lead and canter in the other direction. Looked up and still no sign of Marco—was going to fucking strangle him, that was for sure.

Faced him with a line, and Landrover took it smoothly…nice and round. Quiet and obedient. He could hear Coulder and his clients talking, and the tone of voice sounded good.

And then Jericho looked over and saw what he'd really been trying to avoid this morning. Frankel striding into the ring…a fucking hour early, damn him. That man, he just showed up whenever he felt like it.

"Morning, Jason," Frankel said, walking over to stand next to him. He got a pretty cool response from him, but at least Coulder introduced his customers, and they looked thrilled to be meeting the Show Jumping Chef D'Equip. A minute or two of casual conversation followed, but with Frankel focused hard on Jericho the whole time. Finally he muttered, "Excuse me," and walked further out into the ring. "No, no, no," he bellowed derisively. "You're a good two inches out from the ideal take-off point."

"Two inches?" Coulder snorted to the couple next to him. "He's complaining about two inches? Man, I'd like to be that precise. But actually we're lucky—its not often you get to see Chuck coaching. He's a master at it, and everyone wants on his schedule...till they get there. He's notoriously hard to please and mean as a snake."

Frankel was still yelling. "Do the whole thing again, and stay up in two point, damn it. Don't get lazy on me now, Jericho. Go to work!"

Jericho had meanwhile come around and pulled up beside him—which had done nothing to lower the volume of his scathing remarks. And where the hell was that damn Marco? "For Christ's sake, Chuck," he snarled. "Do you have to criticize every fucking thing I do? I'm showing this horse for sale."

Scornful. "Does that mean you don't have to really ride him? Should he look sloppy or should he look sharp, you tell me?"

Real hardass answer. "Yeah, I figured I'd just park my ass on him and let him go around. That alright?"

Acted like he didn't hear him, or maybe just couldn't care less. "Ride him like a jumper instead of a hunter, and *pay attention* to your mark. How many times do you have to hear me tell you the same thing?" He was already raising the fence closest to him, and lifted his voice to holler, "Marco!" Damned if the little shit didn't suddenly appear. "Marco, get down here and help me change this line." He was hotfooting it down there now—hadn't brought the stirrups with him yet though. Damn, Jericho thought, he was really going to kick his ass for this.

Frankel finished the fence, then gave Marco instructions on a few others. He walked back toward Coulder and the Baylands, calling over his shoulder to Jericho as he went. "Canter. No wait, I changed my mind... *gallop.*" Then to Marco again, but still loud enough for Jericho to hear every word, "I want tape down at the take off point for each of these jumps." Yelled harshly out to his rider. "And I better damn well see an *entire hoof print* on the tape when you go over it—because if I don't, that means you've missed your mark...again. There are no "almosts" here, alright? *Precision,* Jericho. At least try this time through." Smiled at Coulder and his customers.

Jericho just watched him, deep blue eyes treacherous. Chuck standing there smugly with the potential buyers. Fuck, he wanted to go over and tell him where to shove his instructions and his fucking tape for that matter too—wouldn't have hesitated either if it had been just Jason, but he didn't know these Bayland people, didn't want to put them off with a show of temper and harsh words. Snarled under his breath, but then just stomached it.

163

Frankel folded his arms over his chest. He looked fierce, pride in that posture too. He leaned in to Jason and said with some satisfaction, "Did you catch that expression? Jericho's just then? Now, I've got to tell you— there's a real 'fuck you'."

Coulder's mouth dropped. He gave a really censuring answer. "That's for sure. And damn it Chuck, you really deserve that. My people came over here today interested to buy—what are you doing to Jericho?"

Marco had finished laying the tape, and Frankel nodded in approval to him. But then he lifted his voice again, apparently unconcerned and completely overlooking Jason's question. "Hard of hearing today, Jericho? Marco's done, so what's your excuse? I said...*ride!*" And with a growl, man and horse launched into a canter...squeeze from Jericho's legs and up into two-point, and they were galloping instead. Frankel turned back pleasantly to Coulder, and his customers too. "I guess you're looking for a hunter, but wait till you see the jumping talent in this horse. Oh sure, he could be a hunter, but he'd be a better prelim jumper...win some big stakes for you, that's for sure."

Jericho and Landrover bearing down on the jumping line. The horse's head was slightly raised as he sighted the first obstacle, but his back was still up nicely and he was relaxed and round. Jericho's weight balanced easily over him, also sighting...sighting that fucking tape on the ground.

"This is a gallop. Faster!" the Chef D'Equip roared. *"Come on!"*

Sat in for a heartbeat, the horse shooting forward. Measured him. Launched—lifted him sharply. And shit man, Chuck had made the damn fences so wide, the horse was really surprised by it. "Release!" Frankel was screaming, though Jericho already had, and right on cue.

"Oh man, fuck me," Jason said, awed. "That was beautiful." The Baylands were talking among themselves and seemed pretty impressed with what they were seeing too.

Happy smile from Chuck. "I told you this horse was nice."

Coulder turned to him caustically. "Yeah, he seriously is...but I was talking about Jericho. Come on, you've got to think so too."

Too late with the comment—Frankel had already left him to go and check the jumping tape on the first jump, then the second and third. Nothing to complain about on the second or third elements, so he strode back to the first. Jericho was riding back to him just as he ripped it up from the sand and held it up for everyone to see. Beautiful print on it. "Do you want to tell me why it's crooked?" he sneered witheringly. "Marco, lay it again. Redo the line, and come at it *straight* this time."

"God damn you Chuck," Jericho lashed at him, really good and annoyed by now. "You'll have the horse so spent, how's Jason going to try him?"

"*Straight.* Do you know what straight means?"

Dangerous. "Yeah, I know what it means."

"Then can we see it please?"

Jericho took the line again. Frankel stepping back a pace, then laying out a constant flow of instructions in the most insulting tone of voice—as if he were talking to someone who really didn't have a clue what to do. "Sit in…now measure him…sight the damn line, now *face him…lift. Release!*" He strode over and ripped up the tape again. Brought it back to where Jason and his clients were standing, but then motioned Jason off to the side and showed it to him. "Now that's fucking perfect," he said, sounding really satisfied. Then called out to Jericho, "You made me wait long enough, but alright…you got *one.* Want to try for two in a row…maybe without my help this time if that's possible? *Do it again.*"

Got another deep "fuck you" stare leveled hard on him.

Coulder just shaking his head, incredulous. "Jesus, you're completely un-fucking-fair…why do you bust his ass like that? What have you got against him, Chuck? No stirrups, flat out gallop, and a perfect line…he's blowing my socks off here."

"Think I'm hard on him?"

"Damn right I do."

"Screwed him over on the suspension?"

Vehement. "Damn right."

Jericho had come down the line again, and the conversation stopped. He looked very cool atop that green four-year-old, but absolutely ferocious—really wanting it, really putting out, and getting more from this horse than ever before. First fence. Second. Third. Damn near flawless.

Frankel murmured confidently. "Ever see him ride better?"

Paused, conceded the point. "No Chuck, I guess I haven't."

Marco grabbed the three tapes and brought them over. Nice clean hoof print on each of them, dead on straight. Frankel nodded, satisfied, called to Jericho. "Okay, you're done with this horse. Marco, bring QL." Didn't even seem to realize that he'd completely interfered with a possible sale—maybe blowing it in the process for him. He looked at Coulder one more time, hard stare. "Oh, I know what's going on with you riders," he told him coldly. "I know you've got a petition going—that all forty-one participants in that class with Jericho signed it. Every one of them saying they have no issue with him riding, asking for reinstatement. But understand this Jason…he's suspended till January 28th and nothing's going to change it—I don't care how many petitions come through. January 29th? Now that's something different. January 29th I want him in the show ring…he'll shock a few people then, that's for sure."

"Yeah? Well I don't get it. What's one have to do with the other? Granted, he's a major talent and you've really honed him. But why does he have to face suspension to get you to work with him? And tell me this…does he hate you for it?" Jason asked him flat out, really disliking Frankel's attitude—his methods too.

But Coulder's harsh judgment didn't even begin to bother him. "Hate me? Sure he does—but you know what? I don't give a damn if he does or doesn't."

Jericho had ridden over and he pulled up beside them. Vaulted off. He looked unhappy, and really pissed to the core. Ignored Frankel like he wasn't even there, and spoke to Jason. "Jace, you can ride him now if you want to, but hell its not a fair evaluation when he's tired like this."

Coulder nodded, but then shrugged. "It's alright, Jericho. He's not for these people anyway—they want a different type." It sounded like bad news, but he was sporting a lop-sided grin, and even winked at him. "Hell, why should I let you sell him to the Baylands? Truth is, I want him for myself— just plain selfish, I guess. I'll call you later, we'll talk about price."

Satisfied nod coming back from him.

Marco was walking over now with QL. Jericho's sharp stare swung to him. Tossed a stinging and vengeful comment over at him. "Too bad you never managed to find those stirrups like I asked you."

Marco—guilty as hell. Frankel—hiding a grin.

Chapter Twelve

It was 10:01 PM and the night before Christmas Eve. Starbucks' official hours were 6:00 AM to 10:00 PM.

"Welcome to Starbucks, and screw you, we're closed…" Followed by a peal of laughter. "Oh hell, Darien, just kidding. Well…we *would* be closed if it were anyone else, but never with you. What do you want?"

"A Latte, and I came to see you, Brae."

"Cool, drive down."

She appeared at the window about five seconds later, a big smile on her face. Brae opened the window and leaned out it. He had a goofy Santa hat on his head—but somehow on him, it didn't even look weird. Darien laughed merrily and held up a package—covered in beautiful, rich looking foil-trimmed wrapping paper, and a tied around it, a big red bow. "It's for you," she said. "Merry Christmas."

"Oh, man, Darien. Wow." He grabbed the package, shook it. Didn't seem at all embarrassed that she had something for him, but not the reverse.

"Hey, hey! Not until Christmas, okay?" she scolded him—but pretty well sure he'd be ripping the paper off like a two year old the minute she drove out of sight.

"Oh no, I can't wait. I want to open it with you," Starbucks told her. He handed her the Latte and told her, "That one's on me," proud of himself for that. And he did look pretty thrilled about the present, glanced over his shoulder to the other baristas who were starting in on the clean up process that took place every night after closing. Brae hated the clean up anyway—it was too much like real work—mopping, taking out the trash, cleaning the espresso machine. "I'll just cut out on these guys and meet you out front, okay?"

She grinned and shook her head at him. He was pretty hard to resist, and the excited look on his face *was* quite charming. "Oh, okay…come on."

She pulled around to the front of the store, and backed into an empty parking spot. No more than five minutes later he came strolling out the main door, clutching the package and still wearing that stupid Santa Claus hat. Another clerk locked the door behind him while he loped around to the passenger side door and swung inside. He leaned over and kissed her cheek, laid that bedroom-eyes stare on her. "This is really cool," he said, meaning it too. "Are you going to be here for Christmas?"

She shook her head. "No, I'm leaving tomorrow morning for New York. Bob and I are spending Christmas in the city with some friends."

Disgusted face. "Man, that sucks."

"No, it should be fun, Brae."

"Ugh, you should hang with Jericho and me. We're...well, hell, I don't know what we're doing, but I have the day off." Big smile. Shook the package again. Held it up to his ear. "You know, Jericho's coming to pick me up in a couple of minutes. You should stick around. What do you think I should get him, by the way? Jericho, I mean."

"It's a little late to be remembering that, isn't it?" she scolded him. But tired to answer his question anyway. "I don't know Brae...how about framing one of your pictures of him on QL?"

Lopsided grin. "How about one of those other pictures of him...you know, the first ones I showed you?"

She looked embarrassed, punched his shoulder. "Stop it, do you mean to tell me you haven't erased those yet?"

"Nah, I like them. Well, I'd have to lop Ailynn's head off the shot somehow, right? He wouldn't like that part..." Starbucks actually seemed to be considering it...thinking hard about how he could do it. "Hey, that was a great idea, Darien, thanks! I'll tell him you suggested it."

"Brae!"

"No really." Grinned at her. He looked at the tag on his gift and read it out loud. "To Brae, from Darien. Aww, that's sweet." Started pulling at the ribbon around his present. Tugged, and the bow came undone easily enough, but there was still a knot beneath it, still holding the ribbon in place around the box. Started yanking at it, not making much headway—all thumbs, it seemed. Growled, frustrated. Muttered, "Fuck," under his breath.

"Stop that!" she chided. "You're such a child. Here, give it to me."

"No." Still jerking at the ribbon, face screwed up in concentration.

There was a sharp rap on the hood of the car, and both of them looked up, surprised. Three men were standing there. They looked like a group of

Argentinean polo grooms—or RJ's as they were called—a common sight around Wellington. Their leader appeared decidedly drunk. "Hey, you got a little present for me?" he slurred aggressively, pointing at the package Brae held. "Hey you...Santa...get out here and give it to me." He was clearly talking to Starbucks. Threatening tone of voice.

An hour and a half earlier.

Jericho had left the barn late—no surprise there. Showered and thrown on a clean pair of jeans, and hauled a tee shirt over them. And now he was heading back. He was doing the night check himself tonight, covering for the guys who were having a little Christmas party at Marco's house. After he was done he'd swing by and pick up his roommate at Starbucks. He pulled his Mustang into the Brandeis Show Stables driveway. Another car was already parked by the entrance to the barn—a Jaguar XJS, new one. Who the hell was this, he wondered, and swung aggressively out of the car, long strides taking him rapidly to the main barn door. The barn lights were on, and he sure as shit didn't like that.

"Who's there?" he called out, voice sharp and demanding, eyes keen.

Soft lilting little voice. "It's me, Jericho." Ailynn stepped out of the shadows and came over to greet him. She had on low-rise jeans—really low—and a short white crop top that revealed a good two or three inches of slim and well-toned abdomen. "Please don't be angry. I saw one of your guys at Publix tonight, and he said you were going to be here. I had to see you, Jericho. Please don't be angry," she repeated.

Unhappy about it, that was obvious. And completely unrelenting. "Ailynn, what the fuck are you doing here? Christ, I'm afraid to talk to you without having my lawyer present. I'm going to have to ask you to leave." He walked right past her to where two wheelbarrows were waiting, each one set up with enough hay to do half the barn. Laid his hands on the handles to one of them. "And I have to feed."

She wasn't about to be put off by his gruff tone of voice though, and came right up behind him, wrapping her arms around his waist lightly, laying her cheek against his middle back. "Please just talk to me."

"No. You need to go, and the horses have to eat. Get off me." He hadn't moved and he hadn't turned around...and she hadn't let go either. Stalemate for the moment, it seemed. Then he swung around sharply, and

169

firmly put her off to the side. "No. Ailynn, I don't trust you. I'm going to ask you again…leave." Grabbed the wheelbarrow and pushed it angrily down to Monterrey's stall. Jerked the door open, and tossed a flake of hay in to him. Petted him for a moment—not showing him any of the anger inside him, only gentleness—then closed the door again. Refilled his water buckets.

Ailynn, just watching him.

Growled angrily. Knew she wasn't going to listen to him…but his heart was hard against her, and he didn't care how rude or brusque he seemed. Pulled the wheelbarrow down to the second stall where Landrover was, and repeated the process there. The big colt would be leaving inside a week—Coulder had purchased him, and they hadn't even dickered that much about the price. And my god, Jericho thought for the thousandth time in the last few weeks, Jason had been a real friend to him through this past month—never expected it in a million years. Owed him, big time—even wanted to feel in his debt—would find some way meaningful to pay him back for it, that was for sure.

Jericho looked over. Ailynn hadn't moved an inch, it seemed. His eyes on her were hot, and he was really getting angry. Didn't speak though. Just dragged the wheelbarrow down to stall number three. Roué. Darien's hunter—nice damn horse, and teaching her had become such a pleasure. She was a great little rider, and the truth was he loved seeing her, talking to her and working with her daily. To some extent, it was torture…he found innocent ways to put his hands on her during every lesson—nothing overtly sexual or objectionable, but man it turned him on, and she liked it too, he knew that. Things like…"Here look at your leg position…" and his hand on her thigh, the other on the heel of her boot, turning her leg in slightly toward the saddle. Her eyes looking down at him from atop her horse. God, it aroused him. Sometimes it was hard to even remember what he'd been talking about.

Soft voice again. "Please, Jericho. Just look at me."

Did, but only for an instant. "Ailynn, I said leave."

She took a few steps toward him, and he vengefully yanked the wheelbarrow down to stall number four, and Maximus. The Hunter gelding was still with him, though it had been a real fight to keep him there. The owners wanted him shown in the month of January, and there was no way Jericho could ride him in the ring—not suspended like this. In the end they'd compromised—something Frankel came up with. He was putting a working student with Jericho starting Monday, and he knew whoever this bitch Brittany Lange was, she'd be one thing for sure—Chuck's little spy, but who gave a shit? It wasn't like the Chef D'Equip didn't show up any time he damn well felt like it, and there was nothing going on here that he didn't know about. But Brittany would take lessons from Jericho on Rebel and Maximus, and show the horses for the month of January. Didn't like it, but at least they weren't going to be taken away from him.

He topped off Maximus' water buckets and went to move on to Rebel's stall next.

"Jericho, I've really missed you." Ailynn again. She'd come over to join him and was standing only about four feet away. Then only three…two. Pleading. "Cole is…" It seemed like she changed what she'd been about to say to something different. "…out of town. We're basically separated, and we've been separated…I mean he comes and stays with me sometimes, but I don't even sleep in the same room with him. It's been like that for a long time, years even. I don't consider myself married to him. Jericho, I…"

Really biting demand coming back from him. "Stop, okay? I don't give a fuck, Ailynn. I don't care where you sleep or who you sleep with. You lied to me, and then you lied to USAE about QL. Because of you I'm suspended…I could have gone out of business—might still. And from what I hear you were part of the set-up. Where was all this concern you say you have for me when you were helping your husband completely rape me? Fuck you, Ailynn."

Tears on her cheeks. "Alright, you hate me. But just hold me, Jericho. I know I don't deserve anything from you, but I'm so lonesome for you. Please. Pretend…" she whispered. "Pretend I meant something to you. Pretend you cared."

Man, he wasn't giving in to this, though in all truthfulness, he couldn't say it wasn't getting to him. She was making him feel sorry for her, and he didn't want that—didn't want it at all. Growled at her, "Yeah I did care. Did. Past tense."

She stepped around the handles to the wheelbarrow, and came over to him—closed those last two feet. "Please don't push me away." She put her arms gently around his waist, laid her head on him. "At least not for a minute. Just one minute, Jericho. Hold me. I'm so miserable. Please hold me."

"And where's the camera hidden?" he snarled, not pulling away from her, but not returning the embrace.

She held him tighter and just cried.

Muttered a savage curse, but one arm went around her waist, pressing her lightly to him. With that short crop top and those low-rise jeans, it was bare flesh he felt there. His other hand had tangled through that chin-length spiky dark hair and tipped her head back. Deep blue stare meeting her doe-soft, tear-filled eyes. "I don't trust you. Fuck, I don't trust you, and I don't want you here." It wasn't like he didn't remember what it was like to be with her, and though he wasn't celibate, he wasn't really seeing anyone either. And then there was Darien, constantly exciting him…exciting but not fulfilling him. Oh yeah, this act tonight was well done, and yeah, it was affecting him but it was her lies that had almost ruined him for good.

"Jericho, I know you don't want me. Did you ever? For anything more than…" Her hands slid up his back, caressing him and holding him tighter. "…this?" They moved slowly down and then up again…but this time underneath his tee shirt, stroking the hard muscle of his back and shoulders. One hand moving around to the front side of him, lingering over powerful pectoral muscles…lats…abs…and finally curling around his belt buckle.

Stern. "Ailynn, I have to feed these horses." But it was significant that he hadn't pushed her away or even released his own hold around her waist. And he sure wasn't preventing those marauding fingertips from stroking him. And they still were…suggestively fondling his abdomen, knowing exactly how and where to draw a response from him.

She could be so persuasive. "They'll wait fifteen minutes."

"Fifteen minutes?" he snorted derisively. "What do you think is going to happen in fifteen minutes?"

"Oh, you're right, and I'm insulting you," she purred back to him, "You were never done in fifteen minutes. It's one of the things I liked best about you." She took hold of the hem of his tee shirt, and lifted it as high as she could without his cooperation—to about armpit height. He was staring at her, just staring with a look as cold as polished blue steel. Ducked his head with another murmured curse, and let her pull it off him. She dropped it on the aisle way floor. But even so, he took hold of the wheelbarrow and steered it past her, down to the next stall. Finished there, and on to the next, with her moving along side him, touching him, teasing.

He changed over to the other wheelbarrow, and started feeding the second half of the aisle, and she stayed beside him, saying nothing but closely watching him. Ailynn slid her own top off and it landed in a smaller heap on the floor beside her, and man he couldn't help but look at her—

slim almost boyish body, but with beautiful round breasts in a white lace bra—didn't conceal much. Oh he hadn't said "yes" yet, and they both understood that. He was weakening though—and they both understood that too.

One empty stall and then QL was in the last one. Jericho threw hay to her and watered her, then stroked her soft muzzle—maybe looking for some answer there, but not finding it. Looked around and saw that white lace bra lying in the empty wheelbarrow. His eyes traveled up...from the belt on those low-rise jeans, to the perfectly flat stomach, to those beckoning luscious breasts, now unbound. Ailynn came in close to him again, letting herself rub along his forearm where he'd gripped the wheelbarrow's handles. He still appeared to be resisting her, though his expression was fierce, and his body tightening with desire. "Please Jericho," she pleaded with him softly. "Please just pretend that you cared once upon a time."

She was touching him again, then freeing his hair so it fell around and over them both. Her mouth on his chest, her tongue exploring him. Could hear that sound he made deep in his throat—somewhere between a purr and a snarl—and knew how turned on he was just from that. Her hand confirmed it, sweeping over the front of his jeans and his very full-blown erection. Felt his body twitch against her hand...wanting her, though he might not.

Abruptly he lifted her from the floor and into his arms, growling, "Damn you," but carrying her to the empty stall and managing to yank the door open without even setting her down. Brought her inside and dumped her unceremoniously in the thick bedding of clean shavings, then came down on top of her—his mouth finding and immediately plundering hers. His hands went to those low-rise jeans—it wasn't all that difficult to just jerk them down over her hips, without even undoing them. Just yanked until he had them off her, and her little slip-on shoes in the process too.

"You asked for this Ailynn, and I said no, just remember that," he lifted his head to sneer, hair wild, covered in shavings. He was stripping his own jeans open at the waist, shoved them down and over his knees, didn't even bother to take them the rest of the way off before thrusting himself good and hard up inside her—and her body welcomed his, slick and warm and ready for him.

Stroked himself in her forcefully over and over, while she moaned and lifted her pelvis up onto him, taking him as much as he was taking her. Jericho withdrew and grabbed her on either side, easily flipping her over.

He was kneeling in the deep bedding…brought her up onto his muscled thighs, straddling him, but facing away from him. He re-entered her. Ailynn cried out, laid her head back onto this shoulder, his hands running up and down the front of her, fondling, caressing, but not gently…squeezing her breasts, finding her nipples and stimulating them…impaling her onto himself with each upward stroke. And oh yeah, he was really fucking her now, making her feel it, making her acknowledge him. His mouth on her neck, teeth bared and nipping at her almost savagely, his hair like a cloak around both her and himself. Angry, really, really angry. But taking his pleasure with her. Absolutely demanding it. Owning her, and making it so very clear who was master. She wasn't going to play with him this time—that was for God damn sure.

Deep scream from her, and she was climaxing, but he stroked her right through it and kept going. Threw her forward onto her hands and knees, himself mounted powerfully over her, covering her and making her sob with passion. Snarled to her, "Come on, you bitch, come back on me, service me." His arm was around her waist, and he jerked at her, showing her what he wanted. His knees keeping hers so wide open. Her hips pushing up and back, riding him, slowing the rhythm, teasing him. But oh no, he wasn't having that, thrusting against her hard…again, again…until those little hips of hers started pressing back frantically trying to take more of him. Wild thing writhing in his arms, and then she was climaxing with him all over again, contracting furiously around him, and this time he went with her. Pumping himself hard into her, holding himself fully impaled, spurting into her…and wrenching a roar of voracious satisfaction from his throat. Feral beast himself.

Both of them collapsing into the shavings. Yanked her head roughly to the side so he could take her mouth again without withdrawing. He was buried so deep in her, and oh yeah, he was gonna fuck her again tonight…more than once.

He'd spent well over an hour and a half with her in that empty horse stall. An almost faceless encounter…man, woman—need. Would have stayed longer too, but knew he was already late picking up Brae…didn't really give a shit if his roommate had to wait a little while, but the truth was, he had to get away from her. Just plain liked it too much, and she was dangerous for him…so very dangerous.

He'd made her go home alone at the end of it, then swung into the Mustang, heading for Starbucks himself. Top down, long hair whipping like a flag around his face, but hell, he'd lost the elastic band that held it, and maybe the wind would get some of the shavings out.

Couldn't stop thinking about her though. The little things she'd said that made him ache inside for her...*Hold me. I'm so miserable...*or, how about...*Please just pretend that you cared once upon a time.*

Worst part was, he wanted to believe her. Why was he getting his life so entangled? Darien and Ailynn—married, both of them. Totally unavailable. One he didn't want to fuck, but had...the other he hadn't, but did. Man, how screwed up was that? And he shouldn't be thinking about either of them, that was the real truth of it.

Then there was Chuck Frankel telling him he needed more control in his life—shit yeah, that was painfully obvious, wasn't it?

Drove South Shore to Forest Hill, and made a right.

Darien. He'd just been intimate with Ailynn—really intimate. And repeatedly. So why was Darien invading his thoughts anyway? She was leaving for Christmas and wouldn't be back for almost a week—probably good. Still he was seeing her in his mind as she'd been this morning. Wishing him a happy holiday before she left, and putting her arms around him in a "goodbye for a few days" hug. Purely friendship—but not. And him, returning the hug, but not pulling her up against himself the way he wanted to. Nice professional attitude—but not.

Ailynn stripping her clothes off, total come on...Darien a platonic hug. Man, the whole thing sucked.

Pulled into the Wellington Green Mall, and drove around to section where Starbucks was. What he saw ahead of him made his blood run cold with fury. Three RJ's—two pulling Brae out of Darien's car and the Barista yelping like a fool, and the third, having the *mother fucking nerve* to go after Darien herself, his hands on her arm. Stepped on the gas, pealing tire, lurching forward, then jamming the brake on, making the Mustang squeal sideways to a stop. Vaulted out of the car in one lithe movement. Heading evenly but cocksure toward the scene, and pure menace. Stalking lion, wanting to mix it up.

All three RJ's looking over at him now.

Left fist tightening and coming up, stroking it meaningfully with his other hand—nasty looking weapon, and one he obviously knew how to use. Faint swagger in his step, and oh yeah, he was itching for this. Tossed that mass of hair back over his shoulder with a flick of his head. Murmured to them, "You want a fight, look in this direction, *Gilipollas.*"

"*Marna la pinga, perra,*" the obvious leader of the group, and the one closest to Darien said. Little lisp to his voice…yeah, probably drunk. Fall easy. And he was threatening Darien—he'd be the first target for sure.

Jericho coming closer to him, low meaningful tone of voice, and so confident. "Oh yeah, I'll suck your dick for you. Get over here pussy."

"Please, Jericho, be careful," Darien called out, alarmed. "Just let them have the present if that's what they want, it doesn't matter. It's replaceable."

The head RJ sneered, but he wasn't quite stupid enough to rush Jericho. Was letting him close the distance, wasted some time slinging insults instead. "Hey man, you're all covered with shavings. What were you doing, shoveling horseshit?"

Still advancing, circling slowly, and really close to striking distance. Smirked. "No, that's your job, *joto*. This? I was fucking my bitch in an empty stall. And now I'm gonna bend you over too." He stepped in to him, his cool, composed posture a real slap in the face—he barely even had his arms up high enough to be considered a defensive position. The RJ swung at him, and Jericho ducked to the side, easily clear of it, but at the same time he jabbed once with his left hand, connecting solidly with his target's right cheek bone—snapping his head back.

"Oooh, ouch," Brae murmured.

Second jab from Jericho's left almost immediately on the heels of the first one—this time a little lower, and smashing right into the RJ's jaw. Good punishing blows, both of them, but Jericho was still pulling them a little, not really laying out the kind of damage he was capable of. The RJ was still standing, but he was already wobbling, and it was happening so quickly that his *compañeros* hadn't even had time to react.

More commentary from Brae, "Look out! Timber!" Furious, the Argentinean holding the Barista turned to him, arm cocked back.

"*Haga ni trátelo,*" Jericho snarled before that fist could be launched at his roommate. To punctuate his point, he grabbed the RJ leader by his shoulder and drove a short but really powerful right jab to his mid-section then shoved him backwards, and this time his target did just fold and go down with a loud moan. Still talking to the guy holding Brae. "See if you touch him…if you so much as touch him, you're gonna have me in your face so hard. And I…" Drew it out for effect, and man his voice was a low taunting growl. "…will fucking kill you. *Entiende?*" Beckoned to him,

"Come on, bitch...*come to me.*" Started moving toward both of the other two RJ's, stepping calmly but with deadly intent around the front of the car. Flicked a steely gaze to Starbucks. "Brae, get in the car."

They both came to him at once. One tried to grab his arms and pin them to his body so his buddy could pummel him at the same time without having to defend against those destructive blows he laid out. But Jericho broke that hold, and jammed his elbow down the throat of the one who'd tried to pin him. Took a fist to the gut, and ducked one to the head, but it didn't seem to faze him or put him off-balance, as he retaliated with a brutal left-right combination, sending his other opponent slamming back and over the hood of the car.

"Oh man," Starbucks whispered in awe to Darien as he scurried back into the Audi.

Jericho grabbed the RJ up from off the car and spun him around to crash him into his *amigo* like a human battering ram. And Jericho's fist came right along behind the man's body, smashing into the second Argentinean in a deadly package deal—nice clean right hook to the jaw, reeling the man over and to the ground in a heap. The polo groom he had in his grip took the opportunity to launch a few hard body jabs and to shove back at him, wrapping one hand in Jericho's long hair to try and yank him off his feet—and then thrusting Jericho hard into the front grill of Darien's car. But this *gringo* came right back at him, using the heel of his foot against the car's bumper to launch himself onto him, knocking both of them to the ground, Jericho on top...his full weight coming down on the other man, knee pressed viciously into his stomach. Scream from the RJ, and his hands fell away. Jericho grabbed hold of his shirt, scrambled to his feet and jerked the man back upright, then sucker punched him hard in the area of his kidney, wrenching a second agonized cry from him. Still holding him too—ready to finish him off.

Sirens. Lights. Patrol car swinging into the parking lot, and a second one arriving from the other direction. Doors jerking open wide, cops crouched behind them in a heartbeat. Weapons out and pointed.

"They must have called from inside the store," Starbucks guessed. "Man, I hope they don't book Jericho."

"They can't!" Darien cried, and made to get out of the car, but Brae had grabbed her forcefully. "No, wait...those cops have guns. Let it settle down first," he told her. At least he knew that much.

Coming over the first patrol car's loudspeaker: "Police! Break it up! Hands in the air!"

Jericho pushed the guy he was holding backwards and away from himself, ducking out from one last swing from him. Raised his hands to just above his head as ordered, backed away himself, separating himself from any of the three of them. Laced his hands behind his head and just waited—he knew this routine alright.

None of the RJ's was resisting arrest either—of course two of them were down, and the third clutching his side and moaning.

Cops swarmed over the scene. Uniform coming up behind Jericho with a sharp command, "Don't move." Then a sneering, "Haven't I arrested you for this before, asshole?"

Resentful. "Yeah, I've been arrested before. But this time I…"

Unsympathetic and sharply snapped command. "Save it for the station."

The uniform grabbed hold of his right wrist and brought it down and around to the small of his back—slapped a steel bracelet around it good and tight. Took his left wrist and did the same with it. Hand hard between his shoulder blades, "Bend over, legs apart." The uniform kicked at his heels, spreading his feet the way he wanted them. He was putting Jericho over the hood of Darien's car to search him—fucking hated that, but didn't fight it.

Darien was out of the car now. Brae hadn't been able to hold her any longer—not when she could clearly see that Jericho was being arrested. "Please, Officer," she cried. "Don't arrest him, he was protecting us. These men surrounded our car—they wanted to steal from us, and they threatened to hurt my friend over there too. Jericho was protecting us," she repeated fervently.

"Ma'am, we can take your statement and sort this all out down at the station. But my friend here…" He yanked Jericho back upright again. Snarl from his captive, but nothing more. "…has a record of disturbing the peace, so he's going in until I'm convinced otherwise."

Cold and controlled voice from Jericho. "Darien, go home. I don't want you going to the stationhouse. Brae can take my car and come over to give a statement. You don't need to be there and you don't need to be involved."

"Shut up." The uniform gave him a shove toward one of the patrol cars. "Get in the car."

"Brae, you heard me," Jericho ordered over his shoulder. Uniform put a hand on his head and ducked him down and into the back seat. Closed the door, locking him inside.

Jericho laid his head back against the leather upholstery, and closed his eyes, muttering angrily to himself...and thinking about Frankel. Wondering what would happen now.

————————

They'd put him in one cell and the three RJ's in another. He could hear them talking spitefully in Spanish—oh and they knew he understood enough Spanish to hear what they were saying—figured most of it was for his benefit. How they were going to find him and come after him...yeah, like he cared about that. He was pretty damn tempted to answer them too, but didn't. Instead he just paced the cell—anxious, wanting out of there. Didn't seem to be happening though.

He could hear Brae's voice in the next room over from time to time. Wasn't particularly comfortable with it either—who knew what Starbucks was likely to come up with? He could be saying damn near anything. Enthusiastically describing how his roommate had kicked ass. Shit.

Paced some more.

His left hand was good and bruised, the knuckles swollen and even scraped—the right not quite so bad, but also bruised. But that was just indicative of the way he fought...mainly throwing that jabbing left, but when the right lashed out, look out. It was the knock out blow. Those RJ's had to have some really bashed in faces to show for the encounter with him if his hands looked and felt like this. Good for them—served them right, the bastards. But he needed to get his hands in ice and soon if he planned to ride tomorrow. Cops didn't seem to give a damn though—they weren't even coming around, weren't even giving him a hint of what was going on.

Paced to the wall, then back to the bars at the front of his cell. The wall. The bars. The wall.

Turned...and there was Chuck Frankel just standing outside his cell, staring in at him. And man the Chef D'Equip's face looked unforgiving. Jericho paused where he was, let his eyes drop away. Could he look more like a felon than he did right now? Filthy from lying the in the shavings with Ailynn, from fighting and grappling on the ground. Hair down and wild, hands a mess—evidence of the violent kind of action he'd just been through. He blew his breath out. Oh yeah, he looked like a felon alright, but there wasn't a repentant bone in his body. "What was I supposed to do?" he ground out. "Not protect Darien Marx? Fuck me, Chuck...you tell me."

No response at first. Then, "Darien called me. In tears. Says you sent her home."

Lashed back. "Hell yes I did. Should I let her sit down here at the station—maybe wind up with these assholes stalking her cause they think she screwed them? Shit, there're already down there in that other cell talking about how they're gonna fuck me over for good." Murmured in a low dangerous way, "Oh yeah, I'll fight them again...I'll have to. Probably more than just three of them next time out. What do you want me to do when that happens, Chuck? Lay down and let them kick the shit out of me?"

"See you're making me dream that Aachen nightmare again," Frankel sneered. "You think the other teams won't know what your weakness is? Hell, they'll make sure you meet a few assholes in a local bar. It's a waste of my time to teach you, Jericho. Yeah—you have the talent, more than I thought to be perfectly honest. You're a gifted rider. But the Team?" His voice was scathing. "You don't belong on it."

Man that punch hurt a lot more than anything those RJ's had lobbed at him. Ripped him up inside. Chuck was dropping him over this—he didn't have to say the actual words...he'd said it loud and clear without even going there. Jericho turned away from him, just breathed, absorbing that loss. But mother fuck, that guy had his *hands* on Darien. Was he supposed to have allowed that? What? Just sat in his car and dialed 911 and hoped for the best? God damn it. *What?* He spun back around to demand an answer to that...

But Chuck was gone.

Oh man. Jericho walked to the back wall, laid his forearms against it at a height just above his shoulders, then dropped his forehead against them.

Was there anything left in his life that hadn't gone to hell?

Chapter Thirteen

It was the next day, Christmas Eve morning. Early. Jericho was pushing a broom down the aisle way with a vengeance, his mood dark. He looked up and saw Frankel entering the barn, a young woman in tow, and now that was interesting—both the fact that Frankel was here, and the chick. She couldn't be much more than eighteen years old...fresh pretty face, blonde ponytail, buff pair of breeches, white polo shirt, gym shoes on her feet. So who the hell was this, he wondered? But it was still the Chef D'Equip that had his attention. Jericho stopped what he was doing and leaned on the end of the broom handle, laid an ice-cold, deep blue stare on his coach—or more accurately, former coach. Waited. Or maybe laid in wait.

Frankel walked up to him, equally cold. "Christ Jericho," he muttered sternly and with a pretty good dose of disgust as well. "You don't even look like you went home."

Got an even more caustic answer launched back at him. "Well, Chuck, ever think that's because I haven't?" Yeah, he was still wearing the same dirty clothes as yesterday, dirtier now and sweaty—hair still loose and disheveled, unshaven and some pretty obvious beard growth, left hand bandaged—sporting an ice pack, surrounded by tape. A little bit of surprise registering on the Chef D'Equip's face. "Yeah, that's right," Jericho continued harshly. "I didn't get out of there until six this morning, and then Marco comes to pick me up and tells me the guys got trashed at his place last night and none of them's coming in. So I came over to help him."

"So you haven't been home and you haven't slept." Statement, not a question.

"That's right." Defiant and pissed as hell. "They kept me there for damn near seven fucking hours...if you can believe that."

"Kept you where?" The girl speaking up.

His face turned and his eyes swept over her. Still didn't know who she was, and didn't want to answer her. He paused, got a resigned look—was clearly not the least bit happy about giving this up, but finally he did. "Jail," he said. "I was arrested last night. Fucking bullshit charge and that's the truth." He lifted an eloquent and judgmental glare back to Frankel. "They dropped it by the way—after they got done jerking me around."

"Did they now?"

Resentful. "*Yes.*" As if to say…you're the only one who doesn't seem to know how bogus that was.

"Well," Frankel said dismissively, "I gather you're not riding today."

Snapped back at him, "Hell yes, I'm riding. I just haven't gotten that far yet."

It didn't seem like Chuck believed him—or more like he thought maybe he'd just decided that now, or was only saying for his benefit. Totally skeptical. "It just doesn't look like you're riding. Normally you're on a horse by now."

Jericho sighed, and shook his head. Chuck was busting him here, like always—didn't know how to read it either. Why would he care anyway, and what was he saying—that he hadn't dropped him from his schedule after all? It was important enough to him that he tried to clarify it. "Yeah, normally, but I don't normally clean water buckets or muck out stalls. It's not like I thought you'd be here anyway…not after what you said last night."

Shrugged, wasn't acknowledging it. "Well, are you going to ride, or not ride?"

"Ride."

"Get QL then."

God, he couldn't describe the relief he felt. Bellowed over his shoulder, "Marco…QL!" Then to Frankel, sounding more tentative than usual—like asking for latitude, "Just give me ten minutes and I'll be ready with her."

Chuck nodded, looked pleased. Asked, "Which stalls are Maximus and Rebel in? While we're waiting, I want to show them to Brittany here."

That got Jericho's interest in a heartbeat. "This is my working student?"

Another nod of assent.

Jericho held out the broom handle to her. "Finish the aisle then, and don't do a bullshit job either…it's something I'm fanatical about. And Christ, I don't know why you're making a face, Chuck…hell, I was doing it."

Frankel thought for a second, shrugged, conceded the point, and Brittany took the broom from him, getting right down to work with it. Now that he liked. "When you're done, come in the tack room, you can help me," Jericho told her, then turned and walked away from them.

Flurry of activity for the next ten minutes.

Jericho strode into the tack room and exchanged meaningful glances with Marco as his head groom got out QL's tack. He'd told Marco about what happened with the Chef D'Equip last night—had to really—and knew he shared his own excitement that Chuck was here and apparently still working with him.

As Marco walked past him, Jericho stopped him and searched through the grooming box, grabbing the brush that they used on the horses' tails. He began dragging it through his own long chestnut mane, yanking to get the knots out, but wasn't making much headway...it was good and snarled and on top of that, was really tough going with his hands in the condition they were in.

Brittany entered the tack room, saw him struggling with it. She came straight over to him. "Here, I'll do it."

No argument. He dropped down on one knee to make it easier for her. She started at the bottom, just like she would brushing out a tail. "God, your hair's so thick and it's got shavings all through it," she scolded lightly.

He murmured angrily to himself—thought of Ailynn, and what had happened in that empty stall. Spoke angrily. "Just rip the knots out if you have to."

"No, I'll get it." She tsked to herself, but worked that much faster. "There, this is better. See, I'm getting them out."

"Can you braid it for me?" he asked her when she'd finished. "And make it good and tight, alright?"

"Sure."

While she worked on his hair, he jerked at the bandage Marco had put in place around the knuckles of his left hand, and when that wasn't successful, brought it up to his mouth and ripped at it with his teeth.

"Stop that." It was Marco. He'd finished saddling up QL already and was back in the tack room. He came over and knelt down next to Jericho. Pulled out a small knife and cut the old bandage off. Removed the icepack.

"Oh, wow," Brittany said. The hand looked awful. She stopped what she was doing for a second to run a finger over the back of it. "Is it broken?"

"No…maybe…who gives a fuck? It's not like there's anything they can do for it, even if it is—just tape it up like Marco's doing. Goddamn cops. What fuckers," Jericho muttered coldly. "Swear to God, they just let me sit there…wouldn't give me anything to put on it either…forgot, or so they said. Convenient, right? Guess they figured if I'm using my fists, I should feel it the next day."

"Yeah, you're pretty bruised, but think about it this way…imagine the other guys' faces." Marco laughed wickedly—it was pretty clear he took a lot of pride in his boss, and didn't have a problem with the fact that he liked to mix it up. "They have to look like they ran into a Mack truck," he giggled. He had a roll of Vetwrap with him—a self-adhesive bandage that they used all the time with the horses—and began methodically re-taping the injured hand.

"Make it good and snug, Marco."

The head groom did, pushing up from the underside with one hand, and making a figure eight over the knuckles and around Jericho's thumb—ignoring his murmured curse of pain. "Suck it up, boss. When you put your gloves on, I'll tape around the outside again."

Nod of assent from him.

Brittany was still working on the braid. When she got to the bottom of Jericho's long mane, she simply pulled free the elastic band that held her own ponytail in place, and wrapped it around the end. Alright, it was bright red and had a few spangles on it, but who cared as long as it stayed in place?

Looked around at her and nodded in approval. "Thanks," he said, and then rose, yanked his filthy tee shirt off over his head. He could see that Brittany was taking a good hard look at him, maybe staring at the tribal symbol he had tattooed low down at his mid-back. If she was, he didn't give a shit—hell, if she was going to work here, she'd have to get used to him stripping down like this…like this and way more too…cause he didn't have time in his day to worry about it.

Marco tossing him a clean polo shirt. He pulled it on, stripped his jeans open and stuffed the shirttails in, then zipped them up and redid his belt.

One thing he would say about this new working student though—he liked the way she'd just pitched in, and no prima dona attitude either, even though she was here at Frankel's recommendation. That said a lot. Team player. And since she was helping him, he'd do something for her too—it wasn't hard to figure out what she'd consider a reward from him.

"Marco…here's the schedule…" He grabbed his boots, unzipped them, shoved his feet into them, flattened his jeans against his lower legs and then zipped them up again. Then picked out a set of spurs and strapped them on. "QL, Monterrey. Then Maximus. And then Rebel and Roué at the same time."

"Gotcha, boss."

"I'm *riding*?" Brittany nearly yelped with excitement.

Smile, deep blue eyes on her. "Yeah, if you have boots you are."

"Out in the car."

"Get them."

"Oh, and boss…" Marco went on, warning Jericho in advance. "Chuck had me take the stirrups off QL's saddle."

"Oh hell fucking yes, of course he did," Jericho growled. He shoved his hands in his riding gloves, and Marco finished the taping job. "Bastard knows I haven't slept…wants to make it hard for me—little punishment from him. Well, fuck him…it's not like I give a crap."

Marco handed him his riding crop, and he strode out of the tack room. By the time the other two had followed him, he was already gathering QL's reins and vaulting onto her. Leg pressure sending her forward and onto the bit, prancing underneath him, and ready to work. Walked her out of the barn, then an almost imperceptible cue from his leg and she moved into the canter, heading down to the jumping field.

"Wow, pretty intense," Brittany said, staring after him.

"Oh no," Marco reassured her, but with a telling smirk. "This is nothing. He's tired today…usually he's a lot more of an asshole than that."

———————

Frankel had decided they'd work in the grass field rather than the sand arena today. There had been a light rain that morning, and the grass was still wet—a bit slippery too.

Nice argument going on between Frankel and Jericho. He'd ridden QL over and stopped next to him. "Chuck, she's not used to this surface, I wasn't going to start working her out here till next week. But okay, this is fine. Just raise the fences a little."

185

"Well, if you're so worried that she's not used to the surface, I should lower them."

Sarcastic. "You only say that because you don't understand her, okay?"

Hot answer coming back at him. "I think I've seen a fair number of horses in my day, Jericho."

Deep blue stare falling away, snarling frown on his lips.

"Uh-oh," Marco whispered to Brittany. "Watch out now. When he looks like that, it means he's really, really pissed."

She smiled at him—a conspirator's look, already making friends with him. "Then what happens?"

Marco didn't have to say a word, he just pointed. Jericho lifted his face vengefully back to Frankel. "Just mother fuck me, Chuck," he sneered. The Chef D'Equip looked furious, but Jericho just talked right over anything he might have said. "I'll tell you what…maybe we should change places and you can get up here and ride this mare since you know so much. Hell, do you have any respect at all for my ability as a trainer?" He went on and explained his reasoning. "She pays a lot more attention to a larger obstacle, and it needs to look good and solid till she gets used to being out here, okay?" Spun the mare away from him. "Just do what you damn well want to, you will anyway…hell, I'll deal with it."

"Jericho!" Frankel called out sharply. Waited until he'd turned QL around to face him again. Spoke coldly, biting out each word. "As a matter of fact, I have huge respect for you as a trainer." Looked over his shoulder and yelled out, "Marco! Help me with this line. Do you know how he wants them?"

"Sure, Chuck." The head groom was already trotting out, big smile on his face…and Brittany in his wake.

Jericho just sitting there, amazed.

Frankel walked up to him, laid a hand on his thigh. "Alright?"

Nodded. Pretty damn satisfied too. "Alright."

They went to work.

Brittany and Marco sat together for the next half hour…and she got a good chance to watch this guy that she'd be working for. "Wow, can he ride!" she told the head groom.

Nod from him, and the pointed response, "Oh yeah."

"You've been with him for a long time. Is he hard to work for?" she asked.

"You can say that again. But always fair," Marco pronounced. "Perfectionist though…wants everything just so."

"Give good lessons?"

"The best…but judge for yourself."

As they were talking a horse van came rolling down the driveway. Jericho pulled up, and then stood up in the saddle to get a better look. "Now who the hell can that be?" he muttered.

Marco had already jumped up and started over to meet whoever was pulling in.

"Marco, go ahead and take him off," Frankel was calling.

"What's going on, Chuck?" Jericho asked.

Superior smile from the Chef D'Equip. "Well, just hold your horses a minute and you're going to see."

But he wasn't willing to wait…he started trotting QL over to get a closer look. So Chuck had sent this horse to him, that much was obvious. And it had him curious—curious as all hell.

They lowered the ramp, and then Marco and the driver started off-loading the horse inside, backing him out. Gray. Huge round hindquarters visible first…and Jericho saw something else. Nice set of testicles on him. This was a stallion—not a gelding—and Jesus, did he look powerful.

A few more seconds, and the animal was standing in the driveway, the van driver holding him. Gorgeous creature. Over seventeen hands, steel gray with black points. Fine, noble head, delicate little ears pricked forward, "look of eagles" in his eyes. Snorting at the new surroundings, quick on his feet, skittering around in a tight circle at the end of his lead. And proud, too…already thought he owned the place.

Jericho vaulted off QL. "Marco, come and take her."

Frankel, thus far not saying a word.

"Selle Francais?" Jericho asked him, inquiring after the horse's breeding.

Just a nod in answer. Chuck seemed mesmerized with the stallion, he hadn't taken his eyes off him.

Marco took hold of QL, and Jericho went over to examine the newcomer. He laid a hand on him, and the big boy accepted that with little more than just a quick dance of those agile feet of his. Ran his fingers over the stallion's chest and down his front legs, then the hind ones. Turned, and looked sharply back at Frankel. "This is Chasseur de Lion, isn't it?" he asked.

The Chef D'Equip coming up to join him. "I've been calling him Lion as his barn name, but change it if you want to."

Even sharper deep blue stare. "Do you own him now, Chuck?"

Nod. "With a partner."

Christ, he hoped it wasn't Marx. Snarl. "Not *my* patron, I hope."

Frankel laughed. "No, not this time. Someone else—silent partner though, doesn't want his name known."

Accepted that answer just like that, no questions. "Is he back to jumping?"

"No."

He turned to the stallion once again—man, he just couldn't help himself, although he was wary about this whole thing too. This was a horse with a bizarre history—Jericho, like everyone in the industry, knew at least part of it. Chasseur de Lion, or Lion, as Chuck as was calling him, had set the jumping world on fire a few years ago. Big time horse and still a youngster. Olympic quality, and a part of the Belgian Jumping Team. Really, really bold competitor. And then one day he just quit…refused to jump…refused to go over even a simple cross rail twelve inches off the ground. Just planted those feet and ground to a halt in front of a fence— didn't matter how hard you whipped him—in fact, after a while, rumor was he'd become pretty damn dangerous, preferring to rear or buck rather than jump. Since then, he'd gone through any number of different trainers, all of them hoping to get him back in the ring. None had. And he'd also gone from a million-dollar-plus horse, to nothing more than a breeding stallion, worth fifty thousand or less.

"So what are you doing with him, Chuck?" Meaningful look. "And what am I doing with him?"

"Riding him."

"*Bullshit.*" Jericho was vehement.

Frankel shrugged. "You haven't even tried him yet."

Looked really annoyed. "For God's sake, Chuck…now I understand why you tossed me that compliment earlier. That was just you stroking me to get me to get me to work with this albatross. Why in the world would you invest in him?" Really demanding and accusing. "How many other trainers have you had him with? Oh, fuck it—don't even bother to tell me. I'm your last hope, and I was probably the last one you wanted him with too—tell me *that's* not true."

Cold look from the Chef D'Equip. "You just love to spout off don't you, tough guy?" Seemed like he really wanted to dress him down on this. "You know, it's time you try and trust me, Jericho." Lifted a finger and poked him hard in the chest with it. "You want the truth? Matter of fact, I bought him four days ago…and I bought him because you impressed me. I want to try and put him under you. Satisfied?" Paused like he was going to stop there, but then added. "What? Not even curious to throw a leg over him?"

Christ, that little speech took him back a bit…and down a peg too. *If it was true*. Actually, he thought it was though. "Let me get this straight…you bought this horse for *me* to ride?" Couldn't hardly believe it.

"That's right…or more accurately, I talked someone else into buying him. Someone I've been talking about you to. Someone with deep pockets—who'll send the horse to Europe to compete. He'll bankroll it too, no problem…*if* you get him going again. Whatever we want."

"Who gets the bill?"

"I do. Don't worry, you'll get paid."

Deep blue stare on Frankel—thinking about it hard. This horse would be hell to work with and maybe a total waste of his time, no doubt about that. Huge jumping talent in him, no doubt on that score either. But more importantly, this was a…hell, damn near unbelievable show of support from Chuck. Actually, why was he even hesitating? It wasn't a question. Jericho knew he was going to accept this—he was going to try anyway—if for no other reason, to show Chuck his faith hadn't been misplaced.

"Marco," he ordered evenly. "Take QL up to the barn. Then this is what I need. Bring me the bitting rig, a snaffle bridle, jumping boots and bell boots for in front, ankle boots behind, lunge line and lunge whip."

Marco looked pleased for him. He sensed the dynamics and knew they were good. "Yes, boss."

Still talking to his head groom with quiet authority, but looking at Frankel, not at him. "After you untack QL, bring me her saddle…*with* stirrups on it," he added a bit witheringly. His eyes meaningfully on Frankel as he added. "Alright, Chuck. I'll take a look at him."

189

Marco took QL away, and then brought the gear Jericho asked for. He had the saddle with him too, and simply laid it over a cross rail. Then he disappeared again to take care of the big mule-eared mare.

Jericho tacked Lion up, with Brittany working as his assistant—handing him what he wanted as he asked for it.

"How long has it been since he worked?" he asked Frankel. "Looks out of shape. I'm guessing a while—six months or more."

"You're right, they've just been breeding him."

Stroked his neck. "Been living the high life, boy?" he murmured to him. The stallion responding, reaching around curiously to sniff at him. So far, he seemed mannerly enough to work around. But there was quite a bit more reaction when Jericho laid the bitting rig on his back—ears flattening unhappily, tail swishing, good hard stomp with a front foot. Sharp growl to him, "Just stand there." But Jericho was taking his time too, buckling the surcingle around Lion's body just behind the withers—moving slowly so as not to startle him, and not tightening it up just yet. Slid the tail crupper into place—more negative reaction from him. Petted him, talked to him in a low voice. After a minute or so the stallion settled, and Jericho tightened the surcingle one notch.

Wham! One hind leg lashed out wickedly—but into thin air, since Jericho had been standing well clear of it.

"Enough!" He jerked down hard on the lead shank.

Wham! That same hind leg, kicking out again…this time the hindquarters coming partially around, trying to find him.

"Brittany," Jericho said calmly. "Go up to the barn and ask Marco to give you the long dressage whip. Right away," he added needlessly, since she went sprinting off to get it—not wanting to miss out on any more of this than she had to. But that didn't happen, since he was still waiting in essentially the same spot when she returned, just hand-walking the stallion on a 15 meter circle and talking to him—strange, how he could be so intense in some situations, yet so cool and patient with the horses. She handed the whip to him.

He brought Lion back to a halt, gave him a pat on the neck, and then went back alongside him to tighten the cinch again. Left hand on the buckles, right hand holding the whip. As soon as the stallion felt the slightest pressure, that treacherous hind leg came up a few inches. Jericho tapped him on the rump, just once and not that hard, slipping the cinch up tighter at the same time. Instead of snapping back, the leg jerked forward and to the ground. "Good," he said. Tightened the second buckle, using the same process.

"Nice," Frankel said, not a hint of his normal sarcasm. "I liked that. You didn't make it a big deal."

Shrugged. "It didn't need to be." He slipped the bridle on the horse's head and adjusted it, and then snapped the side reins from the surcingle to the bit. Lion tugged at them a little, and swished his tail, but not much else.

Attached the lunge line. "Lunge whip," he said to Brittany—trading the Dressage whip for the much longer lunge whip. "Just set that down over there, and then come over here inside the circle with me."

Excited look in her eyes.

Jericho shook the lunge whip low to the ground and just behind the stallion, sending him out at a walk on a circle, with himself at the center of it. The line attached to the horse's bridle and held by his new trainer, defined the size of the circle's radius. Jericho also walked a circle as the horse moved around him, although considerably smaller, maybe two to three feet in diameter. Brittany waited till the horse went past her, and then ducked in behind him, staying right behind Jericho where she couldn't get tangled or interfere.

Snap of the whip, and Lion was trotting—tugging at the side reins, and not looking happy about it, but not resisting in any major way. For a minute or so, Jericho just observed him. "Alright," he said to Brittany…low compelling voice, touched with a faint trace of humor. "Tell me what you see…besides a horse going around in a circle."

Put on the spot. She took a second, then responded. "Great trot, naturally underneath himself. But really out of shape, especially his back."

"All true," he commented. Flicked the whip once so that it cracked, sending Lion forward a bit faster. Looked back at her. "Is he sound?"

She watched his footfalls—basically they seemed even. Not favoring any particular leg. "Yes."

"No," Jericho corrected her. He raised his voice. "Chuck, this horse is footsore."

"Think so?"

"Know so. Both front feet." And to Brittany. "Yeah, his footsteps are even, and that's what you were watching wasn't it?"

She nodded, then spoke up realizing he couldn't see her. "You're right, but what do you see?"

"Watch the way he tries to get his weight off them." He let her look at it for a little bit longer—knew she probably couldn't see it yet, but if he could fix whatever this problem was, then she'd see the difference, and maybe next time be able to tell it for herself. He lowered the whip, called, "Whoa," and brought the big animal to a halt. Jericho approached him. Ran his fingers down the horse's spine, and Lion winced. Pushed along the top of the pelvis, and got a very angry shake of the stallion's head. Looked over the top of Lion's back, seeking out Frankel again. "This is my quick call, alright?"

The Chef D'Equip looked annoyed. "So in two minutes you've figured out what the rest of the world couldn't for the last two years?"

Shook his head and cursed. "Did I fuckin' say that, Chuck? These are just my general soundness observations—want to hear them or not?"

A bit of a standoff. Then finally, "Yeah, I want to hear them."

Smirk coming back at him. "Well, thank you. What I see is he's using his hind end to carry his weight…keeping it off the forehand, but there's not enough muscle development over his back, so he's strained his pelvis doing it. Fix the feet, spend some time building him up, and the back problems may fix themselves. Anyway, I'd probably inject him…coffin bones, hocks, stifles and maybe pelvis too. And we probably need x-rays of his feet—all around."

Frankel thought about it, then nodded curtly. "Okay."

Gratified nod from Jericho. Then he moved back to the center of the circle, and returned to lunging the horse. Walk, trot and canter in each direction—trot/canter transitions, walk/trot transitions. Not a long workout—fifteen minutes or so at the most. At the end of it he halted the horse, and removed the bitting rig…then laid the saddle on his back instead. Same routine with the whip repeated as he tightened the girth. Pulled his stirrup down on one side, while Brittany did the other. "Stand clear," he told her. Then he put his foot in the stirrup and mounted the horse.

Explosion!

Chasseur de Lion felt the rider's weight coming down on him, and launched himself into a monster leap through the air—like he thought he could fly and was taking off, demons right behind him. Jericho wasn't even seated yet—still had his weight basically on the horse's near side, leg just swinging over, no balance. He grabbed hold of the mane and tried to manhandle himself into place. Lion, twisting in the air, touchdown and straight into a series of hard bucks.

Jericho had lost both stirrups—actually, he'd had only had one of them to begin with, but at least he had hours of work without stirrups to fall back on. Damn close to coming off, but he sure as shit wasn't going to give in and roll. He muscled the stallion's head up, clamped his legs onto the side of him, sat in once but then came up into two point, sending the horse forward like a thoroughbred breaking from the gate. Flat out gallop, legs scrabbling everywhere, but he was riding him now, not just hanging on for dear life. Gave him his head and pushed him—yeah, he was running away, but he'd been out of work and would tire quickly, Jericho knew. He sat cool on him, didn't try to stop him—didn't try to do anything except make sure he stayed inside the sand arena. It wasn't that long before that all out gallop slowed to a canter. Jericho controlling him now, pushing him forward.

"Ask him to lift his back up," Frankel called out to him.

Asked, and the stallion responding, but not getting much. Damn, his back was so tight, that was why. Flying change, and canter in the other direction, then eventually down to the posting trot. Lion cooperating now, and pretty quickly exhausted.

He kept him working maybe ten minutes longer, then pulled to a walk by Brittany and Chuck. Then a halt. He didn't even comment on the explosive beginning to the ride, but went straight to his evaluation instead. "I felt the exact same thing under saddle that I saw on the lunge line," he told the Chef D'Equip.

"Yeah, I could see it too."

"I don't know what other problems he might have, but until we fix those front feet we'll never know."

"Woo-hoo!" The cheer came from the sidelines. Jericho looked up and saw Starbucks strolling over from the gazebo, hands up around chest height and clapping like mad. "Oh, fuck me Jericho," he called out happily. "That was great!" He had his camera banging against his upper torso, hanging from a strap around his neck. "Hey, I got some great shots too."

Brittany was openly staring at Brae in all his disheveled glory. Grungy-looking pair of khakis, long sloppy tee shirt, sandals on his feet. And it was pretty clear that he was looking at her too.

"Damn, I really thought you were coming off," Frankel said to Jericho, but talking low enough that only he could hear.

Deep blue stare on him, telling little half-smile. "You? Hell Chuck, I thought so too for a second there." There was something happening today

193

in the relationship between them, though neither one was mentioning or acknowledging it. Still they both recognized the subtle difference—and considering where he'd been with Chuck last night, Jericho found it pretty damn rewarding too.

Starbucks had meanwhile come over to Brittany. "Hey, so you finally got out of jail," he yelled to his roommate, but not taking his eyes off her. Making it clear that he was interested.

She looked momentarily embarrassed. "Did you know your fly's open?" she whispered quietly—hard to miss considering he was wearing bright orange boxers beneath the light-colored khakis.

"Oh yeah, its broken," he explained unconcerned. He pulled the hem of his tee shirt down a bit, but as soon as he let go, it rode back up—bright orange visible once again. "It's a quick release strategy, you know…express delivery." Goofy grin. Held his hand out. "Hi, I'm Brae…Jericho's room-mate."

She giggled, took his hand in her own. "Brittany. Brittany Lange."

He'd dismounted by now, and was walking with the horse in the direction of the barn. Frankel was right at his side.

Jericho mapped out what he had in mind in the short term. "So Chuck, I want to do a complete work-up on him, and it won't be cheap. X-rays all around…nuclear scintigraphy on his neck, back and pelvis. Injections like I said before. And shit, he'll have to go into the clinic for the scintigraphy anyway, so while we're at it, lets scope him for ulcers too." He looked down, but added rather forcefully, "And I'm not riding him for you till I get a chance to work with him. That's fair, Chuck…give me some time on my own. He's not ready for coaching sessions, and I don't want you breathing down my neck over him."

Frankel's eyes narrowed militantly, but in the end he nodded brusquely. "Agreed. But tell me this, Jericho. How soon are you going to show him a fence? I want to be here for that." He muttered something under his breath. "Just to watch, okay? Not coach. That's fair too."

"Yeah, it's fair. Tomorrow. I'll do him before QL."

"Well, I don't think so," the Chef D'Equip laughed, then corrected him with a touch of his normal condescension back in place. "Tomorrow is *Christmas*, Jericho."

Smile. "Yeah so? Does that mean we don't ride? Horses don't give a shit. Me either."

Brae was walking into the barn now too, sauntering along beside Brittany with long slow strides. They caught up with Jericho and Frankel right at the entrance to the main aisle way.

Jericho was already giving a new set of instructions to Marco. "You'll have to shuffle the horses—stallion's got to be in the end stall," he was saying. "So put Lion in Monterrey's stall…Monterrey in Maximus' and Maximus next to QL."

"Gotcha." Marco led the stallion away to untack and bath him.

Brae came over and clapped Jericho on the shoulder. "Hey dude, didn't get a chance to thank you for last night. Man did you kick ass." He looked over at Frankel and told him wickedly, "I'm telling you, I've never seen anyone more deadly than Jericho here. I mean to tell you, those RJ's fell like stones."

Cold stare from Frankel.

Christ, Jericho thought, sometimes his roommate had the common sense of a pet rock. To change the subject, he asked him, "Did you bring my car?"

"Sure." He went blithely on, still happily driving his roommate nuts. "Hey, what the fuck, Jericho? You've got a chick hair thingy here. Little sparkles in it and everything." He flipped the end of Jericho's braid—got a growl back from him.

"It's mine," Brittany spoke up, chuckling and staring shyly at him—entranced. "It's all we had."

That answer got a giggle from the Barista. "Looks really macho, man. Oh hey, want to see what I did this morning? It's a Christmas present to myself." He turned around to reveal a brand spanking new tattoo at his middle back—a Superman "S"—pretty much exactly where his roommate had his.

Jericho took one look at it, and dark humor lit up the depths of his eyes. He lifted one slashing brow and murmured sarcastically, "Now why the hell would you have that tattooed there?"

"It's pretty cool, right?"

Single bark of amusement—didn't mind busting him back either. The kid sure did it enough to him. "Well, tell me this, Brae…who do you think's gonna look at it back there? I mean, why wouldn't you put it on the front where it belongs?"

"Huh? It's in the same place yours is," he objected.

"Yeah, but mine doesn't mean anything, it just looks good. I'm saying, why would you put a superman symbol right above your ass? Answer that one. Hey, maybe if you were gay…" At Starbuck's look of pure dismay, he threw his head back and laughed out loud. "See now you understand me. Christ, and the mother fucking thing is permanent."

Chapter Fourteen

Jericho brought Monterrey down to the field and they went back to work. After QL, who was talented but tough, and Lion, who was talented but…crippled, maybe psycho too…riding Monterrey was like a present. The big bay tried so hard, he loved his work, and he had power steering and an air-ride suspension. Even after thirty minutes, Frankel was even having difficulty finding things to grumble about.

"I sure can't wait to see this horse go back in the ring," he commented.

Resentment welled up inside of him, and crept back into Jericho's tone. "Yeah, well if his rider hadn't been suspended for being such a dishonest, mother-fucking asshole…"

"Planning on whining about that one forever, Jericho?"

The two of them glaring at each other—Jericho atop Monterrey, Frankel standing next to him on the ground. They were pretty much back at the same place they'd been the night before, the bond they'd been forming earlier in the morning already forgotten.

"Maybe." Cold look, cold tone. "It just grates at me, Chuck, that's all. You know, you…" Dropped it there, and just muttered, "Fuck," to himself.

Frankel pushing it though. "I what?"

"You can't imagine, that's what." And maybe he really did want to say this after all, cause man, he just launched into it. "I'm down here in Florida, and a full third of the season goes by…but I'm not out there, I'm not competing. Everyone else is though. Getting qualified, getting ranked. Hell, I'm not the only one capable of riding a clean round, am I, Chuck? Even when the suspension period's over, think of the pressure trying to catch up." He added acidly, *"And for what?"*

"It is what it is," And he held his hand up. "No, don't interrupt me—I heard you out, now you hear me. Damn right, a sixty-day suspension is a tough penalty, and it puts you behind. Anchor rider on the Team is faced with coming from behind all the time. So deal with it."

"Yeah, deal with it," he snapped back, wheeled his horse around. "Let's work."

But before he could get away, Frankel grabbed a hold of his reins and stopped the horse. "You know what, I figure you for a pressure player...yeah, while you're sitting here on the sidelines it's making you chafe, but in my personal opinion—and granted, it's just an opinion—when you hit that show ring, you're gonna blow some people away. You *will* qualify."

Not buying it. "Will I? How many CSI-W's do you think there are? Everyone else gets eight or nine shows to make it, but I get four or five. Eight faults is only two rails down, more than that and you don't qualify. All I need is to have a bad day here and there—or the horse have a bad day—and I'm out of it."

"Yeah that's right, better learn to deal," Frankel growled, releasing Monterrey's reins with the harsh order, "Take that line again, bring him in a little slower this time." But he couldn't quite leave it there. "And think about this while you're at it...how the hell are you going to ride for me on the Team with that attitude of yours?"

"I ride for you now, Chuck, can it get any worse?"

He cantered off.

Jericho spent the entire day Christmas riding. He'd given Brittany the day off, but she showed up too, and all the guys were back and working. Everything running like clockwork once again.

He was pretty sure Brittany and Starbucks had gone out together—well, his roommate had hung around for several hours amusing her, and then she had that dreamy look in her eyes this morning. Jericho planned to erase it though—just wait till he got her back on Maximus. She'd done a good job with him yesterday, but today, she was really gonna work.

That would be later though. First thing on his schedule was Lion. Frankel already sitting in the gazebo, watching, but they hadn't spoken much after that electric conversation yesterday and didn't acknowledge each other now.

Remembering the wild session with the stallion the day before, Jericho gathered the reins up tight—the left rein considerably shorter than the right rein too, meaning the stallion's head was turned sharply to the side. No more explosions, or at least that was what he was thinking. Didn't even put his foot in the stirrups, this time he vaulted on. But oh man, what a surprise. Lion catapulting forward—he should have been going in a tight circle with his head cranked around the way it was...but he didn't. Giant leap straight ahead and back to bucking, but completely off balance—right shoulder thrust out to compensate for his head position. His feet were all mixed up, and then he was falling right down on that leading shoulder. He hit the ground hard. Jericho had felt it happening—but hadn't been able to lift the horse and keep him going.

Scream from Brittany on the side of the arena.

He didn't want to bail, but he didn't want 1200 pounds of horse pinning his right leg to the ground either. At the last split second he took a dive to the right—away from those deadly hoofs, and got free of the falling, thrashing animal, but hitting the sand hard. Still had the reins though. As Lion jerked back to his feet again, he was shocked to find his rider leaping back on.

Whap!

Whip coming down hard on those massive hindquarters. Squeal of rage from the stallion, but he got moving fast, running for all he was worth. Jericho could feel it—he was going to go down again if he could manage it—it hadn't been accidental the first time either, he knew that now. Threw his weight to the opposite side, jerked the reins and brought the horse's head up, sat in and really pushed him—made him run. Whip coming down hard on his ass again the instant he tried to slow down for even a heartbeat. No way he was going to be allowed to take another dive.

God damn Chuck, was the thought running through Jericho's mind, as he fought to keep the stallion upright, to keep him galloping, keep himself on top. Frankel had to have known Lion did this...and damn it, it was about as dangerous a vice as a horse could have. Hadn't even warned him, the bastard.

And if a horse like this went down on him, he'd be out of the game for good.

Whipped him again. It wasn't the way Jericho liked to operate, but what he did here today would have to be harsh. No, he'd never seriously hurt the animal, but Chasseur de Lion needed to learn in no uncertain terms that falling down was not allowed—that the consequences for trying it were a lot worse than just staying up and doing some work. Forget about the fact that Lion thought he was the big herd stallion—this rider was higher on the food chain…he was the unconditional boss.

Tough ride for the next fifteen minutes, and every second of it perilous. The more the stallion tired, the more he tried to slow down—and the more he slowed down the more he thought about taking another dive into the sand. Jericho, absolutely not allowing it—whipping him, spurring him. In the end, the horse gave in and produced five minutes or so of normal canter work, and that's when he pulled him to a halt.

He turned his deep blue eyes to the gazebo—fire in that piercing stare. Pissed to the core. Didn't see Frankel though. "Chuck!" he bellowed. "Where the hell are you?"

"Here." He'd been looking in the wrong direction. The Chef D'Equip was standing in the middle of the arena—had come out, though there was really nothing he could do to help. "Get off him. Jesus Christ, are you hurt?" Frankel sounded every bit as furious as he did. Worried too. "Those *bastards*, I can't believe they didn't tell me this when I bought the horse, and man am I going to call them on it. But it's my fault—hell, I didn't even try him. I never thought in a million years…" He was over next to horse and rider now. Shaking his head in rage. "Jesus, I'm sorry, you must be ready to slug me. Jericho, just get off—I'll get him out of your barn. To-day."

Stubborn answer, proud too. "Bullshit, I'm not getting off him." Raised his voice and called to Brittany and Marco. "Take the rails down on this fence, and just lay them on the ground."

"Jericho, no."

"Yes, Chuck. It's not even a jump…just two side standards. And he's going to mother fucking walk between them before he goes back to the barn."

Frankel looked really concerned. "Do you want me to lead him through while you ride?"

"Too dangerous. I want you to stand with a lunge whip at the side of the jump, and when I come up to it, if he tries to rear or go down, lay into his hide."

"I don't know…"

Really strong. "Come on, Chuck…you wanted me to ride him."

Stood there for a second, obviously not liking it. Frankel blew his breath out. "Alright, you're the trainer. Alright."

It took them a few minutes to get everything set-up, and to get Frankel in position with the long lunge whip in hand. Jericho trotted Lion around the edge of the ring in the meantime—Lion obedient, but really tuned in to what was happening, mutinously flicking his eyes to the humans and the "jump" they were setting up.

When they were ready, Jericho faced him with it, trotted him most of the way up to it, then brought him down to a walk. He could already feel the resistance in there. Those hindquarters coming underneath him, set to dig in, plant and rear.

"Whip," he said. "And make it crack so he can really hear it."

Jericho squeezed him hard with his legs just before Frankel stepped in and snapped the whip sharply across the stallion's rump.

Lion jerked forward, but he was trying even harder to resist now.

"Again."

Same thing…and getting closer.

"Again."

Same.

The stallion's head was almost even with the standards. This time Jericho asked with his legs, but without calling for the whip again—wanting to see if he'd made the association—legs meant forward, and the whip would reinforce them if he said no. Hesitation on the stallion's part. Squeezed again. More response this time. And then Lion took a jerking leap and passed through the standards. Petted him. "Good."

Brought him around, and did it again. And again. And again. When he'd gone through five times in succession without fighting, Jericho rewarded him by patting him, leaning forward and slipping a sugar cube from his pocket into his mouth, and then vaulting off.

He handed him off to Marco, then turned back around and walked over to Frankel. "Look, don't even say it," the Chef D'Equip was already telling him. "I told you, I'll get him off your property. And I apologize, Jericho. I know you don't believe me, but I really apologize."

Quelled him with that deep blue stare. Then those eyes narrowed militantly—mind very clearly made up on the point. "No," he said. "I want you to leave him. I'll work him for a week, let's see how it goes—eight o'clock in the morning. And come Chuck, come every day if you want to. Truth is, I could use your help." Half-smile from him. "Hell, and I thought QL was difficult."

"Hi. Merry Christmas. Jericho, I've been trying to get in touch with you. I was worried sick."

It was Darien, and she'd called him on his cell phone—and he'd answered it without checking the caller ID. Mistake. Yeah, he knew she'd been trying to reach him, but felt awkward about it. After her seeing him fighting, taking on those RJ's and liking it—oh sure, she'd be grateful for the rescue, but what else was she thinking? Maybe he'd even frightened her with the violence—with the violent side of him. Didn't want to have that conversation, but now he was trapped. "Hi. Merry Christmas yourself. And I'm sorry, you shouldn't have worried. I was fine. Brae gave a statement, and they let me go after a couple of hours. No ticket for disturbing the peace. Nothing." He almost sounded a little defensive, definitely anxious. "How about you? You were okay, and you got your plane okay the next day and everything?"

"I was fine...thanks to you." She sounded warm, not uncomfortable talking to him, thank God. Still, now that she had him on the line, he was going to go ahead and take the opportunity to make sure.

"Darien, I know you've heard that I mix it up a lot, and that cop who arrested me said the same thing to you..." Sigh. "I really hate it that you saw me handcuffed and taken away like that, like some common criminal, and I want you to know, I've been trying to...have more control, and Chuck...he gave me some real shit about it too, and I know he's right."

"Jericho, my God," Darien interrupted him. "You're apologizing. Please stop it this instant. I'm just so..." Meaningful pause, and the next words nearly whispered. "...amazed by you."

Jesus, three little words and she'd completely stirred him, and thrown him off balance. Man he wished she was right there in front of him—he'd have taken her into his arms...where she belonged, God damn it. "No more than I am with you," he murmured back to her, looking around himself self-consciously, and then stepping outside the barn to be sure he wouldn't be overheard.

"Jericho?"

She didn't understand him, or maybe she hadn't meant what he'd thought. "I'm sorry," he said. "That didn't sound appropriate at all, did it?" Actually, he wasn't telling her how he'd meant the words, but then he changed his mind and just came out with it. Deep growl. "But then, fuck, sometimes there's not an appropriate thought in my head where you're concerned."

Pause. Maybe completely stunned. Maybe he'd horrified her.

Soft laugh from him. "Damn it Darien, no wonder I've been avoiding your calls. I'm a fool, I've had a long day…imagine this, I even got dumped this morning."

She was completely stopped by the first part of what he said—didn't even hear the rest of it. "You've been avoiding my calls? Listen Jericho…I know that you're…*oh damn*." She tried it a second time, coming at it the other way around. "I *know* you know how much I'm…oh God, how can I say this?"

"Please, don't try. Believe me, I understand."

Long moment of silence. Poignant.

Darien spoke quietly, and sounded a bit breathless. "I wish I could see your face right now."

"I was wishing the same thing too." There was a harsh undercurrent to his voice, and she had to have heard it. "But it's probably a good thing you're not anywhere near me. Forgive me for this conversation, Darien. I swear to God, I'm not going to act on it."

So hushed. "Not even if I want you to?"

Just dropped his eyes for a moment—man, she's just opened up the door to him, opened it wide. And he wanted her, wanted to feel her beneath him, cover that luscious mouth of hers with his own—just take her, and not even fucking ask. Finally he spoke. "When are you coming back?"

"Two days from now."

His tone of voice was aggressive. "Alone?"

Hesitated, like maybe she was a little bit frightened. "…yes."

"What time?"

Pause again. Whispered to him, an invitation this time for sure. "Eight o'clock in the evening."

"I'll pick you up then. At the airport." Invitation accepted.

"Jericho, you don't have to drive all the way out there."

Murmured to her, "No, and I damn well shouldn't either…but I *want* to."

She'd covered the mouthpiece of the phone, but he could hear the muffled sound of her voice anyway.

Then, deep booming male voice. "Jericho, it's Bob Marx here. Merry Christmas! I really, really want to thank you for taking care of my wife."

Taking care of his wife? Drew his breath in—yeah, he was taking care of her. Talk about a punch to the stomach. And Jesus, this man who'd done so much for him lately. He could hardly have felt more like a heel than he did then. "You're more than welcome...hey, I just did what you would have done if you'd been there." Not really. But it sounded good.

"Frankel give you a hard time?" the investment banker asked him.

"Yeah sure, but he's over it."

"Damn right he is," Marx snorted. "I told him he better get his head on straight."

Oh yeah, Jericho thought, now that explained it. Why Chuck had come around—nothing to do with him...only Marx. "I have to thank you then," he said, voice noticeably tighter. "That night he came in to the lock-up just to tell me he was dropping me, but the next morning he showed up at my place like nothing happened. Wanted to work."

Sure he'd been there—but only because he'd had to. Jericho wondered how much Marx paid to make it so.

Monday evening, the 27th. Darien coming back to Wellington the next evening. But tonight Jason Coulder, his wife Kate, and several other friends including Chip Langdon and his partner John DeWinter were having dinner at Nicole's. Jason just bugged the hell out of Jericho until he agreed to meet them there. He came good and late, but that was expected anyway, and they'd just left an empty chair for him. Kiss for Kate, and he swung into it—and a bottle of beer appeared in front of him in seconds...instructions left for the waiter, obviously. He lifted it in salute to the table, then tossed a long swallow back.

"So...out with it," Jason said.

"Out with what?" All he could think of was Darien, but knew that couldn't be what Coulder was asking about. Or hell, if it was, he'd have to go home and shoot himself.

"Chasseur de Lion?" Coulder mocked him. "Come on, what else could I mean?"

Thank God. "Is anything a secret in this town?" he snorted.

"Well, do you or don't you have him in the barn? From your answer, I guess you do."

"Yeah, Jericho, tell us," Trisha Sommers, another jumper rider demanded.

"Yes, alright, I do have him," Jericho admitted, then twisted the truth a little. "But it's just a rehab gig—something to bring in some income, that's all. Real stallion mentality...stubborn to the core," he added, looking disgusted. "Too late to cut him though, and hell it's all he's good for anyway."

"Liar," Jason accused him good-naturedly.

"Now what makes you say that?"

Laugh from Coulder. "Well, we all go to Starbucks, dude."

He lowered his face into his hand and just shook his head. Damn that Brae. "Swear to God, he's not ridable. Dangerous as hell."

"Not ridable?" Chip tossed out, calling his bluff. "Then why does your roommate have pictures of you on him?"

Yeah, Brae was going to die young, he thought angrily. "Okay, okay...I throw a leg over him every day, but he's really nasty. Already dumped me twice." It had happened again just that morning. Oh but he hadn't gotten away with it, and it didn't matter how many times he threw himself to the ground—cause this human was back on him the minute he scrambled to his feet again.

Chip looked stunned. "Dumped *you*? No way."

"Oh yeah," he confirmed, and his voice was dead serious. "It's his major evasion...he drops underneath you, and you better bail, or he's landing on top of you. I can prevent it most of the time, but it's a big fucking horse. I've started wearing my helmet to ride him, he's that bad."

"Jericho!" Shocked cry from Kate. "How much can they be paying you? Why are you taking that risk?" Her hand had gone to rest on her husband's arm, as if to say, "don't you ever do that."

"Not enough, that's for sure." It was Jason's eyes he sought out as he responded to her question, not Kate's. "I should throw him out of the barn, I know that. But I have to tell you, it really burns my ass to hit the ground." Coulder was the only one there he thought would understand what he meant by that. The challenge just plain called to him, and he hated to lose.

Jason was staring back at him hard. "Making any progress?" he asked.

Cold satisfied smile. "Some."

"Oh, you mother...you *are* going to try and compete him, aren't you?"

"No, Jace." *Oh, hell yes.* "It's just a rehab gig. He's got some serious physical issues on top of the attitude. He's not ridable."

Trisha had lowered her voice, and she was staring over her shoulder. "How the hell does that woman dare to show her face in public?" she asked spitefully.

Jericho followed the path of her eyes. Ailynn. Sitting at the bar, flirting with a well-known polo patron. Oh, and she'd seen him too. Eye contact. He turned away and cursed.

"Just ignore her, Jericho," Kate said, reaching over to take his hand.

"Like I said," he snarled, "It really burns my ass to hit the ground."

The conversation continued in an even flow, but always swinging back to horses, upcoming competitions, and the men and women who rode them. Jericho was noticeably ill at ease, knowing Ailynn was sitting behind him, and after about forty-five minutes, he rose. "I'm just going to grab a quick smoke. I'll be right back."

"Stay away from her," Kate pleaded with him, but only got a cool yet expressive look in return.

Like he was actually trying to make contact with her. Yeah, right. Or was he? He didn't even look at the bar on his way past, and his whole body language was forbidding. Jerked the door open and went outside. He walked to the small fountain out front, and rested one foot on a concrete bench. Shook out a cigarette and lit it.

No more than thirty seconds later. "Hi." That soft lilting voice.

Yeah, and who was he kidding? He'd known she'd follow him out here. Turned his face and stared at her. "New boyfriend?" he quietly mocked her—sounded disinterested, but not quite.

"No, just a friend." She came closer and touched his hand briefly. "You're so angry. You're still so angry. Even the other night. You just did that to show me how little you care."

"That's bullshit, Ailynn. Hell, you tempted the shit out of me till you got what you wanted—you did it to prove you still can, and that's the real truth." He drew on his cigarette, turned his face and exhaled. Looked back around at her again. "It's not like you really feel anything for me, or for any man for that matter. We just amuse you, don't we?"

"Wow, you're hard."

Shrugged.

"Razz is going so great for me, Jericho. You should come and see him some time. Michael says his training's so correct...he really compliments you. I mean, for a jumper rider to make such a nice mid-level Dressage horse." She ran her fingers through the water at the base of the fountain. "I'm always so proud for you when he says that."

"Don't."

"Don't what?"

Sarcastic. "Don't make it personal. It's not personal between us."

She smiled, looked satisfied. Almost smug. "Why can't you admit it? Just admit that you still like me. I'm still available to you."

Laid that deep blue stare on her again, quietly sneered, "Apparently you're available to anyone when your husband's out of town."

Male voice, coming from behind him. "Here you are, Jericho."

Jason. Come to rescue him. Or maybe Kate had sent him.

Tossed his butt into the parking lot, swung his head around to him. "Yeah, I'm coming back in."

"Good. But I wanted to ask you something privately first," Coulder said, giving Ailynn a friendly enough but pointed look.

"Goodnight, Jericho," she said, not minding in the least, it seemed. Took out her car keys and started walking in the direction of that sweet new Jaguar—probably a present from Cole, he thought darkly. Impossible not to watch those slim hips swaying as she left him.

Muttered something under his breath, and looked at Coulder. "Women fucking confound me," he growled. "Thanks for coming out before I let her twist me around inside again. Hell, I'd rather deal with Chasseur than that bitch...yet she draws me in every time."

Nod of sympathy. "I know...I consider myself lucky with Kate, you know?" Paused. "But I really did want to ask you something."

Jericho gave him a quizzical look. "Anything you want, Jason. You know that."

"Suppose I want to leave Landrover with you for another month?"

Oh man, and he'd been counting on that income. But Jason had done so much for him, not to mention the friendship, the support. "Sure. It's no problem. Pay for him when you're ready...you know I'll hold him for you, just tell me you want him."

Embarrassed laugh. "Look, I don't even know how to say this, so I'll say it straight out. You'll get the money this week, just like we talked about. I want the horse, that's not the issue. What I meant was...I'd like to ride him with you for a few weeks...if you're cool with that."

Totally taken back. "You can't be serious."

"I'm completely serious."

Jericho just stared at him. "Let me get this right…you want me to coach you? Come on, Jace, you're a top rider, I don't need income that bad."

Coulder came over and sat along the edge of the fountain. "Smoke another cigarette, Jericho…give me an excuse to stand out here with you."

Didn't question it. Just pulled out another smoke and fired it up. Waited.

Jason wasn't exactly looking at him. "No, I'm not a top rider," he said after a bit. "I'm good enough, sure. But I'm thinking…I could learn something, and maybe watching you ride the other day is making me hungry enough to try." Looked up then. "You and I compete against each other, so maybe you won't want to do this, and I understand that."

Leaned forward with his elbow on his knee. Smoking. "Reaction, okay?"

"Okay."

"It sucks for your reputation, man," Jericho told him. "I'm not nearly important enough to coach you without raising some eyebrows, and you know damn well nothing is secret here." Coulder was nodding at that, but he didn't look happy about it. Seemed disappointed. Jericho went on. "Think about this though…you'll take the horse on trial, and the story is I won't let him off my property till you make up your mind. Makes sense right? You're riding when I'm riding…hell, its natural I'll make comments. Fuck, I have a big mouth…maybe I'll make a lot of them."

Coulder smiling down at his feet. "Yeah," he said. "Big mouth."

Smirk from Jericho. "Complain about it to a few guys…how much it fucking annoys you." Shrugged. "Should work."

Five after eight, December 28th. Today, he'd cut out of work a little bit early, showered shaved and changed into something a little nicer than jeans and a polo shirt—black dress slacks, beneath a lightweight, long-sleeve, white shirt.

Now he was driving, and it was the third time he'd had wheeled the Mustang around the loop that led to the airport Arrivals area, but these days they wouldn't let you stop for more than thirty seconds unless your party was standing there ready to go. Didn't matter though…he stuck a CD in the car's expensive stereo system, fired up a cigarette, and pulled into the line to go past the steady stream of arriving passengers at the curb.

Darien.

Saw her. Little Lily Pulitzer sundress on her, with a buff linen jacket thrown over her shoulders, tiny little sandals. Almost no luggage. She spied him and waved to him. He pulled over, swung out of the car and came around to her. Stood next to her for a heartbeat—towering over her…not by quite a foot, but close—his physical presence, unmistakable next to hers. Deep blue eyes on her. Leaned over her and let his lips brush across her cheek. Eyes intent on her again, reading. Checking…had she changed her mind? "Have luggage?" he asked.

"No, this is it." Smile from her, and that little hand caressing his arm like always. Confident, but excited at the same time…and no, she hadn't changed her mind, he could see that. He put an arm loosely around her shoulders, walked with her to the car door, opened it for her then closed it behind her. Her in his car—such a little thing, but man it meant something to him, stirred him. Felt so incredibly possessive of her.

He went back around and slung his tall body behind the wheel. One last look from him…communicating to her, saying nothing. Then he turned his eyes to the road, and pulled away from the curb.

He drove to the airport exit on Southern Boulevard. Wellington lay to the west and right. He turned left.

The CD still playing, the lyrics so damn appropriate…

> *I can smell the way you taste*
> *I chase every breath you take*
> *And I'll wait*

Truth was, it was one of his favorite tracks on this CD.

> *All you say is that I'm playing games*
> *But if I stay, I'll just go crazy*
> *Throw away the promise that you made*
> *And understand*
> *I just want to touch you*
> *I just want to fuck you*

He reached over and turned it off. "Good flight?" he asked, ignoring the import of that song—or that he'd been playing it because it made him think of her. Never would have admitted that.

"Uneventful."

"Best kind," he observed. Wasn't saying a word about where he was driving, and she didn't ask. "I'm kind of thinking about taking a short trip to Europe one of these weeks soon. Couple of days, maybe three or four at the most," he added, glancing over at her, still heading east toward the city of Palm Beach.

"Horse hunting trip, Jericho?"

He nodded affirmatively. "Believe it or not, I'm almost out of horses to sell…Razz, Laredo, and Landrover are all basically gone or will be soon. That only leaves Illando…so yeah, I need to pick up some more stock."

She seemed interested. "When would you go?"

"Maybe in a week. See what I can get in the way of plane tickets." He shrugged.

They crossed the bridge across the Intercoastal waterway, and out onto the island of Palm Beach itself. He continued driving, around the small traffic circle, and then along the road that bordered the ocean itself. Found a place to park, and pulled over.

"Walk with me," he said to her.

"Alright."

It was about eight-thirty now, and long dark. The beach deserted—just ocean on one side and expensive beachfront homes on the other. Faint lights coming from a few of the houses, but reserved, separated, aloof almost. Sliver of a moon in the sky, lots of stars though. Sound and scent of the surf. Jericho took Darien's hand and led her out onto the beach—the tide had receded somewhat, and the sand was packed down hard and still damp. He walked along slowly, head lifted, just watching the surroundings, taking in the dark solitude. Not speaking, but somehow intimate just the same.

In a bit he stopped, turned to face her, took her other hand in his. "You know, I'm never at a loss for how to handle a situation, especially with women. Me? I've got all the moves, Darien," he told her—really intense low voice. "But with you…those moves mean shit, and I'm so…lost." The last word snarled softly. Lifted one hand and brushed it along the side of her cheek, and then down under her chin. Moved closer, tipped her face up to look into his eyes, his thumb reaching up to toy with that gorgeous lower lip of hers. Lowered his mouth to cover hers. Lingering—almost reverent—kiss…deepening suddenly, and then a lot more aggressive. Hungry.

She just melted against him, slender arms reaching up to circle his neck, no hesitation at all—like she'd simply been waiting for this cue from him. And not backing off either, even though that kiss radiated wave after wave of his claim to her.

His hand coming up to surround the back of her head and keep her mouth captured against his own. His other hand circling her waist, then sliding down over that fine little ass, and bringing her body up hard against him—pressed against his chest, abdomen, pelvis, and upper thighs—letting her feel the hard muscle of him…the hard length of him too.

Reality was, all he wanted in that moment was to lay her down and come up hard inside her—take her. Make love to her. He showed her that, rather than saying it aloud, but it couldn't have been clearer.

And her giving him permission, whispering, "Yes," to him when he eased enough pressure off her lips to allow her to give him that single word.

Sure, he'd screwed Ailynn in the shavings, no problem, but putting Darien down in the wet sand? No…wasn't happening. In fact, he'd pretty much picked this location for that reason—to prevent himself from doing exactly what she'd just asked him to do. He'd intended to talk, not fuck her or even make love—hadn't presumed that far, hadn't dared despite the signals she'd given him over the phone. Confronted with the physical reality of him, it had been entirely possible she'd run like hell instead. He'd been prepared for that actually.

But things had changed dramatically with that one little word. Jericho lifted his head, his eyes sweeping the row of beachfront properties. Third one to the north looked unoccupied, at least at the moment—no lights on in it anyway.

Looked down on her, murmured to her, "Will you come with me, trust me?"

Same word, same soft yielding voice. "Yes."

Took her hand again. Nodded toward the house. "This way then."

She went along with him willingly enough until she realized exactly what he had in mind. He'd come right up to the wooden gate that led into the back courtyard and pool area of the empty house. "Oh, no…we can't," she said, though looking thrilled at the audacity of him. "You don't know these people do you?"

Dark smile from him, and he shook his head in the negative. Put his hand on the gate handle and tried it. It wasn't locked. Opened it a few inches, but didn't try to lead her inside yet…just pulled her back into his arms. His mouth assaulting hers again. Darien sighed with longing, and gave in to him, not fighting him when he swept her up into his arms and carried her inside.

Still no signs of anyone at home—but this house was being lived in. There was an assortment of expensive teak lawn furniture spread around, including several lounge chairs with thick green and white striped cushions. He set her down on one, and inclined it back fully prone, but still supporting her with his hand in a sitting position. Knelt beside her, and removed her jacket, going back to kissing her at the same time. And her kissing him back, excited and wanting him, no question about that. While he slid the zipper down at the back of her dress, she wound her fingers around the long braid at the base of his neck. She wasn't trying to take his hair down, just holding on, wrapping it around her palm in a thick coil— like she didn't want him to get away and had to hold him there.

He kept reading her, trying to find any hint of doubt or fear in her. No matter how much he wanted it, he wasn't going through with this—not unless she was positive. But she seemed like she was, making it easy for him to remove her outfit, then her wisp of a bra and slim thong panty. Seeking his mouth out any time he pulled back to undress her.

He rose abruptly above her. Reached both hands behind his head to grasp the fabric of his shirt, and strip it over his head. Dropped it on the pool deck. Stood proud before her—methodically undid his belt, stripped off his pants, briefs and sandals, letting her look at him as much as she wanted to. Then with purpose he moved over her, and came down onto the chaise with her, laying her back—pretty narrow quarters, but workable. Jericho kept his weight up on his elbows close in by her sides, his forearms around her, supporting her upper back and neck. He was kissing her again, seducing her, making her want him, want more. She moaned as he plundered her mouth, his tongue stroking her teeth, her tongue—nipping lightly at her lower lip. He had one knee pressed between her knees, but hadn't asked her to open to him yet, was just letting her experience the press of his erection from the top of her inner thigh along the indent that led to the point of her pelvis, and sweet Jesus, it was taking all his self-control to go this slow with her.

She was really excited, he could tell—the way she was beginning to buck up against him more urgently…needing…seeking the feel of him inside her. He stopped kissing her long enough to lay that deep blue stare on her while he lifted his weight slightly and his second knee joined the first between her legs, spreading them for him. Held the look with her as he maneuvered to position himself—could feel her nice and wet and wel-coming him—stroked himself up hard into her, filling her and she laid her head back and cried out, and God she was so tight…like she didn't make love that often, and that made him unreasonably satisfied. Though Christ, here he was taking another man's wife.

Moving inside her powerfully, but starting slow, letting her know that this was his territory now, that he was possessing her. One hand sliding down to lift her ass up to him, stroking and stroking her, making her cry and writhe beneath him as he increased the pace relentlessly.

Lights coming on in the house.

Alright, alright…as long as they didn't hear anything, as long as they didn't come out here. The danger, the thrill of how forbidden what they were doing was would only add to the experience—and he didn't stop, just covered her mouth again with his own to stifle her cries. He wasn't even sure she realized what was going on. He lifted his body slightly to increase the friction inside her, and felt her react, pressing up against him desper-ately, her slim body covered with sweat. A deeper cry from her, and then the incredible squeeze of contractions from her climax clasping over and around him.

Voices from the house, and Darien's eyes flying open even while her orgasm was hard on her. Staring into the supremely confident depths of his eyes, fully aware now, but captured by the powerful release she was feeling. Him still stroking her hard all the way through it. He didn't want to cum with her yet, but that wasn't going to be his decision to make, and Christ he just couldn't stop it. Jericho covered her lips with his palm, and laid his own head back growling deep in his throat, but clamping down on the roar that wanted to escape his lips—his own orgasm hitting him full force.

Back porch light coming on.

He lowered his face to the cushion and held both of them still, though it took every mother-fucking ounce of self-control he had in him to stay perfectly quiet while his body emptied with long profound spurts into hers. Sensations taking hold of him like an explosion, violent climax grip-ping him, making his muscles tremble and jerk, and oh Jesus, all he could do was lay there and experience it.

Porch light going back out again.

Lifted his head, eyes closed, lips drawn back in a silent roar…and pressed himself in deep. Chest heaving, gasping for air. It was probably five minutes before he really had full mental awareness back. He just held her, and she was clearly in the same state, only wanting to be within the circle of his arms. Finally he whispered to her, "We should get out of here."

She looked at him and nodded, bit her lower lip, and nearly giggled.

Smiled at her, God she made him feel so warm inside. Just shook his head, and smirked then. Started kissing her all over again. God he wanted more of her, and he didn't want to wait for it.

Porch lights again. Back sliding glass door opening. Crotchety elderly male voice calling out. "Okay, okay…once is enough. Now go on, get out of here."

Jericho's face snapped around. The man was a good thirty feet away, but with the light, it wasn't hard to see his features. Gray hair, weathered face—easily seventy. Wearing a striped silk bathrobe. Eyebrows lifted sardonically.

Oh and the homeowner had gotten a good look at him too. He wasn't angry though—just wanted them to leave now. Jericho lowered his face, but nodded, guilty and with no defense.

Chuckle from the homeowner. Door sliding shut. Lights going out again.

Chapter Fifteen

"Hey Darien, do you think this looks pussy?" Starbucks rose and turned around to show her his tattoo, lifting up his tee shirt. His pants rode so low on his hips, that it was easily visible.

New Years had passed, and also the first week in January…time slowly marching along, the horse show season in full swing…except at Jericho's stable, though the training there had become really intense.

"Well, no Brae…why? Don't you like it?"

They were sitting together in the gazebo, watching Jericho ride. He'd just finished up with Lion. The gray stallion had returned from the clinic just a few days earlier. He'd been evaluated, injected, and now sported special shoes as well. His attitude had also improved somewhat…like maybe he was more comfortable now, and just figuring that out—maybe figuring out that it no longer hurt so much to work. As a result, he'd pretty well given up on trying to throw himself to the ground, though he remembered the evasion, and riding him was still touch and go. And Jericho still wore his helmet when he was on him, ever vigilant. Was making progress in getting him to walk, trot and canter through a pair of side standards without rails too. Lion seemed to understand it wasn't a real jump, and would go through willingly enough now.

"Aw, hell…" Brae was whining, his face as pouty as a spoiled child. "I loved it when I got it, but then Jericho said it looks…you know…faggy or something, cause of where it is."

Darien burst out laughing. "Oh, I see what he's saying, but no, Brae…I'm sure he's just teasing you. I doubt most people would think that when they saw it." She giggled again. "You certainly bust his chops all the time. I imagine he's just getting back at you."

"Oh man," the Barista griped again. "You're laughing…you *do* think it looks pussy."

"No, I don't." What a ridiculous thing to be arguing about. Her eyes swung fondly over to Jericho riding Lion back up to the barn. The last ten days or so with him had been so idyllic. Long hours in the evening with him there in her bedroom, and her there in his arms. Making love, talking about anything and everything, even just watching television lying wrapped up in each other's embrace. And he'd been so circumspect—so protective of her reputation. He even walked over and back from his place to hers nightly, cutting across the Polo Club golf course and entering her house from the back so he wouldn't be seen and his car wouldn't be sitting out front. "Honestly, Brae," she repeated. "I don't think that at all. It looks fine…nice."

Her little world in a bubble with him was bursting today though. Bob was returning to Florida. In fact, he ought to be pulling in anytime now.

Still whining. "Well, is it just "fine", or is it really nice? Here look again." He stood up and pulled up his tee shirt one more time. "And see, here's the worst part," he went right on complaining. "I don't even know what Brittany thinks about it—I mean, she heard Jericho say that and everything. Man, how sucky is that?"

"I think you really need to calm down about this," Darien said sternly. "You'll give yourself a heart attack or a stroke or something." Even so, seeing the tattoo again, hearing him whine, and imagining Jericho's warm laugh at his roommate's expense, did bring another quirky little smile to her lips. She tried to divert him. "Did you get good pictures of Lion this morning? I think he's starting to come around, don't you?"

"Yeah, some really good ones," he confirmed, then finally smiled and looked a bit happier. "I love that new camera you got me for Christmas, and I'm really glad I didn't have to give it to those RJ's." But then he went right back to what he'd been talking about before—like a compass needle pointing north. "And don't change the subject, Darien. I'm trying to find out something here."

"Well, I'm going up to the barn," she announced, and got up to make a hasty escape.

Normally, Jericho would have started in with QL as soon as he finished with Lion, but Frankel wasn't there yet, and no word from him. He waited impatiently, taking the opportunity to step out behind the barn and grab a quick smoke. Hadn't even bothered to yank off his helmet or even lay his whip down like he usually did.

Darien was preying on his mind—being separated from her again, going back to that "look but don't touch" routine. Man, it ate at him, and he couldn't get it out of his head. About halfway through his cigarette she appeared beside him. He just stared at her, and she looked back at him, both of them clearly upset. Marx would be here for probably a good two weeks solid, keeping them apart that long. Longer, if Jericho made the four-day trip to Europe he was planning. She hadn't said anything about joining him there, but he was still hoping she would.

He leaned his whip up against the side of the barn, and came closer to her. He'd never touched her here at the stables, except in the most platonic way. But now he laid one hand behind her head, his thumb stroking gently along her jawline, the look on his face intense. He wasn't trying to kiss her, but he was making her think about what it felt like when his mouth descended over hers. Or when he deepened that kiss, and the animal lust she could feel in him then, his teeth bumping against hers, his tongue plundering. Oh and she *was* picturing it, he could see that in her eyes. Her pupils dilating with budding desire for him.

Marco's voice, raised, and deliberately so. "Hi, welcome back to Wellington. Jericho's out behind the barn grabbing a smoke…I think your wife's with him too."

He dropped his hand and stepped away from her. Looked away also.

"Hello sweetheart." The investment banker came out the rear entrance to the barn, and Jericho swung back around to him. Quizzical look on his patron's face, even maybe slightly annoyed. Even though he wasn't standing close to Darien any longer, Jericho knew that both of them looked guilty as hell.

Darien recovered quickly. Smiled happily, Turned around and gave her husband a quick hug and a light kiss. "Hi," she said, sounding genuinely happy to see him. "I missed you."

And fuck, that grated at him. He dropped his cigarette butt and ground it out with his heel. Nodded curtly to Marx, and then stepped past him and back into the barn—leaving the two of them alone. Not belonging there while they greeted each other, and really, really hating that too.

Chuck was there in the aisle way finally. As was Jason Coulder. "Morning Jericho," Coulder called out and waved as he led Landrover to the exit closest to the ring, preparing to mount him and go down to work.

Brusque acknowledgement to him too.

"QL is ready boss," Marco told him, trying to distract him...and Jericho thought for the thousandth time that his head groom didn't miss much. He knew...oh yeah, he knew—and was protecting him.

"Alright." And to Frankel, "I'll meet you down in the field." Jericho walked over to the mare and took the reins, but then remembered he'd left his whip out back. "Here, hold her for a second," he said to Marco. "I just need to grab my whip."

He started back, but paused as he approached the doorway. Marx and Darien were talking. He couldn't hear what his patron was saying, but his voice was fairly sharp. Then Darien responding, "Don't be silly, Bob. You're reading something into nothing. Sure, I'm friendly with Jericho, why shouldn't I be? But that's all there is to it." Chiding laugh from her. "Come on," she coaxed him. "When you get right down to it, Jericho's really just part of our barn help. Now, do you really think I'd be interested in someone like him?"

Barn help? Oh man, she sounded so convincing...and so completely real. Like that's what she really thought—how she saw him. A paid employee. Those words were a slap in the face...or more like a knife to the heart. And God, it cut deep. Hell, maybe to her it really was just a dalliance. Maybe she wasn't really all that much different from Cin.

Marx and his wife coming back into the aisle—and meeting Jericho face-to-face. She looked totally shocked. "Excuse me," he said harshly, then brushed past them, stepped outside, got the whip, and then went past them again going the other way to get QL. Didn't even look at her.

"Oh my God," she whispered to her husband. "I think he heard me say that."

Marx shrugged. "So what? So you called him barn help. I'm sure he has a big ego, but he'll get over it."

The coaching session started out pretty much like every other session, except that Jason was here today riding Landrover at the same time. Most days he came later, but had a scheduling conflict that afternoon, and Jericho told him it would be fine. He called out comments to him occasionally, or rode up to him and said something more privately from time to time.

Bob and Darien had gone down to the gazebo to watch, and Brae was there with Brittany, taking pictures, and then passing the camera around.

"These are really great," the working student said with adoring eyes.

"Yeah, I have a lot of talent for it," Starbucks answered her, not in the least bit bashful about tooting his own horn.

"Jericho, ride over to me," Frankel shouted about twenty minutes into the session. When horse and rider pulled up beside him, he asked grumpily, "What are you doing? Giving a lesson to Jason Coulder for Christ sakes?"

Jericho's mood was completely dark and unrepentant. Darien and her husband and that scene between the two of them were all he could think about—though oddly enough it had made his riding sharper, not the reverse. He and the horse had been really putting out. Now, however, he sneered out a biting response. "Oh fuck no...why would I do that, and why would Jason want me to? He's just trying that horse for the month, and I gave him a few comments. What Chuck?" he challenged him coolly. "Think I'm opening my mouth too much? Or are you more concerned that a two-bit trainer like me might try to coach?"

"What's up your ass today?" Frankel snapped back at him. "I was only asking."

"Yeah, you were only asking." Jericho looked like he wanted to hurt someone. His eyes were like flint, and his voice like the deep bass lash of a whip.

"That's right."

"Well why don't you "just ask" me to do a line of fences here, Chuck, cause this mare's flatwork was damn near perfect today, and you know you need something to bitch at me about."

Stern. "Okay I'll do that, but I want to know what's bothering you. Are you even concentrating, Jericho? Facing these fences is serious business."

"Do I seem like I'm concentrating? Hell, I just got three "goods" from you in a row. And yeah, maybe something's bothering me, but it's *nothing* you need to know about...now God damn you, let's *work*."

He could see that he was really pissing Frankel off—but who gave a shit? He just went right on glaring at the Chef D'Equip until Chuck finally muttered a savage curse, and then mapped out a short jumping course.

"Alright wise guy, since you seem to need to blow off steam, take it like a timed jump off round. And *try* to tighten up your turns on the back end of it. Yeah you're handy in the turns already, but I want you to *give me more*. Don't lose speed either, because that just negates the benefit." Cold and sharply rebuking tone of voice. "Think you can handle that, Jericho? Or maybe you should just get off…pick it up tomorrow when you've got that temper of yours under control."

Murmured, "Fuck, no, I'll never let my personal life make me dismount." He spun QL around, passing Jason on the way to the end of the field where he intended to circle and come back around to take the course.

"Want me to keep jumping that same line?" Coulder asked him.

Quieter tone with Jason, but still shorter than normal. "Yeah. Deeper on the middle element. You wait too long to measure the stride, okay?"

"Gotcha." And Jason rode off to reface the line he'd been working too.

Jericho ran a hand down QL's neck, quieting her before taking the course. This mare was still a tough ride, and she was green—completely green in actual competition, and still learning on a course at home. Even so, he'd formed a real bond with her, and she with him—loved riding her on a daily basis. And jughead and big ears be damned…to him she was beautiful. Knew she'd love this course Chuck had mapped out, too. She was excited now—had picked up on his own mood and was really looking aggressively at the fences, eyes and ears leveled on them. He sat in, gave her the cue to gallop, and QL exploded onto the first line.

In the gazebo, Brittany had risen to her feet, and was gripping the railing. "Oh my God, look at this," she murmured. "I want to ride like him."

Brae came over in close beside her, circled one arm around her, murmured, "You will," and then started taking pictures rapid fire.

Man and animal eating up this small course…Frankel had mapped it out as two elements in the first line, then hairpin turn, coming across the ring on the diagonal and hitting two more big ones, then pivot turn to a final wall.

Chuck standing between the first two jumps, so he could see Jericho's form on both of them. Really bold approach to the first of them, Jericho up in his irons, sighting and urging the huge moose-like mare on even faster. Lifted her and released, and QL just launched. Touchdown, one stride, and straight into the second element.

"*Yes!*" Frankel was screaming. "Now turn her and don't waste ground."

Darien took her husband's hand and squeezed it. "Bob, I'm so glad we bought into this horse," she told him. "She's wonderful, isn't she?"

"Think about how far she's come since that first time we saw her," he said, agreeing and happy now. Darien was paying a lot of attention to him, and he'd almost forgotten how insecure he'd felt for a minute there.

QL was making the first turn, not even scrabbling for purchase. Jericho just elevated her into it, and she trusted him totally, digging in with her inside hind leg, carrying her weight there, and then swinging her shoulders around to leap forward in a gallop again.

"Nice!" Frankel called out enthusiastically. Man, he'd wanted to bitch about something, Jericho had been right on that score. But the word just jumped out of his mouth before he could hold it back. Beautiful turn, he had to give him that one.

Bearing down on that second short line now. QL moving with such power and beauty, muscles rippling, loving this.

Pretty much everyone saw it at the same time. Collective gasp, and Frankel screaming, "Jason, pull up!"

Jericho and QL were crossing the diagonal from bottom right to the upper left. Jason and Landrover were coming from the bottom left to the upper right—the paths they were making together in the sand arena forming a giant X. And the two horses heading for a collision at the center of it.

Awareness of the situation exploded into Jericho's mind, but his mare was moving with such momentum—absolutely thundering. He yanked her hard to the right, trying to steer away from Landrover, but was only partially successful. Jason reacted slower, and with even less effect. Landrover's shoulder ploughed into the huge mare, who screamed and took a violent and jerking sideways leap. At the speed they were traveling, and up in two point, that maneuver from the mare nearly sent Jericho flying—he was way off balance to the left, but had grabbed QL's mane and was trying to get himself back on top. Second hard bump from Landrover in quick succession—his hindquarters this time. Then shoulder again, and he'd hit Jericho's upper torso, knocking the wind from him, and finishing the job of unseating him. He dropped between the two horses, and right into the thick of those eight scrambling legs with their deadly steel-clad hoofs.

Darien letting out a cry of horror, "Oh Jericho, oh no!"

He hit the ground, tried to cover himself. Searing pain to his left leg. Hard jerk on his shoulder that spun him over. And oh fuck, his arm was tangled in QL's reins, and he felt her dragging him. Then a hard knock to the head. Everything went black.

It was over in a matter of two or three seconds, with Jason manhandling Landrover out of the way and pulling him up. QL and Jericho appeared to be tangled together, and she plowed to a halt, straddling him with her front legs, his right arm still wound in the reins and held above his body at the height of the mare's chest, keeping his shoulders and upper back a few inches off the ground. His head was dropped to the side, and he didn't look conscious.

Marco had started running to reach him. Jason too had vaulted off his horse. Not to mention the group in the gazebo—Brae about to leap over the railing and run out into the ring.

"Stop!" Frankel shouted—or more like hissed. "All of you... everyone...stay where you are and don't move." He spoke with real authority and urgency, instantly taking charge. "Listen to me. If you frighten that mare and she takes off, he's as good as dead."

They all froze.

"Oh, Chuck," Coulder said in an agonized voice. His face looked ravaged, like he wanted to cry. "That was totally my fault, I had no idea he'd turn that fast. And Chuck...*Jesus Christ, Chuck*...I *hit* him..." What he meant was that he'd run him over with his horse.

Frankel had feared as much. "Someone with a cell phone dial 911, and tell them *no sirens* when they approach the farm," he barked. Bob Marx took on the assignment, and started making the call.

Frankel was orchestrating things now. "Jason, get that horse up to the barn where he can't disturb QL. And Marco, come over to me...but very slowly. If you see that mare so much as twitch, stop immediately." He knew the head groom would understand Jericho's imminent peril. "Damn it," Frankel muttered. "His full weight is hanging on that bit in her mouth. If something startles her, she could just freak out. Hell, she might anyway."

Marco inched his way closer to Frankel, keeping his hands at his sides, taking forever to get there it seemed. QL snorted warily. She'd lowered her thick head, her nostrils wide, eyes wild. But she hadn't panicked—at least not yet.

No movement from Jericho—either he was totally out cold...or worse.

"You try and approach her, she knows you best," the Chef D'Equip said, and Marco nodded. He took a cautious step in her direction.

Snort from QL, and her head jerked partway up—the drag of Jericho's body slamming her in the teeth with the bit as she did. Angry squeal from her, and a quick dance with those huge front feet, so treacherously close to the injured man between them.

"Stop there, wait," Frankel told him sharply—needlessly though, since Marco was standing stock-still on the spot. "Try another step," he said a heartbeat later. Marco moved forward again—more sharp negative reaction from QL, her ears lying flat back on her head now—threatening. "Careful, careful," Chuck said, his voice hushed.

Jericho moaned softly—still not conscious, but maybe closer to awareness. His one leg moved.

QL lowered her head again, laying him back in the sand—almost as if she knew what she was doing. Her mouth nuzzling at him, soft worried nicker. Marco tried another step toward her. Wham! That thick jughead lurched back up, ears once again flattened, her expression fierce now rather than scared, even though the movement had slammed her in the mouth with the bit again. Her body tightened, and she swiveled her hindquarters suggestively toward him.

"Back off, Marco," Frankel said. And he did.

Satisfied, QL dropped her head, and Jericho stirred again. She pushed at him gently, sniffing at him, making quiet little horse sounds, just a rumble in her throat.

Darien hadn't even tried to stop the tears that rolled out of her eyes and down her face. She couldn't take her eyes off the scene in front of her. He'd been hurt so badly. She murmured his name in anguish, "Jericho..."

Brae put his arm around her, and she laid her face on his shoulder, shaking all over. "Come on," he said to her without a trace of his normal foolishness. "He's strong. He'll survive this. He'll be alright." Maybe he was just trying to convince himself of that—he was shaking too.

Marx just watched—his wife with Brae holding her...and Jericho. Gripped by what was happening in front of him, frustrated that he couldn't do anything more to help.

They could hear sirens in the distance. Then coming closer. Closer. Then silence.

More orders from Frankel—he was keeping cool and always thinking. "Someone go meet the ambulance. Keep them at the end of the driveway—and don't let anyone come running with a gurney into this ring."

Jericho's tangled arm moved, he yanked at it weakly, rattling the snaffle in the mare's mouth again. She dropped her head even lower, almost to the ground.

"Jericho...Jericho, can you hear me? Don't move," Frankel warned him. No response. He called to him again, trying to reach him. "Jericho, you're wound up in the reins, can you get yourself free?" But the injured man didn't seem to comprehend that, or maybe just wasn't awake enough hear—wasn't responding to Frankel's voice in any event. Instead, he reached up with his other arm...in almost slow motion...and wrapped his hand around the bridle's throatlatch. "God no," Frankel breathed—the mare would never tolerate that, he was thinking—but there was nothing he could do to intervene.

Jericho's hand slipped loose again, and dropped to the sand. He just breathed. His eyes opened. He was on the ground...blue sky above him and QL's face so near. Awareness of what had happened, where he was. Memory of going down between the horses, and trying to protect himself from those flashing hoofs.—then blackness and now this.

He tried to lift his own head, but couldn't, not yet. Lots and lots of pain, but sensation in all his extremities. Right arm tangled somehow, and man it really hurt—shoulder screaming like a mother fucker at him, and his forearm worse—sharp biting pain every time it moved with the motion of QL's head. Fractured, and he knew it. His left side hurt down the length of it with areas of sharper pain, and his lower leg felt like a spike had gone through it—also broken, he was pretty sure, but at least still supported by his boot. He tasted blood, and his head throbbed.

Paramedics were at the side of the field now, and Frankel had gone over to them to explain what was happening. "The mare won't let us near him, and he's twisted up in the tack. If we startle her and she bolts, she'll drag him and step on him. Probably kill him."

"Is he conscious?" the medic asked.

"He wasn't, but it looks like he's coming around. Christ, if we can just get him to free himself..."

"Chuck, he's definitely moving," Marco called over to him, and the Chef D'Equip's face swung sharply around. "Let me get closer to him, try to talk to him," Frankel said. "And please, don't try to approach him. Let us handle it."

Jericho tried again to stir, but the flood of pain blocked him. Christ, the mare was standing right over him, and he could barely see past her and his helmet's rim. Didn't really understand what was holding him immobile—why he was lying here, what he needed to do. He reached with his left hand around and undid the harness that strapped the helmet to his head. Yanked on the rim, and then just let it fall off. Moaned. Damn, his head felt like he'd been hit by a baseball bat. Turned his face to the side and tried to spit out the blood.

Words, someone talking. It was Frankel, calling his name.

Grabbed onto that voice. Choked out a single word. "Chuck…"

"Jericho, can you hear me?"

Weak nod from his head.

Repeated his name with almost every sentence, trying to maintain the connection with him. "Jericho, QL won't let us near you, and you're wrapped up in the bridle. You've got to get yourself free. Can you?"

Wrapped up in the bridle—man, he understood what that meant, knew how much trouble he was in. The more awake he became, the more the pain assaulted him too, and his arm was really in agony. His breathing had accelerated. "I'll try, Chuck." Closed his eyes for an instant and laid some more information on him. "This…wrist's broken…shoulder…left leg too."

Harsh strong voice coming back at him. "Suck it up, Jericho. I know it hurts. Do it anyway. We can't help you till you get free of her."

Couldn't deny the authority of that order. Lifted his head to see. Tried to unravel himself. Sharp stabbing pain when he moved it—gave it a real effort though, just gritting his teeth, snarling and plowing past the searing scream of protest coming from his shoulder and forearm. The leather reins had bitten into the skin and tissue beneath them, and were bloodied, filthy, and deeply embedded in his arm, surrounding that broken wrist. Constant drag from his weight on the arm, giving him no slack to work with. Couldn't get it free, just couldn't. He dropped back to the sand again with a growl of frustration, his chest rising and falling from the torture of making the effort.

"Come on, Jericho…*do it.*"

Reached around with his other arm for the rein, but couldn't quite get a hold of it. He was speaking to the mare now too, and man those huge mule ears flicked forward. Grabbed hold of the cheek piece of the bridle and turned her head to get better access to the rein that held him, and she let him do it—helped him even.

Movement from someone on the sidelines, and QL's thick block of wood head swung up sharply again, mule ears back and threatening. She lurched to the side, jerking the man beneath her hard up off the ground a few inches, and dragging him about a foot—wrenching a deep cry from

him. Heard Frankel barking, "Stay back, damn you!" Then, another command. "Jericho, try again. *Come on.*"

Still murmuring to QL. Damn, couldn't believe it, but she wasn't even
frightened, this animal…no, instead she was protecting him—alpha mare
standing over a downed member of the herd. He knew then she'd tolerate
a lot more than any horse should under the circumstances…had to trust
her. Had to get the pressure off this arm too…stop the damage, cause man
it was bad. He reached up again with his left arm and wrapped his hand
around one of those mule ears, drew up the knee of his uninjured right leg.
Talked to her, asked her to help him, then jerked his body weight up,
pulling against that ear, trying to stand. The mare's huge head, not pulling
away, not fighting back against the tremendous pressure on her ear, but
instead pressing her face against his chest, supporting and even lifting him.
Another cry of pain from him, but his feet came under him and he was up,
but so very tenuously. Released his grip around her ear and wrapped his
left arm around her head now, weight carried precariously on one leg. But
standing.

He just stood there breathing until the pain subsided marginally—just
talked to QL, murmured to her, thanked her. Believing she'd understand.
Then said quietly, "Marco."

His head groom approached them slowly. The huge moose of a mare
stirred nervously, lifting a hind foot and stomping it threateningly. Jericho, working the buckles of the bridle now, then tugging on it. It slid over
her ears and fell to the ground, jerking on his arm one more time, and man
he almost blacked out then, the breath jerked raggedly from his body. Just
held onto her with all he had left in him. "Get a halter," he said so quietly,
he wasn't even sure that Marco would hear him. But then he heard his
voice calling out.

"Halter! He's asking for a halter."

Jericho wasn't even watching. Didn't know when Marco backed away
to take the halter from Brittany who'd run up to the barn to get it. He took
those few minutes just to collect himself, to build strength. His right arm
was hanging limp at his side, and still with the reins wound around it—the
leather good and tangled and still biting into the bloodied flesh of his
lower arm. Wall of pain—arm, leg, torso, head.

"Boss."

Whispered word, and close behind and to the side of him.

Harsh sentence from him…but much more of a plea than an order. "Marco, come and take her."

"I don't know if she'll let me, boss."

"Try."

Jericho murmured again to the mare, told her it was alright, asked her to trust him the way he'd trusted her. Marco coming up beside him, and speaking with soft words. "Move a little, Jericho, you're covering her head." He felt Marco leaning into him from his left side, and released the mare's face to hold onto his shoulder instead while the head groom slipped the halter onto QL.

As hurt as he was, Jericho was the one issuing orders. "Try and get me over to Chuck. Let the mare stay with me. Marco, don't let her get hurt or frightened, she saved my life here. If she'd have run…"

"I know."

He wasn't sure if he could walk or not, but knew he had to try. Marco leaned harder against him, and tightened one arm around his waist. Step. Limping hard and almost going down—yeah the boot was supporting that broken lower left leg, but that didn't stop it from hurting like hell when he put weight on it. Marco just held him upright for a moment. Then step again. All three of them moving together at an absolute snail's pace, Marco guiding Jericho closer to Frankel, the bridle dragging from his arm across the sand—and so much pain from that, it was going to drive him under again.

"Marco, I can't. Stop here. Try and lead QL away."

Squeal of protest from the mare, but Jericho talking to her, telling her to let him, telling her again that it was alright. This had to happen soon cause he was fighting to remain conscious—and he knew he needed to be standing when QL left him…to give her confidence, to let her know her job of protecting him was done. Planted his good leg and tried to balance with the broken one. Pushed himself free from the man supporting him. Upright and unassisted now. Spoke to the mare again. QL seemed to settle then, and when Marco pulled her in the direction of the barn, she let him lead her. Snorting anxiously, and still looking back at Jericho, but following along without fighting it.

Frankel coming to him, his hands on him, strong and steadying. Jericho leaning hard against him, and wavering badly…murmuring to him, "I'm so fucked here, Chuck."

Words of encouragement. "Be glad you're alive. You really kept your cool and I'm proud of you."

Surrounded suddenly by paramedics, laying him down on something. Jason's voice, "Oh, God I'm so sorry, Jericho." Darien's tearstained face appearing above him. World going blessedly black again.

They took him to Palms West Hospital, and Frankel rode with him in the ambulance. Jason, Brae, Brittany and the Marxes came along behind in separate cars and met up again in the Emergency Room.

"He's back to unconscious," Frankel told them gravely. "But maybe that's a good thing, he had to be suffering. They had him on oxygen in the ambulance, but at least they got that bridle unwound. Damn, his arm looks bad."

Brae was the one who'd gone out into the middle of the sand arena and retrieved Jericho's helmet. He laid it wordlessly on the glass-top coffee table in front of himself. Good-sized dent in the front of it, and cracked clean through over the crown. "Good thing he was wearing this," he said.

They all just stared. Man, you could say that again.

Jason paced the room, he was really beating himself up over this. "Christ, I like him so much, and he was going out of his way to help me with Landrover…God, he didn't need to do that, and then I just plow right into him." Slapped the palm of his hand against his forehead in agitation. "My fault, all my fault…I shouldn't have even been on the course when he was going through." Frankel had to take him aside and try to calm him down.

"Come on, Jason, you're not helping anything."

Darien was still visibly upset, and her husband pulled her close, comforting her. "Chuck, did they say anything?" he called over to him.

"Not yet, the doctor's going to come out as soon as he can."

Half an hour passed. Then forty-five minutes. Finally a resident came out and approached them, Frankel going over to meet him. "We're all over here," he said.

"Is this the family?"

Brae rising, his hand still trailing on Brittany's shoulder. "I'm his roommate. He doesn't have any living relatives that I'm aware of, but we're all close friends."

"And I'm Chuck Frankel. I coach the United States Show Jumping Team, and Jericho's one of my riders. We were working together when the accident happened."

The doctor nodded. "Alright, I'll talk to you then." He took Frankel's arm and walked with him to the side, while everyone else waited worriedly. "He's got some pretty good injuries, but from the way you described the accident earlier, I think he was damn lucky to come through it as well as he did. Concussion, and we'll want to keep him overnight for observation to make sure there's no significant swelling of the brain—that's our main concern with him right now. Other than that, there was a dislocated shoulder and we've fixed that. Broken right wrist—the ulna, not the radius, but it's a nasty break...compound fracture."

"Are you going to operate?"

"I don't think we'll have to, but we'll have to wait and see how it heals. There's lots of tissue damage to that arm too. Broken left leg—the fibula— that's the smaller of the two bones in the lower leg. On top of all that, he took a couple of hard body blows and there's plenty of bruising, but we're not seeing signs of organ damage." Shook his head in a bit of amazement. "His body's a wall of muscle—that really protected him. That and the safety helmet."

"Thank God he had it on," Frankel breathed. "But you think he'll fully recover?"

"Yes, I think so as long as there are no complications." Comforting smile from the resident. "Those bones should mend alright in about six to eight weeks."

Six to eight weeks—the season all but over by then. Alright, Frankel thought to himself grimly. Jericho would be devastated by the news...but he'd ride again.

Jericho was sedated although not heavily. But even so he wasn't expected to come around until morning. But no one had been able to make Jason leave the hospital, so in the end the rest of the group just left him there. He'd been chased away from the corridor in front of Jericho's room more than once now, but as soon as he got the opportunity, he returned.

Activity down at the nurses station again. He didn't want to get caught standing there yet a third time, and ducked inside Jericho's room instead.

Knew he wasn't supposed to be there, but too bad. He came over to the bed and sat down at the foot of it.

Everything pristine and white. Jericho looked peaceful. Eyes closed, long hair spilling over the pillow, but the evidence of his injuries all too obvious. Shoulder bandaged up tight. Long casts on both extremities—his right arm encased from the middle of his bicep, around and over the elbow, and continuing all the way down over his palm—thumb sticking out. The leg cast was similar—clearly visible, since they had it elevated. It went from his mid thigh down to and including the ankle and heel of his foot.

"Oh shit," Coulder said, just staring. Jericho was going to hate him for this—and with good reason too. And why? Because he'd been nice enough to help him out.

Jason sat with him a long while, just watching. Didn't seem to mind the fact that he had nothing to do but stare. Got up and paced to the window once, then back again to sit with Jericho.

It was probably a good hour later when his eyes partially opened. Fluttered closed. Opened again. Flicking from Jason, to the room, to Jason…trying to focus, and then to process where he was and what was happening. Then falling on the cast around his arm, and finally the one around his leg. His eyes closed again, and this time the expression on his face was pure desolation. "God, tell me this is a nightmare," he murmured aloud.

'I'm so sorry, Jericho. I'm so thankful too…they said you'll fully recover, but I'm *so sorry* this happened. God, I'm such a fucking idiot. What could I have been thinking? How could I have been on the course when you were taking it?"

"Man, just shut up," Jericho said harshly, despair evident in his voice. Really frail sounding too.

"You have every right to hate me, and I'll be the first one to say it."

Silence.

"Look, I'll leave if you want me to," Jason said with resignation. "I just had to see you and apologize, but I'll go now." He'd already judged himself and found himself guilty—and was accepting the punishment.

"What are you talking about?" Jericho whispered savagely, forcing the sentences out like it was hard for him to do. "Hell, I told you to take the line, I was coaching you. I should have known where you'd be. It was totally my own damn fault."

Coulder reached forward and wrapped his fingers around Jericho's good arm. Said with passion, "No, I'm a professional, and I know better. I should never have been jumping when you were riding a course."

Expressive deep blue stare. "Well, then let's both go home and shoot ourselves...for what good that'll do us." Closed his eyes again and just shook his head, miserable. "Oh man, Jace," he sighed weakly. "Yeah, I'm suspended, but in a few more weeks I'd be out of it, and you saw that QL mare, she's phenomenal. She's strong, she's sound...she's even better than Monterrey is. I had such a shot at it with those two horses...Marx as a patron. Why did this have to happen now?" Looked up at his friend with more strength, as if a thought had just struck him. "The horses are okay, aren't they? Landrover? QL?"

"Yeah, they're fine. Don't worry. Marco gave both of them some 'Bute this evening..."

"This evening?"

"Yeah pal, they had you out for a while."

"Yeah, I *am* out." He seemed completely demoralized. Laid another powerful look on Coulder. "Jace, why am I in long casts like this—are the breaks that bad?"

"Hell, I'm no doctor, what would I know? From what Chuck said, your wrist is the worst of it, and they think it will heal without surgery, so it can't be that bad."

Pause from him. Stubborn look settling over his features. "If I had my knee and elbow free, I could ride."

"You can't mean that."

"Why wouldn't I?"

They sat staring at each other. Jason was stunned at what Jericho was thinking...on the other hand, he understood it all too well. "Maybe you can," he equivocated, though he still sounded skeptical. "I mean, you'll probably have to go a week to ten days in these casts before they'll let you shorten them, but I've seen plenty of guys ride in a short arm cast. I don't know about the leg though Jericho. You'll never be able to put your weight down into the stirrup."

"Chuck makes me ride without stirrups all the time."

Good point, or at least it sounded like it.

"He's not going to agree to this," Coulder warned.

"Maybe he won't, but if so then fuck him. I'll just keep working by myself." Didn't want that though...as bitchy and mean as Frankel was, he was a damn good coach, and one of the most influential men in the business. Jericho was going to convince him to go along with this somehow. If he had to, he'd go to Marx for support.

———————

It was the next afternoon before they finally released him.

Darien never came.

Chapter Sixteen

It was about three o'clock in the afternoon the next day and Chuck Frankel came striding up to Starbucks. He was looking for Brae. Heard someone calling his name out. Looked around and saw Jason Coulder sitting with Chip Langdon. Waved but didn't stop. Went inside—no sign of the Barista. He came back out, and this time did go over to the table. "I'm looking for Jericho's roommate," he said. "Has he been in?"

"Not since we've been here," Langdon told him. "Hey, Jason was telling me about Jericho," he went on, and he looked concerned. "Have you heard anything more today? I feel awful about it. Really bad luck for him…and man, he was having such a tough season anyway. If there's anything I can do for him, let me know, okay?"

Jason was just sitting there, glum and with his head hanging low, fiddling with a straw that he had in his hand.

"Apparently he was released about an hour ago," Frankel told them. "I've been trying to reach him, but he isn't answering his cell." He grabbed a chair and swung it over, straddling it backwards like sitting on a horse. "He was out cold when we brought him into the hospital, and I haven't had a chance to talk to him." Looked at Jason. "Did you?"

Jason nodded. "Yeah, I waited a long time, but I finally got to see him for a few minutes last night."

"And? What's his mood?"

A shrug, looking miserable. "What you'd expect—really low." He lifted his eyes more directly to Frankel. "Hell Chuck, he still thinks he's going to show this season. I'm worried about him, and I feel…oh man, I feel so responsible."

"Jericho blame you?" the Chef D'Equip asked, but knowing differently—he had a pretty good read on the injured rider by now. And although he was burning to ask more about the other part of what Coulder said—about Jericho wanting to compete again this season—he'd get to that. First, he wanted to see if he couldn't help get Jason past this. He had to let go of it, had to stop pummeling himself.

Jason shook his head in the negative, looked vulnerable. "No, Chuck. He let me completely off the hook. Took all the blame himself. But that's just him, everybody knows that. He's just…really big inside…you know what I'm saying?"

"Yeah, I know what you're saying. But if he let you off the hook, then you do the same thing—you hear me? Look, I'm blaming myself too. Jericho was in a foul mood yesterday morning, and I knew that. I even told him to get off the horse, but I didn't make him and I should have."

Resigned nod, though he didn't appear convinced. He clearly still thought he was the one at fault, although Chuck's admission was reaching him. He'd think about it for sure—hopefully come to terms. "You're right, he did seem out of sorts," he quietly agreed.

"But what's this bullshit about him riding again this season?" Frankel demanded. "Six to eight weeks for those bones to mend…and hey he's young and healthy, so let's be aggressive and say it's only six. He'll still be out of condition by then—maybe even need some physical therapy. And the horses will be out of training too. Maybe someone else could ride Monterrey in the meantime, but definitely not QL." *Or Chasseur de Lion*, he was thinking, but didn't mention him.

Coulder looked guilty again, but for a different reason—like maybe he shouldn't have been saying this, like he was giving away a confidence. "You should see him," he said. "He's got casts from here to here," and he pointed. "Elbow and knee both in. He knows he can't ride like that, but he's gonna ask them for short casts as soon as they'll let him…and he thinks he's gonna go back to training after that."

"Ridiculous! I'm not going to allow it." But even though he was saying the words and powerfully, something was stirring inside him. Excitement. Didn't even want to acknowledge it, but it was there anyway. Insidious, wrapping its tendons around him—making him want to change his mind—consider it.

"Yeah, I told him that, Chuck. But he said if you won't help him, he'll just work on his own."

Frankel growled and he looked really intense. "I need to find him. Where the hell can he be? He's not at home, I just went past there."

Langdon laughed fondly. "You're missing the obvious. Have you been over to his stables? Ten to one, he's there."

————————

Yeah, he was there, but not working or even trying. And not talking to anyone either. Marco had picked him up, and Marco was the only one he'd said anything at all to, and not much there either. Just asked him to take him over and let him off by one of the paddocks…then bring QL down to be with him.

Not much Marco or anyone else could say to him anyway…he looked awful and knew it. Not just looked awful—*was* in dreadful shape. Couldn't get anything on over those casts, so he'd just whacked off the left leg of the pair of jeans he'd been wearing, and split the side seam even higher. Similar handiwork on his long-sleeved shirt, plus he was wearing a sling to support it. They'd given him a cane, and at the moment he pretty much had to use it—or hop on one leg, and man he hated that.

Marco helped him get out of the car, and then he hobbled over to the paddock, and took up a position on the inside, leaning for support against the railing at the front corner. Marco returned with QL moments later, turned her loose in the paddock and locked the gate behind the two of them. Didn't stay more than a minute or two either. But before he left he walked over and wordlessly handed his boss a box of oatmeal cookies. Then he was gone. Knew Jericho wanted to be left alone.

But not from this mare. And man, that thick jughead swung around to see him. Big snort, and then she came prancing right up to him. Thrust that huge moose-head out and sniffed him. Sniffed the casts—didn't know what they were, but knew they were something different. Found that cookie box and tried to bite it. He laughed, rubbed that so very plain face with deep affection, laid his own face against it, talking to her, taking in the clean scent of a well-groomed horse, slipping an entire cookie in her mouth. And *that* she liked, crunching happily, big mule ears pitched out contentedly to either side.

Still out there with her maybe an hour later. He'd lowered himself to the ground, and was smoking a cigarette. QL was further out in the paddock grazing.

Chuck Frankel's white pick-up pulling into the driveway, then down to the circle out front. Parking. Both he and Marx getting out of the car, and strolling up to the barn. Jericho watched them, but didn't hail them. He knew they'd be coming out to bother him soon enough. And right now, there wasn't a person alive he wanted to be with. Not even Darien.

Clear enough where she stood, wasn't it? And who could blame her? Who should she choose, who would anyone choose for that matter? A rich, successful investment banker, or a suspended, beat to shit horse trainer—*barn help?* Duh, right?

Tossed his butt away, and just lit another one. He didn't turn, though he could hear them approaching…didn't want to see the mother fucking pity on their faces when they looked at him. Still, he grabbed hold of the fence rails behind him, and levered himself to his feet. At least he was going to be standing.

Frankel's voice first. "Jericho?"

"Yeah, I'm here." Pretty obvious, but who gave a shit? About anything.

QL's head came up, and she turned and trotted over nearer, blowing. Then even closer, looking at the two men aggressively—ears still pitched forward, but ready to step in, if needed. He petted her, spoke to her, and she walked a few steps away again and lowered her head to graze, but she wasn't going far that was for sure.

From Marx and rather awed, "That mare really loves you."

Good thing someone did.

But he didn't say it, and still hadn't looked around. Why were the two of them bothering him anyway? There wasn't a Goddamn thing either of them could say that meant anything.

Frankel again. "Are you going to let anyone talk to you?"

Lowered his head and said forbiddingly, "No." He knew there wasn't a prayer they'd leave though. Jericho sighed…shit, might as well get it over with. Let them go through their "look on the bright side" speeches, and then get the fuck away from him. He grabbed the railing with his left hand, and pivoted on his right heel, hopping around a step or two with his left leg. Knew what he looked like. "Alright, get a good look, Chuck. Yeah, I'm totally fucked-up, so now you've seen it and you can get off my place and leave me fucking alone." Lots and lots of anger there. Inner pain, bitter disappointment. Slightly less belligerent tone of voice. "Please, I'm asking you. Don't ride me right now, alright?"

"You could look a lot worse," Frankel observed, and without a lot of sympathy, although that was what he felt inside. Still, right now, sympathy wasn't what Jericho needed—it might be the *last* thing he needed. "Down between horses, dragged, kicked in the head…I'd say you were damn lucky…*damn* lucky, Jericho."

Raised that deep blue stare to the two of them. "You think I don't know that? Think I'm feeling sorry for myself, Chuck?"

"Yes."

A rush of resentment filled him. "Have some fuckin' mercy."

He didn't seem to. Tossed out an almost mocking remark. "So you think your world's shattered, is that it?"

Gutted out the response. "Don't you?"

Frankel shrugged. He leaned over and pulled a long blade of grass up, slipped it between his teeth and chewed on the end of it. "If you want it to be. If you're done trying."

Instead of a brutal comeback, the fire just went out of him. He raised that right arm with its thick cast, laid it across the top rail of the fence, taking the weight off the sling around his neck. Lowered his forehead down to it, and just blew his breath out. "Please, Chuck...stop."

Even Marx appeared to be uncomfortable with this, and he gave Frankel a look of censure. Their eyes locked, but Frankel seemed completely determined. "Please? From you, a "please"? Don't want to hear it, Jericho? Just want to give up? Maybe I should start looking for some place to put these horses," he pressed on. "And here Jason's got some crazy notion that you want to go back to training as soon as those long casts come off...I told him he must have heard you wrong. Yeah, he misunderstood, that's for sure."

"Come on, Chuck," Marx interjected sternly. "That's enough."

Jericho's head had come up, his expression intent and coldly furious—and totally focused on the Chef D'Equip. "Oh yeah, from you it's always the same message isn't it? I'm such a fuck-up, aren't I, Chuck? Bad temper, no self-control..." Snarling now. "...yeah, yeah, this accident's my fault. You think I don't know that? My patron here and his wife call me a groom behind my back and yeah, I was so pissed about it I didn't realize Jason and I were riding lines that crossed, and that was my fault wasn't it, Chuck? Oh, and you told me to get myself under control or get off the horse. And I didn't, so we both know I only got what I deserved." Really vengeful tone of voice now—though it was probably just himself he was lashing with this speech and not anyone else. "And you just had to come over here and tell me about it, didn't you? Well, too late...I already know it." Paused and then just growled it out again. *"I already know it."* Breathed deeply in and out a few times, then added. "So now I'll pay for it. You want to move the horses? Move them. But...*not...QL.*"

Marx seemed stricken by the import of what Jericho said. He thought they'd called him a groom? That's how he'd taken Darien's comment? "That's not what Darien meant, Jericho," he made himself say.

"Isn't it?" Turned to him now. Yeah, this was his major patron, and that gave him a lot of leeway, but couldn't he dredge up a token amount of respect? Told him about it. "Hell, Marx…I'll never be what you are. I don't even want to try. But at least give me some credit for being a professional, for running my own business, such as it is." Added caustically. "Yeah, I work with my hands, I do a lot of shitty chores you'd never dream of doing. But damn it, its not like I'm without skills, or don't take a risk, or don't provide a service to my customers."

"Listen, I know that, and we do respect you. Darien never meant…and if we caused…"

Jericho cut him off sharply. "Don't even go there, alright? Everyone wants to take the blame for this…first Jason, now you." He swept a disgusted glance over his arm, and then his leg. "But that's bullshit. It's my own fault—my own damn fault, and there's nowhere I can look other than in the mirror, and man that burns me, but that's what it is."

Frankel seemed completely unmoved—ignored the interplay between Jericho and Marx too. "So when do those long casts come off?" he asked, as casually as if neither of them had said a word.

Annoyed and so expressive. "Don't handle me, Chuck."

"Ten days or so?" he asked again.

Jericho snapped back at him. "Yeah, that Jason has a big mouth."

Frankel just seemed to be waiting for an answer to his question—he was ignoring everything else that got tossed his way. Jericho had shaken out a cigarette and was fumbling to get his lighter out left-handed…dropped it, cursed savagely under his breath.

Calmly, Frankel stretched down and picked it up. Leaned forward, cupped his hands, and struck the lighter. Looked inquisitively at Jericho, who hesitated…then bent down and lit his smoke. "Thanks," he murmured.

"Ten days? Longer?" the Chef D'Equip asked one more time.

Stared at him pointedly, and then finally answered the question. "Yeah, ten days…if it's healing alright."

"Gonna try and ride then?" Still completely casual conversation.

Defensive, but pretty challenging too, like just daring Frankel to give him a ration of shit over it. "I want to."

"Is that a yes or a no?"

Drew on his cigarette. Harsher. "It's a yes."

Frankel nodded sagely. "So Jason was right."

"Damn you, Chuck."

Frankel came right back at him, but still in an off-hand, pleasant tone of voice. "Want help?" It wasn't at all what he'd planned to say next; in fact it was diametrically opposite what he'd planned to say next—yet it just slipped out.

Jericho looked away, his eyes traveling up the length of that impossible cast around his leg. Wondering—which direction was Chuck going here? Was he really offering assistance—saying that he'd keep coaching—or just leading him down a path that led to nowhere? "Yeah, I want your help if you're really offering it."

"So now we're down to the truth—and don't try to bullshit your way past me with that crap about how bad you feel for yourself. Yes, you feel bad and I do too, but you're a long way from quitting. You still want to ride, and you think I'm gonna stop you. And I damn well should. Let me put it this way...you riding with those casts on probably won't work out. And it's very dangerous. But, I know I won't be able to talk you out of it. So accept the risk if you want to, just make sure you think long and hard about it, cause we could be talking about the rest of your career here, not just this year." No doubt he was completely on the level now, speaking very seriously. "Look at me, Jericho." Waited until he did, then continued. "Did you hear me? It's a pretty damn dicey thing to do."

He nodded, said fiercely, "Yeah, I know the risk."

"Make sure you do. I know you. You don't think I'll help you. I don't even *want* to help you do something that dodgy, but I will because you'll need help and I don't want to see you kill yourself. But, if I *do*...these are my conditions..."

Yeah, he was tuned in now but good. "I'm listening."

"Are you?"

Sighed, drew on his cigarette again. Muttered coldly, sarcastically, "Yes, Chuck."

Frankel stared at him a moment longer, but then finally started laying them out. "First, you'll promise you won't go to short casts until the doctor says it's alright. You'll get x-rays along the way too—if those bones aren't healing properly because of the work, you'll stop. Are we together on this so far?"

Didn't like agreeing to that, but nodded again. "Yeah, we're together."

"I really mean it."

"I know."

"I don't like this," Marx objected. And it wasn't what he and Chuck had talked about either, and that bothered him. "It just sounds unsafe to me."

Deep blue stare swinging aggressively back to him. "It's not your decision."

"It's my money."

"I don't give a fuck."

"That's enough!" Frankel snapped, effectively breaking that stalemate. "Stick with *me,* Jericho. Control that damn temper of yours for a change."

He murmured angrily, but yielded to the criticism, just shouldered it. Looked pointedly back at the Chef D'Equip again. "Alright, I'll give you that."

"And apologize to your damn patron for Christ's sakes."

Bowed his head and looked mutinous, but muttered, "Fine, I'm sorry."

Marx laid a hand on his shoulder briefly—show of support, apology not really needed—not really given either, and that almost made the investment banker chuckle.

Frankel went back to listing his conditions. "And this is an absolute…you need to have some kind of boot on—I don't know how you're going to do it, but your foot and that cast need protection somehow."

Actually he agreed with that and had been thinking about it. Impossible to get a real boot custom-made in a ten-day timeframe, that was for sure. And nothing he'd buy over the counter was going to work. But he could probably get a half-chap around the cast, and use paddock boots for footwear. Probably have to have the left paddock boot altered too—top cut back or off, maybe even split down the upper center seam. And maybe he'd have to have Marco tape it up every time he rode in it, rig it together. But he was pretty sure it was doable. "I think I have that figured out," he said, and quickly outlined his thoughts.

Frankel seemed to buy them, he listened and nodded his head anyway—seemed to be picturing it in his mind. "Fine, let's take a look at it. But there's one more condition and you're not going to like it. But live with it. I don't want you riding Chasseur de Lion. Monterrey and QL, okay, but not him."

"No, Chuck I'm riding him." Real stubborn on that one.

"No, Jericho, you're not." Even more so.

"Yes, really Chuck, I am." He dropped his cigarette and stepped on it. Lifted his eyes again militantly. "And there's no way you can stop me. Maybe you won't help me, but I'll do it anyway…unless you talk my name-less patron into moving him out of the barn. But man if you do that, then I want the chance to talk to him too. And then maybe you can explain to him why I'm riding every horse in the place except the one you talked him into buying."

Didn't look like he cared for that particular alternative, but said force-fully. "What if that horse goes down on you?"

"That's always been a possibility, so what?" Tried using a little more reason with him. "Man, I've put so much effort into getting him past that, and he is—almost. Come on, Chuck…if I don't ride him for two months he'll be right back at square one, and that's not bullshit. What's more dangerous?"

"Tell me this," Frankel murmured, seduced by the thought of Chasseur de Lion too, or so it seemed. "Do you honestly think you can compete him?"

Some real desire lighting up those deep blue eyes now. Determination too. "Fuck yeah, and I *want* to."

There was a long moment of silence, Frankel's eyes narrowed, really thinking about it. "Compromise then," he said, albeit cautiously. "We'll start…but if I say get off, you get off."

"No way."

"Damn you're stubborn!"

Jericho smiled for the first time that afternoon—an unapologetic smile. "Don't tell me you don't understand. Don't tell me that," he said power-fully. "If I can't compete, then just shoot me now…these last six weeks have ripped me up inside, day by ever-loving day. I'm not giving up a whole year…I'm not. Who knows what next year is, or what it brings? This is a time for me, and I'm not letting it go. I'm fighting for it Chuck."

"Even if you're gambling with your life?" Marx asked him insistently.

Poised, but so potent reply. "Even if."

Frankel nodded. Accepted the response. "Alright…we might argue about this again, but alright for now. So let's talk about this then…how do we handle training for the horses over the next ten days?"

That discussion on the next ten days took about forty-five minutes, and was really detailed. Day by day plans for each of the three horses...Monterrey, Chasseur de Lion, and QL. And Frankel was going to do a lot of the work personally—primarily lunging, Jericho working with him from the sidelines, but it was all they could do right now. Better than time off, anyway.

As they headed back to the car together, Marx looked over at Frankel and commented with sincere admiration, "I have to give it to you, Chuck. You really know how to deal with Jericho, and he's a difficult personality. Strong-willed, aggressive, uncompromising."

Frankel opened his truck's driver's-side door and swung behind the wheel. "You think so? You think I handled him?"

"For sure." Marx got in the other side. "Me? Now, I would just have gotten into an argument with him...actually, I *did* get into an argument with him. But you certainly got him to come around."

A snort of laughter, then a shake of his salt and pepper head. "Bob, that guy completely worked me, not the other way around. I had no intention of agreeing to coach him before those casts came off. And Christ, I even agreed to let him keep working that rank stallion."

Marx looked incredulous. "Well, why did you then, if that's how you felt?"

He put the key in the ignition, and turned it over. "Well, I'll tell you what...he's just so damn hungry, you know what I mean? I don't know another rider who wants it that much, I really don't. And...well hell...I just really want to see him make the Team. I don't think he will, but if he wants to try, I'll be there for him. He showed me that in spades today—and don't think for a minute *that* was an accident."

First lunging session with Chasseur de Lion—just two days after the accident. Jericho was watching from the gazebo while Chuck worked the stallion. The bitting rig was on him, and they'd set him up pretty deep...and he didn't like it. Made him really work that under-developed back of his. To make it easier on himself, the big gray was moving along at more of a jog trot than a real working trot...lazy more so than sore.

Grumble from the sidelines. "Chuck, he needs to go more forward."

Frankel cracked the whip behind Lion. Half-hearted response from him.

Vengeful. "God damn it, he needs to go more forward."

Grumble back from the center of the lunging circle. "Yeah, I'm doing that."

Jericho watched for all of about three seconds, then just hauled himself upright. Grabbed that mother fucking cane from where it was resting beside his chair, and then started out into the sand arena. Closed the distance between himself and the lunging horse a hell of a lot slower than he wanted to, but at a pretty good clip considering.

"What the hell are you doing out here?" Frankel snapped, really annoyed now.

Jericho ducked into the inside of the circle, and limped over behind the Chef D'Equip. "Just give me the whip," he demanded, disgusted.

Withering look. "I think I can do it, and you're not steady enough to be out here."

Laid his hand on the handle of the whip. "Well, let go for Christ's sake." Wrenched it free, gave it a shake and a snap...same half-hearted response from Lion...immediately touched him with it. "Canter," Jericho ordered the stallion. Snapped him again. Lion shot forward into a nice round canter. "Good." Superior look in those deep blue eyes. Lifted his voice and bellowed, "Marco, get down here."

Frankel, really pissed now. "I *know* how to lunge a horse, Jericho."

Acerbic. "Marco and I will do it."

It promised to bloom into a full-blown argument between them, and undoubtedly would have, but at that moment a black stretch Mercedes limousine pulled down the driveway.

From Jericho, "Now who the hell is this?"

From Frankel simultaneously. "Oh, there he is."

Their eyes met. "You planning on telling me something here, Chuck?" The two of them, still lunging the stallion together, an uneasy partnership to be sure.

"Whoa," Frankel said to Lion, pulling him up to a halt. Then he yelled out, "Marco, come down here and take this horse!" Pointless, since the head groom was already on his way down to the arena.

"Chuck?" Jericho warned, still waiting for an answer to his question.

Little smile from the Chef D'Equip. "This is Lion's owner." Innocent look from him. "Well, you wanted to meet him, didn't you?"

Looked amazed first…then completely irritated. "Nice of you to tell me this. He's going to want to watch the animal work isn't he?"

"Sure, but come and meet him first." Marco had joined them and Frankel handed the lunge line to him. "Just hand walk him for a few minutes, Marco," he ordered, and then walked away, heading toward the stretch. Didn't even wait for Jericho, who was standing there muttering angrily to himself. He dropped the whip to the sand and followed him. Christ, what a way to meet a patron—hobbling along, one arm and leg in a cast. Nice first impression, that. Instill a lot of confidence, and damn that Chuck.

He was almost at the Mercedes when the driver loped around to open the right rear door. The chauffeur reached in and helped his passenger out. His unknown patron. Jericho stopped dead.

Gray hair, weathered face—easily seventy. And no…this wouldn't be his first impression. It was the homeowner from Palm Beach—the man whose back yard he'd appropriated that first night with Darien. He just couldn't believe it.

The man appeared to be as surprised as he did. Oh yeah, he recognized him alright. Fuck. Double fuck even.

"Bruce," Frankel was saying warmly. "Thanks for coming."

No, that was me, Jericho was thinking. God, was he embarrassed.

Frankel went on, completely oblivious—thus far. "Armbruster Waverly, Jericho Brandeis." Turned around and saw the look on Jericho's face, and his eyes narrowed suspiciously—they asked the question, "what the hell?" without actually saying it aloud—oh, but he'd be drilling for information once they were alone again.

"We've met," Jericho admitted, then muttered, "Sort of." He stepped forward, and held his left hand out—couldn't really offer him the right in that cast. Didn't have a clue what would happen next—whether this man would dress him down, expose him in front of Chuck or what. Shit. Not like he wouldn't deserve it.

"More like saw each other from across the room," that crotchety voice corrected him, taking the odd handshake. Stern. Good hard grip too. Hint of a smile tugging at the corners of his lips, but he suppressed it easily enough. "Chuck warned me about your accident. Glad to see you're up and around. Be back to your…old self…soon enough, I imagine."

Man, he felt chastised. But no, he thought with some relief, Waverly wasn't going to tell Chuck what he'd done, or at least he didn't think so. Didn't need to. Jericho was good and humiliated as it was, and Waverly had made his point all too clearly as it was. "Thanks," was all he said. Appropriate enough response to the elderly patron's remark—the double meaning clear as well. Time for a diversion for sure. "Let me show you Chasseur de Lion...he's right over here." Looked over his shoulder and called to his head man, "Marco, bring him here."

At least the stallion was a magnificent animal, and thank God for that. Would have greatly preferred to walk over and get him—escape for a minute or two and collect himself, but unfortunately that didn't make sense under the circumstances. It wasn't like he could lead the stallion right now, anyway.

Marco brought him over, prancing at the end of his lead. Thought he was hot stuff, snorting and showing off. Tossing his head and rudely shouldering the head groom, stepping in front of him. Now that annoyed his trainer. "Don't let him do that," Jericho said with quiet authority, tossing the cane to the sand several feet away and reaching for the lead himself. Quick jerk. "Get around here," he rumbled, asserting himself in no uncertain terms above the horse. Piercing look from the stallion, but immediate submission, and a much different attitude now that Jericho was holding him. "Damn stallions," he muttered.

Quiet presence not far behind him, but keeping a respectful distance from the huge animal. "It's been a long time since I've been around horses," Waverly commented, then said wryly, "But I do remember that about the young stallions...always rambunctious, full of themselves. Brazen. Only one thing on their mind, I guess."

Oh man, totally directed at him, that. Had the decency to feel firmly put in his place one more time.

"So true," Jericho said, accepting the reprimand...apologizing too. "They just need to be taken down a peg or two every so often...then they behave themselves."

———

Bruce Waverly hadn't stayed that long. He watched Jericho and Marco working Lion, talking privately with Frankel at the same time. When they were finished, Marco took the gray stallion away...and Waverly sent Frankel off on some made up chore. Jericho knew he'd been cued, and made his way over to the gazebo to take whatever private comments Waverly planned to lay on him.

"Sit down," his new patron invited, and he did. Half-expecting some pretty good words now. Waverly just looked at him for a minute, and he took the weight of that stare, waited. "Am I being hard on you?" Waverly finally asked him.

Rueful smile. "Not at all. I deserved worse."

Nod of approval. "Good, it's between us then." Changed the subject. "This horse I bought…he's a real crapshoot, isn't he?"

"For sure. Like him though."

"And his trainer?"

Looked at him forcefully. "No way."

Laughed. "Good," he repeated. "Very good."

Interview over.

———

Later in the morning, and after Frankel left—and oh yeah, the Chef D'Equip had tried to pry out of him what the deal was with Waverly, but he wasn't giving that up, and obviously his patron hadn't either. Liked the old coot, liked him a lot actually.

This was the part of his day that he'd been dreading, and now it was here. Time for Darien's lesson. She was late—Roué standing tacked up in the crossties and waiting—and she was never late. She was dreading this too, apparently. He wondered if Marx had told her what he'd said yesterday—hoped he'd had the good sense not to, but you never knew. Maybe he had.

Ten minutes past the appointed hour, and he was on the verge of calling to see if she was even coming. And then he saw her Audi TT rolling down the drive. All of a sudden he wished she'd called and cancelled. Just the same, he stood and watched as she got out of the car, and started heading toward the barn. Cute little beige hip-hugger breeches on her—kind of the latest fad in riding wear. Expensive designer belt, nice form-fitting, long-sleeved top in navy blue. Sexy little outfit. Oh yeah, that was going to keep his mind active while he taught her.

She immediately saw him standing near the entrance to the aisle way, and even from a distance, he could read the look of dismay on her face. Fucking casts. Turned away and went back inside. Shock and pity were so evident in her expression, and they were the last things he wanted to see there.

"Jericho?" She was inside the barn now, and from the sound of her footsteps, approaching him. Of course she would be, no avoiding that. "Oh God, Jericho, just look at you."

He so didn't want this. "Hi, Darien." Didn't turn to face her—too awkward and too much effort—only made him look worse. Just swung that deep blue stare around. "Ready to ride?" he asked her.

Perfectly manicured hand on his good arm—that little gesture of hers that so got to him. Concern etched on her face. "How are you?" She reached across him and trailed her fingers over the cast on his right arm instead. "I know I'm late, but can we talk first? Do you have time?"

Stubborn. "No, not really." Those arresting eyes of his unreadable.

"You're really upset with me, aren't you?" She sighed and there was such an expression of sorrow in her eyes. "This is my fault, I know that...and I should have called you last night, but I was such a chicken..."

He interrupted her. Brusque, angry tone. "Damn it, Darien, your husband had no right to tell you what I said to him."

She seemed totally taken back by that...confused. "What are you talking about? Jericho?"

Fuck man...it was so clear that Marx hadn't repeated a word of it...oh but he'd just told her. "Come on, let's ride," he growled back at her. "The accident was my own fault, so let's just leave it at that."

Never going to happen though. "What did you tell him?" she insisted.

"Forget I mentioned it, alright?"

"No, Jericho, I'm not going to."

He wrapped his hand around her arm, and stared down at her hard. Dropped his voice to make sure it was good and private. "Let's not play games here. It's clear enough what you think of me. But even busted up like this, I still make pretty damn good barn help. So why don't you just get on your horse and let me give you a lesson...that *is* why you're here."

Definite score—maybe a two-pointer. Tears welling up in her eyes. She breathed a response. "Please, I asked you to let me talk to you, and I can't do it with all your guys and Brittany walking back and forth. I hurt you, and I feel so terrible..."

"What's the point?" he sneered. "Yeah, you could have broken it easier, so what? Hey, I'm the fucking idiot, anyway. You'd have thought I'd learn after Ailynn." He released his hold on her arm—maybe even pushed her away from himself, but so slightly that it was more of an impression than a fact. Long meaningful stare—the ache inside him naked there, but a stone wall against her too. He pulled out his sunglasses from his shirt pocket and put them on, effectively covering it. "Meet me in the sand arena."

"You're so wrong, I really care for you."

Warning. "Don't go there."

He snatched up the cane; it was close-by as always as much as he hated it. Limped his way over to the golf cart they normally used to get around at horse shows—Marco had gotten it out and brought it out front to make it easier for him to get back and forth between the jumping fields and the barn. "Are you going to ride, Darien?" he tossed back at her.

She almost looked like she'd say no, but then just nodded.

"Then I'll meet you there."

The next half hour was probably the worst horsemanship Jericho had seen in a lesson from Darien. Finally, he just cut it short—truth was, she was doing the same thing he'd done—riding, but thinking about something completely different. Made no sense to keep going—and she could get hurt. Like he had.

"Alright, you're done," he said.

"Really? But I was awful today." At least she knew it.

He was sitting up against one of the jumps in the middle of the arena, taking his weight of that long leg cast. Didn't even argue with her. "Yeah, that's why you're done."

She rode over to him, looked really miserable. "I'm sorry, I just can't concentrate. Why won't you let me talk to you? I'm not like Cin Maitland."

Not much yielding from him, if any. "Are you sure about that?" he asked her. His was a nice casual tone of voice that somehow made the comment more blistering. He'd wanted to say a lot more—like that she was in love with her husband, that she had no intention of leaving Marx, had no real interest in their relationship other than for the thrill of it.

Did he have more interest than that?

Yeah, and maybe. Maybe that's what had him so pissed. But maybe too, that's why he wasn't going to say any more than he had—it only made him more vulnerable. Admitting something, when there was nothing coming back at him.

She kicked her feet out of the stirrups, and jumped off Roué. Came closer to him. Reached out her hand to him and got a censuring look back. Defeated, she just let it drop to her side again. "It's not like you didn't know I was married," she finally said defensively. She was hurting too.

"You're right about that," he agreed so cynically. Then just growled, "So I guess if I'm disappointed about what this isn't or wasn't, that's my fault too. And I'm right back to Frankel telling me there's no control in my life. He's got that number, doesn't he?"

Soft. "No, he's wrong."

Harsh. "How do you figure?" It was obvious that he was into a mode of beating the shit out of himself, shouldering the blame for anything he didn't like in his life.

"Because you put yourself out there more than any person I know, and you don't play games either. How can that be anything but good?" She ran the backs of her fingers along his jaw, wasn't going to let him just brush her away—almost didn't care if he liked it or not, it seemed. And he did lift his face to her—sunglasses hiding the look in his eyes, but she knew what it would be and cherished it—that open, laid-bare expression—rare but striking when something really reached him. "Do I have make a decision about us in less than two weeks?" she asked him. "I'm sorry for what I said, I never meant to hurt you...I was flustered, I was just trying to find a way to...keep everything in a holding pattern, if that makes sense. I'm confused, Jericho, I do really feel something for you whether you believe that, or want to believe it...and can you be so sure about what you want right now either? I mean, what if you..." Whispered the last of it. "...decide it's not right for you, and I've...?"

His left hand came up to her waist, but he had no words to answer her. It wasn't as if what she was saying didn't make sense. Instead of answering directly, he told her something more about what was inside him, "Your husband came out that back door, and the way you looked when you turned to greet him, and fuck, I...man, I *slept* with you the night before." He was just shaking his head, and the anger, the passion, and the sheer denial of that image were palpable. Added heatedly. "But Darien, I didn't belong there, and I had to walk away...and I *didn't want* to."

"And I didn't want you to leave either, but what was I supposed to do?"

She'd gotten her wish, and he was talking to her now despite himself. Still shaking his head, negating everything—wanting it to be different, knowing it wasn't. "Yeah, and he's important to both of us, and he doesn't deserve the betrayal, I agree with you. Impossible fucking situation." His hand had slid behind her now...more of an embrace than before. The horse was effectively blocking anyone's view of the two of them, so he could dare it. He rose beside her, not liking her standing over him. "Not to mention how beat to shit I am here—you think I want you to see me like this?" Glared with real rancor at the casts. "You haven't even gotten a look at the rest of me," he muttered with self-scorn. "Chest, stomach…hell even my back's black and blue. Look what the fuck I've done to myself, Darien."

"It's my fault," she sighed miserably.

"No, you were right before. I knew the situation. I should have dealt with it."

Wanted to kiss her. Thought about self-control, and what that meant. Didn't.

"Can we please just take each day as it comes, at least for a little bit?" she pleaded.

"I'm so territorial, and I have no right to be. But damn it," he murmured.

You're mine.

"Give me some time, Jericho."

Pulled her in close, laid her head on his chest, and his own cheek against the top of it. "No," he said stubbornly—though they both knew he'd just said "yes."

Chapter Seventeen

"I want you to go with me to Palm Beach for a benefit for the Team this evening. Short notice, I know, but do it anyway. Starts at eight." Nine days had passed since Jericho's release from the hospital, and Frankel was on the phone with him—it was early morning, just around seven o'clock. The Chef D'Equip hadn't even said hello, just launched right in with that. Kind of something odd in his tone too—secretive and smirking, and what was that about? "All the short list riders are going to be there," he added.

Jericho and Brae were standing in the kitchen together, drinking coffee and eating bagels—tossing the knife, cream cheese, and Half & Half back and forth between each other as they needed them—harder for Jericho because he was still catching left-handed. But of course it was Brae who dropped his bagel face down onto the floor. "Damn," he muttered. Picked it up and started eating it anyway.

Jericho smirking, trying to concentrate on his conversation with Frankel. "I'm not short listed, Chuck."

"No, you're suspended, but you will be in two weeks on the 29th."

Now that surprised him. "Even injured like this?"

Just glossed right over it. "Yeah, even like that. So are you coming tonight or not?" Frankel demanded, and added threateningly, "No would be the wrong answer, Jericho, in case you had any doubts on that one."

Sighed. "Yeah, if you say I have to be there, then I guess I am. This isn't one of these damn formal things, is it?"

"Black tie," Frankel said, confirming his worst guess. "It's a fundraiser, so I'm going to say a few words, and I might mention you...the other riders too. I'm just warning you now, don't get all shy on me alright? And are you *ever* going to tell me what happened with your doctor last night?" he went right on, moving to a subject they both found a lot more interesting, and away from any questions about that "I might mention you" part.

It worked too, because Jericho was dying to tell him about it, though he was good and annoyed by the way he'd put it. "Well yeah I am, if you ever quit jawing at me." Then murmured with satisfaction. "So he said it's healing up nicely, and yeah, I have the short casts on. God, what a relief that is, let me tell you. I'm going over to see Woody as soon as he opens up this morning to get that paddock boot altered, and I'm gonna stand right there till he gets it done too…but then I can ride right after that. Can you come around ten instead of earlier?"

Frankel grumbled, complaining about it. "Well, that's really going to mess up my schedule for the day," he said irritably—but not covering up his excitement very well. "Should have called me last night," he griped. "But okay, I can probably work it out, I'll call if I can't make it."

Yeah, that was bullshit and Jericho knew it, but he didn't contradict him. "Good," he said.

"Helmet today too, Jericho," Frankel told him firmly. "Did you get a new one?"

"Top of the line model, cost me four hundred, and no argument there," he said. Covered the mouthpiece of the phone and snarled angrily, "Come on, Brae, don't make such a fuckin' mess in the sink…*Jesus*." Then back to Frankel again. "Sorry. Anyway, call me if it's a problem."

"You know what? Can your roommate come with you tonight too?" the Chef D'Equip said suddenly, as if the thought had just struck him—suspicious though, since almost everything this guy did was premeditated.

"You want Brae to come? I don't know, Chuck. I don't have a clue what he has planned."

"Let me talk to him for a minute."

Really suspicious. Definitely up to something, Jericho thought, but held the phone out to Starbucks anyway. "Here, Chuck wants you."

Happy smile on the Barista's face. He took the receiver. "Hi, it's Brae…oh cool…yeah, that sounds like fun." Turned and gave Jericho an excited look and then the thumbs up sign. Screwed his face up in consternation as he listened to whatever Frankel was telling him now. "Oh no, nothing like that…" he responded. "Sports jacket, that okay?" Pause. "Sure, sure I can do that…oh yeah, that too. Oh, nice ones…sure." Seemed to be a discussion of the dress code. Black tie…pain in the ass, Jericho was thinking, and he'd have to stop by the tailor this morning too—have the lower left pant leg on his tux opened up a few inches to make room for that cast—even the short cast was going to be too wide. Hated wearing the damn penguin suit, but needed it for two or three of these functions every year so at least he had one. He'd have to wear a sandal on his left foot though—no dress shoe would fit. "Today?" Brae was saying. "Sure, no problem, I'm off today. What time? Ten? Sure." Listened again. "Gotcha. Want Jericho back again?" Apparently not, since he hung up the phone then. "He says he'll see you at ten. I'm going to take some pictures of you too...training and all that."

Oh yeah, Jericho thought—Frankel would be checking those pictures over thoroughly—checking to see if his leg was slipping as he went over the jump, or if the weight of the cast put him off balance. Damn, he was going to have to ride well today...and he was determined he would. First day back in the saddle after ten days off though. His body also healing, but still badly bruised. Wasn't going to be easy.

None of that mattered. He couldn't wait to have the horses under him again, was so avid for this.

"I'll see you there then," he told his roommate.

Jericho was getting ready to go to the fundraiser, but at a leisurely pace. Brae, on the other hand, seemed hell-bent to get there as early as possible. "What's the rush?" Jericho murmured, struggling with that damn black bowtie that always seemed to confound him, while his roommate watched him impatiently.

"I told Chuck this afternoon I'd help him set up his presentation," Starbucks whined. "Can't you do that in the car, man?"

Annoyed—but not. "Well, hell...I suppose so." Actually, he was in an exceptionally good mood, meaning he was pretty amenable...for once he'd had a damn good day.

Woody—the boot and leather worker of choice in Wellington—had been extremely helpful getting the paddock boot he wanted altered, and had even come up with an idea how to rig together a tall boot that might work, and planned to have something he could look at by the end of the month—amazingly fast turn around. Really had to thank him for that.

But far and away the best thing had been finally getting back on the horses. Decent sessions with them too. Actually, that was putting it mildly to say the least.

It had indeed been a hell of a lot harder than he anticipated. The cast around his left leg was so inflexible and it tended to slide around a bit against the saddle leather, even with the half chap covering it—not to mention the extra weight. So yes, it made riding without a stirrup on that side a lot more strenuous, and after ten days off and as bruised as his whole body still was, it had given him an incredibly demanding workout. He'd been good and tired at the end of it.

Lots of praise and support from Chuck though, and that was gratifying. Unusual too…but, damn it, he'd really earned it today.

And then there was Chasseur de Lion. Great ride on him today, and really a reason to celebrate. After the flatwork, they'd taken him through the two jump standards without rails several times. Then Jericho had called for a simple crossrail—a very low obstacle, twelve inches or less.

"Be careful with this, Jericho," Frankel had yelled out to him, not approving—this was, after all, his first ride since the accident. "Maybe you should wait a few more days."

Didn't want to. He brought the big gray stallion around at a nice round, forward canter. Let Lion see the tiny obstacle, but then just sat in and rode to it like it wasn't even there—like it was no different than those two standards without any rails. Asked for a slightly bigger stride just as they approached the crossrail. Chasseur de Lion seemed unsure—like he was thinking about it. Was it a jump or not? The rider wasn't gathering him… wasn't measuring the stride or guiding him to a spot. Maybe it wasn't. He lifted into the larger canter Jericho requested and simply went over it.

Nope, not a jump.

Came back around and did it two more times. Praised the heck out of him. Pat on the neck, and "Good boy."

"I'm coming through one more time, Chuck," Jericho told him. "Then he's through."

"Alright, you're the boss." Frankel was being pretty agreeable by now— truth was he was as thrilled, if not more thrilled than Jericho at the stallion's performance.

On the sidelines, Brae happily shot picture after picture.

Jericho circled and then brought Lion onto the line one more time, picking up the pace considerably this time.

"Too fast," Frankel complained. "Way too fast for that tiny fence."

Sat in and pushed him—asked for more, and the stallion leapt forward. Not quite a gallop, but a good strong canter. And then as they were almost on top of the jump, Jericho turned the big horse hard to the left, and suddenly they were facing a huge Oxer instead of the tiny crossrail.

"No!" Frankel screamed, incredulous and infuriated by the move. "Jericho, *damn you, no!*"

Sighted the spot. Measured him. Hard squeeze with the legs. Lift—and Jericho threw his own weight forward, powerfully demanding the lift-off. It happened so quickly, the stallion didn't seem to even have time to process the change from no jump to big jump. No time to get his defenses in order. Surrounded by the cues to jump. Felt the launch above him from his rider. Bunched those massive hindquarters and thrust, lifted from the shoulder, huge perfect bascule…and the horse was airborne, flying…

Click, click, click…

…sailing suspended over the big Oxer…leading foot down, and then the hindquarters, push off and continuing on in the same big canter…the stallion snorting excitedly. Jericho still up in two-point, left hand stroking the stallion's neck in rhythm with the horse's huge stride. "Forgot how much fun it is, didn't you boy?" he murmured to him. And man he felt good.

Chasseur de Lion—jumping again.

Oh yeah.

And sure, he'd gotten a ration of shit from Frankel after he pulled up and dismounted. Let him rant on for a minute or so, and then just turned to him, passionate satisfaction in those deep blue eyes—fulfillment. "I'm the trainer here, Chuck. I call the shots," he asserted. End of discussion. "And don't tell me you're not happy with that."

Hard look from Frankel…he really wanted to be angry…really angry. But excitement shone in his eyes, too. He shook his head in denial to hide the little smile pulling at his lips. "God damn right I'm happy," he spat forcefully. "And don't you ever fuckin' do that again without telling me first." Looked him dead on and did smile now. "You son of a bitch," he murmured…but it was amazed approval in his tone, anger evaporated. "You brash son of a bitch." Paused, then gave it to him. "Beautiful job."

He was actually looking forward to seeing Chuck again tonight, though the thought of being put on display at the fundraiser along with the other five short-listed riders made him pretty uncomfortable.

The other five short-listed riders...all veterans with way more experience and credentials than he had. The three reigning Team members—George Strang, Team Captain; Belinda "Bee-Bee" Oxmoor; and Debbie McPherson, and then the first and second alternates—Tim Rawlings and Marc LaCroix, respectively. Really world-class company. Hard acts to follow.

Then of course himself, still suspended, and still pretty much beat to shit.

But, alright, he had to hold his own in that company. He knew all the Team members and alternates well enough to speak to—but none of them personally. Wasn't sure what kind of reception to expect from the group as a whole either. But it would be what it would be, and he'd deal with it, somehow. Had to start somewhere if he wanted to be accepted by them. Actually, he knew he ought to be glad for this opportunity.

The "being on display" part bothered him also. Maybe even more so than stepping into company with the "elite of the elite" of the American Show Jumping world. But he knew what was expected of him—mingle with the rich potential benefactors at the fundraiser. Interest them in his sport. Seek support for the Team.

The benefit was being held at the exclusive club Mar-A-Lago, owned by Donald Trump, and located right on the ocean in Palm Beach. Whether Trump himself would be there tonight or not, Frankel hadn't mentioned. But plenty of other high-wealth individuals would be. Some he'd know, for sure. For example, it was a sure bet the Marxes, Maitlands, and his new patron Bruce Waverly would attend. He'd be expected to spend time with them, but that was the easy part. Talking to strangers was going to be a lot harder. No, he didn't have much experience in that area, but yeah, he'd try it. Least he could do after everything Frankel was doing for him.

They pulled into the Mar-A-Lago drive and a valet took their car—Brae looked pretty self-impressed and puffed up over that one, and pretty damn well pleased with himself too in his rented tux. He had his camera slung around his neck, and a few extra disks stuffed in one pocket. Stopped, posed, laughed and snapped a few shots of Jericho at the doorway. "This is gonna be way cool, huh bra?"

Murmured, "Hell, yeah." The comment was more than faintly sarcastic, and definitely not enthusiastic. Dread rapidly building within him.

They went inside. Brae disappeared almost immediately, and reappeared at the front of the banquet room with Chuck Frankel. The two of them started working over a small portable computer, getting his presentation for the evening in order. That left Jericho on his own, and he slowly wandered out to the patio. The affair began with a cocktail party out there, and then would move inside for dinner and Frankel's pitch. Music and dancing afterwards.

At the moment, the crowd was still thin, but then Brae had made him come so damn early. Hated that.

He saw Marc LaCroix, a stocky guy, later thirties, standing with Bee-Bee Oxmoor, a pretty sun-streaked brunette, small but athletic-looking, and in an evening dress tonight that made her look decidedly more feminine than usual. Jericho walked over to greet them—still a trace of a limp when he walked, but not much. They were watching him approach, and Bee-Bee leaned in and made some comment to Marc, to which he responded intently. Didn't look particularly friendly or complimentary. Still Marc held his hand out as Jericho joined them. "Congratulations, Jericho," he said. "Chuck told us you were about to be short-listed as soon as your suspension's up."

How fucked did that sound, he thought, reaching forward to take Marc's hand in a firm grip. Instead of releasing the handshake, the second alternate held on to him, and ran his free hand up Jericho's arm and over the hard cast beneath his jacket. Rapped on it twice—nice solid sound. "Heard about this too. Sounds like it must have been a horrible accident. Glad to see you looking so well."

Nice of him, considering he was the guy in the berth just above Jericho, and the one most threatened by his addition to the short-list.

Simple, "Thanks," in response.

Chatted with them for a while—all inconsequential nonsense, mostly about horses and riders—the kind of thing they always talked about. The patio was starting to fill up now, as the elegant set slowly showed up, fashionably late but turned out to the nines.

With relief, Jericho saw Darien and Bob Marx arrive—familiar faces, thank God. "If you'll excuse me, these are my patrons," he told Marc and Bee-Bee, and left to go over to greet the two of them. Darien couldn't have looked better, Jericho was thinking—floor-length designer gown of some gauzy material that made you think you could see through it even though you couldn't—off-white with tiny pearl beading, halter neckline that showed off her shoulders. That luscious mouth of hers shimmering glossy red, and impossible not to stare at. And man, he just wanted to go over there and lay his hands on her…he sure wouldn't be acting out that fantasy, but damn, he was aching to.

Platonic kiss from her—*hated that*—and warm handshake from Marx—*yeah so?* Well, not really, but it was hard to care about Marx at the moment, and harder still not to stare at the woman beside him with the kind of hunger he was feeling inside. He cast his eyes down and away, but still they wandered relentlessly back.

"Look at you! No more long casts. And you rode today!" Darien said, sounding excited for him. Long stares from her. Her gaze meeting his, then running over him top to bottom—nice and thorough. "Chuck seemed so pleased when he called to tell us about it."

Frankel had called them and given them a report? Now that took him back, though it really shouldn't have. Obviously there wasn't much Chuck didn't tell them, which explained why Marx was solidly tied into everything. Wondered again how much he contributed…had to be a lot.

"I have to admit three hours was enough to wear me out," he told them. "But yeah, I was happy with it. We did Monterrey last, which made it easier. That horse is the best ride in the barn…tries so hard. Great animal. I'm lucky to have him."

They both looked pleased.

More small talk with them passed away another ten or fifteen minutes. Jericho declined the drinks and hors d'oevres the circulating waiters and waitresses were offering, and instead just held a glass of ice water in his hand.

"You look nervous," Marx laughed as Jericho lit his second cigarette in the short time that they'd been talking. Lucky for him, that's what his patron thought he was seeing—nerves, not him lusting after his beautiful wife. Both were actually true.

Smiled ruefully. "I hate these affairs," he admitted. "And I feel like an idiot dressed like this. But hell, I'm the least known rider in the group this evening, so I'm not expecting Chuck to focus on me, thank God." He was tired standing too, and was more than glad when they called for everyone to come inside for dinner. Frankel appeared beside him as he and the Marxes strolled into the banquet hall.

"The riders are all sitting at a table in the front by the podium," the Chef D'Equip told him, patting him on the shoulder. Show of encouragement. "There's a place for you there." Still a funny little smirk on his face though—just like that odd tone of voice he'd been using this morning. Not to be trusted.

Jericho reluctantly made his way to the front of the room—would have preferred sitting with the Marxes—and definitely with Darien. Worse, the riders' table had been placed where it would draw attention. Set apart a little and pretty much dead center. Fish bowl, with everyone else in the room staring at them. He greeted everyone there, and took the only empty seat—between Bee-Bee and George Strang. Strang was probably ten to twelve years older than Jericho—a real veteran. He clearly had a different attitude from the others at the table too. Where most of the riders were polite but reserved with him, Strang took care to make him feel welcome, though through most of the dinner Jericho remained silent unless directly spoken to.

Finally Frankel stepped to the podium. He rapped on a glass with a spoon to get everyone's attention. Once they'd focused on him, the lights were dimmed in the room. A soft spotlight settled on him, and another one on the rider's table. God, really hated that.

Strang leaned in to Jericho and laughed. "You should see your face," he chuckled. "Smile, Jericho."

Apologetic look. "I can't stand being stared at," he told him. "George, I barely belong at this table…"

From the Team Captain warmly, "Oh hell, sure you do."

Chuck had started into his spiel about who he was, and why they were all there tonight. Brae was right up there beside him, helping him work the computer. Goofy smile and surreptitious wave to Jericho. "I thought the best way to interest you in our Team would be to introduce you to the riders," Frankel was saying. A picture of George Strang appeared on the screen behind him, and he started right in listing George's credentials. More images…of George riding, competing, standing on the podium at the World Games, a silver medal around his neck. At the end of it, he made George stand, and the room applauded.

Fuck, Jericho thought. Remembered Frankel's comment from this morning…*I might mention you…the other riders too. I'm just warning you now, don't get all shy on me alright?*

The Chef D'Equip inexorably went through each of the rider's profiles, one by one. He'd done all five of the current Team members and alternates but didn't start in on Jericho, and that was fine by him—didn't want or need attention on himself. And besides, he understood the reason and wasn't offended by it—he didn't have the list of international championships these other riders did.

Laugh from some business-type at the table beside them. "Hey it's the horses that do all the work, isn't it?" He'd said it to his friends at the same table with him, but had raised his voice just enough that it carried. Polite chuckles from around the room—like maybe there were a number of folks there who secretly agreed with him.

Annoyance flashed on Frankel's face, but if you didn't know him, you probably wouldn't have seen it, he covered it that well. Smiled even. "Well now, remind me that I need to pay you for that remark at the end of the evening," he said warmly. "I couldn't have asked for a better straight man. So the question is—who's the athlete—the horse or the rider? In my opinion, it's both, but decide for yourselves. I'd like everyone here to take a look at this set of pictures."

Image of QL crashing through that first element 7A of the double at this year's National Horse Show.

Jericho's head jerked up. Shit, he thought. Frankel wasn't letting him off the hook after all.

"As you can see, it's pouring down rain in this picture," Frankel told them. "What you can't see is that two seconds before this, it wasn't. Big clap of thunder and lightening, and the skies just opened up. Umbrellas coming up all around the ring, and it scared this mare so badly that she crashed right into this fence. Most riders in this situation would have bailed—jumped off, in other words—before they got hurt."

Next image...QL starting to go down. Jericho above her, up in his irons, short grip on the reins, absolutely powering her head up. Really potent picture. Gasp in the room.

"You want to talk about guts? No bailing here, oh no, not this rider. And do you want me to tell you how dangerous this situation was? No, forget that, I don't have to, I know you can see it," he went on. "But I *will* tell you how much athleticism it takes to maintain your own balance when the animal underneath you has lost hers, and how much strength it takes to lift an 1100 pound horse that's falling, and set her back on her feet again."

Next image...QL launching over that second element, 7B.

"And how about saving that situation, getting the horse to jump in the very next stride, and then finishing out the course in the driving rain...*and* qualifying for the jump off round in the process. Now does anyone here want to tell me that was just the animal?"

Murmur of approval and appreciation. Applause around the room.

Jericho growled under his breath to George. "I guess he's not going to tell them he got me suspended and fined twenty-five thousand dollars for riding in that class."

Strang laughed. "I guess not."

The picture on the screen changed again—this time a close up image of Jericho on QL back in the sand arena at his barn, flat out galloping. And man this one got his attention, cause he knew what day that was—hadn't even known that Brae had taken these pictures.

"Think soccer or football are hazardous sports—something for the real tough guys?" Frankel asked the room. "Hey, they're nothing. Same rider and same horse as those last three pictures. In case you don't know it, in competition each rider takes the course alone, but this happens to be practice and there were two people here jumping. Now these pictures aren't for the feint of heart, so if you're squeamish don't look at the next two images."

Next picture—and Jericho sucked his breath in. It showed the collision of Landrover and QL, close up and in graphic detail. Two huge horses running smack into each other, obviously a hard hit, with QL terribly off balance, himself partially unseated.

"Oh fuck, man," he murmured. Why was Chuck showing this? What purpose could it serve?

"As you can see the horses ran into each other. The rider on the black horse should have given way to my rider on the brown mare, but he didn't."

The screen changed again, Jericho stared at it transfixed. It was himself down between the horses, those flashing hoofs all around him, arm tangled and being dragged. Now that did make the audience breathe aloud in horror.

"Terrible accident here," Frankel kept right on talking. "But I'm showing you these pictures because this is a story of courage, and I want you to understand our Team riders—their heart...what they put into this. And yes, this rider did live and he's right here in the room with us. And the horse was uninjured, but he sure wasn't. And something else I forgot to mention...this accident happened *less than two weeks ago*. Let me show you this rider's helmet." He reached beneath the podium and held it up. The dent and huge crack in the crown were clearly visible. More murmurs of shock in the room.

Damn that Brae and his camera, Jericho was thinking, though in truth he couldn't take his eyes off the pictures, or his helmet for that matter—he hadn't seen it before this, and hadn't asked about it either.

Strang had leaned in close to him again, and quietly commented, "Jesus Christ, Jericho."

"Oh, yeah, believe me."

"This next picture is only *five* days old," Frankel went on gravely, but with obvious pride too.

New image…Jericho standing in the middle of the sand arena in those damn long casts and holding the cane. Fierce expression on his face, proud, chin lifted and he was yelling out something—probably bellowing at Marco. Another really powerful shot Brae had taken.

"Broken arm, dislocated shoulder, broken leg, concussion…and the list goes on. But did this rider quit, or lose his nerve?" Frankel asked the room. "Did he let that horrible injury stop him? Well, you can see he didn't. He couldn't ride himself, but he was still out there working his horses. I couldn't even get him to sit on the sidelines while I did it—nope, he had to be right out in the thick of it. Now that's determination, and that's courage. Of course, he still has to qualify to make it to the finals, and this takes him out of commission during the thick of the show season. There's probably not a chance in hell he can still make it. But you know what…I'm betting he will. Anyone here want to take me up on it?" Smug smile from the Chef D'Equip, potent pause. "No? I didn't think so."

The image changed yet again. Jericho on Chasseur de Lion, going over that huge Oxer this morning. Hushed silence in the room as they viewed it. Such a beautiful picture—both artistically, and from the standpoint of capturing the fierce challenge and beauty of their sport. Huge powerful jump, magnificent gray stallion. Jericho in two-point—mid-release, but still with a light contact. Breathtaking harmony between man and animal.

"And this picture…this picture was taken just this morning," Frankel said with real impact. "Look at it closely Ladies and Gentlemen—this is the same rider you saw with those huge casts in the last picture—the same rider who was trampled between horses less than two weeks ago. You'll see his jeans are whacked off above the knee on that left leg, and that's because he still has a cast on, and will for weeks to come. No stirrup on that side of the saddle either, because he's not allowed to put that much pressure on it yet. You can even see the cast sticking up out of that jury-rigged boot he's wearing, and you'd be able to see the cast that's still on his right arm too if his form over this jump wasn't *so perfect* that his other arm is covering it. Less than two weeks after going down between horses…" Frankel repeated again, really emphasizing it, "…and he's already back fighting for a spot on our American Team. Now that's what I call relentless."

Man, lots of whispering going on then at the riders' table, and Strang said what they were all thinking to Jericho. "Jesus Christ…that's *Chasseur de Lion*, isn't it?"

Deep unhappy murmur coming back from Jericho, because he sure hadn't wanted what he was doing with Lion exposed here—or any of what Frankel had just put up on the screen for that matter. But he nodded. "Yes, it is, George. That's the first jump he's made willingly in the last three years. I was damn proud of him."

"Man, you've got my respect."

Others at the table seemed to second that.

Frankel took advantage of it. "Want to know what my riders over here are all buzzing about? Well, I'll tell you—I'm letting a little secret out of the bag tonight by showing you this picture, and none of them knew it. The horse you see here is one of the most talented, but *most difficult* horses out there—he's a young horse but he was retired because he's just too hard to sit on. In fact, I'll bet there aren't ten riders in the world who would agree to train him—*despite* the fact that he's a top quality jumping horse. But you see, my riders are *that* tough, and they're *that* talented. First day back in the saddle after that terrible accident I showed you, and this rider's taking the rankest stallion you can find, and making him perform like the Olympian he was born to be. Now I ask you…wouldn't it be a shame if this was all for nothing? If we didn't have the funds to support this team—get them over to Europe where they can beat the pants off the competition?"

He just let that sink in there for a moment, before going on and adding with noticeable fondness, "Now I have to tell you, I didn't want this rider making a jump with this stallion today—its too damn early, and quite frankly, I damn near lost him to that accident two weeks ago and that scared me. But if anyone here can tell me…and Ladies, pardon my French here…but if anyone in this room can tell me how to control this *brash unstoppable bastard*…I'm open to suggestions." Genuine laughter from the audience then, and another round of clapping.

God, he couldn't believe this. Wanted out of there, and badly.

Frankel laughing too, and looking totally unrepentant. "Oh, and I know absolutely furious with me right now, because I didn't tell him I was going to say any of this, and he hates being in the spotlight unless someone's hanging a blue ribbon around his neck. But Ladies and Gentlemen, these pictures I've been showing you are all of the sixth and newest member of the show jumping team short-list, Jericho Brandeis, the youngest member of our short-list too. Come on Jericho, stand up for me—give me five seconds anyway."

Stage crew intensifying the spotlight on him. Would have preferred to be on the Moon or almost anywhere else at the moment. Shook his head ruefully, tossed Frankel an expressive look that clearly said, "Man, why the shit did you do this?"…but rose reluctantly anyway.

He was met with an outburst of enthusiastic applause that went on even after he resumed his seat.

Lots more goodwill coming from the other riders around the table than when he'd first joined them, too.

———————

The music and dancing were set up in another ballroom.

Claimed he couldn't dance with the cast on—didn't like to anyway. Asked Frankel if he could be excused now.

Definitely not.

He strolled outside, leaned up against a balustrade. Strang came out to join him there. The most senior and most junior members of the short-list standing together—a total magnet. Balmy night too, great for being outside. It wasn't long before they had a large crowd around them. Darien stood on the fringes, sipping a drink and just watching the two of them. Jericho stood looking down at his feet, embarrassed by the attention, clearly uncomfortable. Yeah, while he could ride in the boldest way possible and be totally unfazed by it…Rich potential patrons…wanting to be with him, ask him questions…he didn't have a clue how to handle that.

Strang—he was probably the heir apparent for Frankel's position in another ten years—out there mainly to lend support, taking care of him.

After a bit, Frankel himself came out with an elderly woman on his arm. She looked physically frail and was tiny—just about five feet tall. Black evening gown with a black silk shawl covering her upper arms—intricate necklace around her throat, all diamonds and big ones. Strong eyes though—even more eye-catching than her jewels—saw and had seen a lot over the years. Inner strength. "Here you are, George…and Jericho," the Chef D'Equip beamed—not at all the irritable, unforgiving coach Jericho knew day to day. "I'd like you to meet someone who was quite a horsewoman in her own right at one time. Lady Augusta Forrester, this is George Strang, our Team Captain, and Jericho Brandeis."

Lady Augusta Forrester? Never met anyone with some kind of title like that before. Murmured hello.

George, doing a lot better…saying he was so pleased to meet her, and sure, of course he'd heard her name before. Won a few championships at the Garden, hadn't she?

Smile lighting up those so wise eyes. "Ladies Sidesaddle Champion, three years running," she confirmed.

Jericho was listening, not talking. Little weathered but perfectly manicured fingers reached over to take his far larger and more powerful hand. No objection to that touch. Incredible deep blue stare swinging up to meet her eyes, one slashing brow lifted, quietly inquiring—arresting yet disarmingly unassuming, made even more so because he didn't seem to realize the impact that had.

"So did your parents buy you a pony when you were little?" she asked, a little grin quirking at the corner of her lips. Hard to imagine this tall, all male creature as a child.

Held her look. "No, not at all, Ma'am."

"Then how did you start riding?"

She really did seem interested…and of course Frankel was staring hard at him—a kind of "put some effort into this, alright?" message in that look.

Yeah, alright, so he did, although this was an area he never talked about. "Started out, I…got a job as a groom actually. Local stable, lesson horses and even a few carriage horses. Maybe I was ten or twelve at the time. I went into it just looking for the money, but fell in love with the horses, and couldn't get enough of them. Used to ride them when no one was around—wasn't allowed to though." Quiet look. Memories of those days lurking in his eyes. "Then a year or two later I lied about my experience and got hired as an exercise rider at the track…" Smiled a little then. "Those days, they gave me all the rank ones—I didn't care though, I loved doing it, but they fired me when I got too tall. After that, I don't know…used to catch rides at shows…things like that."

From George. "Come on, Jericho. There has to be more to it."

Slanted a look at him. "Why would you say that?"

"Alright, maybe you groomed, but somewhere along the line you apprenticed with a real trainer—working student or something."

Was about to answer him, when another voice spoke up—complete change of subject. "Jericho, that's an odd name,"

Shrugged. Pretty used to that reaction.

"Is it a family name?" Lady Augusta asked him.

Hesitated. A little bit more forbidding tone creeping in. "Well, I wouldn't know."

Darien moved closer, she knew that look. Whatever this was, they were treading on something very private. It made her want to be with him. She also wanted to hear what he said.

Frankel grumbling, sounding a lot more like his normal self. "Well it's a pretty easy question, Jericho. Either it is, or it's not."

Irritated now, he let that stare fall on the Chef D'Equip—a lot more aggressive, and more like his normal self too. "Yeah, that's right Chuck, and if I'd ever met my parents I could have asked them that." Backed it way down after that brash challenge. Dropped his face away, and drew on the cigarette he was holding. "Hell, you probably don't know that about me, do you? I grew up in foster homes." Shrugged self-consciously then—everyone in the circle tuned in and listening. Said with some power in his voice, "You know, horses…they were always family to me."

Frankel, turning this conversation to his advantage—Jericho had no idea, but he was raising some money for the Team tonight. "Yeah, you like them, and they just naturally like you. Like to compete too, don't you?" he asked suggestively.

Murmured so seductively, "Oh yeah."

"So then tell me, hot-shot," he baited him shamelessly—might even have to apologize for this with him tomorrow. "We all know you ride like the Headless Horseman, so why haven't you ever made a real run for the Team before?"

Laid it right back on him, statement from the heart, and harsh. "Because I haven't had the money to back me till now, and you fucking know that, Chuck." Murmured something half-apologetic, half not under his breath, then quietly excused himself, took a walk.

"Real temper on that guy," Frankel said casually, unconcerned.

George watching the path he'd taken, asked quietly. "Should I go after him?"

"Nope. Let him alone, he'll come back on his own." Shaking his head, again almost fondly. Grandstanding a little for the group around him too. "So much fire in the damn guy. He could sure control it better, on the other hand I don't want to see him lose it either."

George swung back around to the question he'd initially asked, but in a round about route. "I've seen him on the circuit for years, but never really talked to him before, and you're right…a lot of fire in him. But man, Chuck, those pictures you showed tonight really blew me away. *Chasseur de Lion?* Riding *that horse* with a broken arm…*and* a broken leg? I mean, Jesus Christ, now that takes guts. Who did Jericho actually train with?"

The Chef D'Equip smiled again. "No one, like he said. You know, I think I'm his first real coach, if you can imagine that." And to the crowd, especially Lady Augusta. "I've been watching him ride for years now. Really liked him. But we never had enough Team money to sponsor him, that's the shame of it. This year he's got a real patron, wish he had more too…and you watch, if he makes the Team this summer, I guarantee you, he'll explode on the International scene."

"I believe that," Strang agreed.

Frankel poking Strang in the chest with one finger. "And you're Team Captain. Take him under your wing, hear me, George?"

"Out of sorts?"

Jericho turned around to find Bruce Waverly behind him. Smiled. "No, I'm alright." Sighed, then admitted it. "Damn, I have the social graces of a log."

Little chuckle from the elderly gentleman. "How old are you?"

"Twenty-seven."

Shrug from him. "Explains a lot." Then, sounding pleased. "That was my horse you were riding in that last picture, wasn't it?"

Jericho leaned against the railing, weight on his good leg, the other stretched out straight in front of him—starting to hurt. Ignored that. "It was." Just plain liked this patron's company. "Come and see him again. Anytime. Call me, let me know when you want to be there, and I'll change the schedule around for you."

Nodded, liked that. Another question. "Do you plan to compete him when you get those casts off?"

267

Smile coming back at him, but a tone of voice that was infinitely stronger. "When I get these casts off? No, sir…I'm not waiting for that."

Lady Augusta Forrester, sitting alone at her table, watching the dancing which was in full swing now. Seemed happy enough just to be there, and anyway, people had been fawning over her pretty much all night—the quiet time was nice.

Tall presence beside her, she looked up and saw Jericho there. "Mind if I sit with you?" he asked, his hand on the back of a chair.

"No, please do."

Pulled that chair out and swung athletically into it, despite the casts. Leaned forward, elbows on his knees, chin resting on one lightly closed fist…which brought his eyes down to about her level. Poignant look in that deep blue stare. "I came to see if I…offended you before. I'd like to apologize for it."

Chiding look on her face. "Did Chuck Frankel send you over here?" she asked.

Mild surprise registering, then maybe some resignation. "No. Did he say he was going to? I haven't seen him since." Shook his head faintly. "He'll kick my ass for it tomorrow, I'm sure. Make his morning for him." Didn't even consciously realize he'd cursed—kind of charmingly rough around the edges. "But I did ask my patron for some advice about what to say," he admitted. Smiled quietly. Searching look. The range of emotions in those incredible blue eyes totally undisguised.

She laughed. "And who might that be?"

"Bruce Waverly."

"Bruce?" She seemed interested by that.

Nodded. "He owns that gray stallion Chuck showed in the last picture. Actually…" Eyes narrowing slightly, as he amended that statement for accuracy's sake. "…I'm not sure what the arrangements are. Chuck's pretty well-handled that end. Never used to be that way, but lately he's been…" Aggressive flash of satisfaction on his face, desire there. "…starting to put the mounts under me."

She reached over and took his hand again, just like before. Sweet spontaneous gesture, which basically said, congratulations.

Smiled back at her.

Chapter Eighteen

"I'm still thinking about taking that three-day trip to Europe to pick up some young stock," Jericho commented to Frankel a week later at the end of their coaching session.

"Nope," the Chef D'Equip responded. Case pretty much closed in his opinion.

Derisive. "What do you mean, *nope?*" After all, what the fuck?

"I mean, nope...look it up in Webster's. Nope...as in no, not by any means, forget it." Superior smirk.

Flash of anger, but controlled it. "Yeah, I don't need a dictionary. But Chuck, I've got to have young horses in the barn to sell."

No, you don't.

There was a lot coming out of that fundraiser two nights ago, but thus far Frankel was keeping it all to himself. He wanted Jericho focused on what he was focused on now—not something else. "It'll take too much out of you," he pronounced. "You're not 100% anyway, and don't argue with me on that one—sure you're doing a damn fine job here, I don't deny that. But you're really putting out to get there, and don't you deny that either. Long flight over, hectic schedule jammed into three days, long flight back...too much. Plus these horses need to work, especially Lion." He knew that last point would clinch it for him.

Thought about it. Shook his head unhappily. "Yeah...fuck. But damn it, Chuck..."

"Relax...you're financially alright, aren't you?"

"Yeah. Barely, but yeah."

With authority, "Well then, just cinch up your belt a little. Do with less."

Coldly sarcastic, burned by it. "Oh, and I live so extravagantly, right?"

January 25th. Jericho's suspension would be over in just four more days.

They'd just finished up with Lion this morning, and were moving on to QL. As Jericho was getting ready to mount, Frankel stopped him and motioned him over. "So let's go through this," he said. "Saturday and Sunday you've got the CSI-W with Monterrey, and the Prelim Jumpers with QL. Personally, I think you should scratch QL and just take Monterrey. How many other horses will you have at the showgrounds?"

Shrugged, though he knew exactly. "Brittany's riding Maximus and Rebel, Darien's riding Roué, and I'm taking Artistic in the Open Hunters." And yeah...here would come the explosion from Chuck now.

Wasn't wrong either. "Artistic!" Frankel thundered. "That nag? Why are you wasting your time on the Hunters? You need to be riding *Jumpers*, Jericho. Get more focus in your show string, damn it!" And he wasn't done yet either. "And that's six horses...way too many for this first show."

"Well, I'm only riding three of them." Real stubborn on that. "And Chuck, Artistic is a client horse—I have to show him...otherwise they'll pull him from the barn, and you know I need the cash."

"How many rounds for the Hunters?" Frankel insisted.

Oh yeah, he had him on that one, Jericho knew. The Hunters always had a good three or four rounds of eliminations they went through—sometimes two or more in the same day. "Three...four counting the Under Saddle class."

Snorted. "So that's the equivalent of another horse...more like four than three."

Already in trouble with Frankel, so he might as well just give him the rest. "And I want to take Lion over, to see how he acts. I mean, think about it. He might draw an association with being back on the showgrounds...it could bring back every bad habit we think we've eliminated—I have to know that before we enter him in a real class."

Looked totally unconvinced...disgusted even. "So now we have you with five rides. Totally ridiculous for this first show."

Jericho sighed, even gave in a little. "Yeah, I know, but that's the way it has to be." Chuck wasn't wrong either. He'd be really taxing himself. "And you're going to really hate this, but I'm asking for your help on one more thing too."

Stopped, turned and just stared sternly at him, hands on his hips— knew he had the upper hand here for once and was taking advantage of it. "Might as well come out with it."

"Chuck, I'd like you to get me permission to ride Lion in the jumper class…only as a training ride, not as an entrant." He could see the emphatic "no" coming back at him from the Chef D'Equip, and just plunged ahead, trying to get his argument out before the denial was vocalized. "Hell, they can stick me at the beginning or the end of the class, or during intermission. It'll only be the qualifier, not the jump-off. Come on, Chuck, we've got to see what he does in a real Grand Prix ring with crowds and other horses all around him."

"Too soon—way too soon, Jericho," Frankel snapped.

Not giving up on this. "Look, I know I'm putting a lot of pressure on myself, but if he goes south on me, I need time to work on it—I can't find that out when there are only two or three shows left in the season. Forget about qualifying him then."

Frankel frowned. Clearly really unhappy about it. Saw the point in what he was saying, though. Breathed in deeply, and then just blew his breath out. "Compromise…let someone else ride Artistic. That's a complete waste of your talent anyway."

And get him out of the barn, he was thinking, but didn't say that…yet.

Jericho was remembering that "cinch up the belt" conversation they'd had the other day. He was going to lose Artistic over this…he could feel it. Just a little bit tighter and that damned belt was going to cut him in half. Breathed out, murmured unhappily, "Alright. Get me the slot for Lion, and I'll ask Jason to pick up Artistic's ride."

Thursday the 27th.

Late afternoon, and the Brandeis Show Stables were a flurry of activity, as Marco and the guys got everything ready to go to the showgrounds the following day. Jericho there working with them, an absolute taskmaster, but nothing particularly unusual about that- and actually the process ran assembly line smooth. It was about three o'clock when his cell phone rang. He'd left it sitting on the table in the tack room, and was off somewhere else at the time, but Marco was close by and came in to see who it was.

He picked it up, and looked at the caller ID. "Darien" was the name that had flashed up on the screen. Didn't answer it, but just held it until the message light came on. Marco often retrieved Jericho's messages for him during the day, and dialed his voice mail now to see if it was something important.

Played the message she'd left for him.

"Hi, Jericho, it's Darien. I, ah…just wondered what you were doing later on tonight. I took Bob to the airport about an hour ago. He had to fly to New York, and he'll be back tomorrow evening. But I'm alone tonight, and I was hoping you'd be free. Call me, okay? I miss you."

Marco probably knew more about what was going on in Jericho's life than even Brae did. Understood this message perfectly. Disapproved, even though he'd covered for his boss with her before, and would do so again willingly. Little things, mainly making sure they had privacy when they needed it—finding chores for the other guys to keep them away when Jericho was talking to her, making sure his boss knew when her husband was around. Actually Marco couldn't care less who he slept with—hey, young guy, needed the outlet—just didn't want to see him lose such an important patron. That was all that mattered to him.

Marx had stayed in town this whole month, rather than going back and forth as he'd originally planned to. Marco knew Jericho was plenty frustrated with that, hadn't been out prowling either because of the accident. Knew his boss—also knew he was good and randy—could make him careless. Anyway, he didn't really think he should be screwing around with her two nights before this first show after the suspension and the accident. Should be home resting, saving his strength.

Without a twinge of guilt, Marco simply erased the message. Whistled a tune happily as he went back to what he'd been working on.

It was just before 10:00 later that same evening, and Brae was back in his normal spot at the Starbucks window. A familiar face appeared on the drive-up monitor.

"Welcome to Starbucks, and *yes, yes, yes*…horseshow this weekend! Hi Darien!"

Well now that was about as enthusiastic as she'd heard him sound about anything. Even women. Laughed at him, but not really sounding like her normal bubbly self. "Hi, Brae. You know what I want, I'll be right down."

She drove her TT over to the second window, where he was already leaning precariously out and waving to her, as usual.

Stupid little beaded necklace around his throat, and he'd stuck a pen through it by the clip like a pendant—there to make sure he could find it when customers had to sign credit card receipts. Completely unattractive, but so much like him. "Hey, you look good tonight," he told her. "Going somewhere?"

Sexy little knit dress on her—casual, but short and flirty, showing off all her curves—easy to see even though she was seated and behind the wheel of her car. "No, not really," she answered him. "I'm bored though...what are you and Jericho doing later on this evening?"

Happy about what sounded like an invitation. "Me? Nothing. Jericho...he's home sleeping, I think. Resting up or whatever. Grumpy too," he added. "You wouldn't want to see him, believe me. I don't know, I think he's brooding over some femme or something, but he won't say." Goofy grin from him, and he struck a pose for her that made no sense whatsoever to what he was saying.

She didn't laugh, in fact, she looked unhappy. "Really?" He's seeing someone then?"

"Was," Brae corrected her. He didn't look too pleased either—was surprised that he couldn't seem to draw her normal friendly response from her. Kept talking instead. "It was some kind of every night thing before the accident. Then it just stopped. I thought he'd go back to seeing her once those big casts came off, but nope, didn't happen. Just gets moodier and moodier."

Unexplained relief on her face. "Oh, that's too bad. Alright, well please tell him I said hello, okay Brae?" She waved and pulled away, still seeming out of sorts herself and distracted.

"Hey! What about..." he called after her, but she didn't turn. Finished his sentence despondently. "...me?"

Not more than twenty minutes later Starbucks looked up again and saw his roommate's Mustang sitting at the drive-through ordering station.

"Hola, bro!" he beamed. "Gotcha covered. Come on down and see me, I'm bored shitless," the Barista whined.

Did that. Pulled to a stop where Starbucks was waiting for him, sitting halfway out the window just like he'd been with Darien, hip resting on the ledge where the drinks were usually placed. The car's convertible roof was down, and Jericho had obviously recently stepped out of the shower—his hair unbraided and still thoroughly wet. Best way to dry it though.

"Hey, you just missed Darien," the Barista said conversationally, but then frowned. "I don't know what her problem was though."

Obvious interest there. "Why do you say that?"

"Well, at first she wanted to hang with you and me tonight, but when I told her…" Seemed to be searching for a way to say this that wouldn't get him into trouble. "…that you where home moping over some femme, she just kind of took off."

"Why the hell would you tell her that?" Warning tone of voice.

Innocent look on his face. Played with that stupid looking pen hanging around his neck. "Well, you are man…don't lie about it. Figured you'd be back banging whoever it is by now, but hey, you're not. Oh hell, Jericho, you haven't even been out on a chick hunt lately." Expressive shrug from him. Then a really sage observation. "A guy can only go so long without pussy…no wonder you're in such a shitty mood lately." Smile.

Jericho thought he might just strangle his roommate. "You're saying she wanted to go somewhere with us tonight?" He was trying to process this tangle of facts from Brae. *Could it be that Darien was finally alone?* Reached for his cell phone, but fuck, he'd left it back at the house. "Have your phone with you?" he demanded.

Unhelpful, as usual. "Nah, I never bring it here. Well, sometimes I do…it all kind of depends, you know what I'm saying?"

Just growled under his breath, took his foot off the brake, and jerked the car away from the window, pulling away at a good clip.

"Hey! What about…" Couldn't believe the way Jericho had just driven away without saying goodbye. Really dejected look. "…your Latte?" Shrugged unhappily. Started drinking it himself.

Jericho drove back to the Polo Club, but instead of heading toward his own place, he drove to Darien's street, stopping about a block or so away, and parking his Mustang in a spot that put it in the shadows—inconspicuous. He walked the rest of the way to the Marx residence, staying out of the streetlights himself.

As he approached he could see that both cars were there and parked in the driveway in front of the garage doors. Shit, it looked like Marx was there, just like he'd been all month…blocking the way to Darien, and that really sucked. He was wound so tight, wanting to be with her—wanting to get back to that time when he'd spent hours alone with her every night—hours possessing her and giving himself to her. Now he only saw her for an hour a day while she rode. Yeah, he could caress her body with his eyes, but nothing else. Sure there were little moments—stolen touches of her hand on his.

It didn't even begin to satisfy him.

He ducked around to the back of the house, and quietly entered the screened-in pool area. Like his own house, the master bedroom here had sliding glass doors out to the pool. He made his way carefully over to them. Lights on in the house, but not many. Soft light in her room, but pitch black in the back where he was. He approached the glass doors from the side so he wouldn't be visible. Actually, it would be hard to see him anyway, as dark as it was back here, but he wasn't taking chances. At least she didn't have a dog to give him away.

And he could see her now. Lying on the king-sized bed, the top spread thrown back on that side so that she could stretch out on the silk sheets beneath it. Nothing on her but a slim thong, and man did his body respond to that. He stepped closer, a fierce expression settling on his already harsh features. One slim hand—that hand she used so often to caress his arm—lifted to slide lingeringly over her own shoulder and down her arm, then drifted over to that perfectly toned abdomen. Slightly more pressure, as her fingers drew closer, and then finally surrounded and then touched her breast. Flicked across her nipple—hard little bud. Her back arched partway up in response, eyes closed and head dropping back. And God, how he wanted to replace that little hand with his own.

He watched her for a short while—a minute or two. She was so sensual, not in the least self-conscious, totally uninhibited. Touching herself and loving it. And Jericho was on fire for her—wanted to lift his good arm and use it like a battering ram against this glass barrier that kept him from her. There was nothing else to stop him—only these doors. No sign of Marx either. And man, he wanted in.

He was on the verge of yanking at the handle of the sliding doors, when she suddenly seemed to become aware of the presence—the eyes on her. She sat up abruptly, startled. Her face turned toward the glass sharply, and she cried out—just a brief gasp, frightened—*intruder*. Oh yeah, she could see that tall dark shape directly outside her bedroom, emanating a raw savage power…sexual desire too. Long, thick fall of hair that disappeared behind his shoulders—without question totally male. Unrelenting passionate demand in that hard stance too.

And then she recognized him, and the look on her face was transformed from one of fear to pure joy, and that reached him too—her happiness to see him. Lifted his hand and laid it flat against the glass...wanting entry...into the house, and God dammit, into *her*.

Darien jumped up and ran over to him. She didn't seem to care at all that she had nothing on—or that he'd seen what she'd been doing either. She just wanted to be with him, that was obvious. There were also no signals from her that he needed to be careful, or worse, needed to leave. Her own hand came up to touch the sliding door from the inside, opposite his—mirroring his.

"Thinking of me, Darien?" he asked her forcefully through the glass.

The look on her face was a cross between shy and inviting, eyes wide, gorgeous mouth slack. "I was," she answered him, her lids lowering in a soft sexy enticement—her voice so quiet he could barely hear the words, but watched those luscious lips moving.

His overpowering stare on her. "Let me in," he snarled, tension flowing off him...he truly wasn't that far from taking action to reach her, and it showed. Oh yeah, it really showed.

She reached for the lock on her side, slid it up...jerked the door open...

Security alarm on the house going off...really loud blare in a whoop, whoop pattern. Lights coming on and flashing off and on in the back and front.

A look of shock on her face, and then she was laughing. "Come in," she giggled, then turned and ran for the keypad to shut it off.

He didn't need a second invitation. Just grabbed the doors and pushed them wide enough to admit his tall form, and then closed them behind himself again.

Darien had entered her security code into the keypad, and the sirens went off as quickly as they'd come on.

And then she was coming back to him. Reaching her arms out to him. And Jesus, it felt so right, and so wrong that they'd been apart. His hand and that inflexible cast went around her, jerking her close against his body. His other hand stroked meaningfully up her side, then down again to span her beautifully toned ass—completely exposed to his touch by the skimpy thing. He pulled her powerfully against the front of his jeans and the nicely swollen bulge waiting for her there. Just pressed his hips against hers, rotating her slowly over the hard length of him. That deep blue stare on her saying everything that needed to be said...followed by the immediate assault of his mouth over hers. Seeking, demanding. Finding what he wanted too.

Total acceptance of him from her. A soft cry of hunger for him. Her fingers tangling in and gripping that long damp mane of his. Her kissing him with as much fierce desire as he felt for her.

He didn't even bother with the obvious questions...where is your husband?...why didn't you call me? Is this alright? Totally unnecessary inquiry, that last.

He drew back from her just long enough to lift her and place her onto the bed, following her, coming up over her athletically and with purpose...lion over his prey...fell on her with his mouth, his hands finding her too...that delicate little form that he was driven to lay claim to, to possess for himself...and to protect. *His.* The curtain of his hair shrouding them both, spilling on and around her. No question, she *belonged* to him, and he needed her. *Sweet Jesus, he needed her* and he'd missed her, missed this with her.

Reared up above her, and stripped his shirt off. Came back to her, if anything more demanding than before, and the trail of her fingers across his naked torso...driving him crazy, though fuck, he loved it. Snarl of pure lust from him.

Telephone ringing.

"Ignore it," he growled.

Between kisses. "I can't, it's the Security Company. If I don't answer they'll send the police."

Still ringing.

"Fuck." Sigh of resignation. He reached for the phone, which was on his left side—the good arm side—and handed it to her.

"Hi, this is Darien Marx, I'm sorry, it was my fault..."

He dropped down lower, his lips playing with her stomach.

A deep sensual, "Ohhh..." from her. Then into the phone, "No, I'm sorry, it's just that I..." soft gasp as his mouth moved relentlessly lower, her little thong panty quickly slipped down and off. "...that I..." His tongue seeking out that most sensitive nub at the apex of her legs, and toying with it, and her hips jerking up against him. "Oh, that I..." Really breathy voice now. "...opened the back door, and I...oh God, Jericho..."

Sucked harder on it, tongue moving, his hands spreading her legs, fingers touching.

"Oh no, of course," she moaned, her slim body twisting, wanting more. "I know your name's not...*Jericho*...ooh please." Two fingers inside her now, once from each hand, stroking, knowing exactly how she liked it. He stopped what he was doing with his mouth long enough to nip at and draw his lips across her inner things for a long moment, then straight back to sucking and kissing where he'd been before. Ragged cry from her, "Oh yes...uhm, my secret...password? It's...oh God, oh God...no, no...fine, thank you."

That perfect little pelvis rocking against him more desperately, her eyes closed and head tossed back. "Oh...secret password is...ohhh... it's...ohhh..." Got it out finally, "Monterrey."

Jericho, taking the phone from her hand and laying it back in the cradle, going immediately back to what he was doing—intensifying it— until she no longer just moaned, but screamed instead.

In the Security Company control office, one night officer turned to the other with a puzzled look on his face. "That woman I was just talking to...she had the password and everything, but she was moaning like the dickens the whole time she was giving it to me. Said she was okay though. Do you think that sounds alright, or should I call the police?"

From the other officer. "Well what did it sound like?"

He did his best imitation. "Ooh...ooh Jericho...ohhh God."

Annoyed look. "Well listen to yourself, you asshole, what do you think? That Jericho's a lucky bastard, whoever he is. I doubt he's a burglar though."

January 28th.

He'd stayed the whole night with her, and not sleeping either. Not until the early, early hours of the morning, when he'd finally cradled her next to him, and dozed off briefly with her there in his arms.

Came home around 5:00 AM, got a really knowing look from Starbucks who was up getting ready for the early morning shift. He had to gut it through a trying session where his roommate worked like hell to find out who he'd spent the night with. Brae finally gave up, grousing and annoyed by "all this secret shit."

"Are you coming over to the jog today?" Jericho asked him, changing the subject on him—which usually tended to work.

"Yeah, sure. Chuck asked me." The Barista stuffed half of the muffin he's swiped from the store the night before into his mouth. "Was a jah, anywah?"

"Christ's sakes, Brae, you can't even talk straight, you've got so much in your mouth," Jericho murmured in disgust. "And give me the other half."

"Fuh, no!" he replied as best he could, stuffing even more in his mouth before Jericho took it from him. "An wha is a jah?"

"Asshole," his roommate shot back at him, though not really mad. He went searching in the refrigerator for something edible—defined as anything not rotten or covered with mold—talking over his shoulder as he did. "The jog's a veterinary check. It's mandatory before any qualifying class. Vet examines the horse, and then they trot him up and back, make sure he's sound, things like that." Wasn't finding much in the way of sustenance, grumbled, "Fuck, I'm starving."

The Barista relented, handed him what was left of his muffin…about a bite and a half.

From Jericho, a sarcastic, "Gee thanks." He took it though, and quickly polished it off.

"So are you jogging all your horses?" Starbucks asked.

"No, hell no. It's just Monterrey, and anyway I'm not allowed to do it. I'm still suspended till tomorrow. Chuck got special permission for Marco to jog the horse. I'll be there though." Truth was, he probably couldn't do the jog with these casts on anyway—something to remember for future shows. But he still wished he could.

"Cool. I'll bring my camera. Three o'clock, right?"

"Right."

The morning was really busy. They worked all the horses back at the stables…would have greatly preferred to take them over in the showgrounds and ride them there, but that would have been breaking the rules of his suspension. He had to get Monterrey over early though, since the horse had to be on the grounds for 24 hours before he showed, so Jericho rode him at seven and then Marco vanned him over immediately afterwards. Big coordination game.

At one o'clock, the rest of the horses trailered over—QL, Lion, Maximus, Rebel, Roué, and Artistic. But Artistic would be stabling with Jason's horses not Jericho's, and was going to be staying with Coulder after the show—leaving the barn permanently as Jericho had predicted. Damn, hated that, though Chuck didn't seem fazed by it in the least…then again, Chuck wasn't sharing a muffin for breakfast either. Didn't even talk to him about it—had heard more than enough already about "cinching up his belt."

Lots and lots of people stopped by his stalls to see him, starting as soon as he arrived on the showgrounds. Had to admit it was nice. Congratulations on the end of his suspension…well wishes following the accident. Some just curious to take a look at those casts, and ask if he really planned to ride.

Yes, he did.

One thing was clear though. The news that he'd made the short-list wasn't on the street yet. Not a single person mentioned it. Neither did he.

Shortly before three, he appeared at ringside for the jog, somehow managing to look both excited to be back there and miserable that he wasn't handling Monterrey himself at the same time. Just laid that short arm cast along the top rail, eyes only on the big bay gelding—until Darien arrived to watch her horse go. Then he was torn…looking at Monterrey, then at the beautiful woman standing beside him. She'd already ridden Roué that morning, and was dressed now in form-fitting, designer jeans and a white silk knit top. Good-looking Ariat slides on her feet. Light pink gloss on her lips that made them look wet, and so very kissable.

Special smile from her for him.

Marco was all decked out for the jog this afternoon. Nice sport jacket, white shirt, tie, newly pressed khaki slacks. He had Monterrey on the end of a beautiful new halter and lead the Marxes had purchased for him, and the horse had been groomed till he positively gleamed. Brae took a lot of pictures of both the horse and handler, which made Marco happy—really proud of himself.

"Look at Marco, he's so sweet," Darien murmured.

"Yeah, it's nice for him. He loves doing this."

The jog was over in a matter of a five minutes. No problems there. Monterrey was good and sound, and in perfect health. And of course, Marco had done an excellent job of handling him—knew he would.

Everything cool now for his class tomorrow with him. To qualify Monterrey for the finals, Jericho needed two separate CSI-W shows where he rode the horse with no more than eight jumping faults. This would be

Monterrey's first chance at it. QL on the other hand, was going in the Prelim Jumpers, more for the practice—not a qualifying class, but a better way to start.

With the jog over, Jericho was about to turn and head back to the barn, maybe even catch a few more stolen minutes with Darien, but then he heard his name called out, and turned around to see George Strang hailing him. "I'll meet you back there," he told Darien, maybe letting his fingers linger a little bit too long on her shoulder, then stopped to wait for George to catch up with him. Held out his hand to him.

Warm handshake and greeting from the Team Captain. "How's it going, Jericho? Feel good to be back here?"

"I can't even begin…"

Nodded, smiling. Then inclined his head in the direction of a less crowded area. "Take a walk with me," he said.

Wondered what this was all about, but just answered him, "Sure." Followed him. Strang went further than he'd expected actually, off the beaten path to an area with lots of trees—cover maybe. Man, whatever it was, he wanted it good and private.

George finally stopped and turned to face him. Started out pretty conversationally. "So have you seen Frankel since the benefit?"

Wry amusement lit Jericho's sharp features. Murmured it, "Seen him? I feel like we're married. Every frickin' day, eight o'clock. Seven days a week too, not just six."

George seemed amazed by that. "He comes to you every day now?"

"Like clockwork."

"Wow."

"Tell me about it." Jericho lit a cigarette, dragged on it. "Three hours straight, most of it giving me shit." He snorted. "I'm surprised he has any voice left by the time he's done screaming at me. Not to mention the way he's got his fingers into every damn thing I'm doing."

Strang laughed. "You're lucky Jericho."

Quiet smile. "I know that too." Stared harder at the Show Jumping Team Captain. He knew George hadn't asked him over here just to shoot the breeze, that was for damn sure. It wasn't like they were even really friendly—yeah they'd talked at that fundraiser, but that was different, almost something they'd had to do. "So what's this about?" he quietly demanded.

"Man, you're street smart, aren't you?" Strang asked him, looking him over—as if he was trying as hard to get a read on Jericho as Jericho was on him. He seemed uncomfortable too. "Fact is, I came to warn you."

"Figured."

His eyes narrowed. "Boy…perceptive. You know how to take care of yourself, don't you?"

"Always did." Shrugged. "But it's not like I've got a thing with it…just always had to."

George sighed, as if he hated this whole thing—probably hated anything unpleasant for that matter. Jericho figured him for the prep school type, everything nice and polite. Genteel. "I'm not supposed to know this, but I overheard something in the show office. I need to share it with you."

He just took it in, didn't look ruffled by it, didn't even look surprised —disappointed and scornful maybe. And maybe withdrew a bit—like he didn't trust anyone really, expected the worst from people. Still he said, and genuinely too, "Thanks George, I appreciate it. Hell, I'm used to bad news these days, just go ahead and lay it on me."

Almost imperceptible nod from him. Spoke vaguely. "Watch your gear tomorrow, Jericho. Make sure it's by the book. If it's not, you can almost count on someone filing a protest."

Understood that, but didn't get why it pertained to him—it wasn't like he used any kind of jury-rigged bit set-up, nothing strange or even remotely illegal on the horses' legs either. Every piece of tack he had was one hundred percent legitimate. Muttered something angry under his breath, frowned. "Say more," he demanded. "I'm not following you." Then added with more passion and defensively. "George, my tack is totally clean, and so are my training methods. Hell, ask Chuck. I don't pole, and I don't ever fuck around with their feet."

"I know. Honestly, I've never even heard a hint of that around you." Sighed, looked away and then back again. Stronger tone of voice. "Read the rule book more carefully, Jericho." Seemed reluctant—like breaking a confidence, and man that was suspicious—why would he bring him aside like this, and then not want to come out with it? After a long silence he seemed to change his mind, though. "Ah hell, it burns me, so I'm going to recite a few rules out loud, okay?"

"Yeah good, I'd like to hear them." Inhaled from his cigarette again. He was plenty irritated, offended too. Uneasy damn conversation.

Curt nod. "First rule, and these are straight from the book, okay...riders are required to wear boots. Second rule...saddles have to be fitted with stirrups that swing freely from the bar. Make sure you meet those criteria, Jericho. People are worried about you...people who never considered you competition before. Don't get eliminated for something stupid, understand me?"

He lowered his eyes to cover the flare of anger he felt. "Man," he murmured. "Like I haven't fought hard enough, right George? Like I don't have enough going against me? Someone wants me disqualified because I can't get on a fucking boot? They don't want to beat me, right? Just get rid of the threat?" Lifted his face again, his expression one of harsh derision and aimed at Strang, and with good reason too. Shit, he knew it had to be one of the short-list riders George was talking about—poised to lodge a complaint if he did too well—or maybe even if he didn't do all that well. "Some fucking Team you've got there, Captain," he mocked him. "But thanks, I appreciate the warning just the same."

Strang, looking apologetic, trapped too. "You don't know it's a Team member, Jericho."

Sneered back at him, "Oh fuck me, George. The only people who even know how I've been riding the horses are the ones who were at that benefit a few weeks ago...the way I rigged up a boot...the fact I can't use a stirrup yet."

"Maybe...or maybe it's someone they talked to about it. Does it matter where it's coming from? To me, that's the least important part." Changed the subject slightly. "And yeah, I'm sorry someone's making it even tougher on you, but now you know, so do something about it. And I have to tell you, I haven't been able to get that last picture Chuck showed out of my mind...you on Chasseur de Lion, and hell Jericho...only ten days or so after that accident? You aren't going to let this stop you."

Leaned back against a tree truck, taking weight off his broken leg, a cold look on his face now. "He's here by the way."

"Chasseur?"

"Oh yeah."

Strang looked incredulous. "But you're not showing him...I didn't see his name in the field."

Confidence in those deep blue eyes. Murmured, "Practice round during intermission tomorrow. Right after my ride with Monterrey." He shrugged, dragged on his smoke one more time, then tossed it away. "I would have liked more time between goes, but it was the only slot they could give me, and hey, luck of the draw, right? I got the last ride before the lunch break with Monterrey."

He whistled low, seemed fascinated even though the hostility from Jericho was palpable. "Man, you've got some brass ones. How's he going to react being back on the showgrounds?"

Expression shuttered closed. Aggressive though. "Know what? I haven't got a clue. I couldn't ride him here today. Yeah, I would have loved to try it, just bring him into the practice ring…but I'm still suspended so I couldn't."

Real appreciation. "Oh man. So you're taking him straight into the Grand Prix ring…in front of an audience? Jericho, that is pure audacity, and hell, I know you don't trust me much at the moment, but the plain truth is, we need that on our team—need it badly. I have to tell you…I'm with Chuck…I'd like to see you make the Team too."

Didn't believe him. Challenged him on it. "Are you sure, are you really sure? Three spots on the Team, and we're all fighting for them. And you know what, George? You have to jump-off in the finals just like the rest of us. It's not like you have a guaranteed berth or anything."

That thought, Strang seemed more comfortable with. Smiled even. "Yeah, and if I can't beat you fairly, Jericho, then I don't deserve my scarlet jacket. Alright?"

Thought he might be on the level. Nodded. "Yeah, alright, I'll buy that answer for now." Smirked. Even relaxed the hard guy act a little, but got more in his face just the same and jostled him with one shoulder. Murmured suggestively, "By the way, exactly what size jacket do you wear?"

Bark of laughter from the Team Captain. "It's way too big for you, hot shot."

"Maybe. Maybe not."

Chapter Nineteen

January 29th—and show time. Finally. Damn, it felt good. Suspension over, and going back in the ring.

The schedule for the day today was going to be a bitch and a half. Eight goes. Lots of overlapping. Early morning to late afternoon.

Saturday

Class	Horse	Rider
Juniors - Working Hunter Round 1	Maximus	Brittany
Juniors - Working Hunter Round 1	Rebel	Brittany
The Palm Beach Qualifying Stake, CSI-W	Monterrey	Jericho
Practice ride, Grand Prix ring	Lion	Jericho
Juniors - Working Hunter Round 2	Maximus	Brittany
Juniors - Working Hunter Round 2	Rebel	Brittany
Amateur Owner Hunter 35 & Under Round 1	Roué	Darien
Open Prelim Jumpers Qualifying Round	QL	Jericho

Brittany was first to go, and she'd be riding Maximus around 9:00. Although he was the better of her two horses, she had more trouble with him, and Jericho wanted to spend some extra time with her in warm up first. Her second go with Rebel was later. He'd have some time to work with her on Rebel before she went into the ring, but it wouldn't be very much since his own ride with Monterrey would be immediately afterwards, and no way he was going to short-change the warm-up he needed for that. At any rate, he'd told her to be there around 7:30, and she pulled in right on time...Starbucks, no more than ten minutes later.

The Barista came strolling down the aisle, disheveled as always. Over-sized tee shirt, baggy shorts with the crotch halfway down to his knees. Hair not combed—was it ever? But happy, excited, camera hanging from his neck…and precariously carrying three coffees with no carrying tray—just his long fingers wrapped around the lot of them.

"Wow, this is hot," he whined, making faces. "Brittany, I've got your hot chocolate," he called out, looking for her.

Her pretty face appeared from behind the curtain of the changing room they had set up in an empty stall next to where they were keeping the tack. "One second, okay Brae?"

"Well, hurry up, my fingers are burning," he moaned, hopping back and forth from one foot to the other, like that would help. "Jericho, hey bro, come and get your Latte, my hands are on fire, man."

Ignored him. Jericho was in conversation with Marco about arrangements for the day and not to be distracted.

After another forty-five seconds of increasingly pitiful bleating from Starbucks, Brittany came out of the dressing room to rescue him. "Here, stop that," she told him fondly, reaching for the hot chocolate he'd brought her.

"Yeah, hurry up and take it…ouch…my fingers have third degree burns on them already, yeah hurry up."

Scuffle between the two of them as he tried to turn his hands around so that she could take the right cup. More moaning and an urgent *Come on,* from the Barista. Then Brittany screamed, and cried out, "Oh no! Oh look what you've done," followed by loud squishy sounding splat, as the remaining two drinks hit the aisle way floor.

With a snarl, Jericho turned around to see what was happening, and indeed, Brae had dropped all the drinks—the hot chocolate, complete with whipped cream topping having splattered all down the front of Brittany's light fawn colored breeches. Christ's sakes, he thought vengefully, could that damn Brae do anything right?

He turned away from Marco with a curt, "Get someone down here to clean this up," and then strode down the aisle himself, muttering, "Jesus, Brae, did you have to carry all of them at once?" Stern and short-tempered, he stopped a few steps away from them. Took one look at the damage to Brittany's riding attire, and told her, "Go ahead and change…you're not going to show in those."

"Hey, I brought you a Latte," Starbucks protested defensively.

Disgusted. "Yeah, and I wanted it too."

"But these are the only pair of show breeches I have," Brittany interrupted their little squabble miserably.

Jericho looked stunned. "What?"

"Well, I don't have another pair." She was trying to wipe off the front of them, but it was obviously hopeless.

Jericho, snarling, "How can you come to a horseshow with one pair of breeches? Christ, and you want to be a professional?"

Tears coming to her eyes, and Brae being unhelpful as usual. "Hey it doesn't look that bad."

Sneered. "Yeah, maybe we can slop some pizza down the front of her too." He jerked back the curtain to the dressing room, and went inside—straight over to the smart looking, monogrammed suit bag that Darien had left there the night before. Unzipped it viciously. "See this?" he snapped. "Two pairs of breeches." Yanked one free, then strode back to Brittany and thrust them at her, yelling out at the same time, "Marco, send someone to Hatfields once it opens, and buy a pair of ladies size 24 show breeches—expensive ones. Have them charged to me." Looked back at Brittany and growled angrily at her, "Some future professional. Christ's sakes...*change.*"

"Man, you're really being a prick," Brae griped at him, reaching over to brush a hand against Brittany's cheek, making one of his goofy faces at her that did make her smile a little in spite of Jericho's harsh judgment.

He wanted to tell Brae to stay away from his working student too, but didn't. Settled for an acid, "You think I'm a prick? Maybe it's because I didn't get my coffee this morning." Jericho strode away again.

Five minutes later he was back though. Ducked into the dressing room...Brittany was pulling on Darien's breeches. He didn't care that she was only half-dressed, and in fact, started stripping off his own jeans. She looked upset still, like she wanted to cry and was fighting it. "Come on," he murmured unsympathetically to her. "I know you're tougher than that."

Her eyes swept over to him, to the bruises still faintly visible on his legs and torso, and to the casts that covered his lower right arm and lower left leg. He'd pulled out a pair of snow-white breeches, and shoved his right leg into them, then the left, struggling to yank the tight but stretchy fabric up over that cast. He just yanked until the threads broke that prevented him from getting them up. Tough, oh yeah, no one could argue with that.

"Hey, at least you *can* change," he told her, relenting a bit. "Once Marco tapes this boot on my leg, it's gonna be there the rest of the day."

287

Snorted. "I'm keeping away from Brae with these damn white breeches on, that's for certain."

She laughed at that, seemed to relax a little and told him. "I'm sorry, Jericho."

"Forget it, okay?" Smiled at her. "Think about Maximus and that class instead." When she was decent, he lifted his voice and bellowed, "Marco!" The head groom appeared just seconds later—as if he'd been waiting right outside.

After George Strang's warning, Jericho and Marco had spent time together working on how to get him into a tall boot. In the end he'd bought two pairs—one for today and one for tomorrow…and what the hell was he going to do with all those right foot boots he had left over? Not to mention the cost of it. But to get it on they'd split it vertically all the way down from the top to about an inch above the heel—and both sides too, not just one like a normal zipper. Then they'd continued the cut horizontally, also on both sides of the foot, to just about an inch shy of the toe. The whole front would pull forward, just like the tongue of lace up shoe. Oh, he'd get his leg in there alright. Closing the whole thing up again was going to be the trick. In the end, they'd decided to use black fiberglass casting tape, which was going to make the boot strong and rigid. But then boots were meant to be rigid except at the ankle, and they weren't going to wrap that part. It wouldn't even look that bad unless you got close to it. Thick, but hell, nothing he could do about that.

For the rest of the day, he'd be going back and forth to the rings in the golf cart—no way he could walk too much in this. Still, it was a boot, and ought to stand up to examination. And he had to have it on to walk the course he'd ride later with Monterrey…Lion too. Rulebook said riders had to be properly dressed for that– he'd checked.

Of course, he was going to have a hell of a time getting this boot/cast off again. Worry about that later though.

Brittany's ride on Maximus went better than he expected, despite the rocky start. First the warm-up with Jericho standing on the rail, barking out instructions to her—and her with a look of fierce determination on her face, as if his brief lecture on toughness and professionalism had really gotten to her. Brae took about a zillion pictures of her, but then again, maybe it was just a subject that he liked. In the actual class, she rode like a little champion—cool, thinking out every stride. Jericho was proud of her, and thus far it looked like she was ahead. Lots more rides to go though, including her own go on Rebel in another hour or so.

Darien had arrived too, although she didn't ride till much later. Tall presence coming up behind her. She didn't turn around, but a smile played across her lips.

Deep warm voice, trace of harshness. "Early aren't you?"

Her hand slipped back, just brushed his thigh, felt the muscle in his leg move, and he stepped in even closer. "I just like watching you," she said quietly to him. "You're back in your element, aren't you?"

Murmured response, "For sure." Marx was back though, so he couldn't say or do anything more than that. The investment banker would appear any time now—was probably around somewhere close.

Yup, there he was, standing on the side of the ring with Frankel. Like the Bobsey Twins sometimes, the two of them. And of course, here came Chuck as soon as he spied him, Marx trailing along right behind him too. "Morning, Jericho. Brittany had a nice go," Chuck greeted him—a compliment anyway. Without any further preamble, he fell to examining the boot set-up.

Jericho lifted his leg up to the middle rail on the fence to make it easier for him, and while Chuck did that he took the opportunity to greet his patron. "Ready to see Monterrey in the big ring today?" he asked him. Pretty confident look on his face.

"We saw him once before," Marx answered, he was smiling though.

Yeah sure, that ride with Chip Langdon—not like that had really been a look at this horse performing. "Well today you'll see him really do something," he promised him. Caught his eyes at the same time and held that look. A little brashness maybe, but he could tell Marx loved it. Smirked at him.

Frankel was done examining the boot. "Alright, I like it," he finally said, straightening back up. He added conversationally, "Oh, and just so you know, there's going to be a short announcement before you ride in the arena with Lion."

"Oh?" Suspicious already. He was remembering that benefit. Fished for more information from him. "How's that?"

Frankel looked innocent…as much as he could, that is. "I felt the audience should be warned that this is a training ride, and that some disobedience is expected, but that its an attempt to rehabilitate the horse. The announcer's going to say that. I wrote something up for him."

Looked around at him surprised, but appreciative. "That was a good idea, Chuck," he agreed.

Pleased with himself. "Thanks." He pointed. "Oh say, there's Jason on Artistic. Looks good on him don't you think? Nice horse."

Yeah, and he'd been a nag when Jericho was going to ride him. A nag that paid his bills too. Sighed, didn't even bother to argue about it. "The walk-through starts in about five minutes," he told him. "Interested in going with me?"

Smile. "Absolutely. Oh and here's George too."

Sure enough, Strang was on his way over to join them. Remembering them from the night of the benefit, Strang made a point of saying hello to the Marxes, then Chuck and Jericho. His eyes swept over the boot he'd rigged together and he nodded, approving. Didn't mention it though, although he could have, since Jericho had told Frankel about the conversation. Still, it just slid by.

"They're letting the riders in now," The Chef D'Equip observed. "Let's walk the fences."

Both riders were eager to do that. They said goodbye to the Marxes, little whispered "Good luck," from Darien, and then the three men walked shoulder to shoulder through the entrance tunnel, and entered the Grand Prix ring. The class today would be held in the main jumping arena—huge grass field with bleachers all around for the audience. The more affluent spectators all had covered boxes, and of course there was a large one there for the guests of the Team—catered too.

Jericho had already looked over the jumping layout—big course with fifteen elements, including two doubles at 4 and 6, water jump at 5, and a triple at number 13. Liked it though, nice and technical, the kind of thing Monterrey loved best. Only 57 seconds in allotted time to finish it. He'd need to really move it to make that.

It was a long frickin' course for him to have to step out now too, but somehow he'd manage it.

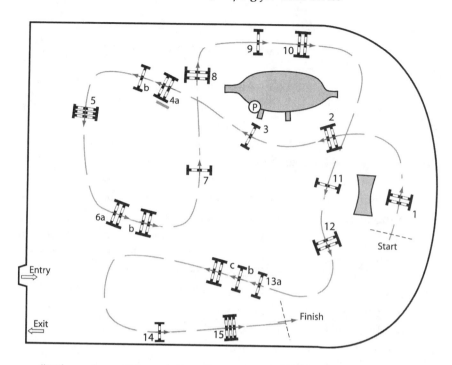

"What place did you draw?" Jericho asked George as they started through it—not easy going for him, since they really had to stride it out to get an accurate reading on the distances between fences.

Looked unhappy about his answer. "I'm early in the go. Four ahead of you Jericho."

Twenty-eight entrants in the total field, and Jericho was twelfth. Later was almost always better—understood why he wasn't pleased with his place in the line-up. Gave him a sympathetic nod.

"So Chuck, did you bring a lot of people with you today?" Strang asked him with some interest, clearly referring to the crowd from the benefit.

"Some," Frankel answered vaguely. "Bruce Waverly's here, I want you to be sure and come over to see him."

Annoyed. After all, Waverly was *his* patron. "Yeah, I'd like to do that too," Jericho grumbled. He saw that George was looking at him oddly, and wondered what that was about.

"And make sure you spend some time with Lady Forrester too."

Ignored that, figured it was aimed at Strang like his other comment had been.

Silence followed, which obviously irritated the Chef D'Equip. Gruff look on his face, and incredulous. "Jericho? I'm talking to you."

"Who me?"

Withering. "Well, do you see anyone else here named Jericho?"

Fired right back at him. "No, Chuck, but I thought you were talking to George."

And from Strang, still looking at him with that puzzled expression. "Jericho, surely you realize that..."

Frankel interrupted him. They were standing in front of fence number 3 now. A fairly simple vertical—airy though. "Well, Jericho, here's a fence your going to have trouble with," he pronounced.

Looked at him like he had three heads. "*What*? Now why the hell would you say that? Jesus, Chuck, it looks pretty straightforward to me."

Sharp. "Exactly my point. You'll probably take it too deep." He turned and gave Strang a censuring look—one that said pretty clearly "keep your mouth shut." They moved on, Jericho still muttering to himself in annoyance. Walked out the rest of the course—he was limping noticeably by the end of it. *And damn this cast of a boot.*

"Are you alright?" the Chef D'Equip demanded.

"You can't imagine what this fucking boot is like to walk in."

"Don't lie to me, Jericho."

Snarled back at him, "Just kiss my ass, alright?"

Really offended, but Frankel didn't respond to the comment. Frosty tone of voice though—really letting him know how little he'd liked it, and how inappropriate he thought it was. "I'm going up to the box to greet the guests there, and then I'll be out to warm you up."

"Yeah you do that." Mumbled to himself, "It's not like I don't hear your mouth every frickin' day as it is."

Frankel stopped dead and turned to stare at him. "I meant *George*, wise ass." Let that sink in for a moment, then added, "It's my job as Chef D'Equip and if you want to be short-listed you damn well won't argue. Like it or not, I'm warming you up too—understand me?"

Alright, he'd been put in his place. Just answered, "Yes, Chuck."

"Well, see that you do." Held that stern pose of his for another few seconds, then turned on his heel and strode away.

Strang watched him go, then looked at Jericho's expression, then back to the retreating form of the Chef D'Equip. When Frankel was well out of both sight and of hearing, George started chuckling.

"What's so funny, George," he demanded, good and irritable after the last ten minutes with the two of them. Marco was waiting on the other side of the tunnel with the golf cart, and bless him for that. Jericho's leg was really hurting him.

"Ah, hell...don't take this the wrong way," Strang said, still smiling. "I don't know...maybe you didn't grow up with a father, Jericho. But you sure as shit have one now."

The remark stunned him. Couldn't even think of an answer. Just laid that deep blue stare on him, trying to process what it meant.

Warm look in response. Strang laid a hand on his shoulder. "I surprised you with that, didn't I?"

Gave him a very open and genuine response in return, "Hell, yes. And you couldn't be further wrong...swear to Christ, George, it's true. Fuck, sometimes I think he barely has the slightest respect for me." Shook his head, seemed unhappy about it. "God knows, I try, but..." Too personal. Left it there. Murmured, "Good luck," to him, then turned and got in the golf cart with Marco. Drove away.

It was getting closer to the time for his ride. He'd watched the first few competitors go through it. Lots of knockdowns. The course was harder than it looked. And oddly enough, fence number 3 seemed to be causing a real problem—the one that Chuck had said would be hard for him. Didn't want to think about that—jinx himself. But still the seed had been planted in his mind.

Marco led Monterrey up. Bob Marx had already gone in to the Team box and was watching from there, but Darien had reappeared. The big bay gelding looked good, and more than that, he seemed excited, prancing and snorting as he came up to the practice ring. For now, the stirrup was missing on the left side of his saddle. They'd have to put it on before entering the ring though. Problem that—either it would be long and swing against the horse's side while Jericho rode him—something the sensitive Monterrey was sure to hate—or he'd have to make it shorter, in which case it would interfere with his own leg position. Still hadn't decided how to handle that.

Jericho vaulted on. Started his warm-up with simple and correct flatwork. Saw Brittany getting up on Rebel in the next ring over and kept an eye on her too—called over a few corrections. Within minutes Frankel was there on the sidelines, shouting out his critical evaluation just like he always did. If anything, he was more caustic here at the showgrounds than he was at home. "*Rounder*," he thundered, making it good and loud. "Damn it, don't you remember anything I've taught you?"

Gritted his teeth, took the scalding criticism, did his best to respond to it.

Sooner than he wanted, they were calling him to the ring. Before going in, he asked Marco, "How did Strang do?"

"Clear round, boss."

Hell, it figured, didn't it?

But as he entered the tunnel on Monterrey, calm just settled over him. Came through the tunnel on the other side and into the arena—and into his zone. Picked up a nice round working canter and waited for the bell to sound. It did. Rode around, and gave his salute to the ground jury—he had both feet in the stirrups at the moment, but as he rode away to begin his go, he simply slid that left foot free. Monterrey reacted a little to the feel of the stirrup iron touching him with each stride, but the big bay seemed to be handling it. Jericho picked up the pace a bit, and put his mount in line with the first obstacle. Passed through the timers, and he was on the course now.

Frankel had taken off for the Team box at a good pace, and entered it just as Jericho and Monterrey flew over that first big Oxer. "Oh yeah, nice," he breathed. Didn't acknowledge the rest of those present, just walked straight to the front of the box—blocking some of the patron's views but not even realizing that.

Strang had moved over next to Frankel at the rail—the two of them together making a pretty solid wall, and Marx moved in close beside them too, wanting to hear what Frankel said. Those behind the trio grumbled and moved.

Jericho guided his mount into a nicely controlled bend around to the left, up to the next element, right on spot and easy over the second spread jump too.

"Man, he's good," Strang murmured. Satisfied nod from the Chef D'Equip.

Coming up now to the third element...the one that Chuck had predicted he'd miss. Said he'd come in too deep. Jericho sighted his spot, then backed Monterrey off a little, launched slightly before it. Felt the rub—the big bay gelding had touched it with a back hoof, and he heard the crowd groan and knew without looking he'd knocked it down. Four faults. Damn

Chuck for being right. Didn't have time to think about it though…huge double in front of him, spread jump first, and then an airy vertical.

Angry comment from Strang to Frankel, "Man, that was totally your fault, Chuck."

Angry reply—angry with himself. "Yeah, I know…never thought he'd pay that much attention to me."

They both watched as Jericho sighted the double, lifted Monterrey, release then touchdown, then straight into the second launch. Release. Perfect form and easily clean again.

"You didn't think he'd pay attention?" George was saying incredu-lously—critically too. "Hell, Chuck, he's tuned in to every word that comes out of your mouth. What? Does that surprise you?"

Jericho and Monterrey were still attacking the course, and yeah, he'd picked up the pace more than just a little. With that knockdown against him, he wanted to be sure his time was as fast as possible. He had to bring himself to the top of the list of riders with four faults if he could. Beautiful, beautiful technical ride—and bold.

Strang just watching transfixed. "Gorgeous animal," he murmured. "Who trained this horse, Chuck?"

Watching the horse and rider, not looking over at him. "Jericho."

Surprised again. "Jericho did all the training?"

Growl of deep satisfaction, as the pair went clean through the difficult triple. "Oh yeah, more than just a good rider. Wait till you see him on Lion."

Jericho called for the flying change of lead, and Monterrey cantered enthusiastically through the sharp bend to the left, back around and facing those last two obstacles. Very solid-looking wall, and then a final Oxer. Man and beast on fire—the bigger the element, the more they liked it. Ate up that wall like it was nothing, and then a huge magnificent leap, stag clean, over that final spread. Through the timers and they'd finished it handily. Jericho leaned forward, patted the big bay on the neck. Slipped his foot back into the stirrup too, just for the appearance of it.

They were announcing it. "…finished their go with four jumping faults, but with the fastest time we've seen this morning. Forty-nine seconds, Ladies and Gentlemen."

Nice round of applause, as he swung around, touched his whip to his cap in the direction of where he knew the Marxes were sitting, in salute to them, and then cantered handily almost to the exit, coming down to a posting trot just before leaving the ring.

"You totally robbed him of a clean round there, Chuck," Strang was still grousing.

"Yeah, I know, I know," Frankel grumbled, taking the blame for it willingly enough, really pissed at himself maybe. Turned around and smiled at Marx then though, like nothing was amiss. "Boy, you must be happy," he told him, and it was clear that the investment banker was. He'd even been standing there when Chuck took the blame for the single rail down, though he didn't really understand what that was all about. "Well, your horse just got the first of his two qualifying rounds. Oh, he'll definitely make the finals for the Team," Frankel beamed. Reached over and slapped George on the shoulder. "Watch out tomorrow, George. That pair's gonna give you some trouble in the jump-off. Snapping right at your heels."

Rueful smile. "I know."

Marx laughed, looked plenty satisfied. And Darien had snuggled up under his arm too, "Wasn't that great, hon?" she asked him, a smile on those gorgeous lips, and he nodded, holding her close.

Back outside the ring, Jericho was vaulting off Monterrey to the congratulations of Jason and a entire group of his friends from the circuit. Everyone seemed happy for him, but Jason was truly ecstatic. Threw his arms around him briefly, then just clasped his upper arm and held onto it meaningfully. "Man, after that accident..." he said expressively. The two men's eyes locked. Powerful smile from Jericho, who murmured, "You'll have to try a lot harder than that to take me out, pal." Coulder laughed. "Yeah, I see that."

But then a buzz started around the warm-up ring eclipsing everything else, as Marco led Chasseur de Lion up, and another of his guys took Monterrey away.

Massive, glorious gray stallion, head up, snorting and blowing. Tail up too, and prancing with huge powerful steps like the entire showgrounds belonged to him. Ears pricked forward, eyes half-wild. Let out a whinny that sounded more like a stallion's challenging scream.

Jason was still holding his arm and his grip around it tightened. "Jesus Christ, you're not riding Chasseur de Lion here, are you?"

Flare of both fierce pride and desire in those deep blue eyes. "Oh yeah, Jason. Let someone try and stop me. It's just a practice ride, but go up to the stands and watch him. You've never seen anything like this animal before. Swear to God."

———————————

The announcer's voice came over the loudspeakers. *"Ladies and Gentlemen, we'll now be on break for the next forty-five minutes, but before you leave your seats you might just want to stay and watch this ride. Our US Show Jumping Team has requested a practice ride, and that's taking place now...for your information, this* is *a training ride, and some disobedience is expected on the part of the horse, but this is an attempt to rehabilitate him, so don't be surprised. It should be very exciting,"* he added enticingly.

Exact words Frankel had told him they'd use. Good, Jericho thought as he entered the tunnel. He wanted the crowd there, it made a better test that way. He could see out to the grandstands now. Didn't look like anyone had left their seats. Probably no surprise there—not after an announcement like that.

Frankel looked casually over at Bruce Waverly, who was happily munching on some hors d'oevres and sipping champagne. Waverly raised his flute in a mock toast, pleased that he was going to be watching his horse go around now. Frankel smiled back at him...like nothing in the world was unusual—like this would be an everyday ride.

And Jericho cantered powerfully into the arena on Chasseur de Lion. Gasp of appreciation for the magnificent horse and rider team from the assembled crowd. What they probably didn't realize was that there were no stirrups on that saddle, or that the rider was up there with casts on his opposing arm and leg. Instead all they saw was sheer animal beauty. Broke into a round of enthusiastic applause.

Immediate reaction. The stallion's head shot up militantly at the noise. Ears twitching, eyes taking in the scene around him. Huge snort. Scream. And oh fuck yeah, Jericho thought, he was in for one hell of a fight. No way this horse didn't remember how much he'd learned to hate the jumping ring.

Petted him, tried to settle him. But no dice. Not even the smallest amount of relenting on the stallion's part. Alright then...fight it would be, cause this man on his back was easily as stubborn as the 1500 pounds of fighting-weight stallion he was sitting on.

Frankel, back at the rail, his hands gripped around it. He could see the signs as clearly as Jericho. "Oh shit," he breathed, then just growled violently under his breath, "*Ride* his ass, Jericho. Make him perform."

Strang saw it too, and spoke with fervor, in strong disagreement. "He should NOT be doing this, Chuck. That horse is totally renegade, he's too damn dangerous."

Vengeful snarl right back at him, "Well, why don't you try and stop Jericho then, George? Hell, he'll never back down from a ride."

Lion was already fighting him, as Jericho cantered him in a circle and around for the salute. His gorgeous head was up and jerking violently against the rein contact, using that massive stallion neck of his like a weapon, hindquarters bunched beneath him and refusing to move smoothly forward over the ground. Tap of the whip and a lash out with one of those murderous hind legs. Oh, and get ready for the dive, Jericho thought. Already a murmur of fear, mingled with the thrill of it, coming from the audience.

Salute.

Acknowledgement back from the ground jury.

Jericho sat in and gave the signal for canter. But instead Lion started backing up, twisting his body to the side, nice challenge to sit on. Cool in the saddle and prepared for this, Jericho gave him a smooth but sharp rap with the whip high on the croup, hard squeeze with the legs at the same time, and the stallion hopped forward. Did it gain…same reaction. Jerking forward now in a sort of canter—sort of not. Huge bounding leaps and getting bigger by the second, front end lifted athletically off the ground, back legs tightly underneath himself. Twisting his neck, jerking his body hard enough to unseat the vast majority of professional riders—and forget bucking, these were absolutely monster lunges, and twice as hard as any buck. Jericho sitting in deep, forcing him, forcing him, insisting on the canter.

Already lots of *oohs* and *aahs* from around the ring.

Fierce battle of wills, the stallion losing. Scream of rage from him, and then he just exploded in a tantrum of fury. He lifted from the shoulder, went straight up on his hind legs in mid-stride, and then thrust with everything in him from behind—rocketing through the air like he'd been shot from a catapult. Jesus, hadn't expected that at all, huge whiplash effect, but Jericho was ready for the very hard landing, still balanced precariously over the horse, but Lion was galloping now and shifting his weight too…and oh mother fuck, out came that powerful right shoulder and this horse was launching himself into a dive for the ground at breakneck speed, and with the force from that violent leap behind him.

On the sidelines Frankel was roaring, *"No! Jesus Christ, no!"* He looked like he was coming right over that rail—could already see his rider down and pinned, though it hadn't happened yet—but it just seemed inevitable.

Brae on the other end of the box—camera in hand and shooting like mad. He was even sporting a VIP badge that he'd scammed somehow.

Jericho threw his weight to the left, he squeezed commandingly with his legs, and he whacked that treacherous right shoulder sharply with the whip to keep him upright.

Didn't faze the animal, and he dove for the ground with a vengeance…couldn't stop him either, he was just coming on too hard. Scream from the audience, Frankel's voice in there somewhere…but Jericho was oblivious, just working like hell to show this stallion once and for all that *he* was the one in charge. Dove himself, hard and to the right. Breath forced from his body as he slammed into the grass, but he didn't stop moving. He rolled quickly right, drawing his right leg in underneath himself at the same time, and when he came back around on his chest again used it to launch himself straight off the ground like a pouncing predator. Lion was jerking to his feet too. Jericho's right hand caught the saddle, and damn it, he wasn't letting go for anything…the stallion taking off in a scramble of legs, lunging into a flat out gallop…and Jericho used the horse's momentum to pull himself into the air…and brute strength and determination to vault back on from the wrong side.

Roar of approval and appreciation from the crowd.

Whip gone. He grabbed up the reins. Sat in deep and really pushed this motherfucker forward, powerfully demanding, but perfectly controlled. Moving fast, taking constant action, but always thinking, never angry. The stallion flying now, and definitely wanting to go down to the ground again. But Jericho got to him sooner this time, shifting his weight hard to the left again, then yanking Lion's head around, facing him directly into the spread jump that was element number 1.

"No, Jericho, no!" Frankel was still screaming.

Launched him. Too far out, but sweet Jesus, this stallion had a powerful stride, and he'd better damn well use it.

Lion lifted into the air—it was simply too late not to—and he sailed like an eagle right over the obstacle. Came down, still fighting. Head thrust way up in the air, almost horizontal, still lurching with his body, lifting those shoulders, monster stride. Jericho tried to power him down into a frame, but damn, even he wasn't strong enough to do it…but this rogue behavior wasn't going to cut it with him. He wanted obedience and he wanted it now. Reached up with his foot and just jammed it down on the rein, putting all his weight into it. Forced that God damn head down, though it had been an insanely dangerous move.

Shocked, Lion came down and round. Jericho brought his leg back into position, and then squeezed him forward…found the closest fence with his eyes and then powered that damn stallion right in front of it…demanded the take-off.

The Oxer at 10, and they were taking it backwards. Could still hear Frankel yelling at him from somewhere, still screaming, *"No!"*

Huge jump, roar from the crowd, and yes they were over it and right on top of the single vertical at fence number 9—also coming from the wrong direction. Launched him, lifted him…release. The crowd screaming in approval once more.

Something was changing in the stallion's demeanor. Less resistance, more excitement. Jericho sat in again, and asked him to come even rounder, even more balanced and in front of the leg. Positive response, and all of a sudden he was sitting atop a monstrous but elegantly rolling canter—fast, but oh so agile and so strong. Probably the most powerful thing he'd ever felt underneath himself, and damn was it incredible—with "to die for" athleticism and length of stride.

Man, just fuck me, he thought, fierce excitement rushing up inside him. Now this…*this*…was Chasseur de Lion.

Oh yeah, *this* was a fucking horse.

Headed him now toward the double at 6, coming in from the correct direction finally—a spread jump, followed by a second spread. Big obstacles, both of them. There was supposed to be a short stride between the two elements. Jericho approached it with that huge and boldest of bold canters…and the audience knew they were looking at something special now.

Sighted that spot, guided him to it, demanded the take-off…a thrust from those hindquarters that was beyond description…giant suspended leap, but still totally forward, the animal rounded in the air in a perfect bascule…so much sheer potency in that jump that it carried him well in between the two fences. Bounce and lifted him right back into the next fence. Mega-effort on the part of the horse. Huge release to help him. Over and clear—in what should not have been possible.

"My God, he did that one-stride as a bounce," George murmured in awe.

Frankel...speechless for once.

Leaned forward. Pat on the neck from Jericho, and fervent "*Good boy.*"

Went ahead and did three more gold-medal quality fences with him— just to cement the association and prove he could. Lion was perfectly in control now—the stallion actually loving it and really putting out. Not so much the partnership he had with QL, but more of a cock-sure, individual pride in his own ability—led and guided by this human. Jericho circled him out of the line of the fences, and continued with that magnificent, rolling, huge canter around the edge of the ring and along the rail...to a standing ovation from the crowd. He rode past the Team box...hand lifted to his helmet in salute to Bruce Waverly, then spun the horse and cantered for the exit gate with him.

Frankel had taken off in search of him, and he'd dismounted, removed his jacket and riding gloves, turned the stallion over to Marco and then went straight up to the Team box, fighting his way through the waves of congratulations, and expressions of admiration and amazement. Either he and Frankel passed somewhere along the way without noticing it, or they took slightly different routes, because they didn't connect.

Jericho entered the box, stripped off his helmet and slid it under his left arm. Eyes sweeping the tables. No Chuck, but of course Bruce Waverly was there. Tossed his patron a cocky smile, something really fierce in those deep blue eyes of his too, then strode powerfully over, albeit with a notice-able limp, to reach down and take his hand in a strong grip. The right leg of his white breeches was filthy with mud and grass stains from that hard slam he'd taken into the ground. Didn't seem to give a damn about how tough that ride had been though. Only the outcome. "Spectacular fucking horse you've got there, Bruce," he murmured in satisfaction to the elderly gentleman. "Tough bastard, but just fuck me, the talent there...grateful to you for the ride."

"Excellent trainer he's got too." Delicate voice, and coming from the table just in front of him. Lady Forrester.

301

Embarrassed that he'd used the 'f' word in front of her—twice in as many sentences. Looked it too.

She laughed quietly. "Bruce, I'm just going to steal him from you for a second. Sit down here, Jericho." She patted the chair next to herself, completely appropriating this virile male animal for herself, and pleased by the coup.

Quick apologetic look at his patron, who shooed him over to sit with her, smiling secretively.

Wiped the sweat from his face against his shoulder, and slung himself into the chair beside her—shirt soaked through too, and probably pretty potent smelling, both of man and animal. Embarrassed about that too. Certainly didn't seem to bother her though. "Bold ride," she complimented him, grossly understating it as only a true horse person could.

Murmured, "Thanks." Man, this tiny little woman really put him ill at ease. Hadn't a clue what the right thing to say to her was.

Which she adored. "But I'm jealous of Bruce," she told him, patting his knee with that perfectly manicured tiny hand. "That's your Gold Medal horse, isn't it?"

Expressive look. "If I get him going. Consistently, that is."

"You will. Three years to work on it." Smiled. "Planning on breeding him?"

"Maybe—probably. Get him more solid in the arena first, then collect him and freeze the semen."

Sage nod from her. Yeah, she knew a lot—a real horsewoman, that's what George had said and he'd been right. And at least that was one thing he understood.

"So Chuck tells me you're going to Europe to look at horses," she went on.

He seemed surprised. Well, after that categorical "nope," he sure didn't think so. "I wanted to, yeah, but he kind of nixed that."

"He certainly did not." Frankel's voice, emphatic, and coming from behind him. And then he simply sat down beside Jericho—didn't wait to be invited, just moved right in. Firm slap across Jericho's back. "I'm gonna yell at you but good for that maneuver with your foot in the reins, but that's later," he threatened, but did so more than warmly. Then just shook his head and came out with it. "Damn, Jericho...I was proud of you." Genuine approval there. "Now go on and get out of here. I need to talk to Lady Forrester."

"Well, I just sat down here," he protested, not wanting to offend either Lady Forrester or his patron.

"Yeah and you're busy with the horses, and that comes before socializing," Frankel said maddeningly, considering that he'd insisted Jericho come up here.

"Yeah, I'm busy…"

Interrupted before he could even get the sentence out. "And Jericho, you need to change those breeches. They look completely unprofessional stained like that—surprised you even came up here before you changed. I mean, I certainly hope you have another pair with you."

Right back to where the morning had started with Brittany. Just exploded at him in irritation. "Christ's sakes Chuck, of course I have more than one pair of breeches with me, but exactly how the hell do you expect me to get them on? This boot's on me till Marco saws it off."

Look of disgust from the Chef D'Equip. "Terrible system then," he humphed.

It was an effective tactic though, since Jericho rose, excused himself with a "I guess I better get back to it," and then exited the Team box, still shaking his head and cursing under his breath.

———————

On his way back to the stalls Jericho saw something that really bothered him. Bob Marx, standing in the shade of a tall tree…laughing and talking to Ailynn McCrae.

God, what the fuck was that about?

Ducked onto a side path so he wouldn't be seen, and just continued on by. Still the image stayed with him. Didn't trust her…not one little bit.

Chapter Twenty

Couldn't have asked for a better first show of the season—albeit a month later than everyone else's first show.

The top eight horses from Monterrey's class moved on to the second round of jumping. Despite his four faults, Monterrey's fast time had put him at the top of the pack of those with knockdowns, and so yes, he was part of that illustrious top eight group. And he'd been clear through the second round—really proud of him. Even so, there were four riders with double clears, including George Strang, so they hadn't made it into the Jump-off. And George eventually won the class. Still they now had one qualifying CSI-W under their belts. One to go, and he'd be eligible for the finals on this horse.

QL won her class hands down, and $3000 in prize money. Really, really thrilled with her. She got lots of attention too—way more people at ringside for that Prelim class than normally would be there—most of them watching Jericho after his ride with Lion the day before. There were a few chuckles when people first got a look at QL—jughead, mule ears and all—but they weren't laughing long—not with her waltzing around the course like it was absolutely nothing, in perfect harmony with the man on her back. Fast, accurate, and utterly loving it.

Both Darien and Brittany had shown well too—with Brittany second in the Juniors, and Darien third in the Adult Amateur class, beating out Cin when the age groups came together in the finals. Cin didn't ribbon, and she looked thoroughly unhappy about that. Served her right, Jericho thought, satisfied.

As for Lion, Jericho rode him one more time in the practice ring, just to work him a second time at the showgrounds. Obedient this time, and drawing quite an audience. Put some more muscle on this animal and he'd be World Games ready without question, as long as his mind held up to the pressure—and that was Jericho's challenge, get him both physically and mentally to one hundred percent.

Only one down note throughout the whole thing, but it was a big one—pretty well ruined the day for him Sunday, maybe the whole show. After his last class, Jericho had walked up to the Team box and was about to push back the curtain that served as a door and go inside. But he heard voices…and his name mentioned—and in a not too pleasant way at that. Paused there, listening.

Female voice, and he recognized it as Bee-Bee Oxmoor. "Chuck, I just don't get it," she was saying resentfully. "Why are you fawning over Jericho like this? It's not like he's all that good. Sure, if you put a great horse under any decent rider, it makes them look a lot better. But how could you possible give him a mount like Chasseur de Lion?"

Frankel, and annoyed. "Why? Did you want to ride him?"

"Well why not?" she asked. "I'm a former Olympian…I deserve the best horses. I don't know, Chuck…you seem to think Jericho's so talented." Real malice in her voice too.

"It's not about talent," Frankel lashed right back at her. "You think I can put you on a horse that takes a dive like that…risk your neck on the most dangerous horse around—a horse that may never straighten up enough to make a legitimate go at a medal? And come on, you have to be really physically strong to sit an animal like that. It's not about talent or technique, it's about brawn."

It's not about talent? Frankel's words cut deep, really hurt. Real sucker punch to the gut.

"Okay, have Jericho train him till he's back confirmed. Then move him."

"I'm not saying it's out of the question," the Chef D'Equip came back, but frostily. "We'll see. I'll make those decisions when the time comes."

"And what about Monterrey? Langley's getting older, Chuck." Langley, her own horse, nearly seventeen now and rumored to be having some leg problems—maybe serious. She hadn't ridden in this show. "You know Monterrey would be perfect for me."

Pause, and then Frankel's voice one more time. "You could be right there," he told her, not nearly as gruff. "That's potentially possible."

Sucked his breath in. Chuck was thinking about taking Monterrey away from him, placing him with Bee-Bee? His best chance to make the Team, also his biggest patron? Now, that didn't just hurt, it ripped him up inside.

It's not about talent. Oh hell no, but he had his uses all right—riding the dangerous ones, making horses for the other Team members to ride. But making the Team himself? Apparently not important.

Didn't stay to hear more, just turned and walked away. But he was going to fight this…if he could make himself care enough. Right now he just wanted to tell them all to go to Hell.

The first load of horses had gone back earlier in the afternoon, and now they were packing up the remaining few, as well as all the gear. Jericho was working side by side with the guys to load up—still in breeches and with his boot still taped on. Removing the one from the day before had taken nearly an hour—a good forty-five minutes anyway. Today it would be the last thing they'd tackle, his own discomfort unimportant to him. And the physical activity was providing an outlet for the bitter anger inside him—or was his anger just a cover up for the face that he was hurting inside? Didn't matter.

He was standing just outside at the far end of the aisle, loading unused bags of shavings and bales of hay into the storage area of the big six-horse trailer like a machine. Not talking and unapproachable, but definitely putting out a lot of work, really knocking down what needed to get done.

George Strang strolled into the aisle to say goodbye and congratulations on a great show. But before he could get two feet inside, Marco stepped in front of him, blocking his path. Pretty good obstacle—no one was getting past him unless he said so, that was for sure. He just shook his head in the negative.

"What's the matter, Marco?" He could see Jericho at the other end of the aisle now, but he wasn't looking around, seemed completely in his own world. Yeah, there was definitely some kind of problem here.

Uncommunicative but forbidding look on the head groom's face. And he wasn't his friendly self at all. "Leave him alone," he said." Then added with noticeable scorn, "All of you."

Whatever the problem was, Marco knew the details…obvious. And he was mad about it personally too.

Frankel showed up at just about the same time. Clapped George on the shoulder happily, obviously in a good mood. "Loved that ride today. Good job," he complimented him. And to Marco, "Where's Jericho?"

But the head groom was still being stubborn and still tight-lipped, maybe even more so now that Chuck had appeared. "Working. Packing up." Some real condemnation in those dark eyes of his.

Frankel lifted his chin and spied Jericho. He was handling those heavy bales like they were nothing, despite the casts, and heaving them with precision into the trailer—and with pretty good force too. Frankel's eyes narrowed with annoyance. "What's he doing that for?" he demanded, not even waiting for an answer. Raised his voice and called out, "Jericho!" Grumbled to Marco again, "Way too much for him to be doing by himself...where are the rest of the guys?" Then called out again, "Jericho!"

He stopped. Just stood there, not turning around. Then went back to work.

"What's this about?" Frankel muttered. Jericho had very pointedly just snubbed him, and even though he couldn't see his face, the tension in his body was easily visible. Really pissed about something, that was for sure, and that attitude disturbed Frankel plenty—didn't have a clue what had prompted it. But the fact that Marco looked equally cold—now that almost bothered him more. He brushed by the head groom, and started striding down the aisle...and Marco right behind him.

"No, Chuck," he all but threatened him. "Leave him alone." And when he couldn't stop him, growled under his breath, *"Corre perro come mierda."*

Jericho had finally turned. *"Me vale,* just let him come, Marco," he sneered. And he was waiting now. Looked like he was ready for a confrontation—or a brawl. To prove it, that right fist of his clenched up tight—that unconscious but warlike gesture of his that said far more eloquently than words what he was feeling inside.

George trailed along behind Frankel at a more circumspect distance. He sure saw that fist and respected it. Stopped a good ten feet away.

Frankel had seen it too, but even so, he came right up inside striking range from Jericho. "I'm going away this coming week," he told him with authority.

Fired right back at him, "Good for you."

"Not even interested where I'm going?" he baited him.

Chuck was trying to draw him out, Jericho realized, but he wasn't buying it. "Couldn't give a fuck."

And from Marco on the sidelines, "That's right."

Stunned by that. "Fine then," Frankel snapped, extremely irritated.

Jericho had been putting two and two together while he'd been standing there working. Stewing over the conversation between Frankel and Bee-Bee. Remembering things like his brief conversation yesterday with Lady Forrester—and Chuck chasing him away when the horse-hunting trip came up. "Going to Europe, Chuck? Sure you are. But I'm not supposed to know that, am I?"

The Chef D'Equip's eyes narrowed at the open hostility. Didn't run from it one bit. "Thought you might want to go with me."

Did you now. Growled at him, "What happened to "*nope*"? Or let me guess…you want to pick up some young stock for the Team."

"Yeah, maybe."

"Forget my fucking sale horses, right?"

"Jericho…"

Really ugly tone of voice. "Need an expendable rider, Chuck? Got a few tough ones you need tried? Ones that need brawn instead of talent, cause talent has nothing to do with it where I'm concerned. But maybe I can work some of the dangerous ones for you—just till they're confirmed and then you can move them where you really want them, how would that be?" Just purred that last…or was it something even more ominous? Turned away from him before he used that fist of his, cause man he wanted to…but then looked back. He just couldn't help himself. Seductive tone of voice that was somehow more accusing and threatening than even his anger had been. "Oh, and I'll bet you've got some suggestions on who could work my horses while I'm gone, don't you Chuck? Like maybe who could exercise Monterrey? Yeah, especially that."

George looked completely confused, but not Frankel. He was taken back for sure, didn't know where Jericho's information was coming from, but he certainly knew what he was referring to.

Really judgmental look from Marco too. The head groom had stepped closer to his boss, protectively. He obviously knew, too.

"Marco, George…let Jericho and I talk," the Chef D'Equip said quietly.

That idea met with firm resistance from Marco—he didn't look like he was going anywhere. Not until Jericho nodded his head sharply toward the other end of the aisle way, seconding Frankel's request.

"Want to tell me what you've heard?" Frankel asked Jericho once they were alone.

"Bullshit, Chuck. No point in my telling you what you already know. And man, if you understood how bad I want to hurt you right now, you'd never go there in a million years." He wasn't exaggerating either. Had lifted that fist up to waist height while he was talking, still clenched. "You ruthless, fucking bastard…you'll do anything to get what you want, won't you? Trample on anyone. Just fucking lie…" He broke off then. It was enough anyway. They both knew exactly what he meant. "I won't take another thing from you, Chuck. Not a horse, not a patron, not your damn coaching either…nothing." Lifted that powerful deep blue stare to him with barely contained fury. "Yeah, I'll be a nobody in this industry because of it, but guess what…that's all you intended anyway."

Stern look on the Chef D'Equip's face, but he wasn't rushing to deny it either. "Who told you all this, Jericho?"

Coldly sarcastic. "You did, Chuck."

Frankel didn't beat around the bush with him either. "So you or someone close to you like Marco overhead my conversation with Bee-Bee," he stated. Pure fact. Had to be.

"Yeah, *I* did. First hand. So we've got nothing left to say, except this…if you set foot on my property again…"

A command. "Enough."

"Maybe it's enough for you…"

Stronger. *"Enough."*

Just shook his head. "You fucker. You motherfucker."

"Want to know the truth?"

Sneer on his face. "Don't you dare stroke me, Chuck. Don't dare presume. Here's the truth…I'm going back to my stables now. I'm going to pack up the few horses I have left after you're done dicking around with my life, and I'm going home to East Hampton for the rest of the winter. Work on my own. Try and find something I still love about this job…some reason why I even care…"

"Jericho, you're one hundred and eighty degrees…"

Acted like he didn't even hear him talking. "Oh yeah, you're right, Chuck. I don't belong in the big leagues. I just don't have the…bullshit and deception in me it takes to play this game."

Frankel just let the bitterness roll off him, potent as it was. "Alright, can I give you a few facts now?" he asked him. "You heard me say what I said, and I'm not denying it. But you're not going back to East Hampton, not by a long shot. That's fact number one."

Well, he'd admitted it—what he'd said, how he really felt. "Yeah, I really am going home—while I still can, while I still own the farm. Do you have any idea how far back in time you've taken my career, Chuck?" Jericho asked him harshly. "Back to the point where I only had three or four rides and struggling to keep them. Just a few customers in the barn…couldn't pay my fucking bills a few months out, and having that stare me in the face every morning. And I have to hand it to you, Chuck, 'cause you've done it single handedly."

"Jericho, I need you to listen to me. Do you ever shut up once you get on a roll like this? Let me get a word in edgewise."

Anger building in his voice again, and no, he really wasn't listening at all. "You know, I weaseled my way into that class with QL, and maybe that was dicey. But you've *just broken* me over it, Chuck—destroyed everything I've worked for. Oh yeah," he added coldly. "You gloss it up real well… coaching sessions, big practice ride with Lion yesterday to make me feel important, but when he's rehabilitated who's going to ride him? What am I, your private exercise boy? Yeah, I'm tough, and if I get hurt, who gives a fuck, right?"

Frankel put a hand out to him and laid it on his good arm—but he jerked himself away, not accepting the gesture at all. "Alright, alright…" Chuck murmured. "You're really pissed. But hear me on this…you're riding Lion, no one else is, and no one else is going to. And yeah, I've dicked around a lot with the horses in your barn. I want to do more too. But I haven't been telling you what I'm doing and why, and maybe that was a huge fuck-up on my part. I promise you this though, your barn will be full."

"With what?" he muttered brutally. "Horses for George and Bee-Bee and the rest of them? No, don't even bother answering, cause I'll never trust a word you say again, so what's the point?"

"Alright, you don't trust me…come to Europe with me anyway."

"No fuckin' way."

"Not even if Lady Forrester authorized me to buy a horse for you? Pretty much open checkbook, anything you want?"

No answer. But that rocked him back pretty good.

"Not even if I have a couple of really spectacular Landor S sons lined up to try? Or how about a younger full brother to Lion—same ability maybe, without the baggage? Any of this interesting you at all?"

He wanted to just say "no", just turn his back on him. Not believe him. But man, Chuck knew how to reach in and grab him by the heart. "Damn you for a liar," he finally said vengefully.

"No, I'm not...yeah, and I can see now I should have said something...maybe not everything I just told you, but enough so you wouldn't start thinking on your own." Shook his head. "And I sure didn't want you hearing that conversation—especially not first, before I talked to you. Yeah, I've got you good and worried now, don't I?" Frankel looked apologetic too, sympathetic even, kind. "Tell me this," he asked him. "Is Monterrey as good as Lion? Definitely a Team quality horse, but can he win an individual medal for you?"

Came back at him hard. "Man, he's the most consistent thing I have in the barn. And I fuckin' *made* that horse."

"Yes, you did, and what's more, you did an excellent job. But what about my question?"

"Hell, Marx even pays for my coaching sessions. Without him..."

"Just stick with my question," Frankel insisted, coming right up next to him now. Making it personal.

Heartbeat of silence, then just growled at him, "Maybe not."

Approval on the Chef D'Equip's face, like maybe he was pleased that Jericho could still think coolly, even though he was anything but. "See, that's my problem," he said, controlling this conversation now. "Things have changed a lot. I've worked with you for two months, and you've shown me something. Want to know what it is?"

Oh yeah, he was being drawn in here, and knew it. He was fighting it. He thought to himself, this must be exactly what Lion had been feeling in that Grand Prix ring the day before...fighting like hell, but knowing he was going down. "No," he said finally.

"Sure you do," Frankel corrected him. Smiled, despite the strength in that deep blue stare that leveled on him. "Or no, maybe you don't want to hear it, because you know. You *know*...it's what you *want* to hear, and that scares the shit out of you, doesn't it? Makes you too vulnerable."

Fuck, put a horse or a fence in front of him, and fear never crossed his mind. But this?

Frankel just kept talking, didn't wait for an answer from him—didn't make him answer. "I want a gold medal team in Beijing in 2008...but I want an individual gold too. And you're my rider." Jericho was shaking his head in the negative, anger flaring up one more time. "Oh yes," Frankel insisted. "And Monterrey's not good enough." Paused. "Lion is. QL maybe. But Jericho, that's just not *deep* enough in terms of mounts, and *I want more*."

Harsh. "Chuck, I don't trust you. I really don't trust you. You'd jerk me off in a heartbeat if it worked for you at the time. And Marx…he's the only thing that keeps me from going under."

Sterner now. "Well, you know what, that's interesting. So you're worried about losing Marx as a patron?" Gave him a really piercing glare, reading right through him, it seemed. "I sure don't need to help you with that. Looks to me like you're working real hard on losing him all by yourself."

Jericho just stared at him, and Christ, for a moment there it felt like he couldn't breathe. The only thing Chuck could possibly be referring to was Darien, wasn't it? But how in the hell could he have guessed? No easing up from Chuck either, just pinning him with that scornful disapproving look.

"Oh god," Jericho murmured with feeling, and turned away from him.

Long moment of silence. "Well, if I wasn't sure before, you certainly confirmed it for me now," Frankel said sharply. "I've just got to tell you just how much I despise that kind of thing."

Strong, hard, heartfelt response—still not looking at him. "Yeah, and I do too."

More silence.

"Even worse," Frankel said bluntly. "Because number one, I believe you and number two, I think you're telling me you're not just screwing around here…you care for this woman, maybe a lot. And hell, knowing you, that means you'll fight for her." Sighed, stern maybe but maybe also resigned. "And you think I'm wrong trying to shuffle the patrons around? Jericho, if I don't, you *will* be back in East Hampton before the month is out."

Wasn't even denying it, powerful tone of voice. "Every time I see her I think abut you telling me I have no control. *Every fucking time*. But I've been so careful," he said defensively.

"Yeah, *you* have been—didn't get a hint from you. But ever seen the way she sits and stares at you? That's not just because she likes to see her trainer ride. Or how about the fact that she's coming with us on this trip when she doesn't even want to buy a horse?" A tone of withering sarcasm creeping in. "And then there's that story I finally weaseled out of Bruce Waverly yesterday evening at dinner."

"Man, just fuck me," he murmured, bowing his head, although on one level, he was also fiercely satisfied—Darien coming with him to look for an Olympic gold medal horse? Man, that was something he'd never dared hope for—it was everything he wanted in life wrapped together for three days straight. *If it even happened now.* Because shit, this entire conversation had been neatly turned around on him. From one about his own anger where he'd clearly been in the right, to one where he was guilty as sin with no excuse to offer for it. Totally at Chuck's mercy, and god damn it, now it would come. He just prepared himself the blistering lecture, asked for immediate sentencing. "Alright, Chuck, what are you going to do to me?"

Last response he expected in the world. Hand wrapping firmly around his good wrist. "Protect the hell out of you," Frankel said, despite the fact he obviously disapproved of it but good. "Tell you to stop first, but fuck, that's gonna be totally ineffective. So just keep doing what I'm doing…put different patrons behind you, take care of Marx in the meantime…hope nothing explodes, but knowing damn well it could. Try to be prepared first." Much stronger tone of voice then. "And yeah, let me answer that question you're dying to ask me…you bet we're still going. And yes, I told her she could come before I knew. But you better damn well keep it cool, and I mean sub-zero. If you don't, I swear I'll go to her and tell her she's ruining your career—and you *know* that'll work, so don't fuck with me on this, Jericho."

———

When Chuck said he was leaving this coming week, he wasn't kidding. In fact, it turned out he meant the very next day. Evening flight out of Miami, straight through 12 hours to Schipol airport in Amsterdam. And he'd wanted Starbucks to come too, which positively thrilled the Barista—take pictures of everything they looked at. Luckily, Brae had a passport, though he'd never been out of the country before.

They all met in the waiting room lounge—Darien, Frankel, Jericho and Brae, with the two roommates being the last to arrive. Boarding started almost immediately afterwards. Darien was in First Class, and the rest of them in Business.

Jericho hadn't told her about his conversation with Frankel either—so both of them were acting like they were nothing more than friends. Sub-zero cool—exactly what Chuck wanted, though when no one was looking, his eyes on her were anything but.

First Class passengers were invited on first, and then Business after that, and Coach last. Jericho and Frankel were seated together, with Brae close by, but on the other side of the plane with a middle section in-between. The stewardesses were already coming around in Business serving champagne, and of course Starbucks immediately began working his charm on them. Clownish outfit on him, as always—rumpled baggy pants, XL long-sleeved polo shirt, black sport jacket and a weird cartoon character print tie just hanging around his neck. He had his camera out already too.

"Sir, would you like some champagne?" an attractive blonde asked him.

He turned his pale blue, bedroom-eyes stare on her, and saw her return look of interest. "Sure." Grabbed the last plastic flute off the tray, then lifted his camera. "Stay right there," he told her, and then snapped her picture. Turned it around so she could see it.

"Oh hey, that's good," she said, really surprised.

"I'm a photographer." Drew himself up in his seat, made himself look important. "Well actually, I'm the U.S. Team photographer," he exaggerated, though it wasn't far from true.

"U.S. Team? What team?"

"Equestrian. Show Jumping…you know, horses," he added needlessly.

"Oh, no kidding?" Dreamy look on her face. "I love horses. I used to ride as a kid."

"Oh hey then, look at these." Brae flipped back through the images on his camera to a few of the best ones he'd taken over the weekend…found what he wanted…a series of shots of Jericho on Lion. The stallion up on his hind legs and making that mammoth lunge through the air, his dive for the ground…Jericho diving too and rolling, then vaulting back on. Then a few of that incredible double he'd gone over—the one-stride he'd done as a bounce.

The stewardess, completely rapt now. Sitting on the arm of his seat, her pretty mouth slack. "Wow, these are absolutely wonderful pictures," she was crooning.

"Yep." Proud of himself.

"I mean, this really looks dangerous. But gosh, I've never seen anyone ride like this…not even in the movies." She had her hand on the camera now, fascinated.

"Oh yeah," Starbucks went on, drawing her in. "That's my roommate… he's an Olympian." In his mind, Brae wasn't even lying; he'd just advanced the timeline by a few years.

"Wow."

"Well, we're not *room*-mates," he added quickly, emphasizing the word but good. Making sure he got that meaning across. "We just…you know…share the same house."

The stewardess laughed. "I'm Annie," she said. "Listen, I better get busy, but I'll stop back. I'd love to see more of what you do."

Not ready for her to leave yet…threw down another enticement. "Yeah, that's him over there."

It worked for the moment too, because she sat back down again, but craning her neck around to see who he meant. "This rider, you mean? The Olympian?"

"Yeah, right there. Standing up there. Can't miss him."

Tall, powerful looking male, long, long, sun-streaked, chestnut hair, tightly braided, sharp arresting features. He'd risen and started pulling off the light sweater he was wearing—wasn't going too well though. He'd stripped it half way over his head, but then it got tangled in the band at the end of his braid, and was hung up on his cast as well. They were close enough to him to hear his growl of irritation.

"Heh! He's kind of a dork though," Starbucks laughed.

Annie jumped up and ran over to him.

"Sir, can I help you?"

Sweater covering his face, and his arms trapped at about shoulder height. Wry humor in that deep warm voice. "Christ, I hope so."

She put her hands up around his broad shoulders and grabbed the sweater—rock-hard body beneath her fingers…nice. Hopelessly tangled though. "Here, let's start over. You've got your hair caught up in it." She pulled it back down into place, freeing him. Compelling deep blue stare falling on her, and right in close, amusement there. Disarmingly helpless male. She could see the cast on his arm and opposing leg now too. "Well, here's part of your problem," Annie laughed, knocking lightly on the cast. She was curious and dying to ask about it—didn't though, at least not yet. She tugged on the sleeve over that inflexible cast, and he drew back his elbow, hiking up the sweater on that side and getting his arm clear. Then she reached around, pulled the braid free from where the stretchy band had caught some of the sweater's fabric, then pushed it under the neckline.

"This should work now." Pulled it up and over his head. Smiled at him. "There."

A round of applause from those sitting close by. Annie took a bow. Jericho laughed. "You're probably wondering who dressed me yesterday, and what the fuck I'm going to do tomorrow," he said—self-deprecating, but not.

Frankel coming back down the aisle from the restroom. He'd missed the whole scene, and could only see Jericho and the pretty stewardess, standing close, laughing and talking. Growled in irritation as he came up beside them. "Christ, take the seat by the window—only way I'm going to have any control here."

Immediate protest. "Come on, Chuck, I'm way taller than you, and there's nowhere I can put this cast." Which was sure true, and he'd been planning on hanging his leg out in the aisle as much as possible.

Grumble from the Chef D'Equip. "We have work to do, and I want you paying attention."

Snapped back at him, "Yeah, I'm planning on that."

From the stewardess, "So your roommate told me you're an Olympic rider." People in the seats close by listening in now, interested.

Shot a censuring look over at Brae, who'd apparently been taking pictures the whole time, damn him.

Frankel, more than just irritated—good and annoyed now. "Yeah, he's on the Team, and I'm the coach, and Jericho, you're definitely sitting by the window so just get in there and shut up about it."

Blew his breath out angrily, and muttering to himself, "God damn it all," but he took orders pretty well, and slid across to the window seat.

———

Once they took off, Frankel got out his briefcase, and extracted a sheaf of papers, some with pictures. "I want to show you the schedule and who we're looking at. And you need to get some rest on the way over, because as soon as we land we going straight to the first barn. Herr Gottemann will meet us at the airport, and you better damn well be ready to ride."

Obviously pretty interested. Murmured back at him, "Yeah, I want to ride."

Fourteen horses to look at over three days—grueling schedule. And Chuck had deliberately put most of the more promising ones on the first day, just in case they wanted to come back and try them again. Six horses, starting as soon as they got off the airplane—three at one farm, and three at another, with a good hour's driving time between the two barns.

Horse Name	Age	Sire	Farm
Fontaine	9	Furioso II	Stahl Gottemann
Landkraft	7	Landor S	Stahl Gottemann
Force de Lion	4	Coeur de Lion	Stahl Gottemann
Lancaster	7	Landor S	Stahl Reisliek
Landkrieg	5	Landor S	Stahl Reisliek
Jouez de Rouet	6	Baloubet de Rouet	Stahl Reisliek

Chuck also had show records on all the horses, where available—although those like Lion's full brother, Force de Lion, were too young to have anything of note. They easily spent an hour and a half talking about them—nice professional conversation, very little bickering.

Brae had the stewardess sitting with him again as soon as they'd finished serving the meal. He was showing her more pictures, including the ones he'd just taken.

"Oh wow, can you email me those?" she asked, and happily gave him a way to contact her again.

Jericho had meanwhile become grumpy, with Frankel effectively holding him captive in his seat. 'Why don't you sleep?" The Chef D'Equip asked him, tired of seeing him restless and miserable.

"Well, yeah I could if I was a sardine." More than just a little sarcastic. Twisted in the small space again—it was way better than Coach, for sure, but still not much room for a man his size—even worse with those casts. Looked over at Frankel and griped to him, "This is ridiculous. Just move out of the way and let me up. I'll be so frickin' stiff by the time we get there it's not even funny. How can I ride like that?" Added angrily, "I'm just going over to talk to Brae a little…hell, I'm not going up to First, if that's what you think."

Stared at him for a moment, then rose and said pleasantly. "I think you should get up and stretch your muscles out before they cramp." Like he'd just come up with that idea on his own.

Didn't argue. "Okay, fine." Just levered himself out and into the aisle, while Frankel sat back down and closed his eyes to try and sleep.

Jericho caught Brae's eye, and nodded toward the front of the cabin, then started moving in that direction himself.

Starbucks smiled happily and got up too, telling Annie, "Come on up with me and talk to Jericho. He's free finally."

"Jericho? Is that his real first name?"

Smirk. "I know, it's gay, isn't it? But don't tell him that, okay? Gets all offended. Truth is, he's actually really wicked in a fight…seen him kick the shit out of a few guys, know what I mean?"

"Really wicked, huh?"

"Oh yeah…saved my ass once, that's for sure." He wasn't the least bit embarrassed by the fact that his ass needed saving—the casual way he said it didn't make it seem like a slur on him.

Brae strolled up to the front, and tossed a fake punch at Jericho. "Hey, bra, what's happening?" he said. "Chuck finally give you a break?"

Sneered, "Chuck's a fuckin' idiot." Smiled then—at the stewardess too.

"Hi Jericho. Hi Brae." Happy little feminine voice. Darien, come back from First Class. "How are you guys doing?"

"I'm great," the Barista said, leaning his arm against the wall in a way that almost put it around the pretty stewardess. "This is Annie," he added. "I've been showing her my pictures and stuff." Bark of laughter from him. "Look at this one…it's Jericho with his head stuck in his sweater." He swung his camera around, and showed it to Darien. She burst out laughing, while the subject of the picture just covered his face with his hand, but chuckling too, and murmuring, "Christ, Brae."

They chatted for a while, with Annie going back and forth between serving the passengers and stopping to listen in and talk with them. Jericho, sighting Chuck every couple of minutes, making sure he was still lying there with his eyes closed.

He was.

Darien was looking at Jericho, warm expression. She laid that little hand of hers on his arm. "You look tired," she said. "Has Chuck been driving you crazy?"

"No, no," he murmured. "We've just been going over the horses for tomorrow." Looked back at him. Sighed. "At least he can sleep in those seats. I can't."

"Change places with me," she offered.

"No, hell no.'

"Please. I'm so much shorter than you are, and the seats in First convert into a full bed. You can stretch out straight," she coaxed him. "And Jericho, I don't have to ride six horses tomorrow. You do."

Man, it sounded like Heaven about now, but still he said no. "I can't do that. Besides, I'm sure it's not allowed."

"Oh sure, Annie will fix it all up, bra," Starbucks chimed in. "Let me go talk to her."

"No, Brae..." But too late, he'd already gone over to ask. Jericho looked at Darien. Reached his fingers out to touch hers—just a brush. She stepped closer. His hand moved upwards, running feather-light over her wrist and lower arm. Sighted Chuck again—still sleeping. Fingers running higher, to her shoulder. Pushed her a step backwards, into the galley between Business and First Class. Then back another step, and well out of Frankel's line of sight.

Annie, of course agreed to what Brae was asking, and anyway, Jericho was a celebrity of sorts, wasn't he? Olympian and all? "Sure, it's no problem, I'll just let the girls in First know." Looked over at he and Darien, still partially visible from where she and Brae were standing. "So is that his girlfriend?"

"Oh no," Starbucks said with confidence, looking around at the two of them. "They're just..." But he broke off abruptly.

Darien was standing with her back to the wall, she'd lifted her face to Jericho—was almost intimately close to him, eyes partially closed, body soft and welcoming. And he was talking to her, arm against the wall over her head, saying something powerful, radiating an animal kind of energy.

His fingers traced her jawline. She whispered something back. Laid that stare of his on her for a few drawn out moments, then murmured ardently to her. And she dropped her head back, eyes closed, sighing, almost whimpering.

Some kind of really intense verbal exchange happening.

Talked to her for just a few more moments, inclined his face down to hers at the same time, mouth just hovering over hers. No real physical contact other than the occasional brush of his fingers along her cheek.

"Wow," Starbucks said, awed. Some technique. Have to practice that.

Jericho pushed himself away from the wall, stepped back a pace. Holding eye contact though. Long meaningful seconds passed. And then he dropped his gaze away. Leaned back against the opposing wall, eyes drifting up, just watching her.

She smiled then, looked warm and happy. Said something final to him—closure. Short sentence, and although they couldn't hear it, it wasn't that hard to read her lips.

I love you too, she'd said.

———————————

Frankel jerking awake in his seat—not sure what time it was. Looked over next to him, but instead of Jericho, he saw Brae sitting there. How the Barista had gotten in past him without waking him was a good question, but obviously he had.

Goofy grin. Wave from him.

"Is Jericho in your seat?" Looked around to confirm it…but no, it was Darien sleeping quietly in Brae's old spot.

"Nah, we kicked him up front. He can stretch out there, get some real rest."

Frankel smiling. "Good idea, Brae. And thanks."

Chapter Twenty-One

Pier Gottemann was probably one of the best-known and most respected agents in the world for the sale and purchase of high-quality Hunters and Jumpers, certainly in Europe. And to him, a customer like Frankel was golden—because he came to buy. No "just looking", no tire kicking. If you put what he wanted in front of him, the checkbook came out.

Pier was waiting now just outside the secure area in the International Arrivals terminal, waiting for the U.S. Chef D'Equip and his party. The monitor showed that their plane had landed, and within fifteen minutes, he saw them walking out. Frankel spied him quickly, waved, and then started walking toward him.

"Pier, good to see you," he said, holding his arm out. The two men shook hands, and then Frankel introduced Darien, Jericho and Brae to him.

Surprise registering on Gottemann's face, probably because the supposed rider was sporting both arm and leg casts. "Let me make a phone call right away," he said, his brusque Dutch accent thickening—the only indication that he was perturbed. "Make sure we have the right riders available so you can see the horses work."

"No, no," Frankel reassured him. "We'll do it just like always. You show us the horses without tack, trot them up and back, then saddle them up. Jericho will ride them." Smirked with a bit of superiority. "Doesn't look like he can with those broken bones of his, but I'll guarantee you he will."

Skeptical look from Gottemann. "If you say so, Chuck."

Jericho, listening, but not saying a word.

The drive to Stahl Gottemann took them about forty minutes, but the place was definitely worth the wait. Gorgeously manicured property, old style but elegantly kept up barn. Nice viewing area for customers to a covered indoor ring, and beyond that a big outdoor jumping field—covered in snow though, given the time of year, and everything was being done inside now.

"Wow, this is nice," Darien said, turning around happily in the viewing room, looking at all the pictures of famous horses that had come through here. One of Pier's assistants brought her a cup of coffee, and offered her some refreshments too. "Thanks," she said, obviously pleased by the attention—but at the moment she looked like she was walking on cloud nine anyway. Probably would have been thrilled with almost anything. Frankel was watching her suspiciously, but didn't mention it.

Jericho had ducked into the stable area proper, taken a quick walk around looking at things and what was being done. Nothing amiss there that grabbed his attention—no odd looking gear, no sign of drugs. Not that he'd expected to find any of that, still it never hurt to make sure. Now he reappeared in the viewing room to join the others. Accepted a coffee, but then sat down with it to pull out his paddock boots, half chaps and riding gloves from a large duffel bag designed to carry all his gear, including tack. Pulled out his saddle too, but set it on the side. Got ready to ride, while Chuck and Gottemann stood on the side talking privately and in Dutch. Figured they were talking about him, at least partly. Hated that— didn't look at them, just kept to himself.

Darien came over and sat on the arm of the chair beside him. "Excited?" she asked him. Really tender look in those eyes of hers.

Deep blue stare running over her. "Hell yeah."

And her, looking away shyly.

Frankel broke up the scene, by snapping frostily. "Alright, Jericho… here's the first horse."

He swung his powerful stare away from Darien and over to Chuck then, and it spoke volumes. Some softening on the part of the Chef D'Equip, a half-smile even pulling at his lips—because he understood. Jericho couldn't really believe this was happening to him, for him.

Jericho rose then, covering that sense of vulnerability by simply withdrawing. No conversation from him. Walked to the viewing window, pulling on his riding gloves—pure detached professionalism.

A positively magnificent animal stood in the indoor with a handler. Huge fiery red chestnut, nice blaze, two little white half-socks in front— and perfectly groomed, gleaming with good health. Recognized him from the picture alright. This was Lion's full brother…Force de Lion. Only four years old.

Jericho turned to Pier—first time he'd directly addressed him after their initial hello. "Tell them to wait there for me, I'm going out. And I need a crew to work fences...I like to be able to change things while I ride." Nodded his head back in the direction he'd come from. "And that's my saddle."

Little show of respect coming from Gottemann's weathered eyes—like he admired a man who knew what he wanted and then demanded it, albeit in a courteous way. Nodded, walked to the doorway with Jericho. Opened it, and then yelled out, "Hans!" His equivalent of Marco, undoubtedly.

Jericho didn't wait for Pier, but he wasn't rushing either. Calm. Moved with authority. Knew what he was doing, oh yeah. In his element and safe there. He stepped through the doorway and walked around to the entrance to the indoor—a pair of double wide sliding doors. Pulled one open and went inside. Frankel wasn't far behind him and Pier right there with Chuck.

Jericho went over to the horse—young stallion. "Approved?" he asked.

"Yes, absolutely," Gottemann told him, and went on to list his scores in the various categories of the stallion evaluations—conformation, gaits, free jumping and more.

Jericho put his hands on him, and the horse turned his head around, sniffing, pushing at his arm with his nose. Curious youngster. Petted him, spoke to him, ran his fingers over his chest, down the slope of his shoulder, over his legs. Picked up a foot first front then rear, looked at the shoes. Stepped back a pace and nodded to the handler, who took up the lead and then trotted Force de Lion away from him about twenty feet, and then back again.

"Again," Jericho asked. And when that was finished, "Alright, tack him up." He lit a cigarette and stood alone and apart from the other two men...tall, silent, not sharing his comments or thoughts, whatever they were.

Pier had come up and was just slightly behind and to the side of him. "Do you want someone to ride him for you first to see what he looks like under saddle?"

"No."

Just five minutes later the handler was leading him back again. Jumping boots on him front and rear. Figure eight bridle, running martingale, Jericho's own saddle. They'd of course made note of the fact that his saddle had no stirrups on it—had brought a pair out with them. But he shook his head in the negative. "Right now it's easier for me without," he said, then asked Gottemann, "What does he know?"

"Not much. He's basically green under saddle," Pier told him, honestly. "And we've faced him with a couple of jumps, that's all."

Nodded, pretty much expected that with a four-year-old and wasn't concerned with it.

"Do you want a crop?"

Shrugged. "Maybe…not yet."

Before mounting, he took a look at the tack and how it fit the animal, and then asked to have the martingale removed. When they were finished, he stepped up to the flashy colt, ran a calming hand down his neck, gathered the reins, nodded to the handler to get out of the way, and then easily vaulted on.

Force de Lion pranced nervously sideways, snorting. Leg on him, and he scooted forward. Petted him. "Good boy." Walked him around the edge of the indoor for a minute or two and then pushed him forward into a nice round and low posting trot, and after about five minutes of that into the canter.

"Nice seat and hands on your rider," Gottemann commented to Frankel.

Who smiled, not communicating much, "Yep."

"Not afraid to ride the young ones," Pier added, trying to draw bit more out of him.

Frankel just chuckled. "Afraid? Well, he rides this horse's brother."

Surprise at that. *"Chasseur de Lion?"*

"Every day."

Knowing look. "So that's how he was injured?"

Frankel was just watching Jericho, who was slowly bringing the big red colt up into a higher frame, but not pressuring him or frightening him, just rounding him up, building…Gradually building the canter up, searching for that huge, magnificent gait his brother had…if it was there. "Nope," he said eventually. "It wasn't his fault, that accident. Another rider ran into him at a full gallop. He tried to avoid it—but couldn't. Knocked him off— went down between horses, hung up, trampled and dragged."

Pier murmured in appreciation of the gravity of that situation. "That could rattle the confidence of even the most experienced rider," he commented. Gottemann, in addition to being one of the top agents for Show Jumpers in the world, was also one of the prime sources of information on what was happening with top horses and top competitors. Chef D'Equip's from around the world regularly talked to him, especially the Dutch Team—serious contenders for the World title each year.

"Sure it could," Frankel agreed.

Force de Lion was responding to the signals from the man on his back. Green and still uncoordinated at his age with those long legs of his, he was nonetheless lifting his back beneath his rider, relaxed and swinging freely along his spine. Naturally under himself, his shoulders lifted athletically—he seemed almost surprised at what this man was showing him he could do. Jericho kept it nice and easy for him. Not asking for that huge stride except for a few moments at a time, then backing off again. Then asking again. Backing off. Infinitely patient.

Then it just bloomed beneath him, that giant, rolling powerful gait. Oh man, he thought.

Beautiful.

He rode him like that maybe a quarter of the way around the indoor, then stretched Force de Lion back down low again, petting him again, praising him. Brought the horse back to a trot and then a walk.

"Crossrail," he called out with quiet authority to Gottemann.

The agent was watching him closely, keenly. He translated the order to his ground crew, who immediately jumped into action. But then he stepped further out into the arena. "Remind you of Chasseur?" he asked casually.

Not really surprised that he knew he was riding Lion—maybe Chuck had even told him that much. Since he'd ridden that practice round it couldn't really be considered a secret anymore. Equally casual answer. "Some." Didn't stop to talk with him at all. Unreadable.

He took the big colt down to the far end of the indoor, then picked up the canter again, came back around at the jump—a simple crossrail, low and a breeze for a horse with this level of ability. Just extended his stride a bit and went right over it. Back to the trot and down to the other end of the arena. Turned him around, making a fuss over the horse anyway. "Two foot rail," he requested.

Same process with that—equally easy for the horse, although his ears were pitched forward, more than interested. New experience for him, and turning out to be fun—eager, happy response from Force de Lion. Went right over it.

"Two foot rail, long one stride to a two by two Oxer," he called the next set-up.

"We're not doing combinations with him yet," Gottemann told him. Not an objection, just a fact.

Deep blue stare falling on him. Confident—completely so. "Fine." Hadn't changed his mind at all though. Just waited for the set-up. When it was ready for him, he put Force de Lion on a big circle at the far end, and as he came out of it, came up into two-point, lifting the big colt's stride at the same time. Sighted the spot and placed the animal dead on it, then quietly launched him…lift and release, then touchdown. Simply sighted the second fence like it was nothing, and Force decided it probably *was* nothing. Ears pitched forward though, more because it was a spread than a combination. Way over jumped the distance, but trying hard, that was for sure.

There was a lot more jump in this horse, and Jericho could feel it. He was way too green to face with a major obstacle yet. More patience needed there—it would be a training mistake, despite the fact that for the purposes of buying this animal, it would be nice to see.

Different test then. "Chuck, lay your jacket down over the first fence," he asked the Chef D'Equip. Actually, Jericho was pretty damn shocked that Chuck was staying so quiet thus far. He'd expected a ration of his normal blistering commentary, and that had been nonexistent today. Interesting, that.

And Frankel was completely cooperative now too. Not asking why…not second-guessing it. He walked over to the simple vertical, stripped off his Team jacket, and slung it across the middle of the single rail. Then stepped back.

Circled again, and then brought Force around to face him with the jump. He saw that jacket and a little tremor went through him. Excitement, shock. Definite monster, dead ahead. Jericho sat in and asked for that huge rolling canter and it appeared like he'd conjured it up beneath him. Little snort from the big colt, lifting up magically from that perfectly sloped shoulder as he approached the monster, flapping just a little bit in front of him. Jericho lifted his front end, and then asked for the launch.

Monster on the fence certainly called for a special effort…and Force just exploded over that tiny fence…enormous leap through the air with probably two feet of clearance above it. He didn't leave his rider behind him, though. Jericho came up high over his back, making room for the huge bascule beneath him, not pinching him or dampening the exercise of those powerful back muscles. Nice release too—keeping the horse perfectly comfortable as he stretched his neck out. Single stride and he went over the spread jump like it wasn't even there. Nothing, after vanquishing the jacket monster at the last obstacle. Really proud of himself too.

Jericho stayed up in two-point until he brought the horse back to the trot again, stroking him and murmuring to him. Pulled him down to a walk, nice and calm. Then a halt. Vaulted off.

He handed the reins to Gottemann's assistant. "Courageous," he commented, off-handedly.

"Nice ride," Pier offered. Small smile. "Are we on the right track with what you're looking for?"

No answer from Jericho, who was lighting another cigarette and stepping away from both Frankel and Gottemann. He'd let Chuck take that one, though the truth was he'd loved the colt.

"He's the right general type," Frankel was saying vaguely.

Gottemann wasn't even looking at him though—his eyes were on Jericho, or more accurately, Jericho's back. "I don't know this rider, Chuck," he probed.

But his fishing didn't catch him much. "Been on the circuit for years," Frankel told him maddeningly. "Good back-up rider. Decent trainer too—makes a nice jumper. Hunters as well. Won the Open Hunters at the National this year." All information Pier could probably have found out by doing an Internet search—which he probably would do. Still, he was leaving the impression that he'd brought Jericho only for the purpose of having a rider while he looked for the Team. Not that he was specifically looking for a mount for him.

Gottemann clearly wasn't sure about that, but he'd accepted the answer for now.

Over the next hour they went through the same process with the other two horses Gottemann had in his barn to show them, Fontaine, the nine-year-old Furioso II son, and Landkraft, the seven-year-old Landor S son. Both horses were confirmed Jumpers and both excellent. The riding had gotten a lot more intense—big jumps, longer jumping lines, tight turns and gallop-throughs.

Gottemann pushing a lot harder for information the more he saw. "This is no practice rider, Chuck," he said, sounding annoyed.

Innocent look on the Chef D'Equip's face. "No? Think so?" He very deliberately acted like he misunderstood. "Think I should have brought someone else with me?"

Stiff. "No, he's fine." He hesitated for a minute…really seemed to be thinking about something. "I've got another horse I want to put him on. If that's okay with you, I'll just call the other farm and let them know we'll be late."

"Sure." Now this would get interesting.

Jericho had gone back into the viewing room to talk with Darien and Brae. The Barista was showing him the pictures he'd taken, but Jericho took the camera from him and started going through them slowly on his own. They really helped cement his impressions of the three horses. As goofy as he could be, Brae could take a picture, that was for sure.

As for the Barista, he'd wandered off, offended maybe that Jericho wouldn't let him click through and narrate each one. Anyway, he was getting bored. He ducked out of the viewing room, and into the barn proper. Heard the sound of feminine laughter. Smiled.

"I thought there were only three horses to look at here," Darien was commenting.

Jericho looked up. Pier's assistant was leading another horse out into the indoor now. One that made him really draw in his breath. War steed. Stallion too. Young horse from the look of him, maybe six or seven. Eight at the most. Young maybe, but already tall and broad with rippling muscle. Coal black, not a white mark on him. "Oh, wow," he murmured. "Nice." He stayed where he was though, waited to see if Chuck would signal him. Whatever animal this was, he wasn't on the sales list they had.

"This horse isn't for sale," Gottemann was telling Frankel. "He's mine, personally. Out of my stallion. I call him Antares."

"Hmmm," was all Chuck said.

More subtle parrying. "I'd like to put your rider up on him."

"Hmmm." Seemed to be thinking about it. "Well, if he's not for sale…"

"One never knows." Quiet smile.

Silence for a few seconds. "Testing my rider, Herr Gottemann?" He'd gone back to a more formal form of address, nebulous message there too.

"Looking for just the right home for him," the agent told him, ignoring the question. "The Dutch Team wants him, but I'm not sure. Wherever I put him, he needs to be showcased…increase my stallion's value for me."

"Ahh."

Standoff.

"Of course, your rider may be getting tired," Gottemann tried. Little insult there to goad Frankel with. "Might not be the time." He nodded to his handler, who trotted the horse away and back again…More enticement.

Shrug from Frankel. "He probably is," he allowed. Looked around and beckoned to Jericho. "Can't hurt to throw a leg over him for a minute or two though."

Jericho came out to join them, stopping just behind where Frankel was standing. He lifted his face to watch the young stallion, eyes keen but expressionless otherwise. He was pulling his riding gloves back on though. Didn't ask what the deal was here, but he was dying to. Another assistant had appeared carrying his saddle. They wanted him to ride, alright, and he wanted it too.

Gottemann had turned to him. "Not an easy ride," he was telling him. "Headstrong. Just turned eight this month."

"Uh-huh." Didn't appear to have fazed him. He stepped past the two of them without another word, and went over to the horse while Gottemann's men saddled him up.

"Where's Brae?" Frankel was asking, craning his head around and sounding exasperated. He didn't mention that he wanted him to take pictures of this horse, but of course, he did.

Jericho shrugged without looking around. Hell if he knew.

"I'll be back in just a minute," Frankel growled, pivoting on one foot and striding back the way he'd come.

Starbucks had meanwhile located the source of that enticing female laughter. A group of three young grooms, or maybe working students, all around Brittany's age. They looked up and saw him standing there, and he drew himself up taller. Pointed to his chest. "I'm an American," he said grandly, like that should mean something.

Giggling and whispering back and forth. Couldn't understand a word they were saying though—and why the hell couldn't they speak English, he wondered—were they dumb or something?

Starbucks spoke slower this time, accenting each syllable—and quite a bit louder too—as if somehow shouting the words would make them more understandable. "*A-mer-i-can,*" he repeated, still pointing, then patting his chest. More giggling from the girls. Tried talking to them like they were simpletons—and hell, maybe they were. "Me pho-tog-graph-er." Pretended to be taking a picture. "Pho-tog-graph-er? Get it?" Pretended again, then punctuated the whole thing with one of his goofy grins. "Me very im-por-tant. You lucky meet me." He walked over to them. Rapped on his chest one more time. "Me Brae...you?" He lifted an eyebrow to the prettiest of the trio. Said it again, even louder. *"Me Brae...you?"*

"Yeah, and me Jane," came a snarl from right behind him. Frankel's voice.

The Barista spun around, tripping and losing his balance in the process, but catching himself before he fell down. "Hi Chuck. Well you know...just trying to improve relations between our countries and all that, okay?"

"No, it's not okay!" Frankel couldn't believe this, actually—that he'd somehow inherited the role akin to that of nanny to a bunch of children with ADD or something. "Damn it, we're looking at another horse here. Don't forget your job. Now get back inside."

Shrug from Starbucks. Smile. He waved to the girls, scooted past Chuck, then turned and waved to them again amid yet another wave of giggles. "I don't think they're too smart," he confided in the older man, cupping his hand around his mouth and whispering, as if they'd somehow be able to understand him now. Seemed completely oblivious to the stern look Frankel tossed at him.

Jericho had meanwhile gone through the same physical examination with this young stallion as he'd given the other three horses. When Gottemann's men were finished tacking him up, he gathered the reins, but the big black skittered away from him.

Oh yeah, tough guy, Jericho thought to himself. And the thing that immediately came to his mind was the memory of Frankel telling Bee-Bee that all he had to offer was brawn—and her reply, suggesting that he be used to correct the difficult ones for the "real" Team members. That whole conversation was still so very fresh in his mind. And here they were putting him on a rough ride that hadn't been on the list for him to try. Man, it fit.

Frankel walked back into the indoor, and Jericho shot a harsh glance over to him. Wondered who he was actually trying this horse for—and who he might be asked to train it for. Resentment rose inside him. Still, he grabbed the rein up close to the bit and made a sharp correction, growling to the horse, "Come around here." The animal started with cautious surprise, and he used that moment to vault on. Clamped his legs on hard and thrust him forward into the bridle and round. The stallion rooted hard on the reins, resisting that way. Dropped him and booted him forward again—more surprise there, like he wasn't used to that correction. Lifted him directly into the canter, and got a light buck or two, but after Lion, this was nothing.

Brae was back in the viewing room by now too. As he picked up his camera to start taking pictures again, he whispered to Darien, "I don't think the girls here are too bright."

"Why Brae?" she asked him, curious.

"Well, they don't speak English for one thing."

Darien burst out laughing. "Well, they're Dutch!" she exclaimed.

"Exactly." Looked smug and added knowingly, "I guess that's why they call you "Dutch" sometimes, when they mean you're nuts, huh?"

She just shook her head. Definitely not worth arguing with him.

After five minutes it was clear that there wasn't going to be a problem between Jericho and this stallion. A nice picture of harmony had developed between horse and rider. And a nice, nice animal, Jericho was thinking. No, he didn't move with that battering-ram strength that Lion had, or that Force showed promise of producing too. He was lighter on his feet, but incredibly versatile—could go from a very collected to a huge bounding stride in a heartbeat, and just floated over the ground. And there was a fire burning inside him, a fierceness in his soul that shown through. It would scare some riders, for sure. Jericho of course loved it.

Jericho started turning him into the fences, and good god, he could jump. *Baryshnikov in grand jeté*—just sailed over the obstacles no matter how sharply you turned him into them, and no matter how fast. Didn't mind coming in from an angle either—in a jump-off, he'd kick major ass. And the stallion seemed to love this light sensitive rider on his back as much as his rider was loving him. No more rooting on the bit either once the pressure in his mouth became soft and even and he'd figured that out. Jericho could see where they'd had trouble with him—difficult type because he felt like you needed to hold him in, when in fact you needed to let him out—but he could also see he'd have no trouble working with him.

If that was even what anyone had in mind. Resentment again.

He pulled up in front of Gottemann and Frankel. "Seen enough?" he asked. Nod from Frankel, and he jumped handily off. Touch of scorn in his voice too—something only Frankel would pick up on. "Done with me?" he asked.

The Chef D'Equip's eyes narrowed, processing that, but he didn't let it on otherwise. "For now, thanks."

Cold smile, and then he stepped past him, returning to the viewing room.

Long, long day for Jericho, and with only a few hours of fitful sleep behind it. When they were done at the second farm he got into the back seat of Gottemann's big Mercedes, laid his head against the window and fell asleep for the entire one-hour ride back to the hotel. Frankel and Gottemann talked together in Dutch for most of the trip too. Brae and Darien looked at the pictures and chatted happily.

"So is he going to make the Team?" Pier asked, nodding his head toward the back seat.

A shrug. "Got a lot going against him," was the only information he gave in return.

Gottemann, a conflicting opinion. "Seems tough."

Frankel. "Hmmm." He was glad to see Jericho sleeping now, because he wanted to go over all the horses with him when they got back to the hotel, and after that Herr Gottemann was taking them all to dinner.

"I'll only sell Antares to a medal contender," Gottemann added, as if the thought had just struck him out of the blue. "Probably wait and see how the World Games come out this year before I make a decision. Had some nice offers on him so far, but nothing that seems quite right."

"Good luck with that," Chuck offered.

End of that particular topic for now. They pulled into the hotel driveway a short time later.

Darien reached over and gave Jericho's arm a little shake as they pulled up to the door. A little shake wasn't enough. She gave Brae a reluctant look. "I hate waking him up."

"Oh, it's not problem," Starbucks said, grinning. He just reached past her, and gripped Jericho's upper arm, jerked him hard. "Hey, bra…rise and shine."

"Oh Brae, how mean," Darien objected, but laughing at him. Mr. Sensitivity, he wasn't.

Jericho's head snapped around, disoriented for a second, and then fully aware. Didn't even realize that he'd been rudely jostled awake. "Are we there?" he asked, maybe sorry to hear that.

"Yeah, man," Brae answered him. "Hey, Darien and I are going to go grab a drink after we check in. Get a shower, and come join us."

"No," Frankel interjected. "He needs to work with me." He'd opened his car door but looked around at Jericho before getting out. "But if you want a drink we can meet in the bar."

Not too friendly sounding. But amenable. "Yeah, Chuck that's fine. I need to call Marco first, check on things."

"We'll meet in an hour then."

They checked in and then all went to their separate rooms. Darien was on the top floor, Brae down two from her and Chuck and Jericho on three—adjoining rooms. No accident, that, and it annoyed the hell out of him. Nothing like having a babysitter sitting right on top of him. Gave Frankel a withering and angry stare as they got off the elevator together. Taciturn and offended.

Didn't seem to bother the Chef D'Equip. "Meet you downstairs in an hour," he said, unlocking his door and stepping inside.

Yeah, and fuck you, Jericho thought.

Alone in his room, he quickly unpacked, called Marco and checked the stables and all the horses—no problems there—then got ready for that shower, started to strip down. Shirt first, then shoes and socks, then the rest.

Faint knock on his door. So light—it just couldn't be Chuck. He grabbed a towel and wrapped it around his waist, then walked over and looked out the peephole. Darien. Unlocked it and quickly pulled her inside. Inclined his head toward the room next door. "Keep your voice down," he warned her, and she nodded, her eyes running hungrily over his all but naked form—hard lean muscle, totally buff. Then she lifted her hand and stroked his face. "You were wonder…" She didn't even get the rest of the word out before his mouth descended over hers. Gave in to him totally, her one arm sliding around his neck, her other hand touching. His kiss deepened more, aggressive, demanding. Man, they had almost no time now, but he was instantly aroused, and God knew, he wanted this.

He backed her up to the closer of the two beds, lifted her and laid her down on it. Came up over her, hands already tugging at her clothing. His mouth still insistently taking hers, and he murmured to her in between the press of his lips on hers, "Forgive me, I'm such a fucking animal here." But no objections coming back at him—she was easily as eager with her mouth and hands as he was, wanting to touch him everywhere at once, to know that he was flesh and blood, stroking him and playing with him till he growled with need, till he rammed himself inside her, reared up and dropped his head back, just snarling. Filling her, stretching her around him, and just holding that profound penetration, fighting for control for long moments to prevent himself from just emptying inside her.

But it almost seemed like she wanted that…her hands on his buttocks and pulling him even deeper, pelvis rocking forward and seeking, creating that incredible pressure.

Man, it was so lame on his part, but he couldn't have stopped the orgasm that hit him even if he'd wanted to, and right now he didn't want to anyway. A deep rumble rose up in his throat—stifled as best he could with Frankel right next door, but not entirely—accompanying his body's forceful release, long…intense…indescribable. Still balanced on one arm above her, purring almost savagely at the satisfaction. Heart beating, and chest heaving. Stayed that way for an extended timeframe, before lowering his face down next to hers and whispering to her, "God that was selfish of me, Darien, I…"

But she was hushing him, caressing him, soothing him. "No, I wanted to feel you, feel that power…like that, just like that." Kissing him too, telling him in so many ways that he was special to her.

"I want to stay with you all night," he said to her, voice a mixture of passion, and something more tender. "Damn Chuck for only giving me an hour of privacy, and damn this whole situation where we pretend we're only friends…where I just lie about how I feel for you." Strong, heartfelt. "Darien, I want to make you mine."

Flash of something in her eyes—apprehension maybe, and man he just knew…just *knew* it wasn't true and she wasn't—wasn't his at all, wasn't ready to be. Yeah, he wanted it that way, but so what? Forget what she'd said on the plane, forget the fact that she was here with him. She was nowhere near ready to go there or commit to anything.

Christ, this situation just didn't seem possible—he had what he'd wanted so badly and for so long—and it wasn't even making him happy. Here he'd spent the entire day looking at some of the best horses in the world, money no object, and was lying replete with the woman who meant so much to him…and both experiences were bittersweet. Both of them, lessons in humility.

These things aren't for you Jericho, something cold and sarcastic inside him taunted him. *Better learn it now.*

And there it came, that invisible wall to shield him…that hardass attitude that had protected him so well for so many years.

Smartass smile to her, brushing the hair from her eyes. "You'll see me tonight, count on it. I'm not nearly done with you."

She laughed in delight.

———————

Chuck was already sitting in a booth in the bar when Jericho walked in there—two beers on the table in front of him, his hand wrapped around one of them, the other, obviously for Jericho. He slid in on the bench facing Frankel, a detached yet confident look in his eyes. Picked up the beer and drank from it.

Brae and Darien were together at the bar, laughing and talking, and the Barista waved to him. Nodded in return. For the next half-hour, Jericho and Frankel traded impressions, working in detail through every horse, the pros and the cons. Swung back around to Force de Lion at the end of it. "Yeah I loved him," Jericho admitted. "But he's only four." They both knew what that meant—horses had to be eight years old to compete in Worlds or the Olympics. Force wouldn't be old enough this time around.

Frankel nodding. "Yeah, I know, but tons of talent there, and he liked working with you."

"I thought so too." He took another swig of his beer and sat back.

Shrewd look from the Chef D'Equip. "But here's what's amazing me…you haven't even mentioned that black horse yet."

A cold, cynical half-smile tugged at Jericho's lips. "You want my evaluation on him, Chuck? I figured you'd make your own judgment, but sure…I'll tell you what I thought of him. Are you going to give me a context to put it in, or just in general?"

"What are you talking about, a context?" Frankel demanded. "I haven't given you a context, whatever that means, on any of these horses."

Wasn't taking that answer. "Sure you have, or at least I thought so. The context was my riding them. Hell, if someone else is going to be riding them, then I take back everything I said."

Thought about that one for a few seconds, then just whistled softly under his breath. "Wow, you really don't trust me, do you?" he observed finally, not happy about it either. "Yeah you told me that, so I better believe it. And damn that conversation you overheard anyway. What's gonna make you forget that?"

"Time," Jericho shot back at him. "Time and maybe how you deal with me between now and the finals." Emotional response though, and he forced the anger out of his voice again. Went on to a safer topic. "Yeah, I liked that black horse, I mean, who wouldn't?"

Seemed like he accepted Jericho's answer on the trust issue. Didn't fight it or mention it again, in any event. "Gold medal horse?" he asked instead.

"I thought so, didn't you?"

Frankel sat back thoughtfully. "Sure did. See here's the problem…" He went on to explain that the animal belonged to Pier, that he was looking for just the right situation to sell him into, that he might just wait until after the Worlds this year to decide. "Not everyone can ride that horse, Jericho," he went on. "He's so sensitive, and complicated too. Pier even has trouble finding the right trainer for him…unless he'd be willing to sell him and forget about it…but to find someone who'll take him for the time being and make him into what he ought to be…not easy."

So he'd been totally and completely wrong about that horse and what was going on with him. Fought it anyway, dropped a hard statement on the table. "Oh, do I understand that. I wouldn't take him either. I'm not making other people's rides for them anymore, Chuck."

"Pier…he really likes you," Frankel coaxed him, but subtly. "That's why you rode that horse—his request, not mine. And he's been drilling me all day, trying to find out more about you. Maybe, just maybe you can have that horse, Jericho. It'll cost Lady Forrester a bundle, that's for damn sure, but man…"

Keenly interested now, and trying a lot harder to be cooperative. Dropped his eyes away too, sorry that he'd challenged Frankel the way he had. "So he's auditioning me, is that what it is?"

"Yeah, sort of…and don't you give him any information either. Make him come to me." He'd seen the turn in Jericho's attitude alright, and didn't make a big deal of it. No lectures, no bullshit, just welcomed the change—made it easy for him. "You were perfect today, actually. So good in fact, that normally I wouldn't have even told you this, but I see I have to treat you differently than with some of the others…I'm asking you to trust me, and so I have to trust you too. Alright?"

Jericho looked across the table at him, expression quiet, way less tension. "Alright."

Still something bothering him though—Frankel knew him that well by now. He could also see where that stare of his kept slipping, and the expression on his face every time it did. Figured he knew pretty well what this had to be about. Leaned across the table toward him, and said in a sincere but low voice. "Now, I'm going to say something to you Jericho, and I just want you to think about it without getting all defensive on me. Look at me, and not her." That intent stare swung powerfully over to him. "Things worth having are worth waiting for, worth fighting for too. Patience and aggression in equal measure—know when to use each of them. Be smart, whatever it is you're after...this black horse, for example...or reaching your goals with the Team." Longer meaningful pause. "Or this woman."

Hung his head, even smiled a little. "How do you know me so well, Chuck?"

He didn't answer that question, couldn't really. Maybe it was just the difference in age and experience, and maybe it was more than that. "Don't be blind though, Jericho. Maybe, just maybe she's not good enough for you...it's not the other way around, alright? I'm here and you can talk to me...if you want to...if you need to," he added, really meaning it. That was clear. Lightened it up then, tossed him a bit of a disgusted look, but somehow warm at the same time too. "And get some sleep tonight, okay? Some. Try."

The next two days were some of the most intense Jericho could remember, the mornings and afternoons filled with excellent horseflesh, great rides...and the evenings with powerful, prolonged sex coupled with tender conversations that went on until the early hours of the next day. Chuck's advice had been so right...patience, let it develop as it would. Not the time to get aggressive about it, and when he backed it down, she came to him on her own. Said she loved him with more and more confidence. And yeah, those two days were the kind of perfect times he'd hoped for on this trip. For once, somehow, he felt some inner peace.

His relationship with Frankel had strengthened too. Between the two of them, they played Pier Gottemann to a tee, and at the end of the last day when they returned to Stahl Gottemann to look at Force de Lion one more time, he brought out Antares one more time too. Jericho rode them both, and really loved both of them. He and Chuck also both liked the six year old, Jouez de Rouet, the Baloubet de Rouet son.

When they were done riding, Chuck and Pier went privately into the agent's office to talk seriously about what they would offer and on which horse. They were locked in there for a solid hour, while Jericho cooled his heels talking to Darien and Brae. Casual conversation but filled with anticipation and tension. Finally, the two men reappeared, expressions unreadable. Business concluded though. But it wasn't until Gottemann had dropped them off at the hotel for the night that Jericho learned the results of that negotiation.

Frankel took all of them into the hotel bar, and ordered a bottle of champagne—still not telling anything, but starting to look pretty damn pleased with himself. He waited until the bartender had poured four flutes of champagne for them, then lifted his own in a toast. Looked at Jericho. "I'm expecting great things here," he said with satisfaction. "So this toast is to Lady Forrester…great patron," he added, dragging out the suspense. "I told her I just couldn't settle on what to do, and she agreed with me."

"Come on, Chuck," Darien pleaded for all of them. "You're killing us here."

He smiled, proud of himself for that. "Alright, alright," he relented. "Here's to Force de Lion…*and* Antares." Could see the look of disbelief on Jericho's face, and said to him warmly, "Oh yes. Took some work, but I got you both of them."

Chapter Twenty-Two

Things started moving very fast. Vet-checks were done on the two new horses, with the U.S. Team vet flown over to Holland to oversee the process. No problems were found with either stallion, and the sale was concluded on both. Arrangements were then made to have them shipped from Amsterdam to Miami—big KLM 747 specially outfitted for horse transportation. Jericho wasn't taking any chances either, so he'd sent Marco over to personally handle the horses and fly back with them. They would be quarantined upon arrival for a few days in Miami and then would come up to Wellington—but still in quarantine for two more weeks before they'd finally be allowed to come home to his farm. But he could start riding them at the quarantine farm as soon as they got in.

Then there was the question of Monterrey. Despite everything, it was hard for Jericho to say goodbye to him—again—see him move to another stable, be competed by someone else. Frankel didn't rush it, but he didn't let it linger either. He set a date, and then just worked inexorably toward it.

The night before the move, Jericho did the night check personally—spent time with the big bay just talking to him. Then got in his car and drove over to the Marx's house. He hadn't called ahead of time, but could see that they were home. Thought about what he was going to say, and then got out and walked up to the front door. Knocked quietly. Bob Marx answered. For a moment, he just stood there looking at Jericho. Then he pushed the door open. "Come in," he said. Then asked, "Is this about Monterrey?"

A shrug. "I need to talk to you…if that's okay."

He could see Darien coming up behind her husband. Look of concern on her face—she was scared—afraid the conversation might have something to do with her, and that hurt him. But man, she looked nervous…sure didn't want him giving away anything about the two of them.

"Sure. Let's go in my office," Marx invited him.

He said hello to Darien, tossed her a reassuring look that didn't seem to help much, but then just followed her husband into the study and closed the door behind himself.

Marx had gone behind his desk, and Jericho sat on the other side from him. Took a deep breath and leveled that stare of his on the older man.

"Look," the investment banker led off before he could even get started. "I didn't ask Chuck for this move, if that's what you think. Are you upset about it?"

"No…yes." Shrug again. "Bob…" Never comfortable calling him by his first name, but did it anyway. "Christ, how can I say this? Chuck's been talking to me about this move for the last two weeks solid, preparing me for it."

"Me too," Marx admitted.

Both of them smiled—that was Chuck alright. Actively orchestrating things.

"Bee-Bee's a great rider," Jericho continued. "She's got super hands and Monterrey's gonna love that, and she's what? At least sixty pounds lighter than I am? He'll love that too." Sighed. "Sure, Chuck got me some really spectacular mounts when we were in Europe, and I…well, I can hardly believe that's real. Maybe I won't believe it till I actually see them standing in their stalls. But I want you to know this…Monterrey's the reason this all happened for me, and no matter what, I'll miss him. I'm not just off moving on to the bigger, better deal."

Soft, appreciative tone from Marx. "No one thinks that Jericho."

Met his look and held it. "Maybe, but it's important to me to say it…to you. Because you gave me this opportunity, and yeah, we've still got QL together, but if there's anything…if I can do anything for you and Monterrey, you just have to ask me." Doubly difficult, this conversation for him—first because it laid him too bare, and he hated that. And second because he felt so guilty about Darien. But still, he'd just had to come here, say this. Wouldn't have felt right if he hadn't. Wouldn't have felt like a man in front of Marx again, if he hadn't let him know. "I don't know if I'm expressing this very well…"

"You're doing a fine job, actually." Really looked like he appreciated it too.

Little murmur of relief that made the investment banker smile.

Jericho continued, almost finished with what he had to say. "You're the first person who had faith in me, and Monterrey's the reason why. Both of you…" Muttered something under his breath and to himself, made himself just say it. "…mean something to me, alright? And that's sincere."

"Thank you," Marx said. "And what you just said means something to me too. And I'm glad…I'm very glad we still have the partnership in QL."

They only talked a few minutes longer. Message delivered. They shook hands warmly, and then he excused himself and left as quietly as he'd come.

Marx pulled Darien close and told her about the conversation. Stared at the door, although Jericho had been gone close to five minutes now. "Really fine character on that young man," he commented.

She smiled at her husband, but extracted herself from his embrace without making a fuss about it. "Yes," she said wistfully. "I'm really glad we were able to help him."

Strange look in her eyes though—happy and unhappy both at the same time. Probably sad that he wouldn't be riding Monterrey any longer. "Don't worry, sweetheart," Marx told her. "He'll still be competing QL for us."

Marco took Monterrey to Bee-Bee's barn the next morning. Jericho didn't go with him…for a really good reason. It was the day he was finally getting those damned casts off. Came out of the doctor's office feeling like a new man. He'd gotten a call from the quarantine farm in Wellington while he was there too…Force de Lion and Antares had arrived and looked well, and yes, he could come and see them…and ride them any time from 8:00 to 5:00 while they were there.

He hopped in his Mustang and drove over to Bee-Bee's. Courtesy visit—he planned to tell her to call him anytime, although he didn't really expect her to take him up on it. Still, he'd make the offer, felt like he had to. Pulled in the driveway…and oh shit, Frankel's big pick-up was sitting there too.

He could see Chuck, Bee-Bee and Monterrey now, and the Marxes too, standing on the sidelines watching. Trim, petite Bee-Bee made Monterrey look monstrous—she looked professional, but cute too, with her sun-streaked brunette hair pulled back in a ponytail, and sun visor shading her eyes. Nonetheless, the whole scene just bothered him.

341

Jericho knew how Bee-Bee felt about him…and he was wondering now if he should even be here. He considered getting back in the car and just driving away again—maybe call Bee-Bee later, give her the same message that way instead. But too late, because Frankel had seen him and was motioning him over. He went reluctantly, stopping first to say hello to Darien and her husband. Showed them his newly healed arm and leg, looked happy about that.

"That must be a relief," Bob Marx said to him, smiling and shaking his hand.

Sincere answer. "God, I can't tell you."

"Well, damn it, Jericho," Frankel was yelling. "I asked you to come out here. Chit-chat later."

Rolled his eyes, and just shook his head, but called out, "Coming, Chuck." Nodded good-bye to the Marxes, and strode out into the ring. Really pretty jumping field Bee-Bee had here.

She was riding over on Monterrey as he approached Frankel, and she sure didn't look happy to see him. Frown on that already cold face of hers.

Chuck, unconcerned with it. "Jericho, why don't you give Bee-Bee two minutes on how this horse is trained? Especially his jumping cues. He's not lifting up the way I want him to." *The way he does with you*, the implied end of that sentence, and she nearly growled at his words.

Jericho looked uncomfortable. "Sure, Chuck." Maybe he could even offer Bee-Bee a kind of olive branch here. "Truth is, she'll figure it out just fine on her own, but I'll tell you how I ride him if that helps." Laid on open look on her, one that tried to express that he wasn't out to screw her, not in any way. No yielding on her part though, and no acknowledgement of it. He just continued talking. "The jumps are so natural for him…I found he didn't always have his mind on his work, so I trained him to look for a light half-halt right before the lift. Really light, nothing to change his stride. Just a 'pay attention, here it comes' type of cue," he told her, talking to her, not Frankel. He laid a hand on the big bay's neck and got a nuzzle in return. Obvious rapport there.

"The Jericho Brandeis method?" she sneered. "Wow, I feel privileged."

Jesus, what a bitch—and jealous too, or so it seemed. So hard to deal with all that rancor coming from her. Tried one more time. "Fuck, Bee-Bee…Chuck holds you up to me every time I ride for him as someone who's better technically than I am." That wasn't really true, but it could have been—he'd done it once or twice anyway. "You'll change his cues, it's just a starting point."

That mollified her some, and she glanced down at him superiorly. "At least you know it," she sniped, before swinging the horse around and cantering off.

Really didn't like her, but hell, she could ride and she'd been on the Team year after year, so that said something. Pretty close to his own age too. He swung his gaze back around to Frankel. "Look, she hates me here, I'll go now. But since I've got the chance to talk to you, let me just give you a heads up...Force and Antares arrived in Wellington this morning. What kind of schedule do you want today...or are you too busy? I might just long-line them."

"No, don't leave yet," Frankel contradicted him. "I'll come to you next. We'll do QL and Lion, and then go over to the quarantine farm together." Smile from him. "I see you got those casts off."

And happy look back. "The doctor said it's completely healed. He took a final set of x-rays. The bones knit perfectly."

Bee-Bee had taken another line of fences. Clear over it, but flat and not especially accurate. She was trying hard to figure Monterrey out, but looked like she'd completely ignored Jericho's suggestion. "No, no, no!" Frankel was screaming. And to Jericho, "Do you have your boots in the car? I might want you to get on him."

Shaking his head emphatically in the negative. "Yeah, I've got them, but that's the last thing you want here, Chuck. I should go—she'll ride better the minute I pull out of sight."

"Nonsense," Frankel scoffed. "Needs to tone down that attitude of hers by a long shot," he added severely. "Get some humility."

"Hey, not from me," he objected, and strongly.

But the more he protested, the more it seemed to cement the opposite idea in Frankel's mind. "Bee-Bee," he was yelling at the top of his voice, just like he always did, and with that same withering tone that Jericho knew so well. "Just bring him over here." Turned to Jericho as she was pulling up beside them, militant look on her face. "Go on and go get your boots on."

"No, hell no Chuck."

Stern stare leveled on him. "I expect you to support the whole team Jericho, now do what I asked."

"God damn it," he muttered viciously, and Bee-Bee looked like she was ready to say the same thing.

"Now," Frankel added with infuriating insistence.

Strode off to do as he'd asked, and really not pleased about it. Got to his car, jammed his legs into his boots, and zipped them up with a vengeance. Slid on a pair of spurs and grabbed his riding gloves. Then returned to the middle of the jumping ring. Bee-Bee had dismounted, she was watching him return, and could see he was good and angry. And so was she.

"Alright, Jericho," Frankel was saying. "Bee-Bee uses an outside leg cue the same way you use that half-halt. Hers is a more subtle cue," he added scornfully. "Of course, you have to have a really steady leg to use it." Implication—Jericho's leg wasn't that steady, and man did that burn him. "So, I want you to get up on this horse right now and show him that."

"Yeah, sure Chuck." Cold tone of voice, obviously offended. Muttered more to himself than Frankel, "I'll just give him a few of my clumsy cues, then show him how it's really done, okay?" He reached for the reins from Bee-Bee, who had the good grace to look apologetic now—albeit still upset herself. Didn't even care at the moment. Jericho adjusted the stirrups on her saddle, and mounted sharply. But no way he'd communicate his own ire to the animal. Petted him calmly, sat light and balanced. Took him forward and into the posting trot, then the canter.

Chuck's scathing commentary began almost immediately. *"Come on,"* he roared. "Show me something here, Jericho." Then as he lifted Monterrey over the first fence, "Use Bee-Bee's cue, damn it!"

Jericho pulled to a halt, looked around, laid a vengeful stare on him and just snarled to him, "Back off, Chuck. I'm using both cues together so he'll associate them. Then I'll drop mine…if that fucking meets with your fucking approval."

"Yeah, well hurry it up."

The next ten minutes were an agonizing exercise, as Jericho worked with the horse and Frankel hounded him mercilessly the entire time.

"This is ridiculous. Stop it now, Chuck," Bee-Bee finally rounded on him and snapped, unable to take much more. "Jericho's a beautiful rider and he's doing a great job."

"Think so?" Frankel responded cynically. "Well, how about you get up there and let's just see what kind of training job he's done."

"Fine." Really stiff answer back from her.

Frankel called Jericho over then, and the exchange was made. Bee-Bee took to the course, and the improvement was immediately obvious. "Better," Frankel called out his reluctant praise, as he headed back over to the fence line, smiling happily at the Marxes. Called back over his shoulder to her, "Do it again."

But Bee-Bee had pulled up next to where Jericho was standing, his expression completely shuttered closed. Man, Chuck had just pummeled him here—in front of Bee-Bee who didn't care for him or respect him much as it was. Really pissed about it.

"I'm sorry for this," she said to him—a lot nicer tone of voice than she'd used with him before too. "You didn't have to take all this shit." She shot a disgusted look over to the Chef D'Equip, then turned back to Jericho, her face softening again. "And don't listen to Chuck...he can be such an asshole. Good ride."

"Yeah, you too," Jericho told her. "I knew you'd get him, no problem."

"Bee-Bee, get to work!" Frankel yelled to her, a definite reprimand.

"Wow, Chuck," Darien said, and her voice was good and scolding. "How unfair you've been to both of them."

Marx laid a comforting hand on her shoulder. "Relax, honey. See, I know Chuck so well by now, I can tell you exactly what just happened here. He made the two of them allies, and himself the bad guy. I'm guessing they didn't get along too well before."

Frankel, smiling, pleased with himself. "Damn straight," he spoke up. "They're going to be on the same team together—time they act like it."

The month of February passed with really intensive training...QL, Lion and Antares. And Force too, though at a much slower pace for the youngster—just getting used to the work. His training would stay light for the next year at least—Chuck didn't even watch him go every day, which probably said something about the way he thought Jericho was handling the big colt.

QL had gone to a second show...entered in the CSI-W this time, and she qualified handily too, making it into the jump-off and placing third in the class overall. No one laughed at her jughead and mule ears anymore...definitely not. In fact, she was actually becoming a crowd favorite with that bold jumping style of hers. She even seemed to realize it, strutting in and out of the ring like the world-class jumper she was proving herself to be.

And Jericho was going to another show the very next weekend…debut for Antares, and it would be the first real competition for Lion too. No more practice rides for him. QL was staying home this time—she'd get her second chance at a qualifier two weeks from then.

Big CSI-W this time around, lots of entries, including all the short-list riders—really competitive. And Bee-Bee would be up on Monterrey for the first time in competition too.

They took the horses over to the showgrounds Wednesday morning. Frankel had scheduled all the short-list riders for coaching sessions that afternoon. Since he had all six of them there—some with multiple horses—he was doing them two riders at a time. Jericho stood on the fence line and watched while Bee-Bee rode Monterrey and then Langley. George was also riding his big-time jumper Tarrytown. Nice workouts from both riders—and man, they were tough competitors.

Toward the end of their schooling session, Marco brought Antares up to the practice area, and Jericho took him to the next ring over to warm him up. Big buzz of excitement as the huge elegant black stallion made his appearance, and people who'd been watching Bee-Bee and George straggling over to take a look at this magnificent animal. Excitement from the horse too—although he was eight, Gottemann had kept him basically sheltered, and he hadn't been to that many shows. All the noise and crowds and unusual sights had him high as a kite. Prancing, snorting, stopping with his tail raised to blow his breath out. Rumbling whinny, ears pitched up. Definite handful to ride today, but that was good—let him get it out of his system before tomorrow and the start of the show.

He mounted Antares, and started stretching him out at the trot. Bee-Bee and George were exiting the ring now, their sessions with Frankel apparently done. Jericho pulled up, and started walking the stallion over. Bee-Bee had dismounted and handed Monterrey to her groom, and seemed to be waiting for him. George was there beside her too.

"Did you watch Monterrey today?" she asked—but of course she'd seen him on the rail, so she knew he had, and her question was really more the unspoken one…how did you think he looked?

"Sure I did," he told her. "Beautiful go today. Good partnership."

"I love him," she admitted. "And this is your new horse, Jericho?"

"Yeah…his name's Antares." He gave the two of them the horse's breeding, and a few words about where he'd come from. Tim Rawlings, the first Team alternate had already entered the ring with Frankel, and Jericho could see the Chef D'Equip searching with his eyes for him. Smiled ruefully. "Let me get in there before Chuck takes my head off. Stay and watch though if you want to, this is a fabulous animal."

Incredible working session with the young black stallion—lots of stinging commentary from Chuck, but it wasn't making Jericho feel any less elated—just took it, used it, and rode his horse to the best of their combined ability. At the end, he vaulted off, made the exchange of Antares for Lion with Marco, and then got ready to get back up for his second ride.

George's voice stopped him. "Jericho!" Both he and Bee-Bee were still there—had stayed for the entire coaching session. They beckoned to him, and Jericho led Lion over closer to the fence. Smile from the Team Captain for him, then just an amazed shake of his head. "Man, that was just a beautiful ride you had with Antares. This is his first show?"

"First over here, yeah."

"Well hurry up and get that damn horse qualified. You've just got to love having a horse like him to compete."

He didn't mind saying it. "Sometimes I still feel like I'm dreaming. And riding him? It's better than sex."

Bee-Bee gave him a friendly look, teased him even. "Oh, come on Jericho…not that good."

Deep blue stare on her, expressive. Murmured it, "Swear to God," and she laughed.

George ran a hand down Lion's neck. "So how's this animal coming?" he asked with interest.

Shrug. "He's a motherfucker, but damn can he jump. Gotta love that."

Frankel had been allowing the conversation, he thought it was good for them, but enough was enough, and he called out sharply, "Am I gonna see that gray stallion work today or not?"

"Right now, Chuck." Made a disgusted face to the other two, who both laughed. "Talk to you later." Gathered Lion up and vaulted on.

"Welcome to Starbucks…and oh man, Darien, does my roommate rock or what?"

Brae, back at the drive through window, Monday after the show. Having seen what he'd seen on the plane—and seen Jericho and Darien together numerous times since then—he knew exactly what the score was between them. And neither of them was trying to hide it from him either, although it was never specifically acknowledged or discussed.

Sweet sexy little voice coming back through his headphones to him. "In so many ways, Brae."

Moan of disgust from the Barista.

"Want to take a break?" she asked him.

Happy voice coming back at her. "Sure! Come get your drink and then meet me out front."

Darien parked the TT and started over to the row of tables. She saw Cin and Richard Maitland sitting there and waved to them as she approached, but picked another table on the far end, and not stopping to talk.

Cin's eyes narrowed. She commented spitefully to her husband. "Ever notice how much time that horrible Darien Marx spends with Jericho's roommate? Good looking boy too," she sniped.

Lift of Richard's eyebrows. "Well, now that you mention it, Cin…"

She took advantage of his interest. "Well, far be it from me to gossip, *but…*" Incredible lie that, but there was no one there to contradict her. "…it's just a little bit suspicious to me."

Richard, openly staring now. "I wonder if I should mention it to Bob Marx."

Wicked gleam in Cin's eyes. "That might be the right thing to do."

Meanwhile Darien and Brae had exchanged a hug, drawing even more stares from the table at the far end.

"Man, Jericho just kicked ass, didn't he?" Starbucks was bragging, as if somehow he had something to do with it personally. Well, he did take the pictures, didn't he?

"He sure did," Darien agreed shyly. "And Monterrey did well too."

Antares had won the CSI-W with a performance in the jump-off that just electrified the grandstands. Lady Forrester, sitting in the Team Box, absolutely delighted as her name was announced as the owner of this magnificent horse. And if that wasn't enough, Chasseur de Lion had been third—with Bee-Bee and Monterrey second. Bruce Waverly, almost as happy as Lady Augusta. George had been fifth—only seconds between his fifth place round and Jericho's first place, but seconds had been enough.

Frankel, totally thrilled.

"Yeah, we're going to Los Angeles," Brae said, pulling his fist from about shoulder height down sharply to his waist in a victory sign. "Yeah!"

Darien laughed as she reminded him, "We still need another qualifier for all the horses, don't forget."

Pooh-poohed it completely. "Oh sure, but that's nothing."

She looked at him amazed. "Nothing! Brae do you know how many riders get into the finals? And with three horses on top of it?"

Still unimpressed. "Yeah, yeah, I know. But he will, okay?"

The two of them had their heads together, talking earnestly.

"Well, that's just disgusting," Cin, said again, unable to stop staring. And from Richard, "Absolutely, I agree."

There were two more big shows during March, and both QL and Antares got their second qualifiers without a hitch. But not Lion. In his last class, the one Jericho had been counting on to get him finished, he'd been completely disobedient. Tossing his head, fighting going into the fences— he wasn't diving, but he was doing just about everything but. Despite Jericho's best efforts, they still finished the first round with three rails down, or twelve jumping faults—not even placing high enough to go on in the competition to the next round.

Worse, it had been the last of the CSI-W's in Wellington. Now Jericho had a choice to make...haul Lion up to Raleigh, N.C. for one of the last qualifiers before the finals, which would also mean taking a week away from training and working the other two horses—or just bag it, and forget about qualifying him this year.

Jericho paced the aisle way in his stables, while Chuck stood close by, trying to talk him out of it. "We gave it a hell of a try, but he's just flawed— unpredictable. Never going to change," the Chef D'Equip was saying. "It's not your fault."

Angry, and not buying it. "Sure it's my fault, I wasn't paying enough attention to him."

"Bullshit!" Frankel thundered. "You and I work with him every single day. You watch these horses like a hawk."

Shaking his head powerfully in the negative. "I know how often we work them, Chuck, but those last few days before the show he seemed stiff...you even commented on it. And I did nothing—not a Goddamn thing. He's uncomfortable, and I think it's a shoeing issue again."

"Pure and utter garbage! You're just making excuses for him."

"No." Good and stubborn.

Standoff for a few long moments.

Frankel and pissed, "Alright fine. There's only one way to know for sure. We'll put him in the trailer and take him over to the clinic...today...right now."

"Yeah, I want to do that." Thought for a second. "Give me a minute to make a few phone calls and shuffle the schedule around. Can you find Marco and ask him to bring the two-horse out front?"

While Frankel went off to find Marco, Jericho went into the small stable office and picked up the phone. The person he really wanted to talk to was Darien. They'd had almost no time with each other recently, and he was missing her—a lot. But Marx was leaving soon for a week in New York. And he could see her, be with her. But not if he went to Raleigh. He'd be away himself while Marx was in New York. How fucked was that?

"Hello," her soft voice answered the telephone. Seemed like she didn't recognize the stable number—either that, or she was just pretending it wasn't him on the line.

His voice coming back to her. "Darien."

"No, I'm sorry, we really don't want any," she said pleasantly, but with finality—as if she'd been talking to some telemarketer. And *click*...she'd hung up on him.

He called back, but this time there wasn't even an answer. Just left a message in her voicemail. Harsh note in his tone of voice. "Darien, its Jericho. I'm taking Lion over to the clinic for some tests. Can I make your lesson late—like maybe three o'clock? Let me know."

They took Lion to the clinic—still no word back from her. Nothing showing on the x-rays either, but yes the gray stallion was definitely foot sore again—positive reaction to the hoof testers, but frustrating lack of a real diagnosis. The vet suggested some changes to his shoeing. Maybe it would work, maybe not. Jericho called his farrier, and got him re-shod that afternoon.

It was five o'clock now, and he'd tried Darien a few more times, but she wasn't picking up. Between that and Lion, he was really out of sorts.

Looked up and saw her Audi TT pulling down the drive. Jesus, about time...he walked out to meet her while she parked. She got out, but she was wearing street clothes—definitely not planning on riding. And she looked like she'd been crying too.

Instant concern from him, no recriminations on the way she'd been avoiding him. "What's the matter?" he asked, reaching out for her. She shrunk away from him. "Darien, please. Are you upset with me?"

Shook her head in the negative. Wasn't answering him though.

"It's about us, right?" he asked her quietly, but not coming near her, not pressuring her.

Simple nod.

Man, he wondered who'd said something, or what had happened—something to alert her husband, that was for sure. Couldn't tell either…was she being so reluctant to talk to him because she wanted to call it off? Had she already been forced to make a choice? Lots of things running through his mind, none of them good.

"Someone talked to Bob," she finally told him. "He wouldn't tell me who it was. But whoever, they said I was fooling around…cheating on him." Expressive look from her. "…with Brae."

"Brae!" Jericho snorted. "Jesus Christ, he's ten years younger than you almost. Come on, your husband didn't believe that shit, did he?" Felt some relief though, hoped that was all it was. Even so, it didn't mean she wouldn't want to back away from him. Be extra cautious for a while…or still even call it quits. Not knowing what was going on in her mind was eating him up inside.

Whispered. "Apparently Bob confronted Brae about it this morning."

Fucking Brae, Jericho thought vengefully. Hadn't even called him to let him know. Was going to kick his ass for this, that was for damn sure. "And?" he asked. There was more, he was positive of it.

"Brae denied it, of course, and I think he believed him. But…he must have said something, because…" She lifted her eyes to him, pleading.

"Because?" he repeated.

"Because he seems pretty sure I'm seeing someone, and he's suspicious of you."

"I'm gonna kill Brae," Jericho muttered harshly.

"Please no, Jericho," Darien begged him. "Bob didn't actually say he thought it was you—he didn't go that far. But your name came up two or three times…more like a 'for instance' than a real accusation. He'd say, like…I don't want to find out that you and someone like Jericho are sleeping together. I told him we weren't…that I wasn't…but I don't think he believes me."

Blew his breath out, sick about it—both for her, and for them—for what they had together. Tried to focus on her, to keep his own feelings out of it. "Did he threaten you?" he asked. "Are you alright? He wasn't...violent with you, was he? Darien, talk to me."

"No, no." A tear running down her cheek. "Nothing like that. He was...decent, really. He said...he loves me. He honors me and wants me to honor him in return. I felt so horrid, so sordid, and he was so strong, so kind. He said...he understands because I'm so much younger." More tears following the trail of that first one. "That he knows men like you would be attractive to me...that he..." Her eyes lifting to him again, begging him to understand. "...doesn't want to do anything about it, just wants me to tell him I'll stop."

Oh yeah, start of a goodbye speech if he'd ever heard one. God, it hurt, and he turned away from her.

"Oh, Jericho," she whispered. "I'm so sorry."

"Yeah, me too." He didn't turn around.

"When he's up in New York next week..."

Here's where she'd tell him she didn't want to see him again. Blocked that, by cutting her off to say, "I'll be away too—in Raleigh. I'm taking Lion up to the CSI-W that week. It's his last chance." Decision made—he sure as shit wasn't going to stay here. Still, it wouldn't change anything. She was breaking it off with him. Confirmed it in a round about way, asked stiffly, "Are you moving Roué?"

Miserable silence. Then, "Yes."

Murmured, "Fuck. God damn it all." He could hear her taking a step toward him, but still kept his back to her.

"I told him I would. I told him if he was so suspicious..." She broke off there, then came back, defending Marx to him. "Bob even said that wouldn't be fair to you, he was worried about you. But I told him I wanted to anyway—to prove it to him." Her hand touching his arm from behind, little caress there. "Jericho, I didn't think you'd want to see me every day like that after..."

Cold statement from him, cynical. "After you told me to get lost, that about right?" Came around then, that deep blue stare falling on her—a range of emotions in it, from hurt to anger to quiet accusation.

Yeah, you love me, that's obvious.

"Jericho, please..."

Emotion pretty well stripped from his voice. "Look, I'm not going to make it hard on you. I get the message loud and clear. Your decision's made, and that's it. Move Roué when you want to…you're taking him to Chip's?"

Nod from her.

"Already arrange it?" he quietly mocked her.

She bit that gorgeous lower lip, nodded again.

"Then there's nothing more to talk about, is there?"

"Oh Jericho," she said, tears near again and making her voice tremble. "You don't deserve this, you've been nothing but good. Honest, sincere."

Perversely, her praise for him only made the anger inside him come alive. "Is your husband waiting for you?" he asked her coldly. "Waiting to take you to dinner maybe? Hear how it went? Comfort you after your difficult experience breaking it off with me? Because, Darien, we both know you admitted it to him." And oh shit yeah, he could see from the look in her eyes that his guess was dead-on accurate—and she'd only been giving him half the story this whole time, been lying about it. Snorted softly to himself. "Well, I got that right, didn't I?"

She reached for him again, but his eyes said absolutely not, made him inaccessible.

"Don't worry," he murmured to her bitterly, "I'll handle it. It's not the first time someone I needed walked out on me. Fuck no, the truth is, I should never have expected differently. It's the story of my life…started the day I was born—when I was only a few hours old. And you know what? All those people can't be wrong."

She looked stunned, stricken too…like she'd never realized how abandoned he must have felt as a child, or that it in any way would carry over to what he was feeling now.

He was sorry he'd told her that too. "Christ, Darien," he muttered in a far quieter tone of voice. "Go on and go meet Bob. I have work I need to get done."

He turned and started walking back to the barn. Heard her car engine turn over. Knew when she was gone.

———

He'd called Frankel that same evening. Told him about it, thought he had a right to know. Brief discussion, Chuck not probing for much, and then the subject was never mentioned again between them. Didn't say any-thing to his roommate either—wasn't interested in the details.

Instead he focused on his riding, and Lion in particular. The stallion remained iffy—some days okay, some days worse. No days really good. A week later a commercial shipper picked up the big gray, and Marco and his gear along with him—heading for Raleigh. Jericho would fly up, he needed to be fresh and on top of his game.

The morning before the start of the CSI-W in Raleigh, he drove to the West Palm Beach airport. No direct flights there—had to change planes in Atlanta. Brae had gotten on the horn with Annie and given her Jericho's itinerary, and apparently she'd made some phone calls too. He boarded the plane, and took his seat in coach, but a stewardess approached him just moments later. "We have room in First Class," she said with a wink. "We're moving you up."

Smile from him. "That's not necessary, really."

She laughed. Put her hand out to pull him up. "Oh, Annie said you were nice. Come on."

He was re-seated in First Class—there was an empty seat beside him too. Nice. He relaxed, had a cup of coffee while he waited for the plane to pull away from the gate…and that's when the activity started. Gate agent coming on board and in hushed conversation with the flight attendants. Jericho looked up and the gal in First briefly touched his shoulders. "It's nothing," she said to him. Went back to his coffee, already bored.

A few minutes later the Captain came over the loudspeaker and made an announcement. "Ladies and Gentlemen, I apologize for the short delay. We have another of our sister flights that cancelled, and we're just waiting for a few more passengers to come on board. Then we'll be off, and we're still expecting an on-time arrival. Thanks for your patience."

Jericho took a pillow, leaned his head against the window, closed his eyes. But no more than two minutes later, the stewardess was shaking him lightly. "I'm sorry to bother you, but would you mind if I moved you over across the aisle? We have a husband and wife getting on from that other flight and I'm trying to seat them together."

"No problem, hell put me back in Coach…"

She smiled warmly at him, silencing him. "No, you're fine. I'm just moving you up a row and across the aisle, okay?"

Smiled back. "Sure." He rose, sliding his tall body out into the aisle way. "So exactly where do you want me?"

"Right here."

Started moving to the seat she indicated. The husband and wife party were being escorted on at the same time. Jericho stopped and for a moment he just stared at them, a cold look settling on his features.

Bob Marx and Ailynn McCrae.

Marx, with his arm around her...Ailynn cuddling close. Nice expensive outfit on her too—black slacks—made from a beautiful, supple, leather that fit her like a sensuous second skin. Silk blouse that was almost transparent, nothing but the tempting movement of her breasts underneath it. Matching black leather jacket. Luscious mouth glossed bright red. God, she looked stunning. Jericho growled under his breath with pure fury, but moved to his new seat without a word.

Oh, but they'd both seen him, that was for sure.

"That was nice of you to move," the woman next to him in his new spot told him. Mid to later forties, executive looking type—business suit, briefcase, laptop and all. Attractive in a very professional and mature kind of way.

Looked at her, tried to force himself not to dwell on the irony of catching Bob Marx cheating on his wife with Ailynn. Lifted one slashing brow to his new seat partner, shrugged. "You can put me about anywhere," he said. "I don't really care that much."

Smile from her. "You strike me as the rock-climbing type."

Keeping his voice neutral, and being pretty successful at it. "I ride and train show jumpers, actually."

The plane had taxied away from the gate and out onto the runway. Not a peep from Marx, and Jericho hadn't looked around at him either.

"Oh sure," the woman beside him continued. She seemed to know exactly what he meant—not surprising on a flight that originated from this airport. Horses were a big part of the economy here. "I was just down visiting my aunt. She rode years ago. There are pictures of horses all around her house. But she doesn't ride anymore of course, she's close to seventy. Although actually, she told me she's sponsoring some Olympic hopeful or something now."

The plane had turned the corner at the end of the runway, and was picking up speed. Seconds later the nose came up and then they were in the air.

He seemed clearly more interested, his arresting blue eyes narrowing. "Not Lady Forrester?" he asked.

"Why, yes, exactly. Do you know her?"

"Christ, I ride for her," he answered, sounding pretty astonished himself.

"Then you must be…" She hesitated. "…Jericho, is it?"

"This is amazing. Yes, I know it's an odd name, but yeah that's me. Jericho Brandeis." He offered her his hand, and she shook it, clearly more than interested in him now too.

"Camille Forrester," she introduced herself. "So my aunt told me that she just purchased two horses, and one of them is qualified for some big show in June."

Explained it. "The show she's talking about is the finals of the selection process—it pretty much determines who'll ride for the U.S. at the World Games this summer. Your aunt's horse is right in the running. In fact, I'm pretty confident he'll make it." Brash statement, maybe. But then a softer look came into those expressive eyes. "If you get the chance to mention it to her, please tell her again how grateful I am for the ride."

"I will," she promised. "Although from what I hear, you're one of the best and boldest riders my aunt's ever seen. I think she's delighted…and hoping for a medal maybe too."

"I'm doing everything I can to make that happen."

Nice conversation, almost made him forget the scene behind him and across the aisle. Almost.

The seatbelt sign had gone off. And like clockwork, Marx had risen. He stopped meaningfully next to Jericho, then indicated the front of the cabin with a sharp nod of his head. Walked up there himself.

"Oh you know him?" Camille asked in surprise, recognizing him as the husband Jericho had given up his seat to.

Sarcastic, but said in a quiet, low tone of voice. "All too well. And that's not his wife he's sitting with either. Probably what he wants to tell me about. I'm sure he's unhappy they cancelled his flight and moved him to this plane."

Appreciative laugh. "I'm sure that's true."

He unbuckled his seat belt and rose. "Excuse me for a minute, let me get this over with." He walked up to join Marx, said nothing, just leaned against the wall, waiting for him to begin.

"You didn't see this today, Jericho." The investment banker told him. Authoritative, superior and cold tone of voice.

"Bullshit, don't talk to me like that," Jericho purred. Dangerous sounding. "I damn well saw it. That doesn't mean I'll tell Darien, but don't ever presume to tell me what to do or not do, and be clear on that."

Uncomfortable silence.

"Darien is my wife." Laying claim to her.

Jericho snorted. "Yeah, right. I see that."

Silence again.

From Marx, and he'd sure modified his tone of voice. Still hard, but no longer condescending. "You came to my house the other day, do you remember what you told me?"

"I remember it."

"You came to thank me for what I've done for you." Marx nearly sneered. "What I've done for you while you've been screwing around with my wife behind my back."

Calm, powerful, and not repentant either. "That doesn't nearly say it, and I think you know it too. And I can tell you, if I'd had my way I'd have told you way sooner."

Indifferent shrug. "Actually, I believe you, Jericho. Guile isn't what you're about. You love her or think you love her, and for all I know, she even came on to you. But she'll never leave me for you." Emphasized it. "Never. Not even if you tell her about this. She'll just think it's her fault too—that it was my reaction to finding out what she did."

He knew it was true…all of it. Didn't even bother to argue. "Fine, then what are we standing here for? Doesn't seem like there's anything left to say."

"Just this…stay away from her. Ailynn too."

"Oh, Ailynn too now?" Jericho murmured back to him. What a greedy, self-impressed prick bastard he'd turned out to be. "Ailynn…Christ, I've fucked her, Brae's fucked her, and now you've fucked her too. Want to take a poll around Wellington and see who else fits that bill?" he mocked.

"Enough, Jericho…now I'm going to tell you something, and you better hear me because I know it's important to you."

"Backing out of the QL partnership?" he guessed, still quietly taunting.

Laugh from Marx. "No way. She's half mine by contract, and I still pay her bills—your coaching expenses too. I want a medal horse, and for my money you're still the rider I'm counting on. Nothing you can do about that."

But it surprised the hell out of him—he couldn't read this Marx at all. He did whatever the hell he wanted, that's what it boiled down to. Ruthless when he felt like it. "Fine, Bob," Jericho said again. "It's your money, do what you want with it. But you had a threat for me before, and I guessed wrong. So lay it on me."

Smug. "Believe me, I'm going to. See, I don't want children, and I had an operation years ago to make sure that never happened. Darien doesn't take the pill. And now that she's seeing me, neither does Ailynn." Superior look on his face again. "Maybe you think it's an odd form of control, but believe me it's effective. And if either one of them gets pregnant, Jericho, I can promise you how I'll handle it." Nice dramatic pause, then out came the real threat—one he was pretty certain would mean something to Jericho. "If either one of them gets pregnant...I'll eliminate your child in a heartbeat. Abortion. You won't even know about it till it's over. But I'll damn well make sure you find out then."

Flare in those deep blue eyes that was so potent that Marx even stepped back a pace. That left fist had tightened with aggression too. "Has that happened?" Jericho demanded brutally. He hadn't raised his voice—hadn't done anything that anyone other than Marx himself could see. Even that menacing fist was hidden from Camille and the other passenger's view by his body. Still the command in his question was not to be denied. And just to be sure he repeated it. "I'm fucking asking you, and I want to know."

"Back down," Marx hissed at him. "Or maybe this will help you." He reached into his suit pocket, pulled out what appeared to be a slip of paper, and handed it to him. It was a check written out in Jericho's name, and had today's date on it—meaning Marx had just drawn this up before asking him over here.

The amount was $100,000.

Jericho stared at it, felt utterly hollow for just a moment...and then violent enough to kill. Was this supposed to be his answer?

"No," Marx said forcefully, understanding his own mistake almost immediately, and frightened by what he was seeing on Jericho's face. *"No.* I'm telling you no. Are you even listening to me?"

Didn't trust himself to speak, wanted to hurt someone and badly. Breathing slightly accelerated, eyes as keen as a peregrine falcon sighting his prey and ready to dive from the sky, talons extended. That left fist of his still hovering there at his side. "Then what's this for?" he warned.

Unconvincing answer. "Lost income on Roué...your silence about Ailynn."

Looked at it, quietly ripped it into pieces, gave it back to him. "Like I said before," it was his turn to threaten, "we have nothing left to say here, and there are no deals between us."

"No, Jericho, you're wrong...I still own half of QL, and I'll never sell."

"That didn't look like a pleasant conversation," Camille commented as he resumed his seat.

Calm, quietly controlled, but powerful. "No, it wasn't. Threatened me, then tried to buy me off." He shrugged, eyes cold. "I have no intention of telling anyone what I've seen anyway. For what?"

"Most people love to gossip."

"Never had much use for it."

Look of approval, but dropped the subject. "Do I detect a hint of a New York accent there?" she asked, teasing maybe.

He nodded. "Queens actually."

"Street kid?"

"Yup." She was gathering facts for her aunt, he decided, but didn't see any reason not to give her the unaltered truth.

"But you grew up okay. Took care of yourself."

"I had to." Looked at her again, gave her an honest and more complete answer. "I've done alright for myself. But I'll be the first one to admit that I've had a lot of help recently—things I could never have gotten on my own. And if I bring a medal home from Aachen this summer, it damn well belongs on your aunt's shelf."

Smiled at him. "You know what?" she said warmly. "I think you will."

Chapter Twenty-Three

Raleigh, N.C.—Jericho arrived there just after 1:00. Rented a car and drove to the showgrounds. Found his stalls, with Marco and Lion safely ensconced there.

There'd been no further conversation on the plane with Marx, and none at all with Ailynn, and when they'd arrived in Atlanta, they went their separate ways. But the little bitch had left a message on his cell phone.

"Hi, Jericho. It's Ailynn. I just had to call and tell you how great you looked on the plane today. Damn I know they're just jeans, but a man should never look that gorgeous. You've got one fine ass on you, darlin'. It made me really want to see you again. Call me...oh I better hang up, here comes Bob. Bye for now."

And he was just pissed enough at Marx that he even considered it. Didn't act on that though, at least not yet.

They tacked Lion up and Jericho took him up to the practice area. To his surprise, he saw Bee-Bee there, working her older horse, Langley. Waved to her, rode over. "I wasn't expecting to see you here," he told her.

"Spur of the moment decision," she said and shrugged. "I mean, Monterrey's already qualified and everything, but Langley still needs another go, and I thought, hey...why not give him one more shot at it?"

"Same thing with Lion here."

"Where are you stabled, Jericho?" And he told her. "Oh, not too far from me, maybe I'll stop over later on today." She smiled, and then went back to work.

Major change in her attitude, nice though. She'd accepted him finally.

Lion's training session went so-so...some good moments anyway, and he didn't seem as stiff as he'd been a few days ago. Maybe the new shoes were helping him. When he was done, Jericho took him back to the stalls, and he and Marco iced his legs, gave him a nice bracing wash...threw him some hay and made up his dinner, working quietly together. Even when they were finished, Jericho just hung around.

"You're down, boss," Marco observed, not really prying, but making himself available. "Been that way all week."

"Yeah, well she dumped me." He didn't have to say who, Marco knew all too well.

"Who dumped you?" Pert feminine voice, and Bee-Bee came around the corner. Really beat-to-shit pair of cut-off jean shorts on her, tee shirt, visor, sandals, ponytail—pretty much her normal uniform except when she was riding.

He looked up at her from where he was sitting on a spare bale of hay. "The woman I've been seeing."

"No way."

"Yes way."

She smiled and came over to sit beside him. "Well, then she's an idiot, right Marco?"

"Totally," the head groom humphed—like he was saying he'd thought that for a long time now.

"Hey, will you school with me tomorrow?" she asked Jericho. They had the jog in the morning, but wouldn't actually start the jumping rounds till the following day. "You can watch me and I'll watch you."

Little smirk from him. "Missing Chuck, are you?"

"Well, I hate to admit it, but yes, I actually do."

"I can't yell like he does though."

"Oh sure you can," she laughed. Then imitated his voice almost perfectly, "Bee-Bee, don't you remember anything I told you? *Do it again!*"

"Hey, that's pretty good." Amusement in his eyes now, and he bumped shoulders with her. "Just substitute Jericho for the Bee-Bee and you've got it knocked. Or how about my personal favorite...*Come on!* Show me something!"

She giggled. "He says the same things to everyone. We should just tape him sometime, and play it at the side of the practice ring. Now that would really piss him off."

Nice easy conversation, rambling and about nothing in particular. Felt hungry, looked at his watch, and was amazed to see that two hours had passed that way. "Are you in the mood for dinner?" he asked her. "I was just going to go and get some pizza and beer maybe, then come back and spell Marco so he can get away."

"Sure or we can just order in. I've got beer."

Looked at her like she was nuts. "Now that's dedication…you want to eat dinner at your stalls?"

She burst out laughing. "No silly, my two-horse has living quarters—shower, air-conditioning, television, everything. I never go to a hotel when I bring that rig—it's a lot nicer." She indicated generally behind herself with her hand. "It's not far, just right over there where the hook-ups are."

Marco, scowling at him. Knew exactly what the bastard was trying to say too. Something on the order of…don't you have enough trouble with women as it is? Don't go getting mixed up with another one. But Jericho doubted very much that Bee-Bee thought about him that way—or him about her for that matter. She was just being friendly, and maybe trying to make up for the way she'd snubbed him when he first made the short-list.

"Okay, that sounds good," he told her, standing up, and then extending a hand to her to pull her to her feet. "Marco, I'll be back in two hours. That okay?"

"Thirty minutes would be better," the head groom grumbled to him.

He leaned in close to him and murmured, *"Todavía tiempo de sobras,"* dark humor lighting up the depths of those deep blue eyes.

"Malperida." Disgusted, disapproving, and saying it.

Ended up they did spend most of the evening together, though only talking casually, watching television, walking around the showgrounds—nothing remotely romantic, just buddies more or less. There was something about her…she had a way of drawing the conversation right out of you, and Jericho found himself telling her things that he'd never told Darien… some things even Marco didn't know.

While they ate dinner, Bee-Bee sat cross-legged on her bed—Jericho on the floor at her feet. "So George told me you used to be an exercise rider at the track," she said, then took a bite of pizza, looked curious.

Wasn't offering much. "For a while."

"Oh, is it a secret?"

Smile lurking at the corners of his mouth. "No, it's not a secret. But do you really want to hear this?" At her affirmative nod, he shook his head, amazed that it would hold any interest for her. "Alright, if you say so, but it's not my fault if you get bored here." No backing down from her—she was still waiting, looking expectant. He gave her a Cliff-Notes version. "It was years ago. I exercised...oh maybe from when I was about thirteen till about sixteen—that time frame. Lied about my age—I think you had to be eighteen or something, but the truth was no one gave a shit. Lied about my experience too, because basically I didn't have any. I didn't live near the track either. Got up in the dark, snuck out and took the train to Belmont. Or a lot of nights, I'd just stay there. It was easier. I was lying to my foster parents about where I went too—that was the Sullivans, I think, or maybe there were two sets—doesn't matter, none of them allowed it. But nothing could stop me. I wanted to be a jockey back then."

"Really?"

Tipped back his beer bottle, took a long swallow. 'Oh yeah, but that was about six inches ago." He ran that deep blue stare over her. 'Now you...you'd be the perfect size."

"Maybe, but I'm not crazy, Jericho."

Surprised. "Like me, do you mean?"

"Exactly."

Bark of laughter from him.

She was going to make him admit it too. "Well, Jericho, just go out and look what you have here with you. Chasseur de Lion? And you want to tell me you're not?"

"Come on," he murmured to her. "That's not a fair comment. I am what I had to be." Scoffed at her, teasing—but not. "Now you...someone paid for you to have riding lessons. You had your own Hunter pony too, I bet."

Didn't get it. "Yeah, so?"

"Yeah so...I could only ride what no one else wanted to get on. Understand?"

Soft look for him, something dawning in her eyes. "I guess I do." She leaned down on her elbow, stretched her legs out, took a drink from her beer too. "So you were either tough or you went home. But Jericho, you had no fear?"

"None." Sounded dead serious, too. "That was always true—from the first time I rode one of those damn hacks at that barn where I groomed, and shit...I was *not* allowed to ride them. Did though." From his amused expression it wasn't hard to imagine what the quality of those horses had been. "You couldn't show me something rank enough that I wouldn't get on it. Didn't matter what the vice was...bolt, rear, buck, bite. But it was good though—because of it, I can ride a horse like Lion now when no one else even dares to try.'"

"And you never fell off?" she asked, amazed.

Humor in those deep blue eyes. "Sure I did. I hit the ground more times than I can begin to count."

"And you got right back on?"

"Of course." Smiled at her, polished off the rest of his beer.

Later that same evening they took a walk in the dark, did night check on the horses together. Bee-Bee turned to him and asked, "So did you ever try and find them...your parents, I mean?" She had a way of just making the question sound so ordinary, like it was the most natural thing in the world to ask.

Maybe it was.

He was answering her, too. "No...would you?" He strolled along beside her, lit a cigarette, seemed thoughtful, introspective. "I mean, think about the likely scenario. I doubt they were married, and my mother..." Didn't really want to say it, but Bee-Bee wasn't stupid—she knew. "Either she was on drugs or she was a prostitute...or both. For all I know, I was addicted when I was born too...makes sense really. Explains why I wasn't placed as an infant, and then when I got older...well no one wants to adopt an older child."

"So how many foster homes did you live in?"

Shrugged. "That I remember? Six, I think."

"Wow."

"Yeah, it's a lot. But none that I've stayed in touch with—probably more my fault than theirs." Said a little bit more, tried to explain it—what it had been like for him all those years. "I was a loner. Angry. For me it was always about the horses. I'd stay at the barn at night...come home every few days or so...get yelled at...leave again. When I was eighteen, I walked out for good." Snorted. "No one came looking for me, that's for sure."

After the first round of jumping, Bee-Bee and Langley were standing ninth with one rail down—four jumping faults. Jericho and Lion had a clear go, but with time penalties—Lion had been fighting him through the first few fences while precious seconds ticked away, but after that he'd settled, and had a good second half of the course. They were fifth thus far. Both horses looking like they might have a chance to qualify. Excited, Bee-Bee called Frankel and told him about it.

Of all places, he was sitting at Starbucks, having a coffee with Darien. Trying to see what was going on in her head, but without mentioning it— just a general temperature reading.

"That's great, Bee-Bee," he told her. "Good for you and Langley." Darien looked completely uninterested. "Even better," he continued, not saying what had prompted him to add that. "Fifth place? I sure would never have guessed that." Darien was throwing crumbs from the cake she'd ordered to the birds instead of eating it. "Well, maybe he was right and those new shoes made a difference. Tenacious son of a bitch, I'll give him that."

More interest from her now. Eyes stealing over to watch him talking.

"Hell, you're making me wish I'd made the drive up there," Frankel grumbled. "I'd really love to see both those horses qualify." He listened for a second, and then started laughing. "Yeah, you better not play a tape with my voice on it—I'll spank both of you if you do." Smiling now, listening again and nodding. "Okay you do that…you call me as soon as the second round is through." Hung up the phone.

"So that was Bee-Bee?" Darien asked him innocently.

"Yep." Not telling her anything, stony look on his face too.

"I really like her," Darien continued. "She does a great job with Monterrey. Well, so did Jericho." Obviously she had no idea the extent of what he knew.

"I'm glad you're happy with the arrangement," he said, deliberately vague.

Tried again to get more information. "So she took Langley somewhere to try and get him qualified?" she asked. "Sounds like she might make it from what you were saying." Then she got clever. "Is she in fifth place? You mentioned that."

Didn't take the bait. "No, she's ninth. Four faults so far."

"Oh, because you said fifth."

Really annoyed look starting to settle on his face. "No, that's Jericho, and don't you dare call him."

She looked stunned. "What are you saying, Chuck?"

"I'm saying he's got a good chance to qualify Lion and he doesn't need to be distracted…and yes, Darien, Jericho talks to me. I know all about you two…have known for a long time. Who else is he going to tell? Anyway, I guessed it on my own."

She looked mortified. "Oh." Then even a little angry.

"No, I wasn't the one who said something," he went on, defensively. "I might have to you, but not to Bob."

Looking down, nodded, as if to say she believed him. Maybe she did, maybe she didn't. She knew her husband and Frankel talked a lot.

"Just don't start stringing him along," the Chef D'Equip went on sternly. "If it's over, it's over—let it stay that way."

Little voice. "I miss him, and he was so angry with me."

"Fine, and you are going to let it stay that way," he repeated, unrelenting. "He's handling it, but he won't if you start popping in and out of his life. That's just selfish, Darien, unless you really plan to leave your husband. And if you make that decision, then make it loud and clear, understand me? Jericho's going to make the Team—he could even be National Champion this year with Antares…but not if you go getting his head all turned upside-down, and that's just not right."

She gnawed on her lower lip self-consciously. She understood him alright, but still looked miserable.

"If you miss him, it's because you decided to send him away," Frankel pressed on, making her face it. "He's not your personal toy, Darien. You can't just pick him up and put him down anytime you feel like it."

"That's not fair, Chuck."

"It's exactly fair. Now promise me."

She didn't want to, but eventually, under constant insistence from him, she did.

Darien sat there for a long time after Chuck had gone. "Hey what's the matter?" It was Brae standing behind her, and she looked around, tried to smile. "Aww, I know you and Jericho are on the outs," he said, sitting down beside her. Tried to coax a smile to her face. "Man your husband…now there's one heavy dude. You should have seen him shaking his finger in my face." He giggled. "I was tempted to bite it."

Little chuckle from her, still she was staring at the ground.

"So he says…are you sleeping with my wife? And I said no, but I want to."

She laughed at that. "Stop it, Brae. You did not."

"Sure I did."

Lifted her face up finally. "Really?"

"Scouts honor." Goofy grin. "I was never a boy scout though, how lame would that be?" Deep mocking tone of voice, "You know, pack meetings, the *Den*, merit badges…duh!"

"Well, you seem to know a lot about it."

"Yeah, well, I was a *cub* scout, but only for a year, okay? Hey, my mother made me do it."

Despite herself, he was lifting her spirits with his ridiculous banter. "Brae, it's not something to get defensive about."

"I'm not defensive. Okay, I spent a *few years* in the scouts, and yeah, I was pack leader for a little while, but that doesn't make me a dork."

"Don't be silly. No one said it did." Another impossible discussion with him. Time to change the subject, distract him. "Brae what are you doing tomorrow?"

"Well, you know...nothing."

"Here's another question...what time do you get off today?"

Smiled at her, seemed proud of himself for absolutely no good reason. "Right now."

"Feel like taking a drive?" Real speculation in her voice. Definitely something on her mind.

"Oh cool, to the ocean or where?" Happy, and the boy scouts completely forgotten.

"How about grabbing your camera and let's go up to Raleigh, N.C.?" she asked him. "Chuck said it looks like Lion will qualify after all."

"Oh man," the Barista breathed. "That would really be awesome. I know Jericho would love to see you...he's been moping around for days. Not mad, like he was after Ailynn, you know? I mean, more like someone stuck a knife through his heart." He saw the look of dismay on her face, and quickly amended what he'd been saying. "Well, I don't mean you." That didn't work either though. "Well...I guess it had to be you, huh? Otherwise it would be some other chick."

"Oh, Brae, was he that bad?"

Tried again to make her feel better. "You know...it wasn't like a *machete* through the heart or anything." He dramatized it by pulling both hands into his chest like falling on a sword. "Maybe more like a penknife or...you know, a butter knife or something." Little slashing motion in the air.

"He *was* that bad, wasn't he?" she said fondly, gently.

"Yeah, he was rough." Smiled at her. "So are we going?"

She nodded. "Go pack a little overnight bag and I'll pick you up in forty-five minutes, okay?"

___

Marx was meeting all week with a very well known entrepreneur, and the deal they were cooking up promised to be more than lucrative. Unfortunately though, it meant that Ailynn wasn't getting much attention, and he could easily see that she was getting bored—cranky too.

"It's just one night," he was telling her, explaining that he and his client still had things they needed to discuss—and planned to do so tonight over dinner. He'd be home late no doubt. It was four o'clock in the afternoon, and he had a few hours free before dinner. He'd come home for a little diversion—only to be met with a pouting and uncooperative mistress. "Here's a suggestion," he offered, enticing her. "David has a private plane, and he won't be using it while he's tied up with me. How about if I arrange to have his pilot take you up to Martha's Vineyard? I'll give you my credit card and you can spend some obscene amount of money on yourself to get back at me…have a nice dinner, stay over night, go shopping in the morning and then come home. How would that be?"

Happy little smile from her, and she came over and curled up in his lap like a contented cat. Kissed his cheek. "I'd like that, Bob."

"Fine, it's settled then."

Of course she had no intention of going to Martha's Vineyard. Raleigh, N.C. sounded more like the ticket to her.

After he left Starbucks, Frankel went over and worked with George Strang. Told him about what was happening with Bee-Bee and Jericho.

"Hey! That's great news, Chuck," George told him, clapping him soundly on the back. "This could be the strongest Team we've had in years, and I just know you're thinking about Gold at the Games."

Admitted it. "Yeah, I am." Shook his head though. "I'm sorry now I didn't just go up there. I'd really love so see both Langley and Lion as alternate horses. So much can happen, and we need that depth. The Dutch and German Teams always have it, why shouldn't we?"

"We definitely should." Pensive for a moment. "Well, hell, Chuck…if you and I left right now, we'd be there in plenty of time for the second round tomorrow. We'd have to drive straight through, but we'd be there by midnight…sleep a few hours and then find Bee-Bee and Jericho in the morning."

Shook his head as if to say George was reading his mind here. "I was thinking that same thing. I mean, I think they'd both like it...don't you?"

"For sure. What a shot in the arm for both of them to have you come up there personally—to care that much. I'd love it, I can tell you that."

"Want to go?" the Chef D'Equip asked him.

Smile. "I was hoping you'd ask me."

Mind made up. "Why don't I just go gas up the truck then, and I'll meet you back here in an hour?"

"Sounds perfect, Chuck."

————————————

Bee-Bee had gone out with some other friends for dinner, and Jericho was hanging out with Marco—had spelled him from four to seven that evening, and then when he came back, just sat with him for a while, shooting the breeze.

"I think I saw a pool hall next to the hotel," Jericho mentioned. "Dive of a place, but maybe I'll stop in there anyway. Get my mind off things."

Marco was smirking at him. "Looking for a fight, Jer?"

Shrug. "Not really."

"Bet you wouldn't mind it."

Leaned up against the side of Lion's stall, laid that deep blue stare on him, said lazily, "I wouldn't run if it came my way, if that's what you mean."

"Chuck hates you fighting," Marco warned him—didn't seem like he was against the idea though. Maybe thought it was a good release for a younger man—he'd probably punched his own way through a few bar brawls years ago.

"Yeah, well Chuck doesn't need to know everything."

Marco, whistling a little tuneless song. "Go on, get out of here," he said.

Nodded. "See you in the morning."

"Call me if you need someone to get you out of jail."

"Will do."

Yeah, the place was definitely a dive, he knew that the second he walked in there. A real Bubba bar—ninety percent guys in there, and if you discounted the chick barmaids, even higher. All locals, seedy looking sorts. Jericho got a beer and took a pool table in the back corner—beat up felt top, and lousy cue sticks, but who cared? Played by himself, and no one bothered him—he looked tough enough to dissuade that, at least for now.

Wasn't putting much effort into playing. Lined up a pretty easy shot and missed it. Set it back up again, and dropped it nicely into the pocket the second time around.

"Hey cowboy, want to play a game?"

Recognized her voice even before he looked up. Bee-Bee, wearing a cute little denim jean skirt that only came about two or three inches below her little ass, and a cropped tee shirt that showed off her waistline too. Gorgeously toned legs from hours of riding, and tanned. Hair in that ever-present ponytail.

Lots of the Bubbas staring.

Leaned on his cue stick, held a hand out to her and drew her over close. Making it real clear that no one was to mess with her. Maybe that would be effective—maybe not. Couldn't call these guys a bright lot.

"I thought you were out," he told her.

"Well, I was, but I got bored." She took his cue stick. "Hey can I hit one? I'm horrible at this," she confided in him.

"Yeah, I suck too, but it passes the time." He looked around the table, found a pretty easy shot that would keep that tempting bottom of hers toward the wall rather than the Bubbas. Lined up the cue ball for her. "Here, take this one."

"Oh, that's cheating, isn't it?" She walked around to the other side of the table, thwarting his best efforts, and then pointed to a striped ball. "This is better, isn't it?" She bent over, but Jericho had moved in right close behind her. She felt his presence, looked over her shoulder, surprised…then with dawning comprehension. Stood back up again, and said tentatively, "Jericho, is this a rough bar?"

Expressive eyes on her. "Yes. Want to go?" Strong suggestion from him, and he knew she understood him.

She nodded, eyes a little wide.

He smiled at her, confident. Took the cue from her and was about to lay it on the table.

Gruff, surly voice, coming from behind him. "Let the little lady shoot."

And here it would come now, Jericho thought. Wouldn't have minded it at all, except for Bee-Bee. This wasn't her scene—not even close.

He turned slowly…let that brazen and condescending stare of his run over the hick who'd spoken. Fat, slovenly, but big too—strong. Farm hand type. "You know what?" he drawled insultingly—had even let that trace of a New York accent thicken. He'd also flipped the cue stick in his hand, holding the handle end up suggestively like a billy club. "She can't stand it here...and neither can I." He'd heard her suck her breath in at his taunting statement. She'd think he was asking for a fight, when in fact, the only chance they had to avoid one was to look so badass that these guys would just let him walk. Faint hope, that.

"Fuck..."

The Bubba never even got the "you" out before Jericho bopped him hard in the chin with the cue stick handle, grabbed his shirt and shoved him backwards. Took an aggressive step forward himself. Purred to him, "Now either you're gonna let me pass peacefully, or I'm gonna beat the ever lovin' crap out of you...your choice."

Bubba tried to swing at him, but he'd definitely picked the wrong opponent. Jericho jabbed a vicious right to his mid-section...but still just standing there calmly, in command, while the big man doubled over, expelled his breath and groaned. Held him up though, eyes scanning those around him, looking for anyone else who was thinking about stepping in. "Bee-Bee, walk to the door," he told her. And she immediately obeyed him. Good girl.

When she was almost at the exit, he thrust the big man away from himself, and hard, reeling him over and to the floor. Dropped his cue stick on the table with cold practiced cockiness, turned his back on the crowd very deliberately, and then just walked away himself. Opened the door and held it while Bee-Bee preceded him outside.

No one had followed them—damn lucky there. Almost regretted it—throwing that punch felt good.

"Jesus," she breathed.

Jericho just smiled at her. "Bunch of wusses...could have been a lot worse, believe me. Where's your car?" And she pointed. "Go on, I'll follow you back to your trailer, alright?"

She nodded in agreement, then spontaneously leaned up and kissed his cheek. "I'm sorry I caused that—I guess I wasn't even thinking."

"No, it wasn't your fault." Well sure it was, but he wasn't going to tell her that. Now she knew...no decent girl belonged in a redneck bar. Live and learn. "Marco should have warned you," he added—and that was true too. Couldn't believe he'd let her come over there—especially not dressed the way she was.

Ten minutes later they were both parked in front of her trailer. He got out and came around, escorted her to the door of her unit. Just stood there while she unlocked it.

"It's early, want to come in for a while?" Bee-Bee asked him. "Hey, I've got some movies and a DVD player. I even have popcorn."

Yeah, he did, and his blood was running hot after that oh so short interlude at the pool hall. And that meant he wasn't entirely sure what his behavior might turn out to be. Knew he shouldn't…knew it was just a flood of adrenaline talking to him, but man he wanted some kind of outlet. He leaned one hand on either side of the doorway, just about shoulder height—half-in, half-out.

"Are you sure you want…" he started.

"Well there you are, Jericho."

Christ, he knew that voice—didn't even have to turn around to identify it. And didn't turn around either. "What the hell are you doing here Ailynn?" he asked her, but eyes on Bee-Bee—dissatisfaction, even annoyance in their depths. All he was getting back from Bee-Bee was gentle support for him—like she knew he didn't want to see this woman—the offer to come inside, still open. That made his mind up. Smiled at her quietly. "Yeah, I'll come in, just give me five minutes here."

Bee-Bee winked at him.

He walked over to Ailynn. "I don't know how or why you're here, but you wasted your time if it was to see me," he told her bluntly.

She ran a teasing finger down his arm. "So is Bee-Bee your new flame?"

"No."

Didn't believe him, obviously. Asked again, mocking. "No? Are you sure?"

"*No she's not*, and yes I am," he repeated, stronger this time—powerful, suggestive. Telling her to let it go, because she was really pissing him off.

"Jericho, you're always so fierce," Ailynn laughed. "But I love that about you. So I know I can't interrupt whatever you have going on here, but give me your room key. I'll just wait for you."

"You can't be serious."

Radiant smile from her, lighting up that gorgeous face. "Well, if Bee-Bee's not your flame, then aren't you going to be nice and horny by the time you go to bed?" She moved in close to him, almost purring. Laid both hands on his chest—played with a button on his shirt. "Come on, Jericho…we both know what there is between us…and it's really, really good, even if that's all it is. Anyway, imagine how it would burn Bob's ass to have me standing here, begging you for sex." Looked up at him with so much promise. "Give me your room key. If you don't, I'll just bribe the kid at the front desk anyway."

Took it out, laid it in her palm. "I may not even go there tonight."

She laughed at him. "We'll see."

Smug but unreadable. "That's right, we will."

He turned and just left her standing there. Walked back over to the trailer, opened the door, and went inside.

Bee-Bee, curious as always. When he didn't tell her what the score was, she just asked in that unassuming way of hers. "So Jericho, it that the woman you've been seeing? The one who dumped you?" She'd made a bowl of popcorn and laid in on the fold out dining table between them. She'd switched on the television too—popped in a DVD—comedy thing.

Shaking his head over the situation. "No. I dated her for a while, but she neglected to tell me she was married. I broke it off when I found out, but she's never accepted that."

"Have you?"

Raised that deep blue stare to her. "Boy you're perceptive, aren't you? Or am I just that transparent? The answer's yes…and no—being married means so little to her, it's hard to take seriously. But I try to avoid her. I don't have a clue what made her come here tonight either…I haven't even talked to her for probably two months."

"So it's a twisted game to her, then." Sage observation.

"Totally."

She smiled, tried some of the popcorn. Licked the butter from her fingers. Innocent little gesture—mild turn on though. "See, I don't see you mixed up in something like that."

Heartfelt response from him. "Christ, I don't want to be."

She nodded, sympathetic, and just dropped it.

They watched the movie together. After a while Jericho got down on the floor, back propped against the foot of her bed, knee drawn up and his one elbow resting on it. And pretty soon she joined him, sitting inside the circle of his legs, her back on his chest, and his arms eventually going around her. No touching beyond that though, just comfortable. Her ponytail was an uncomfortable bump against his body, and in a little bit, he pulled on the band and let it fall free. Sun-streaked brunette hair, and almost as long as his was. Smelled of a shampoo that made him think of evergreens.

"Hey that's not fair," she complained, laughing and teasing. "If I show you mine, then you have to show me yours too."

No argument. Did the same thing with his own hair, shaking his head a few times till the braid just ceased to be.

She turned partway around, just far enough to run her fingers through that long, straight curtain of chestnut hair, shining with good health—highlighted with blonde from hours in the sun just like hers was. "Wow, you could be in a Breck commercial."

Smirked. "It's reassuring to know I have a career alternative in case I fail at this one," he purred back to her.

Amusement in her eyes. "You won't," she told him.

Poignant moment. He could have kissed her then—really, really wanted to.

But he didn't. Had to prove he had some control over himself, for Christ's sakes—Ailynn waiting for him back in his hotel room. Man, he just couldn't disrespect Bee-Bee that way. Instead, he brushed the backs of his fingers against her cheek. And it seemed she liked that, leaning her face into his touch, caressing him back that way. Turned around happily to watch the movie again.

He only stayed a short while after it was over. "Rest up tonight," he told her. "I'll run by Langley's stall later when I go to check on Lion—don't worry about that. See you tomorrow in the warm-up ring."

"Goodnight, Jericho," she said fondly—no recriminations whatsoever in her voice either. But still she told him, "You know, I'd say the same thing to you—get some rest. But then you're not planning on resting, are you?"

Didn't answer her. But obviously, she knew.

He let that thought just wander around his mind as he checked the horses, and then drove back to the hotel. It sure seemed like he was heading to his room and the woman waiting there, though he'd deliberately left it up in the air with Ailynn. And he still felt reluctant—dissatisfied with himself. But it didn't seem to be stopping him.

He pulled the rental car into the hotel parking lot. Just could not believe what he was seeing. Right there in the front circle was an Audi TT, and he didn't even have to see the license plate to recognize it.

First Ailynn, now Darien?

Impossible, just impossible. But hell, now that he'd seen the car, he could also see through the glass entryway and up to the reception deck—and there she was in the flesh, standing with Goddamn Brae, checking in. He pulled into a spot and turned the lights off. Shut the engine off too.

Yeah, and who was he kidding? Because his heart had leapt in his chest at the mere sight of her. She was here because she did care…or at least he was hoping like hell, and damn sure interpreting it that way. On the other hand, damn it, if all she said was that she still couldn't decide but that she'd wanted to see him again—how was he supposed to handle that one? Didn't have a clue. Open himself up all over again? Get destroyed again too?

And what now? Go in and confront her? And shit, what about Ailynn?

And then all of a sudden he knew exactly what to do with Ailynn. It wasn't rocket science. *Brae.* Of course. Starbucks had his uses for sure, and they weren't all related to taking pictures.

Jericho waited for a minute or two while they checked in and then disappeared in the elevators, then dialed his roommate's cell phone. Didn't even wait for Brae to say hello, just growled to him, "If you mother fucking let on who this is I'll kill you."

"Jericho?"

Slitting his throat seemed entirely possible.

And of course his voice was immediately replaced by a decidedly feminine one. Breathless. Excited. "Hi, it's Darien. We're here…in Raleigh. We're in Raleigh, Jericho."

Not happy. "I know. I'm sitting in the parking lot looking at your car."

Boy, she'd picked up on that tone of voice. "I'm coming down."

And he was so aching to see her. But his tone remained forbidding. "Why would you come here? Christ, Darien…I have to ride tomorrow, and I have to ride well. Because…unless you came here to tell me something's changed…" Stopped, caught his breath. So hard, so hard…it wasn't what he wanted to be telling her at all. "Just let me talk to Brae for a minute, okay?"

"I'm coming down," she repeated.

Then Starbucks was back on the line. "Uh-oh, fucked up, didn't I?" Didn't sound concerned about it though. Far from it.

Snapped at him. "Can you just shut up and listen?"

"Ah…sure."

"My room is 525. Ailynn's there. Go in and entertain her for the night, will you?"

Thrilled about that one. "Oh cool, no problem, dude."

"Later, bro." Hung up on him. Question was…what was he going to do now? If Darien had decided she was going to leave her husband for him, wouldn't she have told him that immediately? Would she have passed the phone back to Brae without saying it? Didn't think so.

And he had visions of spending the night in long angst-filled conversation with her—heart ripped to shreds, wondering why…wondering why he loved her the way he did, why she could say she loved him with the same intensity…and yet Marx with his money and social position still held her.

He saw her getting off the elevator, and she looked so beautiful, eyes already searching the parking lot for him.

Couldn't and didn't want to face the situation.

Jericho turned the key in the ignition, flipped the lights on…and pulled away.

———————

Frankel and Strang pulled into Raleigh just around midnight right on track with their time estimate. "Lets run by the stalls and check on the horses," Chuck suggested. "I know it's superstitious, but I like to see them."

Frankel was driving anyway, and he was already heading in that direction, so it really didn't matter what George said.

"Sure, Chuck," he replied anyway, smiling.

At the showgrounds, they met with some resistance from the night security man. "Sir, I can't allow you into the stable area without a competitor's pass," the older gentleman objected. But after a ration of Frankel's shit, and after having his identification card as Chef D'Equip of the U.S. Team thrust in his face, the poor man eventually gave in and let them enter.

"Ridiculous," Frankel was muttering.

They parked and then went looking for Bee-Bee and Jericho's stalls. Found Langley first—he appeared to be sleeping and looked fine. Moved on to find Lion, and luckily he was close by. As they stepped into the aisle, Marco came out of the tack stall where he'd been resting on a cot, staying overnight on watch. Chuck nodded in approval.

"Everything good here, Marco?" he asked.

The head groom held a finger to his lips, hushing him, then beckoned him closer. Pointed to Lion's stall, and Frankel looked in. George too. The big gray stallion was sleeping much like Langley had been, but in his case, he'd stretched out flat on the ground, completely relaxed...and there was Jericho too, also asleep, lying half in the shavings, and half sprawled right across the horse's body—his head on Lion's shoulder.

"Shouldn't you wake him up, Marco?" George whispered.

But the head groom just shook his head in the negative. "No, I'm keeping an eye on him, but no. He does this every once in a blue moon. Usually it means he's upset about something. Crazy, I know, but sleeping with the horses...it brings him peace when nothing else can."

Chapter Twenty-Four

Frankel and George had breakfast early and were out at the showgrounds by eight o'clock. Bee-Bee saw them almost as soon as she came out of her trailer. She was already dressed in her white show breeches and shirt, but had thrown a pair of overalls over them to keep them clean.

The top twenty riders from the previous day would go into the second round today, in reverse order of their current placing. Since Bee-Bee had been ninth, she'd be the twelfth to go today, and Jericho, who had been fifth, would be the sixteenth rider. The class started at 10:00 AM.

Bee-Bee waved happily, and immediately came over to join Chuck and George. "I can't believe you're here!" she exclaimed, giving Frankel a hug.

"I couldn't stay away—I just wanted to see you make this so much," he replied, and with feeling. "And Jericho too." He looked at her a bit sternly, half-expecting some kind of deprecating remark from her.

She didn't even seem to notice it though, and came right back with, "You should have seen him force that nasty stallion of his to behave yesterday. Lion was being such a pig, but Jericho just sat in and showed him who makes the rules."

Frankel beamed like a proud parent—for Jericho's ride, and for Bee-Bee's warm description of it. Nice to hear his Team sounding like one for a change.

"Hi, Chuck!"

They all looked around, and there came Brae strutting up in all his rumpled glory, camera slung around his neck like always. Having had an excellent time with Ailynn the night before, he was in great spirits too. He was carrying a large coffee from one of the local vendors and took a big drink from it. "Wow, the coffee here's terrible," he said, making a face.

"Brae, I wasn't expecting you," Frankel said, voicing his surprise. But he sounded pleased to see him just the same—his pictures were always useful, that was for sure.

"Hi, I don't think we've met, but I'm Bee-Bee Oxmoor," she said to him. "I've seen you on the rail before."

"And I'm George Strang," the Team Captain piped up, just to be sure Brae remembered him, though they'd already been introduced several times before.

"This is Jericho's roommate, Trevor Braeden," Frankel told George and Bee-Bee. "He's a great photographer...well, you'll see."

"Brae for short," Starbucks corrected him. "No one calls me *Trevor*—duh. How queer would that sound?" He rolled his eyes. "Anyway," he told Frankel, going back to his note of surprise about seeing him there, "Darien and I decided to drive up yesterday afternoon." Smiled. Obviously didn't have a clue that Chuck knew about Darien and Jericho, or that it should have been a secret that she was with him too.

"Darien Marx!" Bee-Bee exclaimed, as Frankel scowled furiously. "How wonderful. Well, she owns my horse, Monterrey. What a lovely person."

"Oh yeah," Starbucks agreed. "She's great. Hey, smile Chuck," he added, throwing an arm around his shoulders. "You're frowning. You should get some sunglasses before you get those crows feet and shit. Hey, and then you'll need that Botox or whatever. Some kind of paralyzing squid juice." Hooted with laughter. But it didn't change the Chef D'Equip's expression one bit. And Brae just went right on talking anyway. "So, has anyone seen my roommate? He didn't come back to the hotel last night."

"He didn't?" Bee-Bee asked, looking suddenly pleased. Maybe he'd stayed away from that woman after all. If so she was proud of him.

"No, listen to this," George interjected. "Guess where Jericho..."

Brae talked straight over him. "Nah, he never came back. I think he was trying to avoid the uhm...avoid the uhm..." He nodded his head toward Bee-Bee as a general example of what he meant, then described an hourglass shape with his hands. Added, "Oh, yeah, pretty sure."

She laughed—Brae had just confirmed what she'd been thinking.

George tried yet again to get a word in edgewise. "Well, I was trying to tell you where he spent the night. Get this, Bee-Bee...Chuck and I walk into the stalls around midnight, and there's Jericho and Chasseur de Lion sprawled out together, both asleep. Jericho's lying half on top of him, and that miserable gray beast is actually allowing it, just like a giant teddy bear."

"*Lion* let him do that?" Now that stunned her.

"Sure did. Wasn't objecting to it a bit."

Shaking her head in amazement, affectionate smile as she imagined it.

Brae, making a face though, really screwing up his nose. "Eeww," he whined. "In the horse stall?" At George's affirmative nod, he said it again. "Eeww. That's disgusting. I mean...doesn't the horse crap in there and everything?"

Bee-Bee and George burst out laughing. But Frankel wasn't paying that much attention...his eyes were scanning the crowd, and when he found Darien Marx he was going to have a *serious* talk with her. No wonder Jericho hadn't gone back to his hotel room last night. Smart move on his behalf.

"So where is he this morning?" Brae was asking again.

Shrugs all around.

Truth was, Jericho had been up for some time now—showered and shaved in the common showgrounds men's room, rebraided his hair and had Marco fold it under and sew it into place like he always did for shows. Dressed in some spare jeans and one of the shirts he kept around the barn for when he needed them. After that he'd gone to see if Bee-Bee was up and had coffee made, but no sign of her at the trailer, so he went looking for the vendor booths and bought something to eat for both Marco and himself. He already knew from Marco that Frankel and George were there, and he was grateful. Chuck's mere presence would make both Darien and Ailynn stay away, at least until after he rode. He didn't need that distraction—hell, just knowing they were both here was distraction enough all by itself. But maybe he could deal with that.

Darien had also gone to the vendor area. She'd lost Brae while they were walking, and was looking for him now. No telling what...or who...had distracted him. He sure was in a good mood this morning, but she had no idea what that was about. Maybe nothing—maybe he was just being his goofy self.

"Well, Darien...is that you?" Soft lilting voice.

She looked around. And there was Ailynn McCrae.

A million thoughts going through her mind all at once...the cold tone of voice Jericho had used with her last night...the fact that he and Ailynn had once been lovers, and maybe they were again. Felt horrible, out of place...like she'd intruded on something Jericho had rekindled. And man, he moved fast, she was thinking. Though she had no right to be critical. None at all.

Ailynn had walked over to her. She looked great in a tight pair of Capri pants and light sweater. Sexy little sandals. Darien felt grungy in comparison in her jeans. "Uhm...hi," she muttered.

Ailynn laughed. "Well, no wonder Jericho didn't come to see me last night. Now I see why." Unconcerned by it apparently. "You and I need to learn to share better," she added, then winked.

"Share?" Darien was stunned. Had Jericho told Ailynn about his relationship with her? Apparently. And what did Ailynn mean, he hadn't come to see her last night? Where *had* he been, if not with either one of them?

Little cat claws coming out as Ailynn fell into step with her. "Well, sure. Share Jericho, of course. We'll have to coordinate our schedules." Laughed merrily. "With Bob too, for that matter."

"Bob?" Darien was just completely lost...or maybe she didn't want to understand.

Ailynn held out a hand, sporting a newly purchased diamond horseshoe ring with a two-carat center stone—courtesy of Bob Marx's credit card. Great vendors at this show. "It's pretty, isn't it?"

"Yes, it's lovely...but what did you mean about Bob?" Sounding good and defensive now, really worried.

"Well, just that he bought this for me..." Purring. "...among other things." Absolutely loved that stunned look on the face of her lover's wife. Changed the subject on her too before she could think long enough to react. "Oh look, there's Jericho now...I want to say hello to him. Don't worry, honey," she added sweetly. "I won't let Bob know you were here chasing him."

As for Jericho, that little duo was absolutely the last thing in the world he wanted to see. Ailynn and Darien—together. Ailynn already waving to him. No way he could escape them. Just stood there and waited while the pair of them walked over to him. Darien had a kind of horrified expression, while Ailynn looked smug—really pleased.

"So look who I ran into," Ailynn said suggestively as she neared Jericho, lifting her eyebrows as if to say, "you can't hide anything from me." She linked arms with him.

Not much good will coming back from him, and no hello's either—that deep blue stare falling on Darien. He was asking her...really appealing to her not to drag him down into some miserable scene. "Look, I have to take this food back to Marco, and Chuck's waiting for me…" Lie that, but who cared? It was close enough to the truth.

"Chuck!" Darien burst out.

"Well, sure. He came in last night to coach Bee-Bee…and me too."

Her dismay was complete. What a horrifying trip this was turning out to be. After that conversation with Frankel yesterday, she really didn't want to run into him.

"How can you know that for sure, Jericho?" Ailynn asked him. "Have you seen him already this morning? Because I haven't. And weren't you and Darien…"

"No we weren't," he snapped, cutting her off. Really pissed-off tone of voice. Man, she was just fishing for information—didn't give a shit about Frankel, that was for sure. "I slept here at the stalls last night, if you want to know so badly." Cold stare for both of them, and especially Ailynn. "And I'm going back there now. This might be a shock to you, but the reason I'm here is to ride in this show, not service you." Reached out then, brushed his hand along Darien's arm in a gentle gesture, letting his eyes fall on her and her alone for a second—maybe excluding her somewhat from that last harsh statement of his. Then turned and walked away from them.

"Aww, now that was sweet," Ailynn said. "You know, I really think he likes you. Or maybe I should use the past tense…liked you. Don't let go of him, he doesn't really want to leave." She looked at her watch. "*I* have to go though," she said nonchalantly. "That private plane Bob arranged for me takes off an hour from now. Talk to you soon."

She looked back at Darien and waved as she hurried down to the parking lot and her rental car.

———————————

Bee-Bee was standing in front of Langley's stall with her groom Santo. "Does he look right to you?" she asked him. Santo stood there for a moment, just scowled. Langley had his head down some, and hadn't finished his hay from this morning. He wandered a bit listlessly in his stall, didn't come over to greet her or look for treats like he normally did.

"Maybe he's tired," Santo finally said.

She opened the door and went inside, walked up to the older gelding, petted him. Still got very little response. "Well, lets take him out and tack him up. We should take his temperature too, just to be sure. If he doesn't look any better, then maybe I should scratch him from this class." She looked around anxiously. "I wonder where Chuck is," she asked, wanting his advice.

Twenty minutes later they had him ready. Still no sign of the Chef D'Equip—but he could just be waiting in the warm-up ring. Langley still seemed lethargic, but his temperature was normal, and there was no heat in either his legs or feet.

"Well, I'll take him up and then we'll see how he goes," she fretted. They took him outside, and Santo helped her get on.

Frankel had meanwhile gone to hunt for Darien. He'd really planned to give her a piece of his mind—couldn't believe she'd driven up here after their conversation yesterday. But apparently she was hiding from him—her car was still here, but no sign of her anywhere. Looked at his watch and saw that he was running late. Grumbled under his breath, and then started back to the warm-up area. He'd have to find her afterwards and hope she didn't get to Jericho first.

Jericho too had mounted up, and was slowly making his way over to the jumping arena, but was taking Lion on a round about route, letting him just relax. Almost like a hack. He could see the warm-up in the distance, saw Bee-Bee come in and pick up a posting trot. Frowned at the way her big gelding seemed to be moving. Picked up a trot himself, and started heading over there.

Bee-Bee had already dismounted, and she and her groom were standing there talking as Jericho came into the ring. Marco had walked up too and was waiting at the fence line holding a bucket filled with last minute things—a towel to wipe down Jericho's boots before he went into the ring, little odds and ends they sometimes needed, like a hoof pick and a leather punch.

"What's up?" Jericho asked as he pulled up beside Bee-Bee.

Worried look on her face. "Does he look right to you, Jericho?" she asked. "Maybe I'm just being a mother hen. Santo thinks he might just be tired. But he seems wrong to me somehow. Am I crazy?"

Vaulted off. "No," he said. "You're right, something's bothering him. I was way over there, and I could see it when you started trotting." Looked around then, and hollered, "Marco…come and take this horse. Hand walk him for a few minutes, alright?" The head groom appeared like magic and quietly led Lion away.

"Oh God," Bee-Bee murmured. "Did he look lame to you when you were watching?" Rumor was he'd had a lot of soundness issues this year.

"No." Ran his hands down the horse's legs anyway, feeling the tendons, letting his palm lay over each joint. "He's got a little splint here," he told her, fingers trailing over his left fore.

"That's old…do you feel heat in it?"

"No." He stood up straight again. Stroked the horse's neck. "But I don't like this…see he's a little bit sweaty, and you just barely started to work." Jericho felt along his side. "Lets get the saddle off him." Undid the girth himself and handed her saddle to Santo, then he laid his ear against the horse's gut. Serious expression, but didn't say anything. Instead, he moved around to the front of the gelding and opened his mouth—pressed his thumb on his gum. Pinched the skin on his neck and watched as he let go again.

"What's going on here?" Frankel's voice, and pretty demanding. It was pretty obvious that there was some kind of problem with the horse.

"Something's not right, Chuck," Bee-Bee was saying, a tremor in her voice. One thing for sure, she loved this animal. "I saw it and Jericho saw it too, we're not both crazy."

And from Jericho, "He might be collicking."

"Oh God, please don't say that," she whispered. Colic could kill a horse in a matter of hours if it got bad.

Frankel stepping in now. He pretty much repeated everything Jericho had just done. "Not much gut sound," he commented, moving away from the horse's side.

"That's what I thought too," Jericho agreed. "And he's a little dehydrated on top of it."

Chuck looked at Bee-Bee. "Well, you've got two choices…try and ride him through this class, and then look at him again and get him over to the nearest clinic if he doesn't improve…or take him back to the stalls now and we'll get the show vet over."

Clearly she was torn. "Man, I'll just kick myself if this turns out to be nothing…but Chuck, how can I ride him through this class if he's not feeling well?"

"We don't know that," Frankel reasoned. "I mean, at the moment, he's just a little lethargic, right? Maybe he's tired from yesterday. It's been a hot weekend too. Strange place, he might not be drinking quite enough." It seemed clear that he was in favor of the first of those two options, but still he was leaving the decision up to her.

Bee-Bee walked up to Langley, petted his face, looked into his eyes. Soft affectionate look from him but unsettled too. "I guess I could try it," she said finally. "If I don't like the way he's going, I can always pull up and excuse myself from the class."

Santo put the saddle back on him, and Bee-Bee gave him a very light warm-up. Jericho got back on Lion, and started some flatwork with him, keeping an eye on her the whole time. Didn't like it. He hadn't voiced his opinion, but if it had been his decision he'd have taken the horse to the clinic now. Not his place to say though, so he stayed quiet. Unhappy about it, worried too.

Minutes later, she entered the arena. The way things were set up at this showgrounds, Jericho couldn't see her after that. He heard an enthusiastic applause though after just a little bit—apparently she'd finished the round, gotten through it.

She came back out, and George was there to greet her. Still had an apprehensive look on her face as she dismounted and they led Langley away. But by now, Jericho was only minutes away from his own ride, and was concentrating on that—Frankel there with him coaching.

"How did Bee-Bee do?" he asked as he walked up, ready to enter the ring for his go.

"Clear round," Chuck told him, and smiled. "Now you get one too."

Jericho knew he wouldn't ride in a jump-off round today—and it was because of his time faults from the day before. Either all the horses above him would have a rail down, and he'd win the class assuming he was clear now…or someone or ones would have a double clear and beat him—no way around that, not with those time faults dragging him down. In any event, he wouldn't ride in the jump-off…he didn't need to save his horse's strength—he could give this everything.

The competitor before him was riding out, and he cantered in.

Mutinous tug on the reins from Lion. He leaned forward and petted him reassuringly, then sat in and asked him to come round. Indecision on the stallion's part, then surprisingly, he obeyed.

He pulled to a halt, saluted the ground jury, and got their return acknowledgement. Then quietly took to the course with Lion. Aimed him through the timers, and then into the first fence.

The ride was just amazing. That huge rolling canter appeared out of nowhere, and there was nothing in the arena that the big gray even thought about knocking down. Chasseur de Lion was so tuned in to him, seemed to be eagerly awaiting every single cue. Lifted him into fence after fence, and the stallion just soared. Tight turns, lead changes, combination jumps…nothing even made him hesitate. Jericho couldn't believe it, they were just eating this course up as if it were all three-foot jumps. When he went through the final timers, he knew he'd been clear—also knew it was the fastest time they'd see here today.

The audience knew it too. The applause was thunderous. And Lion was qualified for the finals. He rode from the ring elated, the big gray stallion prancing and oh so full of himself.

No sign of Frankel, George, or Bee-Bee when he came out…not even Marco. And oh man, he knew that couldn't be good. Cantered his stallion all the way back to the barn.

The head groom was there. "Go back up to the ring," he told him. "You have to be there when they pin the class."

"What's happened?" he demanded.

"Langley's worse." Marco looked grave. "You were right…it's colic. I helped load him on the van. Now go back," Marco insisted. But he knew his boss all too well—knew what he wanted. "I'll bring your car up and you can leave from there as soon as you're through."

"Alright."

God, he wanted to get down right now—go to support Bee-Bee. But it was mandatory for the winning horse and rider combinations to be in the ring when they pinned. Knew that—knew he couldn't risk disqualification or even a disciplinary action—having already been suspended once this year, they might just decide to throw the book at him. Damn sure couldn't let that happen. He pivoted the horse, and cantered back the way he'd come.

Turned out there was a jump-off between the top two horses, and he had to wait till they set it up, ran through it, and then finally pinned the class. Marco drove the rental car up, and Jericho dismounted, muttering impatiently. While he paced, Marco took Lion, threw a light cooler over him and walked him out. Darien appeared by the warm-up.

"Jericho, you're third!" she said happily, coming over to him timidly. Happiness for him so apparent in her eyes.

He told her what was happening. Barely seemed to care about himself right now.

"I'm so sorry. Poor Bee-Bee…will he be alright?"

Little hand on his arm, and man did he love that. His anger with her forgotten, just glad that she was there. Concern in his eyes though. "I don't know," he told her. "This will sound really strange—maybe even bizarre. But that's the best ride Lion's ever given me, and I just feel like…I don't know. Like it was a tribute or something."

"Oh God, don't say that."

Expressive look from him. "I know, I know, Darien. Just fuckin' a, I hope I'm making that up."

She put her arms around his waist, and he pulled her close. To have Langley—or any horse for that matter—in serious condition, just reached in and grabbed him. Darien's presence and her obvious feelings for him were so incredibly comforting. It was so right, and she just felt so perfect in his arms. He laid his cheek against the top of her head, giving in to what he felt for her. Murmured to her, "I'm sorry about last night. Swear to God, I was so damn happy you made the trip, and without my even asking you to. But Darien, if you'd said to me…"

Her arms tightened around him, and she sighed with longing for him. "I'm so confused," she whispered. "Everyone's upset with me…Bob, Chuck…you. But I love you, Jericho. I know that much."

I love you.

One little sentence, and it washed all the doubt away. And in return, he told her how he felt too, and said it without fear—and without conditions. "And I love you. Nothing's going to change that."

He tipped her chin up to look at him. No, she wasn't his, but even that indisputable fact didn't alter what was inside him. Didn't care who was watching them either. Leaned down and laid his mouth over hers.

Jericho pulled into the clinic—he'd had some trouble finding it, and a good hour and a half had passed. But he could see Frankel's pick-up parked there, and knew he had the right place. Darien and even Brae were with him, none of them saying all that much. He parked and they went inside together.

The group inside looked grim, and Bee-Bee had been crying. She was controlling herself pretty well now though. Still the expression on her face was miserable. "I should never have ridden him in that class," she muttered to no one in particular.

"No way you could have known," Frankel told her firmly. "Don't go beating yourself up, he didn't look that bad." His own expression was pretty frazzled and he didn't even scowl at the fact that Darien was there—or that she was holding hands with Jericho when they walked in.

"What's going on?" Jericho asked Chuck.

"They took him into surgery about fifteen minutes ago. Looks like an impaction of the small intestine."

Shit, sounded serious. Jericho went over to Bee-Bee, while Darien and Brae took seats off to one side. Dropped down onto his heels beside where she was sitting. "How are you holding up?" he asked her.

"I'm okay." But clearly she wasn't.

He took both her hands and just held them in the protective circle of his own.

Grief-filled eyes turning to him. "I rode him in that class...I *rode* him."

"Come on," he murmured back to her. "You know keeping them moving is important when they're collicking. Maybe what you really did was give him a chance. Was he fighting you?"

"No." Whispered, and her face looked so grateful.

"Then he wanted to jump."

Long minutes passed. They couldn't see into the operating area from where they were sitting, but there was a sudden flurry of activity—doctors and assistants with bleak, harried faces, rushing in and out of surgery. Bee-Bee, just watching them, looking shell-shocked. Jericho, right beside her. Silence in the room.

And then the rushing stopped.

Everyone there in the waiting room just looking at each other, no one daring to say a word, to speculate. The head veterinarian appeared, still in his greens, taking his mask off. Blood covering his surgical gloves, and his arms up to the elbows. He stared at them all, then just shook his head in the negative.

Bee-Bee let out a moan, and began sobbing, hard. Frankel came over, and laid a hand on her shoulder almost awkwardly, and George rushed over too and was hovering right there beside her. "Oh Bee-Bee, I'm so sorry," he said to her.

Jericho had also risen. His expression was open, understanding, pain-filled too. He still had her hands in his and pulled on them lightly—a suggestion or invitation, no more. And she accepted it, got up and went to him, laid her head on his chest while great heaving sobs took over her whole body. He wrapped his arms around her, held her tightly, one hand lightly stroking the back of her head.

"What happened?" Frankel choked out. He almost looked like he was teary-eyed too. Had to brush the moisture from his cheek.

The doctor gave a clinical answer, but delivered in a compassionate tone of voice. "There's a major blood supply that lies across the top of the small intestine. It was corrupted by the impaction beneath it and ruptured during surgery. The horse bled out and was dead in just a few minutes. I'm sorry, there was nothing we could do." He looked really upset and frustrated by the situation—knew he'd been dealing with one of last year's Olympians as a patient—could see the terrible grief on Bee-Bee's face.

"Oh Chuck," Bee-Bee was saying, gulping for air, "I promised him he'd be alright. Right before he went into surgery, I promised him. Oh God, Chuck, I lied to him. He isn't alright…he's…"

"Stop it," Jericho hushed her. "He knows you love him, he knows that." Still very deliberately using the present tense. Wondered if he ought to be handing her over to Frankel now, but she was clinging to him so desperately he just couldn't push her away. Held her tighter instead.

Finally, embarrassed, she pulled away from him, took a stumbling step and then fell back down into her chair. Chuck and George closed ranks around her, and Darien was there too. Somewhere in all of this, Brae had stepped outside.

Jericho walked around the corner and into the surgery. Horrible image…Langley lying on his back on the stainless steel table—brought up there by a series of chains and pulleys, long incision across his stomach. Tongue pulled to one side, and an oxygen tube taped in his mouth. The surgeon was standing there looking at his lost patient miserably, and an orderly was hosing blood on the cement floor down a central drain.

Deep sigh, and the doctor turned around to him. "I'm sorry," he said.

Jericho nodded. "I want to bring her in here," he told him. "Can you close his mouth, take that tube away?"

"Yes, of course. Give us two minutes to get it done."

He went back out, and Bee-Bee had started to settle. She also looked numb. Lost. He moved in beside her again, and the others gave way to him—he seemed to be the only one who knew what to do. Murmured to her, "Come with me, I'll take you to see him."

A new rush of tears streamed down her cheeks, eyes imploring. "I don't know if I can do that."

"Sure you can, and you'll be mad at yourself later on if you don't." His voice was soft, coaxing, had no judgment in it, just gentle guidance and infinite strength. "I'll be right there with you. It's the last chance you'll have to say good-bye to him." Held his hand out to her one more time, and her fingers slid in it, trusting him.

She knew what to expect, had seen colic surgery performed before, but still the sight of her beloved companion on that table was shocking. She stopped, but Jericho was right behind her, and simply led her into the room and around to the horse's head. Eyes still open. He wasn't breathing but didn't exactly look dead yet either. She gasped, but was reaching out toward him tentatively. Jericho's hand covered hers, and then stroked down the animal's glossy side. Still fairly warm, but he wouldn't be for long.

He dropped down on one knee, and brought her down beside him, just started talking in a voice so low that only she, and what remained of this beautiful animal's soul could hear him. Told Langley he'd been loved, that he wouldn't be forgotten. Thanked him for his courage, his devotion, and his heart for all those years. Told him he'd been a competitor in a million, had carried Bee-Bee to the Worlds and even the Olympics, and had never let her down, never faltered. Thanked him for the privilege of knowing him. Told him that she knew he'd always be near.

Thanked him too for that one last ride today for Bee-Bee—that perfect round over the fences, and his final farewell to her.

She was whispering to Langley now too, her tearstained face next to his face, speaking directly in his ear.

Frankel peeked in the doorway for a second, but immediately backed out of the room again. "Leave them alone for a few minutes," he told the others. "Jericho's taking care of her. I couldn't do what he's doing in there," he admitted. "It's good he was here."

No one thought Bee-Bee should drive that empty trailer home, and although Santo could drive it, he didn't have a driver's license, and it wasn't good to have him on the road that many hours alone. In the end, Jericho volunteered that he and Marco would load Lion in it and drive together back to Wellington. Bee-Bee would go with George and Frankel, and in fact, they were ready to leave.

But not before she said a private goodbye and thank you to Jericho. She'd come back over to the trailer, asked him to come inside for a minute with her. They stood now at the foot of her bed, only maybe twelve inches separating them.

"What you said about him...*to* him...was so beautiful," she told him. "It was like you knew him personally, and for years." A little dampness in her eyes, but she was no longer crying—well, maybe off and on, but nothing like before. "There's no way I can thank you for that, or for making me go in to see him. You're right, I would have hated myself if I hadn't. But if you weren't there with me insisting, I probably would never have had the guts." Soft voice. "You've lost a horse before that you really loved, haven't you?"

Nod from him. Then said quietly, "More than one."

She sighed, "It's so hard."

Powerful look from him. "It's about love...what they always say," he told her. "The risk. The more you love, the harder you fall, and I guess it's true. But would you really miss it? Would you really want to do without?"

Whispered it. "No."

"Me either." Little look of self-scorn then. "Though God knows I get myself in more trouble that way." Shook his head.

"As in Darien Marx?"

Reached out and ran his fingers along her jawline, deep blue stare wandering over her face, searching. "Yeah, I've made that painfully obvious, haven't I?" It hadn't been true until that visit to the vet clinic, but the way they'd walked in together—and the way Darien had come up to him when they were ready to leave...well, it hadn't left much question as to what was going on between them.

"Is that a bad thing?" Typical Bee-Bee questions, asking the important things, not cloaked in anything—just laid them out there.

"I haven't got a clue." Honest answer too. "But I don't see it going anywhere, much as I want it to. So probably yes."

He hadn't removed his hand, thumb sliding now across her chin.

"Can I ask you for something, Jericho?" She was a little tentative about whatever it was she meant to ask him for, but was making herself go ahead and do it anyway.

"Of course. What's that?"

Her answer was not at all what he'd expected—if he'd had any expectation whatsoever—but it still got to him, really got to him. "Will you kiss me, Jericho? Not because it means anything, and not because I'll ever mention it again…I won't. But just because…right now, I really…want someone to just kiss me. Someone I can trust."

Wasn't at all sure exactly how much kissing she was talking about, but the request, or invitation, or whatever, wasn't unwelcome, that was for sure. What he had with Darien was super-intense…and rife with the potential to really hurt him, maybe over and over again. And a dead-end street too maybe. This was different, not so raw, just quietly comfortable.

He closed that one-foot distance between them, his hand moving from her cheek to around behind her neck. His eyes open, and hers too until the very last instant. Then contact, his mouth over hers…light, deepening slowly but not intense. Then ending it.

"Please," she said softly.

Something starting to smolder inside him. More aggressive kiss this time, mouth open and wanting. His tongue finding hers, coaxing but demanding too—the response delicate, but welcoming. Innocent almost, but learning. Leaning into his mouth. Little moan from her. Tentative touch with her tongue, wrenching a return snarl from him, and causing a tightening of his muscles, like a claw gripping his lower abdomen. He pulled back, deep blue eyes powerfully on hers. Knew she hadn't meant the response he was feeling. Knew she was just looking for an emotional outlet—friendship too. Someone's arms around her when she needed them. Growled at her, "Looks like your trust was misplaced…"

"Don't. I asked you to."

Lowered his head again. More kisses from him, slower now but consuming…commanding. In command. Seductive. And if he'd laid her down on that bed right there and then, God knew, she might have let him. Total turn-on, that.

Wrong of him though.

Stopped himself…stopped them, already hating the way he was taking advantage of her. Made her look at him. "Bee-Bee, I like you. I like you a lot. You're nothing like what I'm used to, but so damn nice. Over the last couple of days you've been more of a friend to me than anyone I can remember…" Dropped that train of thought, it made him way too vulnerable. "But don't let me…don't let me come to you that way…not while I have

Darien in my life." Stroked her cheek again, murmured deeply to her, "Because right now *I want to*. But Christ's sakes Bee-Bee, make me be a man. Make me choose."

Gentle comment back from her, not a reproach, or hardly one anyway. "You're so spoiled, Jericho. Not every woman wants you that way, and it's not what I was after. Not at all." It was her turn to touch his face now, five o'clock shadow rough beneath her fingertips. "I like the way you're thinking though."

"Shit," he murmured to himself. Boy, she'd put him in his place—not harshly, not even close, maybe not even trying to. But oh so thoroughly, and he backed away a pace, feeling pretty stupid. Shallow too. Street kid, no couth. "Forgive me, then." Just wanted to get out of there. Felt a little baited on top of everything else, and resentful of that. Soft growl to her, "I'm just so clumsy, forgive the advance. I was never raised to..."...*give a woman like you what she wants or expects*. Turned and put his hand on the doorknob, yanked it open.

"Wow, fragile male ego," her voice trailed after him. "I wasn't trying..."

"I know you weren't."

And just like that, he was gone.

Chapter Twenty-Five

Only three weeks remaining after the end of that Raleigh show and before the start of the finals. Plus Frankel wanted all his riders to go to the Los Angeles venue a week ahead of time—to get the horses acclimatized. So what that really meant was three weeks was more like two. Lots of work for Jericho to get done in the interim. He'd sent Brittany and all the horses except Lion, QL and Antares back to his farm in East Hampton, along with two of the guys. Hated the fact that he couldn't bring Force with him, but not much he could do about that. He was in constant communication with her, making sure everything was set up how he liked it—she was even picking up a few clients of her own, which brought him more income too. Yeah, maybe that was working out.

"Here's the problem. You need two working students," Frankel told him. They'd done his sessions with the horses late in the afternoon that day rather than early morning, and had stopped at Backstreet's to have a beer afterwards. No accident, that, Jericho knew. Chuck wanted to talk with him, and this was obviously going to be one of the topics. "Brittany is good, and I'm going to find you another one like her—not just any starry-eyed kid, mind you. I want to put someone with you who has real promise, someone who's worth your time…because you don't have time to spare. Build your business the way it should be—not that you have to do all the riding personally. You need to be free to compete…like this."

Admitted it. "Yeah, Chuck, you're right."

"So you're not going to object or fight me on this?" Seemed suspicious that it was going too easy.

Looked at him, smirked a little, just shook his head. "Would it do me any good?"

"No."

He shrugged. "Then why argue? Truth is, it never mattered in the past and now it does, and…well hell, you're just right and I like the idea."

Now that made him happy. More confident too. Moved right on to the next subject, one that probably wouldn't be so simple. "So what's the deal with Darien Marx now?" Frankel asked him more sharply, knocking back some of his beer, maybe expecting Jericho to clam up on him—refuse to answer.

That wasn't the case though. Chuck hadn't mentioned his relationship with Darien since Raleigh, but Jericho knew he was watching the situation. He even understood why—Marx was an important patron, and Chuck had to be on top of it. It wasn't like he was prying. Jericho knew him better than that by now.

He answered him truthfully, but in a harsh unhappy tone of voice. "The deal is, there is no deal. Show season's over here in Wellington. Darien's back in New York—she left right after Raleigh. But you probably know that." Truth was, they'd had one night together before he left the Raleigh showgrounds. One fabulous night, uninterrupted by the rest of the world. Long passionate hours spent with her—no commitment though, and no promises. "I haven't called her since I got back and she hasn't called me either. I guess they'll be out in L.A. for the finals, but both of them... together." Bitter look in his eyes as he spoke. "So the deal is...her winter fling's over." Scornful sneer for himself. Lifted his eyes, found Frankel's. "I'm the only fool who thought differently."

Frankel looked down, seemed thoughtful. He hesitated, like he wasn't even sure he wanted to say this. Finally he did. "No, actually I thought so too. I thought there was more there. But alright, now you know it...just remember it next time you see her and stay away, you hear me? From the husband too, that's just trouble waiting to happen."

Stay away from her? He wished he could say he was going to do that—yeah, he wanted to, but his track record sucked. And he admitted it too. "I'll try, but she doesn't make it easy, and that bastard husband of hers likes to come around and bait me too. Boy, he's shown his real colors, and I can't guarantee..."

"You let that be my job, understand me, Jericho? Your job is to ride those three horses, nothing else. Here's what I want...I want you to be National Champion this year. Focus on that for me, will you?"

"Oh, National Champion?" he mocked him. "Well, you don't set high goals, do you?" But no way he was taking it lightly. *National Champion.* Flare of desire in those deep blue eyes of his—and he wasn't kidding anyone about how hungry the mere thought of it made him.

Frankel leaned forward on his elbows, worked him over a little. "I haven't spent all season coaching you to get second place, Jericho. What did you think I was doing, just stroking your friend Marx to get his patronage? Well maybe you did, but if so, you were dead wrong. I picked you—picked you right out at the beginning of the season. And even with everything you've had thrown at you, you haven't shown me anything different. Not once. Hell, I got you suspended myself, but you didn't back down for a minute. And you didn't ride for damn near two months in casts to be third or fourth either, now did you? So hear me...I want that title, and any one of your three horses can do it. No excuses, no distractions. This is your year and you bring it home."

Silence. Potent look.

Frankel, pushing it. "Did you hear me?"

"I heard."

Really pushing it. "Nothing less than National Champion, Jericho."

"I said I heard you."

"Fine, then you do it."

Powerful statement in return. "Yeah, I'm going to."

The Manager of the Forest Hill Boulevard Starbucks was a middle-aged man named Donald—kind of a dour sort. He disliked a lot of the antics that took place at his store, and especially had his eye on that tall blonde guy, Trevor Braeden.

He'd tolerated a lot while the show season was in full swing—also knew this damn kid Brae drew in a ton of his friends and those of his roommate—that rider, whatever his name was. But now that the season was over, he was finding Brae more and more irritating. Came in late all the time, took too many breaks, chatted up all the customers...not to mention his incredibly annoying personality. Dressed like a pig most of the time too, though to be honest, the female customers liked him.

Anyway, enough was enough, and today he was late again—he wasn't even there yet, but had been supposed to clock in a good ten minutes ago.

Looked up and saw the Barista strolling in casually. Brae paused at the doorway to take one last drag from his cigarette before throwing it away and sauntering in. He exhaled the smoke inside the building though, nice little cloud hovering right there where customers came in.

Donald stepped around the counter, motioned Brae over. The Barista took his sweet old time getting around to it, stopping to trade smartass remarks with another friend along the way.

"You're ten...well by now it's fifteen minutes late, Trevor," Donald told him sternly.

Starbucks looked around himself trying to figure out who the Man-ass-ger was talking to. Got a look of surprise on his face—nice pose—lips pursed up like the letter O. Then he pointed to his own chest, but with a question mark. *"Trevor?"* he said, obviously offended. "My name is *not* Trevor. Well...actually it *is*, but that's just a legal thing, alright? I mean, it's almost like calling someone "hey, you"...it's not a real name, get me?"

Completely lost by this sudden and rather bizarre turn in the conversation. "Huh?"

Hands on hips. "How would you like it if I called you Donald?"

"Well, that's my name."

"Exactly my point," Brae replied with feeling. Smiled. Lifted his eyebrows superiorly.

Just staring at each other.

"You know what?" Starbucks continued after a few long moments. "You're making me late, I need to get to work before the Man-ass-ger gets all worked up and everything. High blood pressure, you know? His face all red and shit." Laughed. "Oh, that's you. Nah, you're face looks okay." Clapped him on the shoulder. "Ugly as a monkey, but then that's nothing unusual." Laughed again at his own joke. He brushed past the older man to retrieve his Barista apron, with Donald trailing in his wake, mouth open but no sound coming out—somewhat desperately trying to gain control of the conversation.

"I really need to speak with you, Trevor." Donald tried again.

Stunned. "See, I'm not Trevor."

"Your name isn't Trevor Braeden?"

Exasperated. "Yeah, it *is*..." Gave him a really strange look, pulled back. "Hey, could you get away from me? You seem retarded or something."

The Manager shook his head to try and clear it. He thought to himself that the best thing might be to just start the conversation over. "Here's the point," he said emphatically. "You're late."

Starbucks gestured toward the Manager himself from head to toe, then just murmured, "Duh!" Laying full blame on him for his tardiness.

Testy tone of voice from the Store Manager now, and tapping his watch. "Yes, well you were already late when you first got here."

Really offended. Shook that mop of blonde hair out of his eyes, pointed to Donald's chest with his finger. "Why didn't you *say so* then? Huh? Gotcha on that one, didn't I?"

"I most certainly did say so." At least he thought he had—although by now, he couldn't really even remember for sure.

"Nah, you were just calling me names and shit."

Stunned. "I was calling you by *your* name." Obviously he wasn't too experienced in dealing with Brae's circular logic and was letting himself be dragged deeper and deeper into an impossible argument with him. "Anyway, you're fired."

"Fired!" Now he had his attention. "Oh man, I'm not listening to you anymore. I'm just going to go to work."

"No, you can't...well, you're fired."

Really loud conversation—totally disrupting the place, and getting worse. Starbucks—who had been planning on quitting anyway when they left for L.A.—fighting like mad to keep his position. "Who said you can fire me? I mean, aren't I a stockholder or something? Maybe I have to vote on it." Put his apron on anyway, and stepped behind the counter. Said to the next customer, "Welcome to Starbucks, want your usual, Sam?"

Smile from the elderly gentleman. "Sure, thanks Brae." Nasty look for the Store Manager too.

Donald threw up his hands and walked away. Figured he'd better call his boss, the Territory Manager. Maybe he'd know what to do.

———

Darien and Bob Marx were having lunch at a fashionable New York restaurant. Their relationship had been pretty strained lately, but she'd never mentioned that she knew about Ailynn, and was trying hard to get along with him—make him happy, be happy herself too. She'd dressed up to meet him, and looked especially nice in a chic, slim-fitting, black knit dress—kind of upscale-casual.

Her cell phone rang and she hesitated, but then finally answered it.

"Well, hi Brae," she said, hoping Bob wasn't going to mind this—Brae wasn't someone he held in very high esteem. She tried to keep it brief. "No, I'm not really free...I'm at lunch...oh it's important? Well okay, go ahead."

Seemed to be listening for a moment, confusion on her face. "Well, no he can't fire you because he doesn't like your name...of course not...a lawyer? Gee I don't know, Brae, weren't you going to quit anyway?" Listened again. "Oh, another week? Well, exactly how much are your one-week's wages?...No, I'm not trying to pry...well, I just mean in comparison to the cost of an attorney." She shrugged helplessly at her husband.

"Oh, for God's sake," he muttered. "Just give the phone to me."

Darien shook her head in the negative. "Well, okay, that sounds like a good idea...well, yes, I know, I'm sure it was very upsetting...no, I think you have a lovely name."

Of course the conversation went on for another five minutes before she was finally able to extricate herself. Then she burst out laughing.

"What's the problem?" Marx demanded.

"Brae's upset," she told him, shaking her head fondly. "Well, I guess he got fired, but he's refusing to leave. He claims he's going to get a petition going. But here's the crazy part...he was already planning to quit when they go to L.A."

"Frankel actually hired him, didn't he?" Marx inquired. "Team photographer?"

Darien nodded.

The investment banker shrugged. "Well, then it's simple. I'll just call him and tell him to find Brae something to do pronto...so there will be some hope the rest of us can survive the rest of the week."

———————

The day had finally arrived to ship the horses to Los Angeles. The plan was they'd be trailered down to Miami airport—only a one-hour or so trip, and then flown from there to L.A. Jericho and Marco and his second groom, Juan were all going with the horses. Monterrey and George's two horses, Tarrytown and Phantom, would also be on the plane with QL, Lion and Antares. Their grooms too—full load.

He was pretty sure Chuck, George and Bee-Bee were taking a commercial jet together—could have gone with them, sure, but had decided not to.

As for the other current short-list riders, Debbie McPherson had failed to make the finals—someone else would be moving up to take her spot. Tim Rawlings was sitting about ninth in the standings and had already shipped his two horses out—teetering on the brink of dropping off the short-list too. Pretty much ditto for Marc LaCroix—he was eighth with his nine year old mare, but still looked like he could move back up. Marc was also already in California, but then he hailed from there, and had gone back weeks earlier.

No problems getting to the airport in Miami, and the ground crew started right in loading up the plane. First, all the gear they had with them was stowed on board the aircraft—saddles, bridles, and all the rest of their tack trunks and supplies. The horses came next. They were led into portable stalls at planeside, and then the stalls themselves, along with their occupants, were raised and slotted into place in specially designed fittings built right into the floor of the huge jet. Jericho spent time with each of his three horses both on the ground and after they'd boarded, talking to them, making sure they were comfortable and not afraid. Stopped over and spent a minute with Monterrey too.

Long flight, and not particularly comfortable quarters for him, but he didn't mind it. He checked the animals regularly, and they were all doing well. Passed the time playing poker with Marco and pretty soon the other grooms joined in with them. Most of the conversation was in Spanish, but that didn't really bother Jericho…he knew enough to follow the bulk of it. Interesting too—hell, you could learn a lot from what the grooms had to say. Turned out Santo was pretty fond of Bee-Bee but considered her a little aloof. George's groom, Reynaldo made a lot of fun of him—had a good sense of humor too, really got the group chuckling. Reynaldo called his boss *Limpie Uñas*, or "Clean Fingernails"—apparently because he didn't like to get his hands dirty. Jericho had to laugh at that.

He learned that Marco had a pet name for him too, something he hadn't known before…*Puño*. Took that as a compliment…it meant fist. Of course, Marco probably had several other names for him that he wasn't mentioning—names that wouldn't be considered flattering one bit.

Four hours later they touched down in LAX. Offloading was uneventful, and the local shipper was there as scheduled to pick them up. Pretty much everything had run like clockwork. Jericho tipped all the grooms, even Bee-Bee and George's. Insurance, knowing he'd get anything he wanted from them in the future. Maybe Frankel and others had spent a comfortable few hours compared to his trip…but the time he'd invested had been productive, and the horses were safe—couldn't put a value on that.

Jericho oversaw the unloading at the showgrounds, then helped Marco and Juan take temperatures, fill water buckets and throw hay to his crew. When all of the animals were settled in, he finally called Frankel.

"Jericho, how did it go?"

"Everyone's fine, Chuck." Told him about the flight, the horses, and general status on everything.

Frankel sighed, relieved. Brightened up his tone too. "We're just about to go out to dinner," he told him. "Why don't we come by and take a look at them, and then you can go with us?"

Jericho tried to beg off. "Nah listen, I'm filthy, I stink like horses, and I'm really tired. I'm just going to find my rental car, go back to the hotel and get a shower…turn in early."

Not having it though. "Ridiculous. I want you to join us. We're not going anywhere fancy, and you need a decent meal—I doubt you've eaten. We won't stay out late, we all had a long day. Just wait for us at the stalls, and we'll pick you up. You can get your rental car in the morning."

Jericho cursed softly under his breath. Would have argued, but he could already see that Frankel wasn't bending. Truth was, he didn't feel much like spending the night with Bee-Bee and George—or Chuck for that matter. But especially not Bee-Bee. Hadn't seen her since Raleigh, and didn't want to now either—not after that last uncomfortable scene between the two of them. Gave it one last shot. "Look, you'll see me tomorrow morning…"

Pretty firm reply. "No, I'll see you in twenty minutes." Then Frankel just hung up on him.

Man, wondered what the fuck was up Chuck's ass that he was so frickin' insistent, but hell, it didn't seem like he had much choice. Yeah, he could still walk out now if he wanted to, but would it be worth the ration of bullshit he'd have to take tomorrow? Probably not. And he was going to have to face Bee-Bee sooner or later anyway. Wished it was later. But typical Chuck—always thought he knew best.

Ten—not twenty—minutes later, Frankel, George, and Bee-Bee showed up at the stalls. As the little group started strolling down the aisle, Marco appeared, moving to stand in front of them. Smiled. "Little bit early, aren't you, Chuck?" he asked.

"What? Do I need an appointment?" the Chef D'Equip grumbled. "And we want to see the horses, so what's the problem?"

The sound of water shutting off, and then Jericho's head, his muscled shoulders and his upper torso appeared from out of the wash stall—sopping wet, and soap worked all through his hair and dripping down over his body. "Well Chuck, I'm standing here buck naked, but I don't give a fuck, so come on if you want to. You said I had twenty minutes, and Hell, be glad I'm taking a shower—I couldn't even stand myself." Head disappearing again, and the spray coming back on.

None of them moved.

Marco, smirking little shrug. He grabbed a couple of the towels they used to dry the horses, and walked down to the wash stall with them. Water going off again. Pitched the towels in to Jericho with pretty good force. Little exchange between them in Spanish, sounded like Marco was laughing at him from the tone of voice he used. Then Jericho getting the last word, a darkly amused, "Yeah, but it's not my problem, you know?" Said low enough that it was obviously not meant to be overheard—but the words distinct anyway. He came out then, water from his hair running in rivulets over his shoulders and arms, chestnut mane streaming thickly down his back…towel wrapped around his waist, sandals on his feet. Tossed a disgusted look at Frankel, avoiding eye contact with the other two. Ducked into the area they'd set up as a dressing room—a stall drape covering the door for privacy.

Five minutes later he was back out in the aisle way, dressed in battered black jeans and black tee shirt—the tee shirt already soaked both front and rear and clinging to him—and trying to blot the water from his hair in one of the towels. Bee-Bee and Frankel were standing in front of Monterrey's stall, and George a little further down with Tarrytown. But everyone seemed to be watching surreptitiously as he reached over into the grooming box, and extracted a mane and tail comb—not having a lot of success getting it through that snarled mess though.

Marco came to the rescue. Made him sit on the edge of a large tack trunk, then sprayed a de-tangler they used on the horse's tails through the mass of it, combed it out and braided it up in about two minutes flat.

Thanks from Jericho, and then he rose and went to join the rest of the group.

Bee-Bee was watching him approach and feeding bits of apple to Monterrey. Chuck had moved on and was looking in at George's horses now. She had a nice pair of casual khaki slacks and a bright turquoise top on—looked fresh, relaxed, and comfortable. Pretty too. "So Jericho," she asked him. "Do you do that often? I mean, how does it work?"

Man, she just had to rub in it—make him feel like a field hand. *"How does it work?"* he snapped back at her, incredulous. Disgusted too. "You put water on yourself and then rub some soap around and the dirt goes away...Christ, Bee-Bee."

Peal of delighted laughter from her. "No, I meant that mane and tail spray. I heard that's great for your hair and I saw you use it. I always wanted to try it."

He came up and leaned on the stall door beside her, one hand reaching in to lightly pat Monterrey. Nice comfortable pose, but somehow he just looked poised and dangerous. "Well, fucking try it then," he replied.

She turned her head away coolly, muttered, "You're a jerk."

George was meanwhile wandering back toward them, and Frankel following in his wake. He paused for a second in front of QL's stall. "Boy who would think this mare..." But he didn't get one more word of that sentence out. QL's mule ears went flat back on that big jughead, and she lunged for the front of her stall, teeth bared—like something out of the movie *Alien*. Squeal of anger to accompany the threatening movement, followed by a sharp kick of the wall with a hind foot. Luckily for George he was safely outside in the aisle way. Still QL had made her point. "My God!" he said, shocked.

"Damn it, George, can't you leave her alone?" Jericho snarled at him viciously. Crossed the distance to QL's door in less than a heartbeat. Opened it and went inside. She immediately came to him, thrust her head against his chest. Nickered, unhappy—intruder bothering her. He cradled her face against his body, spoke quietly to her. Marco there beside him seconds later...putting something in his hand, which he offered to QL. Happier now, she took it and munched on it.

"What's that you're giving her?" Frankel demanded. "You know you have to be extra careful—if she fails that drug screen..."

"For Christ's sakes, Chuck," Jericho said, with growing irritation. "It's an oatmeal cookie...that's not a controlled substance, is it? I mean, hell... Bee-Bee gave Monterrey an apple...bitch about that, why don't you?"

"Alright, alright," Frankel said testily. "So all of you are short-tempered, and we all know why. Just relax."

"Yeah, like you're not," Jericho muttered.

And George was protesting too. "Hey, what did I do?"

And from Bee-Bee, "Jericho's the one being the asshole."

"Oh right, Jericho's an asshole," he sniped back at her. "Yeah, you've all been sitting around relaxing, while I babysat your horses on the way here…and Dad over here…" He nodded derisively at Frankel. "…decides I'm not even allowed to go to my hotel room and clean up."

Santo, close by him, murmured suggestively, *"Si, Puño. Usted los dice"* Bumped forearms with him.

"Santo!" Bee-Bee scolded, her voice shocked. Couldn't believe he seemed to be siding with Jericho against her.

"Enough!" Frankel growled, absolutely furious. "Now I said it's enough, and it's enough!" He turned sharply, finger leveled hard at Jericho's chest—effective move even though there was still probably five feet separating them. "And not another Goddamn word from you, understand me? Just get in the M-F-ing car, and shut up. Then we're all going to go and have a really nice dinner."

Positively snarling under his breath with irritation, didn't trust himself to even look at Chuck—would have loved to give him a few choice words, that was for damn sure. Predictably, the bastard had cuddled up next to George and Bee-Bee—with Jericho blamed for all the squabbling. Couldn't even begin to imagine what kind of "really nice" dinner this was going to turn out to be.

"You know what?" Jericho murmured.

"Don't you dare even say it."

"What's the matter, Chuck? Think I'm gonna tell you to go get fucked? I wasn't," Jericho enticed him, stepping closer, just baiting him into a full-blown argument. "No, I just wanted to tell you that I'm out of here. I don't need this. And you can go have your *really nice* dinner with people you really…"

"No." Frankel, closing the rest of the distance and coming right up into his face. Had to look up at Jericho, and that ruined the effect somewhat, but still his voice was rife with authority. "I said it was enough." Jericho was the one he had to control here—the others…well, they'd fall in line, they never challenged him…not like this wiseass did. "Now, I know you had a long day, and you stayed with these horses…you didn't have to, and no one made you, but I was damn glad to have you there, and they all look great." Could see those powerful blue eyes on him, just watching him, lying in wait…waiting for the "but" that was sure to come after those positive words. Deliberately didn't give him one, though he easily could have started the next sentence that way. "I have a reason I want you to

come to dinner, and I don't intend to explain myself either. So you just *give in.*" Pointed at his chest again—nice imposing obstacle in that black tee shirt. "Just do what I asked you to and don't fight me on this, okay?" More of a demand than a request.

Thought about it for a moment, just breathing, expression guarded. Wasn't going to completely knuckle under. "Then get off my case."

"Fair."

Yeah, good answer on Chuck's part—hadn't left him with anything he could latch onto. Meaningful pause...then he just nodded. Gave Marco a look that said "I'll call you later," and got a return nod from him.

Frankel took complete advantage of the capitulation before it vanished. Threw an arm around his shoulders, starting moving with him toward the car—Bee-Bee and George trailing along behind the pair of them. Asked him a question to distract him. "So what does Brittany say about Force?"

It worked too, because he came along willing enough. Murmured unhappily, "Yeah, he's there and they're just lunging him this week in side reins. Fuck, I hate not having him with me."

Sympathetic. "I know you do. But he's a young horse, time off is good for him...good for his mind."

"Yeah, you're right on that."

"He'll be five next year...throw him in a few Prelim classes maybe."

Compelling look in return. "Oh yeah."

Bee-Bee whispered to George, "Don't you just hate the way Chuck fawns over him?"

And Strang, taking on the big brother role, "Come on, he's an okay guy, and he was there for you in Raleigh, remember?"

Pacified somewhat. "Well, you're right about that...he was."

"And he's younger than we are Bee-Bee."

Didn't want to be classified in George's age group. Really objecting. "Hey, I'm only thirty!"

Insistent. "He's still younger. And sure, he's been in the finals before, but never as a real contender. It's a lot of pressure. Chuck's just watching over him...and you be nice to him too, okay?"

Barely meaning it, "Okay."

Frankel had rented a big Lincoln Continental, and he'd successfully herded them all over to it—finally. Jericho grabbed the front passenger-side door handle, yanked it open and just stood to the side, holding it for Bee-Bee obviously—unconscious gesture on his part, just being courteous.

Testy little look from her, but she got inside and he closed it behind her. Smile of approval from Chuck as he went around to the other side to drive. Jericho and George got in the back.

The place he took them for dinner wasn't exactly the casual joint he'd made it out to be. Nice oceanfront steakhouse, and busy. Turned out they had reservations, and were meeting some other people there too…Frankel being deliberately vague on that score, although it turned out Brae was one of them.

As the hostess led them over to the table, Jericho could see him already there and waiting with Marc LaCroix and another man that he didn't recognize. Brae jumped up at the sight of his roommate. They hadn't seen each other for several days.

"Hey bra!" he said happily. Bumped fists with him in greeting…head on, then top to bottom, then bottom to top. "Here, sit next to me, okay? You look tired."

Started right in grousing, "Yeah, I am, and I…"

But he didn't get any further before Brae just started talking right on top of him. "Guess what happened to me," he whined.

Bored with this story already. "Yeah, I know, you got fired or whatever."

"No, it wasn't official last time I saw you," the ex-Barista objected. This had obviously been a traumatic event in his life, cause he sure seemed to want to dwell on it. Really distressed expression on his normally smiling face. "But now it is—official, I mean." Looked around at the others sitting down at the table. "Seriously, can you imagine this…" Jericho looking like he wanted to slit his own throat, so damn sick of this particular topic. "I was fired because the Manager didn't like my name," Brae continued pathetically. By now the story was pretty hopelessly twisted around too.

"Well, that's illegal, isn't it?" the unnamed guy at the table spoke up, then rolled right on past the subject and on to something of much more interest to him. He rose and extended a hand to Jericho. "Actually, I think I've met about everyone else here tonight except you. You've got to be Jericho Brandeis…I'm Chris Lomas…reporter for the LA Times, Sports Desk."

Jericho had been reaching his hand across the table, but stopped short, tossed an accusing look at Frankel, then went ahead and took Lomas' grip in his own. "Yeah, I'm Jericho," he said, not a particularly inviting voice.

"Hell yes, it's illegal," Brae was still complaining. "Spanish surname or some such non…"

Frankel cut him off—especially considering that Brae didn't have a Spanish surname, but that their guest at the table certainly did. "Let's save that for later, Brae," he said in no uncertain terms.

But Lomas had turned back to Brae. "Oh, you're Latino?" he was asking, more interested—although he couldn't actually remember thinking that when he and Brae were introduced. Couldn't recall his last name though.

Completely confusing answer. "Well, not really…I guess so."

The Chef D'Equip stepped in again, carefully redirecting the conversation back where he wanted it. "I'll tell you one thing, Chris…you're probably sitting here with this year's Show Jumping National Champion, and any one of these three…George, Bee-Bee or Jericho could do it. All of them are in the top five in the standings right now. George has two horses qualified, and Jericho has three."

"Three, wow…" Lomas had started taking notes.

"Brae…show Chris a picture of Antares," Frankel asked him—almost afraid to direct any remark toward him. But once he got him showing off his pictures that should be safe enough ground—end this whining about the Starbucks thing. That was, after all, why he'd invited him tonight. And to the reporter again, "Brae is our Team photographer. I asked him to put together a disk for you with pictures of all the horses George, Bee-Bee and Jericho are riding. Then you can use them in your article if you want to."

"Perfect."

The ex-Barista had scrolled through the images he had with him, and put a really breathtaking shot of the coal black stallion going over a huge obstacle in front of Chris.

"Wow, this is a great shot," Lomas said in appreciation. Looked over at Jericho. "This is you riding him?"

Brae jumping back in. "Don't ask him anything, ask me. Yeah, that's him on the horse."

The waitress had arrived and was taking drink orders.

"Jericho always has a beer," Bee-Bee piped up, but managing to make it sound like a bit of an insult. She was still apparently annoyed at him—maybe even more so with Chuck seeming to focus the reporter's attention on him.

Purred to her, "Well, if you want to knock back shots of Tequila, I'll be right there with you."

"Why? Do you think you can drink me under the table?"

Really good and sarcastic, low tone of voice. "Oh, hell no, bitch like you?"

Sharp evil eye from Chuck for both of them, cutting off Bee-Bee's spiteful return remark.

"Oh look at this horse," Chris was saying. He clearly knew something about show jumping, but not a great deal. Enough to do an occasional story, that was all. "Or *is* it a horse? Almost looks like a donkey, but with an especially large head."

Jericho's eyes narrowed coldly, "Just mother..." Kick under the table from the Chef D'Equip to quell the rest of that unfortunate statement. Murmured unhappily to himself, then said with some feeling, "No she's not traditionally beautiful, but she jumps like a gazelle. And that mare you're calling a donkey saved my life a few months ago—she's beautiful to me."

Human interest story, for sure. The reporter's ears perking up immediately. "Jericho, could you tell me about that, I'd love to hear it."

"Oh here, I have a picture of it," Brae said excitedly, digging around in his camera bag for his other disks.

"Yeah, Chuck, you tell the story," Jericho muttered. "Excuse me, I'm going out for a cigarette."

Lomas watching him leave, and looking a little stunned at the show of bad manners. But Frankel smoothed it over like the expert he was, "He seems brusque, I know...brash athletic guy and really powerful, but underneath that he loves these horses, and they love him too. Let me tell you what happened with that mare, cause it's so amazing..."

"You know, I really can't take this," Bee-Bee whispered to George, then got up with a soft, "I'll be right back." Frankel was so involved in telling his story now, he merely nodded and smiled at her.

Bee-Bee strolled outside, but with intent...saw Jericho standing up against the railing near the front door smoking. Walked over to him. "Want to try that Tequila now?" she dared him.

Barely looked over his shoulder as she approached him. "Sure, why not? I'm not the one who'll be throwing up tomorrow while Chuck is coaching," he mocked her right back.

Came up right beside him. "You think you're so cool, Jericho."

"Do I now?"

"Yes, you do." Defiant.

"Funny," he murmured. "I was thinking just the opposite."

Stalemate.

He rounded on her. "Why did you come out here, Bee-Bee? To pick a fight with me? Hell, I haven't bothered you. I mean, so far tonight, you've called me a jerk...an asshole, and God only knows what else."

"Well, you called me a bitch."

"Yeah, but that was after. You started it."

No answer from her for a few long moments. Then she giggled. "We sound like three year olds...I hope you know that."

There was a deep rumble in his throat that might have been the start of a laugh. "What does that make my roommate Brae then?"

"Oh my God," she blurted out. "He's a total idiot. I mean, be thankful you were with the horses...I've had to listen to that garbage about his job at Starbucks all afternoon."

Yeah, he was definitely laughing now...then harder. Then just tossed his head back and roared. Tears in his eyes, choking on his cigarette smoke. And Bee-Bee joining in, his uninhibited humor contagious. The two of them howling like fools for a minute there. He put a hand on her shoulder, a spontaneous gesture, and she came into his arms, hands sliding back and around his waist. Pulled her close, both of them still rocking with laughter.

"What are you two cackling about?" It was George Strang asking. He'd come outside to find them, at Frankel's request. Looked more than a little surprised at the way they seemed to be embracing. And they didn't act like they were in a hurry to pull apart either...Jericho just holding her comfortably up against himself.

"George, who's this?" Bee-Bee asked, drew herself up tall, then did a pretty good imitation of Brae's voice. "Oh, you won't believe it...I lost my fabulous job as a *counter clerk* at Starbucks three days before I planned on quitting anyway. Don't you feel sorry for me? Should I sue?"

Jericho and Bee-Bee cracked up all over again. And George burst out in a loud guffaw too.

"Hey, Chuck says get your asses back inside." It was Brae himself talking, still had that whiny tone of voice. "And what's everybody howling about?"

The three of them looked at each other and then just dissolved with laughter...tension release in equal measure with hilarity.

———————

The next morning an article appeared in the L.A. Times, covering the upcoming selection trials for the U.S. Show Jumping Team. Stating that it was also the National finals, and that this year's National Champion would be named as a part of it—whoever won the event.

Picture of Frankel with everyone at the table the night before, except Jericho who'd once again found a way to escape. But Lomas had also used the picture of QL jumping, and done a paragraph or two about his accident, the relationship between Jericho and QL and how she'd very possibly saved his life…and the way he'd fought back from all of that to qualify three horses, and now had a very good shot at taking the National title for himself.

Man, just hated the publicity.

Frankel really pleased though—bound to increase donations, he said.

Chapter Twenty-Six

Practice sessions with the horses the day following the article in the L.A. Times—Bee-Bee's go with Monterrey would be later, but she was there early anyway, sitting on the fence line watching. Marc LaCroix and Tim Rawlings had just finished up with their horses, and Jericho and George would be next. Gorgeous day out, and she was really enjoying it…light breeze ruffling her ponytail, dressed in a lemon yellow polo shirt and expensive buff breeches…still didn't have her boots on, just sandals on her feet.

"Uhm…excuse me." Quiet voice coming from beside her—tentative.

She looked around and saw a woman standing there…mid to later forties, tall but slim, features weathered from the sun—handsome rather than pretty. Long brown hair, straight and streaked with gray, but thick and lustrous. She was wearing jeans, a sleeveless blouse and sunglasses.

Bee-Bee smiled at her. "Yes?"

"These are the riders that were mentioned in the paper?" the woman asked, still sounding fairly unsure of herself. Didn't seem like she knew much about it.

Happy nod from Bee-Bee. The public wasn't really supposed to be here in the practice area, but the show didn't officially start for another two days, so she couldn't see what harm there was.

"Hey Mom, there you are." A young girl, pre-teen or early teen came up to stand beside her, sipping on a can of coke. Looked a lot like her mother, actually—sharp features on her, gorgeous hair, slender but tall for her age—taller than Bee-Bee already. Same uniform—jeans, top, sandals, sunglasses, and carrying a Barbie purse. She looked over at Bee-Bee and then smiled. "Hey, I saw your picture in the paper didn't I? Mom, she was one of them, right?" Friendly, out-going.

"I think so," the woman said, friendly too, but quite a bit more reserved—like she realized she really shouldn't be there, even if her daughter didn't.

"Sure, I'm Bee-Bee Oxmoor. Nice to meet you." She pointed to Frankel. "And there's the coach for the U.S. Team, Chuck Frankel. His picture was in the paper too." She waved at Chuck, who looked confused, but waved back.

"I'm Meagan Rhys. But no "nutmeg" jokes, okay?" the daughter told her with a grin, holding out a hand importantly. Bee-Bee laughed and took it. Nice firm grip on her for a young girl, confident. "And this is my Mom, Jessica."

Jessica Rhys smiled tolerantly, proud of her child though. She muttered, "Nice to meet you too." Patted her daughter's arm, as if to say, "Now, don't bother this nice woman too much."

But Bee-Bee seemed to be enjoying it. Little PR for the Team.

"So do you like horses?" she asked Meagan, assuming that was probably why the pair was here.

She shrugged. "Sort of." Not too enthusiastic. "I mean, they're really big—I'm kind of scared of them," she admitted, and wrinkled her nose up a little. "I never thought they were all that nice, you know? We used to live by where they had some of those carriage horses, and most of them would bite you. You had to be careful. The drivers were always mean to us kids too. But then my Mom read me that story in the paper about the guy whose horse saved him and all that. That was cool."

"Oh, that's Jericho," Bee-Bee told her.

Typical child's honesty. "That's a weird name."

"Honey, don't say that," Jessica Rhys chided.

Bee-Bee made it easy though. "Well, you're right, it is a different name. But I like it, don't you?"

"It's okay I guess."

Marco had arrived at the side of the practice ring, and was leading Antares. Magnificent black stallion, snorting and shaking his head at the unfamiliar surroundings.

"Wow," Meagan said.

Bee-Bee had jumped down to open the gate for him, though Marco could easily have gotten it himself. He nodded to her and said, "Thanks." Walked in, leading Antares a little bit further out into the ring.

"See," Meagan was continuing. "That horse is awesome looking, but he's gigantic. I'd be terrified to get near him."

"Actually, that's one of Jericho's horses," Bee-Bee was explaining. Jessica had looked over with more interest, and was listening now too. "He should be here any minute. Maybe I'll ask him to bring Antares over so you can see him—see what a good boy he is. Would you like that?"

"I don't know." Meagan had moved unconsciously closer to her mother, who put an arm around her, gave her shoulders a squeeze.

"We don't want to bother you...or him," she said.

"Honestly, it's no trouble at all." Bee-Bee—the little goodwill ambassador, and proud of herself. She sat up straighter and looked over her shoulder, then smiled and pointed. "Oh, look...here he is right now."

A golf cart had pulled up next to the fence line a little ways down from them, carrying a bucket filled with supplies...and Jericho. He flipped off the key and jumped out—tall and hard to miss. In keeping with the regulations at this show, he was dressed in breeches rather than jeans—nice black pair, relatively new looking—and white polo with his farm's logo embroidered above the left front pocket. His back was to them at the moment, though—broad and imposing. Thick braid swinging between his shoulder blades.

"Woah, hottie alert," Meagan muttered, eyes wide.

Her mother's hand had gripped the side of the fence tightly, and she'd leaned forward, but scolded softly, "Meagan."

"Well, he is!"

Grabbed his riding crop and helmet from out of the golf cart. Looked around the arena keenly, sighting Marco and the big black. Signaled him. Then started walking toward the entrance gate where Bee-Bee and the mother-daughter pair were standing.

"Jericho," she beckoned to him.

He detoured a little to approach her, nice swagger on him this morning, feeling cocky maybe. Looking alive, healthy, and so very athletic. Came over and leaned comfortably up against the fence from the inside, smiling down at her. Just murmured, "Hi."

And from her back, "Hi. What's up with you, big guy?"

Smirk from him. "Oh, so I'm not an asshole this morning?" He liked teasing her...when she was in a decent mood, anyway.

"Well, you weren't until just now."

Bark of laughter from him. "So I got about thirty seconds in first."

"True, but at least it's an improvement." Merriment in her eyes.

Tossed a mock punch at her shoulder.

Frankel, yelling at full voice from the center of the arena. "Jericho, let's get going! I don't have all day."

Disgusted murmur from him. "Want to talk about assholes…"

Meagan was watching him, enraptured.

Bee-Bee called back to Frankel, "One second, okay Chuck?" He was grumbling out there, but seemed to be allowing it. Satisfied, Bee-Bee turned back to Jericho. "Jericho, I just wanted you to meet my friends here, the Rhyses…Jessica and her daughter Meagan—but no "nutmeg" jokes, okay?" she added, repeating Meagan's little phrase. Made it sound like she knew them pretty well, though that hadn't really been her intention.

Looked charmingly awkward then, embarrassed in front of people he didn't know maybe. Expressive deep blue stare. Murmured, "Hello, nice to meet you."

Meagan stepping toward him. "Hi." Her mother's hand still holding her back a little.

"Jericho, could you just show Antares to Meagan for a second?" Bee-Bee asked him. "I know you have to ride, but just to let her see him?"

"Sure, I'll get him." He seemed grateful for the opportunity to step away actually, but willing enough. Took a few strides in the direction of the stallion, but then just lifted his face and bellowed, "Marco!" Motioned him over. Talked with him for a second when he drew near, and then Marco handed him something that he slid into his shirt pocket. He took the reins from him then, petted the black's neck, murmured to him. Friendly nose butt from the horse, little gesture of welcome.

Jericho led Antares over to the fence close to Meagan. Curious, the big stallion lowered his head and stretched his neck out toward her. Sniffed softly, then blew his breath out in a big snort.

"Oh!" Meagan jumped back, startled.

Antares ditto, tossing his finely sculptured face up high in the air, taking a little scrambling hop with all four feet.

Deep yet soft, seductive voice. "Whoa, now." Jericho drew his hand down the stallion's neck all the way from poll to the point of his shoulder. Insecure little nicker. "Easy, boy." Encouraged him to come forward. Antares pawed once, uncertain, then just gave in and walked willingly toward the fence again. "Good boy." Jericho slipped a sugar cube from his pocket into the horse's mouth. Seemed happy with that, crunching on it then looking for more.

"Alright, give me your hand," he said to Meagan.

"Oh, no, I couldn't."

"Come on." Smirk from him—warm though, and accompanied by that powerful yet open stare. "Come on...*Nutmeg.*" She sighed in mock exasperation, one hand on her hip, admonishing him, and he chuckled, pleased with himself. "Give me your hand. Flat, like this." He showed her.

Cautiously, she put it out.

He placed a second sugar cube in the center of her palm, and she looked really dubious about that, but before she could change her mind, he simply captured her hand with his own underneath it. "Keep your hand flat," he repeated. Brought it right over to the stallion's mouth.

Wide-eyed, Antares brushed her palm with his feather soft muzzle, making her giggle, but Jericho held her hand in place, and in just a second the sugar cube vanished.

"Wow," Meagan said, awe in her voice. "He feels like velvet."

Smiled at her.

From the middle of the arena Frankel's voice rang out, just stinging with criticism. "Jericho!" he screamed at his withering best. "How about getting over here and taking this line of fences!"

Tossed a scornful look over his shoulder and snapped back at him just as loudly, "How about kissing my ass, Chuck?" Muttered irritably, turned around again, and looked at Meagan's mother, and murmured, "Sorry."

Little reprimanding smile from her, but understanding—appreciative for the way he'd been with her daughter.

He slapped on his helmet, then vaulted onto the horse in one lithe movement—cat-clean and graceful. Gathered up the reins and spun his mount on a dime, his feet finding the stirrups like they'd been born there. Took off at an elegant and beautifully round canter. Didn't even bother to circle, just sat in, asked for speed and got it, then aimed for and positively flew through a line of three big obstacles, the horse like a magnificent black stag—bold, beautiful, soaring. Right on mark.

"Alright, fine," Frankel was still screaming. "But come around again. Come on! I want more! *Show* me something here, Jericho!"

"Jericho's nice, isn't he?" Bee-Bee was saying—well, she wasn't always so sure of that herself, but it wasn't necessary to go into that with these people. "He's a great rider too. Everyone thinks he'll make the Team."

Meagan was still looking at her palm where the sugar cube had been—little expression of wonder. She reached up then, and lifted her sunglasses for a second to wipe a few beads of sweat from her face. "Thanks for being so nice to us," she said to Bee-Bee, her eyes on her as she was speaking, friendly and innocent…and a deep blue shade that Bee-Bee immediately recognized.

For an instant, she couldn't answer. Her lips had parted slightly in surprise.

"What's the matter?" Meagan asked.

"Wow, your eyes are so blue," she managed to get out.

Giggle in return. "Yeah, everyone says that…they're just like my Mom's." Shrugged like it was nothing. "I don't know if you noticed," she went on blithely, her face turning toward Jericho and Antares, "but his were too."

"Time to go," Jessica Rhys spoke up, taking her daughter's hand and holding it. "I can't thank you enough for how great you've been," she told Bee-Bee. Seemed apprehensive again, almost like she'd been in the beginning, and already starting to move away.

Bee-Bee took a step toward her. "Please come back again." Almost pleading with her. Couldn't help herself. She even said it again. "Please. You can't imagine…you can't begin to imagine how much it would…"

But Jessica had already turned, and was walking away.

"Mom, that's rude. She was still talking," Meagan was protesting as they left.

Jessica looked around over her shoulder one last time. Found Bee-Bee's gaze and held it for a second, shook her head in the negative, her face pleading as well. Then took one long last look at the black stallion and his rider, eating up that practice course like it was absolutely nothing for them.

———

There was a small bar in the hotel—a larger one attached to the restaurant too, but this one was quieter and Jericho was sitting alone…drinking a beer, contemplative. Also hiding from Brae to some extent. He'd finished up his rides, then come back to the hotel to shower up and relax for a few hours—had changed back into his normal jeans and tee shirt. Was chatting off and on with the bartender—all nonsense relating to the night before's baseball game.

Good practice sessions with all three horses today—predictably, Lion had been the most on edge—every time he came into a new horseshow venue, his insecurities and bad memories would kick in. He needed lots of reassurance from Jericho, as well as an equal measure of authority and insistence to get him going. Had fought hard today for the first half of the session, settling in a bit after that, but not totally. Hopefully, by the start of the show he'd be ready.

As he was sitting there, his cell phone rang. He almost turned it off without looking at it, assuming it would be Brae, but pulled it out, flipped it open and checked the caller ID.

Darien. Man, that surprised him.

"Jericho," he answered it.

"Hi, it's me," she said.

Disgusting, the way her voice made the joy shoot right through him. Tried to kill it, but wasn't really successful. No matter what, he was happy to hear from her. "Hi, you," he replied—neutral sounding but not unfriendly. "Where are you?"

Little sexy laugh. "About a mile from you. Bob got us a room at the Four Seasons, well a suite actually. It's nice. He's not coming out until tomorrow...want to come over? Say hello in person?"

Thought about it for a few seconds. Hell yes, he wanted to...and fuck no, he sure didn't...not the way she'd described the circumstances...Marx coming out tomorrow, nothing changed between them. On the other side of the competition, yeah then for sure, regardless of circumstances, but he didn't need his head fucked with right now. "I don't think that's smart," he said, real regret in his voice, longing also apparent.

She sure wasn't giving up that easily. "Alright, then I'll come where you are...where are you?"

Should stick to his guns, and knew it. "Little sports bar in the hotel," he told her anyway. Then tossed in, "Nothing you'd like...just me and the bartender and some baseball talk."

Teasing voice. "Oh, I know a lot about baseball...uhm, home runs, bases loaded, tenth inning...how am I doing?"

"Lousy," he chuckled.

"May I just come over and listen then?" she asked him, soft voice, leaving it up to him, but enticing. "I promise to leave my mitt at home."

Meaningful tone of voice. "I'll be here a while." God, he really missed her, and every bit of that came back through the phone line to her.

"Alright...it'll take me a half hour to get there, probably." Long pause then. Whispered, "I love you, Jericho."

He just closed his eyes for an instant, savored the sound of it. Didn't answer her though...just disconnected. And that could easily have been interpreted several ways...but he knew she'd read his feelings flawlessly. There was just nothing to say after that simple phrase...it was perfect and complete all by itself. Anything more would simply take away from it.

It was more like forty minutes before she actually pushed the door open and came into the bar...soft gauzy flowing dress, knee length with spaghetti straps—it just clung to her as she walked, outlining her slim figure to a tee. Black and white print, but not loud—so pretty with her short sassy blonde hair and lips glossed bright pink, like candy. She paused...saw him...smiled.

Nothing coming back from him. He planned to let her make all the moves—if in fact, there were any moves to be made. Didn't get up when she came in the room, drank from his beer instead—eyes hard on her though.

And she wasn't upset with his lack of greeting, didn't seem to have any expectations. Just smiled at him, no judgment. She walked around and took a seat at the bar, leaving a pretty good distance between her barstool and the table where he was sitting—two empty beer bottles pushed to the side of him, and a full one in his hand.

But for all their lack of words, their expressions were saying pages full.

"Want anything?" the bartender asked her.

Her eyes flitting to him, almost surprised that he was there. "Just an iced tea."

He filled a glass with big cubes, and then poured tea over them from a pitcher behind the bar. Set it in front of her.

Smiled at him. "Thanks." She squeezed the lemon wedge on the side of her glass into the tea, then slipped it between those gorgeous lips and sucked on it.

Murmured softly but almost fiercely to himself—desire for her flaring inside. Hot...so very hot. Rose with the deadly grace of a stalking great cat and moved to the end of the bar closest to his table, beer forgotten on the table behind him. Even there, at least five feet separated them. She'd swiveled her chair around to face him, her left side pressed against the bar now, and his right the same. Deep blue stare watching her, powerful hunger there...exciting, dangerous.

The bartender moving discreetly to the far end of the bar. So much for baseball talk.

"It's been over two weeks since Raleigh," she told him. "You haven't called me." Not a reprimand at all, just sad. Missing him.

Countered her. "You don't pick up when I call. And I don't leave messages anymore…I never know who's listening to them."

"I know." She'd extended her left arm along the bar's polished surface toward him, just reaching for him, an invitation.

And he'd laid his right hand on the bar too, not reaching for her—at least not yet—but there, mirroring her move but to a lesser degree. "See…you're over there in your suite at the Four Seasons…and I'm here."

Darien tilted her head in a gentle inquiry. "So?"

His hand sliding forward, reaching but not stepping closer. "So, it explains everything that's going on between us, doesn't it?" he said, intent tone. Accusation too. "You're there, in a luxury room…with him. And I'm here…okay place but nothing special. And Darien…that's where you'll spend your time…most of your time. Spa treatment in the morning maybe. Limo to take you to the show. Maybe steal over here once or twice to fuck me."

"It's not like that."

"Sure it is." He came one pace nearer to her—still about eight inches separating their hands. Repeated it powerfully, *"Sure it is."*

Again the denial. "No."

"Your husband…he's what I'll never be," Jericho continued, almost angrily. "He offers you what I'll never offer, never can offer. Buy you anything…cars, clothes, houses…anything. Like that hotel suite. Only the best." Another step closer, their fingertips just brushing now. "Me…hell, I work like a dog, but I've got no complaints on that score, because I love what I do. And things are happening for me…I'll be someone in this industry. No, I'll never have your husband's money, but I have a good life. And I have a future."

Soft look from her—proud of him, happy for him. "I believe that, Jericho. I watch you ride, and you're…so talented, and only just coming into your own. You have so much in front of you."

Closer. Slipping her palm into his palm. "Share it with me," he invited her. "Yeah, maybe you'll wear jeans instead of Gucci and Armani…and maybe you'll do your own laundry. Fuck, maybe we'll go to McDonald's sometimes. But there wouldn't be anything in my life that you wouldn't part of. And Darien, I love you." Her eyes tender on him. Closer still, bringing her hand up off the bar. "Does he cherish you the way I do...the way I will? Is he even faithful to you?"

She chided him softly, "Jericho, you have Ailynn."

Powerful response. *"No."* Heartfelt and real. "Never, since I started seeing you. Never once. Not with Ailynn, and not with anyone else."

Quiet joy in her eyes. She believed him...hadn't known it before though. Her lips parted with a kind of open innocence. "Really?"

"Really." Moved in even closer to her, right in front of her, placing her hand over his heart and covering it with his own, capturing it there. "I'd give you everything I have. You'd be my world...you are now. I'd love you, care for you, protect you." His other hand was stroking up her arm, playing with the jagged ends of her chic haircut, brushing across her cheek, her mouth. "Darien, you say you love me...make a choice to be with me. I want to marry you...no more backdoor romance. I want to tell people I love you, and I want to show you—I want to show you how much."

She put her free arm around his waist, laid her head against his body, held him with a kind of desperation. No response though.

"I'm asking you to marry me," he said again, making it as clear as he could.

Still silence.

Just breathed out. Waited for long moments. Closed his eyes then, laid his cheek against her head.

Knew her answer, even though she'd said nothing. That was her answer...nothing.

Stepped back half a pace, brought her fingers to his lips and kissed them. Released her hand, backed away a few more steps. "Alright," he murmured, the hurt inside him like a silent shadow in his voice. "Alright."

"Please understand," she pleaded with him. "Please..."

She'd just ripped his heart out, but there was strength in him, fortitude. And he accepted it. "I do understand."

Fear in her eyes. She understood too...he was ending it—ending it right there and right now. Tears coming to her eyes. "Please, spend the night with me. Just tonight. Jericho..." If he'd do that much, he'd give in again too and she knew that.

Soft reproachful question from him, "What do they call a male mistress? Is there a word for it?"

Darien gasped so delicately it was hard to hear her. Shock at his query had registered on her face though. Was that actually the way he felt? She tried to deny it, to reassure him. "Oh Jericho, I'd never, ever treat you like that."

Just the faintest trace of ridicule entering his voice—maybe for himself, maybe for both of them. "Think not?" He looked away then, felt empty inside—couldn't believe that he was doing this—that he was actually going to say what he was about to say to her next. "Don't call me again, Darien." He hadn't even qualified it—hadn't even said, "Unless you change your mind." She wasn't going to. Raised that deep blue stare to her—the depth of emotion there shattering. "It doesn't mean that I don't love you...just that I won't dishonor what I feel that way."

Didn't wait for her answer, just turned and walked away.

And she let him go.

They had all agreed to meet in the lobby for dinner. George showed up first, then Frankel, and then finally Bee-Bee. Brae—fashionably late as usual. "Hi, everybody," he said as he got off the elevator, but at his whiny tone of voice, everyone quickly found something else to do, leaving him standing there looking around himself with no one to moan to. "Hey what's everybody doing?" he said pitifully. "Chuck?"

"Be with you in a minute." The Chef D'Equip seemed to be looking through a restaurant guide at the Concierge's desk with George, although they already had reservations. "Why don't you give Jericho a call, see what's keeping him?"

"Okay," he said unhappily. Bee-Bee was the closest one to him. She was pretending to be looking at some clothes in the window of a shop in the lobby. He sauntered closer. Confided in her as he pulled out his cell phone, "Normally, I'd be clocking in at Starbucks around now."

She hurried inside.

Miserable look on his face as he dialed.

No answer.

"He's not picking up, Chuck," the ex-Barista called out.

"That's funny," Frankel said. He tried using the house phone to call Jericho's room—no response that way either. Concern on his face now. Got his own cell phone out and dialed Marco instead. When he came on the line, he asked him, "Is Jericho there by any chance, Marco?"

"Haven't seen him, Chuck."

They wasted thirty minutes trying to locate him, but to no avail...finally giving up, and leaving for the restaurant without him. Frankel kept trying though, leaving multiple messages for him on his cell phone, his voicemail at the hotel, and at the showgrounds.

He'd driven to the shore, found a deserted stretch of beach—or nearly so—enough so that he felt alone anyway. Just sat there, smoking...watched the sun go down and the moon come up, the sky grow dark, the stars come out. Listened to the gulls' cries—nice desolate sound to suit his mood.

No thoughts at all for a long time, just an empty husk. One word starting to form in his mind.

Alone.

Started out his life that way. Still true.

Didn't understand why...wanted to believe there was more worth to him than that...couldn't prove it to himself though.

Stayed there for hours—didn't really know how long. But finally around eleven o'clock that night he called Frankel, feeling guilty, knowing he'd be worried.

"Jericho, where the *hell* are you?" Frankel demanded, really sounding upset...angry too. "I've left messages for you everywhere, and I was damn near ready to call the police."

Short answer. Short and to the point. "I asked Darien to marry me, Chuck." Derisive pause. "She said no." Brutal tone of voice then. "I'll see you in the morning. Don't wait up for me."

Hung up. Turned his cell phone off.

It was well after midnight when Jericho returned to his room—tired, and soul weary too. Unlocked the door, stepped inside, flipped the light switch on, turned around...

And there she was, lying asleep on his bed.

Nutmeg.

Recognized her immediately. *What the fuck?* The sudden light was rousing her now.

He went to her, dropped to one knee beside her. Put a hand on her shoulder, shook her lightly. "What are you doing here?" he asked her, though she probably wasn't awake enough to answer him yet. It even ran through his mind that he should call Bee-Bee or Chuck or someone else—anyone else—that being here alone with a minor, and a female minor at that, might not be the best idea in the world. She was already rubbing her eyes though—deep blue eyes. Didn't register as anything special with him though. "Nutmeg, why are you here?" he asked her again.

She was just staring at him—so very intently. Reached up to touch his face, but he backed away from the touch, still good and nervous about having her there.

"Nutmeg…" he started sternly one more time, using a tone of voice that was intended to sound like an adult reprimanding a child.

She just plain interrupted him. "Are you my brother?" she asked him flatly. Defiant too.

Now that positively stunned him. *"What?"* Then with some force, "No." Stood up straight, backed up a step. "I don't know what you're doing here, but you need to call your mother right away, and I'm going to call the…"

Meagan interrupted him with another potent question. *"Are you sure?"*

Moved well away from her now, took out his cell phone. Cold tone from him. "Yes, I'm more than just sure—I'm positive. I don't have a family, alright?"

"Your family is dead, or you just don't know who they are?" she insisted, sitting up now, brushing down her top, and flipping her hair to smooth it out. He didn't seem to be responding, or maybe it just wasn't fast enough to suit her. *"Which one?"* Dead, or you don't know?"

Dialed his cell phone. Then said powerfully into it, "Chuck, get over to my room and now." Pause. "Just do it, damn it. I'll explain when you get here." Was staying away from her, but she was up on her feet now too, and not accepting his lack of cooperation.

"Dead, or you just don't know?" she reiterated, her voice easily as forceful as his. When he refused to answer again, she cried out softly in exasperation. "Look in the mirror, damn it." She reached out and grabbed his arm.

He pulled away, angrily. "Stop it." Went over and threw open the door, looking outside for Chuck. Saw him coming and murmured to himself, "Thank God."

"Look…will you just *look.*"

"No, I'm not going to look."

Frankel was walking into the room now, and Jericho just gestured to Meagan. "Hell, Chuck…she was waiting here when I got back. I don't even know how she got in here."

Frankel staring at her transfixed, then at Jericho. "Who is she?" he asked cautiously.

"Some friend of Bee-Bee's," Jericho told him. Still really furious tone of voice. "I'm trying to get her to call her mother, but hell, Chuck…"

"I don't even know Bee-Bee," Meagan was insisting, hands on her hips.

"Sure she does. Bee-Bee introduced…"

"I just met her today, okay?" she said adamantly, stomping her foot, talking right over him when he contradicted her. "My mother read that article in the paper about you and she wanted to go to the horse show and see you. We met Bee-Bee there just before you came over." Went on desperately now, suddenly looking so frustrated that she might actually start crying any minute now. "Then tonight I heard her talking on the phone to her best friend, and she was talking about you."

Jericho, listening despite himself, shaking his head emphatically in the negative, but listening anyway.

"She said…'I saw Jericho today.' She was describing you. Then she said…'I can't believe I finally saw him after all these years.' She sounded so sad, but proud too." Meagan came over closer to him, staring at him like she'd bore holes right through him. "Why would she say that? *After all these years?* Then I started thinking about how you have the same color eyes that Mom and I do, and I…" A tear on her face now, but she brushed it viciously away, not wanting to cry in front of him. Looked at Frankel then. Said in an accusing voice. "He *is* my brother, isn't he?"

"I don't know," the Chef D'Equip said, looking from Meagan to Jericho to Meagan to Jericho again.

"Christ's sakes, Chuck," Jericho snapped. "Don't encourage her."

"Look in the mirror!" Meagan all but yelled at him. "Can't you even do that much? What are you? *Chicken?*"

He didn't need this…couldn't take it either. Had to make it stop. "Alright, I'll do this much," Jericho growled at her. "You call your mother and tell her where you are—and you tell her we're bringing you home *right now*. You do that first, and then I'll stand in front of the mirror with you. Deal?"

Thought about it for a second. Negotiated. "You stand in front of the mirror with me, then I'll call."

"No fucking way."

Frankel nodding, agreeing with him.

"Alright," she snapped, holding her hand out. Lifted one clean brow expectantly, said with some disgust, "Cell phone?"

She made the call, and from the side of the conversation they could hear it was obvious that her mother had been really worried, and was more than a little bit upset with her. Meagan started crying, and Frankel took the phone and stepped out into the hall with it. He had some questions he wanted answers to—questions he didn't want Meagan, and especially Jericho to hear him asking.

"Okay, I called her. Now it's your turn," Meagan said to Jericho then, sniffling a little, but brushing the tears from her face—and absolutely demanding. Strength in this little girl, that was for sure.

Really, really didn't want to do this. He hesitated…almost looked like he wasn't going to do it, but then just muttered viciously under his breath and stepped over to the dresser and the mirror above it. Meagan came right over next to him. They both looked.

Resemblance for sure. How strong…up to interpretation.

"Let your hair down," she pleaded. "Come on…please. Don't you want to know?"

"No, I don't," he sneered, but yanked at the band that held his braid in place just the same. Dragged his fingers through his hair till it hung loose around his shoulders.

Resemblance a lot more noticeable now. Hair color and type, height and general build, eyes and eye color…those sharp arresting features of his—softer and more feminine on her, but so similar.

"Am I wrong?" she said, looking up at him with certainty on her face.

Jericho had turned away from the mirror, emotional to the point where he couldn't even speak. A sister? Full or half, he had no idea—*if it was true at all.* Could he *actually have a sister?*

And a mother…a mother who'd deserted him twenty-seven years ago. A mother who'd come to see him ride today…and left again without acknowledging him. Left him, deserted him—both then and now.

Oh no, she hadn't discarded this daughter…just him.

"It doesn't matter either way," he said coldly—totally forbidding. And thankfully Frankel had stepped back into the room. "Take her out of here, Chuck." Violent look on his face, barely leashed fury. That fist of his tightening and coming up to his side, threatening…threatening someone, maybe anyone. "Just fuck me, Chuck…just…"

"Alright," Frankel jumped in, coming to him, laying a hand on him, wanting to calm him down. And for once, the gesture was accepted—didn't even flinch, needed the contact from him even. Jericho had turned that deep blue stare on him—a cry for help—panic in him, finding outlet in brutal anger. "Alright Jericho," Frankel repeated. "Just don't go out again. Stay here, wait for me…I'm coming back."

"No, don't."

"Jericho…"

"Don't."

Poignant moment, the two of them staring at each other. Frankel wrapping his hand around that bicep, the muscle clenched now—so tight. "You'll stay here, you'll be alright?"

Nodded.

"Alright," he said to Jericho again. "I don't like leaving you alone, but Lord knows you've had enough today. If you want to be alone, I'll let you. But you call me if you need to talk…I don't care how late it is, okay?"

Nodded again.

The Chef D'Equip turned and held his hand out to Meagan. "Let's go."

"But…"

Sterner. "Meagan, let's go right now, and no "buts" about it."

She looked equally as distressed as Jericho. Stared at him for another long moment, then cried out in frustration and stomped out of the room, with a final, "I hate you."

The show had started, but it was all a blur to Jericho. He was just going through the motions—convincingly, but numb. Frankel was shielding him from everything—contact with the other riders, the media, his patrons…everyone. It wasn't that hard to do…after all, he was a contender for the top honor this year, and everyone seemed to understand that he needed to be left alone, at least for now.

The jog was no problem at all. And the following day, Jericho had clear rounds with all three horses. Getting harder to keep the press away from him—almost unprecedented what he'd done thus far…three horses in the top twenty…all placed in the top ten…Antares sitting in first place.

QL had been seventh after the first round, and Lion sixth.

And now the second round had started. Beautiful day—breezy, crisp and clear.

He watched the first few goes from the fence, staying well away from the Team box and all the patrons…including Darien and her husband. Hadn't seen or heard from her since that last miserable conversation. That was good—but it hurt too. Turned away to go and warm-up QL…and Lion would go immediately after her. Antares, being in first place, would be the last to go today.

Nice course for the second day of jumping. One double, one triple—some pretty strange looking obstacles that were sure to throw some of the horses off. All three of his animals were bold spirits though, wasn't too worried about that. Some tight turns too. He liked that even better. Antares could turn on a hair, and Lion pretty much the same thing. As for QL, she'd power her way through anything.

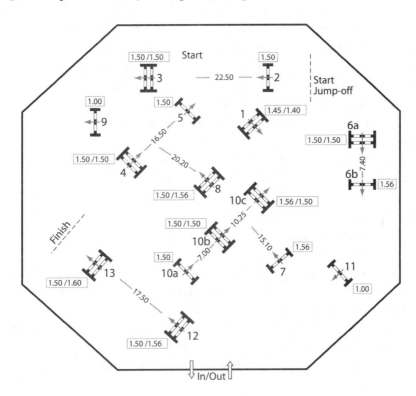

Good warm-up with QL, and she was ready to go for him—eager. He cantered her into the arena…lots of applause and audience noise. Everyone had read that article in the paper, and QL was so recognizable with those ears and that head of hers. The crowd noise only seemed to make her high, and wanting to go even more. Gave his salute, brought her through the starting timers, and aimed her at that first big Oxer. Big snort and those mule ears pitched keenly forward, and man she just started jumping for him, giving him everything she had in the huge heart of hers.

Look out…alpha mare on course!

Beautiful tight turn between fence number one and fence two, right on spot and over it cleanly. And so it continued, nothing they'd thrown at her fazing her a bit. Just eating the course up, one fence at a time. Jericho was so with her—if any of his horses was more special to him than the others, it was QL and when she performed like this there was nothing else to compare it with. They came out of the big triple at fence number ten, still clear and flying at a good clip that was sure to give her an excellent time. They came around, navigating between the elements of the double at six to head into the wall at eleven, the wind gusting. Beautiful jump there too and with an easy margin over it…yet Jericho heard the crowd groan with dismay. Tossed a look over his shoulder, but it was still standing, and he looked back around, concentrating now on finishing the last two fences. Both of them easy for her…man, she'd just taken this course like a veteran, not like a mare with less than a year's worth of jumping under her belt. Through the final timers, and he was so fucking proud of her.

Looked up at the board and saw her scores coming up. Her time had really been excellent. Eighty-four seconds was the allowed time, but she'd finished the course in seventy-nine. But they were showing four faults, and she hadn't had a rail down, had she?

He exited the ring, saw Chuck waiting right there for him.

"What the hell happened?" he demanded. "What's that four faults for?"

Frankel shaking his head and swearing. "The rail at nine went down. Not when you went over it…not till after you passed through the triple. Damn it, I think the wind brought it down."

"She never touched it," Jericho growled, springing off to make the switch for Lion. "Not even a rub."

"I believe you…I thought that too, but they're counting it against you."

Man, just so much pressure over the last few days, and he felt ready to come unglued.

"Fuck!" he snapped sharply. "I want a ruling." His voice, a deep threatening demand. Standing there like he wasn't going to move until he got one either.

"Not now," Frankel insisted. "We'll talk about it after you ride Lion." Jericho wasn't moving though. Got really aggressive with him. "Get on him. Now. *Do it!*"

"Yeah, fuck you, alright? He grabbed the reins on the big gray stallion, and vaulted onto him, the tension and anger in him tangible.

And no doubt about it...Chasseur de Lion felt it too.

Head straight up in the air, and a huge snort and then a scream from him. Jericho clamped his legs on pushing him forcefully forward and through the entrance gate to the jumping field. Brought his crop down with force on the animal's hindquarters—and Lion scrabbling and leaping ahead in a bounding stride, eyes wild now. Mistake, huge mistake, and Jericho knew it immediately. His own anger had transmitted perfectly to the stallion...scaring him, taking away his already tenuous confidence in the ring. That thick stallion neck was already fighting against him. Tried to relax his own legs, seat and body, petted the horse as he came around to the salute, but could tell it wasn't having much impact. Fuck...his own fault, his own fault.

He saluted. Return acknowledgement.

Asked for the canter, and Lion picking it up, but twisting his body and still with his head up...barely cantering, barely at all. Wanting to buck, wanting to rear, wanting to stop...maybe even dive. Jericho urged him toward the timers and through them, and they were on the course now, but Lion fighting him so hard as they headed directly into that first Oxer. Sat in and just pushed for all he was worth...Lion in so deep to that first fence and not even preparing to jump...and oh God, Jericho just knew he was going to get a refusal. Trusted his horse—had to. Lifted him anyway. Hesitation...more hesitation, almost stopping...and then the big gray stallion committed, literally throwing himself into the air like a rocket taking off. Released to him...and by the grace of God, and the incredible power of this animal, they went over it with an enormous lurching leap that jarred every bone in Jericho's body on the landing. Clear, unbelievably...but precious seconds slipping away in the process.

On the rail, Frankel let out a curse. Screamed, "Come on!"

Lion, clearly upset. Jericho asked for the flying lead change and got it, but the stallion was so wound up, he was still fighting, body already covered with sweat, mouth as hard as lead and pulling like mad.

Jericho cleared his mind of everything but this ride—knew he had to be cool, strategic, not just reacting. Alright then, alright…fundamentals first. He had to calm Lion down. He wouldn't get anything from him if he didn't do that much. Took the longest possible turn into the second obstacle, and came slowly, slowly toward the fence…more time slipping away, couldn't worry about that though. It was a simple vertical—planks. Planks that fell easily. Let him take a good look at it, one hand forward on his neck, petting him…his pace as slow as a horse on an outing in the park. Big round jump though, Jericho well up over him. Clear again, and his confidence slowly returning. Same story at fence number three…still going at a snail's speed. Time just vanishing, but clear again.

By four and five, he was starting to come back up to a normal speed—Jericho still had one hand forward on Lion's neck the entire time. Murmuring softly to him, "Good boy." Through the double at six, and by now he had his horse back, could feel that he'd finally settled, that he trusted again…and the joy coming back to the way he was jumping. But man, Jericho knew he was facing a huge time penalty. Made a decision…sat in and gave the signal for speed, lifting that front end, asking him to come up into that massive rolling canter.

He made a sharp turn into fence seven, drawing a gasp from the audience, and oh yeah, Lion was flying for him now. Asked for more speed. Then even more. Flat out, breakneck gallop. Seven, eight and nine, taken in a totally unsafe manner—form gone to hell, and they were attacking the second half of this course like it had never been designed to he ridden. Instead of skirting around fence thirteen to get to the big triple at number ten, Jericho pivoted his stallion on a dime and came at it from the inside—approaching that massive triple at an incredibly sharp angle and at a speed that had the audience on their feet and screaming. The triple…a one stride to a two stride. But not when Lion and Jericho came through it. He asked…asked…and then launched him…and like a guided missile the stallion took off, his tremendous athletic ability catapulting him up, up and forward through the air with incredible momentum. *Bounce to a one stride*…instead of the intended one stride to a two stride. The horse just plain airborne. Deafening roar from the crowd.

A flying lead change and a turn back to fence number eleven so tight that it could only be called suicidal. Then fences twelve and thirteen, and through the final timers, the stallion with his neck stretched out and giving it every ounce of speed and strength he had in him. Jericho had to gallop him half way around the arena before he could even begin to bring him back to a normal pace. But he was already up in his irons, searching for his time on the electronic board. And up it came.

Eighty-three seconds...inside the allowable time. Lifted his crop in the air fiercely—the crowd going wild for him.

Frankel on the sidelines, laying his head back and just letting out a whoop of joy.

Jericho searched out the Team box with his eyes. Found it. Crop to his helmet for Bruce Waverly. More fervent applause, and the audience coming to their feet as he cantered the big gray from the ring. One section actually picking up a chant..."Jericho, Jericho, Jericho..."

Frankel waiting for him at the outgate with the passionate comment, "Jesus Christ, I'm going to kill you for that ride...and I couldn't be prouder of you and this horse than I am right now."

———————

The show came down to a jump-off held later that afternoon. Both Antares and Lion were in it. The rail down against QL held up, even after appeal, and she was out of it. Jericho rode both his remaining horses like they were his number one mount—giving each of them everything he had to give. It was close, but Antares ultimately won, Lion second—an unprecedented event for a single rider to be both Champion and Reserve—with George third on Tarrytown, Bee-Bee fourth on Monterrey, Tim Rawlings fifth, Robin Smith, a West Coast rider who hadn't been in Wellington for the winter nabbing sixth place, and Marc LaCroix seventh. And that was the Team.

Meagan Rhys watched the little snippets that were broadcast on television—thrilled and miserable at the same time. She even taped them so she could see them again.

Microphone shoved in Jericho's face along with the question, "Tell us how it feels to be National Champion. And to take both first and second place, that's an amazing feat."

Answer: "Oh *Bleep*, I don't even know yet." Really happy but dazed look on his face. Laughter from the newscasters, slapping him on the back and shoulders in a warm way. Frankel standing approvingly in the background.

"Jericho, tell us about that ride with Chasseur de Lion…what happened there?"

Jericho shaking his head. "That was my fault…totally my *Bleep, Bleep* fault. I was upset over that rail down with QL and he felt it. Really threw him—he's so sensitive. I had to settle him down again, and then, *Bleep*, we'd lost so much time, I just had to ask him to gallop out the rest of it. He's an incredible animal. I don't know another horse who could have done it…not even Antares. Really tough ride, but the most talented *Bleep, Bleep* horse I've ever been on."

Chapter Twenty-Seven

Two weeks back on the farm in East Hampton, and after that the horses would ship over to Europe. Short round of shows at the end of July, and into the beginning of August…and then the World Equestrian Games. Brae came with him—he was almost like family to Jericho now, and stayed with him at his East Hampton house. Happy reunion with Brittany too, and a brand new audience for his Starbucks story. If Jericho heard Brittany say one more time, "Oh, Brae, I feel so terrible for you," he thought he was going to shoot himself right between the eyes. Throw up for sure.

Chuck had located a possible second working student, and the two of them flew out for a day trip to a show in Ohio to take a look at him. "Now, he doesn't have any idea that we're going to be there, or that you're looking at him to come and work for you," Frankel warned him. "This kid's only sixteen, but when you see him you're gonna recognize the attitude for sure." A bit of a withering look from the Chef D'Equip. "Might be special though, and he's doing a working student gig right now for a local trainer, so I'm pretty sure his parents would let him come…for the rest of the summer anyway."

Understood all that. Nodded.

They got to the showgrounds no problem, and were making themselves as inconspicuous as possible—not easy considering that Frankel was one of the best-known figures in American Show Jumping…and that Jericho's picture from the National finals had appeared in almost every horse-related magazine. Still, in jeans, wearing a ball cap, and with dark sunglasses, he could fade onto the sideline easier than Chuck could.

Frankel led the way around to the warm-up area. Nodded his head toward the center of the ring, and a big, ugly pinto. Young guy standing beside the horse—shaved head, left ear pierced three times, sharp, almost savage features—several inches shorter than Jericho, maybe five foot ten, but well built, muscular—rough looking. Watched him leap up onto the horse—athletic anyway. Did some flatwork that wasn't half bad, then took to some fences. Bold rider but his form needed a lot of work. From Jericho's perspective, yes, he had some promise, but was he special the way Chuck had been talking about? Couldn't see it.

Looked at Frankel, shrugged—annoyed even. "Yeah so?" he said.

Seemed pretty confident. "Keep watching."

The local trainer this guy was working for had come out and was raising the fences on him, and now he could see more. The kid had a way of lifting his horse that was pretty exciting…the ugly pinto starting to soar, even though the horse itself clearly wasn't talented at all.

"Alright," Jericho murmured. "Alright."

They watched his class together—kid had entered the Open Prelim Jumpers, even though he was still young enough to ride as a junior…and he came in third. Smart mouth on him though—telling off the ring steward, and almost getting tossed out on his ear in the process. Slight sardonic curve to Jericho's lips as he watched that—and yeah, Chuck was right…he recognized the attitude alright. Himself, ten years ago.

"Terrible form on him though, Chuck," Jericho commented, getting pretty interested in teaching this young badass. "And it's not like I'd be around all summer to work with him. Better if he came in the fall."

Nod of agreement from Frankel. "Well, who knows, maybe that's possible."

"What's his name?"

"Rick or Richard Sommers, I think," the Chef D'Equip told him. "Goes by Race though. Race Sommers." Frankel stepped up to the rail and motioned to him. Jericho, remaining a few steps back from the fence, leaning comfortably against a tree, smoking. Frown on Race's face—sneer almost, but he came over, leading the pinto. Insolent swagger to the way he walked. "Race Sommers?" Frankel asked.

Smartass reply. "What's it to you?"

Withering look from Chuck. "Either you are or you're not," he said coolly.

"Yeah, I am, and you're Chuck Frankel. So what?"

Jericho murmured in irritation under his breath…oh yeah, real cocky this one.

"Well, I don't know," Frankel was saying smoothly. "Maybe so nothing. But me, I like to go around the country…keep an eye out for developing talent. Try to put promising riders in the right situations. But then maybe that's not you."

Dark, almost black eyes on the kid. "No?" Sharp, defiant. "Then how about you go jerk someone else off, okay?" he sniped—probably a defense mechanism more than anything else. And man did Jericho understand that—had lived it. Unacceptable behavior though.

He stepped forward out of the shadow of that tree aggressively, with a kind of brutal grace. "How about shutting the fuck up and listening when Chuck's talking?" he snapped.

The kid just staring at him. Some acknowledgement there of the fact that he was a powerful guy and looked capable of beating the crap out of pretty much anyone. Then dawning recognition. "You're Jericho Brandeis," Sommers said…much more respectful tone of voice. Still a pretty good defensive wall of badass attitude, but yeah, he was gonna show some deference to Jericho.

Knew just how to handle him too. Laid some pretty heavy eye contact on him. "That's right." Tossed his butt away, leaned both arms along the top rail, stared down on him. "Turns out I'm looking for a working student, and Chuck told me I should come here and watch you…and yeah, maybe I'm interested, but I can't stand a fuckin' mouth."

Interest there for sure—flare of desire in those dark eyes, and he liked that. Hunger. Hunger plus talent. Loved the combination.

Quieter tone but still arguing, and still defiant too. "Like you don't have a mouth."

"Sure I do." Smug, totally in control here and knew it. "And if you come to work for me you better fucking understand that my mouth's the fucking loudest. Got that?"

The kid staring back at him, lots of excitement in his eyes although he wasn't willing to admit it. Scared a little bit that it wouldn't turn out to be real. But man the truth was he'd kill to get the chance. Dropped his gaze away, nodded.

"Good," Jericho went on. "And just one more thing, and remember it. Don't ever disrespect Chuck Frankel in my presence again, and that rule can't be broken, it doesn't even bend. You should be so Goddamn lucky that he'd lower himself to coach you someday, cause there's no one better." Lightened his tone some, made a bit of a joke of it. "Maybe I talk back to him, but you…never…do."

Dark eyes back on him again, giving in, nodding.

"Alright," Frankel said. "Go put this animal away and then meet us back here. We'll grab some lunch together, then we'll talk."

———————

"So what's the possibility that you could spend the winter in East Hampton?" Frankel was asking Race. The three of them had grabbed a burger, and were walking together, talking. Stopped and leaned against the fence line.

"Or what about this?" Jericho suggested. "I'd still like to pick up a couple of sale horses in Europe. Maybe I'd leave Juan in East Hampton and take Race with me instead, let him start them. Have something salable by the time I got home."

Frankel, disapproving. "I don't want you distracted, Jericho. You don't know this, but I do…those European teams are going to mark you, and they'll be gunning for you. Jostle you in the warm-up, cut you off at the fences in the practice ring…anything to rattle you. You're going to have your hands full, I'm telling you." Had been planning to talk with him about this anyway—warn him. Yeah, Jericho was one hell of a rider, but he was completely green in International competition. Had no idea how cut-throat it was.

Thought about it. "Don't think I can handle it, Chuck?" he asked, unconsciously turning more aggressively toward him.

Race, watching keenly. His own future being discussed here, but he wasn't going to step on Jericho—was letting him run with it.

"I know you can handle it," Frankel came back at him. "But sale horses on top of it? Lesson responsibilities that you're trying to keep up with? Spending time looking at horses?"

Shrugged, not brushing it off though. "Race will do that. He'll pick two young prospects, and I'll buy them. That's one day of my time to approve his choices. And he'll get lessons when and if I have time." Looked at him harshly. "And he'll take every order I give him like it was straight from the mouth of God."

Dark eyes on him again. Nodding in agreement, an intense promise there, because man, he really wanted to go.

Frankel nodding too. He controlled Jericho best by giving him a little rein—knew that from experience. "If it works just like that…*just* like that."

Paused, then said powerfully, "And don't fuck with me on this, Jericho. I'm the Chef D'Equip, and I call the shots."

"Understood."

And a warning then too. "Because if you're not riding well, I'll drop you to alternate rider in a heartbeat, and then you're out of the Games. Understand that too."

Man, didn't like that. Really didn't like it.

"Say yes to that Jericho, before I agree to this," Frankel insisted.

Hard, expressive look on him. "I hear you, Chuck."

"Make sure you do."

Dropped his gaze away, unhappy. "Alright...alright." Forceful statement then. "No way that's happening. No way."

"Good."

And from Jericho to Race. "So, you heard that, and you know. No leeway for you. None."

Accepted it unconditionally. "I'm not going to fuck with your shot at the Games, Jericho."

Chain of command...pecking order too...clear between the three of them.

"Fine, then it's settled," Frankel pronounced, satisfied.

———————

Brae and Race hated each other. Bickering between the two of them beginning almost at first sight.

"Yeah, I used to work at Starbucks," Brae was saying the day after Race's arrival.

The kid obviously didn't have much in the way of personal possessions—had only brought one large duffel bag with him, plus boots, and a beat to shit saddle which he was putting with care on an open saddle rack in the tack room now. "So?"

"But get this..." the ex-Barista went on. "I was fired because of prejudice...you know, hate crime sort of thing." The story getting wilder with the retelling. "And just because I'm Latino...which I'm not."

"Why don't you shut the fuck up? You told me this crap yesterday."

Jericho, walking into the tack room at exactly that moment—he had to choke back the bark of laughter that sprang to his lips. "Jesus Christ, knock it off," he muttered harshly, dragging up some real scorn to emphasize his words. Took a look at Race's saddle. "And you're not riding in that," he added.

Snapped back at him. "Why the hell not?"

"Because you'll ride in my old Hermes, and tell Marco I said so. This is a piece of crap, that's why the hell not."

Superior look from Brae. "Yeah, real crap."

Race turning on him, arm cocked back, and lunging toward him. But he never got a chance to connect…Jericho had grabbed him from behind, spun him, and slammed him against the wall, pinning him there before he even knew what was happening to him. "No," he said sharply, threatening. "Yeah, I've got a temper too, but I control it, and you'll do the same. Hear me?"

Fierce dark eyes on him.

Shoulder into his shoulder, and jostled him hard. "I said…*hear me?*"

Resentful, and trying to jerk himself free, but no dice. Jericho pressed him harder into the wall, making it uncomfortable. "Is this fucking kindergarten?" he sneered. Then looked viciously over his shoulder at Brae who was smirking happily at the scene. "And what are you laughing at? Race could kick your ass in a heartbeat. Now, both of you…*cut it out.*" Looked at the teen in his grasp. Murmured to him, "You. Give in to me… *now.*"

It didn't get any better over the next week, with Jericho even threatening Race that he wasn't going to Europe if this continued—and that backed him down some. Tough kid—really tough. Jericho was the only one who could handle him, and forcefully more often than not. Liked what he was seeing with his riding though. Got on his ass and stayed there…made the damn kid work, only thing that tamed him. And he was starting to understand what Jericho wanted from him. Frankel had one hell of an eye, that was for sure, cause this kid could ride and he was fearless. Impressive- real talent there.

And Race hung glued to the fence during Jericho's coaching sessions with Frankel…watching every move he made hungrily. Didn't care if he had to work late into the evening to make up the time he spent watching…he wouldn't miss a ride Jericho made. Idolized him.

Bored with no competitions and no pictures to take, Brae had put together a website for Jericho's East Hampton farm. The night before they were ready to leave for Europe, he came strolling into the living room. Race was staying there at the house now too…where Jericho could sit on him but good at night. He was sprawled out on the floor there, looking through some of Brae's pictures from the Wellington season—now that was one use he had to admit the ex-Barista had…maybe his only use. Jericho not far from him, sitting on the couch drinking a beer before finishing up his packing.

"Hey, Jericho," Brae said, holding up a piece of paper. "Look, you got an email on the website. I printed it out for you. It's from some girl named Nutmeg…what kind of queer name is that?"

Looked up at him sharply. "Throw it out," he snapped.

Interest from Race.

"Well, it's just like a fan mail thing," Brae protested. "Want me to read it to you?"

Really vengeful. "I said, throw it out." He got up furiously and left the room.

"Let me see it," Race demanded, standing up and coming over to Brae, hand held out.

Little bit scared of Race when Jericho wasn't around—let him have it.

Dear Jericho, it read. *I found this website, and I hope you get this note. I just wanted to wish you good luck in the World Games. See? I've been reading up on what you do. Please, let's be friends, okay? Love, Nutmeg*

"It's just fan mail," Brae said again. "Some chick with the hots for him."

"It's someone he knows, okay, asshole?"

Starbucks gave him a condescending look, shook that disheveled blonde mane of his out of his eyes, sneered. "Hey, I'm his roommate, Race. I know who he's met and who he's never met, okay? You're new…you don't know shit, okay? *Okay?*"

"No…*you* don't know shit…" Then imitated his voice, *"Okay?"*

"Shut up, both of you." Jericho had returned to the room. "Give it to me," he said, and Race brought the note over to him. Read it. Stood there, looking damn forbidding. Took out a cigarette and lit it.

"Give me one." From Race.

Handed the pack to him, but snapped at him, "You're too young to smoke." Handed him the lighter too.

"Me too," Brae said.

"Christ, don't you have a pack?" Jericho said coldly.

"In my room."

Shook his head in disgust, but looked at Race meaningfully and nod-ded his head toward Brae. Race tossed the pack to him, deliberately making him reach to catch it. It fell on the floor, of course, Brae muttering angrily to himself as he picked it up.

"How do I write back?" Jericho was asking.

Smile from Brae. "Cool. The computer's in my room, I'll show you." He turned in that direction and Jericho followed him...Race trailing along behind, curious but not asking.

Showed him how to type out an email—addressed it for him, and then let him type out his message, which he did...slow and with one finger.

It took him a long time to decide what he was going to say. First he typed out, *Don't write to me.* But then erased that and typed a different message instead.

What do you know...or do you know anything more? Jericho

Pretty cold little note, he knew—but right now, it was as much as he could give her.

Uneventful trip over if you discounted the constant sniping between Brae and Race. They flew with the horses, Brae complaining that he should have called Annie and gotten them a nice flight in a commercial jet—he might have been right on that score. Ten hours in a plane fitted out for horse transportation was pretty miserable. But QL, Lion and Antares weath-ered it well, and were safely transferred to the barn that Chuck had rented for the Team right in the heart of German Show Jumping territory. Beau-tiful place. And this would be their base of operations for the next month between now and the Games.

The rest of the Team and their horses arrived either the day before or the day after Jericho and his crew. And their first show would be the very next weekend. Outdoor show in Lanaken, Belgium.

Jericho was taking QL and Antares, leaving Lion behind at Frankel's insistence. "Too much for this first show," he insisted. "And besides, he's not the one you'll be riding in the Games. He's got bad memories here too, Jericho. Less is more with him right now."

Couldn't argue with that.

He'd received another email from Meagan upon arrival.

Dear Jericho—I'm not allowed to tell you this, but I will anyway. I dragged it out of Mom finally—she's really scared that you'll just hate her, I told her you won't. But anyway, I was right and we are—brother and sister, I mean. Well, we have different fathers, but they're both dead. I never knew mine either so I'm like you that way. What do you like to do besides horses? What's your favorite color? Write back, love, Nutmeg PS: I sent you my picture with this email. I found lots of you on the Internet, so you don't have to send me yours.

Showed it to Chuck. "Yeah, I knew," he said. "You knew too...figured you'd come and ask me about it when you were ready to."

"Did you actually talk to..." Couldn't bring himself to use the words "my mother", so just said, "...her?"

Frankel nodded. "Couple of times. Want me to tell you this?"

Thought about it, shook his head in the negative. "Not till after." The World Games, he meant.

Smiled, put a hand on his shoulder. "I'm fine with that, whatever you say. I can bring them over here for the Games if you want it—you won't have to see them either unless you want to."

"Let me think about it okay?"

He wrote back too—couldn't seem to help it. He was bad at it though—never read or sent out email—and didn't know how to deal with a young girl like Meagan. Couldn't very well tell her that his hobbies were brawling, drinking beer, and chasing women, now could he? Instead he wrote:

Horses are all I do, and my favorite color is blue (as in blue ribbons), or maybe gold, (as in gold medals). I probably shouldn't say that—jinx myself. How old are you? I'm 27. What grade are you in?

Didn't know why, but he added one more sentence.

The Team will pay for you to come and watch me ride. Want to? If so, call Chuck Frankel. Jericho

Gave her Chuck's number—warned him about it too.

They packed the horses up, and made the drive with them over to Lanaken. Gorgeous showgrounds, and promising to be a huge crowd in the stands. But nothing Chuck had said could have prepared him for the way things were there. Yeah, the other Teams had totally marked him, especially the front-runners...the Dutch, the Germans the Swiss and the Belgians. Horses were big business in Europe, and especially in those four countries, and if this nobody American was to actually beat their best riders...well, it wouldn't be good for the industry there, that was for sure. And so they hung around and watched him practice...made derisive comments and made sure he heard them, bumped into him when he was walking back to the barns—always apologizing, looking innocent. They crowded him when he was riding, even cutting him off at the fences. Anything to throw him off-guard. And they were doing well- it was getting to him.

He'd brought Race along to this first show, and they were together, heading for the stalls after the morning workout. And he was complaining angrily about the unsportsmanlike treatment, having just been crowded right into the rail while riding Antares in the practice ring.

"Man, just kick their asses for them, Jericho," Race was saying grimly, liking the idea too. "You know you could."

"Truth is, I love a fight," he murmured back to him.

Laugh from Race. "Yeah, I could tell that about you."

"Problem is, I'll be the one who gets the disciplinary action," he growled, really burned by the thought, but knowing it was probably true—because once he got going, he wouldn't be just jostling…he'd be re-arranging some unlucky bastard's face for him but good.

Three members of the Belgian Team walking toward them. They saw Jericho, and then spoke among themselves. Looked up at him, smirked… like they were just waiting for him.

Cold glare back from Jericho, squared his shoulders in a rather obvious threat—like saying, don't even dare to mess with me again. And Race, imitating his posture—only sixteen maybe, but an imposing figure even so.

Three against two…maybe the Belgians were feeling cocky. They kept coming, taking up the entire aisle way. The distance between them and Jericho narrowing rapidly. Neither group looking like they'd give way to the other.

Bee-Bee had just entered the far end of the aisle too. Immediately saw what was about to happen, and called out to him, "Jericho!"

He turned partway at the sound of her voice, and that's when the Belgians plowed right into him. He didn't go down though…but that right hand cocked back…caught himself in that split instant and didn't throw it, shifted his weight, and moved one foot handily, tripping the guy who'd smashed into him and sending him to the dirt hard. Jericho's arm had snapped out too—straight-arm in front of Race, blocking him and holding him back. "Any of you want to come to me, you're more than welcome," he purred to the two remaining Belgians.

Hesitation. Jericho had dropped their comrade so easily, and he was getting up good and slow—like it really jarred him…and Jericho, looking more than willing to mix it up further—even take on the other two all by himself. They murmured words in Belgian that he couldn't understand, but that sounded like a demurral, and then they were lifting their team-mate to his feet—wanting to get out of there now—the brash American's attitude maybe more than they'd been counting on.

"That's right. Get out of here, you bunch of..." Race had started.

Barked order from Jericho. *"Shut up, Race."*

And Bee-Bee coming down the aisle now. "I'm sorry," she said sweetly to the other Team. "That was my fault. I called his name out and he wasn't looking. Sorry you guys bumped into each other." And to the guy who'd hit the dirt. "You're not hurt are you?"

He was brushing himself off, and moving away from Jericho, plenty wary of him now. Muttered that he was fine, and then all three of them just kept on walking—Bee-Bee having given them a graceful means of escape.

She linked arms with Jericho and Race too. Tipped her face up to each of them in turn and smiled. "Come on you two hoodlums, before you get into more trouble." Then giggled. "Wow, Jericho, you really sent him spinning."

He'd relaxed again, and was letting her lead him away from there. Knew what she was doing too, but he was okay with it—had made his point without throwing the fist that would have gotten him into trouble with Chuck, and possibly the Federation too. Proud of himself for that.

The word of that little confrontation got around pretty quickly too, because although some of the Teams still harried him, they'd backed it down quite a bit.

Decent show for him, despite the constant harassment and pressure. QL making the jump-off and finishing fifth, and Antares eighth, even with one rail down. Frankel was damn happy with that result, and said so. "Way better than I expected, Jericho. I wouldn't have been surprised, or even unhappy if you'd finished somewhere between fifteenth and twentieth. But you showed me something here...about control, self-control. Maturity. This is what I've been looking for from you for a long time—proof that I can put you in the anchor spot for the Team."

Glad he hadn't thrown that punch at the Belgian—really, really glad.

———————

Two weeks in between the end of the first show and the next one. The final Team for the Games was going to be named coming out of that—four horse and rider combinations, plus one alternate. Unlike the shows he'd been participating in up till now, only one of his two horses—QL or Antares—would be allowed to compete for the U.S. on the Team. Ultimately Chuck was the one who'd make the final decision, and right now Antares was the likely pick. Of course there was Lion too, but basically he was only there as a back-up—he was the least consistent of the lot. They'd only use him in a pinch, and that wasn't probable, considering Jericho had two other mounts ahead of him. Even so, he worked all three horses daily, building them to be at peak condition just in time for the start of the Games.

There were weekly Team meetings too, going over everyone's standings. Frankel ran them like a drill sergeant—pretty stress-filled too. As it was right now, the Team would be George and Tarrytown, Bee-Bee and Monterrey, Jericho and Antares and Robin with her horse Montaldo, with Tim and Marc still fighting to make the team proper…and duking it out between the two of them to see who would be the alternate, at least.

After one such session—two days preceding the final show before the Games—Jericho came out of the small office at their farm that served as Team headquarters, stretching the tension out of his body, and just shaking his head.

"Holding up okay?" Soft, female voice. Bee-Bee.

Looked around at her, tried to smile. "God, it's pretty intense, isn't it?" he asked. Though the Team meetings were always civil, there was an electric current in the air that really sapped the strength from him—he was more than grateful when they ended.

"It's always that way," she told him. "But a lot worse this year, because Chuck can see that medal dangling in front of him…well, and the Committee can too, and they're really pushing him."

Hadn't thought about it that way.

"You're really on edge though, Jericho," Bee-Bee continued, probing the way she normally did. "Want to go someplace and talk?"

He was shaking his head in the negative, but then said quietly, "Yeah, okay."

They drove to a nice little German pub close by the stables, Jericho not saying much along the way. And Bee-Bee wasn't rushing it—at least not until they got inside and both had ordered a tall glass of German Lager. They sat in a booth, facing each other. Silence for a moment. Then she just looked at him intently. "Okay, spill," she said.

Hard for him to begin, but somehow he found her easy to talk to—maybe the only one other than Chuck who listened without critiquing. "I'm so off-balance right now," he said, sighed, and just slugged a swallow back. Then wiped his mouth across the back of his hand. "Did Chuck tell you the story about Meagan?"

Really sympathetic tone of voice. "Yeah, he did."

"You probably know more than I do."

She nodded again. "Probably." Reached along the table with her hand toward him, and his fingers slid across from the other side to twine with hers. "He wasn't talking behind your back, Jericho," she went on. "He thought I was involved in getting them to come to the show in L.A. and he pulled me aside to ream me out about it. Then, when he found out I had nothing to do with it, he just went ahead and told me the rest."

Face cast down, but his deep blue eyes looking up to make contact. "Tell *me* the rest," he asked her. "She's my half-sister...I know that much. And the woman with her, she was my mother, I guess. That's what I know."

Her hand reaching past his fingers to stroke his arm, soft little caresses. "She told Chuck that she was a runaway. She'd gone to New York to be an actress or model or whatever, but of course was starving, and then she got pregnant. Your father was in the Army or maybe the Navy or something. The service anyway. But like you guessed, they weren't married and he'd shipped out...I don't think he ever even knew about you. And then he was killed."

No response from him, but he was definitely listening.

Bee-Bee leaned forward and touched his face. "It's not that hard to understand. I think she was seventeen or something when she had you. You weren't put up for adoption, because she intended to come back for you. But eventually when enough time passed and she still couldn't, she just gave up. Didn't try to find you after that. And now..." She paused, just stroked his cheek lightly. "...now you're a grown man, and she's afraid. Afraid to meet you. Afraid you'll hate her. But when she saw your name in the paper, she just had to come—to see if it was you...what you looked like...who you'd grown up to be."

He took her hand and held it there against his face, five-o'clock shadow rough against the back of her fingers. "Why am I named Jericho? Did she tell Chuck that?"

Bee-Bee shook her head. "No, or he didn't tell me anyway. Her name wasn't Brandeis either—that has to be your father's last name."

Closed his eyes—really hard question for him. "Does she want to see me now?"

She smiled softly at him, then got up and came around to sit beside him. He hadn't released her hand yet either, but when she snuggled in next to him, he did—putting his arm around her shoulders instead. She tipped her head back to rest on his chest. Eyes intent on his eyes. Their faces so close. "I think so," she finally answered him. "That's why she was there at the show. But maybe she's looking for a sign from you—that you'll let her talk to you. Otherwise, she might stay away." Teased him a little. "You can be pretty imposing you know, Jericho."

Derisive look on his face. "To who?" he scoffed. "Did Chuck also tell you that I asked Darien to marry me out in L.A....and that she refused me?"

Sorrow for him in her eyes. "No."

"Well, it's true." Powerful expression, lots of emotion there. "Between all that, and the Games, and the way it feels around the other Team members...man, Bee-Bee, I've just lost my center. Nothing feels right to me, especially not myself. I mean...who am I?"

Little bit of an affectionate smile. "You're Jericho Brandeis, just like you have been. Big tough guy, super athlete..."

"...whose world feels like it's been through a blender."

Her other hand lifted up to trace down his nose, brush over his mouth, touch his chin. She seemed to have something to say to him, was watching him closely. Started slowly. "Do you remember that time in Raleigh? When I asked you to kiss me?" she reminded him timidly. "I told you I wasn't interested in you that way and you got mad at me?" He was nodding, one slashing brow lifted in a kind of...yeah so? "I was lying to you Jericho. I just didn't want to get hurt, and you made it so clear...about Darien. So I just said that."

Lowered his face till his mouth was no more than two inches from hers. "Is that why you're here, why I'm here? Why you asked me here? Not to talk, but because you want me to kiss you? More than that? Because I won't lie, I do want to kiss you, and I want a lot more too. But it wouldn't be the kind of kiss that..."

She put one finger over his lips to hush him, then let it drop away. "I know exactly what kind of kiss it would be—and what kind of kiss it wouldn't be." Took a chance then. Lifted her mouth to press delicately against his, trembling a little.

He pulled back from her a few inches. Forceful look. "Oh? And what kind of kiss do you think it would be?" he asked her with feeling.

Little murmur of unhappiness from her. "Maybe you're right, Jericho. Maybe I'm kidding myself, or maybe the real reason I wanted to come here was just to find out if…"

"If?"

She looked nervous, but went ahead and answered him. "Just listen to me for a minute, okay? Look, I lied just a minute ago too—Chuck did tell me you proposed to Darien. He said it was over between you. So maybe I did come here tonight to find out if you're still in love with her."

Lowering his head again. Dragging his mouth over hers in a slow kind of torment—turning her on, and himself too with a vengeance. "Am I? Still in love with her?" Kiss deepening, becoming real. Devouring kind of force to it. His mouth open, and hers opening to him. Hungry pressure of his teeth against hers, probe of his tongue over hers. Demanding kiss… wanting her, wanting sex, wanting it badly. Public place, but man he could have laid her back in that booth and thrown a leg over her, claimed her right there. "Am I?" he murmured to her again, almost savagely this time.

"No," she whispered back.

Snort of scorn, but not for her, only for him. "How wrong you are." His mouth attacking hers slowly again. "Do I want to sleep with you to-night?" Answered that question between more enticements of his lips over hers. "Oh yeah. All night, Bee-Bee. Over and over. But don't think I'm over her. Don't think that."

"Alright, I won't think that." Kissing him back. "But pay for our drinks and lets get out of here."

Pretty damn sure she felt something more than just desire for him— had to, if she'd say all that. Wrong of him to take advantage of it…but pretty damn sure he was going to anyway. Because he needed…to have someone right now, he really needed someone to hold on to. Wrong of him. His hand on her waist, thumb stretching up to graze along the side of her breast. Felt her shudder with desire, wanting him too. Drew back, took some money from his pocket and laid it on the table meaningfully, eyes on her, making sure she understood—that he meant to come inside her, take her. Not just kissing, no stopping short tonight.

But no hesitation coming back from her.

Pushed her out of the booth and came up to his feet after her. Standing possessively over her, looking down on her.

They'd come in her rental car, Bee-Bee driving. "Car keys," he demanded, and she gave them to him.

Wordlessly took her hand and walked back out to he parking lot with her. To the passenger side of the car. He didn't open it though, but instead pushed her up against it, her back to the vehicle. Laid both his arms across the top of the car, and his body up tight against hers—something to feel there, for sure, and not just hard muscle. Leaned his mouth down to capture hers—deep violent kiss, rife with emotions repressed too long. Hadn't been with a woman since Raleigh with Darien…had been keeping that night as something almost sacred in his mind. Outlet now. Right now.

And her…she was letting him behave like a rutting animal here. She was going to get that too, and he wasn't waiting long. Not long.

Reached behind her to find the door handle. Yanked it open and lifted her back, through and down into the seat, him over her—knee pressed into the seat beside her, pushing her body over the console, mouth finding hers again. Long kiss, assaulting.

Growled with mounting desire. Barely in control. He threw himself backwards, shoved her feet in through the opening, and closed the door. Came around to the driver's side and jumped in. Started the car up and peeled out of there, heading fast for the farmhouse where they were all living. Thinking hard—no way he could take her to his room right there in the middle of everyone else. No way he wasn't having her though.

And Bee-Bee was still touching him, her hands on his muscled thigh, stroking, higher too, urging him on—not reproaching him in the slightest for his almost mindless need for sex with her.

He pulled into the farm, but drove around to the back where the grooms lived in a row of small rooms—barely more than a shed with a few separate compartments, common washroom. Jerked the car to a stop in front of the second unit—Race's. Jericho got out, every movement sharp and aggressive. Came around and got her out, held her hand and brought her with him up to the door.

"Jericho, what…"

He didn't even answer her, just lifted his foot, and smashed it against the door, spending it flying inwards. Race and Marco were sitting there at a small table, playing cards—they both looked up in shock, Race jumping to his feet. Jericho came into the doorway, the hunger in him voracious now—talking to him…demanding from him. His expression raging, severe, unstoppable. "Out," he ordered sharply, and when they didn't move fast enough, he repeated it even more harshly, *"Out!"*

Stunned look on Race's face as he processed what was happening. Marco, completely understanding it though. He rose quickly, grabbed Race by the wrist, and jerked on it. They circled around Jericho who'd come further into the room, bringing Bee-Bee behind himself—circled around him the way they might around a poisonous snake in their path. Hurried out the door.

Jericho lifting Bee-Bee and laying her down on the bed—joining her, coming down over her as Marco closed the door on them.

Male smirk settling on Race's face—still not really believing it. "What? Is he going to…?"

And Marco laughed fondly—he didn't answer…well, the answer was obvious. *"Puño,"* he said, shaking his head. Then passed a quiet verdict. "Good. Too long."

The next morning, and one day away from leaving for that final show before the Games—Frankel and George were walking together before the start of George's coaching session, predictably talking about the line-up for the Worlds. They strolled to the jumping arena, thoroughly engrossed.

Suddenly Frankel's head popped up. "Now what's this?" he muttered.

Bee-bee was sitting on the top rail of the fence around the jumping field, and Jericho leaning along the fence beside her. Her ever-present ponytail was gone, and instead she'd made two long braids, one on either side of her forehead, then pulled them back with a ribbon at the back of her head. The rest of her long sun-streaked brown hair was loose and falling in soft waves around her shoulders—pretty. Nice, tight-fitting pair of breeches on her, and a top that was more revealing than anything she normally wore. Lip gloss highlighting her mouth—sexy, hard not to look at it. Even odder, Jericho's long chestnut mane was loose too, and Bee-Bee was doing the same thing to his hair that she'd done to her own. He was patiently permitting it, talking while she worked. Soft laugh from him.

"What, Chuck?" George asked, not seeing anything strange in the scene.

Annoyed. "And you want to be Chef D'Equip someday?" he asked witheringly. "Well, tell me this, George...have you ever seen Jericho's hair any way except pulled back in that braid of his?"

"Actually, no."

"Actually, no," Frankel repeated, disgusted—hard to tell if he was more irritated by George's lack of insight, or Jericho and Bee-Bee. "I should have been watching for this," he grumbled. "They just fought too much...should have realized they liked each other."

"Oh no, Chuck," George protested. "I mean, Reynaldo was making some smartass comments this morning, but I don't ever listen to groom's gossip."

"You don't?" Frankel asked, amazed. "Can you think of anyone who knows more about what's going on with Jericho than Marco...or even Race? And who do you think Marco sits around and bullshits to when he's got some free time?"

"Well sure, Reynaldo and Santo." Still didn't seem to totally get him.

Frankel stopped and just looked at him. "Well what do you think Marco, Reynaldo and Santo talk about...the weather? Or maybe the fact that their bosses are banging each other hot and heavy?" Just shook his head. "Which would you find more interesting?"

Sheepish look on George's face. "I guess you're right. Anyway, that actually *is* what Reynaldo was hinting at, now that I think about it."

"Now that you think about it," Frankel murmured furiously. "Just wait till I get my hands on that Jericho."

Time for Jericho's coaching session, and Race led Lion up to the ring. Look of pride on his face. "Hey Jericho, do you see this? Lion let me tack him up, and bring him up here...I think he's starting to trust me."

Frankel, good and nasty tone of voice, from the middle of the arena, "Get the stirrups off that saddle!"

"Whoa," Race murmured. "What the fuck?"

Sharp glance from Jericho to Frankel, and an unhappy murmur to himself, but he said, "Just do it." Vaulted on as soon as that was done, and took up the reins. And the Chef D'Equip started in on him immediately. "Come on...get out here!" And then a snarled, "Get up in two-point!"

Came right up into position. Thought to himself, oh fuck man—Frankel was on the warpath…not hard to guess why.

"Gallop!" Chuck ordered—really severe. "Get those toes forward, and put some damn muscle into this. Oxer!"

Lion obviously startled by the command to gallop and then take fences without even a warm up. Head up and fighting, tossing that powerful neck, yanking hard against his rider—it was taking all of Jericho's strength to stay balanced and not let himself be pulled forward. Lifted him to the fence, and got a really jarring jump from him.

"No, no, no!" Frankel was screaming. *"What the hell was that?* Stay centered, and *rounder! Work*, Goddamn you, and don't you dare grip with those knees! Take it again, and add that vertical first."

Sat in just a second to get him round.

"Two-point, damn you! Get up off your ass!"

Positively brutal session. Jericho took every bit of shit Chuck handed him and put out with everything he had. By the end of twenty minutes the back of his shirt was soaked through with sweat and clinging to him—the muscles of his back and shoulders clearly visible and sharply defined beneath it, working constantly.

Brae was there now too, taking pictures. "Oh, this is cool," he said happily.

"What, are you an idiot?'" Race snapped at him, then muttered to Marco. "What an asshole that Frankel is…he's killing him. He can't keep this up."

Quiet answer coming back at him from Marco. "Oh yes he can."

By the end of the first hour, Lion was covered in sweat as well, and Jericho's shirt soaked clean through front and back—the waistband of his jeans too. Pretty much all of the other riders had come out and were watching now—the session so intense they were just plain drawn there—awed and horrified at the same time, and hoping like hell they weren't going to get the same thing, especially Bee-Bee. But one thing for sure…they were seeing some incredible jumping coming out of this pair, because anything short of absolutely incredible drew viciously caustic corrections from Frankel.

No let-up in sight either.

Marco had led QL to the ring, and Chuck screamed out. "Marco, take the stirrups off that saddle. Jericho, get off this horse and get on QL. Do it! And don't waste time either. I want you *right back out here!*"

Jericho cantered over to Marco and made the exchange of horses, to the tune of Frankel yelling, "Hurry it up!" His breathing had accelerated, and that long mane of his clinging to his neck, his face, and his back. Angry, expressive look at Marco, shaking his head vengefully.

Fierce question from Race, "What the hell does that bastard think he's doing?"

Harsh response as he vaulted up onto QL. "I'll live, don't worry." A militant, unrepentant sneer from him. "It's his form of punishment. Took him about thirty seconds to figure out what I was doing last night."

"Jericho, gallop and up in two-point, right now!" Frankel was shouting again, scathing tone of voice—to the max. "Move it!"

Three and a half hours straight for all three horses—without a doubt the hardest series of lessons Chuck had ever put him through. His thighs burning deep through the muscles, not just a surface pain. Arms, back, abdomen—the same. Sweat running in rivulets down his face and over his torso. Drawing breath in great gasps by the end of it.

Frankel tossed a threat at him when he was finished too. "Jericho...I want to see you in my office when I'm done coaching here."

Didn't have to be close to him to know what he said in response to that...easy enough to read his lips and the ferocious expression on his face.

"Yeah, see this instead."

The meeting with Chuck took about three minutes, maybe less.

Sneering question from Frankel. "Tired?"

No answer.

"No? I can try harder."

Still no answer—didn't trust himself.

Already found guilty. Then came the sentence. "You'll work that hard every day between now and the Games...and if I think you're involved in any..." Withering. "...*extracurricular activities*, it'll be worse. Get me?"

Nothing.

"*Get me?*" he demanded again.

Just murmured it. "Man, *fuck you*, Chuck."

"I'll take that as a yes...now get the hell out of my sight."

Chapter Twenty-Eight

The show they were going to was the Indoor Brabant, in 's-Hertogenbosch, Holland, and once again Jericho was taking both QL and Antares. Marco would be with him as always, and that was all the support he needed with just two horses to go in the ring.

Race was staying behind to watch over Lion—and there was more going on with him too. He'd already picked out one sale horse, and Jericho had reviewed his choice and agreed to buy him—he'd be arriving at the farm while they were gone. And when they got back, they'd go to see the second prospect Race had in mind. The kid was pretty happy with all of that—ecstatic even. Staying out of trouble too—not even picking on Brae too much.

Jericho was looking forward to this show—famous jumping hall, and he'd never been there before, only seen it in pictures. Basically all the horse-and-rider teams that would be at the World Games would be at this event. Excellent test of where he'd fall in the overall rankings. Really eager for it too.

Frankel was still hot and heavy on his case the next day, and even in the practice ring when they got to the showgrounds. Chuck wasn't worried about him and he knew it—no, he was worried about Bee-Bee...that Jericho would do something to get her upset and spoil her ride. And yeah, he was so fucking tired by the end of the day it should have been an effective strategy.

Should have been.

Wasn't.

And not necessarily his fault either—though God knew, he wasn't objecting. Bee-Bee...little wild thing, she'd turned out to be. And here he'd thought of her as some sweet little mid-western girl—apple pie and all that. But not in private—no, there she came to him like a little sex kitten, just stroke her and she purred. Claws on her too, drove him crazy even though he was exhausted and aching from the brutal coaching sessions—made him forget all that, the only ache he felt, the need to be inside her. Her given name was Belinda…liked it…called her that when he had her there beneath him, hot words of passion spoken in the drive for release, and in the tender moments afterwards.

It was hard to hide what they were doing from Frankel, but maybe he knew too, because those daily sessions with him were brutal. One thing for sure though…if this kept up, Jericho was going to be as fit as he'd ever been by the time the Games came around. Stamina like no one else had.

Liked it actually—the challenge, and the sheer strength he felt building in himself, almost as fulfilling as the nights he spent with her.

Male animal in his prime.

As for the show at 's-Hertogenbosch…bring it on.

's-Hertogenbosch. Maybe those three days there were the worst three days of his life.

And it started almost as soon as they arrived.

Antares came up slightly lame before the jog. Probably just a muscle soreness, but Frankel decided not to risk him this close to the Games, and they scratched him from the show. Man, it sucked, but Jericho totally agreed with the decision. He and Marco spent hours with the big black, taking care of him—icing down his legs, then putting magnetic boots on him. Tending to those joints and ligaments, fussing over him. Chuck supervising everything like a mother hen, and criticizing nonstop 'till everyone wanted to string him up and leave him for the crows. Seemed like Antares was coming out of it, still it worried them all sick. He was the real gem on this Team and everyone knew it.

On the bright side, QL got through the jog without a hitch, and so did the other horses from the American squad.

In the early afternoon, Bee-Bee stopped by to see how Antares was doing—and since Monterrey was only stabled a few stalls away, she could look in on him at the same time. She'd ridden in the morning, and had already gone back to the hotel to shower and change. Now she was dressed more like a spectator…low-rise beige mini-skirt, a light fabric but with jean styling, and a white halter-top. Pretty little beaded sandals, and she'd even taken the time to paint her toenails pink. Her mass of hair pulled to one side and held in place with a decorative comb. Barely recognizable as Bee-Bee...sure looked like Belinda though.

Soft voice, sympathetic. "Hi, how's he doing?"

Frankel came out of the tack room as soon as he heard her there—already on edge, what with the big show and the problems with their star piece of horseflesh. Took one look at her outfit. Anger—maybe uncalled for—flaring on his face. "He's fine...now go see to your own horse and then get out of here and let us work," he snapped.

"Come on, Chuck, she's just asking," Jericho said wearily, also keenly on edge. He was down on one knee beside Antares, putting standing wraps on his legs.

Just snarled at him, "Am I the Chef D'Equip here or not?"

Sighed miserably, looked raw. Chafing, and sounding bitter, but at least he wasn't arguing. "Yes, Chuck, no one said you're not." Gave her an apologetic look, really getting tired of the abuse from Frankel today—like this was his fault, or worse yet, like it was somehow Bee-Bee's.

"Then just shut your mouth."

Looked away, cursed acidly under his breath.

"Sure, I'll just go," she said, trying to smooth things over before they exploded. Light touch on Jericho's shoulder, smile for him, and then she passed on down the aisle to look in on Monterrey.

Frankel stood there frowning until she was gone, and only then did he turn to Jericho again. Nodded brusquely toward the tack room. "You. *Get* in here."

Jericho swore again. Finished up the last leg wrap on Antares, then rose sharply.

"I said *right now,*" Frankel growled at him again.

The two of them entered the tack room—both looking grim and really pissed at each other. The curtain that served as a door had barely closed behind them, when Frankel rounded on Jericho. "You're a total disappointment to me," he lashed out. "Some National Champion you are...are you supposed to be someone our young riders can look up to? Hell, you're nothing more than a disruption to this Team, and a waste of the time I put in. No self-control, just like I said from the beginning." Sneered at him, "Without Antares, what are you?" Cold, harsh judgment. "Nothing."

Man, those words hurt him, cut him good and deep—especially considering the source. *A total disappointment. Nothing.* Jericho turned sharply away, anger and resentment rising up and surrounding him like a wall. Kept his back to Frankel, because if he didn't…

"I'm talking to you," the Chef D'Equip shot out at him, demanding attention, demanding a response.

"Are you?" Jericho snarled. "Who gives a fuck?"

Frankel really getting down and dirty. "And on top of it all, just look at the way you run your life. Sleeping with married women…and when that doesn't work out, where do you turn instead?" Really nasty and sarcastic answer to his own question. "To the most naive female you can find, of course—and a teammate, right? Just make a shambles of the Team, why don't you? You can't perform, and you're bringing the rest of us down with you."

Christ, he just couldn't listen to this any longer. Body tight like a whipcord, still not looking at Chuck. Murmured savagely, "Oh, I don't perform now too? Why don't we cut this short and just agree I'm one big fuck-up. That about sum it up for you, Chuck?" Couldn't really believe Frankel was saying this, had turned on him so viciously lately. He tried appealing to him one last time. "Man, I've put everything into this…worked my ass off, worked my way up from…"

Cut him right off. "Yeah, here's what you are…just a lousy bastard from Queens who had a few good rides, and now you think you're someone special. Well let me tell you something, mister…you're not." Frankel wasn't using the word "bastard" in the literal sense—wasn't even thinking that it could be taken that way. But man it sure came across with that meaning to Jericho…especially now that he knew his own history.

Exactly right—he was a bastard, and he'd grown up in Queens. He knew Chuck knew it too.

For a minute Jericho couldn't speak or breathe, just standing there facing the wall, head hung but feeling ferocious inside. Didn't know which emotion was stronger at the moment…his murderous rage or the abject bitterness inside him. Chuck, voicing every doubt he'd had about himself—making them real. Giving them validity.

A happy "Hello," drifted in from out in the aisle, followed by. "How's everyone doing over here? And how's Antares?" It was George.

Frankel stepped to the doorway. He forced himself to use a civil tone, pleasant even, though he felt anything but. "He's coming along, and thanks for asking. But we're a little bit busy here right now, George." Obviously wanting to get rid of him.

Get back to reaming his ass out, Jericho thought.

George didn't seem to be leaving though. "Well, actually I need to speak to you, Chuck."

Irritable, forbidding. "Does it have to be now?"

"Yeah, it really does. Just for a minute, okay?"

He grumbled under his breath, and then turned to Jericho. "I'll be right back, and don't you dare walk out on me, you hear me?" Then stepped out into the aisle with a look on his face that said to George in no uncertain terms...this better be important.

George took him by the elbow, walked him down the aisle and around the corner. He lowered his voice, but still spoke forcefully. "Jesus Christ, Chuck, what are you doing to Jericho?"

Snapped an answer right back at him, rapid-fire. "You stay out of it."

"No, I'm Team Captain, and I won't." Tightened his hold on Frankel's arm. "Chuck, did you know that you were yelling so loudly that I could hear you plain as day in the next aisle over?"

Looked a little bit embarrassed about that.

George continuing, "For Christ's sakes, Chuck—a total disappointment? Then you throw Darien in his face? Tell him he's worthless without Antares? Young guy, first time in International competition, and you completely destroy his confidence? How can you expect him to ride for you after you batter him like that?"

Frankel blew his breath out, ran an agitated hand through his hair. "I wasn't that bad, was I?"

"Hell yes, you were." Really severe look from him. "And you know perfectly well what Jericho thinks of you...how he takes everything you say to heart. Now damn it, that's my anchor rider...what are you going to do about it Chuck?"

Not giving in. "He's got no business screwing around with Bee-Bee."

But George clearly wasn't buying it. "Bee-Bee's thirty years old—that's her decision, not yours. Now I've been keeping my mouth shut while you worked Jericho's ass into the ground because I thought he was actually thriving on the challenge. But when you make it personal and start calling him things like a lousy bastard from Queens..."

Protesting. "I didn't say that."

"Well, you damn sure did."

"Those exact words? I actually said, *a lousy bastard from Queens?*"

"That's a direct quote, Chuck...a lousy bastard from Queens who's had a few good rides."

"Oh man," he muttered, slapping his forehead with the heel of his hand. Looked down. "I'm so frazzled, I don't know what I'm saying or doing anymore. Well shit, I was just shooting my mouth off, but yeah, that's way out of line." Turned his face to George trying to explain himself. "Here's the truth, alright? I've been fighting this battle for the last week or more. Bob Marx has been making trouble for Jericho with the selection committee…saying he's too inexperienced, that he should be named the alternate. And Bob Marx is a big contributor. I've been pointing to Antares and the job Jericho's done with him—what he can do in the show this weekend, for example. And now Antares turns up lame…worse thing that could have happened before the Team is finalized. I know I'm on edge, there's just been so much pressure. Pressure for a Team medal, pressure against Jericho…and then to have him fucking around while I'm fighting for him tooth and nail…"

George looked sympathetic, slapped Frankel on the shoulder. "I know you take a lot of shit that we riders never see. And I'm grateful to you for it, I really am. But…telling Jericho he's nothing—that Antares is all he has going for him? I see now what made you say it, but that's not the way it came out. You just slaughtered him, Chuck."

Exhaled. "Well, I'm gonna have to fix that, aren't I?"

"Yeah you are."

Nodded, heaved another deep sigh, looked really harried. "Let me go find him then." And his next sentence was heartfelt. "Thanks George, thanks for stepping in."

Frankel walked back around to Jericho's area. Marco was there with Antares, putting him away in his stall. Pushed open the curtain to the tack room, but it was empty. Came back out looking up and down the aisle way for Jericho. Didn't see him anywhere.

"Where's Jericho, Marco?" he asked—sounded tired, unhappy with himself too.

Condemning and not very informative answer coming back from the head groom. "He left."

Frankel stared at him. Easy enough to see what the story was here. Marco had overheard every word he'd said to Jericho, just like George had—and he was upset about it, didn't want to be cooperative. Close-lipped and hostile attitude. "Where did he go?" Chuck asked him pointedly

Antagonistic. "I have no idea. He didn't say."

Sighed again, just slumped. "Yeah, I know you're pissed at me, and I'm pretty pissed at myself too. I was wrong, Marco, and I need to tell him that. Now help me. Where would he go...back to the hotel?"

Paused. Seemed to be thinking about how he was going to answer—*if* he was going to answer. "I doubt it," he said finally.

Pushed it. "Then where? Come on, Marco...tell me. You know better than anyone how to find him. Help me. I need to apologize...make it up to him somehow."

Shrug coming back at him. "I'd just be guessing."

"Guess then."

Looked at the floor, reluctant. Kicked some dirt around with his foot, wasting time. Finally he said quietly but grimly, "Somewhere to hurt somebody."

Just blew his breath out, defeated look. "He'll go pick a fight?"

Nodded, pretty smug about it too. "Ever see him fight, Chuck? He's good enough, he could have been a professional. Bare knuckles like that? Really dish out some damage. KO power in that right hand of his."

Frankel murmured a curse to himself. Then to Marco, insistent now. "Where, Marco?"

"Anywhere. You won't find him. First place he winds up where he can taunt another guy...or maybe two or three...into taking him on. Watch out then."

———————————

Marco knew Jericho, that was for sure.

Got in his car and just drove, feeling so empty, and almost savagely angry too. Temper in complete command of him. Hating...someone, maybe everyone. Frankel and himself for sure.

Knew exactly what he was looking for—not the best neighborhood, but not the worst either. Local pub, hangout place. Still mid-afternoon ...wouldn't be too crowded yet. Just enough...local workers, guys getting out from a mill maybe. Tough sorts.

Took an exit from the freeway that seemed promising, and oh yeah, this was where he wanted to be. Didn't take long to scope out a corner tavern either. He pulled over and parked, got out and went inside. Strolled up to the bar, leaned one elbow on it, his tall frame balanced comfortably there. He ordered a beer. Picked it up, drank from it.

Turned his back to the bar then, hooked one heel over the brass rail at the bottom, eyes roving dangerously around the room. Insolent blue stare, like an invitation…just begging someone to try and mess with him.

Yeah, a total disappointment. Planned on proving it.

He was definitely creating some interest—one guy in particular who really seemed to resent the attitude. Big man, heavy build, thick meaty arms—stocky, five foot ten or so—truck driver maybe. He was looking at Jericho, then down again at the table in front of him. But his eyes were drawn relentlessly back up again—really, really couldn't stand the way he was just daring the entire room. Ugly sneer growing on his face.

Eye contact. Jericho reached behind himself, and picked up his beer again. Sucked some into his mouth, but didn't swallow it—instead he tossed a challenging look across the room, sneered, then maliciously turned his face, and spat the liquid out onto the floor. Totally deliberate insult, that.

Irritated cry from the behind the bar, and the angry question, *"Wat doet u?"*

But Jericho simply let his eyes slide in that direction…a very obvious, "Fuck you," in them for the bartender. Clear threat too. The man backed away, not happy at all. Worried.

Eyes back to the trucker across the room—the one he'd marked here. Smirk for him. Pushed himself away from the bar aggressively—not really going anywhere, just not leaning anymore. Looking more poised than comfortable now.

"Come on, motherfucker," he murmured. "Come to me."

Finally, unable to stand the arrogance of this unmistakably American asshole for one more second, the man rose, stripping off a light jacket. Rolled his sleeves up. Harsh, violent movements, intended as a warning.

Started coming on.

Yeah, he wanted to fight.

Jericho walking slowly toward him. Everyone in the place watching the two of them.

"Geen, geen!" the man behind the bar was shouting. *"Ik roep de politie!"*

Used the only Dutch phrase he knew, *"Flikker op."* Just slurred it. It meant, "fuck off," and worked equally well with the bartender and his intended opponent. Jericho laughed softly, taunting—lifting his middle finger crudely to the man now advancing on him, making a joke of it.

The man was circling him slowly and with deadly intent, but they weren't coming together fast enough to suit Jericho's taste—they'd only get

a limited amount of time before the police arrived to break it up anyway—
the bartender looked like he was getting ready to dial now, one hand on
the telephone. Jericho grabbed a chair in his path, and shoved it to the
side, advancing belligerently and very directly with long strides—just aching for the confrontation and looking like it too. He got in tight, inside
striking distance, and tossed a really insulting left hook—not a punch, just
a poke…hard…in the chest—as if to say, this is how easy it is for me to get
past your guard. Had the nerve to laugh contemptuously as he did it.

Return swing from the trucker—right fist to the body and not just a
poke, a real blow. Didn't even attempt to block it—wanted to see how
hard it was, feel it. The fist connected solidly, jerking him. Expelled the air
from his body too, but not moving him much more than a fraction of an
inch. It was followed by a left aimed at his jaw, and that he ducked cleanly
out of, just swinging his upper body a few inches backwards and to the
side. "Never to the face," he purred.

He jabbed just once then—quick in and out—hard punch to the chest,
right over the heart. He'd pulled it too—a blow to that area could kill if it
was hard enough, and he wasn't going there—just wanted to hurt. Loud
choking grunt from the trucker and he fell back a step, but Jericho didn't
take advantage of it.

Oh sure, he could have, just didn't want to…yet.

Dropped his guard a little…smirk and that insolent deep blue stare
accompanying the move. Making himself into a nice target.

And the man seized it. Another hard body blow from the trucker—
again with no attempt on Jericho's part to stop it. Oh, no. He *wanted* it.
Sickening thud and really hard connection, although just like before it
barely seemed to move him, barely fazed him. It was followed by yet another blow from the man, equally punishing. Same reaction, same result.

Flare in those deep blue eyes, like he was really warming up to this.
Then a double tap from Jericho against the man's jaw, neatly snapping his
head to the side. Making him stumble a bit. Still no follow-up though—
just left it at that. Waited.

And uncertainty starting to grow in his opponent's eyes. The trucker
swung harder this time and with both fists in rapid succession—both connecting, and with force—the first, square in the abdomen and the wall of
hard muscle there, the second, glancing off Jericho's shoulder, although
he'd been aiming higher.

"I told you, not the face," Jericho sneered again, and drove a punishing blow to the trucker's midsection—not pulled this time, and it really sent him backwards, groaning. They were getting closer to the wall, and a measure of fear was dawning in the man's eyes replacing the uncertainty. Starting to know that Jericho was just toying with him…but inexorably moving closer to causing serious damage.

Vicious intent building in those intense blue eyes. Loving it—and that might have been the scariest part.

Lightning fast left-right combination from Jericho now—starting to follow up on his advantage, both fists smashing into the man's chin but each from a different direction, making his head bob back and forth like a punching bag.

His opponent was looking unsteady on his feet now. Jericho backed down, inviting another return attack. "Come on," he sneered. "Hit me. *Try.*"

He got what he was asking for too, and this time the man was able to connect with his jaw and with bruising force, followed by a pounding fist to the ribs.

Instant response, not even contemplated, just reacting…that powerful right lashing out like a striking snake, crashing brutally into the trucker's temple. His whole body slammed back against the wall, and he started sliding down it, losing his balance—still conscious, but wobbling. Jericho moved in closer, launched a series of stabbing punches to the gut—holding the other man upright by the mere force of the blows, jerking him back erect with each plowing fist. Getting really nasty now.

The sound of the door bursting open and a shout coming from behind him. *"Het einde! De politie!"*

He stepped back away from the man, held his hands up, knowing they'd be on him in seconds…the trucker starting to slump. Final sneering gaze to him from Jericho, and then the local cops had him, grabbing him, slamming him down over a table to search, cuff and then arrest him. Firing questions at him—couldn't answer them, didn't understand them. "I don't speak Dutch," he said, then fell silent.

It was all taking place around him now—he wasn't really driving anything. Had no say in what was happening. The bartender had come around from behind the bar, was gesturing broadly and speaking in an agitated voice. Some other witnesses having their voices heard too. Both Jericho and the trucker being taken into custody, but put into separate vehicles.

Didn't fight it—didn't fight it at all. Cooperating, letting them take him. Fatalistic smile on his face now. Frightening. Truth was, he didn't really give a shit. Had known all along he'd probably wind up in jail. Who cared?

———————

Hard to say who'd actually started the fight. Clearly Jericho had provoked it, but the trucker had thrown the first real punch...was the one who'd risen and started advancing first too.

And Jericho was, and had been, cooperative. Allowed them to process him. Provided what information he could when asked, or at least when he could figure out what they were asking. The trucker apparently was causing a lot more trouble—making himself look guilty instead of merely the victim here.

Cops starting to act a bit nicer toward Jericho.

His temper was beginning to quiet as well, the beast inside him returning to that hidden place where it normally lived—lay sleeping. Replacing it, a self-destructive, embittered resignation...waiting, just waiting for the next fist in the face—but it would be figurative this time, not literal. And he knew who'd be delivering it.

Chuck.

Hatred, still alive and well. Self-hatred too.

They were keeping him isolated in a cell. After a bit one of them came and unlocked the door, brought him to a room with a telephone. Indicated that he was allowed to use it. Showed him one finger—he could use it once.

Nodded at that.

The cop staying in the room with him, but stepping over to one side to give him some privacy. It wasn't like he spoke English anyway.

Jericho had already thought about this, knowing eventually they'd let him make a call...damn sure wasn't going to contact Frankel. But unfortunately he didn't have a way to reach Marco either. Marco would have been the best choice.

Settled on Brae instead. Dialed the hotel and asked for his room. Late enough in the day, he ought to be there—and early enough that he shouldn't be out to dinner yet.

Three rings, and then he picked up.

"Hello."

"Brae."

"Oh man, bra!" Sounded really happy to hear from him. "Where are you? Chuck's been looking everywhere for you." Paused. "Well, I guess it's about Race. You heard that, right?"

Just growled it, "What about Race?"

Silence, and although he didn't voice it he might as well have said, "Uh-oh," because it was damn sure hanging in the air between them.

Jericho, getting really demanding. "*Goddamn it,* Brae. Tell me." The cop looking around at him, curious, watching now.

The ex-Barista sounded nervous. "You didn't hear about Lion?"

Jericho turned his whole body toward the wall, like he'd just been hit with really devastating news. Murmured it, "No, I haven't heard anything. I'm in jail, alright? Just please…fucking tell me Brae. What happened to Race and Lion?"

"Oh man, you're in jail…"

"Brae."

"I never liked that Race," Starbucks told him, hedging—sniping a little too. "He thinks he's so tough and so cool—and now look what's happened." Hesitation, but at Jericho's impatient murmur he finally went on, just said it. "Alright, look…while you were away, Race tried to ride Lion, but Lion had a fit. He threw himself on the ground, and Race was pinned. They had to take him to the hospital. Well, no one else was there, so I guess it took a while, and he had to get himself to a phone…"

"Holy shit," Jericho snarled, really tortured by the news. Man, should he have seen this coming? Done something? Talked to Race? He felt so responsible, and so heartbroken about it. Terrible, terrible fall…to be pinned under a horse of that size. Race could easily have been paralyzed, even killed by it. The damage had to be bad, it almost had to be. "How is he now?" he breathed.

"Lion?" Brae asked him. "I think he was really upset, and he was running loose in the jumping arena all tacked up and everything, maybe for a few hours before someone got there who could…"

"Race first!" Jericho interrupted him furiously. "Tell me about Race, *then* tell me about Lion. Christ, he was pinned you said? How is he, tell me his condition…damn it…*damn it!* Why wouldn't he come to me if he wanted to ride Lion so bad?" Covered his eyes with his hand, and just

leaned his head back. How much more, he wondered? How much more was he supposed to take? Just prayed that Race would be alright.

Brae starting to sound as upset as he did. "Jericho, I'm sorry…I wasn't really in on the details. I just heard Chuck and Marco talking about it, and then Marco left and went back…"

"Marco went back?" He'd started to pace as far as the phone cord would allow him—the Dutch police officer still watching closely, but not cutting him off—he could see that something critical was going on, and gave him some leeway. Shit, Jericho was thinking miserably, Race had to be really bad if Marco had gone back to the farm…he'd never leave QL otherwise. Other than Jericho, no one else but Marco could get close to her. Who the hell was feeding her, bedding down her stall? And what about Antares?

The very last person in the world Jericho had wanted to talk to right now was Chuck Frankel. But he was beginning to realize he had to…to get information on Race's condition…to find out about Lion, who'd apparently been traumatized too, *damn his ugly gray hide*…and to make sure QL was being cared for, because hell, she was all he had to ride in this show…*if* he rode in this show.

Big "if" right about now.

Plus he had to get out of here…had to get back to help.

Closed his eyes. No *fucking* way in *fucking* hell he wanted to talk to *fucking* Chuck—still he wished he'd called him instead of his roommate. Mistake. "Brae, this is my one and only phone call, so I'm counting on you to let Chuck know where I am. Look, tell Chuck he can decide what to do with me. I don't give a shit if he wants to let me sit here and rot…or if he wants to send me back to the farm with QL and Antares…doesn't matter as long as the horses are taken care of and someone's there with Race. Race comes first, then the horses…I'm way down the list from them. You tell him I said that too. But let me give you the phone number here, alright?"

Brae took it down, they said their good-byes, and then Jericho was returned to his cell. Several hours passed—long hours during which he tortured himself about Race almost constantly. Remembered him bringing the big stallion up to the ring—so proud that Lion was letting him take care of him. Maybe he should have known then—known that Race wanted to ride him…and that he'd try. Hell, he would have at that age, with or without permission—why hadn't he realized Race was the same? Race was his mirror image, just younger. Sixteen, and to have a terrible accident like that? Would he want to ride again?

Would he even be able to?

The thought ripped him up inside.

A total disappointment.

Hadn't needed to prove it with that fight…he'd already proved it. Something inside him, feeling like it was dying right there in that jail cell.

It must have been seven o'clock or later the next time the cops came to get him. They unlocked his door, then indicated he was to follow them. He nodded, went with them down a long hallway—flanked on either side by them. They came to a door, and one officer opened it and motioned Jericho inside. He entered the room, and the door closed behind him, leaving him alone again.

A few minutes later the door opened from the outside. Jericho turned to the sound…and in walked Chuck. He looked old, haggard, and beat to shit. Still dressed as he'd been earlier in the day and rumpled, dirty even, like he'd been doing work around the horses personally, and maybe he had.

They stood just facing each other for a long minute, and then Frankel walked nearer. Closed expression—impossible to read what was going on in his mind.

"Tell me about Race," Jericho finally asked him, emotion heavy in his voice. Didn't care at all what was going to happen to himself in that moment, just needed to hear about his working student. Desperate to know how he was.

"He's in the hospital," Frankel responded, his voice sounding every bit as bad as he looked. "His leg's broken in three places…compound fracture, lots of muscle damage too."

Jericho dropped his eyes and just turned away. "Fuck, why didn't I realize it?" he lashed at himself. "Am I just so fucking wrapped up in myself?" Breathed for a few moments, then asked the most important question. "Will it heal normally?"

Straight answer, and he looked so tired. "The doctors think so, but I won't kid you, it's an ugly break. Eight weeks easy, and long cast the whole time…break in the femur. Might as well send him home."

Man, that said it all. "Damn." So soft, he'd almost whispered it. Alright, now he knew. Made himself go on to the horses next. "Brae said you sent Marco back to the farm…what's happening with QL? And what about Lion?"

Another factual answer. "QL's not happy, but she's alright. I took care of her myself tonight. Tried to bite me…tried to kick me too, damn alpha mare. She's looking for you, but I'm sure you guessed that. A little bit anxious. As for Lion…" Seemed he really didn't want to go there. Did anyway. "Pretty traumatic experience for him. He was running around in that jumping field with the saddle turned halfway around for at least an hour. Wouldn't let anyone catch him—all lathered up, frantic. That's why I sent Marco back, try and settle him."

"Fuck me. Just fuck me."

Neither of them speaking for a moment, then Frankel went on—asked some questions of his own. "Turn around here, Jericho, let me see that jaw of yours. Witnesses told the police you took a lot of hard punches. What kind of condition are you in?"

Just sneered. His attitude slowly changing, as the topic swung around to himself. Half-turned, where Chuck could see the purple bruising along his jawline, reached up and felt it himself. "This?" he murmured, resentful, disrespectful. "This is nothing. I chipped a tooth, but it doesn't hurt. I'll get it fixed when I get the chance." Purred, "Maybe I'll have time tomorrow…am I even still riding?"

Weary sigh from the Chef D'Equip. "Yes, if you're not hurt. You pulled an early spot in the draw—fifth to go. And I've got this mess covered, I did some fast-talking with the magistrate. They're releasing you, and it won't hit the press."

Smartass question, just daring him. "Was I fined, Chuck?"

"Yes, and I've paid it—my own money, not the Team's."

Frankel not nearly condemning him like he should be—like he normally would be. Didn't get it. Didn't trust it either. Sniped at him again. "Yeah, well don't worry, I'll pay you back."

Quiet voice, taking control back, or at least trying. "I don't want you to pay me back, Jericho. But I do want to know that you're not hurt. Now do I need to get the Team doctor to examine you, or are you going to tell me about it?"

Jericho laughed—humorless—nothing more than a deep sarcastic rumble. "Hurt, Chuck? You want to know if I'm hurt? Not the way you're talking about. I was *letting* him hit me. Giving him all the time in the world. Not even blocking him—you don't think I couldn't have dropped him anytime I wanted to? Truth is, he wasn't hurting me nearly enough to suit my taste…because I *wanted* to feel it. Those fists pounding my body. Physical pain, understand me?"

Frankel's eyes starting to look haunted now, like he did understand it, and all too well. He nodded miserably. "Yes, I think so."

"And good thing those cops showed up when they did," Jericho taunted him, tone suggestive, holding a bitterly derisive eye contact at the same time. "Because once I was done letting him hit me, I planned to do some damage—real damage. I wanted to hurt him, Chuck. Make him suffer. Damn good thing they pulled me off."

Frankel staring at him straight on, laying out a bald statement of fact. "That's me you were hitting."

Dark satisfaction in his eyes, stinging commentary too. Mocking. "Well, you're not stupid are you? I couldn't very well slug my Chef D'Equip, now could I?"

"No." Frankel sighed and mumbled a curse—a curse at himself. "Think I don't know I caused this? I've been winding you up, winding you up for the Games…and then I just lit the fuse, didn't I? That's why I'm paying the fine…this is my fault, not yours."

Not buying the attitude of understanding, still just poking away at him. Sparring. "Well, I'm glad you know that, because you know what? Here's the truth…I thought you deserved that Aachen nightmare of yours, Chuck. So I gave it to you, proved it for you, made it come true. Jericho Brandeis…a total disappointment—disgrace to the Team…hell, to the U.S."

"No you're…"

Just talked right over top of him. *"Nothing."*

Moment of silence.

Wretched expression on Frankel's face. "Are you going to let me tell you I'm sorry for that?"

He shook his head coldly in the negative—just once, then came out and voiced it. "No. Because it *is* what you think of me, don't lie. And you're right, you're so fucking right. Just look at the way I've let Race down. Look what I've done to him."

"That's not your fault."

Lashed back at him, "Don't tell me that, Chuck."

"If you'd had any inkling…any inkling at all, you would have…"

Stepped right on top of what he was saying one more time. "Two days ago he was telling me how proud he was that stallion was letting him tack him up. I should have known from that…"

But Frankel was the one cutting him off this time. "Stop it! Will you just listen to yourself? You're not clairvoyant, Jericho."

"Race is *me*," Jericho snapped right back at him. Flash of something just aching in those deep blue eyes...something in trouble, needing help. Drowning. Blew his breath out, slumped and turned away from him. A little bit more controlled, not much. "Race is me, Chuck. Maybe *I am* nothing, but does he have to be nothing too?"

The Chef D'Equip came over to him, laid a hand on his shoulder, and not about to be shaken off either. Wanted to tell him that he was sorry he'd hurt him this badly, but couldn't—it just wasn't something that could be said between two men. Tried to express it through the quieting touch instead. Stood there with him silently for a short time, then said simply. "Let's get out of here. I'm taking you to the hotel."

The next morning, Jericho rode QL to a flawlessly beautiful clean round—the big brown mare with her donkey ears and block of wood head drawing ohhs and ahhs from the crowd at almost every fence, and a nice appreciative round of applause at the end of her go. There were a fair number of Americans in the stands too, and they waved the flag and chanted for QL and Jericho.

He rode from the arena to the happy cheers of his teammates, nodded to them, but only barely. Tried to smile, but really couldn't. Took QL back to the stalls, bathed her, started wrapping her legs.

Bee-Bee showed up pretty quickly after his ride. She didn't go with Monterrey till much later in the line-up. "Well, you sure made the second round," she said brightly as she came down the aisle. "That was really great, Jericho."

He looked up at her from where he was sitting on his heels next to QL. Mumbled, "Thanks."

Gentle, concerned question. "Are you okay?"

Jericho rose, came toward her, pulled her over close. He stared down at her, then shook his head, saying no—he wasn't nearly alright. Drew her the rest of the way into his arms, and held her. "I'm going back there, Belinda. I have to. It's less than a two-hour drive. If I leave now, I can be there and back in time to take care of the horses this evening. I don't know...Chuck may kill me for this, but then he's wanted to anyway, so..."

"No, actually Chuck was going to suggest the same thing too." It was Frankel's voice and he was standing right behind them. Didn't even flinch at the fact that they were embracing. "Go clear your mind, Jericho. Don't rush either, take your time on the roads. If you're not back in time, I'll feed QL…hell, I'm starting to like the way she tries to kick me every time I get near her." Little humor from him—giving it a shot anyway.

Jericho turned to him—their relationship terribly fragile at the moment—lots of suspicion, distrust. Just nodded. "Thanks, I appreciate that," he said.

Race had been taken to the *Universitätisklinikum Aachen,* or the University Hospital of Aachen. They weren't going to let Jericho in to see him, but then he insisted that he was Race's legal guardian, and that ended that dispute.

Found his room, pushed the door open. Walked inside.

Semi-private room. Race was closest to the window. He looked up and saw Jericho coming toward him, turned away. Afraid, ashamed maybe too. Really unsure of himself, and dredging up some anger to cover it all. Sullen face.

Yeah, knew that attitude.

He walked over, didn't challenge him. Didn't say anything at first, just half-sat up against the bed. Reached over. Laid a hand on his arm.

Race's face slowly swung back to him, and he looked up with those dark eyes of his. Said gruffly, "You're really pissed at me, aren't you?"

"I should be." Calm voice though, gentling. "But hell, I'm so happy to see you sort of in one piece…"

Eyes casting down, hint of joy in them. But to a sixteen year old, what had happened to him seemed like the end of the world. And being sent back to the States in disgrace…and a failure…"It wasn't Lion's fault," he said, defending the big stallion, not himself. Tried to explain. "Man, you ride him and it looks so easy. I didn't realize that I'm so lousy that…"

"Race, I've got ten years riding experience on you," Jericho told him, knowing exactly where he was going with those self-critical comments of his. "And Lion's still thrown me off a bunch of times…only difference is I know how to get out of the way if he goes down, and I know better how to save it. This is the truth…he dove on me, just like he did to you, in the middle of the jumping arena in Wellington—stands full of people watching it happen too. No way I could stop him either." Getting a reaction back, that was for sure. Race was definitely tuned in to this. Jericho wrapped his fingers tighter around Race's arm. "I know you weren't showing off, alright? And I'm not going to send you home either."

Really grateful look lifting up to him.

Tested to find out where his head was. "Man, do you want to ride him that bad? Him? Or just a horse of that caliber?"

Just silence.

"Come on, you can tell me."

Expressive. "Him."

Jericho understood that too—he so understood it, but he warned him. "He's really dangerous and this could happen again, Race. He's got so many bad memories...he'll never be stable. Never. Understand me? Don't think different."

Nodded.

"Fine, then you'll ride him. Look at me, Race, don't turn away. I'm making a promise to you here, and I don't lie and I think you know that." He waited right there till he got what he wanted—full attention. Continued, told him how it was going to be—how it had to be. "When your leg's healed and you and I have a chance to work together first...then I'll let you ride him. But before you do I'm going to teach you how to take a fall, and that's not going to be fun, and it's dangerous. But if you want it, then tell me."

Really firm about it. "I do."

Accepted the answer. Hell, nothing would have stopped him when he was sixteen, and nothing was going to stop Race either—better he learned under real supervision, than going off half-cocked like he'd done. "I'll map out a program and you'll follow it. We'll do things when I say so, not before. At least give me that much."

"I'm sorry Jericho."

Just murmured to himself. "Yeah, don't tell me you're sorry, cause I'm not done here, and I want you listening." Point made and he kept speaking. "If you want to ride Lion, and it's really about him...and I mean *really*, okay? If that's what you want, then you'll ride him and you'll compete him, and I'll get you the permission. But now hear me on this, Race...it's not the best thing for your riding or your career right now. Understand that too." Expressive look from Jericho for him. "Some guys...hell, *most* guys don't have either the balls or the ability to ride a horse like Lion. You do. But put a horse like Antares under you...man, you'll go so much farther."

"Like that's gonna happen," Race breathed, frustrated, wanting.

Laughed softly at him. "Not today, maybe…but yeah, it is. Prove yourself, Race. I'll get you mounts. And trust me for Christ's sakes…have I given you a reason not to? You don't have to lie to me, alright? Don't do this again." Repeated it, and emphasized it too. *"Don't* do this again." Slid his hold down to Race's wrist, warm, accepting look for him. "Now you can be sorry."

But Race was looking at Jericho's grip on him. Reached over with his free arm, and traced the bruised and swollen knuckles on that powerful hand around his wrist. Little smirk from him. "What's this?" he asked suggestively.

Jericho growled—guilty and caught at it. He'd just told Race he didn't lie either—needed to prove it. "Yes, damn you, I was fighting. That's the straight story, no BS. But I'm not proud of it. Completely lost control of myself—went out and hurt someone over it. Satisfied? Race, you and I are too alike that way—don't make my mistakes. Learn from them…be better than me."

"So that's where that bruise on your jaw comes from?" He'd been listening, but was still getting a kick out of Jericho's dangerous streak. Liked it—liked hearing about it too. And more…he knew that repentant speech Jericho had just given him was only one side of it. Pushed it with him. "What's the other guy look like?"

Just shook his head ruefully, but smirked himself. Guilty again—yeah, part of him had loved it. Bemusedly, "A lot worse than me."

Special meeting of the selection committee. Normally, this wouldn't be happening, but Marx was working hard behind Frankel's back, undermining him. He was there in the special session too. And it was all about Jericho. Marx wanted him named alternate.

But Marx was losing here tonight…that clean round with QL really working against him.

"Why are we discussing this?" Frankel demanded harshly—he was way too tired to put up with this shit, didn't need it. "Jericho's our National Champion…our Reserve Champion too. And he's leading the Team standings. What difference does it make that this is his first year? Why are we second-guessing him? We've never done this before."

Of course he knew the answer to that question, and it had nothing to do with riding ability. It had to do with one thing and one thing only.

Darien Marx.

Cold answer from Bob Marx. "Because he'll fold under the pressure."

"Bullshit!" Frankel snorted. "He's best under pressure. And if you want, I'll get George Strang in here, and he'll tell you the same thing."

The rest of the committee agreeing with him, but still disturbed that such a major patron—and Jericho's patron on QL too—was making such a stink. Unprecedented.

"Let's not make a final decision tonight," Marx was saying. "Let's see how QL does tomorrow, and then decide." Little smirk from him.

That made Frankel *very* uneasy—something amiss there.

But the rest of the committee seemed to sigh in relief. Fine, they expected Jericho to do well the next day, so that would settle it.

And so it was agreed. If QL and Jericho had a decent showing, he was on the Team. If not, he was alternate.

He'd gotten back late from Aachen. After the hospital, he'd stopped at the farm to see Lion. Marco had been fussing over the big gray stallion, but still he seemed upset and off-balance—spinning in his stall, pacing constantly. Jericho spent time with him, just talking to him, feeding him treats, running his hands over him. And yeah, it was helping some, but not nearly enough. He knew right now that the next time he rode him, there was going to be a major fight on Lion's part. It had to happen though, and soon...to get him past this and through to the other side of it.

In one sense, he wasn't looking forward to it, but in another, he couldn't wait. Wished he could ride him the very next day, even. Anyway, it had to be as soon as he got back—the longer he waited, the deeper the behavior would take root.

After that, he'd driven back to 's-Hertogenbosch, looked in on QL and Antares, then finally went back to the hotel and turned in. Didn't call Bee-Bee, didn't call Chuck. Long day...and right now he just wanted it to end.

The next morning, he got up early and went out to the showgrounds. Went to see QL—to take care of her, and more, just to be with her. Found peace there with that big mule-headed mare—she had that consoling way about her, or at least she did where he was concerned. Talked to her, asked her to help him get through this show…asked her for her strength.

After that clean beautiful round with her the day before, he was sitting high in the standings…fourth. Which meant he wouldn't ride till late in the second round. He walked the course with George when they opened it up to the competitors, avoiding Frankel, and Chuck just allowed that. Then went back to the barn, waiting for the time when he'd get ready and go up to the warm-up ring. Not looking forward to that, especially not to the coaching session that would come along with it. Yeah, Chuck had taken it pretty easy with him yesterday, but still there was a pretty good rift in their relationship—hard to span that gap right now.

Without Marco at the show, Jericho did all the work with QL personally—grooming her, tacking her up. When it was time, he led her on foot to the warm-up ring, located just outside the indoor jumping hall.

He heard a feminine voice calling out to him as he got there. "Jericho!"

Looked around, surprised. Recognized who it was that was talking to him even before he saw her. Cin Maitland. Hadn't known she was there in Holland, and hadn't seen her the day before. He acknowledged her greeting with a curt nod, but then prepared to mount up, not intending to go over and speak to her.

"Jericho," she called again. "Come here and say hello."

Shit, he didn't have time for this, and sure didn't have the interest. Still, he swung up onto QL, and guided her over toward the fence line—force of habit maybe, putting up with Cin Maitland and her whims. "So you came to the show, Cin," he said. Not really unfriendly, but detached maybe. "Is Richard with you?"

Frankel watching, not happy with this—it was an unneeded distraction. But he didn't try to stop it. He'd been treating Jericho with kid gloves since that argument two days ago. He just needed to get him through this round today—not to win or even rank in the top five—just a respectable showing, that was all. Then maybe they could all relax for the next week or so.

"Sure, he's here," Cin was saying happily. "He's up in the Team box with Bob Marx…well, too bad Darien couldn't be here—to watch you compete her horse and everything. Well, but then you know where *she* went." Little bit of a naughty and reproachful tone to her voice there.

"No, actually I have no idea," he replied—dangerous undertone creeping into his voice. "I didn't know she was here either...I haven't seen her, or him for that matter."

Cin lifted her eyebrows. "But Jericho...you do know..."

Darkening look on his face, and QL dancing beneath him, feeling the tension that was rapidly building in him. "Know what, Cin?"

"Well, where she is today."

"No, why would I?"

She tried again, hinting rather than just coming out with it. "Today's the day she went to *Geneva*, surely you knew that?"

"Geneva?" Something really sinister hanging around the fringes of his mind—just a suggestion. God, and he better be wrong. He better be.

Frankel finally called out to him. "Jericho, let's get going." Man, he didn't like the dynamics of what he was seeing. Jericho was starting to look angry enough to explode.

He turned and called, "Coming," to Chuck, but still wasn't moving. QL prancing nervously from side to side and snorting...Jericho holding her there, not letting her move more than a few feet in either direction. "What's in Geneva, Cin?" he demanded.

She was looking pretty anxious herself now too. "Well, uhm...*you know*...the clinic."

The clinic. Man, he knew...he just knew. Closed his eyes for an instant, as cold fury swept through him, just ground out the next sentence. "Cin, are you telling me she went to an abortion clinic?"

Soft voice, scared too. "You didn't know?"

Positively snarled back at her, "I didn't even *fucking* know that she was pregnant. My child, Cin? *Was* it?"

Hesitation, then a little half-nod, backing away from the fence a step. "That's what I understand." Whispered it. "A boy, I think."

Couldn't think, couldn't breathe. Rage, pure rage. Forced out the only important question. *"When?* What time? *What time* is it supposed to happen?" Couldn't believe Darien had done this to him. She hadn't even told him, hadn't even discussed it with him. Christ, did he have any chance left? Any chance at all to save his unborn child...and a son? A son who'd die before he even took a breath, or let out his first protesting yell?

Cin glanced at her watch, then looked back up again frightened—she actually looked sorry for him too, like she sure hadn't meant to be the one to break the news—had just come down to tease him and maybe gloat a little about what a bad boy he'd been. "It should be over by now," she said in a small voice. "I really apologize, Jericho. I was under the impression you knew."

"Jericho!" Frankel was calling out again. He was walking over in that direction now too…then trotting. Whatever Cin Maitland had said to Jericho, he looked like he wanted to kill.

And he sure did. He didn't answer Cin, just pivoted QL and took off at a canter, going almost mechanically into his warm-up, but totally ignoring Chuck—couldn't even hear him over the roaring in his head. An unvoiced scream, but inside his mind it was positively deafening. Nothing in his world at that moment but hatred…hatred intermingled with pain. Not even forming coherent thoughts, just feeling that venom eat him up from the inside out.

Utter blind rage.

Frankel talking to Cin now. Didn't matter, changed nothing. And then the ring steward was beckoning to Jericho from the in-gate. Time for him to enter the jumping hall. Fine, fucking fine…he'd go through the motions. And when he got out of there…when he got out of there…

He was gonna find that mother fucking Bob Marx.

Oh yeah, find him. Punish him. Rip out his heart.

A bitter and oh so lethal calm coming over him as he cantered in and pulled around to give his salute to the ground jury. Everything seeming so incredibly crystal clear to him in those moments—senses on hyper-alert, like somehow he could see every grain of sand in the footing, even the tiniest ding in the rails on the fences, feel every muscle in QL's body, even hear her breathe.

Came around to take to the course…no, to *assault* this course. Attack it. To ride for the son he'd never had the chance to protect. This performance, done for him somehow…every movement, every cue, every fence for him. For his life that hadn't been, that wouldn't be.

In one sense, Jericho didn't even know what he was doing, but at the same time his ride was so intense to him…sighting the first fence, lift, release. Again at the second. It had to be perfect, and it had to be fast. And it had to be dangerous. Lift, release. Faster still.

Coming around into the first combination. He asked QL to slaughter this obstacle—bear down on it and soar. And the mare was like an extension of himself—every bit of his fierceness coming right back at him from her. Huge magnificent leaps from her—bigger than what Lion gave him, more agile than Antares. And so fast, flying. Her heart joined with his—delivering what he needed from her. Understanding him in the way that only an animal such as this could—at the fundamental, intuitive level. Loving him too. His partner. Carrying him.

Came over the last fence. Couldn't remember a thing he'd just done or how he'd gotten this far. Didn't even know…had he followed the course as laid out? Had he been clear or not? Had he even done a full round?

Roar of applause though. American flags waving madly.

Didn't look up at the board. Instead he just turned QL boldly, and rode her from the hall. Escape.

Couldn't seem to see anymore—the ring outside the arena was just a blur to him. He rode almost to the far side of it…vaulted off…then realized he didn't have Marco to take QL for him. Just stood there beside her and buried his face against the big mare's neck, her head coming around to nuzzle at him gently. Lost in his own world. Suffocating.

Hand on his shoulder. Ignored it.

Heard voices, whoops of joy. "Way to go, Jericho! Oh Jesus Christ, man!" George Strang's voice.

Ignored that too.

Frankel talking…right there behind him. Frankel's hand, the one touching him too. "Stay away, George. Keep everyone away from him. Do it right now. Everyone. Bee-Bee too."

Anger—just a tidal wave of ferocious anger slamming into him. But rational enough to be grateful to Chuck for isolating him. Grateful to him for not talking and not asking questions. Moisture there between his face and QL's body—her sweat maybe, maybe his tears. Both.

Soft purring threat from Jericho, and man it was poisonous. "I'll kill him." He spun around then, murder just pouring off him. Lips pulled back in a snarl, those deep blue eyes flaring. Body coiled, one hand still holding QL, the other clenched into a fist and drawn up aggressively—like he meant to do it now, and with his bare hands.

Frankel was smart enough not to tell him to calm down. Didn't contradict him at all, just hoped that he could maybe refocus him. "You'll be in first place going into the jump-off," he told him. "No one's going to beat that ride you just had."

Understood that, nodded. Just breathing, growling under his breath without even realizing it. Marx…wanted to see him, go to him. Lay his hands on him. Oh yeah, Chuck was there in front of him, blocking his path—take about two seconds to get past that though. Still he was allowing the Chef D'Equip to contain him—for now. Just for now.

And Frankel intended to stand right there with him until they called him into the ring for the jump-off. Only three horses going into that last tie breaking round…Jericho in first place and the last to go. At worst, he'd be third in this competition. No way he'd be named alternate after that kind of showing. Lousy set of circumstances though. Cin had told him about her conversation with Jericho, scared that she'd made a terrible mistake. And Chuck had a pretty strong suspicion—he was betting Marx had somehow wound her up to come down there and tease Jericho about it, trying to destroy his ride. The reverse had happened instead.

Tortured sentence from Jericho, voracious anger there in his voice too. "Nothing I can do about it, Chuck." He was already assuming Frankel knew everything—hell, he'd seen him talking to Cin. "Nothing I can do to stop it. It's over, it's already over."

"I know."

Repeated what he'd said before. "I'll kill him."

"Look at me, Jericho. No, really look at me." Got the full weight of that deep blue stare…almost sorry he'd asked for it then. Spoke to him passionately. "He made sure you heard that right before you went in to ride—to hurt you, to ruin your go…and keep you out of the Games too." Another flare of anger in that already intent stare, and Frankel took advantage of it. "You go into this jump-off, and you *deny* him. Hear me? You *deny* him. Win this thing, Jericho. Shove it down his throat."

Murmured vengefully, nodded.

"Alright. Get up on this horse now, trot her out a little, keep her muscles warm and loose. Do you remember the jump-off course?"

Shook his head in the negative.

"Good," Frankel said, patting his shoulder as if he'd said yes instead of no. He stood there with him until he'd remounted and started back working QL.

George came over to Frankel once Jericho had moved away, asked him, "Is Jericho alright?" He was pretty well expecting a negative answer to that question, but still he was surprised at the power in the Chef D'Equip's expression when he turned to him.

"No," he said. "And just fuck that Darien Marx."

It wasn't long before they were calling Jericho and QL back into the ring for the jump-off. He was pretty much oblivious—didn't have any idea how those who'd gone ahead of him had done. Wasn't even sure that his was the last ride, although Chuck had said it would be. He was just wound so tight—only knew one thing…he was going to hit this course like they'd opened the gates of Hell and let him out, cause man, that's exactly how he felt.

And then he was going to find Marx. There had to be a reckoning. Marx would pay for this.

Only six fences in the jump-off, one a combination, and the name of the game here was agility because it was set up for incredibly tight turns. The only way to really have speed was to thread your way thorough it, taking the shortest possible route—there wasn't enough room between most of the fences to gallop flat out.

Salute, and he was on the course. The first obstacle was a spread jump, nice long approach to it, and he cantered in boldly, QL eager and ready for this. Lifted her and she sailed over it effortlessly, even tossing in a little buck of happiness as they landed and made a hard bend around to the right—three strides and right into a second spread, this one with planks hanging from it. He launched her from further out to get a nice big jump from her, but at the same time keep her from gaining too much forward momentum, because the very next element required a 180° turn and immediate launch over a very airy looking Liverpool. And she turned on a dime at his command, thrusting into the jump and lifting that powerful forehand in a gorgeous bascule. Beautiful jumping effort, and a gasp from the crowd as she went over it clear.

Flying change and around to the left now, picking up speed coming into the course's only combination—a short one stride between two big Oxers. Lifted, then lifted again, those mule ears twitching excitedly as she went through it. Still clear, and still eating up this jump-off course.

Continued on around to the left, making almost a full circle back around to the Liverpool, but turning just short of that, and cutting in at an incredibly sharp angle to go over a simple vertical—and damn, she was coming at it steep, but this alpha mare couldn't have cared less. Just rocketed off the ground at Jericho's order, almost diagonal across the top rail, drawing more cries of appreciation and encouragement from the audience.

Flying change again, and then back around to the right—gallop now for a few strides, heading into the final huge spread jump. Jericho checked her just a little bit to hit his mark, then lifted, came up over her, and those massive hindquarters bunched and thrust, throwing her up into the air. Slight rub there with a hind foot, but the rail held and they were past it and clear—racing through the final timers, QL starting a series of joyous bucks to celebrate her accomplishment.

Roar from the crowd as he pulled back to a trot and then exited the ring. Knew he'd been clear and with a good time—if he wasn't first, he was second—almost had to be with a go like that.

His teammates were running toward him, Frankel too, and they were cheering and waving their arms—wanted to close ranks around him, congratulate him. But that ended quickly when QL flatted those long ears of hers and started swinging her quarters around threateningly. Appreciative laughter at her from the little group as they scattered, but they were much too happy to care—loved her for it even. She was just being QL.

Somewhere through the noise he understood he'd won the competition—gotten back at Marx in that much at least. Numbness settling over him then. He badly, badly wanted to get out of there. Wanted to go search out his enemy, but couldn't. Not until they'd pinned the class and gone through all of the fanfare.

Lived through that, made himself go through the motions. Robot… mindless…a shell of a man sitting on a horse. By the time he'd done all that, taken QL back to the stable area, and pushed his way past everyone who wanted to talk to him on his way up to the Team box…there was no sign anywhere of Marx. Or the Maitlands either.

Of course not—if Marx was smart, he knew he'd be coming for him.

Turned around, and there was Frankel right behind him. No judgment either. Just a very strong, commanding voice, instantly taking charge. "Come on," he said. "I need you to help me bathe QL and put her away here. Then Bee-Bee and Brae are driving you straight back to the farm—Brae's packing your things now. No reporters, no interviews, no nonsense. And no argument from you either, Jericho, alright?"

Jericho looked back at the empty Team box with longing, his right hand just clenching and unclenching at his side. Man, he'd wanted to lay his hands on that smug asshole. Fuck him over long and hard. Hadn't gotten what he wanted here, not at all, not even a little bit. But there wasn't a reason to hang around now either. The chicken-shit bastard. He wouldn't be back.

Fine…but he'd have his time with Marx—wouldn't rest till he'd done it.

Looked at Frankel finally. "Alright," he said, just giving in.

Chapter Twenty-Nine

Brae and Bee-Bee collected him at the stalls—neither of them knowing what this was all about, but having followed Frankel's orders and certainly aware that something was wrong. But Chuck was leaving it up to Jericho how much he'd share with them—felt it was only fair, such an intensely personal subject.

Brae was behind the wheel when they came to get him. Jericho just slung himself reluctantly into the back seat—as much as he liked both of them, this long drive would be hard for him. Bee-Bee opened the opposite side rear door. "May I sit with you, Jericho?" she asked. "It's alright if you don't want me to, just say so, okay?"

Held a hand out to her, inviting her. Wanting to hold her in his arms, if nothing else. Just feel her there. She slid in beside him, and he drew her in close.

"Isn't anyone going to sit with me?" Brae asked, already whining.

"No." Jericho and Bee-Bee said it simultaneously.

"Oh man," the ex-Barista sighed. "I feel like a chauffeur here."

"You'll live," Jericho snapped.

"This was such a great weekend," Brae was saying happily. Figured he'd just pick a happy topic to occupy Jericho with. And he had to be pleased with those rides he'd had on QL, right? And hell, winning a huge show like this right before the Worlds—fantastic confidence booster. "I got some great pictures of both of you," he went on, just chattering. Bee-Bee had finished twenty-third, and Frankel had been happy with that. George, sixteenth. The others had been eliminated after the first round. "Yep," Starbucks went on, turning onto the main highway between 's-Hertogenbosch and Aachen. "And you know, some of those jerk Belgian guys were talking about you…well, the bastards were talking in *Belgian* so who could understand them?" He said it with disgust, like it must have

481

been some kind of deliberate covert move on their part. "But anyway, I heard them say your name. Bet they're scared, huh?"

"I doubt it," Jericho murmured, trying to answer him, though sounding totally unenthusiastic with this conversation. "They have a great team."

"Yeah," Bee-Bee sighed. "Really great. Still…I bet it burned them that you won."

"You had such a great show personally…you must be happy," Brae continued, semi-oblivious, although Frankel had told them Jericho was going through some difficult personal things and to be careful with him.

No answer to that.

"Of course," the ex-Barista chuckled. "You did go to jail and all."

Now that stunned Bee-Bee. "Jericho?" she said, amazed. "You were in jail?"

"For a few hours, but I'd rather not talk about it," he said quietly in response, closing that subject.

"I know," Brae chimed in miserably. "That's exactly how I feel about being fired…I'd rather not talk about it. I mean, there's the Man-ass-ger saying he doesn't like my name and all, and that I have to leave *right then,* even though I didn't want…" He seemed to be preparing to launch into a full-fledged bitch session about it.

"This sure is beautiful countryside, isn't it?" Bee-Bee spoke up desperately.

"Well, for God's sakes," he protested vigorously. "I was talking about something important—unemployment and all that. And you want to talk about the scenery? Here's the thing," he continued with feeling. "Older guys are getting fired and shit from their jobs, okay? And then they come around and take *our* jobs—you know, the jobs college kids are supposed to have. Hey, I'll bet they hired some gray revolution guy or something to replace me."

Bee-Bee looked at Jericho frantically. Were they going to listen to this the whole way back?

"Man, you've got some real problems there," Jericho growled irritably.

"I know!" Really getting into it now, and totally missing the sarcasm. "I mean, like I was a stockholder and all that too."

"How many shares did you have, Brae?" Bee-Bee asked, curious in spite of herself.

"Uhm, well, I don't know."

"They can't take them away from you, can they? After they gave them to you?" she asked again.

"I don't really know," he said and shrugged, then added defensively. "I mean, I think I had three or four shares or something."

"Oh, a real fortune," Jericho said sarcastically. "Worth about twelve dollars or something."

"Yeah, right?" Brae said, lifting his hand in the air dramatically, as if that had proved his point.

It didn't let up either. And thank God the ride was only about an hour and forty minutes. Eventually, they pulled into the farm driveway, and not a minute too soon for the pair in the backseat. "Drive me around to Race's place, will you, Brae?" Jericho asked him.

Grumbling about that. Something about "...fucked up royally..." which Jericho ignored.

"I just want to spend some time with him," he told Bee-Bee. "Can I stop by later..."

Kissed him lightly. "I'd love that."

He got out and went up to Race's door, knocked on it.

Gruff answer from inside. "Yeah?" Kind of a, *what the hell do you want, whoever you are?*

"Jericho." He'd been about to come straight in, but waited now to be invited, would have wanted that himself.

A couple of bumping sounds from inside the tiny apartment, and then the door swung open. Race standing there, happy look in those dark eyes, trying to hide it and look cool instead. Right leg in a cast, foot included and all the way up to the top of his thigh—wearing jeans with one leg whacked off.

Weary smile from Jericho. He nodded toward Race's leg. "Yeah, I've got a whole set of jeans just like that from when I broke my leg. I'd give them to you, but it's the wrong leg."

"Wear them inside out," Race laughed, opening the door wider. "Come in. How was your show?"

He walked inside the small room—pathetic little quarters, but yeah, he knew Race didn't care about that. It was a place to sleep. But how to answer his question? Truthfully, he guessed. "It totally sucked...and I won."

Amazed look on the kid's face, ecstatic for him too. He just breathed it. *"You won?* Oh man...Jericho." Didn't care about the "it sucked" part, obviously. "So you made the Team...you had to."

Nodded. Added coldly, "Apparently my patron Marx didn't want it to happen, but he's overruled now. And sit down. Tell me how you are."

"It's hard for me to sit." He half-hobbled, half-limped over to the wall, and banged on it. Yelled, "Marco! Jericho's here and he *fucking won!* He won, man!" Looked back at him, just shaking his head. "God, I'm glad my fuck-up didn't…"

Interrupted him. "It didn't, okay?" He was growing amazingly fond of this kid…knew him so well.

He stayed with him probably an hour or so, and Marco joined them too. Jericho had a few beers with them, he regularly bought a case for Marco anyway, made sure he had plenty so he didn't feel guilty taking a few from him…and yeah, he didn't say anything when Race grabbed one for himself either, beyond a flat, "Drink if you want to—I can't stop you anyway, but don't let me catch you drunk." Left it at that.

He was happier here than almost anywhere else, to be honest. But eventually he got up, said goodbye to them, and went over to the farmhouse where his own room was…but more importantly, where Bee-Bee's room was.

Spent the rest of the night with her—he hadn't told her about Darien yet and still didn't. Wasn't ready to. Just needed her. He'd tell her soon, probably. Needed that too. Strangely enough, she hadn't asked the way she normally would either—seemed to sense that it would take him time, whatever had hurt him so much.

He was starting to feel deeply attached to her too—more than just sex. No, the truth was she was just different from anyone else he'd been with. Maybe she'd hate this comparison—but she quieted his soul the same way the horses did—maybe the first human he'd felt that way about. To him, it was a compliment.

Frankel officially named the Team for the Games the next day. Early morning meeting, and there'd be no coaching sessions that day—the horses were all getting time off after the show. Jericho was planning on riding Lion, though.

The Team was him on either Antares—first choice as long as the big black stallion was sound, and they had up till the day before the start of the Games to decide that—or QL if not, George on Tarrytown, Bee-Bee on

Monterrey and Robin on Montaldo. No surprises there. Tim was named alternate. Marc pretty despondent, and not in the room when the announcement was made—Chuck had obviously told him first. Felt for him, really did.

Just to leave his options open, however, Frankel had officially submitted the names of all the riders and horses as possible Team members—they were allowed to identify up to ten riders and twenty horses. Fair amount of leeway there.

When the meeting was over, Frankel called Jericho and Bee-Bee aside. He was looking at Jericho while he talked though, not her. "Look," he said. "I'd like to see you take today and tomorrow off and spend some time away from here. You need this." He looked awkward, like he didn't feel comfortable with what he was about to say. "There's a nice spa in the town of Baden-Baden. It's about a three-hour drive, or you can fly there if you want to." Looked at Bee-Bee apologetically. Added self-consciously, "Or not."

She was smiling, not in the least offended by the suggestion. Poor Chuck, he was still having a hard time dealing with the fact that she and Jericho had a relationship. Hated it probably. "I'd love that, Chuck," she told him, making it easy for him by looking really happy and grateful. "You could use a day off too, you know."

"Tell me about it," he breathed.

Jericho was looking at Bee-Bee apologetically too, but for a different reason. "I don't think we can do that. I need to ride Lion," he reminded him. "And unfortunately it can't wait. It has to be both days too. But hell, if we could just stay in town overnight…spend the day away from here after I'm through with him, that would make me happy." His eyes were still on her, and she nodded to him warmly, telling him she understood, didn't mind. After all, horses were her life too. Jericho smiled, relieved. He even tried to be friendlier toward Frankel. Joked a little. "Save the Team some money."

Didn't argue with him at all, accepted what he wanted without questioning it. Tentative question then. "Want help with Lion?"

"If you have time…if you will."

"You know I will."

Both of them being cautious with each other, but trying. Not easy after this last weekend. Lots of fences to mend.

Chasseur de Lion was fighting as hard as he ever had—almost mindless resistance.

It started in the crossties, as soon as he'd seen the saddle coming out, and that wasn't totally surprising considering the way he'd run around in the jumping field for an hour with it hanging halfway around to one side of him. Jericho laid it on his back, but didn't tighten the girth up. Just petted him, talked to him. Took it off again. Petted him some more. Then back on. Repeated the process a good four times—Race watching miserably from several feet away—knowing this was something he'd caused. Huge setback in Jericho's training program with him.

Finally Lion settled down a little bit—not much, but it was something. Jericho tightened the girth, with the stallion humping up his back and stirring mutinously, popping up off all four feet, little mini-bucks right there in the aisle.

Thought to himself that this was going to be one hell of a ride.

Marco put the bridle on him, but Jericho was the one who led him up to the jumping field, talking to him the whole time, trying to reassure him. Man, someone had really traumatized this horse, he knew that much. Not Race, it had happened long before that—and would never go away, the scars just part of him now. Whoever it was needed to be shot.

Race had reopened old wounds for sure though—that was also true.

Chuck was waiting, watching him approach.

Just getting Lion into the ring wasn't easy because he sure didn't want to go, planting his feet and yanking backwards. Jericho reached behind himself, keeping the whip on the same side as the stallion's body, not really letting him see it, but snapping him sharply every time he balked.

Chuck held the gate open, frowning as the massive gray finally lurched through it, hoofs flashing. "Big risk riding this horse right now, Jericho," he commented, reproachful—not telling him he shouldn't do this, but wishing he wasn't, that was clear.

"I'm not being a cowboy, Chuck."

"I know…I know." Not fighting it…just hating it.

Little crowd starting to gather at the fence line—Bee-Bee, Brae, George and Tim. Race also came up to take a place by the gate, a little bit separated from the others, ashamed maybe that he was the one who'd caused this turn for the worse in Lion. Not really close with any of the rest of them either.

Jericho led Lion in a little ways from the gate, called over his shoulder to Race, "I want you watch what I'm doing here, and if you're not strong enough to do this easily put a chin up bar in your room and work on it. Sometimes what you really need with a horse like this is just plain, old-fashioned physical strength." Looked at Bee-Bee and just smirked. Murmured, "You didn't think this was a sport for girls, did you?"

She put her hands on her hips, tilted her head to the side and gave him a fake annoyed look.

Liked it. Winked at her. Turned to Frankel. "Chuck I'm going to mount him, and you need to stand at least five feet away, maybe off the point of his right shoulder." Then called Marco in to help him. "Be careful man," he told him. "Watch out for those front feet."

Nod from the head groom, and he stepped up to hold the reins while Jericho moved back next to the saddle on Lion's near side.

Everyone holding their breath.

He placed one hand on the cantle and another on the pommel of the saddle, then simply lifted his weight till his arms were straight, his waist about even with the topline of the horse—didn't make any attempt to swing his leg over. And Lion was already dancing, swinging his hindquarters around, and trying to jerk his head free. Jericho stayed up, poised where he was, saying quietly again, "Careful, Marco." After about five to ten seconds he lowered himself to the ground again. Waited a little bit more than a heartbeat, then lifted himself up again. Like the saddle—desensitizing the stallion to the idea of him mounting. And just like the saddle, it was having some effect, but not nearly enough with Lion still fighting hard and swiveling his body—trying to get free, really jerking on Marco and lifting both front feet into the air to paw simultaneously. Ready to explode.

This time when he lowered himself to the ground, Jericho gathered the reins up tight. "Stand clear of him. I'm getting on this time," he warned both Marco and Chuck. When they'd both stepped back, he vaulted on.

His full weight coming down onto the saddle…instant of surprise on the part of the stallion, and then the reaction. Lion swung viciously around in a half-circle, then lifted his powerful front end with both feet off the ground, pulling hard on the reins. He lunged forward, and then he was trying to get his head down so he could start bucking…to get rid of this human any way he could. When he couldn't get his head free, he simply erupted—bucking after a fashion anyway, head in the air. A series of really jarring hops, flinging his hindquarters up into the air at the end of each one. Jerking his body forward, and picking up speed as he went now, already half way around the jumping field in an incredible string of malicious bounds. Jericho sitting in and pushing him, getting whipsawed up there with each leap and the pounding landing, but he was driving with his back, pressing his seat down into the saddle...demanding that the horse come into a normal canter.

Frankel, just watching and cursing at first, then he started yelling. "Don't ask him to come round yet," he shouted, stepping further out in the field to get involved. "Keep that head up and get him forward! Really, forward, Jericho!"

Bee-Bee and the rest of them, staring transfixed and somewhat horrified.

"Push him!" Frankel screamed again.

"Man, only Jericho would do this," George said to Bee-Bee. "No way you'd get me on that horse."

She looked worried, anxious, but nodded in response to him. "Me either. But believe it or not, he really loves Lion, and remember that ride on him at the finals in L.A.? This horse has so much talent. Jericho's right, he had to do this today...Lion's still an alternate for the Games. Hopefully we won't need him, but what if we did?"

Brae had his camera as always and was taking pictures non-stop. Still he'd managed to wander over next to Race. "Wow," he breathed. "Major fuck-up on your part, huh? Worst he's looked in a long time. Good thing Jericho's such a fucking good rider...yeah, and he likes you." Little complaint there at the end.

"Just get the fuck away from me, before you eat that camera," Race warned.

It took Jericho twenty minutes of fighting with Lion before he even got the horse into a real canter, both man and animal soaked through with sweat by then. Fifteen more minutes of simple flatwork, with the stallion basically behaving, but not wanting to. Still Jericho was pleased, it was headway, anyway.

He pulled Lion up near the gate again. Petted him, made him stand there quietly before vaulting off. "Race," he called out. "Come over here to me."

"No, Jericho," Frankel objected. "Not today, not yet." Concern on his face as he looked over at the injured working student on the rail.

"Race!" Jericho barked. "Chuck's objecting because what I want you to do is dangerous, and it is. Still want to be part of this?"

Growled back the answer, "Hell yes."

"Then get out here."

Frankel not saying anything more, but thin-lipped, unhappy about it.

Looked at the Chef D'Equip, spoke only to him. Maybe in his own way he was telling Frankel that he did value his opinion—just disagreed with him on this. Tried to convince him. "Come on, you know damn well if I don't put the two of them together and make it a part of bringing Lion back around, then he'll never trust Race again. You know that, Chuck."

From Frankel, and really questioning, "Would that be such a bad thing?"

"Yeah, I agree with you, and it would be safer not to. But is it a good thing? It's what he wants...I've got to help Race, that's why you put him with me, isn't it?" Race had hobbled over beside him. "Just do what I did in the beginning," Jericho said to him. "Pull yourself up over the saddle for a second, then back down. Maybe three or four times."

Flare of desire—gratitude too—in those dark eyes of his. While Jericho held Lion, he grabbed the saddle, eager and not afraid. Lifted himself— pretty strong too, not a huge effort. And the gray stallion allowed it, trembling but exhausted by now. Did it three more times.

"Good boy," from Jericho and with deep satisfaction, then he handed Chasseur de Lion over to Marco. "Take him back to the stables, he's done for today." Nod of approval for Race too. Smile for him.

Chuck looking at him quietly. Came over and patted his shoulder briefly before leaving the ring.

They'd made reservations to stay the night in Aachen proper. The hotel was a five star place called the Dorint Aachen Quellenhof, and was located right on the Kur Park and only minutes from the casino. There was also a spa with a swimming pool, Turkish bath and a Finnish sauna. After the morning's ride with Lion, it all sounded like heaven to Jericho.

They checked in, spent the first hour and a half just exploring the room...showering together, making love and then laying together afterwards, just talking between kisses.

And maybe he could talk to her now—about Darien, about his son. Wanted to, before she dragged it out of him anyway, which she eventually would. "I want to tell you about this past weekend," he said, quiet voice but strong.

She turned in his arms, her slim, well-toned form fitting there so very well. She slid one leg comfortably between his, laid her head on his shoulder, facing him. Stroked him lightly, tipped her face toward his. "And I want to listen," she told him. "I'm glad you trust me enough."

"It has to do with Darien," he warned her.

Light smile. "I assumed that."

He ran his fingers through that long, still-damp mane of hers, tracing a blond streak that started at her temple and ran the length of her hair. "You're wrong then—at least in part. It's not so much about her as…" Couldn't quite go there yet. Torment re-surfacing in those deep blue eyes of his. "One of my former clients…Cin Maitland…I guess she and her husband are staying here somewhere with the Marxes. Anyway, I saw her in the warm-up—right before I went in for the second round."

"I know who Cin is," Bee-Bee encouraged him. Didn't push it though, didn't ask any questions either.

"Cin just loves gossip…she also loves to give me a hard time. For as long as I've known her, really. Anyway, she'd come down there to toss a few digs my way."

"That bitch."

Murmured laugh from him, still playing with that long blonde streak. Pushed it back off her forehead. Touched his lips there for an instant, and then laid his cheek against the same spot, meaning she could no longer see his face, and maybe that was deliberate. Continued talking right next to her ear. Low voice, aching. "She told me something…she thought I already knew about it, but Belinda, I had no idea…none at all." Sighed. "She told me Darien was pregnant. My child. A boy."

Bee-Bee pulled back surprised, but she smiled at him, not acting jealous—not reacting at all to the way news like that might impact her relationship with Jericho. "But Jericho, I know you—well, I know that much about you anyway. You'd love that. A son? God, look at how you are with Race and even Brae. You'd be a wonderful father."

He put one hand on either side of her face. So much hurt in his eyes, just breathing.

"You have a right to see him, to know him," Bee-Bee said, second-guessing the issue. "If it's your son, they can't keep you away."

"He's dead," Jericho murmured back to her. Repeated it, still hadn't come to grips with it himself. "He's dead...she killed him." Closed his eyes, then reopened them, more aggressive look there. "Aborted him. Didn't even have the decency to tell me, talk to me about it first. Just took my child...our child...and scraped him out..." The words so angry now, and then he couldn't even continue speaking. A few deep breaths. "Defenseless little thing, and she..." His voice caught again, and the rest of that sentence just came out as a tortured growl. "If I'd known, maybe I could have...oh fuck, I don't know. Maybe as a man there's something wrong with me that I care so much..."

Her arms were around him and she was holding him, soothing him. And not making light of it or trying to tell him he'd have another someday. "No, there's something very right with you that you care so much, Jericho. And believe that, please believe that."

"He was...I loved her, Belinda. Understand? He's...because I loved her, and she threw both of us away in the same gesture. That's what I meant to her, mean to her. Yeah, I know, she would have had to carry him for nine months, but I would have taken him, raised him, because...he was mine, ours."

Devastated for him. Nothing she could say or do for him. "And Cin told you this right before you had to ride?" Couldn't believe that either, wanted to kill her for that. "Oh, Jericho. No wonder Chuck wouldn't let anyone near you. I'm so sorry, so very sorry."

Powerful voice from him. "My own mother...she abandoned me, never came back. But at least she had the...*courage*...to give me life. And she had nothing, she was starving. The Marxes...they can have anything they want, but Darien..." Real anger in his voice now. "...wouldn't risk her life as a *princess* to protect him. My son. Our son—wasn't worth that. But think about it, she'd have to acknowledge me for that to happen, wouldn't she? Let people know it was mine if she'd given him to me." Forced another rage-filled thought out. "He was conceived in Raleigh, had to be—and she came to me there, I didn't invite her. In L.A. I asked her to marry me, and she said no, and I just wonder...did she know then? Did she know about him then? Know what she was going to do with him...and she never told me?" Just spat out one more final sentence. "Thank God she said no then, if that's what she is."

Almost afraid to say this, but she went with what she felt in her heart. "Jericho, have you thought about this? Have you thought about naming him? Maybe doing something for him? Something that would make you feel more closure…it could be anything. A memorial…plant a tree…I don't know. Something that would mean something to you?"

He obviously hadn't considered it, but from his expression it wasn't an unwelcome suggestion. In fact, it was like a lifeline. "Thank you," he said with feeling. "Thank you. God you're so beautiful…inside, not just outside."

Kissing him now, and he was returning the act. His mouth seeking against hers. And Bee-Bee, just opening up to him, showing him that he mattered, that she cared. Inviting him to come back inside her, letting him cleanse his soul that way. Find some measure of oblivion…and peace.

———————————

Later that evening they took a long walk through the park, not holding hands, but fingers almost constantly brushing. Something inside him avoiding any real attachment to her or to anyone. Something inside him desperate for it at the same time. And she seemed to understand, was trying to give him both things together.

Special woman. Becoming a best friend. Way more important than just the incredible heat of sex, though she gave him that too.

Flowers blooming around them, perfuming the air. Not talking much, but lots of eye contact, meaningful looks. Eventually they made their way back to the hotel and the outdoor patio there. Both of them had dressed up more than they usually did—Jericho in dark casual slacks and a white dress shirt, and Bee-Bee in a pretty soft pink summer dress. Both had let their hair down loose around their shoulders too—Bee-Bee had stolen a flower from the thousands in the park and threaded it through hers. She'd wanted to do the same to Jericho's, but he hadn't let her. Thankfully, as it turned out.

They strolled in—little bit of concern from the maitre d' that he wasn't wearing a jacket, but they got past that and were eventually seated at a nice table for two in the corner. A waiter took their drink order—beer for him and white wine for her, and then left to get it. Jericho lit a cigarette and sat back comfortably. "You know…what you said earlier. About naming him?" he began thoughtfully. "I've been thinking about it, and would it be totally queer to…"

But he was interrupted by, "My God…I thought that was you."

Looked around, tossing that long chestnut mane over his shoulder in the process. Recognized the woman standing there…tried hard to dredge her name up. "Camille Forrester," he said, as it just popped into his head.

The woman from the plane…and Lady Forrester's niece. His patron very likely here too then, and his eyes swept the tables on the patio for her.

"Are you looking for my aunt?" Camille asked. "She'll be down in just a moment."

Jericho rose then, hated these social situations and really felt awkward. Put a hand out to Bee-Bee, and she stood also. "This is Bee-Bee Oxmoor," he said, moving almost protectively one half step in front of her. "She's on the Team too. Well, Chuck let us out of our prison, and sent us to town for a little R&R after the show last weekend. Bee-Bee this is Lady Forrester's niece, Camille. Lady Forrester owns Antares."

Smile from Camille. She'd certainly noticed the dynamics between the two young people—they were a couple apparently. Evident from Jericho's protective posture, and the fact that he hadn't released Bee-Bee's hand. "Well, I'm sure the two of you want to have dinner together," she said. "But please stop over and just say hello to Aunt Augusta. I know how much she'd love to see you."

Soft expressive look from him. "Of course."

Camille pointed to a large table. "We're right over there."

"We ordered drinks," Jericho told her. "We'll come over as soon as we get them."

That seemed to please her, and she waved and turned back toward her table with a happy, "We'll see you in a few minutes then."

The waiter returned with their drinks, and Jericho paid him. They walked together over to the large table Camille indicated, and Lady Forrester had arrived by then. Bruce Waverly was there too, as well as several other major patrons of the Team that he recognized but didn't know personally. All here for the Games, apparently.

Went over to his two patrons and said hello to them, introduced Bee-Bee too.

Lady Forrester took Jericho's hand almost immediately. "I'm going to steal him away for a second here," she announced, and tiny as she was there wasn't a person there who would have contradicted her. "Come and talk to me, Jericho," she said, leading him back in the direction he'd come, and to the small table where he and Bee-Bee had been sitting. Didn't have a clue what this was about, unless it was Antares coming up lame. Nervous about that, but she was a horsewoman—hoped she'd understand.

She took a seat, and he sat next to her—he pretty much had to anyway, considering she was still holding his hand. "So that's what all that hair looks like when it's down," she chuckled. "Pretty."

Looked embarrassed. Couldn't very well say he'd done it for Bee-Bee.

"Chuck tells me you had a tough weekend, but congratulations on winning the Indoor," she went on. Kindly voice, inquiring.

Sure, okay, she had to be referring to Antares. Ignored the congratulations and went right to the heart of what he thought he question was. "It's just a minor lameness," Jericho told her. "To be honest, I could have shown him...he'd have passed the jog, but it just wasn't worth risking him with the Games so close. Magnificent animal," he added. Man, she always made him feel so uncomfortable. Imposing little thing.

"So you think he'll show in the Games?"

"God, I hope so."

"What about Bruce's horse?" she asked. "You haven't been showing him."

Soft laugh from him. "That stallion? So talented. But he's a little bit *loco*, you know what I mean...well, you saw him in Wellington there." Complimented her own horse for her. "Antares—he has the same kind of ability, but his head is screwed on tight, not like Lion." Slow burn of real desire building in his eyes then. "Wait till you see Force...God. What an animal. He'll beat both of them."

Happy smile coming back at him. "Too bad about Lion," she said, though not looking sad at all that her horse was ranked over Waverly's. What she'd wanted to hear, obviously.

"Lion...his problem is that someone destroyed his mind. Handled him roughly when he needed understanding instead." Figured she'd seen situations like that with horses before.

Thoughtful look on Lady Forrester's face. "Now that sounds a lot like what Chuck told me he's done to you, trying to peak you for the Games—handled you too roughly. Beating himself up over it, too."

Surprise registering on his face, open vulnerable look. "No," he said, denying it. "That's not true."

"But he says you're strong, that you're handling it. That you were still able to come back from his mistake and win that show. He's very proud of you."

Damn, these patrons sure had their sources of information. It always caught him totally off guard. "No," he said again. "Chuck's too hard on himself...way too hard. All he wants..." Looked her dead on—not sure why he was saying this to her, but like Bee-Bee she seemed pretty good at drawing the truth out of him. Maybe he just didn't lie very well. "All he wants is to see me be a better man, live up to what I should be."

"Hmmm," she said pointedly. Suspicious too, the way she'd paused there. Definitely going somewhere with this. "That does bring up another topic. I assume you know Cin Maitland?"

He drew his breath in, lowered his head, really stunned, shamed too. God...Cin and her big mouth. But sure—she'd blabbed to everyone she could find who'd listen. Sure she had. "I know her," he murmured.

"She told me a story."

Way too soon for him to be discussing this with someone like Lady Forrester. The wound, still raw and bloody. He lifted his face to her, the emotion in those deep blue eyes naked and exposed. Tears rising to fill them, but unshed. Strength there and a powerful anger too, co-existing with the pain. Murmured it harshly, "She told me that story too."

His patron's face immediately softening, genuine sympathy for him there. "You didn't know?" Framed as a question, but she'd already surmised the answer. Or maybe Cin even told her.

At first, he just shook his head. A tear even escaping to run down over his cheek. He didn't brush it away. Fervent voice, not excusing himself, but stating a fact. "Not until after. I swear to you," he said forcefully, "I'd have stood up to it. Stood up for him if I'd had the chance. Any chance at all. And I'll live with that..." Bitter. "...*failure*...my whole life. It...no, *he*... means so much to me."

She patted the back of his hand gently. "Yes, I believe that. I'm sorry to have brought up such a painful subject, but thank you for reassuring me. I knew my feelings about you were right. Actually, Cin defends you too, but hearing it from you means a lot more to me."

Still looking her in the eyes, not shrinking away from her judgment. Nodded. Hell, she was supporting his career, she had a right to know what his character was. Closed his eyes briefly and just asked her, "Forgive me."

"Nonsense," she said firmly. "You're a young man, and you make mistakes like we all do, but actually I'm very proud to be connected with you. Proud to be a part of what you're doing, and what you will do in the future.

Now do me a favor. You go out there and ride your best for the Team, will you?"

"With everything in me," he promised her.

Lady Forrester leaned forward, brushed the tear track from his cheek, then gave him a little kiss there. "Good," she said. Gave his hand one final squeeze.

Jericho and Bee-Bee only stayed a little bit longer after he and Lady Forrester returned to the table. They said goodnight to all the patrons, promised to give their regards to Chuck, and then started walking toward the building. Sapped by his conversation with the elderly woman, Jericho was anxious to be alone with Bee-Bee. Wasn't sure whether he'd tell her about it or not—he probably would given a little time and encouragement.

Opened the door to go inside.

And there they were…face to face with Bob and Darien Marx. Not surprising—all the other big patrons were here, and sure, they were too.

Marx looking elegant in an expensive silk and wool blend suit, and Darien resplendent in a fiery red cocktail dress. Both of them horrified to see Jericho and Bee-Bee.

Oh sure, he knew they both thought he'd go ballistic on them. But he had what his son would never have…all the time in the world. Harsh, threatening, and utterly derisive look from him, as he opened the door for them and held it. Darien's delicate and sympathetic return look, so filled with longing, like she wanted to speak with him…only making him sick. Hated the pair of them.

And Bee-Bee, bless her heart, having faith in him, not saying a word to try and control him.

"After the Games," he just snarled to Marx as the pair of them walked hurriedly past. "After the Games."

The next morning Chuck handed out the Team jackets, two for each of them, even Marc—still an off chance that he might ride, although he was second alternate, and basically out of it.

Jericho worked Lion again—pretty much a mirror image of the day before, with one small crossrail jump thrown in at the end of it. Lion was very slowly returning to earth.

Chuck caught him in the afternoon, pulled him into his office. "Lady Forrester called me," he told him, and yeah Jericho knew what that conversation had been all about.

"I would have told you about it today," he replied.

"No, it's fine," Frankel said. "I'm not scolding you for it. I just want to ask you this…if you need someone to talk to, Jericho, I can make that happen. A professional, I mean. Counseling."

Not embarrassed that Chuck though the event had been that traumatic to him—hell, it had been. But he shook his head in the negative anyway. "I have someone to talk to."

"I know you do."

Fine, and topic closed. Almost.

Looked down, did feel embarrassed about this part. "I thought I might wear an armband for him, Chuck—if that's okay, and the rules allow it and all. Belinda suggested I might want to do something…make some kind of gesture. I don't want to cause an issue, and if it is, I'll drop it."

"It won't be an issue," Frankel promised him. "I'll make sure it's cleared. You'll get questions though, people asking about it."

"Then I'll answer them truthfully…but my word on it, Chuck, I won't mention the Marxes…that's private between him and me, and it'll wait till after the Games. My word on that too."

"Alright."

Pretty good conversation between the two of them—the most comfortable they'd had in days.

Jericho rising, going to the door and placing his hand on the knob there. Pausing. Still looking at the floor. "Belinda thinks I should name him. I mean, it won't be official or anything, but just for myself. Would it freak you out totally if I called him Charles?"

The Chef D'Equip, positively stunned. Got up himself and went over to stand by Jericho. No physical contact, but close. Really soft and amazed look on his weathered face. "I'd be…deeply honored," he said.

Chapter Thirty

The two weeks before the Games were a time of relentlessly building pressure, and especially from Chuck, whose coaching sessions with all of them were getting tougher and tougher. Antares went back to work and was doing fine, seeming to love the increasing challenge and not missing a beat physically. The same was true with QL. As for Lion, he was slowly returning to normal—normal for him. And he was back to jumping. Race—unable to do that much around the barn—spent hours with him every day, and Lion was starting to enjoy those daily visits, thrusting his gorgeous head out into the aisle and nickering to Race much the same way he did to Jericho.

The Games themselves were being held in San Patrignano, Italy, the first time they'd been held at that locale. The Equestrian Center there included a 100 x 60 meter outdoor grass jumping arena, a 60 x 40 indoor warm-up arena, and a 75 x 50 meter training area. In preparation, the horses were taken to a farm near San Patrignano a week ahead of time, and the whole team said goodbye to the stable in Aachen that had been their home base for the last month. The new farm was an old estate with a rambling farmhouse, a large thatched roof barn and a Grand Prix jumping field.

Late in the afternoon on the second day there, they all decided to go into town and get a look at the jumping venue. It was around four o'clock and would still be light outside for several hours yet. Brae, Race, Bee-Bee and Jericho were in one car together, Jericho driving, and were following Frankel, George, Tim, Robin and Marc. As they pulled into the town of San Patrignano proper, Brae suddenly sat up straight in his seat, and yelped, "Oh my God! Pull over! Pull over right here!"

The reason was obvious once they looked around…there was a Starbucks on the corner.

Collective groan from everyone in the car, but Jericho was already swinging the car into a parking spot, and Frankel…seeing the move in his rearview mirror…did likewise.

"I could use a Latte," Jericho announced.

"Oh man, this is so cool," the ex-Barista was saying.

And from Race, "I think I'm gonna throw up."

The bickering, completely predictable. Brae shooting right back at him, "Hey shut up, asshole."

And Race, turning to shove aggressively at him. "Yeah why don't you make me?"

Bark from Jericho, "Both of you, put a lid on it. *Now.* Jesus Christ, you'd think you were brothers the way you pick on each other."

Now that thought disgusted both of them. Ended the arguing though.

As he stepped out of the car, Frankel called out to him, "Why are we stopping?"

Smirk from Jericho. "Hey look, Chuck…it's Starbucks."

The Chef D'Equip tossed his head back and roared.

The entire group trooped inside.

You might have thought that Brae was giving them a guided tour, the way he began explaining the entire operation to them. "Yeah…there's no drive-through here, and that's kind of low-class, okay? But see, they take your order right here, and then you wait for it down there." He was pointing excitedly.

"Brae, that's every fucking Starbucks in the world," Jericho said, exasperated. Still he stepped up to the counter and ordered a Latte for himself, and a Mocha Frappuccino for Bee-Bee, his roommate leaning so far over the counter to watch, it looked like he might actually fall across it and onto the floor on the other side.

"Oh no, that's wrong," he was telling the Italian baristas. "You have to draw a star on the drinks for inside…well, you don't have a drive-through, but do it anyway because you're supposed to."

They seemed to be mumbling in confusion among themselves.

Frankel covering his face, trying to pretend like he wasn't associated with this.

"Yeah, a star," he was continuing. "Well, don't you have a black marking pen back there? You know…like my roommate ordered a Latte, so you have to put a big "L" in this bottom box where it says "Drink." Yeah, then you make a star at the top…hey, that's how it's done. I mean, I didn't make up the rules or anything, but I should know, right? *Right?"* Getting a little bit more aggressive now. He reached over and grabbed a pen, and then Jericho's still-empty cup, and dramatically made the star. "See? You know, sometimes we make smiley faces instead, but that's like a refinement. Better start with the basics."

The group was all trying to order as fast as possible, and get the heck out of there, although Jericho seemed to be enjoying the show, standing to one side with Bee-Bee and laughing.

"Is he retarded or something?" Race sniped, coming over to be with him.

"Or something."

To pacify him, the baristas behind the bar were listening and nodding, though they seemed to be making some pretty good comments in Italian about this weird American guy who had a thing with stars.

"Now here's a tip for you," the ex-Barista went on, passing on some of his vast technique with customers. He said it that way too…like he was imparting some great marketing secret to them. "For the regular customers, sometimes I write a little message on the cup." He grabbed Jericho's empty cup again, and wrote "Hi, Jericho!" next to the star. "See, the customers like that."

Some murmuring back and forth between the Italian baristas. Nodding their heads. One picked up the marker and started adding stars to all the cups waiting in line for orders, Brae smiling with approval.

"God," Race said quietly to Bee-Bee and Jericho. "Remind me to never get a job at Starbucks—I think it's contagious."

Jericho smirked. "Here's the truth," he said. "They should have promoted Brae, not fired him."

Couldn't argue with that.

Brae was in the process of trying to communicate with the guys behind the bar. "Do you have any…" He made his fingers walk up to the ordering station, "…chick customers", and then drew the outline of a woman's form with both hands. Not a very good pantomime, but since it was a pretty good bet these guys spoke decent English they were nodding, and repeating the gesture for the female shape. "Oh hey, Chuck," Brae said happily. "I might stay here for a while and help these guys…"

"You most certainly will not."

Bitter disappointment. "Oh man."

After that, any time you couldn't find Brae in the evenings, there was a pretty good shot that he'd snuck into town for a little Starbucks fix. The guys even gave him an apron with his name on it, and a pen of his own, and he definitely liked that. Had even learned a little Italian... *"Benvenuto a Starbucks!"*

Turned out it was one of their highest weeks for sales since the place had opened six months earlier.

Two days before the start of the Games, and the horses that were expected to be on the Team—Antares, Monterrey, Tarrytown and Montaldo—were taken over to the American stalls at the Games venue. Frankel also had Marc and Tim's horses sent to the showgrounds so he could continue to coach them there—just in case. And all of the grooms moved over to take care of them, with the exception that Marco came back to the farm at night to handle Lion, QL, and George's second horse Phantom, and fed them breakfast every day before he left.

The next morning coaching sessions began, Jericho's scheduled as last among the four. But he stood on the rail and watched all of them. By now, Chuck had him so fired up...talking to him both inside and out of the sessions they spent together like a private devil on his shoulder, alternately building him up mentally, lighting his desire for some kind of medal, and riding his ass unmercifully for the slightest mistake...the Games, this show...making his blood boil for this. He was doing the same thing to all the Team members, peaking them both mentally and physically, but was especially concentrating on Jericho because he would be anchor rider, because this was his first time in the Games, and because he had a good chance of medaling individually as well as with the Team. And also because his personality was such that he thrived on the pressure, really needed it to be at his best.

Twenty-four hours left to go before the jog. Frankel—an expert at this. Jericho could barely sleep at night now. His days, pure adrenaline.

Just bring it on. Wanted it badly. *Needed it.*

Standing there on the rail now, while Robin rode. Could feel every stride with her, nerves burning, itching to ride himself.

Soft, cautious little voice. "Jericho? Hi."

Swung his head sharply, aggressively.

What he saw there really surprised him. His half-sister…Nutmeg. She was dressed casually, carrying her Barbie purse, hair in pigtails, and sporting a family member's pass around her neck.

She took a small step backwards under his heavy scrutiny, but still couldn't hide the fact that she was thrilled to see him. "Hi," she said again.

Tried to soften his expression, but it was hard and he wasn't sure he was all that successful—he was just feeling so fierce. Said hello to her, then made an effort to be friendlier. "When did you get here?"

"Yesterday sometime." She smiled, more at ease already and not at all appreciating where his head was—probably a good thing. Giggled. "I'm so confused about what time it is."

He came over closer, to within two feet or so of her, drawn there, curious—this half-sister of his. Had to be nice to her, he told himself. She was there for him, there because she wanted to know him, and man, he sure couldn't fault that—more courage than he'd had with her. Felt really awkward around her though. "I'm glad you came," he said.

"Me too." Smiled at him, but maybe she felt unsure too—looked a little nervous, fidgeting with her badge. "Mr. Frankel's been really nice to us." She looked over toward the Chef D'Equip and waved, though he was so wrapped up in Robin's session that he didn't seem to notice her. And to Jericho, "Have you been getting my emails? I write every couple of days or so."

Expressive look coming back from him, again surprised by it. Hadn't even thought about her in weeks. He shook his head in the negative. "I'm such an idiot with computers," he admitted, knowing that was a lousy excuse but using it anyway. "If my roommate doesn't show your emails to me, I don't even know they're there. Sorry." It was true too, although he sure could have followed up with Brae if he'd wanted to.

"It's okay. Uhm…" She was digging around in that Barbie purse of hers now, and pulled out a tiny package, wrapped in paper with horses on it and tied with a blue bow—jewelry box size. Thrust it out at him. "This is for you," she said. "You can open it later if you want to. It's for good luck. See the blue bow…you said it's your favorite color."

He closed the remaining distance between them, wordlessly. Laid his hand around the little wrapped box, pretty moved by the gesture. Dredged up a teasing grin for her though, and flipped one of her pigtails as he said, "Thanks."

"Hey!" she scolded, but secretly liking it.

Laughed at her.

"Typical boy," she muttered, and he laughed again.

He toyed with the box in his hand—it looked pretty small there. "Can I open it now?" he asked. Wanted to.

"Well sure."

Leaned up against the fence line. Long fingers trying to deal with the small bow, yanked it off eventually, tore off the wrapping paper. Inside, indeed a jewelry box, containing a gold medallion on an 18-inch chain—the medallion marked on the front with a raised horseshoe, and engraved on the back with his initials. Maybe not expensive, but not cheap either. Apparently she knew his middle name too, since that initial was there along with the other two.

JAB, for Jericho Aaron Brandeis.

Speechless.

"Well, do you like it?" she asked impatiently.

Like it? No, he loved it. Told her so, just murmured it. "Yeah a lot." Really sincere sounding, bringing a smile to her face. He took it out of the box, struggled with the clasp, but it was eluding him—tiny in those powerful hands of his.

"Here let me."

He didn't even question it. Turned the medallion over to her, smiling ruefully—knew when he was beaten and admitted it—bent over a little, and Meagan slid it around his neck and fastened it. Stood up again, and just ran the fingers of one hand over it. "You know, no one's ever done that for me before—for a show like that."

"Really?" Her smile broadening.

Warm look from him, and he reached over and touched her face lightly. "Really."

"I'm thirteen and my favorite color is pink," she told him. Little facts about herself for him. "You asked me how old I was in your email, remember?"

Nodded. He remembered it. Still fascinated with her gift to him. "You know my middle name?"

She nodded. "Well, I asked."

Sure she had—it wouldn't have been volunteered. Question in return. "Is *she* here?" No need to specify which "she" he was talking about.

Still she verified it with him. "You mean Mom?" Nervous affirmative shake of her head—not sure where he was going with that. "Yeah, she is, but she wouldn't come out here with me."

Man, he wished he'd taken a better look at her in L.A., but he hadn't known who she was back then. He really felt driven to just see her, even if they didn't speak. But he also wanted her to show some interest in him—something. Was that a lot to ask? "Don't look around at her…just tell me where she is," he said to Meagan.

"Well, right behind me…by that door to the indoor." She looked up at him, barely intimidated, if at all by this tall and very grown-up half-brother of hers. "Are you going to talk to her…I wish you would, but don't be mean to her, alright? Please." Defending her. "She's not a bad person."

Maybe she wasn't—couldn't prove it by him though. Adrenaline starting to pump through his blood again, because man he wanted to see her—didn't want to wait either. "I'm not going to be mean to her." He looked around sharply for someone to stay with Meagan, keep an eye on her. Saw Brae taking pictures of Robin and called out to him.

He looked over, waved, goofy grin.

"Wow, who's that?" Awe in that girlish voice of hers—and naturally, Brae was having his usual effect on her.

Jericho motioned to him, and he jumped down off the fence where he'd been sitting and started strolling over. Looked especially happy today—the newest member of the *Barista Italiano* team—maybe they weren't paying him anything, but sometimes a guy had to give up a few things in pursuit of his dreams. "That's my roommate," Jericho told her. "His name's Brae. Talk to him for a few minutes, okay? I'm going to try and find her."

No objection from Meagan—she seemed to accept the fact that he wanted to, and was also mesmerized by the tall, blond approaching her with the disheveled hair and that incredible bedroom stare—maybe more the latter than the former. "Wow," she said again.

When he got close enough, Jericho said to him, "Brae, do me a favor, will you? This is Nutmeg—the one in the emails, remember? Well, her name's Meagan really. She's my sister…half-sister. Stay with her for a minute, okay? I'll be right back."

"Your sister!"

Didn't even answer Brae, just spun and took off with long strides in the direction Meagan indicated. And oh yeah, now he could see her—his and Meagan's mother—she looked shocked that he was heading over to her. Turned like she'd try to get away before he reached her, but he stepped up his pace. Close enough now that he knew she'd hear him, though he'd only raised his voice a little. Bark of an order, aggressive. "*Wait.* Christ, don't walk out on me." Almost threw in "again" but didn't.

And that stopped her, but she looked off balance—really nervous. Just watching him with dread as he closed the rest of the distance between them, not stopping until he was right up next to her.

No words from either of them.

But those deep blue eyes of his were on her, and hers on him too—drinking in every detail—this powerful man, her son. That fact—almost impossible to comprehend.

He reached out and wrapped his hand around her arm, strong grip, but not enough to hurt. Knew Frankel would be watching him—Chuck knew every fucking thing he did, psychic that way—but he didn't care. "Not here, okay?" he said with feeling. "That's my roommate with Meagan, he'll take care of her for a few minutes. She'll be alright. Walk with me, give me that much."

Jessica Rhys, cautiously nodding.

Some reassurance in that commanding look of his. Potent though.

He found a concrete bench not far away, where he could still see the practice area, but separated enough to provide a measure of privacy. Sat himself, and pulled her down beside him. But as soon as he released her, she scooted back a few inches from him. Allowed that. Drew one booted foot up onto the seat of the bench close in to his body, and wrapped an arm around it—just totally at ease with that athletic body of his. Radiating strength. Some of the aggression Chuck had stoked in him, also more than evident.

For a minute, they were just looking at each other—she seemed awed there in his presence. Timidly, Jessica lifted one hand, and touched the embroidery on the pocket of his polo shirt...the words "Brandeis Show Stables." Allowed that too.

Impressed wonder in her eyes.

His too.

When she was done and her hand fell away again, it was his turn to touch her. He reached across and brushed his fingers over her hair—a sprinkling of gray running evenly through it, and a darker and browner shade than his own, but the same thick, sleek texture, and straight like his. Wanted a more direct comparison though. He reached back and tugged the band off the bottom of his braid, then shook it loose—letting her see it, looking himself.

His eyes finding hers again—deep blue meeting deep blue. His stare powerful, but not openly threatening, although maybe there was an accusation there for her—something that said...*oh hell yeah, just look at us.*

She got her courage up. A mouse toying with a lion would have been a good comparison as she dared to touch his hair like he'd done with hers, threading her fingers through it—then dared even more, tracing her hand along his jawline despite his forbidding expression—his face slightly rough beneath her touch even though he'd recently shaved. Just looking at him. A kind of wistful longing in her expression.

Not getting much in the way of feedback from him other than the fact that he was drawing some pretty clear but unspoken boundaries about how much of this he was going to allow. And she'd basically reached that limit.

She gave in to him, hands moving nervously back to her lap.

Silence for a while, his eyes on her, looking for something. After a bit, he reached around behind himself and quietly rebraided his hair, fingers working automatically, and with a precision born of practice. Wrapped the band around the end of it, and let it swing between his shoulders again. Only then did he speak, the first words between them since he'd brought her over there...and she had yet to say anything at all, but he was going to get past that and now. Dose of sarcasm. "I'm not that bad, am I?"

Jessica brought her hand up to her mouth hesitantly, almost a young girl's gesture. Said with some feeling, "No, no...just...a little daunting." Rushed to explain that. "I always think of you as a child. Not an infant, but maybe four or five years old...and you're a man instead. A grown man. It's so unnerving. My God, how can it have been so long?" More trepidation coming to her expression, but she said what she was thinking...feeling. "How alone you must have been all those years. You must despise me."

"I'll be honest," he admitted. "I have a thousand feelings about it, and yeah sometimes I feel like that. It can haunt me, and at the worst possible times. And I just wonder...if I'm worth anything. And if so, to who?" Stronger tone, caustic. "And I've also got to wonder why no one ever gave a damn. But that's not what I'm feeling right now, and that's not what this is about either." He took her wrist in his powerful grip, and lowered her hand away from her face—wanted to *see* her. *"Come on,"* he pressured her irritably. "You must have some desire...to know who I am."

Her fingers wrapped lightly around his forearm in return. Regret intermingled with the tremulous quality to her voice. "You can build a wall in your mind," she groped to explain. "And it just gets bigger and bigger and after a while, it doesn't seem like there's any way to get over it. And then you stop trying. I know that's not a very good excuse...there's really no excuse, Jericho..."

Had to make her stop. Couldn't face her guilt. "Enough. Don't go there. I hear you anyway." Truth was, he didn't know if he wanted to get to know this woman or not. But there were things he had to find out about himself, and she was the only one who could tell him. Changed the subject—to the question he'd waited his whole life to ask. "Why am I called Jericho? Why that name?" Not that it was so important in and of itself—but it was a fundamental part of the "who am I?" question. Something unique to him that he didn't know shit about.

She wasn't looking at him, but a soft expression came over her face. A fond memory, maybe. Maybe him as a newborn, and her naming him. Still, she was apologizing too. "I was seventeen. I guess I didn't realize it might be a difficult name to live with. I'm sorry if you..."

Interrupted that, didn't want her sidetracked. "Actually, it's fine. I've just always wondered, and people always ask me, and I can't ever answer them." Intense look in his eyes—really wanting to know.

"Your father's name was Ricco, and my name's Jessica." She looked down softly. "I just put them together, and well...Jericho came out." She moved her hand further up his arm—all hard muscle and so fascinating. Just still couldn't get over the reality of him. Only hours old when they'd taken him away from her, red-faced and screaming...and now this imposing creature—tall, panther-like grace, and very much an adult. "It sounded like a strong name to me—that walled city in the Bible story."

Bark of derisive laughter. Smirking a little even. "Yeah, but the walls came tumbling down, didn't they?" Trace of self-scorn. "Could be appropriate at that."

Jessica Rhys shrugged nervously. "Well, I ignored that part. Anyway, I figured you'd just change it to Jerry."

Shook his head strongly in the negative. "No, I've never shortened it or used a nickname. I mean, it's the only link I have to my past. Think about it…if my name had been John or Dave, would you have even come to that stadium in L.A.? But Jericho? Now that's different."

"You're right. But I won't claim I was that smart or forward thinking. I just wanted to pick something that tied you to the both of us…"

Interrupted. He was just that impatient—had to stop himself from grabbing her by the shoulders and shaking her to focus her where he wanted her. "Tell me about *him*." Expressive and really asking, with all the longing of growing up without a father and the years of wondering about it.

She shrunk back a little more, sensing the demand in him, hearing it in his voice. "That dark red in your hair? That's his. He was tall too…" Little sigh. "And handsome. You look something like him…around the nose and mouth, but you're more intent. You always…look like you mean business."

Pushing it again. Hard voice. "Yeah, well I do."

She nodded, understanding him. Embarrassed look on her face. Hesitating. "I have to be honest with you because you deserve to know this, but please don't repeat…"

"I won't." Tightening his grip on her arm. Pretty intolerant.

"I only met him once."

Now that shocked him, set him back a little and he eased off on her a bit. Protested. "But I thought he shipped out and was killed in action."

Jessica sighed. "I told Meagan that, and your Mr. Frankel too." Tried to explain why she'd altered the truth. "Jericho, she's only thirteen…how can she understand? And your coach…well, I just don't know him all that well. But I'll tell you the story—the real story. I was only sixteen at the time I met your father—seventeen when you were born. A runaway, desperately trying to get by and not doing very well. We met at a nightclub—I'd lied about my age and was a waitress there. And he…he was a Navy pilot, in town on leave for the night—just one night. By the time I knew I was pregnant…well, I had no way to find him."

Jericho, really keenly interested in this and leaning toward her. "And his name was Ricco Brandeis?"

Her eyes cast down guiltily. "Well, he told me his name right at the beginning when he asked me to dance, but you know how that is…you're introduced to someone, and the very next second you've already forgotten their name, and then you're too embarrassed to ask? And of course, young girl, drinking champagne for the first time…anyway, I couldn't remember it afterwards—not his last name anyway. But I knew he went to Brandeis

University…he was proud of that, mentioned it more than once. You know, he had a college jacket that he was wearing too—all his friends were wearing their flight jackets, but not him." She looked back up at him finally, a lost feeling in her eyes then. "Maybe I was just fantasizing, but I liked him so much. I always hoped he'd come back again…that we'd find you, be a family. But those were just a young girl's dreams. That's not how life really is."

Very human story…had to admit he understood her better now that she'd told him this. Jury still out for sure, but at least deliberating, thinking about it. "So who's Aaron?" he asked her, the final piece of the puzzle of his name. "Or does it mean anything?"

"My younger brother."

Startled again, and finally angry. "Fuck, I have an uncle too? And what about your parents? *Come on,*" he snarled again, "None of you could find a way to…?"

Drawing back a little at the harsh note entering his voice. "Jericho, I'd never have let you stay with my parents," she said firmly. "Jesus, *I* ran away from them."

Demanded it. "Fine, then my uncle…*does he know?*"

"About you?" she asked, pleading a little. "Aaron's…he's seven years younger than I am—he was only ten when you were born, and of course I'd run away from home, so no. And I never told him. But I did right before Meagan and I came over here. If you want to meet him sometime…"

Backing away from that—way too much to even think about.

"Anyway, he's not here. There's time for you to decide."

Just murmured. Fell silent. Lit a cigarette and smoked it.

Resignation in her voice. "You do hate me, and I understand that." Stroked his hand but he jerked it away.

Finished the cigarette, tossed it away. Lit another. Expression harsh and bitter. Blew his breath out and just cursed. Finally answered her statement, although minutes had already passed. "No, I don't. I'll give you this much…you had me. I'm alive, at least." Eyes hard on her, unyielding despite the words. "And my sister…seems happy, and you're doing that by yourself."

She leaned toward him and touched the gold medallion hanging from his neck. "You know, she earned all the money for this herself—wouldn't take anything from anybody else because she said it had to be from her. She's so thrilled…to have a brother, and she's so proud of you."

"Yeah I like her too, but I haven't got a clue how to…"

"Jericho! How's it going over here?" George Strang's voice. He was approaching them on foot, although he'd been the next to ride after Robin. Jericho had seen him get on Tarrytown a few minutes after they'd sat down.

Looked around at him in surprise—knew damn well Chuck had sent him, and annoyed about it too. Sarcastic. "What did you do, George? Have a ten-minute coaching session? Chuck must really think I need babysitting if he's willing to cut your ride short the day before the Games."

"No Jericho, I did a full hour." But admitted the rest of it too. "But you're right, Chuck's over there fretting up a storm about you."

Hard to believe he'd been sitting there that long, covered it up though by standing up sharply, deep blue stare sighting out into the middle of the practice arena and landing squarely on the Chef D'Equip. Grumbled irritably, "That doesn't seem right to me. And how the hell am I supposed to ride without a horse anyway?"

George just smiling. "Well, I don't know Jericho, but Marco's been standing at the in-gate with a black stallion for the last five minutes. Isn't that what you usually sit on?"

Murmured self-consciously to himself, "Yeah, usually."

Something cathartic about having that conversation with her. Purged his mind of the distraction, sharpened his focus on riding even more. He mounted the big black, felt strong, good—ready for this. Signaled Chuck, and then went into a warm-up with Antares, his partner, this huge athletic animal. Full of fire today, too.

Frankel left him alone for the first few minutes, simply watching. Nodding, liking what he was seeing. Eye on the other competitors in the ring—other Chef D'Equips too, especially them. They were all sharing this training area together—had to coordinate who was jumping which line of fences and when. And that was all working pretty smoothly this morning. He sighted the others and barked out which line he was taking…no objections there, and he passed the instruction along to Jericho.

"Jericho…long line with the Oxer and the Liverpool!" he ordered.

The highest and most difficult of the practice lines out here, and yeah, he wanted to hit it. Just burning up inside to jump.

Bee-Bee had arrived at ringside. She'd been the first to ride this morning, but was still dressed in fawn colored breeches and riding boots. Sidled up to George, said, "Hi."

"Hi, yourself."

Jessica and Meagan Rhys standing close-by too, watching, but Bee-Bee hadn't noticed them, and they didn't approach her either—Jessica holding Meagan back.

But Brae and Meagan had hit it off predictably well, and he was entertaining her, watching while Jericho rode and snapping pictures. Even tossed in a happy "Hi, Mom!" when Meagan introduced her. Held his hand out. "Hey, I rent a room from Jericho when we're down in Florida, and I'm the Team Photographer." Went right into his normal routine, but with a new twist. "I used to work at Starbucks..." Bee-Bee and George taking a few steps further away, and hurriedly. "...but now I've been opening up this new store here in San Patrignano. You should stop in...it's pretty cool, and you know, I've got most everything straightened out now so it's running pretty smooth."

Jessica, impressed to be meeting someone on the International Starbucks management team...or at least that was the impression he gave.

"Man, will you look at Jericho," George was saying, as his teammate lined up to approach the line of fences. "Chuck has him wrapped so tight you can just feel the fire rolling off him."

Jessica Rhys, inching closer to them, hoping to hear some tidbits, but staying out of the way.

Soft laugh from Bee-Bee. "Well, tell me about it. He's not even sleeping anymore. Sometimes I wake up, and he's just lying there. His eyes will be open, and George, I swear to you they're just smoldering."

"Wow."

"Yeah."

They both turned back again to watch.

Jessica, processing that. Little bit different slant on Bee-Bee—Jericho, sleeping with her apparently.

Jericho and Antares were about four strides out from the first fence now. He sighted his mark, but suddenly saw another rider bearing down on him out of the corner of his eye—on a direct path to cut across in front of him, and really close—way too close...maybe even on a course to run into him. Jerked Antares hard and to the side. The black stallion stumbled and had to scramble fast to keep his feet beneath him...and in that second, another rider, teammate to the first one, buzzed him from the other side. Antares startled again and snorting in fear now, Jericho struggling to keep him from bolting—his line at the fences in utter shambles.

He roared in fury at the pair of them, and pulled out to come back around.

The first rider looking over his shoulder, calling out sweetly, "Sorry," in an accented voice. One of the Belgians. Oh yeah, recognized him.

Click, click, click…Brae taking pictures of everything.

"Jericho! Ride to me!" Frankel shouted, really, really angry.

"Oh my God," George said horrified to Bee-Bee. "That was totally deliberate."

She was gripping the fence line, scowling. "I know it was. Damn it, George, are they trying to hurt him?"

Grim. "Not hurt, unnerve."

He'd ridden up to Frankel, deep blue eyes hawk-sharp, every muscle in him flexing…man, wanting to fight. And the U.S. Chef D'Equip took that, played it to his advantage. Laid his hand on Jericho's boot, and spoke harshly up at him, "These guys know all about your accident…don't think for a minute they don't. And they think they can scare you by riding right at you…but then they didn't see that trucker's face in 's-Hertogenbosch…I did. They don't have a clue what kind of fighting son-of-a-bitch they're challenging. Now I'm telling you something, Jericho." Tightened his grip around that booted ankle. "I'm telling you…*don't you dare give up that line again.* Understand me? Don't you dare back down. You ride right over top of them if you have to, but you…*don't give up the line.*"

Oh yeah, liked those instructions. Powerful nod.

Fierce look coming back from the Chef D'Equip too. "And you've got a crop in your hand, don't you?"

That violent beast inside him, rising. Just growled it. "Fuckin' A."

"Alright." Slapped that booted leg one more time—firing him up, but with just enough reproach there—like maybe he should have done this on his own—guaranteed to motivate him even more. "Now I'm gonna clear that same line for you again. When I signal you, you take it…and when you take it, you make sure it stays yours. You hear me, Jericho?"

"Yeah, I hear you, Chuck."

"You don't back down."

Eyes narrowed, vengeful, *"No way."*

"Alright then…*ride.*"

Took Antares and cantered him down to the far end of the training arena. Waited for the signal.

"What did Chuck say to him, I wonder?" Bee-Bee asked, sounding anxious. "George, look at Jericho…Chuck really pissed him off."

"Oh no, you're wrong," the Team Captain told her. "They couldn't be more together. Christ, watch out for this though—Chuck's putting an end to this hazing Jericho bullshit once and for all."

Brae coming closer and asking, obviously interested, "How do you mean?" He liked the sound of it, even before he heard Strang's answer. Reset his camera, getting ready for some cool action shots.

George, and speaking pointedly. "I mean, Jericho's the hand grenade, and Chuck just pulled the pin."

Signal from Chuck.

That same deadly calm settling over Jericho that he normally felt before a fight. Something violent living inside him, but so perfectly controlled. Controlled—not as in contained—in fact, let loose to do it's damage. But always thinking, strategic…brutally cold-blooded.

Didn't get more lethal than that.

He gave the cue for the canter, brought Antares straight out onto the same line as before. One big Oxer—4'6" high x 4' wide, then two strides to a vertical, and then finally three strides into another big spread—a Liverpool, also 4'6" x 4'. Sighted those two Belgian riders—both of them doing flatwork, looking innocent, not on a path with him at all.

Four strides out…no change in that. Then three, everything still fine, and maybe they weren't going to try it again, not twice in a row like that. He marked his spot, checked Antares to hit it. Beautiful lift when they got there, the black stallion launching nicely from behind. Elegant athletic jump, rounded in the air, then touchdown and heading into that vertical…two strides and cued for the jump again. His mount working confidently, coming up from the shoulder, clean, perfect bascule in the air.

And that's when he saw it—poised there in two-point going over that second jump…one of the Belgians spurring his mount to cross straight through the line between that second vertical and the final Liverpool. It made the rage flare up inside him—how fucking dangerous was that? One thing for sure…that bastard Belgian was about to find out.

Hell yeah. Loved it. Violence etched in those deep blue eyes.

Shouts of anger coming from Frankel, and from his teammates on the fence as they realized what was happening. Ignored them, focused only on his target. On punishing him.

Antares touched down with a front foot, then his hindquarters landed, thrusting powerfully forward. Jericho stayed up in two-point, squeezed with his legs asking for speed, aiming dead for the collision—flipped the crop in his hand too, so that it was facing up and forward, rather than down and back. Up and forward like a weapon, and man, that's exactly how he intended to use it. Made eye contact with that Belgian, letting him know he was coming for him. Surprise on the bastard's face that he wasn't desperately trying to pull to the side—surprise too at the aggression coming at him from this brash American. Then terror. The Belgian trying to turn his own horse aside, but way too late for that. Hard bump as Antares' shoulder hit the other rider's leg. Scream from him, and then...whack! ...Jericho's crop slicing into his thigh, and damn hard too, tearing the fabric of his breeches as it bit into his flesh.

He'd been so ready for the impact—it was much less forceful on his side than the Belgian's, he'd made sure of that by picking the angle to suit himself. Yanked Antares clear of the other horse and rider combination, back onto the line, and into the path of the jump, then lifted him...and God, the courage and heart in this animal, because despite the bump, he followed the cues from the man on his back boldly—launching himself into the fence...up and over that big Oxer clean.

Turned at the end of that line, and now Jericho was coming back for him. And yeah, he'd fallen and was on the ground, grasping at his leg and groaning—hoped like hell he'd broken it. Slowed Antares and rode past him, sneering and cocky. Called out to him, "Sorry," then just laughed darkly. Eyes on the rest of them surrounding the downed rider, just daring them, challenging. No takers either.

Spun Antares and headed him back over to Chuck.

Dangerous smile from the Chef D'Equip as he got there, and an approving hand stroking the horse's neck. "Nice form, Jericho," he said, coldly pleased. So there was a little nasty streak in him too, and Jericho could sure relate to that. "Now give this horse to Marco," Frankel told him—praise for him there, satisfaction. Powerful eye contact. "That's enough for you today. You're ready for these Games."

Oh sure, there was a stink about the incident in the training arena. Frankel kept Jericho well out of it—took Brae with him into the hearing instead. And that settled it—the pictures clearly showed Jericho on a line, and the other rider interfering—not only once but twice. The Belgian, disqualified from this competition, and fined handsomely. He'd been their alternate though, no real blow to them as a team. And undoubtedly planned that way as well.

And yes, there'd been a hairline fracture of his leg. Served him right, the prick.

Chapter Thirty-One

Probably 2:00 AM, and Frankel banging on the door to his room, and shouting, "Jericho, get up! I need you right now!" Then began banging across the hall on George's door as well.

Never heard Chuck sound like that before, and hell, he'd been awake anyway. Jumped out of bed, leaving Bee-Bee still mumbling and trying to figure out what had woken her so abruptly—rammed his legs into a pair of jeans, strode to the door, and stepped out into the hallway. And man, Frankel looked about as bad as Jericho had ever seen him. "What is it, Chuck?"

Straight answer, and right to the point. "Sabotage with the horses."

Just murmured it. "No...Oh fuck me...which ones?"

"I don't know...could be all of them."

All of them?

George coming out into the hallway too, dressed in sweatpants, and within a few seconds the others appearing too...Bee-Bee's small form coming up behind Jericho wearing just his shirt.

"What's going on?" From George.

Frankel repeated it, little bit more information this time, but he clearly didn't want to stand there talking—wanted to get going. "Santo called... hard to understand him. He was on duty watching the stalls, and someone hit him from behind—he didn't know how long he'd been out. Woke up pretty groggy, but it looks like they might have drugged the horses—he couldn't tell me for sure which ones, but maybe all of them. Probably Antares...Monterrey..."

All of them talking at once, really upset...asking questions to which Frankel had no answers. "Let's just get down there," he snarled. "We'll find out then."

Just impossible to believe, but starting to sink in. If it was true...*if it was true*...then the Games were over for them. God, let it not be.

516

They all piled into their cars—for the most part taking separate vehicles in case they needed them, but Brae and Bee-Bee went with Jericho.

"Well, you've still got QL," Bee-Bee was saying miserably, close to tears. "Maybe you can ride as an individual, Jericho."

"No!" he insisted powerfully. "Chuck will come up with something." Didn't know if that was true or not…Chuck could only do so much. Yeah, he worked miracles sometimes, but this? Well, they didn't know the facts yet, didn't know and he consoled himself with that

It was closer to 3:00 AM by the time they arrived at the Games venue, got through Security, parked and finally got over to the stalls. All the grooms were standing there except Santo, who'd been taken to the Emergency Room in the closest hospital for evaluation, and Marco, who was still back at the farm. They were talking in angry tones among themselves.

"Reynaldo," Chuck barked, addressing him as the most senior of the grooms in Marco's absence. "Tell me exactly what happened and what's going on now."

All the riders had gone down the aisle to look at their own horses, though they were listening, too, and coming back pretty quickly to hear what Reynaldo said. Jericho, standing in front of Antares' stall, and his heart just sunk. The big black had his head down, looked completely lethargic, and as a stallion, had dropped—a sure sign that some type of tranquilizer had been used on him. He barely glanced up, not looking for treats or companionship like he normally would. Jericho just slumped against the stall door. Felt so cheated. Hard to believe someone had wanted to eliminate them this badly. To go after the horses? And man, they'd even had someone standing guard. Just heartsick about it.

He turned and went back to listen. Reynaldo had described about the same thing Chuck said earlier—Santo had been on watch, and had been hit from behind—he'd seen nothing before or after that, but woke up face down in the middle of the aisle. "When he checked the horses, they were just starting to look drugged—not like they do now…now you can really tell," Reynaldo was saying. "Someone Aced them, or something like that."

"Oh sure," Jericho said, rage just building inside him. "I guess I should be glad it was nothing to really harm them, just an illegal substance so none of them can pass the drug screen. They'll all be fine tomorrow by mid-day, but it'll still show up in blood and urine samples. We won't be allowed to compete them, will we?"

Frankel shook his head—he could barely trust himself to speak. "Probably not. I'm going to ask for a special exception, but don't hold out a lot of hope for that." Just too devastating…his entire team, gone. The entire team. Everything they'd worked so hard for…months of preparation, his riders, so ready for this, medal contenders. All blown away in one vindictive act.

George slammed his arm against the side of the stall. "Bastards," he snarled.

"Those Belgians," Brae said, voicing what they were all secretly thinking.

"If we can prove that…" Chuck began, voice harsh and filled with bitterness. *If.* He'd get them thrown out of International competition for a long, long time, that was for sure. But that wasn't his first priority at the moment—it was pretty high on the list, but nothing came before trying to salvage the rest of the Games. "I'll get on the horn with the Organizing Committee right away," he said.

Brae went around and took pictures of all the horses. At least they'd have a record of what they found.

Bee-Bee was still standing with Monterrey, hadn't moved from there. And Jericho came up behind her—knew how excited she'd been about riding him in the Games. After Langley's death, it had taken on a special meaning to her. Fury, just pouring off Jericho, but still there was a good measure of tenderness in him as he wrapped his arms around her, and she turned around in them, burying her face against his chest, her shoulders shaking quietly.

Maybe it wasn't going to do a lot of good, but Frankel got on the phone and stayed there, stomping in and out of the stabling area like an avenging angel…calling the Organizing Committee, the Police, the Team Vet, the American Selection Committee members, the FEI President himself. Tremendous shock and sympathy coming back at him…not a lot of answers though.

The Police showed up inside twenty minutes of being called. Took statements, taped off the area, walked the aisles looking for evidence, interviewing grooms in neighboring aisles.

And then there was Security. Tim and Marc went out and talked to them. No, they didn't keep a log of who came in and out, but it could only have been other grooms or another competitor—at this hour they were the only ones allowed in the stable area, and yes, any number of people had come and gone, and some slept overnight there too. Not much information to help them.

The Team Vet arrived, checked all the horses, and drew blood work on them. He confirmed that it appeared to be Ace or some other tranquilizer. He'd know for sure once the results of the blood work came back.

Ace Promazine—definitely a forbidden substance.

Face it, Jericho thought to himself, every animal in this aisle would be disqualified. Game over.

Or was it? Something taking root inside his mind.

He waited until Chuck was finally standing alone, and went over to him. Nodded meaningfully toward the end of the aisle, and the Chef D'Equip gave him an affirmative look in return. They walked all the way outside together. The sun was coming up now, but the place was still quiet—just the occasional soft nicker of horses. Jericho paused…lit a cigarette.

"Chuck," he said with conviction. "You know damn well they'll never bend the rules and let us compete with horses that don't pass the drug screen. It sets a precedent, opens the door for abuse."

Just miserable about it. "I know it."

"But we still have three good horses back at the farm."

Yeah, obviously Frankel's mind had been working in that direction too, because he said regretfully, "Sure, and if I could clone you and have you ride both QL and Lion we could still compete as a team. But that's not going to work, is it?" Just shook his head—of all the things that might have happened, man this was sure the last one he would have expected. And he could hardly be any more despondent than he was now. "Anyway, that damn Lion is nuttier than a fruitcake and too dangerous to show here, especially after that accident with Race. No, you and George can still ride as individuals, but there won't be any U.S. Team this year."

Drew on his cigarette, just thoughtful. "Lion has just as much talent as Antares. On a good day he could medal—hell that's why you got Bruce to buy him for me. And if I ride him, why can't George take QL?" he tossed out.

"Come on, Jericho." Almost irritated by this, didn't need it right now. "Get real, alright? And what's the point in that? George will ride Phantom."

"No, Chuck, I'm serious. Why can't he?" he insisted again. "And *come on* yourself…you're not even thinking about this, not even giving it a chance. Hear me out, will you? George is a damn fine rider. Maybe he's not going to want to do this because QL can be a bitch, and he knows it, shit, he's seen it. But he can ride her—he's strong enough. Bee-Bee isn't. But Bee-Bee can ride Phantom, can't she? And then we'd have a team again, maybe a strong one."

Not liking it at all. "Oh bull, I have to go with my best shot, and that's you and QL. I'd be crazy to put anyone else on her. And why wouldn't you want to ride her?" Getting really annoyed about this now. Too much tension, finding an outlet. Started sniping at him. "Are you scared to have the U.S. hopes focused on your ass? Is that what it is?"

Snarled back at him. "Is that what you think it is?" Dropped his cigarette and ground it out with his heel, taking out his anger that way.

"Well, I don't know."

Challenged him heatedly, "You're calling me a coward, is that it?"

"Maybe."

Voices getting raised now, drawing interest from the rest of the group who'd started staring.

Just lifted up that right fist of his. Nice threat. "You know, Chuck…I've wanted to cold-cock you so many times, it's like a fantasy to me. Here's the truth…sometimes I even jerk off to it." Jericho not relenting, derisive and daring. Deliberately offensive. "So keep it up. Because, I swear to you…you keep going at this rate and you're gonna feel it."

Frankel, glaring at that clenched right hand, remembering that trucker's face maybe. "I've seen what you can do with that fist, and so no thank you, Jericho. And as for jerking off, I don't believe it…Christ, you're like a damn rabbit as it is. How can you have the time or energy left, or hell even be able?" Smiling, even snickering a little bit at his own scornful humor, although he was obviously trying not to. "Now Goddamn it, Jericho, shut up for Christ's sake, alright? I'm thinking here."

"Yeah, I'll shut up. God forbid I might have an idea, right Chuck?"

"Now listen to me and listen good, cause here's what's happening…I'm thinking—you're shutting up." Smirk pulling his lips up, quickly stifled it.

"Go ahead, just laugh at me, you bastard." Half-turned. Maybe he didn't even know he was going to do it himself, and maybe he was just that upset by all that was happening, but man, he lashed out with that fist…*lightning strike*…slamming it into the side of the barn…and oh fuck man, explosion of pain all the way up his arm, cause that barn wall was solid. Grabbed his right hand in his left, biting back a howl of pain, and cursing viciously, "Fuck…*fuck*."

Frankel automatically stepping back into the Chef D'Equip role again. "*Damn you* and that temper of yours. Now let me see that." Pure demand. He reached out for Jericho's hand, but he'd pulled it up tight to his chest, still cursing, and sure as shit wasn't surrendering it.

"Fuck, why didn't I hit *you*?" Jericho ground out, just sucking his breath in and snarling. Long string of bitter curses.

Frankel had the nerve to chuckle again, this situation so ridiculous, and the Team's situation so fucked. Trying to act angry. "Let me see it right now. I'll kill you if you broke that hand."

Deep blue stare swinging around to land slap on him. "It's not broken…just fuck me, Chuck, and you're *still* laughing. Man, I was trying to say something to you." Smile tugging at his own lips now too, despite the shooting pain in his hand and arm. Couldn't even keep a straight face, and growled angrily, "Fuck you, don't make me laugh. I swear to Christ, I'm really pissed at you."

Frankel chuckling harder now, covering his mouth with one hand. "Yeah, and I'm pissed at you too. How stupid was that move? Come on, let me…" Had to stop for a second as a wave of laughter shook his body. "No, seriously Jericho…let me see that."

Moaning. "Ow…it fuckin' hurts." So close to laughing himself now, couldn't stop it. Gave in, threw his head back and just howled.

"I'm glad you two think this is funny," George said hotly, coming down the aisle toward them. Real reproach there.

"Christ, *I* don't," Jericho managed to gasp. "He's such a prick…and I'm ready to kill him because he's being so unreasonable." Turned his face away, dark amusement lighting up that powerful stare of his. Still holding his one hand in the other. He doubled over it, cursing in between waves of laughter. "Damn it, George…I really hurt my hand here. I need Marco."

"Let me see that," George said firmly, reaching his arm out, grabbing Jericho's right wrist.

Sucked the pain up, and let him have it—enjoying the fact that Frankel looked really irritated that he'd let George take a look at it, and not him. George staring at the damage, amazed. "Jesus Christ, Jericho. How childish are you? Isn't this situation bad enough without you hurting yourself too? Will you look at this?"

"Give me that." Frankel, grabbing it.

Knuckles, bruised, already swollen, the skin scraped off and bloodied, a few small wood splinters evident too.

"Yeah, well he provoked me into it," Jericho growled, jerking his hand back now that Frankel had it, and massaging it, wincing as his fingers worked over each of the bones. Lifted his head to Reynaldo, and just bellowed, *"Obténgame algún hielo!"*

"Bueno, Puño." Little smirking grin there when he said it. He set off to fill a bucket with ice for Jericho.

"Seriously, George," Jericho said between gasps of pain while he waited. It was subsiding slightly, but still ached like a son-of-a-bitch, and he pulled it back in to his stomach again. "I was *trying* to tell Chuck we have three good horses left. We can still mount a team. I mean…if we do that I'll ride Lion, no one else can. But that leaves QL and Phantom."

"I'll ride QL."

Soft feminine voice. Bee-Bee. Coming down to get involved in this discussion, wanting it so much.

But that definitely wasn't what Jericho had in mind. QL was one strong ass mare, and if she decided to test you, you'd better be tough enough to handle her. Sure, Bee-Bee was an excellent technical rider—better than he was even—but to sit a horse like QL and make her behave?

Frankel staring sharply at him. "Can we make it work?" he murmured. Then more forcefully, "Can we?" Only Jericho knew for sure what QL would do for another rider, and only he could prepare the teammate who'd be giving it a shot. "I need to know this—and a really honest assessment. I've got two choices…let you ride QL and go for an individual medal, and then George rides Phantom and does the same. And there's no Team score. Or…we try to ride all three horses as a Team, and Jericho moves over to Lion…and maybe gets blown away in the first round if that stallion throws a fit—and if that happens, then we're really fucked. And, if knowing all that we're still stupid enough to try it…then who rides Phantom and who rides QL? And remember, we have six team members to pick from, not just you three." Looked from one of them to the other. "George, you're Team Captain. You think about it for a little bit…talk among yourselves maybe. I'm going to have to make a decision in an hour or two at most."

By now, the first member of the Organizing Committee had arrived and Frankel left to go over and speak with him.

The other three riders just sitting on the floor at the far end of the aisle watching them.

And Jericho was looking at Bee-Bee now.

She was trying not to let his scrutiny make her nervous, it was hard though. "Listen, I agree with Chuck," she was saying. "George and Phantom are a great combination already, and we know they can do a solid round—we so desperately need that. And you have to ride Lion, because you're the only one who can. But I've seen you ride QL, and I know…listen, *I know*…she's really bonded to you. But I'm not afraid to ride her."

George was looking at her and nodding like he agreed. But maybe he wasn't convinced, and his eyes wandered down the aisle toward Tim and Marc.

What a horrible situation, Jericho was thinking. Didn't know who was going to make the final call, and hoped like hell Chuck wasn't going to dump it on him.

Reynaldo had meanwhile come down the aisle with a bucket that was filled with ice about three fourths of the way up, and then water poured over it all the way to the top. He set it down next to Jericho, who dropped to one knee beside it, and tested it with his fingers…It was freezing cold. Grim look on his face.

"Feurza," Reynaldo said. Light touch on his shoulder.

Harsh but expressive look in return from Jericho. *"Del dolor que surjo."*

Appreciative nod from Reynaldo. *"Ah, sí."*

"Reynaldo, me trae un par de riendas, lo hacen?" Jericho said to him. Turned to Bee-Bee, going back to that discussion. "You've got a great position. Maybe you *can* ride her. Let's try something," he said to her. "I just asked Reynaldo to bring me a pair of reins. But while we wait, let me get this over with." Looked at that bucket of ice, drew his lips back in a snarl, anticipating that fierce biting cold. Balled his injured fist up, and then just jammed it into that frigid mix of water and ice and held it there. Laid his head back and groaned.

Shock on George's face. "Jericho, I thought ice was supposed to make it hurt less, not more."

Teeth grit and forcing the words out between sharply drawn breaths. "Yeah, it does *in a minute*, George. But man, it's so cold…just burns like hell."

Smirk from Reynaldo, as he walked off to get the reins Jericho asked for. Called back over his shoulder, *"Limpie…qué un tonto."*

Bark of laughter from Jericho.

"Why does he call me that?" George snapped irritably. "I always know he's talking about me when he says 'Limpy'."

Dissolved in laughter then.

And it really seemed to piss George off. "Jericho what's the matter with you…this isn't funny, none of it."

"*Limpie*…it doesn't mean what you think, okay?" he chuckled. Lied a little, and conveniently didn't mention the fact that Reynaldo had also just called his boss a fool. "It's a nickname he has for you…a compliment, not an insult…he just thinks you're a perfectionist." Then told the truth about the rest of his question. "And damn, George…forgive me for laughing. I'm just so tight…swear to God, I'm trying not to cry here."

Soft from Bee-Bee, and protective of him too. "We all are, Jericho. George, you too."

Strang nodded, admitting it.

Reynaldo had returned with the reins, and handed them to Jericho. Left that right hand where it was, submerged in the ice—and yeah, it was totally numb now, pain all but gone. He took both ends of the reins where they would normally be attached to the bit in the horse's mouth, and closed them in his left hand. "Stand like you're balanced in two-point, weight on the ball of your feet," Jericho told Bee-Bee. "And take up the reins." She did that, not questioning him, shortening the reins till she had a light contact. Jericho applied pressure, rocking his arm back toward himself in an easy rhythm, creating the feel of the horse's mouth for her.

"Wow, that's good," she said, surprised.

"That's Monterrey, right?" he asked her. "How he feels in the bridle?"

"Well, sure." Smile on her face. "Exactly."

"And this is him into a fence." Drew his hand smoothly up and back, little jerk at the beginning of it to simulate the launch.

She laughed and gave the release to his imaginary horse. "That's so perfect, Jericho. That's just what he does."

George watching with interest,

"Alright," Jericho continued. "So that's Monterrey…and this is QL." Relentlessly increased the pressure, little slower rhythm to his imitation canter, jerked the left side of his hand a few times.

"Wow," she breathed. "She takes that much contact?"

"Oh yeah. Makes those little tugs on the right rein too, that's normal. And she expects you to maintain that much pressure. She doesn't want you to drop her, feels insecure without it. So, this is a fence." Much sharper jerk with the reins, imitating the way the mare stretched her neck up and out, and easily pulling Bee-Bee forward out of position with the sudden pressure. "Come on," Jericho murmured to her. "Try it again. I'm not even making her pull yet, and she will. If you come forward like that, she'll fall on the forehand, and then you're fucked, okay?"

He patiently spent the next twenty minutes with her that way. And she wasn't acting like it was a stupid exercise either—taking it seriously, really putting an effort into getting used to the feel, being able to handle the powerful contact with losing her balance. He'd gotten pretty into it too, pulling that right hand out of the ice to hold the reins with two hands to produce the effect he wanted.

Conclusion at the end of it…"You better be prepared to push this mare hard with your legs to keep her hind end coming on, but if you do, and you ride her with this kind of contact…I think it could work."

Huge smile on her face, and she threw her arms around his neck. "Oh please tell Chuck that," she breathed.

Looked at George. Thought the message should come from him.

The Team Captain nodded. Yeah, he'd talk to Chuck for them.

Nine o'clock that morning and a special session of the U.S. Selection Committee—most of the major patrons in attendance also. Frankel had outlined his proposal to them, and he'd gone with what his riders were asking for…a three-man team instead two individual riders. Most teams had four members, but then they dropped one score and only counted the top three rides. With only three on their team, every single score would count, increasing the pressure on them. The pairs would be Bee-Bee on QL as the leadoff rider, George on Phantom, and Jericho on Chasseur de Lion at anchor.

"I object to this," Bob Marx was saying, though he wasn't a committee member, and had only been invited as a courtesy. "Jericho won the show at 's-Hertogenbosch on QL. That's our best pair and our best chance at a medal. Chasseur de Lion is…well, he's crazy. He damn near killed Jericho's working student, or at least that's what I heard, Chuck."

"Why can't we do some tryouts of all the riders on QL?" someone else was asking.

"Okay, one question at a time," Frankel said, trying to keep the irritation from his voice, but not doing very well. "Look, our riders are fighting mad—they're upset that someone tried to eliminate them from competition as a Team, and they want to go in there and win a medal—prove they can't be taken out that easily. And to be honest with you, Bob…" Really starting to dislike this damn Marx. Yeah, he was a great Team supporter, but he thought his money gave him way more power than he ought to have. Not good. "…it's a lot tougher to win an individual medal than a Team medal. We could get a Team Silver or Bronze, and not have any of our riders be in the top three or even the top five. That's just the way the numbers work out."

Marx grumbling about it, but even he could see the logic in that. Still he took one more shot. "Yes, but if Chasseur de Lion flips out then that's it for the Team, and we'll have given up our shot with Jericho and QL."

Didn't lie about it. "That's true."

Bruce Waverly, also not a committee member, cutting in to defend his stallion. "Yes, but Lion was Reserve National Champion, and he beat QL."

Frankel, feeling like he was babysitting a bunch of spoiled millionaires—maybe because he was. "That's also true, Bruce."

"Why can't we do some tryouts of all the riders on QL?" That same question coming up again.

"Well, first of all QL would have a fit," Frankel explained, trying to remain patient. "And secondly, we have to jog her today, and she has to be on the showgrounds—we've already taken her over. Only one rider can sit on her once she's on the grounds—and that's the person who's going to compete her. Now I'm suggesting we go with Bee-Bee. Next to George she has the most experience, and she's been the third highest of our riders in the standings on a consistent basis. Plus Jericho believes she can ride her, and that means a lot."

Dry comment from Marx. "Jericho's sleeping with her, isn't he?"

Now that pissed Frankel off. "You're gonna have to ask Jericho that question…want me to call him in here?" He rose, turned like he was going to the door.

Backpedaling pretty quickly on that one. "No, no. I just mean, can we really trust his opinion?"

"Actually the recommendation comes from our Team Captain, George Strang," Frankel countered him again. "And I asked Jericho to confirm it. I can get both of them in here." He was still standing there by the door, and flung it open. "George, Jericho!" he bellowed.

The Team Captain stepped into the room, pretty unyielding look on his face after all they'd been through in the last seven hours. And right behind him came Jericho…and if George looked unyielding, then Jericho looked completely forbidding. Sharp aggressive step, deep blue stare sweeping the room. Tall commanding presence.

"Yes, Chuck?" George said. No nonsense voice on him for sure.

Jericho, eyes resting on Marx. Just purred. "Is there a problem?" Took a step closer to him even. Man, hated that fucker, and really wanted to hurt him…just looking for an excuse. And didn't that come through loud and clear? Tension positively popping in the room.

Marx, looking at the floor, definitely not wanting the challenge.

"Well, I don't know," the Chef D'Equip said, smiling cynically. "Anyone have any questions for either of these two?"

None voiced. Pretty well settled it.

And Frankel submitted the revised Team list to the Organizing Committee shortly afterwards.

———————

All of the horses, and most of the grooms, were sent back to the farm. QL, Phantom and Lion were brought over, with Marco, Race and Reynaldo staying at the showgrounds now—almost exactly the opposite of what they'd had the day before. Lots of buzz around the venue about what had happened to the American Team's horses, and it hit the news too, so reporters were hanging around everywhere, trying to get information. Frankel and the Selection Committee issued a press release, but that seemed to draw more information seekers, not less.

Other Teams stopped by too, offering their sympathy and expressing anger—for what good that did. Nice of them though, but another unwanted distraction as much as anything else.

The jog would be held at 1:00, and Jericho spent the rest of the morning trying to introduce Bee-Bee and QL.

Alpha mare was not very happy about it.

Took one look at Bee-Bee entering her stall behind Jericho. Immediately laid those mule ears back flat and stuck an unfriendly head out in an "I want to bite you" posture. Tail switching angrily.

Jericho went to her, got an unhappy mare head pressed to his chest, and sad "bad person in my stall" eyes looking expressively at him. Stroked her, talked to her, asked her to trust him. Held a hand out to Bee-Bee. "Take my hand, but slowly," he told her, and she did. He pulled her closer, over right next to him…QL's head jerking up in objection. Still talking to her, wrapped his arms around Bee-Bee, trying to show QL that Bee-Bee had his protection, that she should accept her. Huge front foot stomping, and she jerked away, snorting. Eyes suspicious, unforgiving. Really disliked the other human. Said "no" to having her there.

Jericho sighed. This wasn't going to be easy. "Alright, move back again, almost to the door." With Bee-Bee well out of the way, he stepped over to QL again, the mare nuzzling his shirt gently. Gave her a cookie. Really happy now—with one exception…icky human still in the stall. Swung that block of wood head toward Bee-Bee one more time angrily.

"Jericho, is this going to work?" Poor Bee-Bee was already getting discouraged, and sounded miserable. She had to lead QL in the jog in just a few hours, and the big moose-like mare wasn't even letting her get close.

"Christ, I hope so." Pulled a cookie from his pocket, but keeping it palmed where QL couldn't see it, and stretched his arm out to hand it to Bee-Bee. "Try showing her this…offer it to her."

Bee-Bee took the cookie and came forward again, but slowly, with the cookie held out in front of her like a cross before a vampire.

Alpha mare with a major dilemma…wanted the cookie, hated the cookie-carrier.

QL took a lunge forward, neck extended, teeth bared, and Bee-Bee jumped backwards, dropping the treat. Problem solved. The big mare happily nosed around in the shavings until she found it, lifting it in her teeth and carrying it back over to Jericho to "hide" behind him while she munched on it.

"Oh God," Bee-Bee sighed. "How in the world am I going to jog her?"

"Yeah, stop worrying about the jog, will you? Hell you've got to ride her this afternoon," Jericho reminded her sharply.

"Well, you act like it's my fault."

Turned and snarled at her, "What? You're saying it's mine?" His irritable sentence was punctuated by a furious squeal and another nasty head lunge from QL. Bad small human, making her God unhappy. Insufferable.

Murmured to QL, tried to make her happier.

Loved Jericho, slung her head over his shoulder, rubbing on him. Nasty "get out" look for Bee-Bee from the corner of her eyes.

"Well, Jericho...you're just making it worse telling her she's a good girl!" Bee-Bee cried. She turned and stomped out of the stall, muttering, "This is ridiculous. What a horribly spoiled animal!"

"Damn it, get back in here!"

The partner human, yelling angrily. Small horrifying human daring to return to the stall anyway. Squealed again, objecting vigorously. Started to swing those deadly hindquarters around. Hard slap from Jericho, along with the correction, "None of that!" QL utterly confused and miserable. Butting him softly again, needing reassurance, and him stroking her. Much better, liked that.

"So how's it going here?" Frankel's voice, trying to sound chipper despite how unhappy he was over everything, and how much pressure he was feeling now. And then he appeared in the aisle way in front of QL's box.

The big mare's head swung toward him. Recognized him. Really irritating human who'd tried to come in with her at the last horse show when the God human was missing. Lunged at him too for good measure.

Just murmured to her, "It's alright. Quiet down now." And maybe he'd screwed up trying to do this in her stall like this—give it a minute, try again in the aisle maybe.

Bee-Bee sure didn't want to tell Chuck she was having a problem. "Well, we're just starting," she said brightly. "Jericho's introducing me to the bit...to QL." Smiled. "I don't think she likes you, Chuck. Maybe better if you're not around," she suggested.

He looked suspicious, but nodded. "Alright. But you'll be ready for the jog, right?"

From Jericho. "Sure, Chuck. We're doing fine."

———————————

Well, it depended on how you defined "ready."

Jericho, Bee-Bee and George had all changed into the Team provided beige dress slacks, blue blazer, white shirt, navy tie, and matching navy riding gloves that they'd wear during the jog. And Marco and Reynaldo had show-groomed the horses. Phantom would go first, and he was on his best behavior.

Well, that was one.

QL really balking at the continued presence of the dreadful small human, and obviously unhappy and upset about it—dreadful human, hanging around while she was being groomed too—really annoying.

And Chasseur de Lion...one step short of being out of his mind. It was the first time he'd been on a showgrounds since the Nationals in June, and that, coupled with the incident with Race had him good and lathered up. Screaming, fighting for no reason...needing Jericho's presence to restore confidence in him, but not getting enough attention because of the time spent with QL. Even Race wasn't making a dent in calming him down.

"Jericho, get over here and deal with this stallion," Frankel reprimanded him sharply. "And I mean, right now. Bee-Bee can take care of her own horse."

Yeah, right.

"What a fuckin' show this is going to be," Jericho muttered to Bee-Bee derisively.

"God, I know," she breathed.

"Listen to me...you let Marco take her up to the ring," he told her. Gave her a quick hug of encouragement. "Then you take her in for the jog. I had Marco put the stallion halter on her. You'll have leverage—use it. Be strong with her, then she'll behave."

Yeah, right.

Little parade of champions going up to the veterinary check. Phantom, looking like an angel, QL pulling against Marco and alternately looking around jealously at Lion and glaring at Bee-Bee, and then Chasseur with Jericho on the lead...the stallion's eyes popping out of his head, snorting, prancing, giving voice to an occasional scream.

Jericho talked to him, stroked him...getting a response too, the big gray pressing his shoulder desperately against him. Hard to hold on to him the way Lion was shaking his head and jerking against his lead—worse with that damn right hand of his hurting the way it was, apparently that was his punishment for losing his temper earlier. Figured he deserved the pain—just sucked it up.

There were lots of spectators on the rail there watching—all interested because they knew all the top horses had been drugged, and that this was the replacement crew—among them, other Teams who'd considered the Americans direct competitors, wanting to see what the substitute squad was going to be—and if they were still the threat they'd been. The Dutch,

Germans, Swiss, French and Belgian Teams all in attendance with their Chefs D'Equip. Pier Gottemann also standing there.

Plus the rumor mill had spread the word like wildfire...Chasseur de Lion was here, and he was going to show...everyone fascinated by that. He was pretty well known in Europe—had been at his greatest here—pulled some of his worst stunts too.

Phantom was the first to go into the jog, and Jericho used the time to walk out Lion, calm him. Knew QL would be okay with Marco, at least for now. It wasn't long before he felt a presence beside him, looked around and was surprised to see Pier Gottemann falling into step. Just murmured to him, "I'm sorry."

"Not your fault," the Dutch horse trader said unhappily. "I know you took precautions...I heard what happened. Terrible thing."

Nodded. Low passionate voice. "I really wanted to win with him." Of course, they both knew he was talking about Antares.

Shaking his head. "I was hoping that too. I've been very impressed. Nice win at your National Championships," he complimented him.

"Love that animal, he..." Had to stop what he was saying as Lion struck out with his near front foot, and then lurched forward in a springing half-rear. Just kept a firm hold on him, didn't make a big deal of it. "Whoa now," he soothed the big gray, gentle with him. Free hand laid quietly against his neck. Looked back at the horse trader. "Sorry...what was I saying?"

Gottemann murmured appreciatively. "This stallion...is his head going to hold together?"

Knew he was fishing for information, didn't mind though. Saw Chuck looking over suspiciously too—just tossed him a nod to say he understood—*be careful what you say.* Gave Pier kind of a roundabout answer—tried for a little information of his own. "I love this animal...huge talent in him. I always wonder who abused him and how."

Soft humph. "Well, my friend, I'll tell you this much...I can't prove anything, but my best guess at the guilty party is standing on the fence line watching you now. Don't let anyone come near this stallion, not if you want to be able to show him. *No one.* More than that, I can't say."

Expressive look of gratitude for the warning, and then that deep blue stare sweeping the group of spectators. Lots of people looking at him—and sure, Lion was drawing lots of stares. The Belgian team—their eyes on him, and talking among themselves. Man, it would fit if it were one of them—hated the way their horses jumped too—oh yeah, big and clean, but they had a way of popping over the fences that just smelled like poling to him. Illegal as hell, but then obviously they wouldn't do it on the grounds here…but who really knew what they did at home.

Maybe Lion.

Phantom was finishing up his jog—no problems there. Jericho walked Lion closer to watch what was happening with QL. Two pairs of eyes turning to him with desperation…one that beautiful hazel shade that he was beginning to know so well—Bee-Bee's…the other a deep rich brown—QL's.

The big mule-eared mare had been happy enough—not perfect, because the God human was paying attention to other equine—a rival for his affections—but the groom human was standing with her and feeding her tiny cookie tidbits. He was acceptable. Small icky human way too close though. And now as they opened the gate, and Marco began leading her forward, the much-disliked small human coming over right next to her. Gave her a nice warning squeal, and stomped a hind foot.

Bite you.

Icky human taking the lead line from acceptable groom human, and jerking it. Irritating high-pitched voice saying, "Come around, you!" Really indignant about that. Ears flat back and snapping at her, and entering the ring snorting and just dancing off those quick-as-lightening hoofs.

Jericho watched, feeling bad for both Bee-Bee and QL. The huge mare was on her worst behavior. But good for Bee-Bee, she was keeping her in some kind of order at least—despite the fact that QL was trying pretty hard to latch onto her with those wicked teeth of hers. Some pretty perplexed stares from the officials at this ill-mannered beast, and they were plenty cautious as they took a look at her.

"Up and back," the lead official requested.

Bee-Bee turned QL—not easy to do with the mare shaking her head as hard as she could and lunging at her. But she had a tight hold on her right up close to the halter where QL couldn't reach her. They trotted up, with the horse hitching up those hind legs trying to buck, trying to swing them around, and radiating animosity. Pretty hard to tell if she was sound or not given the jerky way she was moving.

"Again," the official asked.

Oh man, Jericho thought, poor Bee-Bee. They were making her go again to try and get a better look.

Icky human snapping the lead chain again, and more of that high-pitched growl from her, "Straighten up here!" Tried really hard to chomp down on her, but it wasn't working. Little kick too. Finally gave in and trotted, but plotting how to get back at this appalling creature.

Wanted the God human back, whinnied pitifully to him.

And he felt bad for poor QL too, she was hating this. But eventually they got through it—some pretty good snickers from on the rail, but at least she'd passed. Marco took QL back again, and started leading her back to the barn—looked a lot happier anyway. And hell, what was he worried about QL for...it was his turn with Lion now, and no horse was crazier than this one. Calming hand on him, and then Jericho led him into the ring. Oh, Lion knew this routine...and he knew what it meant too... jumping competition coming up.

His eyes were completely wild, head straight up in the air...so nervous he couldn't even walk, just prancing—knees so high when he moved they were almost up to his chin, skittering nervously sideways. Lots of murmuring on the fence line. Scream from Lion, and then a big blowing snort. The jog officials looking anxious about even getting close to him. No one really wanting to examine this dangerous looking nutcase.

The stallion struck out with a foot hoof as the vet approached, and he jumped backwards, startling Lion even more. Jericho threw his weight into the big gray's shoulder, unbalancing him just enough to steady him back on his feet. Spoke to him softly, and he settled a bit, standing there but shuffling all four legs in an edgy little dance.

He got what was probably the fastest examination of any horse at the Games, and then the order to trot him up and back. Did that—although it was like holding onto some kind of turbo-charged racecar, and trying to control it with a brass chain attached to a one-inch strip of leather. So much power in that gait that only someone with Jericho's strength could have possibly kept him in hand. Turned him to trot him back and got a miserable little head butt from him.

Reassured him. "Good boy."

Could hear some of the comments from the rail too...things on the order of..."he'll never ride that animal."

Sighted those damn Belgians as he brought him back, and just sneered at them. Wait and see, Jericho thought. Just wait and see.

Excused from the ring, and Lion had successfully passed the jog. Jericho slipped a piece of sugar into his mouth. He was even starting to calm down a little bit as he brought him back out the gate.

The Belgian contingent had wandered closer. Their lead rider was in the front of the pack, but closely flanked by his teammates.

Huge snort from Lion, and his head shot straight up, yanking with all his power on that injured right hand of Jericho's, and damn that hurt. Fear radiating through the big gray stallion like a bolt of electricity, eyes wide as he stared, horrified at the Belgian team. All four legs scrambling desperately, trying to spin and run or to back up when that wasn't happening—the move so sudden that it really threw Jericho off balance and to the side, swinging him hard, and he nearly lost his grip on the lead. Hoofs flashing dangerously close to his own legs, the animal's whole body trembling. Everyone on the rail turning in shock to watch.

Lion leapt frantically in a small circle around him, as Jericho struggled to regain control and settle him.

"Get a hold of him!" Frankel was yelling at him.

It probably took him thirty agonizing seconds to get through to Lion enough to even have any measure of control over him. But once he did, Jericho swung his head around furiously toward that group of bastards, and the fuckers were having a nice laugh over it. He moved Lion as far away from them as he could, but he still needed to go past them to get back to the barn. Tightened his grip and just plain powered that big animal on by. But even though he'd opened some distance between them and himself, he was close enough to hear the smartass comment they made as he went past.

"Sorry."

Oh yeah…well, they were going to be. Sorry as hell.

Chapter Thirty-Two

Frankel had asked for, and had been granted a special private two-hour session in the practice arena, for the exclusive use of the American Team. Although it was an inconvenience, most of the other competitors seemed pretty understanding, and they'd turned out in fairly good numbers to watch. Of course, tales of the rather...*interesting*...jog for the American horses were already circulating, and that increased the number of spectators as well.

Chuck had planned that Bee-Bee would ride first, and Jericho right after her. George would overlap both of them, coming in about a half-hour after Bee-Bee started, and staying about a half-hour into Jericho's slot.

Jericho and Bee-Bee had already gone up to the arena. Saw the nice crowd forming, and Bee-Bee just slumped. "What's QL going to do when I get on her?" she was asking, wishing like hell that she'd had a chance to do this back at the farm—without the audience.

Little smirk from Jericho. "Well, the first time I rode her she was pretty rank, but hopefully her manners have improved since then."

Look of dismay on Bee-Bee's face.

He laughed and put an arm around her. "Look, she'll try to bully you, but just keep her really forward, and here's the secret, that mare loves to jump. Keep your flatwork to a minimum and go to the fences as soon as possible. She'll like you much better if you do."

Pretty dubious about the whole thing, but said, "Okay, if you say so."

"I do."

The crowd on the fence line thickening. A number of the patrons seemed to have dropped by—Bruce Waverly, and now that was predictable since his horse was going to be worked. And there was Lady Forrester right beside him—the two of them in a golf cart, in a great spot where they could see the whole ring. Looking happy and ready to watch.

Deep blue stare sweeping further down the line...the Dutch Team with their Chef D'Equip, the Germans right beside them. Pier Gottemann back again...and oh yeah, those motherless Belgians were there too, just leering, the bastards.

And if that wasn't enough to make his blood boil, there was Bob Marx with Darien right beside him...his arm around her, heads close together while they talked. Soft, lightweight, wide-leg pants on her, fluttering in the light breeze, and a sexy little top—both cream colored, and gorgeous, really flattering to her slim shape.

Refused to allow himself to stare at her, dragged his eyes further down the line instead.

Not far away he spied Brae with Jessica and Meagan. Caught his half-sister's eye, touched the medallion around his neck...saw her delighted smile, and tossed a return grin at her.

Couldn't help himself though...eyes drawn relentlessly back to Darien. Vortex of emotions, none of them healthy. Murmur of something purely animal, and plenty mad. Forced himself to look away.

Light touch from Bee-Bee. "You just noticed her, didn't you? I was hoping you wouldn't. Try to ignore her, Jericho."

Couldn't quite dredge a smile up for her, but a warm look anyway.

"Alright, are we ready to roll here?" Frankel was coming up beside them. Plenty of pressure on him right now, and man it showed. But he was keeping it together, thoughts only for his riders. But irritable as all hell.

"Ready, Chuck," Bee-Bee said bravely.

"Good, because here's Marco with QL now. Let's not waste time here."

And oh yeah, Marco was leading that huge alpha mare into the arena. She seemed excited, prancing but eager. Big mule ears twitching from the crowd to the jumps to Jericho. Happy mare. The hated small human there in the ring, and that was annoying—little irritable snort for her. But filled with joy at the sight of the partner human—ugly snort turning into a soft nicker of welcome. Raring to go.

Jericho went over to her, checked the tack. Bee-Bee's saddle was on her, and he tightened the girth a notch. Little "alright, already" dancing action from QL, wanting him to vault on as he usually did, and he laughed and stroked her. Murmured to her, "Be good, okay?"

He reached out for Bee-Bee's hand, and she came over to him. QL glancing sideways at her, not liking this development. He gathered the reins up, then slid Bee-Bee into position in front of himself. "I'm just going to lift you up onto her," he told her. "She'll think that's normal since I always jump on."

"Oh right, the superman approach," Bee-Bee snapped.

Forgave that in a heartbeat…knew she was nervous. He put his hands at her waist—she was so small and light anyway. "Take the reins from me," he said and she did.

Lifted her easily, put her up on the horse.

Huge objection, mule ears flattening. Really militant look in those dark eyes. Small icky human in the saddle. Not allowed. Not allowed at all. Humping that back up.

"Get her forward, and I mean *right now*," Jericho warned her, his voice a whiplash of an order and probably way too harsh, but he absolutely didn't want to see her get hurt.

"Hey, I'm riding her," Bee-Bee retorted, sitting in and putting her legs on.

Difference of opinion from the alpha mare.

Lurching forward, then a crow hop, picking up speed and launching into a series of full-fledged bucks.

"Forward!" Jericho barked. "Goddamn it, Belinda…*forward!"*

And she was trying to do that too, but QL already had that block of wood head down, and each jarring leap and landing was inching Bee-Bee further out of position.

Something straight out of the rodeo.

"Use the crop on her ass!" Jericho was yelling.

Way too late though. That smart alpha mare could feel her going…just a few more good strong bucks should do it. Yep, definitely. Going…going…Gone.

Bee-Bee sailing through the air, landing hard on her shoulder, the air expelled from her body in an audible, "Ohh!"

Frankel came right up beside Jericho, and snarled at him vengefully. "God damn you Jericho…just God damn you."

Turned just his head sharply. Growled at Chuck that he could go fuck himself, and then took off at a trot to help her get up. Bellowed, "Marco!" at the same time—a shorthand order meaning catch QL and bring her to him—knew his head groom would understand.

Bee-Bee was already standing and dusting herself off by the time he reached her. "God damn you, Jericho," she said, furious and embarrassed to have been bucked off in front of this large crowd.

He bristled. How fair was that? Hell, she'd wanted to ride QL, had damn near begged him. Wasn't offering her much sympathy. Sniped at her, "Yeah, Chuck cursed me out too—exact same words."

The two of them, glaring at each other.

When Marco led QL up alongside them, Jericho grabbed Bee-Bee and unceremoniously tossed her right back on, ignoring her gasp of protest and cry of, "I'm not ready yet!" Stepped back, growling at her, "Now *ride* this goddamn horse."

Alpha mare, totally shocked. Detestable small human back in the saddle—knew just how to handle it too. Mutinous switch of her tail. Already popping those hind feet off the ground as she began to walk.

"Forward!" Jericho barked again. "I told you—get her moving, then get her over a jump. *Face her!"* Then turned vengefully to Marco, just snarled at him, "Go back to the barn and bring me a lunge whip." The head groom nodded and took off at a run. Knew that tone of voice for sure. *"Canter!"* Jericho shouted at her, pretty much at the top of his voice.

Bee-Bee glared over at him, just tossing daggers at him with that stare. She gave the cue for the canter, and the crow hops started almost immediately.

"Faster!"

Frankel coming over beside him again. "Damn you, Jericho."

Cursed viciously at him, then really let him have it, "Just kiss my ass, alright? I heard that crap from you already—her too. Bee-Bee's a professional rider. And Chuck, you know this mare as well as I do. If she doesn't sit in and get her forward, then QL's gonna dump her every time she gets on."

Furious and really arguing, "I should have never let you talk me into this."

Snarled at him—a really cogent and compelling argument. Or maybe not. "Just fuck you, okay?"

Nice squabble with everybody watching too, and Jericho doing nothing to lower his voice. Frankel was absolutely livid with him. "No, it's not okay…"

Walked away from him before he decked him. *"Come on!"* he screamed at Bee-Bee again, striding across that practice arena toward her.

Tiny rider on a monstrous horse, and the horse having a field day misbehaving. With every stride, the height she flipped up those hindquarters was increasing, really snapping Bee-Bee back and forth. She'd grabbed a hold of QL's mane for balance and for the moment that was keeping her on board. But the situation wasn't getting any better—pretty unnerving. Not to mention the way Jericho kept roaring at her.

"Fence!" he ordered harshly.

What, was he nuts?

Small icky human, pretty tenacious. Alpha mare trying harder to get rid of her. Leaping through the air with that front end, landing with all four feet on the ground at once. Icky human slipping to one side...*oh, good.* Made a ninety-degree spin in the opposite direction. Parting company with the loathsome human. Happy alpha mare, on the loose now and running tail up, snorting and pretty pleased with herself.

"Chuck, grab that horse," Jericho demanded, covering the distance between himself and the downed figure of Bee-Bee in mere seconds. Scooping her up onto her feet again.

"No, I can't, Jericho," she was already pleading with him.

Frankel had more trouble catching QL than Marco, so that gave her a little breather—but not much. In five minutes or less, he was leading that irascible mare back over.

"Oh yes you can, and you will," Jericho said, without a trace of pity in his voice. When the horse came alongside again, he tossed poor Bee-Bee right back onto the saddle, to the tune of her telling him, "I hate you. You're such a jerk."

Didn't seem to faze him. "That's fine, Belinda...now stop giving me shit and *ride.*"

Marco had returned by now, and handed the lunge whip to him.

Snap! He touched it right to the mare's powerful hind end. "On a circle around me!" he commanded Bee-Bee, and when the mare tried to get her head down...*snap!* He cracked that whip on her butt again.

Alpha mare flying forward now, on a circle around the partner human—something familiar in that—almost like him lunging her, with the notable and miserable exception that the small detested human was on top of her. But no time to think about that...partner human pretty demanding and mad sounding too. Jumped forward into a huge round canter for him.

"Good."

The people on the fence line absolutely buzzing. This American rider Brandeis...what a hard-hearted bastard he was. Running roughshod right over his own Chef D'Equip, and brutal when he coached his teammate—a small female rider at that.

Didn't give a fuck, and yeah he knew they were talking about him. Just kept right on cracking that whip until he'd forced QL to give in, come round, and mother fucking carry her rider like she should. Better picture developing—not much control, but at least the horse was cantering instead of lurching around like some kind of equine kangaroo from hell.

"Now, pull out of the circle, and *fence*, damn you!" he yelled at Bee-Bee.

Still getting that "I hate you" look from her, but she'd totally accepted the fact that he was the one running the show here, that Chuck wasn't coming to her rescue, and that Jericho was going to keep throwing her up on this horrifying animal until she found a way to ride her, or got killed in the process. Riding for survival now…turned the mare into the nearest obstacle, and *Ohmigod*…monstrous jump! Hadn't expected that. Came up in the irons in a heartbeat. Desperately released to her. Sailing through the air. Touchdown and clear!

It had to be the most miserable hour of riding Bee-Bee could remember, but at the end of it she'd taken QL through a small course, managed to get her into something of a frame, and had finally gotten some small amount of obedience from her. But Jericho had been there the whole time with that whip too, cracking it in the air even when he wasn't close enough to touch QL with it—the sound alone having a powerful effect on her after he'd popped her several times but good. Hard to imagine what might have happened if she'd been trying to do this on her own…

…like she'd have to do in the ring tomorrow.

Terrifying thought, but right now she was just grateful she was finally being allowed to dismount. She basically slid off, legs wobbling, and turned QL over to Marco. Refused to even look at Jericho.

And man, that pissed him off. He sure hadn't been tough on her because he was trying to be an asshole—in fact, just the opposite—it was the only means he'd had to keep her safe. Gutsy little thing though, he had to give her that much. Really gave it her heart.

George was out in the ring now with Phantom. Very normal looking schooling session, and Chuck had moved over to work with him.

"Poor Bee-Bee," George was saying to Frankel.

Nod from the Chef D'Equip, pretty angry—maybe angriest of all over the way Jericho had just stepped in and taken charge, making Frankel feel foolish in front of his peers. "Yeah, but don't forget, now's my turn with Jericho." Nasty look coming over his face, and vindictive suggestion, "Might be a tough hour. Let's just see how that goes."

Enter Chasseur de Lion.

Pier Gottemann talking to the Dutch Chef D'Equip. Laughed, "They could have sold tickets to this. Made a bundle for the American Team, heh?"

"Here's what amazed me," the man said right back to him, shaking his head to punctuate it. "That ill-mannered mare won the Grand Prix at 's-Hertogenbosch…eager, beautiful jumper. Nothing like this…" Snicker. "…little performance."

"Brandeis," Pier murmured. "Really elegant rider. Strong too. Tough on his teammate, wasn't he?" Chuckled, thinking back on the last hour. "The way he kept throwing her up on that horse." Pretty amused by the whole thing. "But now *this* is actually what I've been waiting to see…him on Chasseur de Lion."

Appreciative look in the Dutch Chef D'Equip's eyes. Cold murmur. "Let's just see if he's as hard on himself as he was on her."

Gray stallion, just shaking, snorting and pawing as he walked…if you could call it a walk—Spanish walk maybe. More on edge than he'd been at the vet inspection, if that was possible. Looked at the crowd on the rail. Screamed, veins in his finely chiseled face popping out. Huge muscles in his hindquarters wound tight as springs in a cuckoo clock. Yanking so hard on the reins that Marco was really struggling to keep control of him.

Belgian lead rider on the rail, snapping his fingers and calling softly, "Chasseur."

Wild eyes falling on the Belgian. Another scream, and then he began twisting that head back and forth, desperate to get free—to be anywhere else. Jerking Marco around on his feet like some kind of child.

Jericho striding over, and quickly. Snatched the reins from out of Marco's hand. Lion running backwards and Jericho with him, the stallion ignoring any soothing words on his part, only getting worse. Striking out, half-rearing.

And Frankel yelling out caustically, "Jericho, get a hold of that animal and settle him down!"

Jericho swore under his breath in response. Yeah, he was gonna settle him, in fact he planned on getting on him. Got his hands on that near side stirrup and snapped the iron into place. Although Christ, this stallion was a powder keg right now. Something had really set him off.

From the Dutch Chef D'Equip, "Surely he's not going to ride till he quiets that animal. Lunge him, maybe."

Gottemann snorted knowingly. "You wanted to know how demanding he'd be on himself—just watch," he said.

Jericho knew what had to be done…he had to mount Lion, and right now too. Before this crazy stallion exploded and hurt himself…and he had nothing left to ride. Dodged those deadly hoofs and jumped in close to the big gray's body. Utterly fearless, despite the peril of those churning legs. Lion, wanting to bolt now, feet beginning to scramble and finding purchase in the sand. Jericho, gathering the reins at the same time, running two steps alongside him, grabbing onto the pommel, then powering himself up on. Came right into position, too…back straight, thighs draped athletically over the flaps, calves on. Pulled the other stirrup free, jamming his foot into it.

No sooner seated than both of Lion's front feet came up off the ground simultaneously…and at the same time lurching forward on those powerful hind legs…bunching them underneath himself to absolutely catapult through the air amid cries of shock from those watching. Tooth-jarring landing, and the huge gray was thrusting forward, running for all he was worth—head straight up, nostrils flaring, and legs moving like 350 horsepower instead of one. A mad gallop—literally. No lucid thought in him. The animal completely irrational.

Knew it in his heart…with the stallion this upset, the dive was coming, and at this speed it could easily be fatal. *Not happening.* Absolutely *was not* going to allow it. Planned on stopping it before it even began.

Made the decision. Headed that sucker right into a fence—only thing that was going to reach him. Either the precision required for an obstacle of this size was going to straighten him out—force him to think for a moment instead of just running blindly…or the two of them were going to die right here and right now.

Bee-Bee had turned around and was watching the scene, horror etched across her face.

Fence. Big fence. Really coming into it fast. Frankel yelling—tuned that out. Marked the spot and yanked back hard to check him, then just mother fucking launched him. Scat! Legs stampeding. That massive hind end rushing underneath him. Some sanity left in that tenuous stallion brain of his. Lifted his front end like a rocket. Airborne! Long moment of suspension. Then landing. Lion realizing that he had work to do, understanding that, and knowing that this human wasn't one of the ones who'd hurt him. Marginally calmer. Grip on reality returning. Second fence coming up. Took that one too.

Both of them still alive.

Little tug on the reins and push with his seat, and now the horse was coming back to Earth—soft landing. Jericho took him on a 20 meter circle, praised him, then came around and straight onto another line of fences... huge, rolling, to-die-for canter, soaring beautiful jumps, hitting his spots like a magnet.

Really appreciative murmuring from the fence line.

"Suicidal," the Dutch Chef D'Equip told Pier with disapproval—but a touch of awe, too.

Difference of opinion. "Perhaps, but so beautifully salvaged. Unstoppable rider—why do you think I sold him Antares? He'll make the final four. I'll put a thousand dollars on it."

Shrug, not really wanting to admit it—or to acknowledge the threat it might pose his team. Said quietly, "You're on."

Deep blue stare swinging back to the fence line. The Belgians... mysteriously gone. And man, he was sure gonna corner Pier and find out more from him when he got out of here.

Frankel starting to breath again, pulse racing though. Oh, he'd wanted to give Jericho a hard time in this hour, but the courage and heart in his anchor rider had changed his mind. Couldn't do it. Mind racing too.

Crazy but oh so talented frickin' horse. Unbelievable jump on him. And a crazier but oh so skillful rider mounted over him. Guts to spare, couldn't argue with that...too much, maybe. Had to love him for it though.

But that was just Jericho being Jericho.

"You've got him now!" Frankel called out powerfully, the earlier tiff with him all but forgotten. "But rounder and coming on more from behind. Lift that front end." Got closer to him and watched, while miraculously it happened. Something really stirring inside the American Chef D'Equip— first time he'd felt this way since that fateful phone call at 2:00 AM this morning. Called his rider over to talk with him privately—Lion settled enough now to bring him down to a halt. Laid a hand on the horse's mus-

cular shoulder, said with real passion, "Yeah, Antares would have been easier, but Goddamn you Jericho, let me tell you something…don't you give up on a medal yet."

Satisfied look coming back at him, then aggression flaring into those deep blue eyes of his. "Swear to Christ, Chuck…something those Belgians said or did set him off. Guarantee you it was deliberate."

Frankel agreed with him too, really starting to hate that Belgian team. But he thought the best way to get back at them was to just beat the pants off them, humble them—and if they could prove anything against them, well all hell was gonna break loose. But that was later. For now, he was just going to wind up his personal Terminator, and turn him loose. "Then you ride them into the ground, you hear me? You slaughter them in this round tomorrow. *Nothing* they do can stop you. They eat your dust!"

Understood him perfectly. Confirmed it. "Oh yeah, bury them. Last rites…the whole nine yards."

When he was done riding Lion, Jericho went back and untacked him. After Marco and Race finished bathing the sweat off the big gray, Jericho took him for a walk on the showgrounds…let him eat a little grass, maybe relax that screw-loose head of his.

No sign anywhere of Bee-Bee. Jericho knew she'd stayed and watched while he rode, but she'd disappeared pretty quickly afterwards—maybe gone back to the farm to clean up. Get some rest too. Or maybe she was just still pissed at him and staying away.

Walked along with the stallion, thinking to himself. Smiled—he ought to tease her…she needed to learn to take a fall better than she did now—well, pretty much like Race did. Maybe he'd set up a little lesson for the pair of them. But man, then it struck him. No, he wasn't going to be teaching her anything. They'd all be going back to the States next week when the Games were over, and once they did…his farm was in East Hampton, New York…hers in Virginia somewhere.

The fact was, he was only days away from being separated from her. Very likely wouldn't see her again until they returned to Wellington later in the fall. November maybe. Just hated that. Wanted to talk to her about it…explain that he'd only just now realized it. Christ, what must she be thinking? That he didn't give a shit?

Soft female voice calling his name.

And how much he wanted it to be Belinda…but knew it wasn't. No, instead it was the last female voice on Earth he wanted to hear.

Darien's.

Couldn't look at her, couldn't even acknowledge her. Turned with Lion and started walking away.

Delicate little plea. "Jericho, won't you even talk to me?"

Didn't answer that, still walking, angling the stallion's massive body like a wall between the two of them.

But she hadn't given up, and was walking along with him on the opposite side of the horse—talking to him from there. "I know you're really upset with me," she started. She stepped a little faster, ducked under Lion's neck around to the same side with him. Got in front of him, stopped him…long moment of pause, the stallion's head dropping down to graze. "Jericho, you're not even giving me a chance."

The nerve of this…yeah, face it…*bitch.* Just thought the whole world revolved around her. Snarled at her. "Like you gave *me* the chance, right Darien? The chance to be a part of the decision…about my *own son?*" Fury on his face, and man he looked dangerous. "Just get away from me, and I mean it. God, I'll never forgive you for that. As far as I'm concerned, hell, you murdered him—and you killed anything I ever felt for you along with him. My child…our child…" Trace of grief entering his voice along with the bitter rage, cutting off his breath.

Little hand on his arm. "Oh Jericho, how precious," she breathed softly. "You really cared about it."

Just felt brutal, body shaking—had to turn his face away from her, jerked his arm free of her touch too. "It? *It?* Is that what you called him?"

"Be reasonable," she coaxed him. "Come on, it was only a tiny thing, a clump of cells, not really a person. And you know I couldn't be running around next season carrying your child." Little reproach entering her voice. "And Jericho, we don't even know your background…there could be some kind of hereditary…"

Swung that piercing deep blue stare around to pin her with it, quelling the rest of what she was saying, though it had been clear enough where she was going with that.

He murmured to her, such an obvious tone of warning. "Why are you here? Stay away from me. Go back to your husband."

She bit that gorgeous lower lip of hers. "You wanted more from me, I know. And you didn't get what you wanted, and I'm sorry. But now things are different, and well, we both know it's not going to happen." Certainly was making it sound more like "you're not for me" than the reverse. "But Jericho, you threatened Bob...back in Aachen, remember? And I came to ask you...let it go. For me. Just let it go." She reached over again, clearly not intimidated by his anger—maybe she thought he'd never hurt her...maybe she thought he'd always be in love with her. Stroked that powerful forearm of his—so enticing, so strong. She added regretfully, "You're a beautiful man, Jericho."

Stared at her, a lethal calm coming over him. Man, talk about the final insult. Yeah, she'd used him like most men used a mistress—wasn't kidding himself about that. And she was here now, not to apologize, and not because she gave a damn about him—yeah she'd lived her little fairytale—had fun. Nothing ugly had touched her...or if it had, she'd taken care of it. And now, all she wanted was to protect her lousy bastard of a husband. Quietly snarled, "Sorry Darien, it doesn't work that way."

He lifted Lion's head, turned with him and led him away from her—shock that he hadn't said "yes" to her request, apparent in her eyes.

"Wait," she said, starting to come after him.

Pivoted back around to face her, expression totally forbidding. "Come near me again, and I promise...you won't like the consequences."

Looked quietly at him, smiled too—even a little amusement. "My God, you really got your feelings hurt," she told him gently. Slowly started backing away herself. "But I know you, Jericho...you're good, you're real...and you'll never hurt my husband, because that would be hurting me." Possibly just trying to convince herself of that.

Bark of laughter, truly malevolent sound. "After you aborted my son? Are you kidding me? It's what I dream of, Darien—hurting you and hurting him."

———

Happy little reunion going on at the farmhouse. Bee-Bee's parents and her younger sister, Teri, all sitting around in her room, talking. Adjoining doors in this place to the room next door—Jericho's. But then, they didn't know that and she'd made sure it was locked—avoid any embarrassing situations.

"I can't imagine how you must have felt," Teri was saying, referring to the news that Monterrey had been drugged, taking him out of competition.

"But honey, we're so very proud that they picked you to ride one of the horses they had left," her mother piped up. "And you're going to do fine, just fine." She knew her daughter was nervous about it—that was easy enough to tell.

Tug on the handle of the adjoining room door from the other side. Murmured male voice accompanying it.

Guilty look on Bee-Bee's face, quickly covered. Just ignored it—hoped he'd be smart enough to figure it out.

"Thanks, Mom," she said. "And all of you, please don't be disappointed if we have a few rails down tomorrow. It's so hard to ride a horse that you don't…"

Tall, partially clad male figure striding into the room, grumbling irritably, "Hell, Belinda, I know you're pissed at me, but I need my…" Stopped dead. Jericho—shirtless, barefoot, jeans zipped about three-quarters of the way up but the snap undone and belt unbuckled—body still damp, obviously fresh from the shower…arms above his head rubbing a towel briskly through his long mass of wet hair. Took in the room full of people—real family look about them. Mumbled something about being sorry, retreated pretty quickly the way he'd come.

Bee-Bee jumped up. Looked apologetically at her parents. She knew they weren't stupid—it would take them about ten seconds to figure it out. Good thing she'd had the door locked though—it was a good bet he'd only thrown those jeans on because he'd had to go out into the hall. "Well, that's Jericho," she said. "Let me introduce you to him."

Teri snickering, and getting a sharp "quit it" look from her sister.

Bee-Bee ran into the hallway after him, called his name, and he turned. She held her hand out to him. "Come on. At least meet them." Smile from her, saying it was alright, they wouldn't bite him or anything.

He chucked the towel into his room, then came back over to where she was standing, but not further. Took her hand, drew her closer to himself instead. "I thought you'd be snapping my head off."

Soft reprimand. "No, that was you this afternoon."

Pushed her back up against the wall, himself standing in front of her—quick look in the direction of her door, but no one there—smartass smile, lowered his head to tell her, "I had to."

"I know you did."

Man, something about that answer…she so understood what he was…Jesus, she *was* what he was.

Traced her face with his fingertips, deep blue eyes seeking something in her expression—some answer. Cursed softly, then just said it. "I couldn't get it out of my mind all afternoon…"

"What, Jericho?" She was glancing over at her doorway too now. The coast still clear—the family waiting inside for her. Eyes back on him again.

Thumb sliding slowly over her lower lip, tender caress. "Belinda, I kept thinking, what a life we'd have, if…"

"Bee-Bee?" Her mother's voice calling her.

"Just a minute," she called back. Then to him, "Jericho, let me just send them downstairs for a minute." She said it a bit desperately, so much wanting to hear the end of that sentence he'd started.

Stroked her hair. Expressive. "No, I have to finish this now."

Catching her breath.

Went right back to what he'd been saying, the thought so clear in his mind that he picked it up exactly where he'd left off. "…if we decided to have a life together. If you wanted that."

Whispered. "Do you?"

"I keep telling myself…wait. How can you say this to her when she knows…everything about you. Darien. Everything. She'll just think that's why. And God, I don't want to taint it with that for you. I want you to know that's it's true, so I've kept how I feel to myself. Waiting for the right time." Hoping like hell he was saying this so she could appreciate it, and more importantly, believe him. "Then I realized today—we're all going home next week, and…I want you to come with me. To East Hampton, Belinda. I built that house, most of it myself, and I want you there. To complete it. It'll be so empty…I'll be so empty if you don't."

Wonder on her face, happiness growing in those hazel eyes. Not the kind of retreating sad look Darien had always given him when he expressed or tried to express how he felt about her. No, this was open, and so embracing. Made him feel so needed, cared for. Loved.

"You built your house?"

Smiled at her. Lips just touching hers for an instant, brushing against hers. "Most of it. The barn too."

Could just see him doing it too. Her hands had crept up to his muscled shoulders—broad, strong, smooth beneath her fingertips. "I'll bet it's beautiful."

Soft to her. "Come and see."

Kissing him now, little kisses. "I'd like that."

His question, her answer—neither one specific enough to suit him. But she'd opened all the doors up wide. Time to go through them. He made it real this time around. "Come to East Hampton, Belinda. Come and live there with me…as my partner…as my wife, that's what I'm saying."

"Are you sure?"

"Completely."

Her hands slipping the rest of the way around his neck, and she whispered in his ear, "Yes." Conviction in that one little word though. Heartfelt, happy beyond expression.

He leaned his head back just far enough to stare into her eyes…eyes that shared a look, communicating the promise—the joining of their futures, the deep passion between them, their love.

Someone close by clearing his throat.

Startled, they both looked around, broke apart. And of course there stood her parents—little sister too. Little sister smirking. Parents looking more than surprised at the sight of their daughter in the arms of this compelling and rather aggressive-looking male. He'd moved possessively in front of her, taking her hand. Bee-Bee whispering something to him, and smiling. And him returning her look, embarrassed smile, said something low yet powerful to her…then stepping back toward his room…holding her hand until the distance forced him to release it. He disappeared inside.

"Uhm, that's Jericho," Bee-Bee explained again. She had that "feet not quite touching the ground" happiness about her. Eyes positively shining. Said brightly, "Well, let me get my purse and let's go out to dinner. I need to be back early, but we have time to grab something quick."

As they walked out to her parent's rental car together a few minutes later, Bee-Bee's mother hooked arms with her and said with interest, "That looked fairly serious between you and…what was his name? Jericho?" Little confiding girl talk.

"Yes, Jericho." Had to share it with someone, and who better than Mom? "This is a secret, okay? Just until after the Games, then you can tell Dad, well tell anyone who'll listen." Dragged out the suspense for a second, squeezed her mother's arm. "Jericho just asked me to marry him. I said yes."

"When? Just now?" Amazed. Tentative but thrilled too. "Oh honey, are you happy?"

Nodding. Excited enough to burst. "Right there in the hallway." Admitted it too. "Mom, I'm absolutely crazy about him."

"Well, good morning, Melissa," the co-anchor from ESPN said brightly. "Seems like we have a great day for the opening round of Show Jumping, here at the World Equestrian Games in San Patrignano, Italy."

"That's right, Roger. And what an interesting day it promises to be."

Melissa Pepper was the acknowledged equestrian expert in this pair—the one who'd give all the knowledgeable answers. Roger Lucas, her partner. His role was more to ask the kind of questions the audience might want to know…create an interesting dialogue.

"So our American Team has got quite the challenge in front of them," Roger went on happily, queuing up the discussion for the viewing public.

"Exactly right. As you know, it's been quite a scandal. Nothing like this has ever happened at the Games before." She went on to describe the incident with the malicious drugging of the top American horses, and the new line up with Bee-Bee on QL, George on Phantom, and Jericho on Chasseur de Lion.

All of the riders had walked the course earlier. Nice big scopey set of jumps—a few odd-looking and airy. The design required the horses to stretch out between some of the fences and then really pull in tight almost immediately afterwards. Antares and Monterrey would have totally eaten up this kind of course, and QL too, with Jericho aboard her, but it was going to be tough going for the line-up they had today.

"So Melissa," Roger clarified it. "You're saying *yesterday* was the first time Bee-Bee Oxmoor rode the horse she'll be on today?"

"That's right, first time ever. So you can see it will be quite a challenge for her. This mare, named QL, is a nine-year-old Westphalian. She's normally ridden by Bee-Bee's teammate, Jericho Brandeis, and she won the Grand Prix two weeks ago in 's-Hertogenbosch, Holland, so she's an excellent jumper. But we're told she's difficult to ride, so this should be exciting. And of course, Bee-Bee will be the first of our U.S. riders to take the course.

Actually, QL has a fascinating background…she stared out as a Dressage horse, not a jumper, and we're told that Jericho first saw her running loose at a show in Florida, having thrown her rider. But he recognized the potential in her, and bought her on the spot." Not completely accurate, but close enough.

"Wow," Roger laughed. "Guess he's happy with how that gamble turned out."

Huge competition in this first round, over 100 competitors all told. Bee-Bee was early in the go at 27th, George would be 53rd, and Jericho 87th. Still, Jericho had gotten up early and gone over to the showgrounds, taping a message on Brae's door to bring a Starbucks when he came. And thankfully, Chuck had hired security guards who stayed all night with the horses, so it wasn't really that he was worried about any more sabotage. He just felt a need to be with them, especially Lion. Anything to build the stallion's confidence, cement their partnership.

Melissa Pepper had been narrating as the first horse and rider combinations had their rounds. Lots of rails down, no one clear.

"Melissa, we've been told that all the U.S. riders are going to be wearing black armbands during this show," Roger continued. "What do we know about that?" he asked her, this dialogue already planned.

"Well, precious little, Roger," his co-anchor responded, getting into this now since it was a juicy little tidbit and something the audience was sure to resonate with. "We know it's a tribute from the Team to Jericho Brandeis' son, Charles Aaron Brandeis, who died recently, but the press has been asked not to question him about it before he rides. Apparently the loss of his son was very difficult for him."

"Gee, I'm sure that was tough, but what a great show of support from his fellow riders."

"Yes, well Jericho's the anchor rider for the Team even though he's the youngest member, and even though these will be his very first World Games," she said, repeating information she'd given the viewing audience earlier, and also expanding on it. "But he's done very well here in Europe over the last month. The Team will be counting on him today, and we also understand he's very well liked by the other riders. Here's another interesting fact…apparently Jericho named his son after the Chef D'Equip of the American Team, Chuck Frankel."

"Well that says something about how close this Team is, doesn't it?"

"Yes, it does Roger."

This broadcast was being shown live in the U.S. Team box, though it wouldn't be broadcast on U.S. television for several weeks. All the patrons were present and having a nice catered champagne breakfast. At this last exchange, Darien Marx drew in her breath sharply, and looked over at her husband. He looked plenty mad as well.

Lady Augusta Forrester, turning around and giving her a rather pointed and censuring stare, then looking away again.

Jericho had walked up to the warm-up arena. Marco would be bringing QL up in about ten minutes or so. Bee-Bee had arrived at the showgrounds, and was dressed in her Team uniform, but she was keeping to herself, getting mentally prepared, and he understood that totally— gave her her space.

"Hey, bra!" Happy voice from the fence line. Brae, his normal disheveled self, but in a Team provided blazer and beige slacks that almost made him look presentable—almost even fashionable. Camera slung around his neck, like always, and carrying a Venti Latte in his hand. "Here's your Latte…special delivery, dude." Big grin, proud of himself.

Amused, Jericho sauntered over. Took the Latte, drank from it, sighed. It was fantastic. Turned the cup around in his hand, those slashing brows knitting as if something was wrong.

"Hey, what's the matter?"

Kept a straight face when he answered him. "There's no star on my cup," he complained.

Shock, consternation. *"What?* Let me see that!"

Showed it to him. "See, no star…I mean, you did buy it inside and everything right?"

"Well, sure…*oh man!"* he wailed. "Oh, I gotta talk to the store manager. That new guy he hired…total idiot." Really looked exasperated. "Keeps forgetting the stars…doesn't smile at the customers…not even the cute chick ones…"

Felt almost guilty for making his roommate so upset—almost. Dark humor tugging at his lips. "Oh, hey man, that sucks," he prodded him. "Real loser, huh?"

"The worst."

Marco and QL had arrived in the warm-up, and Bee-Bee right behind them with Chuck. Marco, bless his heart, had the lunge whip with him too—just in case.

Handed his Latte back to Brae, and started walking toward the group of them—the Barista Italiano, fishing out a black marking pen from his pocket, and surreptitiously adding the star. Felt better then.

Frankel was giving last minute instructions to Bee-Bee, feeding her encouragement, putting a little pressure on her too. She didn't even look over as Jericho approached, just listening, nodding.

Ran his hands over the mare. "Looks good," he commented to Marco.

"Yeah, boss. She's raring to go this morning."

Smiled. Took the lunge whip from him, and oh yeah, QL picked up on that. She sure looked happy though, lots of fire in her...little nuzzle for the partner human, searching for a cookie bit. Got one. Even happier. Deep brown eyes flicking over to the small icky human—laid her ears back for just an instant, then tried to look innocent again.

Jericho rubbed her forehead. "Yeah, I saw that," he admonished her. Laid his head against that huge railroad-tie head of hers, murmured to her. Asked for her best effort, asked her to take care of Bee-Bee. Told her Bee-Bee was special to him. Man, didn't know if she understood.

"Alright, I'm ready." Determined little voice. And she came right over to him and that huge alpha mare—took up those reins. Strong heart in her, he was thinking. Proud of her.

He came around behind her to lift her into the saddle, but leaned his head down before he did. Brushed his lips against her hair behind her ear and below her helmet, whispered to her, "Ride like hell."

Little smile, but she didn't answer him.

Tossed her up there.

Difficult warm-up session—alpha mare pretty upset about it. Trying hard to listen to the partner human, and to keep going forward in response to his unremitting demand. But somehow he didn't seem to be noticing this completely objectionable situation...small icky human sitting on her back again.

Fix that.

"And Melissa...here comes Bee-Bee Oxmoor now!" Roger was saying with enthusiasm. "Wow, she looks tiny on that horse!"

"Yes, well QL is almost 18 hands, Roger. She's a really huge and powerful mare. And Bee-Bee's only five-three and weighs 110."

Bee-Bee had headed around and saluted the ground jury, wanting to get this started—and over with—as soon as possible, and while the mare was still remembering Jericho and that lunge whip. Nasty little head shake from QL, and mule ears pressed aggressively flat back as Bee-Bee asked for the canter and headed around to face the first obstacle.

They passed through the timers, and then were on the course.

"Well, she's off, Melissa!"

"Yes, Roger, and here they come into that first big Oxer, and…oh my goodness, that was a huge leap over that fence!"

"Well, they're clear, but wow, this pair is really going fast," he observed.

"Yes, you can see that Bee-Bee's trying to check her." Little tone of concern in her voice.

Second fence, and easily over it. Nice run to the next obstacle. Alpha mare clearly having a really good time out there. Big fence coming up, loved to jump…icky human sawing on the reins though. Didn't like that one little bit…just tossed that huge head up and back. *Whap!* Hitting small human in the face, pleased with that…no more sawing either. Then just launched at the next vertical, picking her own spot. Huge soaring leap, big touchdown. Leapt forward again.

Oops…small human gone. Just started bucking and running in front of the big crowd. Really having a blast.

Standing at the in-gate, Jericho and Frankel had seen it happening. "Just fuck me," Jericho swore viciously—he knew what it was like to have that big head slam your face, saw Bee-Bee wobbling, dazed by it, and then that gigantic leap over the vertical on the mare's part, and the hard landing on the other side…and in the next stride, Bee-Bee going limp, dropping off…just crumpling to the ground.

The gate was opened for them and he and Chuck went running—Chuck straight to Bee-Bee, Jericho, after the horse. Couldn't tell how badly she was hurt, just sick about it. But if she was going to get back on—allowed in a World competition like this—then the clock was still running, and they had to get her back up as soon as possible—inside 45 seconds, or she'd be eliminated. Really conflicted about that—whether he should even let her continue, but his actions were automatic. Lifted two fingers to his lips, and let out a piercing whistle.

Alpha mare…stopping, snorting…then turning. Sighting the God human, knew he was calling her. Welcoming return nicker for him. Ran to greet him.

"That's Chef D'Equip Chuck Frankel helping Bee-Bee stand back up," Melissa was saying excitedly. "It looks like she's okay, but wow that blow to the face had to really hurt. She might have even blacked out for a second there."

"And is this Jericho Brandeis, Melissa?"

Voice of infinite knowledge. "Yes, that's Jericho, Roger. Look, he just whistled to the horse, and she's cantering back over to him."

Jericho grabbed those reins as soon as QL got over to him. He jerked on them hard—severe correction, and just growling at her.

Uh-oh…alpha mare in a lot of trouble. Tossed her head up, snorted, but tried to look repentant too. Little "I'm sorry" sheepish expression, though not really sure what the God was upset about. Went obediently with him, tried to make up for whatever had made him so angry.

He ran alongside QL back to where Chuck and Bee-Bee were standing. Frankel telling his rider gravely, "Your own safety comes first."

Expressive look exchanged between Jericho and Bee-Bee. Almost imperceptible nod from her. God, she was brave. Just grabbed her and tossed her right up there—handed her the reins. Murmured, *"Ride…don't try to stop her, just let her run."*

Melissa Pepper was still narrating animatedly. "And Roger, here she's taking back to the course. You've really got to admire the courage in her—being slammed in the face like that, and then a hard fall. But Show Jumping certainly isn't a sport for the timid."

Awe. "You can say that again." Really sounded like he meant it too.

Jericho and Frankel went back outside the arena, both of them fretting, watching anxiously…Jericho swearing under his breath the whole time. Asked Chuck more than once, "Did she seem alright to you?"

"Yeah, you asked me that already," Frankel snapped. "I told you before, I couldn't tell."

But one thing for sure, that little slip of a girl was out there riding—competing her heart out for the Team. And QL, duly chastised, was jumping for her. Maybe not quite controlled, but big and clean.

"No rails down, Melissa," Roger said when her go had ended. "That's amazing, isn't it?"

"What an unbelievable story," his partner said, clearly agreeing. "Second time she ever rode this very difficult mare, and to complete the round without a single rail down…of course, she'll get eight faults for the fall, and then there'll be time penalties on top of that, but all in all, it was just an astonishing ride. We should all be very proud of her."

As Bee-Bee exited the ring, Jericho was there to grab her, lift her off that big mare, and then carry her in his arms to where the Team doctor was waiting. Laid her down on the ground, but her arms stayed around his neck and she was trying to smile, despite the way her face ached.

"She was clear wasn't she?" she asked. Happy rather than sorry for herself.

"Belinda, you were incredible..." Way more than just affection in those deep blue eyes of his. "...and yes, she was."

A number of hours later and after the lunch break.

"So let's just recap where we are," Melissa Pepper was saying. "Bee-Bee Oxmoor, our first rider, had no rails down, but fell early in the course after her horse hit her in the face. She also had three time penalties, for a total of eleven faults."

"And George Strang, the Team Captain and a real veteran, had a rail down on the second element of the triple combination, for a total of four faults," Roger chimed in.

"So the Team has fifteen faults so far," Melissa said, doing the very obvious math so the television audience wouldn't have to. "And in just a few minutes, our anchor rider, Jericho Brandeis will be entering the ring on Chasseur de Lion, an eleven year old, eighteen-one hand Selle Français stallion."

"Tell us about Chasseur de Lion, Melissa," Roger asked her—another of their planned dialogues. "Why is everyone so shocked that Jericho's riding him?"

"Roger, this stallion is one of the largest animals in these Games, and he's rumored to be so difficult to ride that he was actually retired to stud a few years ago. So you've got power, combined with a very sensitive, fiery spirit, and unfortunately also, some serious vices." Said that last part pretty gravely. "So it takes a very strong and bold rider to work with him. Now, Jericho was able to ride him to the U.S. Reserve National Championship earlier this year, so that's encouraging. But I know Chef D'Equip Chuck Frankel hadn't intended to show him here."

"Here he comes now, Melissa!"

Jericho cantering into the Grand Prix arena on Chasseur de Lion. Huge bounding stride—incredibly beautiful animal, gleaming with good care.

Gorgeous dapple-gray coat with dark points, muscled body—utterly fit. Tall powerful rider, scarlet Team jacket, the black armband vivid against it, white breeches, and black boots with a "see your own reflection" shine on them—Marco's work. Elegant equine head lifted and those fierce dark eyes sweeping the field, the grandstands. The stallion's back rounded and swinging freely, tail flowing behind him, relaxed—or relaxed for Lion anyway.

Jericho had kept him very isolated during the warm-up. Isolated and away from the fence line…and especially far away from those damn Belgians, who'd been there watching, but thwarted from getting too close. It was true, the animal's brain was still pretty well scrambled from the jog and that practice session yesterday, but he seemed to be clinging to his partnership with this human—dealing with his insecurity that way, which was more than acceptable. This might just work.

Now Jericho brought him around for the salute. Nervous dancing and snatching at the bit as the horse came to a halt, snorting excitedly too, but otherwise obedient. Oh yeah, being in the Grand Prix field itself was riling him up, and though he wasn't actively fighting, it was like sitting on the equine equivalent of C4 explosive.

"They're certainly looking strong this afternoon," Roger said with feeling. "But that horse sure seems volatile, doesn't he?"

"Yes, let's hope they can keep it together. I know the Team is really counting on this pair to get a clean round."

Return signal from the ground jury, and Jericho picked up the canter again, swinging his horse around in a circle to go through the timers and into that first obstacle. Pat on his neck for a moment to calm him, but had to give that up pretty quickly because he had his hands full here—Lion pulling, shaking his head, and moving with a monstrous, ground-eating stride.

"Way too fast!" Frankel was screaming, not that Jericho could hear him.

Couldn't stop that stride anyway—and wouldn't have. At least it was willing on Lion's part and Jericho didn't want to do anything to jeopardize that—just had to react that much faster himself, be totally cool about it, get the stallion to the spots before each fence and launch that crazy animal over them. And this wouldn't be the first time Lion had carried him at such a breakneck pace. That was an advantage too.

"Melissa, I can hardly breathe here," Roger was saying, after they came through the first two fences. "That pair is just flying, and time doesn't count in this phase of the competition, does it?"

"You're right, Roger. Having a fast time in this round won't give Jericho and Chasseur de Lion any advantage, but it looks to me like he's trying not to interfere with the horse's state of mind. But let me tell you, this is a technical course—its not meant to be attacked at a pace like this."

Coming into the water jump now, and just stretched him out...Lion easily clear of it, but oh Jesus, that big combination was next and it was tight...really, really tight for a big-gaited horse like this. Sat in hard, pushed that hind end under and lifted the front end. Lion responding. So much power underneath him now, tried to contain it—jump the moon with a thrust like this...but tight four-foot-six verticals? A lot harder. The first element of that combination jump dead in front of them. Hit that spot and lifted sharply to bring him higher, instead of long. Way, way over that sucker—man it could have been six foot, and they'd have cleared it just as well.

"Oh my God!" Roger was crying out, not at all the calm announcer's voice. "Did that horse even touch the ground between those two fences?" he shouted in amazement.

Even the very professional Melissa sounding spellbound. "Well, yes he did, Roger, but it happened so fast, no wonder you're questioning it. And I'm with you, I'm gripping my seat here. Clear so far and now they're facing up to that final triple that's tripped up so many other competitors."

Huge triple combination...lead change first, then Vertical, short one stride to an Oxer, longer two strides to the final Oxer, then through the timers to end the round.

Lead change—didn't happen. Counter cantering around the bend to that big airy Vertical. Couldn't get the stallion to check at all, so he launched him early at it, hoping like hell he'd keep that hind end up. Touchdown and madly scrambling stride then positively blasting-off over the Oxer. Way up over him, touchdown again, and now huge bounding stride to that final spread, just staying up in two-point.

"Clear round, Melissa!" Roger, having lost a bit of control here, really exuberant.

Jericho, cantering past the Team Box, giving his traditional crop to his helmet salute to his patron, and Waverly waving at him, positively thrilled.

Chapter Thirty-Three

At the end of the first round of competition, the U.S. Team was standing in fifth place, and still had the opportunity to medal...much of the pressure sitting squarely on Bee-Bee, and her ability to successfully compete QL the next day. The blow to her face had created a pretty good black and blue around her left eye and extending down her cheek, but beyond that, the doctors had ruled her healthy and cleared to compete in the second round.

Frankel suggested that she spend the evening with her parents, and be back at the farmhouse by 10:00 PM. "And no alcohol either," he added needlessly.

"Yes, Daddy," Bee-Bee told him sweetly.

And she wanted to have Jericho go with them too. Predictably, her mother had blabbed the news instead of keeping it secret, and her entire family was dying to spend some time getting to know him. She wasn't at all sure how he'd respond to that news.

Actually he surprised her. Yeah, he wanted to go—had some pretty old-fashioned views about getting her father's approval too, which she found incredibly endearing.

"If you don't mind, I'd like to invite my mother and sister to join us," he told her. He needed to do this, no matter how uncomfortable it was making him. Hell, give it some kind of chance anyway. "That is, if you can explain my situation to your folks ahead of time, and they'll be cool with it."

She laughed. "My parents are so laid back, almost nothing bothers them. And sure, I'd love to see Jessica and Meagan again."

He had no idea how to contact them, but Frankel had that information, and Jericho called and left a message for them at their hotel, giving them the name of the restaurant and the time.

Much later that night, Jericho and Bee-Bee were in bed together, neither one sleeping though they'd been lying there a while. The dinner had been fine and not too stressful, both families getting along well together. Jericho friendly enough to both of them, but quiet most of the time.

"Something's bothering you," Bee-Bee finally said to him—he was just too withdrawn, even given the situation and the pressure of the Games. "Do you want to talk about it?"

"I don't know," he answered reluctantly, but then gave it up anyway. "I just keep thinking about the final four."

The final four. Something he'd never done before—and maybe he wouldn't make it that far in this competition either. But right now he definitely had to be considered in the hunt.

The World Games were held under "Nation's Cup" rules—and the top individual honors would be decided the day after the Team Championships, with the four highest ranking riders returning for a grueling four rounds of jumping…one round on their own horse, and one on each of the other three competitors' mounts. The rider with the best overall score for those four rounds became the Gold Medalist, the next best, Silver, and the third, Bronze. The fourth rider went home with nothing.

"Jericho, you have a good chance to make it," she encouraged him. "And how great would that be for you and the Team?" Really sounded excited about it. Proud too.

"You don't understand," he murmured unhappily. "I'm worried I *will* make it…not that I won't."

She turned around in his arms to face him. "Huh?"

"We're in fifth place right now," he said. "To have any chance at a medal, I'll need a clear round. And if I'm double clear, I'll probably make the final four—or at least a jump-off for the final four. Well, a jump-off I could handle."

She reached up and brushed a hand over his cheek. "You're not making any sense to me," she told him—but she knew him well enough, he definitely had this analyzed and re-analyzed and knew what he was talking about. It was just a matter of getting it out of him.

"Lion," he answered her simply. Rolled over on his side and looked into her eyes. Concern in his expression. "Damn, he's so insecure, but he's trying really hard for me. Can you imagine what it will do to his mind to have three unfamiliar riders get up on him, one right after the other? Christ, he'll be wild…and dangerous as hell. Look at what happened with Race."

Comprehension dawning on her face, yeah now she saw the issue. "God, how fair is that, Bee-Bee? To him? To everyone else?" Sighed. "Hell, I guess I should have known all along it was a possibility, but that's just my inexperience showing. I've never ridden in a Nations Cup before. I wasn't even thinking about the final four until after we went clear today. But damn it, Chuck should have brought it up. He's after an individual medal—don't tell me it's never crossed his mind."

"I see what you're saying." How like Jericho, she was thinking—to worry about the horse and even his fellow competitors, rather than seeing his very difficult mount as an advantage that would almost surely get him a medal—maybe gold. Couldn't answer him about Chuck though. Sure seemed like he was right.

"So I ride for a clear round for the Team, and where does that leave me?" he asked in a miserable voice. "It's damn sure Chuck isn't going to scratch me. But maybe I'll get lucky. If there's a jump-off to decide the final four...now, that would be ideal. Clear round for the Team, then just..." Mumbled it. "...blow the jump-off." Shook his head unhappily, sighed. "But I hate that the thought of that too—not trying to do my best? Christ Bee-Bee, I've never deliberately gone for a knock down. Never."

Stroked him, kissed him, then laid her head on his shoulder, their bodies nude and all intertwined. "Don't drive yourself crazy tonight," she told him. "Wait and see what happens...maybe it won't even come up. Maybe George or I will do poorly, and none of it will matter." She laughed then. "Well, probably not George."

"Yeah, don't say that. You were great today," he contradicted her. "Man, I was so fucking proud of you."

Huge smile.

And him covering that beautiful mouth with a passionate kiss.

———

"So Melissa, tell us how this is going to work today?" Roger asked her, the broadcast having resumed for the second round.

Tolerant expert smile. "Well Roger, the order of go here today will be first all the individuals who's teams have been eliminated, but who are still in the running for an individual medal, and then after that the top ten teams. The first rider for the tenth placed team will ride first, then the first rider for the ninth place team, etc. Once the lead-off riders for all the teams have gone, then the second rider for the tenth place team will go, followed by the second rider for the ninth place team, and so on."

"Okay, I get it. So the anchor rider for the team that's in first place after yesterday will be the last to go, right?" he asked, clarifying it one more time for the viewing public.

"Exactly, and that will be the anchor rider for the Belgian team, Marcel Damien. Naturally, that gives him the advantage of knowing exactly what he needs to do to win this competition."

"Right. So, our American team is currently sitting in fifth place, and the order of go will be the same as yesterday...Bee-Bee Oxmoor on QL as the lead off rider, George Strang, Team Captain on Phantom next, and our anchor rider will be Jericho Brandeis on Chasseur de Lion."

They cut over to some footage from the day before, showing one more time QL smacking Bee-Bee in the face and her fall, and Melissa described the event. "Bee-Bee told me she's not discouraged at all by that fall, and that she's feeling fine and excited about riding again today," Melissa added. Now, of course, she hadn't really spoken to Bee-Bee, but Frankel had given her that tidbit, plus one more that she threw in now. "She's sporting a black eye from that accident, but it doesn't seem to be bothering her at all. What a great competitor."

"I'll say."

Since all the individual riders would be going first, there was plenty of time before the teams started in, and Jericho had wandered up to the Team box—urged to do so by Chuck—to say hello to Lady Forrester and Bruce Waverly. All the patrons were sitting around sipping coffee or drinking champagne, just like the day before, but then he hadn't come up here yesterday. Darien and Bob Marx were a few tables down, but he very deliberately ignored them, stepping with long strides over to the table where both his patrons were sitting, chatting together amiably, Camille Forrester with them too.

"Good morning, Jericho. How's Lion today?" Waverly asked him as he approached.

Grabbed a chair from a nearby table and swung it around to sit between the two of them. "He looks good," he told them. "Not tired at all." Little smile. "High as a kite though." None of his concern over the situation with the final four evident.

The voice of Melissa Pepper came over the large screen plasma TV set up for the patrons. "So Roger, I understand you have some interesting news about our riders on a more personal level," she said brightly.

Conspirators look from Roger Lucas. "That's right. Now, I don't believe in spreading gossip, but I have this on very good authority, so I think it's okay to talk about it…" he said with just enough enticement in his voice to catch the attention of everyone in the Team box. All of them listening avidly now. "Apparently there may be wedding bells in the future for two of our riders."

Stunned look on Jericho's face. Head jerking up to the screen.

"Well, don't keep us in suspense," Melissa prompted him.

"Let me put it this way," he said. "Miss Bee-Bee Oxmoor will soon become Mrs. Bee-Bee Brandeis."

Flashing their official team photographs up on the screen.

Voice over from Melissa. "So she's going to marry our anchor rider, Jericho Brandeis?"

Said with authority. "That's right."

"Do we know the date?"

"We don't know the exact date, Melissa, but I believe its intended to be sometime this fall. I'm told he asked her right here at the Games."

"How wonderful for them, and how romantic," Melissa commented, then closed that segment with, "Well, congratulations and best wishes to Bee-Bee and Jericho from all of us at ESPN."

Just couldn't mother fucking believe it. Every head in the box turning to look at him. Speechless…how in the hell? But then he saw it…oh yeah, right next to the male announcer's right hand was a Starbucks cup—complete with star if you looked closely enough. And Goddamn that Brae…yeah, Jericho had told him about it last night.

Lady Forrester looking thrilled. "Oh Jericho, do tell us…is it true?"

Deep blue stare falling away, charmingly embarrassed. Finally nodding.

Everyone at the table expressing how thrilled they were to hear it, and what a wonderful match it was.

Murmured thanks…told them in a low powerful voice, "She's incredibly special to me—like the part of me I've been searching for but couldn't quite find—the part that's truly good."

Darien Marx getting up from her chair abruptly…upset, close to tears even…leaving the box in a rush.

Alpha mare confused and forlorn today. The happy, happy routine of life seeming to have changed on some kind of permanent basis—small icky human showing up with the God human yet again, and the God human acting very stern again too. Pitiful horse noises and head butts barely having an impact on him.

Small human producing an oatmeal cookie—the whole thing, not just pieces—holding it out. Soothing murmurs from her too in response to miserable horse whinny. Hmmm. Alpha mare needing some love. Tried taking the cookie from her like a "good girl" instead of snatching it aggressively.

Amazing result. The God human praising her and petting her for it. Loved the God human. Adoring mare eyes for him.

Alpha mare thinking and thinking hard. Ears twitching, trying to figure this development out. Two facts. Small not-quite-as-icky-as-before human seemingly accepted into the herd by God human. All herd members...protected by alpha mare. Conclusion obvious. Nuzzling her, memorizing the scent.

Positive reinforcement from the partner human—affectionate pat from him, accompanied by those soft mutters of his that alpha mare loved. Cookie piece from him too, along with powerful, "Good girl." Really happy with that.

Lifting that huge head proudly, taking on this new assignment, taking it seriously too. Alpha mare role—very important responsibility.

QL—more than up to the task.

"And here's Bee-Bee Oxmoor...soon to be Bee-Bee Brandeis...on QL!" Roger announced.

Alpha mare cantering boldly into the Grand Prix jumping arena with very solemn duty of carrying small belongs-to-God human around safely. Huge bounding stride to show power of a mare on a mission.

Bee-Bee brought her around for the salute. QL was certainly trying a lot harder for her today than yesterday, and she was pleased with that, although maybe the big mare was trying a bit too hard—and QL certainly considered herself in charge of the situation, as opposed to the other way around. Still, it was a relief not to have her threatening to buck constantly. She picked up the canter, remembering Jericho's advice from the day before, "...don't try to stop her, just let her run."

Okay.

She headed her through the timers and toward the first fence.

Nice big fence—happy alpha mare making a gigantic leap to be sure and keep small belongs-to-God human out of harm's way, but pretty much ignoring signals from this bottom-of-the-totem-pole herd member on her back. Putting up with them though. Probably a foal—making special allowances because of that.

"Wow, Melissa, QL sure is a big jumper, isn't she?" Roger was saying, not sounding like he was sure that was such a good thing.

"Yes, we saw that yesterday. See how she's missing her spot and just powering over? Still well clear though." Sounded a bit worried with that wild style. "Has to be a jarring ride," she added dubiously.

Alpha mare seeing another fence and heading for it, ready for another big jump. In high spirits. Confident. Bottom-of-the-totem-pole herd member picking a different fence instead. Bit of a struggle going on.

"Melissa, isn't she going off-course?" Roger asked with horror.

Equally horrified response. "It looks to me like she's having a hard time steering QL."

Talk about horrified...Bee-Bee was yanking on that block of wood head for all she was worth.

Very tolerant alpha mare finally giving in, humoring brand-spanking-new herd member. Jerking at the last second into the fence she wanted, and just launching over it.

"Oh thank goodness," Roger blurted out.

Still cantering boldly around the field. Bee-Bee desperately trying to make sure the next fence QL noticed was the correct one. Her arms were already aching.

And Jericho was standing on the fence line, just gripping the top rail, and growling, *"Come on,"* viciously under his breath. Frankel and George were right there beside him. The tension in the air between the three of them just crackling.

Alpha mare coming into the triple combination. Oh goody! Taking really good care of belongs-to-God human, bunching those hindquarter to sail into the air...whoopee!

Uh-oh, next element really close, feet scrambling, head up, taking off too close and just twisting those hindquarters to the side...made it!

Third fence...wild leap. Hind foot rubbing hard.

"Will you look at that!" Melissa yelped, calm expert exterior thrown to the wind. "That rail popped up a good two inches out of the cups, but it came right back down without falling over. Just listen to this crowd cheering, they really seem to be behind this very unorthodox pair."

Truth was, you just had to love the exuberance of this moose-like mare—ungainly creature, super athlete, jump any obstacle from anywhere, so obviously loving her work despite the fact that she appeared to be anything but controlled.

And through the final timers at last.

"A clear round, Melissa!"

"Oh, this is really great news for the American team!" She was actually laughing with delight as she spoke now. "I'll be honest, that had to be one of the most *unusual* rides we've seen here in these Games...but the horse certainly wasn't resisting at all. I think it's fair to say that QL was having a wonderful time. And good work Bee-Bee."

Out in the warm-up area, Jericho, Frankel and George were yelling and slapping each other on the back. They were still in the running here! Little Bee-Bee had just opened the door for them.

Really proud of herself alpha mare exiting the arena at an excited, springs under her feet, prancing trot. Belongs-to-God human needing a lot of supervision, but carried as only an experienced protector of the herd could.

Alpha mare getting a lot of pats and praise too. As it should be, really.

Life not quite back to normal, but definitely good.

The jumping continued. None of the teams below the Americans were threatening to move up in the standings. George had one rail down again, just like yesterday—a solid round. Their total faults, now sitting at nineteen.

At the conclusion of the first day's worth of jumping, the teams above them had been the French in fourth place with 12 faults, the Germans and Dutch, tied for second and third with 8 faults each, and the Belgians in first place with only 4 faults—two of their riders having gone clear.

But as the day wore on, that was starting to change. And now, with only the anchor riders for each team left to go in the competition, the French had slipped to fifth place with three more rails down today, and a current total of 24 faults. The Germans had two rails down, and were still in third place with 16 faults. The Dutch had one rail, and were in second place with 12 faults. The Belgians, all clear thus far today, and still in first with 4 faults.

"Well, what does our team need to do here to get a medal, Melissa?" Roger was asking for the benefit of their audience.

"It's certainly not going to be easy," she told him. "First, our anchor rider Jericho Brandeis needs to go clear. If he doesn't, we'll be out of contention. But even then, we're going to need some luck. The Germans need to have at least one more knock down, or the Dutch two, for us to get the bronze. And if both of those things happened, we could get the silver, but that's unlikely. And of course the Belgian anchor, Marcel Damien, would have to have an absolutely disastrous go for his team to fall out of the gold medal slot—it pretty well looks like they've got it clinched."

"Alright then. So what we need right now is that clear round from Jericho on Chasseur de Lion. How difficult will that be?"

Melissa smiling, infinitely wise. "One thing we need to remind our viewing audience is that the horses our team members have been riding in this competition are all horses that they hadn't planned to use. And of course that's because our top horses became ineligible for competition when they were maliciously drugged the night before the start of the show in what was probably the biggest scandal in equestrian competition in recent years. So to get any medal at all here today would really say something about the quality of this American team." Roger was nodding gravely as Melissa spoke. She went on, repeating what she'd said the day before about Lion. "Now, Chasseur de Lion is a very talented horse, but so difficult to ride that he'd actually been retired several years ago, so yes, it's going to be difficult. Still, Jericho had a clean round yesterday, so it's certainly possible."

And man, that's what Chuck had been telling him—feeding it to him, really driving it home.

When the French team fell down to fifth place, and the first two German riders ran into problems, Frankel could see they had an opening. And he'd started in on Jericho...isolating him, talking to him, relentlessly pushing him—really stoking that fire inside him till he just burned. And damn, going into this he'd been so conflicted about the final four and Lion…but by the time Chuck was through with him, he couldn't even remember that issue any more. Only the goal. A clear round—the entire team depending on him.

"Now you show these bastards they can't refuse us," Frankel was saying to him. "You *show* them. They started this fight—they came after you, the cheating pricks. They tried to *take this away from you* by eliminating Antares. But they can't stop you. Nothing stops you. *You don't bow.*"

No answer, not speaking at all anymore. But oh yeah, he was taking it in, had gone inside himself. And Chuck knew exactly how to ignite him, rousing that violent side of him and focusing it on one objective and one objective alone. A perfect ride.

A "take no prisoners" ride.

Needed it.

The warm-up with the stallion surprisingly strong. Something about the coldly calculating and violent beast awakened inside him now… resonating with the animal's dangerously wild spirit—mind meld on some unknown level, and the two of them working as one unstoppable entity— absolute precision combined with inexorable power. Authoritative, swaggering too, uncompromising.

The other anchor riders who would come behind him, taking note. Tension rising among them. Too good. The American, looking too good.

"Wow," George commented to Bee-Bee. "I've never seen Lion look that mentally and physically connected. Now *that's* what he was meant to be."

But she was shaking her head unhappily. "They do look great—really great. Best I've ever seen them. But it scares me what Chuck's doing to Jericho, putting so much pressure on him. What happens if things don't go well? He'll be devastated. Chuck's never done that to me, and boy I'm glad."

Agreed with her. "Me either, but you need to trust Chuck. He's a great coach. And he knows Jericho. He told me Jericho really thrives on pressure. He soaks it up and turns it into performance. And you have to admit, he sure looks like he's in the zone."

Shrugged. "I hear you, I'm just worried, that's all."

Opening the in-gate. Calling him to come inside.

"So, Melissa…what should we expect here?" Roger was asking.

The patrons in the team box, all leaning forward to hear the answer. Really wanting to know—especially Bruce Waverly.

"Well, Roger, yesterday as you recall, this pair took the course at an incredibly fast speed, and Jericho told me afterwards that Lion, as he calls him, was very nervous but willing, so he decided to let him gallop rather than interfere." Another make-believe conversation, and more information she'd weaseled out of Frankel. "So lets see if he's settled down...Oh wow," she murmured.

"What?"

"Let's let our audience get a look at this picture." Cut to a live view of Lion and Jericho coming into the ring and around for the salute. Lion at his finest. Huge and utterly commanding, rolling canter...beautifully round and soft in the bridle...intelligent eyes in that exquisitely chiseled face ...small ears pitched forward keenly. The rider, relaxed, self-assured...but also fierce. Razor-sharp pair. "Now this is a different picture," Melissa was saying. "You don't really need to know anything about Show Jumping to see what a beautiful horse-and-rider combination we have here. So obviously Lion's a lot more comfortable today."

Understatement that. *They owned this ring.*

Took to the course. Thirteen obstacles in all, including a double, a water jump and a triple...simply disappearing one by one behind them. Effortless. Form...picture perfect, the horse...magnificent. "Ride of a lifetime" good.

Frankel was standing by the in-gate and watching...more like "glued to the scene in front of him" would have been a better description of how intent he was—not even talking to George or Bee-Bee, not even knowing where they were standing. Still, his head turned for about a nanosecond when Pier Gottemann came up beside him. They stood together for a moment in silence, mesmerized.

"Mistake," Gottemann predicted quietly.

"What's that supposed to mean?" Frankel snarled at him, but without taking his eyes off Jericho.

"Too early," the horse trader told him. "That's your gold medal ride...should have saved it for tomorrow."

Obstinate moment of silence, then, "I needed it right now."

Difference of opinion. "Even as good as this is, you could still walk away with nothing—you'll need mistakes from either the Dutch or Germans to get the team bronze, and silver's out of the question. No," he insisted again. "You peaked him a day early, Chuck. Better think about how you're going to recover from that." Soft laugh. "Actually, I have a few decent-sized bets on him, so I'd like him to do well."

No answer, but the American Chef D'Equip had obviously heard. Continued to watch as one elegant jump after another just totally captivated the crowd filling these grandstands...hushed silence replacing the normal wall of sound.

The final triple combination coming up. This just might be the most satisfying ride of Jericho's career so far—it had a kind of raw, unspoiled purity to it—even more so, coming from Lion. The whole world gone away...no noise registering to him beyond the steady beat of his own heart in absolute rhythm with that of the huge gray stallion beneath him—and in time with the powerful beat of his canter. Nothing to see except each jump coming up—*sighting the spot with precision, putting the stallion on it, lifting him*—and then leaving it behind in their wake, untouched. And the same with this triple. Stag-clean jumps into and out of the three elements of this combination, Lion's feet barely seeming to touch the ground in between fences, the animal reveling in his own power and ability—right now, today.

Lion, like he'd once been...in the beginning. So alive.

The round concluded. Having a hard time making the transition from that almost ethereal experience, back to the reality of these Games. Cantering to the outgate, salute to his patron forgotten until the very last second. Pivoted the stallion, found Bruce Waverly with his eyes. Crop to his helmet.

Return roar from the crowd.

———————

And maybe Chuck wasn't stupid after all.

The German anchor rider, seemingly unnerved by the ride that went before him had two knock-downs, taking his team score to 24 faults, and dropping them to a tie for fourth and fifth place.

And moving the Americans to third.

The Dutch anchor went clear, as did the Belgian, leaving the results: Belgium, gold medal...Netherlands, silver medal...and the good old U.S. of A. nabbing the bronze.

Patron box, going wild.

As for the individual medals, which would be contested tomorrow, there were five riders who'd had a double clear over the two days...two of the Belgians, Marcel Damien and his teammate Luger Andres...the Dutch anchor, Hans Gutsch...one more rider who'd competed as an individual after his team was eliminated, hailing from Ireland, named Ian McAlister, and Jericho. Five riders—four slots in tomorrow's competition, meaning there'd be a jump-off today to determine who would ride.

A jump-off. How perfect was that?

A gift from the Gods.

With the goal of the clear round successfully behind him, and the passage of about a half an hour's time, something closer to normalcy had returned inside him, and he was thinking again—thinking about Lion and the final four. And Frankel wasn't whispering to him anymore either, hadn't been trying to keep that fire alive—maybe he'd just been too caught up with the press and others. Maybe never suspected that Jericho might have an agenda of his own.

The plan was straightforward...rail down on the last fence, maybe even a refusal...just get in too deep where the stallion couldn't maneuver, then let it happen on its own. Should be easy enough.

He really hated the thought of deliberately blowing the jump-off, and yeah, there was a good chance he was giving up an individual medal too, but Christ this animal had given him so much today. That absolutely phenomenal ride. He'd never felt closer to him than he did at this moment. No way he was letting those Belgians get on him. Especially Damien. Felt pretty sure he was the bastard who'd blown the stallion's mind in the first place. There was going to be a reckoning for that one of these days—maybe not here and not now, but oh yeah, someday...soon.

The jump-off was being held immediately prior to the awards ceremony for the Team Competition. Short run—only six obstacles. Jericho got back on Lion, and worked him quietly as far away from the other four riders as possible—away from his own teammates too. And most definitely, away from his Chef D'Equip.

The order of go was determined by a special draw, and would be McAlister, Andres, Brandeis, Gutsch, and finally Damien.

Jericho saw McAlister going into the ring...and oh sure, Frankel was beckoning and calling to him now. Pretended he hadn't seen him. With only six jumps, the rounds were going to be good and short—easy enough to avoid him, and man he needed to because he sure as hell couldn't look him in the eye with what he was planning to do. Totally concentrating on Lion now…and the stallion right there with him. Marvelous animal despite his tenuous grip on reality. Still plenty strong and ready to jump.

Looked up a minute later and saw McAlister coming out—and congratulations for him from his Chef D'Equip. Another clear round apparently. Andres had disappeared inside the Grand Prix arena for his go.

"Jericho, ride to me," Frankel called out, good and irritable at being ignored—not fooled either.

Yeah, alright…thirty seconds. No sense pissing him off more. Trotted the stallion over, not rushing to get there. Pulled up next to him, but fiddling with a spur, not making eye contact.

Good and suspicious tone of voice. "What's going on in that head of yours?"

Mumbled, "Nothing."

"Bullshit…Goddamn you, Jericho, don't lie to me, I…"

Interrupted by the ring steward calling him to the in-gate.

Tossed a condemning look at him…maybe hating this so much, or on the flip side, maybe wishing he'd talked to him about it. And maybe too, just plain angry that Chuck had done nothing, acknowledged nothing, leaving him to do it all.

Jericho spun that big gray without another word and cantered him to the Grand Prix field. The in-gate opened. He went inside.

Frankel stood watching for an instant, and knew something wasn't right. Bee-Bee was still with George, and he turned to her, demanding of her, "Tell me."

Really guilty look on her face. "Tell you what, Chuck?"

"Don't you dare pull that on me," he snapped. "Tell me right now." He motioned to her to follow him as he ran to the in-gate to watch. Eyes on Jericho as he came around for the salute, but still growling at her, wanting to know. Definite intimidation routine, *"Damn it, Bee-Bee…"*

But she wasn't about to say a word. Played innocent. "I don't know what you're talking about. Honestly. What's the matter?"

"Oh yeah, like I believe that." Really, really mad at both her and him.

Jericho and Lion were on the course already. "Well, this pair is looking excellent again, aren't they, Melissa?" Roger was saying, up in the ESPN broadcasting booth.

Enthusiastic. "Yes indeed. Very impressive. And here they go over the first fence…just lovely. Smooth, fast and the horse so tuned in to his rider.

With the way he's going today it's hard to believe he's as difficult to ride as we're told he is. Oh…just perfect over that second obstacle too."

Also lots of excitement in the Team Box. Bruce Waverly positively beaming as his horse sailed cleanly over the third fence—a big spread jump. "I'm really proud of that Jericho," he was telling Lady Forrester.

She reached over and squeezed his hand. Said good-naturedly, "Well, I'm very jealous of you, Bruce. And just look at this…fantastic!" Jericho and Lion had made a tight turn to face directly into a very solid looking wall, and the stallion launching over it bravely.

Frankel relaxing a bit, but still muttering under his breath, "He sure as hell didn't look like himself going in." Watched as his rider came in dead on spot to that fifth jump—a set of planks with no ground rail—unsettling to many of the horses. But Lion taking it without question, and still clear. Mumbled it again, still uncomfortable. "He damn sure didn't look like himself."

Approaching that last fence now, and this was where Jericho planned to do it. Sat in and pushed the horse forward instead of checking him…got him in nice and deep. Undercurrent of shock coming from the grandstands—huge pilot error. Could even pick out Chuck's voice screaming over top of the crowd.

Melissa, just beside herself. Totally stunned. "Oh no, oh no! *Way, way* too deep to this fence, Roger. They'll *never* make it."

Fiery, screw-loose gray stallion…after all these months, finally joining forces with this human…finding something so kindred in him in the warm up before that last round. And stallion's job was to jump, he understood that clearly. But this was a very, very difficult obstacle—high and no room to gather himself and thrust. Any other time he would have just stopped or even crashed right through it. Not today. Instead he tossed his heart and soul over that fence, lifted straight up from the shoulder, and lunged with all the power in his body to rise up into the air at an impossible angle, then tucked those hind feet in tight and flew.

Squealing gasp from the ESPN expert. *"Oh my God!* What a *mammoth effort* on the part of the horse!"

Through the final timers, and man, Jericho just felt miserable. Lion had foiled him. They were over and clear.

573

"Would you mind telling me what the hell that was supposed to be?"

He'd barely gotten back out the in-gate and Frankel was on him, demanding, and just God damn knowing that "mistake" had been deliberate …either that, or Jericho had completely lost it for a moment, and he knew him too well to buy that.

Jumped off and handed the stallion to Marco. Stepped away from the area where most of the riders were standing. Could see Marcel Damien smirking at him too—still waiting for his round.

Prick.

Frankel still following after Jericho, and wanting an answer. "I asked you a question. I knew God damn well something was wrong when you went in there, and don't you dare walk away from me."

No one in the warm-up area surprised at Frankel yelling at his anchor. Inexcusable rider error, and his Chef D'Equip giving him hell.

Got far enough away—to the fence line—turned on his heel and just snarled back at him, "Yeah, I did it on purpose, you're not wrong about that."

Chuck about as coldly furious as he'd ever seen him. "Then you better tell me why…and if I don't like this answer you're dropped from the Team after these Games, and you won't be back."

Man, just drew his breath in—hadn't considered that possibility. Had to fight to keep his anger coming. Needed it to carry him. Just lashed right back. "Don't give me your crap, Chuck. You know exactly why I did it…or why I tried to do it, cause it didn't work, did it?"

Their argument interrupted by a loud groan from the grandstands.

"Well, there you are," Frankel taunted him, good and smug. "Gutsch just had a rail down. You're in the final four."

"Then scratch me."

"Absolutely not. And if you want to ever ride for me again, you'll take my decision and swallow it, no questions asked." Stuck a finger hard in his rider's chest—that really annoying gesture of his. Threatening, lethal tone of voice. "And Jericho, if you don't show up tomorrow, or if I see a hint…even a *hint* of you throwing a round on purpose…I won't just drop you from the Team…I'll have you suspended for the next year—maybe longer. Better believe I can make it harsh."

Knew Frankel meant it too, the ruthless bastard. But Jericho never even considered backing down. "You know what? That's an empty threat. What good would it do me to blow a round tomorrow? And how *greedy* are you?" he barked heatedly at him—way too loud, but who gave a shit? He only toned it down marginally as he continued—really harsh and aggressive. "Do I have to destroy that stallion to satisfy you? Want me to see if I can go find you a gun someplace, Chuck? Fucking shoot him between the eyes…save us all a lot of bother?"

Astonished. If anything, even angrier. "That's what's bothering you? And you didn't even come to me? God damn you, I really want to kick your ass."

Purred it. "Well then come on, Chuck. Just give it a try." Really let him have it. "Don't tell me you didn't know Damien's the one who ruined him, but no, you weren't going to tell me that. You want to let that motherfucker get on him. Think he'll ever be sane again after that?"

Heads turning from the other end of the enclosure. Whatever was going on between Jericho and Frankel, it wasn't a normal ass kicking for making a mistake. Way too much anger there, and American anchor—seen after the last three days as being hard on himself, not the reverse—really fighting back.

Bee-Bee and George watching, heads close and her talking to him.

Marcel Damien was inside the arena now. Huge cry of dismay from the audience. Frankel and Jericho, just staring at each other. Then a second groan from the grandstands. Two rails down…had to be. Gutsch back in—Damien out.

"There, satisfied?" Frankel sniped at him. "Problem solved. Now I want you to tell me right now what I want to hear." Barely even gave him a second to respond before he snarled it at him again, *"Right now,* Jericho, or just go home and start to pack."

Still three unfamiliar riders getting on the horse—but at least not Damien, at least not him. And either he agreed, or he was saying goodbye to the Team, his horses, his patrons…his career. Saying goodbye to Bee-Bee too, cause man, he couldn't drag her down like that with him. Desperately torn.

Never got the chance to answer though. Derisive snort, sharp comment, "I said it from the beginning—you're not dependable enough for international competition. Never will be either. Think you know everything, don't you? Too good to be part of the Team like everyone else is…doesn't bother you at all to do something as unethical as deliberately take a knockdown…doesn't even faze you that I'm responsible for this Team, not you. Well, let me tell you this, I can't coach a rider like that. I'm through with you. Get out of my sight. Go home," and Chuck spun on his heel, walked away from him.

Yeah, he could have gone after him, but wasn't going to. He turned his back to the warm-up area instead, just staring out at nothing. Ripped apart inside. Couldn't deny Chuck had a damn good point too—yeah, he'd fucked him over by not including him. And yeah, he lived by his own rules— couldn't promise it wouldn't happen again. Didn't change a thing about how he felt about Lion either. Really unhealthy mixture of rage and something bitterly fatalistic, telling him that this had been inevitable. All he deserved—all he'd ever get. Street kid—didn't belong on this National Team with its wealthy patrons. Maybe couldn't find anywhere to fit in.

Didn't know how many minutes later. Calm voice, sympathetic. "Come on Jericho, get back on your horse." George Strang.

Having a hard time comprehending him. Get on the horse? Couldn't think of a reason why he would.

"The awards ceremony," George reminded him.

Really ugly smile as he turned to him. Low, dangerous tone. "How could I forget?" Just walked past his Team Captain to where Marco was standing with Lion. Vaulted up onto that sucker, face blank. Got into formation, deep blue eyes so forbidding that even Bee-Bee didn't ask— she'd wait.

Cantering into the arena. Dismount, and standing with the rest of his Team on the podium. Medal hung around his neck. The Belgian national anthem played. Remounting, victory gallop. Going through the motions.

Disappearing after that.

Social held that night for the entire Team and their families, even those Team members who hadn't ridden—and of course the patrons too…really more for them when you got right down to it. A few members of the media had also been invited, including Melissa Pepper and Roger Lucas. The function was held in a private banquet room in a local five star hotel. Decorated, of course, with red, white and blue banners…also with beautifully done murals placed around the room, sporting pictures Brae had taken throughout the Team event—pictures so good they were startling. By the end of the evening, Melissa had asked for a copy of them.

Frankel had gotten there early. But he wasn't himself at all—didn't even look well. And keeping away from everyone, not talking—not orchestrating things with the hotel, not setting up a presentation like he normally would.

The Team members came as a group, but minus Jericho. Bee-Bee also missing. And then the patrons began arriving, decked out to the nines—designer gowns, jewels. Black tie formals for the men.

The event began with cocktails and circulating waiters with hors d'oevres. George had tried to mingle, but the conversations were just too hard. After a little while he wandered over to Frankel. Murmured to him miserably, "Tell me what to say and do here, Chuck."

Almost broken stare coming back at him. "Did you go in Jericho's room?"

"Yes."

"And?"

Hesitated. Sighed. "Packed and gone."

Just breathed it, "Oh, fuck." Waited a few seconds and asked the second most logical question. "And Bee-Bee?"

"She's there in her room, but her door's locked and she's not coming out. She said she won't be here."

Little defensive snarl from the Chef D'Equip. "Yeah, you think I was wrong . You think I'm an asshole…too hard on him, right George?"

Hesitating again. Then just stepped up to his question. "Want to know what I think? If you really do, I'll be glad to tell you. But then don't turn on me."

Frankel's expression aching. "Yes, I want to hear it."

Quiet question, accompanied by a hand placed with friendship and support on Frankel's arm. "Is he that much like you, Chuck? That much like you were at his age? 'Cause man, you're so hard on him sometimes, it's like you're screaming at yourself. Yeah, he did something stupid today and without telling you about it, but his motives weren't selfish, and maybe… just maybe, you make it impossible for him to come to you. I'm not defending him, Chuck. You had every right to get after him. But man, you don't know when to stop. And here's the crazy part, I know you like him. I think you like him a lot."

Admitted it too. "You're right, I do."

"He thinks the world of you too. And you want to see him ride tomorrow, and you want him to stay on the Team."

Nodded, not denying it.

Taking charge, because nobody else sure was. "Alright, here's what we're going to do then. I'll run with this affair. And I'll call Bee-Bee and make her get her ass over here too. That's my job. Here's yours...go and find him, Chuck."

Fighting back a little. Look of scorn. "Apologize to him?"

Strang just shook his head, even laughed about it. "Yeah, you're both assholes, to answer that question you asked me originally. It's probably why you fight so much...probably why you like each other so much, too. Apologize to him...talk to him...you figure out that one."

Didn't even try to respond. And still pretty defeatist underneath it all. "What do you want me to do, George? Start combing every jail in a fifty mile radius?"

"Guarantee you this much...he's somewhere you can find him. Maybe not the rest of us, but you? Absolutely. Consciously or unconsciously he'll have made sure you can reach him...if you look hard enough. If you care enough to hunt for him."

George's prediction...true.

But it had not been easy. Frankel started at the most logical place...the horses. Reynaldo was there on duty for the night—the security guards too.

"I'm looking for Jericho," he told Strang's groom.

Cold reception...more like sub-zero. Stiff answer. *"Puño? Ah, sí.* He was here earlier...picked up his saddle, said goodbye to the horses. Leave after that."

"How long ago, Reynaldo?"

Shrug, not wanting to tell him much. "Couple of hours maybe."

Pushing it. "Did he say where he was going?"

"To Marco, I think."

Frankel drove to the hotel where they'd put the Team grooms who were working at the showgrounds—small place, the Italian equivalent of a "Motel 6" or something similar in the States. The rooms all opened onto a concrete balcony. Metal steps leading up to it. Found Marco's door and knocked on it.

The door opening a crack, and a grim face appearing behind it. It almost looked like he was about to slam it shut again, but then threw it wide open instead. "He isn't here," Marco said. "See for yourself."

Came into the room. "But was he here?"

Little sneer, and then almost the exact same words as Reynaldo used, "Couple of hours ago maybe." Dropped another little bombshell on the table. "He came to say goodbye...then he fired me. Said I needed to get a secure job, said he probably couldn't afford to keep me anyway. Wanted me to stay with QL."

Talk about feeling like shit. "Marco, you'll have a job, and the Team is going to pay you till we get this straightened out."

Turned his back on him, very pointed insult. "It wasn't *my* job I was worried about, Chuck." Slung another hard comment at him too. "He's a good man, good rider too. Try an find another one like him."

Truth was, he agreed with that, still he thought Marco needed to face a few things too. "Marco, he deliberately tried to blow a round today—are you going to defend that?"

Not really wanting to acknowledge it. Shrug. "No. But he's not like that." Defensive again. "It wouldn't have been for money. Never for that."

"Think he should just make decisions himself? Ignore the Chef D'Equip? Maybe everybody can do that."

Didn't like answering that either. "No." Tried his own question then, said it harshly. "He grew up hard Chuck—had to take care of himself. See, you don't understand that, but I do. One mistake, and you want him off the Team?"

"No, I want to try and find him."

Nasty little laugh. "Then better get to the airport."

Did that. San Patrignano had a small one. Walked the whole thing, checked every counter, but none of the attendants remembered selling a ticket to him.

Race.

The name just came to him. Sure, why hadn't he talked to him while he'd been at the hotel? No way Jericho would have gone without seeing him first—the two of them so alike, no telling what he might have said to him. Went back and got his car, drove back the way he'd come but a hell of a lot faster. Back up those metal steps, but this time going to Race's room.

Knocked.

Threatening voice coming through the door to him. "What do you want?"

"I'm looking for Jericho." The door opening, and Race hobbling out onto the balcony. Shutting the door behind himself. How suspicious was that? And Frankel started to hope. "He's here, isn't he?"

Defiant answer. "What if he is?"

"Let me in, Race. Let me see him."

Race wasn't looking directly at him, but his expression was totally unfriendly. And maybe nervous too. "Yeah, well you can't talk to him."

"Why not?"

Lifted those dark eyes up to him, a powerful accusation there. "Cause he's barely coherent."

Stunned by that, but maybe he shouldn't have been. "Drunk?"

Shook his head in the negative, mouth turned sullenly down.

Insistent. "Then what?" And Christ, he sure hoped it wasn't drugs.

Paused—seemed to be really interested in something on that concrete floor, staring fixedly at it. "He came by to say goodbye to me. Then I don't know where he went, but he got in a fight with some guy wherever it was. Bet he was winning it too," he added defensively. "But then four or five of his buddies jumped in. Worked him over real good. Dragged himself back here afterwards." Uncertain look about him again. "I was just about to go get Marco."

Frankel remembered 's-Hertogenbosch all too well, remembered Jericho telling him he'd wanted that trucker to hurt him then. Tonight he'd made sure it happened—didn't have a doubt in his mind about that. "How bad is he? Damn it, this isn't something to play around with. Let me see him right now, Race." Pretty demanding about it too, taking advantage of the insecurity on Race's face. And unfortunately fairly certain he knew the answer to his own question.

Reached behind himself and opened the door. Mumbled it. "He's wrecked."

Small room, the main feature the bed, and that tall form sprawled across it. Face badly bruised and bloody—small cut over one cheekbone, but mainly coming from his mouth. His own knuckles really raw, and yeah he'd gotten some blows in. Dirt ground into his clothing, like they'd had him down on the ground, and worked him over there. How much other damage there was, Frankel wouldn't know till someone examined him.

Sat down on the edge of the bed. No reaction. Called his name, asked if he could hear him.

Eyelids—one almost swollen shut—opening just a crack, but even so, those deep blue eyes flaring with scorn, aversion. Couldn't quite get the words out. "...you."

"Yeah, fuck me, I know. I'm fine with that."

Major effort, but he managed to choke out a sentence. "Race, get him out of here."

"He's not going to do that, and I'm not leaving." Glanced over at the working student. "Race, go to Marco. Tell him to get the Team doctor, get him over here. Do it right now." Just waited till he left them, then ground out his main question. "Damn you, Jericho...how badly are you hurt this time?"

Resonant deep bass growl, "Not badly..." Chest rising and falling, teeth grit against the pain. Spat out the last word. *"...enough."*

"Don't give me that bullshit again. Not this time, okay?"

Sneer of satisfaction. "Might not look like it, but I...beat the..." The rest of the sentence garbled. Blood seeping from his mouth. Tipped his head back, just sucking up how much he hurt. Sarcastic murmur from him. "Liked it...couldn't hit me hard enough. Man, just...tore into..." Stopped. Breathed.

"I know that too." Remorse—wrong or not, Jericho had already shown him how he handled that bitter self-scorn that haunted him—should have known this would happen. Wiped the fresh blood tickling down over his jaw away with a towel that Race must have laid out on the bed. "Where's this coming from?"

"Mouth."

"Alright." Better than the alternatives.

Frankel got out his cell phone, rose and started pacing the small room as he called George. Skipped the "Hello" part and went straight to, "I found him." Could see that Jericho was listening, though he was trying to look like he wasn't. "Beaten up pretty bad...no, you heard me...well this time they got him." Listened for a minute, expression resigned. "No George, isn't it obvious? Problem solved...got himself pummeled, so now he *can't* ride, can he? Doesn't have to face the issue with me either—the question of who makes the decisions here. Didn't have to leave yet either."

Jericho really looking at him, those words hitting home. Too close to the truth, maybe. Dragging himself up onto his elbows. Interjecting harshly, disagreeing, "No. That's *not* what I did."

Not even giving that denial an answer. Instead, Frankel's face hardening at something George said to him. "What do you mean?" Listening, considering it, looking even angrier. Eyes swinging to Jericho. "Where did this happen?"

"Parking lot."

Frankel drawing in his breath, just growling. "Here?"

Nodded.

"He's saying yes," Chuck told George. Then another question for Jericho. "They were waiting for you?"

Nodded coldly again. "Or followed me. Didn't matter, because I *wanted*...them." Sank back to the bed again, expression brutal—remembering the fight maybe.

"Are you hearing this?" he was asking George again. "Said they might have followed him." Eyes back to Jericho. Really pointed question this time, and just furious. *"Were they Belgian?"*

Silence.

Replaying the scene in his mind...those fists and booted feet smashing into him. And him, fighting his way back off the ground, lethal machine and doing serious damage. Knew he'd hurt them in return and a couple of them badly—that right hand lashing out like a pressure hammer again and again. Couldn't withstand the brute force of their numbers for long though, and yeah, he'd taken it pretty good then.

What language had they been speaking? Couldn't remember that. Not English, anyway.

Frankel, still talking to him. Not George. Him. "Because it makes sense, and it sure fits with everything else we think they've done. See if you're out, Damien's back in. Maybe he'll get that gold medal after all. And yeah, he's scared to death of you...sees you on Chasseur, knows *he* couldn't ride him...knows you can beat him. But now? He wins."

Jericho, gone dead quiet.

And his Chef D'Equip, finding that button and pushing it. Pushing it hard. "And you're right...you're so right, and maybe I was wrong risking Lion...to get back at them for drugging the horses, for roughing you up in that practice ring. For taking the Team Gold, when we should have had it...when we *worked* for it." Murmured it to him, seductive. "I told you these teams over here would know your weakness. Sure they did. Yeah, they knew they could get you to fight...sent five guys to make sure they hurt you too—chicken shits. And why? To take you out of the running, and *you...you* specifically, not anyone else. Because you're the one he hates, you're the one who's *scaring the shit out of him."*

Knew Chuck was playing him, and God, he had it down to a science. Knew something else too—he wasn't off this team, no matter what had been said earlier. Not if he didn't want to be.

And maybe he'd always known that, but it would have meant facing Chuck...being wrong and admitting it. Being vulnerable. And yeah, maybe Chuck was right and getting roughed up had been easier.

Marco and Race coming back in the room, and the Team doctor with them. But Jericho and Frankel, ignoring them, eyes locked.

"Fine," Jericho murmured dangerously. "I'll give you what you want. I'll ride tomorrow."

Protests immediately coming from the doctor—no one paying any attention to him. But Marco wasn't looking at all surprised.

The American Chef D'Equip, not happy yet. Making an issue of it. "See you and I, we keep having the same argument—have since day one. Let me ask you this question. Would you ever put Force and Lion out in the same paddock?"

Didn't understand where that question came from—right out of the blue. "Of course not," Jericho ground out—hard for him to talk with his mouth cut up inside and the sharp pain in his body, and irritated by the stupid question. "Two herd stallions...bound to fight. Hurt each other."

"Yeah, they're gonna fight, till one of them acknowledges the other. Only one can be leader. The other *gives way* or he gets driven out. That younger stallion...he's got to bow to the one with more experience. Learn from him till it's his turn to rule. Now I run this team. *I* make the decisions. Better understand that. You disagree, you come and tell me, but then I decide and you just live with it. Can't be any other way, Jericho." Expecting confirmation too.

Totally understood that, said it flat out, "No argument."

"Sure, no argument right now, but what about next time? Can't just go on making up your own rules. Yeah, you grew up that way, and you had to. And I'll give you this much...most of them are good. But damn you Jericho, sometimes you remind me so much of Lion. Damaged a little bit maybe, but so much heart in him...that stallion never once stopped fighting no matter what they did to him—but now he has a hard time telling the difference between you and Damien. Maybe these last few days he's figuring it out. You figure it out too."

Comments finding the mark, and really personal. "Jesus Christ, Chuck."

Still not letting it go. "Because this destructive behavior has to stop, you hear me?"

Tried to defend himself. Yielding. "I didn't go looking for that tonight. Yeah, I loved it when it found me, and you were right before…" Stopped to spit fresh blood from his mouth. Didn't go on to finish what he'd been saying either, but he knew Chuck understood—getting pounded in a fight did solve a lot of things without being forced to come to terms with them. New tack. "But I'm trying, Chuck. No bullshit. It's not like I don't hear you." Laid his head back, taking in the physical pain, using it to block the rest. Murmured it. "Man, it's not like I don't respect you."

"Alright." Just accepted that. Turned sharply to the doctor, "And no drugs for him." Seemed to be taking some very obvious and smug satisfaction in that, although it was also a valid concern the way they were screening the athletes these days.

Had to admit Frankel was smart—offering him an excuse to mouth off with this drug thing—and done only because he'd given in, obscuring that fact, keeping it between the two of them. Took him up on it too, just slurred a response. "Like I give a shit, I thrive on pain."

Superior stare. "Good. Works out perfectly then."

Chapter Thirty-Four

At George's insistence, Bee-Bee had gone to the social—late, but present and accounted for. She was pretty impressed with how he was handling things too. He'd given a nice little speech right after dinner, introduced the whole Team, and then Brae too, pointing out his photographs to a round of applause—the ex-Barista thrilled.

Made a decent excuse for Jericho's absence, what with him riding in the individual competition the next day and how grueling today had been, and everyone understanding that. Mumbled something about Chuck helping him that didn't make sense, but no one questioned that either.

Then Brae showed a slideshow of all the shows they'd been to here in Europe—nice way to get all the riders in. Not surprisingly, he was quite a ham—drawing lots of laughter and participation from the audience. George disappeared during the middle of the slide show and could be seen talking on his cell phone over by the windows. When he returned, he passed a note to Bee-Bee that said simply…

CF w/J
K & M-u

The first part was easy enough to interpret. CF w/J…*Chuck Frankel with Jericho.* Good, thank God. But she really had to struggle with the second line of that message. K&M-u…then finally it hit her, and her smile broadened again. *Kissed and Made-up.* Huge sigh of relief and a smile for George. Now she could relax and enjoy herself.

There was dancing again tonight after dinner, and Bee-Bee found herself very popular…for several reasons probably—her rides during the competition, and of course, her engagement.

The elderly Bruce Waverly, swinging her out onto the dance floor for a waltz—something she could barely do, but he was so elegant that it was easy to follow him.

"Congratulations," he told her. Then made a sage observation, "I really like your future husband. Bit of a wild streak in him though." Tipped his face to look at her, little bit serious expression, knowing. "Can't tame it."

She smiled at him, not at all offended by his word of caution. Just nodded in agreement. "I know."

And of course, not to be outdone, Lady Forrester also came over and sat with her. Complimented her on how well she'd done—touched that black eye she had fondly. "Really gutsy," she pronounced—a huge accolade from her. "And now we'll all be counting on you to take care of Jericho." Little laugh. "That might be even gutsier." Seemed happy about the match up though. "You know I might just have a few ideas for the two of you next year. We can talk about that later though."

Finally the last dance was playing. Bee-Bee was standing on the fringe of the dance floor, when she realized that Bob Marx had moved over next to her. Her own patron, so of course she had to be nice to him—had taken time out to say hello to he and Darien several hours ago too, and how awkward did that feel?

"Since you're not riding tomorrow, Darien and I would love to have you sit with us in the Team Box," he invited her.

Really ill at ease with that one, but what could she say? Lied—just a little white one. "I'd love to." Tried to smile at him.

"I have to tell you how thrilled I was with you and QL—both yesterday and again today," he continued. And that was natural, since he did own half of that crazy mare. "We were so disappointed about Monterrey, but that really made up for it. So I got that picture for my office after all." Warm smile.

She gave him a stock kind of answer. "She's a wonderful mare…quite a challenge, but very talented." Something about the way he was staring at her that didn't feel right. A little too bold. Giving her the creeps.

"Yes." Marx took her hand and squeezed it briefly. "The spirited ones are always the most interesting, I think."

The four rounds of the individual World Equestrian Games championship began at 1:00 in the afternoon. The Team box filling up nicely well before that, and Bee-Bee arriving around 12:30. She hadn't seen Jericho at all since yesterday. George told her Chuck was keeping him with Marco and Race, but didn't mention that he'd been attacked last night. Not a damn thing she could do about it anyway, and Chuck would never let her in to see him. No sense getting her all upset.

"Well, good afternoon, Melissa." Roger started the broadcast. "So here we are down to the wire on these individual championships. Today's the day we'll see who's going to capture the medals this year."

"Yes, it's very exciting because this year we have an American rider in the final four." She went on to list all four participants in today's competition, and then to describe what had happened in the last two days of jumping, finishing up with the American's winning the Team bronze. There was footage of that incredible round with Jericho and Lion to clinch the medal, and then more from the jump-off, including that final fence and Lion's heart stopping jump. "Now Jericho told me he'd lost concentration before that last fence, and that his horse got a bit away from him, but that when he asked for a major effort, Lion was there for him. He was very proud of his equine partner—gave all the credit to him." That little tidbit, totally made-up. "It's really wonderful the partnerships that develop…"

Roger interrupting her. "Excuse me Melissa, but we've got a major development here. I've just been notified that Luger Andres, the Belgian rider in the final four, had a car accident last night, and is unable to participate today. Following International rules, he'll be replaced by the rider in the fifth place position—his own teammate, Marcel Damien."

Back in the American stabling area, things were busy, and they'd yet to be told the news. George was patrolling up and down the aisle, keeping everyone away. Reynaldo and Race had taken charge of Lion, and were beginning to tack him up. Jericho was isolated in the stall they'd set aside as a dressing room and had been for the last hour, Marco with him, still working on the injuries to his hands and face. That left eye had been swollen shut last night, but now was open. But it kept puffing up again as soon as they took the ice away. And nothing was going to change the deep purple bruising surrounding it and along his jawline. The cut on his right cheekbone was an angry red slash too. Marco had bound his ribs for support, though none were broken. But at least his hands were flexing and gripping alright.

Jericho himself wasn't thinking much about it—because Frankel was there with him, and he was totally focused on him. Already going inside himself. Everything but this competition blocked out.

Out in the aisle way a Show Steward approached George. Handed him a printed piece of paper. "Here's the order of go. And you should know, the Belgian team just scratched Luger Andres. Car accident last night they said, and he's not fit to ride."

George just murmured it. "And Damien's replacing him."

"That's right, you'll see it here." Pointed to the sheet. "That's why we're late with this." Odd look on his face too, and they were probably both thinking the same thing...if the accident had happened last night, then why were they just scratching him now?

Said okay. Understood it. Went back down the aisle to tell Chuck. Ducked his head inside the dressing room, nodded behind himself, beckoning him.

And Frankel came out. Knew it had to be something, or George would never have interrupted him. George very quietly told him the news, handed the line-up to him too.

The Chef D'Equip looked positively vengeful. "Well here's what that means," he said, eyes narrowed and hot. "They were waiting for us to scratch, and when that didn't happen, they decided to pull Andres in favor of Damien. Now maybe this Andres was one of the guys that hit Jericho last night, and maybe he got a few good punches back, but it's a damn good bet they were still planning to start him if we withdrew."

"I think so too."

Really calculating look on the Chef D'Equip's face. "Too bad about that car accident. File a complaint anyway. Ask to see a police report. Even if they rigged something up, that should unbalance them. Do it right now...make sure they know about it going in."

"Alright, Chuck. You've got it." George looked tensely back at the dressing room. "Are you going to tell him?"

"Oh hell yeah. Have to, and that's gonna be ugly."

"Want help?"

"Nope." Seemed like he meant to do it immediately too, because he strode right back over to that dressing room, pushed the curtain aside and ducked through it—purpose in his step. Jericho's face snapped around to him, intense—the bruising only adding to that impression, not taking away. Pretty much a reflection of what Chuck had been building up in him for the last month, and culminating today. "What is it?" he asked. Wanted it laid on him and right now too.

"Well," Frankel sneered. "Our friends the Belgians had one more trick we weren't anticipating. They've scratched Andres, claim he had some kind of car accident and can't ride. That puts Damien back in. We're filing a protest, but don't count on that for anything. Assume he'll be there."

Jericho rose, eyes just flaring. Already so fired up, hating those bastards for everything they'd pulled and this only making it worse. Remembering how they'd gotten him down and gone after him, and yeah that memory really made him hot. This ride today wouldn't be just any competition—and World Games and medals be damned, it wasn't about that any more. No, this was payback, and that thought consumed him. Wanted it. Thought about Lion...wondered vengefully if the stallion wanted payback as much as he did. "What's the order of go?" he demanded.

Frankel handed him the sheet. Said nothing.

	Brandeis	McAlister	Gutsch	Damien
Round 1	Chasseur de Lion (USA)	Angelica (Ireland)	Tour de France (Dutch)	Oakley (Belgian)
Round 2	Oakley (Belgian)	Chasseur de Lion (USA)	Angelica (Ireland)	Tour de France (Dutch)
Round 3	Tour de France (Dutch)	Oakley (Belgian)	Chasseur de Lion (USA)	Angelica (Ireland)
Round 4	Angelica (Ireland)	Tour de France (Dutch)	Oakley (Belgian)	Chasseur de Lion (USA)

Malevolent flash in those deep blue eyes. "So Damien's last to go on Lion, now that's fitting. Get the stallion when he's at his craziest...and you think he's scared now? Just wait." Thought about it. Grim satisfaction... realism too. "But you know what he'll be trying to do," he added coldly. "Get the stallion so upset that he'll explode with one of the other riders and be eliminated...and me along with him."

Chuck moved in close, voice strong but convincing. "First of all, Lion can be difficult if he wants to, as long as he isn't so dangerous that he's unfit to ride, or doesn't hurt himself to the point he can't continue." Meaningful look at Jericho. "And the other two are up on him first. If we keep Damien away from him, they should be alright. He's a hard ride, yes, but not impossible, especially not after you've ridden him first."

Maybe, maybe not. Still he countered. "We'll all be in that enclosure together, and Damien's going to be trying his damnedest to get to him."

Ruthless comeback. "Know what? McAlister and Gutsch will help you keep him away."

Oh yeah...good point. They damn sure would. Their Chef D'Equips too. Jericho still had reservations, but man, he had a lot of rage inside him—didn't want to let this fucker do what he'd connived so hard to do...manipulate a victory for himself. Felt really fierce about stopping him. "So do I ride or not?" he asked Frankel. "I honestly can't predict Lion's reaction. You call it."

Gratifying for sure to have the decision turned over to him—for once. Didn't have any trouble making it either. "You'll ride, Jericho. You'll ride for yourself, you'll ride for your Team, and you'll ride to beat this asshole. He goes home tonight and he's lying there in bed, and he knows...you're better than he is—can't even win by cheating. You're his nightmare. And you'll be back every year to do it all over again."

"So Melissa, we now have the order of go for these four rounds."

Flashing it up on the screen.

"And you can see that our American rider is first up," she cut in, not wanting Roger to steal any of the important material from her. "He'll be riding his own horse first, and that's only about ten minutes away."

Shooting her an irritated look, but staying professional. "So tell us about this special enclosure they've built at one end of the Grand Prix field," he asked.

Back in the expert role, and pleased with that. "Well Roger, after each rider goes, he and his horse retire to the enclosed area, and will remain there while the riders behind him take the course. Then of course, they'll switch horses for the second round, and each competitor has three minutes to school the new horse they'll be riding. There are two jumps in the enclosure..." Switching to a picture of it. "...and they're allowed to jump each one once, but no more than that. Then they have to come out and take the course again."

"Wow, sounds complicated."

Little knowing laugh. "Yes, but it won't be hard to follow once we get going."

Jericho and Frankel walked up to the warm-up ring together sharing a few last words between rider and coach. Marco following along behind with Lion, and Race bringing up the rear with the golf cart and all the last minute items. They were still a little distance from the fence line, when Jericho looked up, eyes running over the area. And oh yeah, there he was alright...Marcel Damien.

Target marked, and in his sights.

"Don't walk in with me," he said—pretty much an order.

Frankel not fighting it. No, one thing about Jericho...he'd be totally controlled no matter how hot he felt inside—actually the angrier he was, the more calculated he'd be. Didn't have to worry about him blowing it with Damien. Knew how to intimidate too. If he wanted to walk in alone, he damn well had a reason. Frankel simply turned aside, and started back toward Marco and the horse.

Jericho walked in to the enclosure, on the surface just minding his own business. Pretty well expecting Damien to start something with him, although if he didn't he'd provoke it himself. Not looking at Damien either. Just lit a cigarette and quietly stood there smoking a couple of feet inside the fence.

Hard bump from behind, someone plowing into his shoulder with enough force to rock him forward a step, and that hurt. Swung around sharply to face him. And sure enough, it was that mother fucking Belgian—who else would it be?

Damien, backing away, lifting his hands to about shoulder height, and sweetly saying, "Sorry." But his eyes were traveling over the very obvious bruises on Jericho's face...his apology, more of a taunt, and very subtly but clearly referring to the attack last night...not just the bump.

Coldly confident return look for him. Reached up and unsnapped the harness on his helmet, then just stripped that mother off.

Race pulling up in the golf cart and parking outside the enclosure. Frankel, Marco and the stallion walking into the ring and onto a large circle. Stallion looking plenty hot. Huge and powerful too.

"Race," Jericho called out sharply, then just launched that helmet at him hard. The kid caught it easily, although the force of his throw still moved him. Race sneered, loving it—oh yeah, street fighter in that kid for sure, just drawn to the smell of violence—and so tuned-in to Jericho.

And Jericho stepping closer to Damien...nice slow, cocky swagger, poised aggressively like he was about to act. Tossed his cigarette away to prove it. Turned his face both ways so Damien could see it—not embarrassed by the bruises, hell, if anything proud of them. "Get a good look," he snarled. Low voice, but almost savage...also darkly amused. "Five of your pussies, and this is all they could do?" Stripped off a glove then too, let him see those damaged knuckles—let him think about what that damage meant. Sinister and smirking humor, touching first those deep blue eyes...and then followed by a soft threatening laugh. Barked out, "Marco," without ever once looking around. Eyes still pinning Damien...and yeah, for sure, he looked unsettled, had even jumped at Jericho's unexpected shout.

Cruel eyes on this fucker though. Liked to hurt when he thought he couldn't be hurt back.

Wouldn't be the case today though, wanted him to know it too.

Marco came up behind him with Lion. Jericho turned and vaulted on all in the same movement. Not even a hint of the pain that shot through his battered torso as he mounted, though man, it hurt. Jammed his feet in the irons and took up the reins...Lion recognizing Damien now, eyes wild...screaming in rage. All four legs churning, half-rearing, but held almost on the spot by Jericho—making sure this Belgian saw what kind of hellion he'd be sitting on later today. Spun that stallion sharply, one hand forward and petting his neck at the same time—dirt and sand from the arena footing spraying in the wake of his hoofs...hitting Damien's boots and snow white breeches.

Rode to the fence line to pick up his helmet from Race, calling the Belgian's favorite taunt over his shoulder. "Sorry."

Went straight into his warm-up, concentrating now on Lion—trying to find that unity he'd had with him the day before. And not trying to calm him down either—wanted him fierce.

Nice course for the jump-off. Eight obstacles in all, one combination. Good sized jumps, all five feet or better. All the spreads at least five feet wide, including element "b" of the combination jump. Three changes of lead required, and some pretty tight turns, especially between fences 3, 4, 5, and 6. Two big spread jumps at the end, the last one five feet high by five feet two inches wide. Fifty-five seconds to complete the round.

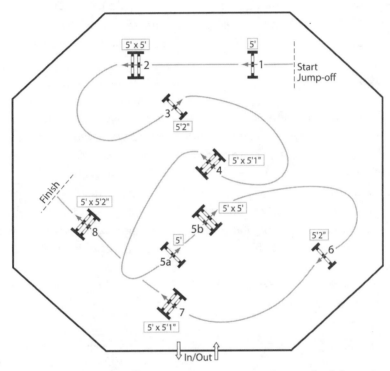

"Wow, tough course," Bee-Bee was commenting to the Marxes, more than happy that she wasn't going to have to try to steer QL through it.

Bruce Waverly had moved over to the table beside them. "Mind if I listen in to the expert here while my horse is going through?"

"No, of course. Please do," Darien invited him, maybe hoping to get back in the good graces of Waverly and the other senior and most affluent patrons like Lady Forrester. "In fact please join us Mr. Waverly so you won't have to crane your neck around." Little deference for him too.

Polite but not more, and not asking her to call him by his first name either. "Oh, I'm fine," he said, then looked at Bee-Bee—much softer expression when he turned in her direction. "Will Lion like this course?" he asked her. It wasn't like he really knew much of anything about it, certainly not from a technical standpoint. But he was picking up the terms, and starting to know what questions to ask.

"That's going to be a really interesting question, Mr. Waverly," Bee-Bee started.

Big smile. "Please call me Bruce."

Happy little reply. "Alright, Bruce then." Darien not looking pleased. Bee-Bee continued. "You know a week ago, I would have said this would be very difficult for him because he has a huge stride, and he's not easy to handle, and there are lots of tight turns here. But now this week is different."

"Really?" Bob Marx asked, trying to get into the conversation. "Why is that?"

Smiled at him—he was her patron after all. "Well, this might sound vague, but this week something's happened between Lion and Jericho. Before, I think he got performance out of Lion because he was able to make it happen…because he's such a strong rider and so physically strong, too." Marx frowning slightly…hadn't really intended to create the opportunity for a commercial on how great Jericho was. Bee-Bee, completely oblivious though, and still chattering happily. "Lion was pretty wild when we first brought him to the showgrounds—afraid I think. Maybe he got strength and confidence from Jericho, felt more dependant on him, and sees him more as a partner now. Anyway, they've really clicked, and Lion's settled down a lot. Think of that beautiful ride yesterday…" Dreamy look in her eyes.

Little chuckle from Waverly. "Now which are you remembering? The horse or the rider?"

Guilty look. "Well, probably both."

Excited voice filling the patron's box, coming from that large screen TV. "And here comes our first rider, the American Jericho Brandeis on Chasseur de Lion, Melissa! What a gorgeous animal!"

Really nicely set-up here…you could see the actual field in front of you, but then easily look over to the plasma monitor for a very crisp close up shot. Jericho had come around for the salute, swept his helmet boldly off his head, brisk nod in the traditional manner.

"My God, Melissa," Roger blurted out in shock. "I wonder what happened…Jericho looks like he was hit by a Mack truck."

He did too. One entire side of his face pretty much varying shades of purple, the other side to a far lesser degree, but with that vivid gash over his cheekbone. Made him look fierce though, combined with his potent expression—like some kind of jungle camouflage, or war paint.

Everyone turning to Bee-Bee for an explanation, but her sharp intake of breath and look of shock and then dismay clearly showed she had no idea. *"What?"* she gasped.

Melissa, responding to her co-anchor. "You're certainly right, Roger. Let's see what we can find out, and if we get any news we'll be sure and share it with everyone watching."

Malicious chuckle from Marx though. "Looks like your husband-to-be has been fighting again." Said it loud enough that it pretty well carried through the whole Team box.

And Darien nodding, agreeing.

"Incredible temper on that guy," Marx dug at him again.

Helmet already jammed back on his head, the harness strapped handily, and he took to the course. Through the timers, and he and Lion went into and came out of the first fence, just soaring. The stallion looking just as good as the day before, if not better—real unity between man and animal. Yeah, Jericho had felt it even in the warm-up, almost from the moment he vaulted on.

Over that monstrous five by five spread at fence number two, into a turn so tight it could have been the start of a working pirouette—but aimed so that their approach to fence three was still at an angle, giving them a better exit line on the other side. Really big vertical at three, standing a solid five feet, two inches. Touched that spot, came up in the irons, lifting at the same time…a gazelle-like take-off, so elegant, barely looking like an effort despite the height. Flying lead change on the landing, and really cutting that curve short to come back around into fence number four.

"How's that form look to you Melissa?" Roger was asking, vocalizing the question she'd slipped on a piece of paper to him.

"It's just textbook perfect," she answered, voice that careful balance between awe and professionalism. "And the horse is jumping so bravely. Jericho's really keeping him on the inside of those turns, like this one we're watching into that big combination. That'll shave seconds off his time." Pause. "Oh, and nicely clear through both elements there."

Nothing changing in that description as he rode through fences 6, 7 and 8, picking up speed at the end of the round where the line straightened and those two big spreads sat one right after the other. Roar from the crowd as he went over the last one. "Clean round for our American rider," Melissa pronounced in delight. "Won't that put the pressure on?"

Rather than exiting the arena, Jericho rode as required to the enclosure. Both Marco and Frankel waiting for him there. Perfect scene for the television camera. Jericho jumping down, enthusiastic slap on the back from his Chef D'Equip…then nice close-up of him handing the stallion a sugar lump, petting his neck, and getting a gentle head butt back. The companionship obvious. The stallion looking like a complete gentleman, not the nutcase of three days earlier. Major, major behavior change.

Melissa turned the microphones off and said to Roger, "I can handle these next few riders. Try and find that Starbucks guy…he'll know what those bruises are from."

Roger exiting the broadcasting booth.

Brae had what Race wanted—as Team Photographer he had a Press Pass and could get into the restricted area next to the enclosure, where the views of the jumping field were excellent. And Race had what Brae wanted—control over the golf cart, and the ability to get back and forth quickly. Long walks from the stalls to the practice ring to the stands and back again were certainly not among the ex-Barista's favorite things.

And so an uneasy truce was cut between them. Race drove, and Brae got them inside. "This is my assistant," he said, pointing to the frowning Race as they entered. But standing along the fence line now, there was finally something they could agree on—Jericho had laid out one bitchin' good ride. High fives and a few healthy whoops over that one. And now, Ian McAlister was entering the ring.

Little tap on the ex-Barista's shoulder. "Uhm, Brae? It's Roger from ESPN, remember?"

Pretty impressed with those initials. And yeah, he remembered him. Gave him kind of a nonchalant look though—showing off in front of Race more than anything else. "Hey, how's it going?" he asked.

"Oh, you know…taking a little break," he said unconvincingly—then again, it didn't take all that much to string Brae along. Said the magic words that clinched it in the next sentence. "Still missing that really good java, you know?"

"Oh, yeah man, I know." Sounded like he was missing it too, though he probably made it over to the Starbucks in town at least twice a day or more.

"So hey, what happened to Jericho's face?" Roger tossed out casually. "We could even see it on the camera's from our booth. Must be really something up close. Looks like a steamroller ran over him."

Race bristling, just listening.

"Here's a better look." Brae was already flipping through the shots on his current disk, and brought up one he'd just taken in the practice ring. Jericho cocky and coldly amused—taken during the interplay with Damien, although the Belgian couldn't be seen in this particular shot. Just Jericho, the gray stallion in the background but deliberately blurred, and dressed in scarlet jacket, white show breeches, and tall black boots buffed to a mirror-finish shine. Helmetless, face lifted—powerful expression—the evidence of the recent violence against him just vivid purple and red on his face.

"Jesus Christ," Roger gasped.

Voice of authority from Brae. "Oh yeah." Actually, he wasn't really in on what happened—hadn't been there last evening, and Chuck hadn't let anyone near Jericho today except himself, Marco, and George, and of course Race.

Roger probing. "What happened?" Holding his breath, hoping he'd get something here.

Shrugged, laughed a little. "Oh, he probably picked a fight or something…"

"Bullshit," Race interjected.

McAlister had just finished his round…also clear, and got an enthusiastic applause as he too headed over to the enclosure.

"What do you mean, bullshit?" the ex-Barista snapped back sharply.

And Race taking a hobbling step right up into his face. "Because that's not what happened, *Trevor.*"

"Hey, that's not my name!"

"Yeah, get out your driver's license and lets see what your name is," he sniped.

Roger interrupted them—their argument, seemingly slipping into the realm of the ridiculous. Tried to get them back on track. "Were you there when this happened?" he asked Race.

Shook his head in the negative, but a lot of anger in those dark eyes of his. Just glaring. "No, but he came to me afterwards."

"Race is Jericho's working student," Brae interjected, drawing a harsh look from him—the "shut up" message unmistakable.

Race seemed to withdraw for a moment, then reconsidered. "Look, I'll tell you this much, but it's all I can say…a group of guys followed him… from the showgrounds he thinks. Attacked him in the parking lot behind our hotel. Five of them," he added defensively, making sure this guy understood the odds against him, and why Jericho looked the way he did. "Anyway, Chuck filed a police report last night—it's all there. More sabotage. That's what Chuck thinks anyway, but he can't prove it."

Roger looking stunned. His eyes flew over to the enclosure and Jericho. "Jesus, and he's trying to compete like that?"

Race had turned to stare at Jericho too—not hard to guess that he idolized him. "Yeah, and you're only seeing his face," he growled vengefully. "That isn't the half of it. But he'll never scratch. Not while he's still standing. Not him."

Hans Gutsch had entered the Grand Prix arena for his first round now.

And in the enclosure, Marco had prepared an ice compress for Jericho—to keep that left eye open. Then he took Lion from him and started walking him at the far end of the area. Jericho held the compress to his face, and of course the ESPN and other broadcasting cameras were focusing in on that, trying to get a shot. Photographers from the adjacent press area too. He ignored all that, walked over to where McAlister was dismounting.

The Irish rider took one look at Jericho and just whistled low. "Damn," he said with that lilting Irish accent. "I was hoping like hell you wouldn't make the final four…" he nodded toward Lion meaningfully, nervously, but tried to smile. "Looks like I almost got my wish." Reached up like he'd actually touch Jericho's face, but stopped short, the gesture more demonstrative than real.

"Yeah, well they tried," he drawled derisively. His injuries would show when he walked too—movements stiff and restricted. The round had been harder on him than he'd expected, and his body already ached. It would get worse too, with each successive ride. Nothing he could do about that except live with it. Changed the subject instead. "You're next on Lion. There's a way to ride him and a way not to."

"I'm listening." Definitely looked attentive, and definitely not offended by the advice.

"Come and meet him," Jericho invited. Yeah, maybe McAlister was surprised he was doing this, but hell if Lion was eliminated before the fourth round, so was he. And maybe a lot more importantly, the stallion desperately needed it…for his sanity. "Two things to remember…first, be as fearless as he is, he respects that and it settles him too. And second, keep him the hell away from Marcel Damien…hates the guy."

Mumbled answer. "Not surprising."

Show steward entering the enclosure to talk to Frankel, motioning him over. Both of them turning to look at Jericho. Some words exchanged— didn't look like a pleasant conversation.

The Dutch rider, Gutsch had finished up his ride. One rail down over jump number 7, one of the big spread jumps. He was riding to the enclosure now, and Marcel Damien had come into the ring and around for his salute.

While Damien took the course, Roger hurried back to the ESPN booth. Couldn't wait to get his information on the air.

Everyone in the Team box was good and excited. The first round of the competition was just winding up. All of the riders had been clear, with the exception of the Dutch entry, Hans Gutsch, with one rail down.

"Well, a very close competition so far," Melissa was saying. "But that could start to change rapidly as the riders begin taking the course with each other's mounts. It's a real test of horsemanship for them to get up on an unfamiliar horse, and jump these very difficult obstacles."

Roger had slipped back into the seat beside her, and the camera angle widened to include him again. Very animated look on his face. "And it's going to be even more difficult for our American rider, Jericho Brandeis, Melissa. Of course everyone in our viewing audience remembers the drugging of the top U.S. horses earlier this week that eliminated them from competition—almost certainly a deliberate act of sabotage. And now, we've been able to learn that a second malicious incident occurred just last night, when five unknown assailants followed Jericho from the showgrounds and attacked him, and that's what all that bruising we noted earlier is about."

"That's just horrible, Roger, and really disheartening to think that these Games have been marred by such inexcusable acts."

"Well, just look at this, Melissa."

Flashing the picture that Brae took of Jericho in the warm-up onto the screen. It was much clearer and more graphic than the limited view they'd had earlier.

Gasps of shock in the Team box, and especially from Bee-Bee who half-rose from her seat murmuring, "Oh my God."

Several of the patrons moved closer to her, lending their encouragement. Especially Lady Augusta Forrester. "I guess you were wrong," she said sweetly to Bob Marx—admonishing him for his earlier comment with a trace of polite disgust in her voice. "Now don't you worry," she told Bee-Bee, taking a seat at the table with Waverly. "You know how tough he is. And you rode with your black eye too," she laughed. "You're like book-ends." And that drew a little smile.

Roger continuing. "Melissa we're told from a very reliable source in the U.S. camp that the injuries we *can't* see on Jericho are just as bad, but that this very brave competitor refused to withdraw from competition. That ice we see him holding to his face is because his left eye keeps swelling shut. The Ground Jury is apparently worried that he'll lose depth perception, and they've been threatening to declare him unfit. And that's why the Show Stewards and the American Chef D'Equip Chuck Frankel have been in constant dialogue—looks like some pretty strong words being exchanged there."

Bee-Bee's little smile quickly erased by that commentary. Lady Augusta, reaching over quietly to take her hand.

"But so far he hasn't been eliminated," Melissa said to clarify it.

"No, as you can see, he's getting ready for the second round."

The television image moved now to the best picture they could get of him in the enclosure—taken from a distance, but with a lens that provided a decent close up shot. Jericho…removing that ice compress from his face and handing it back to Marco, slamming his helmet back on, then taking up the reins of the horse he would ride for the second round, Marcel Damien's gelding, Oakley. Really unpleasant look exchanged between the two of them, then Jericho stepped with his left foot into the stirrup, and swung up and on. The fact that he hadn't vaulted on, probably only apparent to Bee-Bee. Worried sigh from her.

"So he's got three minutes to school this horse, and then he'll come out and take the course," Melissa explained. "You can see there's a timer running on the board, counting down the time."

Nice animal, Jericho was thinking as he rode him, concentrating on that rather than the throbbing injuries to his body, or the fact that he actually could see better with that left eye closed. The gelding had tons of athletic ability, much like Antares, but man, he'd been intimidated, felt really insecure in the bridle—no surprise there either. Tried to show him no one was going to hurt him. Popped him nice and easy over one of the practice jumps, maintaining that light contact, giving him confidence.

Three minutes up, and the enclosure gate opened. Jericho cantered out into the Grand Prix field and around for the salute. Fifty-one seconds later he sailed over that final giant Oxer—bringing home another clear round.

Next to ride, McAlister on Lion.

Jericho came back in the enclosure, and dismounted with a lot less energy than after his first round. Hurting, but still covering it up pretty well. Frankel was right there with him, talking to him, keeping him fired up. "If you want to beat this bastard then suck it up hard, Jericho. Those Stewards are watching you. They'll pull you in a heartbeat if you look badly hurt to them."

"No way," he snarled back. Just dug down and broke away, striding over to where McAlister was mounting Lion. Wild look in the stallion's eyes. Petted him, talked to him while the Irishman got settled. Feet flashing in little crab steps, lifting that head up and snorting…but nothing worse than that so far.

Jericho told McAlister one more time. "Give him confidence."

McAlister and Lion came out into the Grand Prix field. The stallion was tossing his head and appeared to be tugging on the reins fairly hard, but he was going forward, and in a pretty normal canter. Salute and they were on the course.

"Wow, Melissa," Roger narrated. "I guess now we can see why they say that Chasseur de Lion is hard to ride."

"Absolutely. We can certainly see over these first few fences that Chasseur de Lion is pulling pretty hard, and his back is hollow, so he's not getting that lovely round jump we've been seeing from this horse thus far…*oh*, rail down at three," she said, not sounding too sad about it either. "And the horse is fighting much harder here between fences three and four, Roger. He's really not wanting to make that turn. *Oh*, and there goes another rail."

Jericho watching from the fence line of the enclosure and snarling to McAlister, even though the Irishman wouldn't hear him, *"Come on. Don't wimp out on him. Ride."*

Hans Gutsch had come over beside him. Spoke perfect English. Little laugh, "Who are you rooting for?"

Just murmured it, "My horse."

Laughed again. "You gave Ian some advice. I'm on Chasseur next…"

"Yeah, I'm gonna help you."

Gutsch nodded quietly. "For what it's worth…you've got my respect."

Didn't look around, just murmured low, "Thanks."

One more rail fell by the time McAlister and Lion had finished the course for a total of 12 faults. But the stallion had held together—snorting and nervously hopping along sideways all the way back to the enclosure…eyes on Jericho and calling anxiously out to him. Met him at the gate, petted him while McAlister jumped down, told him how good he'd been. The horse pressing fretfully against him, but starting to settle again.

The second round concluded with Jericho and Damien tied for first place, both of them double clear. Gutsch was in third with 4 faults, and McAlister trailing with 16 faults…but then he had his go on Lion behind him, and couldn't be counted out yet.

Bee-Bee was closely watching the television monitor. More trouble in the enclosure with the Show Stewards, apparently. The Belgian Chef D'Equip had gone over to them, urging them to take action, and then Chuck had joined the group, and was arguing vigorously. "Well, he's double clear so far," he said hotly. "So I guess he's seeing well enough." Turned to the Belgian. "And I don't know what you're all worked up about—he's already ridden your horse, no problems."

Not satisfied, the official show physician had been called in, and Jericho, angrily protesting, was called over so he could examine him. Short recess in the action while that was happening.

Looked like Damien had tried to get over closer to Lion—maybe to rile him up before the next ride. But McAlister and Gutsch made sure that didn't happen, blocking his path—harsh words exchanged there too.

Marx leaned over to Bee-Bee. "Could you take a short walk with me while we're waiting?" he asked. "I'd like to chat with you about next season. I'll be brief, I promise." Nice reassuring smile on him.

Didn't want to—hard to say though. "Uhm, okay," she said. "But I really want to see Jericho ride."

"Oh, it won't take that long," Marx said again.

They got up and went over to the buffet table, down to the end of it where coffee and drinks were being served. He was still looking at her pleasantly, kindly almost. "Darien and I are very pleased with how Monterrey is doing," he complimented her. "And we're even considering buying another horse like him…or maybe like Antares," he suggested.

Bee-Bee knew that Antares was a lot harder to ride than Marx understood, but the principle was there, and she sure wasn't arguing. "That would be fantastic," she told him, obviously happy about it.

He reached in his pocket and pulled something out. Took her wrist in his other hand and turned it over. Laid the item from his pocket in her palm. She looked down, somewhat stunned. She was looking at a room key.

"This is a suite I got to use as an office while I'm here," he told her. "I've got all my papers and computer equipment set-up there. Come on over tomorrow afternoon, and I'll have a contract put together. You can take a look at it, and we can discuss it then. I can be very, very generous. Naturally, I'll include Monterrey in the contract too…since I know you wouldn't want to lose him."

Had that last been a little threat? It had almost sounded like it. For a second she was speechless.

"Now, this is just between you and me. I want to make it a surprise for Darien, and well…I'd rather not include Jericho either, it's just easier when you don't have to satisfy a whole group, isn't it?" Marx continued, smiling again—hint of something suggestive in his voice. "I think you're going to be very happy. I know I am."

The end of the third round saw a change of positioning. And yeah, Jericho's injuries were really starting to get to him. Holding himself up and balanced over the horse in the air…the act of lifting to the fence, and leaning forward in the release…the strength required to check the horse and put him on spot…all were making his sides and abdomen just scream. Tried to block that out during the round, but at the end of it, pain hit him like a wall. Even worse, his left eye was almost closed again, and his depth perception faulty—exactly what the Ground Jury had been afraid of. But man he'd done this so often, and Chuck was such a perfectionist that he was still hitting it close enough most of the time. End result…two rails down.

Damien was still clear and sat comfortably in first place, but with Lion yet to ride. Jericho in second place with eight faults. McAlister had gone clear, and was in third place, still with 16 faults, and Gutsch brought up the rear, having a pretty tough time with Lion, and adding 16 faults to his existing 4 for a total of 20 faults thus far.

The Ground Jury was still concerned, but with only one round to go and Jericho clearly in medal position…gold still possible…they weren't going to stop him unless he was clearly unable to ride. He stood with Frankel waiting for his turn again, leaning up against Lion, worrying about the big gray stallion and what was ahead of him. Petted him and murmured softly to him, while Chuck kept talking. Listening, but also holding that ice pack to his eye.

"Last round, Jericho. And you hear me now. You have no pain, and you've been through this course three times…you know where to take off, forget what you can't see. I won't accept anything less than gold from you. Are we clear on that?"

"I hear you, Chuck."

"This bastard thinks he's got your medal, yeah, but he folds under pressure—we saw that yesterday. And that's when you come alive. You're clear this time through…no rails down. None. *You don't even have a rub.*"

"Alright." Just mumbling a response. Totally focused, absorbing it. Lifted that deep blue stare to Frankel, voice aggressive, hard. "Time to ride."

Hand on his shoulder. "That's right."

This round, he was up on McAlister's mare Angelica. Looked over at her, then at Frankel. "Walk with me," he muttered.

No questions asked, Frankel came along with him.

Jericho gathered up the reins. Quiet voice. "Chuck…put me up on the fucking horse."

No acknowledgement that he'd asked. Just waited until Jericho lifted that left boot off the ground, then grabbed hold by his ankle and gave him a leg up. Powerful look exchanged between them—knew how bad he must be hurting if he'd asked for that, but the sheer determination in his eyes said more—that he'd saved himself for this, that he didn't mean to fail.

He wasn't going to waste his remaining strength on a schooling session. "Open the gate," he called to the Ring Steward. Picked up the canter, and exited the enclosure—out into the Grand Prix jumping field.

"Now this is interesting," Melissa was saying. "We just saw Chef D'Equip Chuck Frankel assisting our American rider Jericho Brandeis mount his final horse. And now he's given up his right to work the horse for three minutes before competing her. I'm guessing these four rounds of jumping have been very hard on him physically. Let's just hope he can hold on, Roger."

Bee-Bee stared fixedly at the television monitor as Jericho came around to the Ground Jury, gave his salute, then brought the Irishman's mare on a circle heading for those timers and the first fence. "Come on, Jericho," she whispered. Hers hands clenched into fists as she watched.

Nice mare too, though she felt like she was tired to him. Really needed to hit those spots with her to keep her clean over these fences. *No rails down.* That's what Frankel had told him. *You don't even have a rub.* The goal—clear enough. Lifted her into that first vertical, and then the Oxer that followed it. Damn…sides, ribs and chest hurt like a mother. Just grit his teeth and turned her into fence number three. Then four. Then the big combination at number five.

"Alright, nicely through that combination," Melissa commented. "Change of lead now, and he's coming back around to that plank jump at number six." Pause while she was watching. Then Melissa cried out sharply with disappointment, and the audience in the grandstands groaning too. *"Oh no…*rail down at seven."

Jericho knew it, dug down even deeper. He rode boldly to that final fence and clear over it. A roar of approval went up from the crowd.

"Well, Roger, one rail down, but Jericho's clinched the silver medal at the very least. What a gallant effort from this injured rider," Melissa breathed.

They flashed up that picture Brae had taken of Jericho again to remind the audience what he'd been up against.

"Boy, I'll say, Melissa. Considering his physical condition, it's nothing short of amazing. What a show of determination. And congratulations, Jericho."

He rode through the gate and into the enclosure—had to make it back inside—but once there, he just leaned forward over the neck of the horse. Hurting. Hurting a lot. Frankel was there with him in a heartbeat, taking hold of the reins. Jericho just breathed it to him, half the words missing. "Chuck...sorry...couldn't...you that clear round."

Powerful support coming back at him. "Come on, get down. And don't you dare apologize, understand? That's the best finish for an American rider in one hell of a long time. You be proud of that."

Jericho climbed out of the saddle, landed with both feet on the ground, but then just stood there facing the mare for a moment. Searched inside himself one more time for strength and found it. He needed to get to Lion, prepare him first—then get Damien onto the horse and out into the arena— at least that far. The devil take him after that, the bastard. Let him get what he deserved. Justice after all.

McAlister and Gutsch were still battling it out for third place and the bronze. Each one took to the course in turn. When both had finished McAlister was still sitting in the top spot, and all that was left of the competition was Damien's final ride...on Chasseur de Lion.

Marco had been keeping the gray stallion as far away from the Belgian as possible, although Lion had been looking over at Damien off and on the entire time. Stomping his front feet, lifting his head and snorting at the merest glimpse of him. Eyes wild. That back humping up in anticipation—remembering, hating. Jericho came to him now, spoke to him, laid a gentling hand on him, turned the big gray's head aside as Damien drew near.

Fear on the Belgian's face.

And how poetic. Jericho's deep blue stare fell squarely on him—grimly satisfied. He held onto the bridle, though Lion was pulling hard now, trying to look around at the despised one, the one who'd hurt him in the past...*but never would again.* Stallion was strong now. Stallion didn't intend to bow. He stood amazingly steady as Damien took the reins up, dancing on his feet a little bit, but eyes alert...proud. Only skittered to the side a few steps as the hated one mounted. Jericho still talking to him, pressing into him, trying to let him know he'd be alright.

But stallion knew that. He'd found a rock to lean on, a partner, had a life now. Something worth defending, like he would have defended his herd in the wild. And stallion wasn't afraid to fight—wasn't even afraid to die if it came to that either. He was more than ready for whatever might come.

Like Jericho, Damien waived his warm-up—clearly wanting to get on and off this horse as fast as possible. While he shortened the reins to head out of the enclosure, Jericho looked up at him coldly, and in a low voice only he could hear, threw the Belgian's own taunt back at him one last time, "Sorry." Then murmured to him harshly. "No, actually I'm not."

Damien didn't answer, and there was something close to panic in those cruel eyes of his as he put his legs on, and Lion jerked through the gate.

The pair entered the arena, and Jericho could see the big gray tightening the muscles all along his torso. Oh, he was ready to explode if the Belgian so much as twitched up there. They halted for the salute—just barely. Then started forward—Lion picking up a huge bounding canter, legs way underneath him, sticking that nose out in the air and locking that powerful stallion neck against his rider. Damien sitting scared on him and sawing desperately on the reins. Lion acting like he wasn't even there, ignoring him.

Through the timers and onto the course.

The powerful stallion was picking up speed now, each stride larger than the one before. The first fence already on them. Damien urgently trying to contain him, but no way. Lion didn't even jump. Just crashed through that vertical like it was made of pick-up sticks, the rails flying, the Belgian covering his face with one arm, and ducking low over to one side.

Jericho ran to the fence line of the enclosure, the pain in his body forgotten. Afraid for Lion. Eyes locked on the scene in front of him. Couldn't get close enough.

Shout of fury from Damien as he righted himself in the saddle. The second Oxer dead ahead of them, and the stallion absolutely barreling. Huge lurching leap, the audience gasping in horror, as Damien gave up his contact on the reins to throw his arms around the big gray's neck—holding on for all he was worth. Over it, but rail down again...almost as if Lion had deliberately knocked it and brought it tumbling to the ground.

Touchdown, and a hard buck, Damien lifting a good six inches out of the saddle. The stallion if anything, going faster, completely out of control. Mad pivot on the horse's part, almost as if he remembered the course from the previous three rides. He was heading toward that third fence with a vengeance. Damien muscled his way back into place as Lion lunged wildly into the air again, but far too early...his front feet sending the top rail flying, and his hind feet demolishing the rest.

This time when he landed, he started shaking his head violently, slowing down dramatically too...that right shoulder popping out, heralding the dive. The Belgian didn't seem to understand that threatening signal—only knew the animal was wasn't racing wildly any more—knew too that Lion's defiant mad dash had cost him the gold. Furious to the point of irrational, he raised his crop in the air all the way above his head, and brought it smashing down on the stallion's hindquarters, a welt rising up on that fine gray coat in a long slashing line tinged with red. Did it again equally hard, but against Lion's side this time—with no real purpose there other than to punish and make the horse underneath him cower. The stallion screaming in rage instead.

And Jericho screaming too, "You *bastard!*" He lunged at the fence, intending to go over it, but Frankel and Marco grabbed him, forcibly holding him back, while he fought to get free of them.

A bell went off—the Ground Jury—wanting Damien to pull up. But he either ignored them, or was too worked up to even hear it. Lion was fighting even harder now, and that crop came down on him a third time. The stallion, starting to stumble, and then in what seemed like slow motion, going down on that right side...Damien's leg pinned underneath him. He let out a shattering shriek of agony that seemed to echo through the arena. The horse crying out too, and rolling partially onto his back. Second long tortured scream from Damien...and then nothing more.

Both of them lying in the dust now. Damien motionless, the stallion thrashing but not getting up.

Nothing was stopping Jericho this time, and no one tried. He was over that fence, and the Belgian Chef D'Equip right behind him. Frankel and Marco too.

"Jericho, get the horse," Chuck was calling to him. "Try to hold him still while they get Damien out."

Damien? Who gave a shit about Damien? Whatever happened to him, he'd brought on himself. Lion was all Jericho cared about. Blaming himself, cursing himself, feeling like he'd caused it. Praying the big gray stallion would be alright. At least he wasn't screaming now, he didn't seem to be in agony.

And God, don't let a leg be broken.

Jericho dropped down on one knee beside the animal's head, touching him, speaking to him. Soft little horse noises coming back at him, but irregular and weak. Recognizing him though. Lion's nostrils working, taking in air and the scent of him—his head caught up somehow. Now Jericho could see that the stallion had stepped through the reins as he fell. The leather was wrapped around one front pastern, holding him captive and on top of Damien. From what he could tell, the bastard was alive but still trapped and probably badly injured. He was also out cold. Called out to Frankel, "Chuck, if we cut this, maybe I can get him up."

Marco was there now beside him, and thank God—he always had a knife. While Jericho soothed the horse and kept his head still, Marco slit the rein that held him down. Jericho tugged on the cheek pieces of the bridle, encouraging him to get up—hoping like hell he even could. Those keen intelligent dark eyes staring back at him. But he wasn't moving. Christ, he wasn't moving, wasn't even trying. "Come on, boy," he called to him. Reached over and stroked him, asked him to try. Tugged again.

This time there was some effort on the horse's part, and he rolled over onto his stomach, freeing Damien. The Belgian was still unconscious and medics had arrived with a board to take him out. And now Lion's legs were moving too. He was trying to get into a position where he could rise.

"Come on, Lion," Jericho urged him again. Just knew in his heart that the horse was injured. Felt so responsible and sick inside.

The stallion shuffled his front feet again, lurched forward with his body. Groaned and sank back into the sand again. Waited, gathered his strength. Another lurch, and this time he was able to come all the way up off the ground, but just standing there at first, head lowered, body trembling. Then he took one tentative step, limping badly. Stopped. Lifted that right front foot, taking his weight off it. Snorted softly. Jericho got in close to him, leaned against him, holding him up, helping him balance. The stallion's head touching him, lips twitching, nuzzling him—almost as if to say…it's alright, this was my fight. "Find the Goddamn vet," Jericho ordered Marco, pain for Lion flaring in his voice.

The fall was ruled an accident, caused by the stallion slipping after fence number three and stepping through the reins. No official mention of Damien's abusive use of the crop—no mention of Lion's wild run through the fences either. Jericho took home the gold in perhaps the most trouble-ridden World Equestrian Games ever, McAlister the silver, and Gutsch the bronze. The awards ceremony had been bittersweet, but the three riders deeply bonded—something between them now, something that wouldn't be forgotten in years to come.

Marcel Damien had broken his leg, and also his pelvis. Maybe he'd ride again—more likely not. Not many people in the riding community were sad about it. The general consensus was that the horse show world was better without him, without his corrupt tactics, and without the kind of abuse he regularly dished out.

And Chasseur de Lion would never compete again either. A muscle had been badly torn in his right forearm, and yes it would heal in time. But the vet predicted he would always be unsound on it, and even if he wasn't, would probably never be strong enough to jump. Didn't matter, Jericho wanted him. He asked Bee-Bee, and she agreed. Wanted to give him a permanent home—big box stall, large run-out paddock. Breed him. Spoil him. Cause man, he deserved it. He was a gold medalist, a super competitor.

He was more than that too. Like Chuck said, there were a lot of parallels between himself and this stallion. Both of them had come through dark times, and both had made it to the other side—with the help of someone they could believe in. Both ready to find roots, share a life with that special new partner. And he meant to see that both of them got that now.

Went to Bruce Waverly about it the next morning, dropping in unannounced in his hotel. If anything, Jericho looked worse today than he had yesterday, that purple on his face tinged with yellow and almost black in spots too. He called Waverly on the house phone and asked to see him. The two of them met in the coffee shop. Warm greeting from his patron and congratulations too. Thanked him for that. Then came straight to the point. "Bruce, I guess you heard the vet's report on your stallion."

Grave nod.

"I'm here because I'd like to buy him from you."

Waverly's expression softened. "He means that much to you?"

Looked down at his coffee. "Yeah, he really does. Look, I don't know how much you'd want for him, but I'll find some way to pay you."

Little laugh. "Would a dollar be too much?"

Jericho's head jerked up. "Bruce, he's worth way more than that. Ask Chuck to put a value on him. God knows, you've been nothing but good to me and I…"

"And you what? Can't accept a gift from an elderly gentleman who's watched you bring that horse from renegade to champion, and enjoyed himself handsomely in the process? Call it a wedding gift."

Now that made it harder to refuse. "I owe him a lot. He's taught me so much—about my riding…about myself too. He trusts me, and I promise you I'll take care of him. Make him forget the hard times. Let him enjoy the rest of his life, be a horse."

His patron looked happy. "I know you will. Frankly Jericho, there isn't another home I'd want him in." He reached across the table and patted the back of his hand lightly. "Anyway, you already own his heart…it's time you got the rest of him."

Marx came down the hotel hallway looking pleased with the world and with himself. He stopped in front of the door to a large suite—his temporary office while they'd been here at the Games. Bee-Bee should already be inside—he'd timed it that way. Put his key in the lock, and pushed the door open, came inside.

The sound of water running. Was it the shower? Sounded like it. A smile touched his face. So maybe this was going to be really easy. So much the better. He walked toward the sound. And yeah, it was definitely coming from the bath attached to the main bedroom, and he went into the bedroom now, heading for the bathroom door. "What are you up to, you little minx?" he called out, both arousal and amusement evident in his voice. "Are you in the shower?" He was even thinking about joining her…probably what she'd had in mind anyway.

The water going off.

"Now, what a way to tempt a man," Marx chuckled, reaching out for the doorknob.

"Yeah, I thought you might like it." Resonant, deep male voice.

The investment banker stood stunned as the bathroom door swung open, and Jericho came into the opening. Not a very pleasant look on his face—made so much more threatening by those savage bruises. Body loosely

611

poised, just balanced to strike. Superior look in those deep blue eyes. Marx fell back a step, one arm coming up in front of himself defensively.

"What's the matter, Bob?" Jericho baited him softly. "Afraid I'm going to lay into you? God, would I love to. Truth is, I've wanted to beat the crap out of you since the first day we met, remember? Even then, you just had to goad me…you must like flirting with danger. Well, here I am—want to try your luck again?" Just let that thought sit right there for several long moments. Took a step closer. Real fear springing up in the other man's eyes.

"Jericho, I…"

Voice harsh, and snapping like a whip. *"Don't* interrupt me."

Silence.

"Better." Right up in Marx's face now—and watching him cringe. "Oh yeah, I'd love give you a feel of this." Brought that powerful right fist up, menacing. Then just dropped it. "But that's not what I have in mind, and that's not what this is about."

Marx expelled his breath hard. "Jesus Christ, Jericho…" he muttered. Really relieved, but shaking and still not sure.

Jericho turned away from him and walked to the door between the bedroom and the front sitting room. Looked back over his shoulder. "Come out here," he ordered. "I've got something I want to say to you, and you're damn sure going to listen. And believe me, it's not bedroom talk." Watched him for a moment, then spoke sharply. "And don't toy with me, Bob. Get your ass out here. I can always go back to Plan A if you don't."

He went into the sitting room. Waited. And Marx followed, still plenty unsure—hovering just inside the doorway, but not daring to refuse him. Jericho approached him again, but stopped while there were still a few feet between them. "Alright, cards on the table, Marx." Authority in his voice. "You told me that first day we met to stay away from Darien, and I didn't. And that really pissed you off. I'll concede the point, you had a right to be angry…forget the fact that I didn't go looking for it, that I wasn't playing a game with her and that there was nothing in what I did that was deliberately aimed at hurting you. But okay, I was wrong, so no excuses." His expression grew harder. "But Bob, since then, you've done everything you could to get back at me. And you're still trying—first Ailynn, now Bee-Bee, and don't tell me you have any real interest in either of them—you just want to take away anything that's remotely mine."

Denying it. "That's not true."

"Bullshit." Fierce look coming into those deep blue eyes, right hand clenching unconsciously, but his temper still well under control. "Be a man—stand up to your own actions. That's exactly what you're doing, and I have to hand it to you...you've already hurt me more than I thought possible, and Christ, I'll never forgive you for that...to destroy my child like he's garbage..." Had to cut off that thought, the wound still raw. Went on instead. "Be satisfied...be satisfied knowing that what you did haunts me every single day, and will for years, maybe the rest of my life. Because I swear to you...if I have to stop you again, it won't be a civilized like this."

"So you want me to go away. And just what exactly are you proposing, Jericho?" Marx came back at him, a lot more confident, coldly arrogant too. "That Darien and I disappear from the world of Show Jumping?"

"You know what? I don't give a damn what you do. If you want out of the QL partnership, talk to Chuck, I'm sure it's possible and I'd like that. If you want to move Monterrey, then do that too. Just don't fuck with me, Bob—I'm so tired of your attitude. You and your money mean nothing to me—I've got no use for it, or you." Laid out his terms, and they were pretty simple. "This is what I want...you won't get anything but civil treatment from me publicly. My word on that. And I expect the same in return. And as for the rest of it? It's through. Finished. I'm giving you this one chance. Get out of my life. Don't make me come after you."

Didn't have to think about it long, not with that threat and the physical reality of Jericho facing him. "You're right...you've done your damage and I've done mine. And maybe I should consider myself lucky you're willing to end it here," he said. "But I need a promise that you'll stay away from Darien...*even if she comes to you*—I know she did before, and she might even try again." Had to be a hard admission for him. "A real promise from you Jericho—one that means something to you."

It really pissed him off, his tone, good and biting. "You've got that right...she's the one who came to me in Raleigh. I even slept that first night in the stable to stay away from her—not that she'd accept that answer. But now I know her better—know she used me pretty much the same way you used Ailynn. No, I won't let her come to me, you damn sure have my word on that." Didn't bother telling him he knew now he'd never loved Darien. No, he'd loved the woman she created for him...the one that wasn't real.

The investment banker hesitated, looked down, then answered him. "One thing about you, Jericho, you're honest and I believe you. And the truth is, I wish we'd never come down this road. But we have and nothing can change that—even so, maybe we can live without going after each other. Draw a line in the sand and each one stay on one side of it. Doesn't mean we like each other, and you and I never will. But my word on this agreement? I'll give you that and it's good."

Jericho looked at him squarely, said with feeling—bitter. "You can't begin to understand how I'm reining myself in, how badly I want to come after you and how much I think you deserve it. I just hope your word is good, Marx, and that you stick to it like it's sacred, because here's another promise…you won't like the alternative."

Didn't need to say more, and couldn't stand being there with him. He turned, grabbed that door and jerked it open…walking out, leaving that part of his life behind him for good.

Epilogue

It was three weeks after their return from Europe, most of that time taken as rest. Light work for the horses, just getting their heads on straight. Mid-September already—making plans to return to Wellington in a little over a month. The winter horse show season, almost ready to start again.

Frankel had gone home to his own place in Virginia, though oddly enough, he and Jericho still talked every day. At first, one or the other of them finding an excuse to make the phone call, but after a bit, just giving in and calling for no particular reason at all.

Tonight, Frankel was just getting back from dinner at a local diner. Kicked his shoes off, strolled into the living room, grabbed the clicker and turned the TV on. Got nice and comfortable on the sofa, and of course that's when the telephone finally rang. Grumbled about it, but jumped up pretty quickly to go retrieve it.

"Frankel here," he answered it.

Warm male laughter from the other end. "Christ, you sound so surly— bet a lot of telemarketers just hang up."

Tried to keep right on sounding grumpy too—hard though, just loved it when Jericho called. "Jericho, how do you always know exactly when to phone me? As soon as I get good and settled, I can almost count on the telephone ringing so I have to get up."

Not very sympathetic—not fooled by the grumpy routine either. Just went right on with his news. "So the vet did another ultra-sound on Lion's leg today."

Really interested, and not hiding it. "And?"

"It looks great, Chuck. Way better than he expected," Jericho told him. "He said not to get my hopes up yet, but anyway, it's good news. And if you could see him running around the paddock…man, he's so happy. Any of the guys can handle him now too, he really seems content."

"That's super…" He wasted some time by sitting on the sofa again, and switching the sound on the TV off. Didn't know if he should ask this, but finally did. "So are you thinking you might be able to compete him?"

"Maybe, maybe not. I think I'll bring him down to Florida with me anyway—hell, I just like having him around." Wasn't sure how he felt about that one himself—figured Lion would tell him what to do, when and if they got to the point where they needed to decide. Changed the subject on Frankel instead. "This is kind of short notice, but what are you doing October first?"

"Probably nothing. Why?" Not really all that hard to guess.

"Belinda and I thought we might pick that day to get married. It works for her family…mine too. Hell, I might even get to meet my uncle. And Chuck…" Little pause. "…I kind of thought…I mean, I'd like it…if you were best man."

Quiet. "You don't have to ask me that."

"No, I'm serious, Chuck. It would mean a lot to me." Kind of hard for him to say this, but felt really strong about it—and maybe it was easier over the phone like this. "I…hope this doesn't offend you, but…you know, you're the closest thing to a father I have. No…I want to say that differently. I want to say…I never had someone to look up to before, to learn from, till I met you. You've changed my life in a lot of ways." A little intense maybe, and he tried to lighten it up. "Yeah, I know I'm a pain in the ass sometimes, but I figured you'd stand beside me. Hoped you would anyway."

Frankel smiling warmly to himself. Yeah George had said it over and over—there was just something there between the two of them—something so similar. "You never had a father, and I never had a son," he said. "But if I *had* a son…and he'd turned out like you have…I'd consider myself damn lucky." Paused, then chuckled, "And yeah of course I'll be there, and I'd be proud to stand with you."

Strange goings on at the Brandeis Show Stables in East Hampton, New York. Beautiful fall day, and all the equine heads sticking out of the barn, trying to see what this was about.

Happy alpha mare standing in one of the nice front paddocks, lush with green grass. Sun falling on her glossy hide. Rest day—taking it easy.

Funny thing…the groom human had braided flowers through her mane and tail this morning. Lots of them, some ribbons too. Felt happy about it—pretty. Looked over coyly at attractive gray stallion in the paddock beside her. Little tail swish to interest him—flowers in his mane and tail too. Calling to him, and him answering. Stallion trotting over to the fence line—had been weak before, but getting stronger all the time. Him snorting, tossing his head and showing off.

Stallion…pretty interesting.

Little squeal and buck from alpha mare, head lifted proudly. Showing stallion what a strong herd protector she would be. Trotting with him to the front of their adjacent paddocks.

Many, many humans on the side lawn today. Sticking her head out and sniffing. Stallion doing the same thing, whistling in challenge just in case. Didn't know what all the commotion was about, but had to be something.

The God human standing in front of all of them, and belongs-to-God human beside him. Flowers in their hair too, just like alpha mare. Liked that. Eat the flowers later maybe if she got the chance. Something gauzy and white covering belongs-to-God human, flowing in the breeze around her. Maybe eat that too.

Others that she recognized from her day to day life also nearby—the groom human and assistants—liked the groom human, hated the assistants. Annoying human who stood in the jumping field barking while she worked—especially liked lunging at him and seeing him jump. Tall goofy human with small metal clicking gadget—neutral on that one, but harmless. The shaved head human with the hard leg—but hard leg gone now, replaced by normal leg. Some connection between he and God human that she didn't understand, but definite herd member. Seemed to have a special relationship with stallion too.

Ah…something happening.

Fat stranger human in black moving in between God human and QL—facing him, not alpha mare. Making noises for a while.

Then God human speaking…deep voice, loud and clear. Loved the sound. Called out softly to him. Other humans laughing.

And then belongs-to-God human responding to God human, turning to face him—her voice higher, more musical. Starting to like this little herd member—almost always had cookies for QL.

God human and belongs-to-God human embracing. A little bit jealous about that—certainly used to seeing it though. Tried a diversion to get God human's attention. Reaching nose over to stallion, nipping at him, and him spinning, galloping away with tail up, and then back again, sliding to a stop—oh definitely much stronger. Very suitable for mating too.

All the humans getting up now, crowding around God human and belongs-to-God human. Friendly noises from them, but QL on guard anyway. More commotion for a while…took time out from guard duty to chomp grass and flirt with stallion.

And finally, at long last, God human and belongs-to-God human coming over to the fence line. Annoying barking human with them. Laying ears back and lunging madly at him, and him scooting out of her way. How much fun! Pats, soft murmurs and treats from the God human. Nuzzling him and belongs-to-God human.

Alpha mare happy. All was right with the world.

Give the Gift of
In & Out
to Your Friends and Colleagues

CHECK YOUR LEADING BOOKSTORE OR ORDER HERE

❑ **YES**, I want _____ copies of *In & Out* at $22.95 each, plus $4.95 shipping per book (Ohio residents please add $1.66 sales tax per book). Canadian orders must be accompanied by a postal money order in U.S. funds. Allow three to four weeks for delivery.

My check or money order for $_____ is enclosed.

Please charge my: ❑ Visa ❑ MasterCard
❑ Discover ❑ American Express

Name _____

Organization _____

Address _____

City/State/Zip _____

Phone_____ E-mail _____

Card # _____

Exp. Date_____ Signature _____

Please make your check payable and return to:
BookMasters, Inc.
P.O. Box 388
Ashland, OH 44805
Call your credit card order to (800) 247-6553
Fax (419) 281-6883
order@bookmasters.com   www.atlasbooks.com

DATE DUE